BEETLE & THE HOLLOWBONES

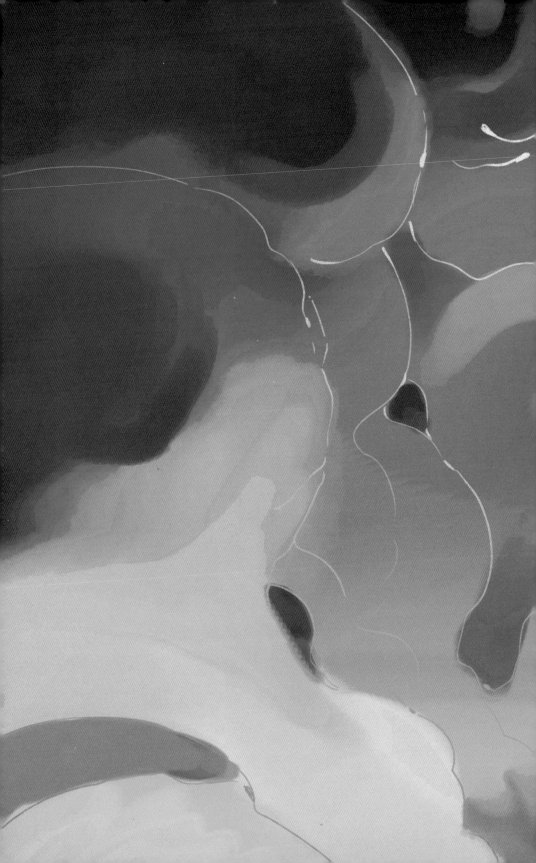

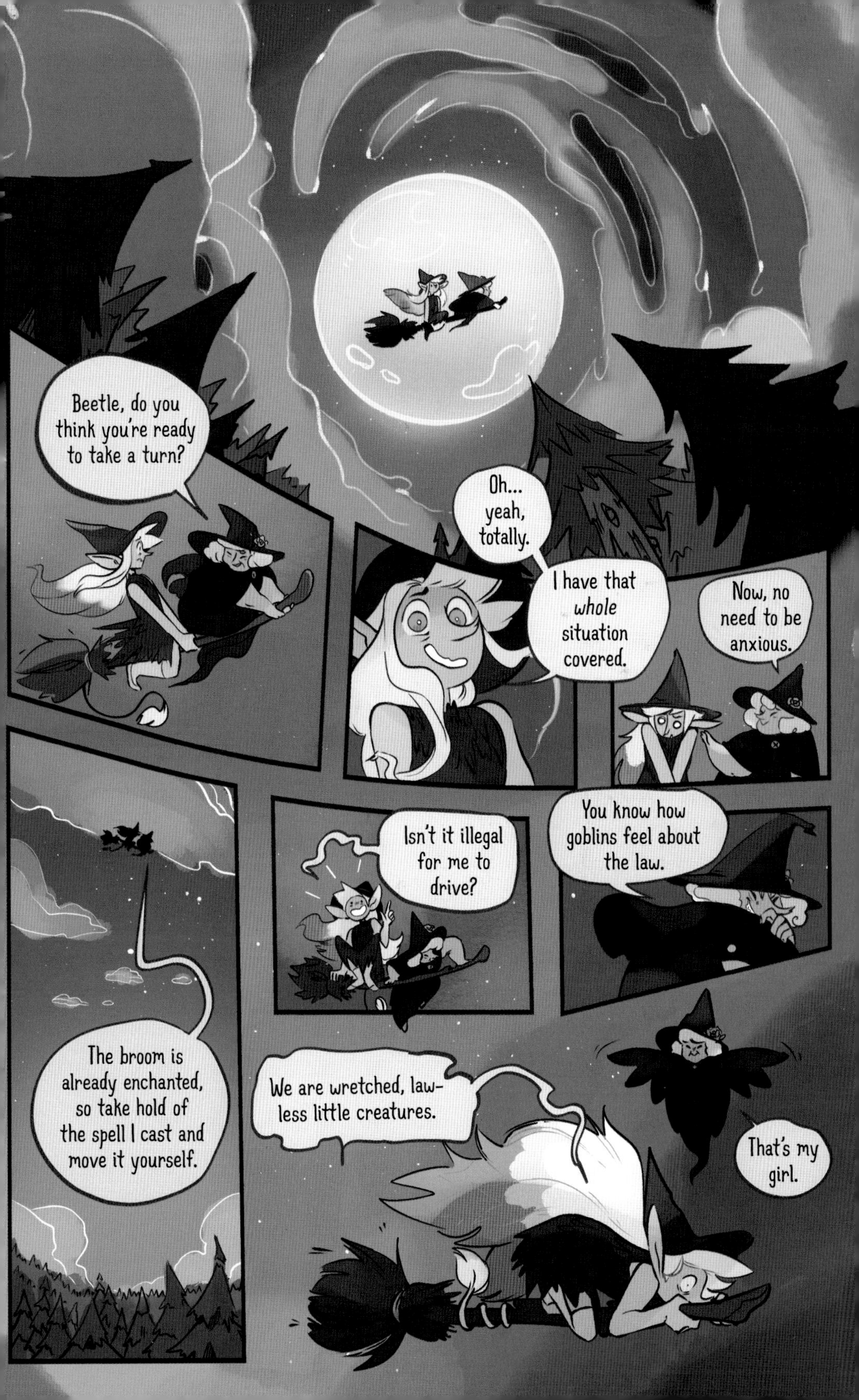
Beetle, do you think you're ready to take a turn?
Oh... yeah, totally.
I have that *whole* situation covered.
Now, no need to be anxious.
Isn't it illegal for me to drive?
You know how goblins feel about the law.
The broom is already enchanted, so take hold of the spell I cast and move it yourself.
We are wretched, law-less little creatures.
That's my girl.

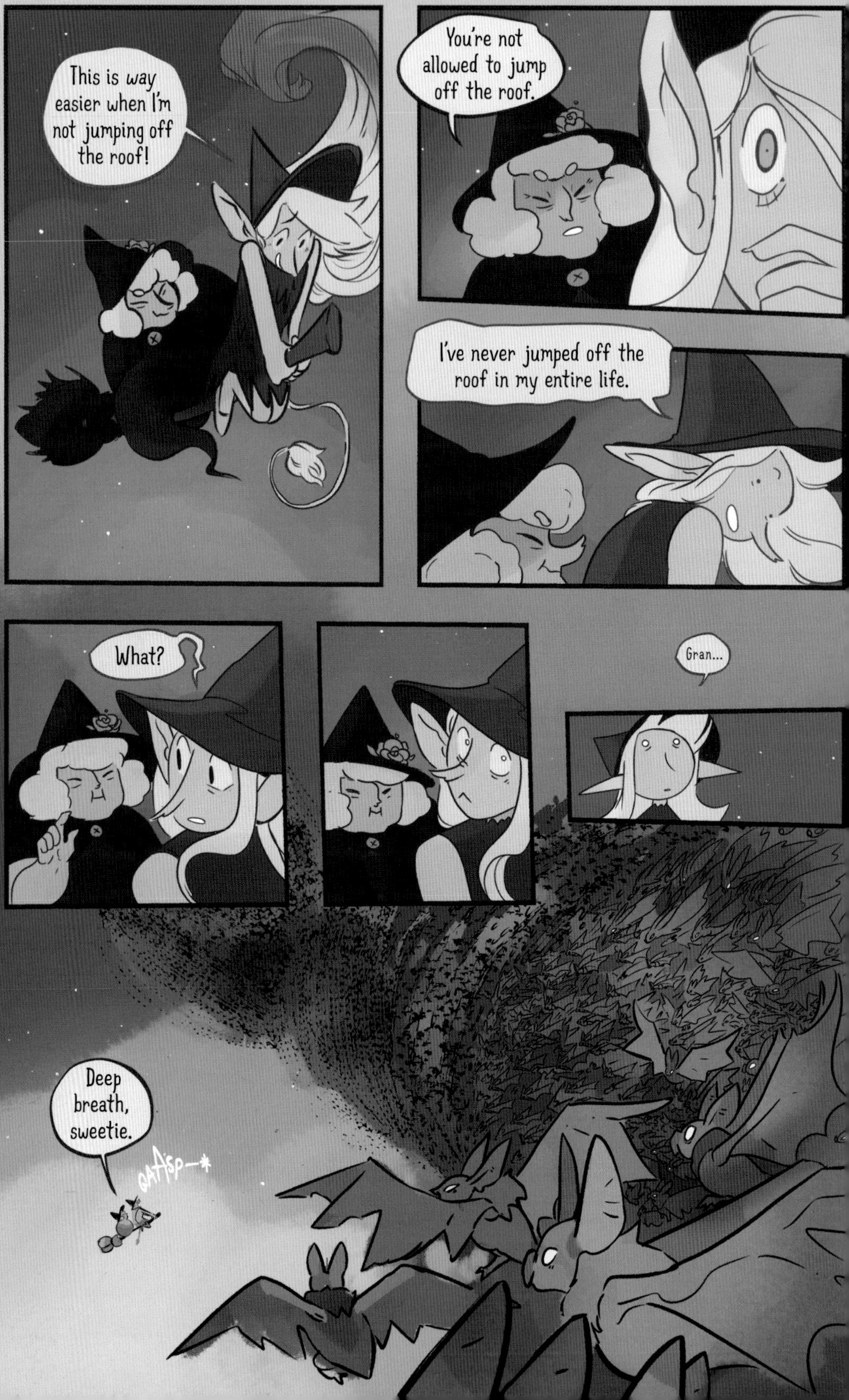
This is way easier when I'm not jumping off the roof!
You're not allowed to jump off the roof.
I've never jumped off the roof in my entire life.
What?
Gran...
Deep breath, sweetie.
GAAASP—*

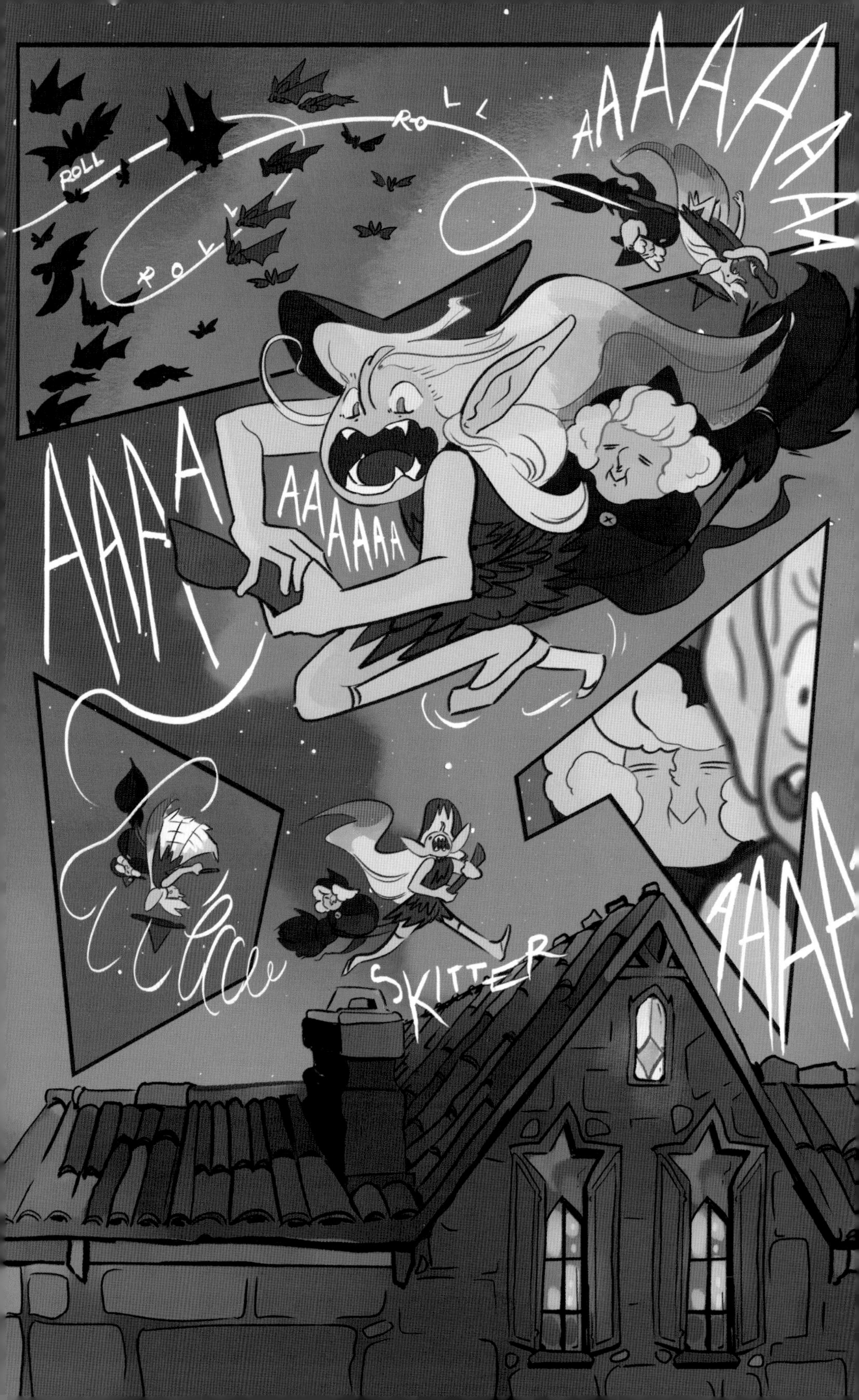
ROLL
ROLL
ROLL
ROLL
AAAAAAAAAA
AAAA
AAAAAAA
AAAA
SKITTER

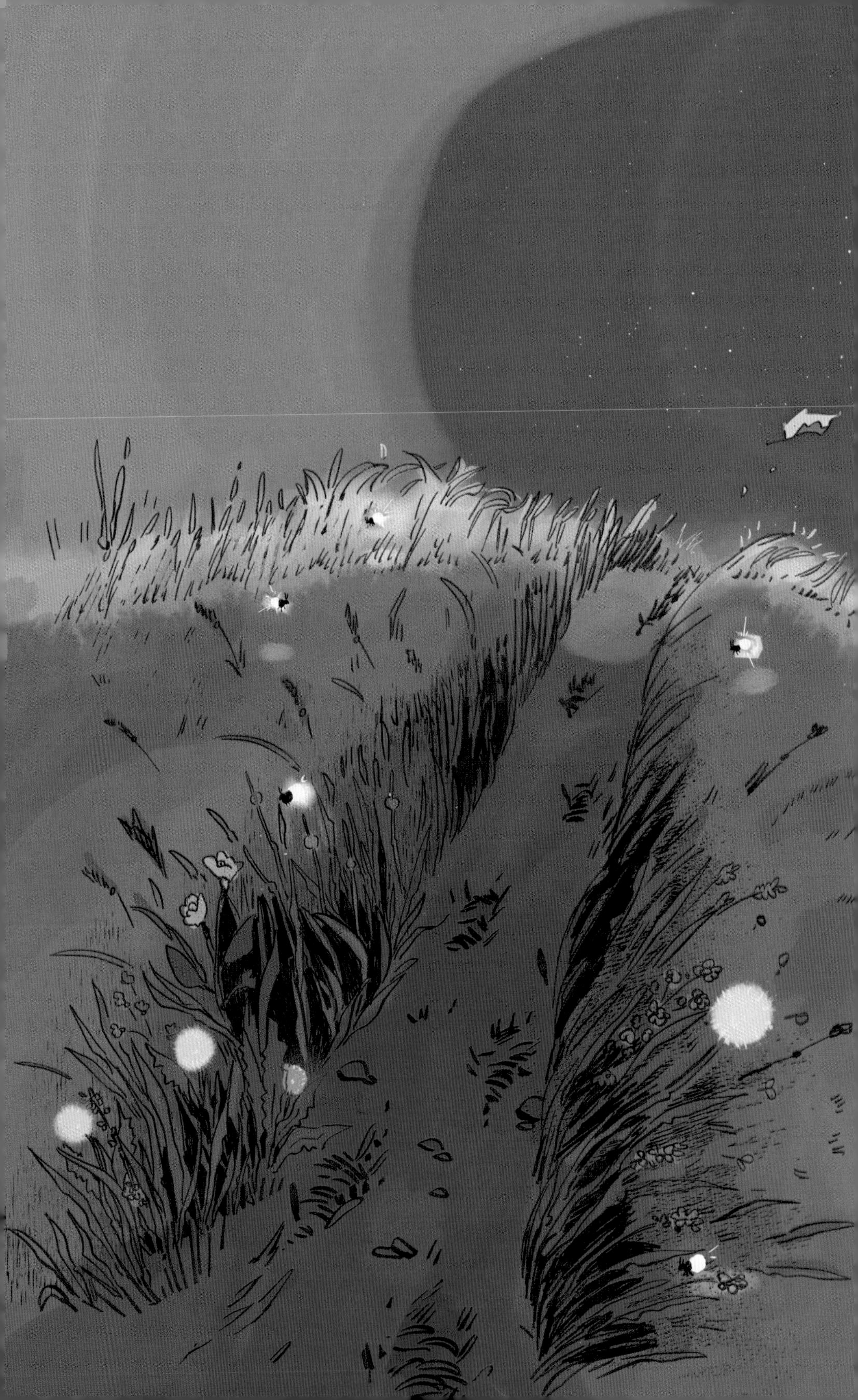

Beetle & the Hollowbones

ALIZA LAYNE

COLORING BY NATALIE RIESS
AND KRISTEN ACAMPORA

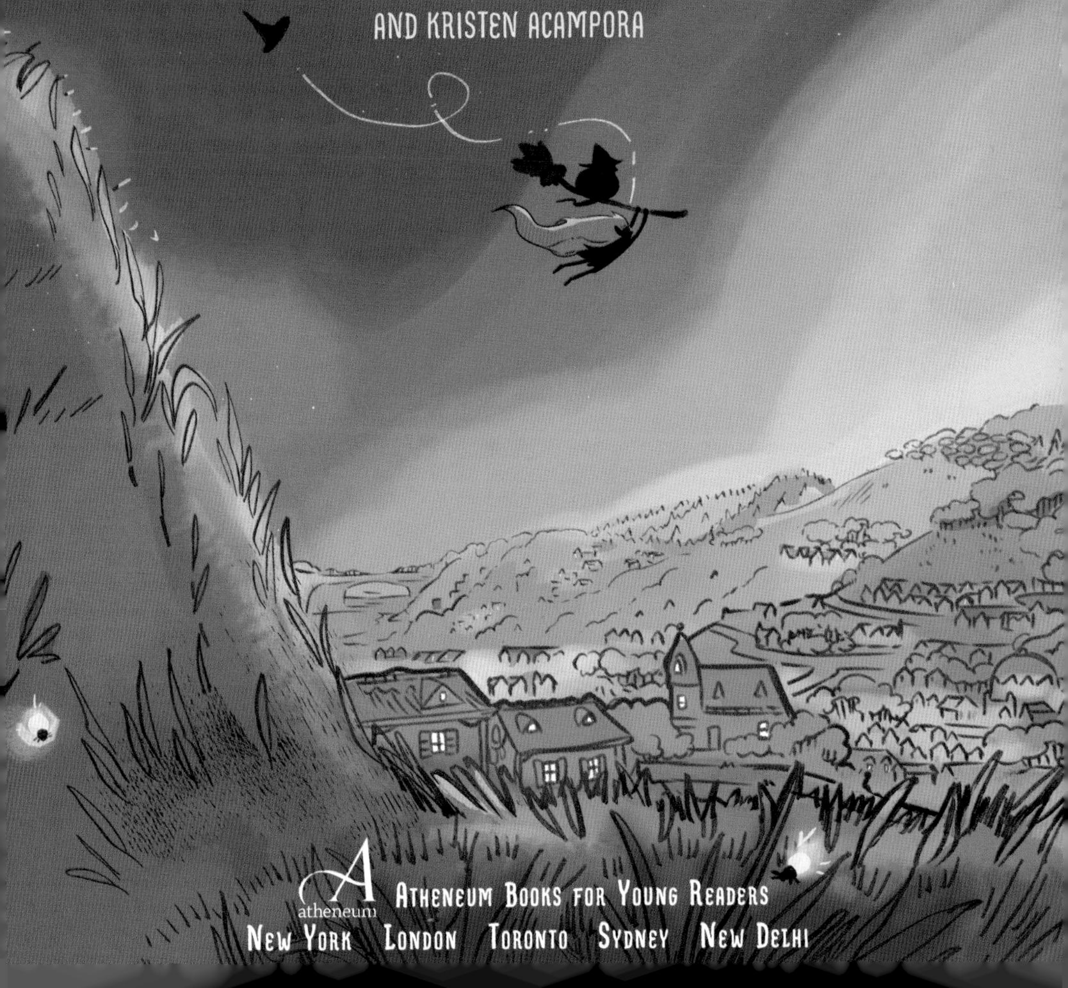

atheneum
Atheneum Books for Young Readers
New York London Toronto Sydney New Delhi

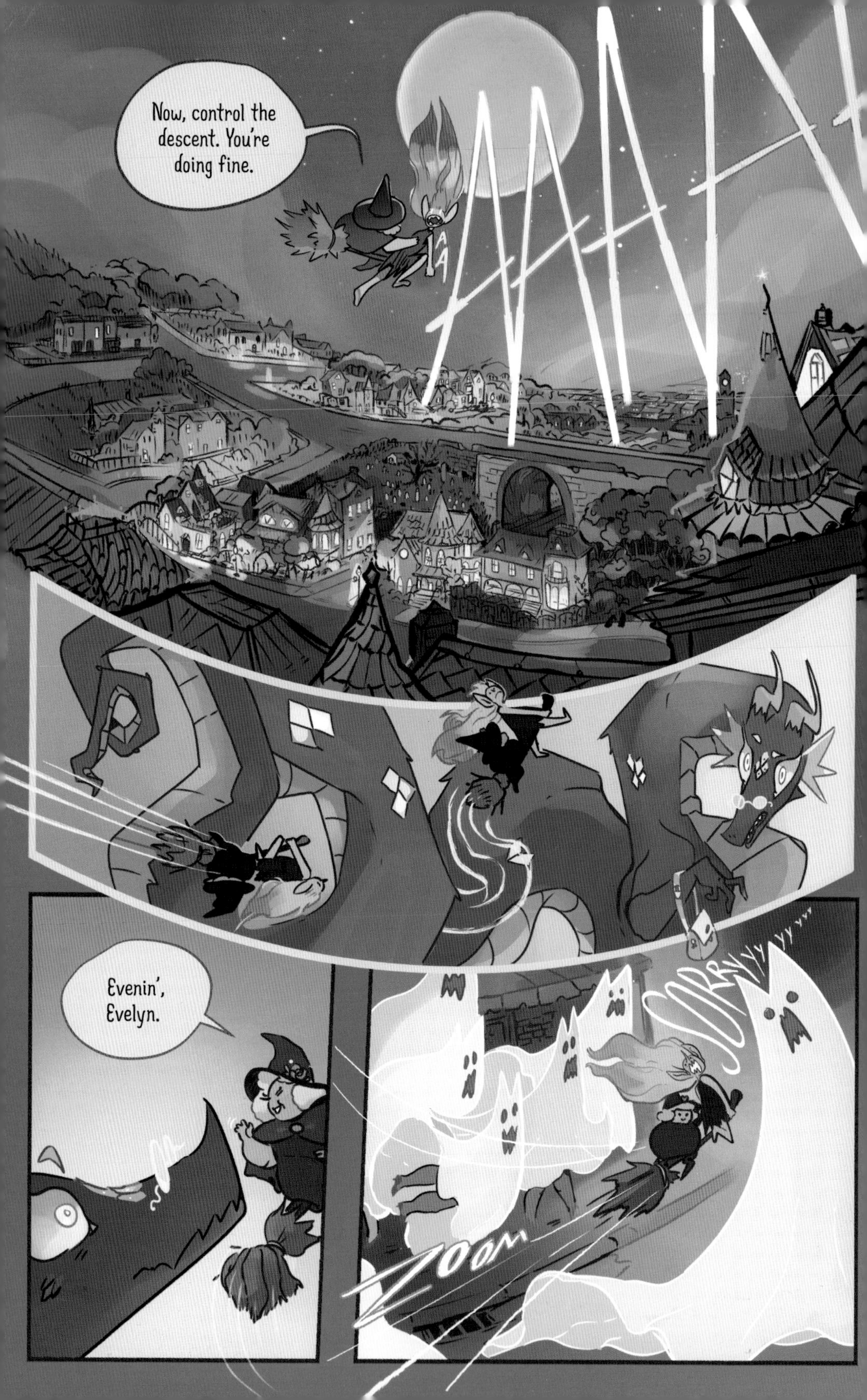
Now, control the descent. You're doing fine.
AAAA
Evenin', Evelyn.
SORRY
ZOOM

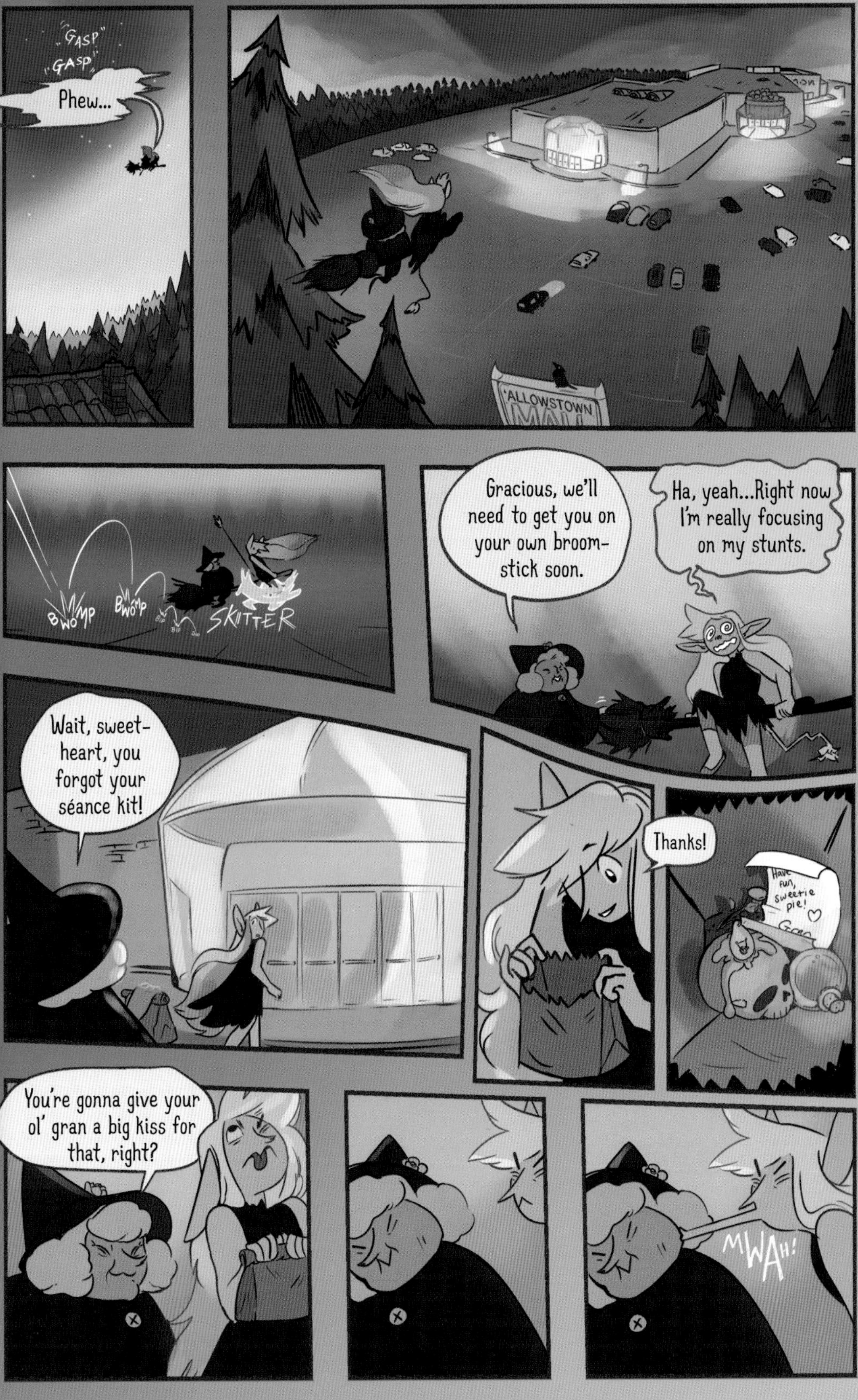
GASP
GASP
Phew...
ALLOWSTOWN
MALL
BWOMP
BWOMP
SKITTER
Gracious, we'll need to get you on your own broom-stick soon.
Ha, yeah...Right now I'm really focusing on my stunts.
Wait, sweet-heart, you forgot your séance kit!
Thanks!
Have fun, sweetie pie! ♡
You're gonna give your ol' gran a big kiss for that, right?
MWAH!

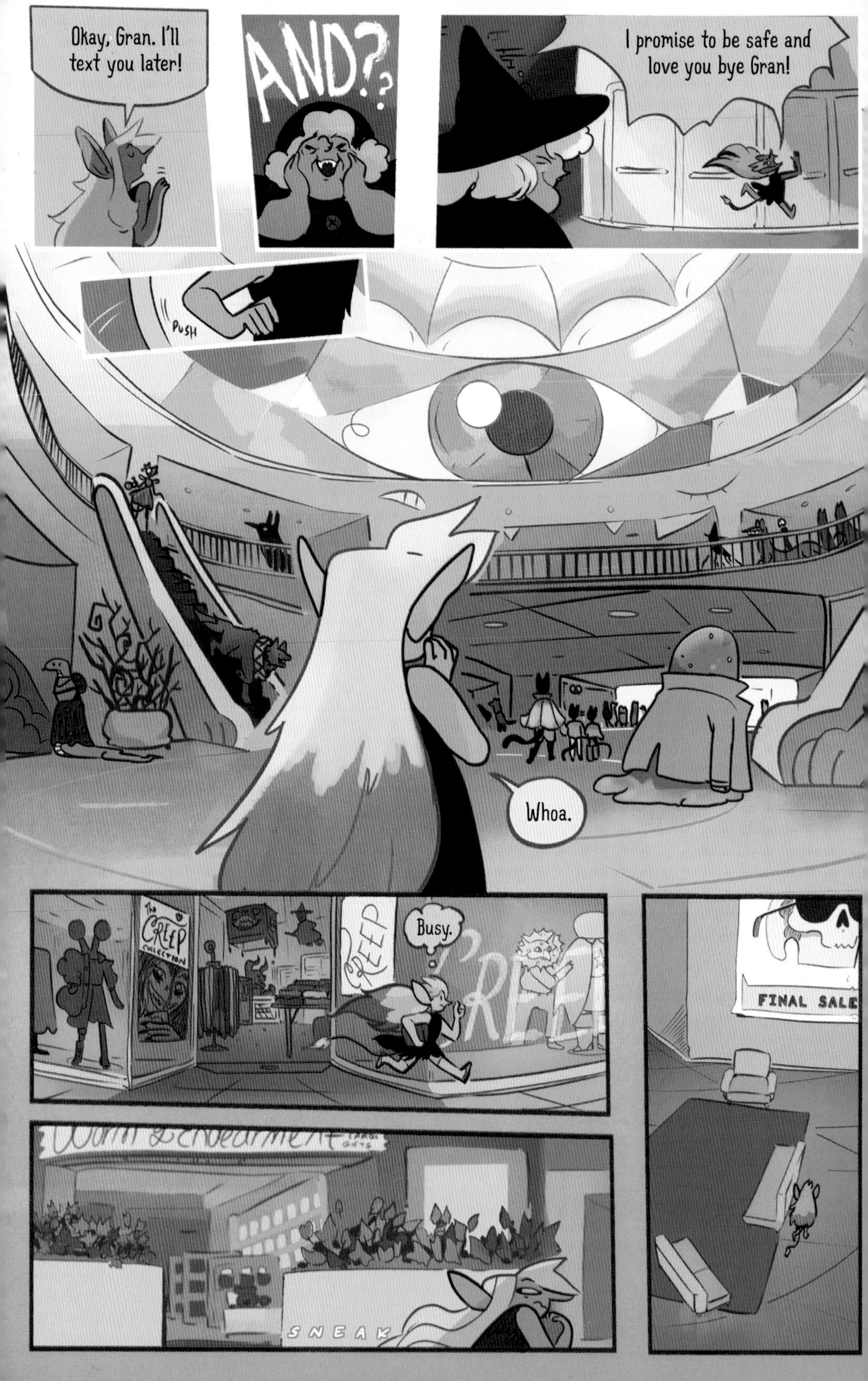
Okay, Gran. I'll text you later!
AND??
I promise to be safe and love you bye Gran!
PUSH
Whoa.
The CREEP COLLECTION
CREEP
Busy.
FINAL SALE
SNEAK

CLICK!

Okaaay.

Blob Ghost of this mall, hear my darque message across the veil...

Hey, what's up? I'm here!

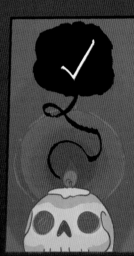

RISE

EEEoEEoEEoooOOOooooo

CRAK!

SQUEAK!

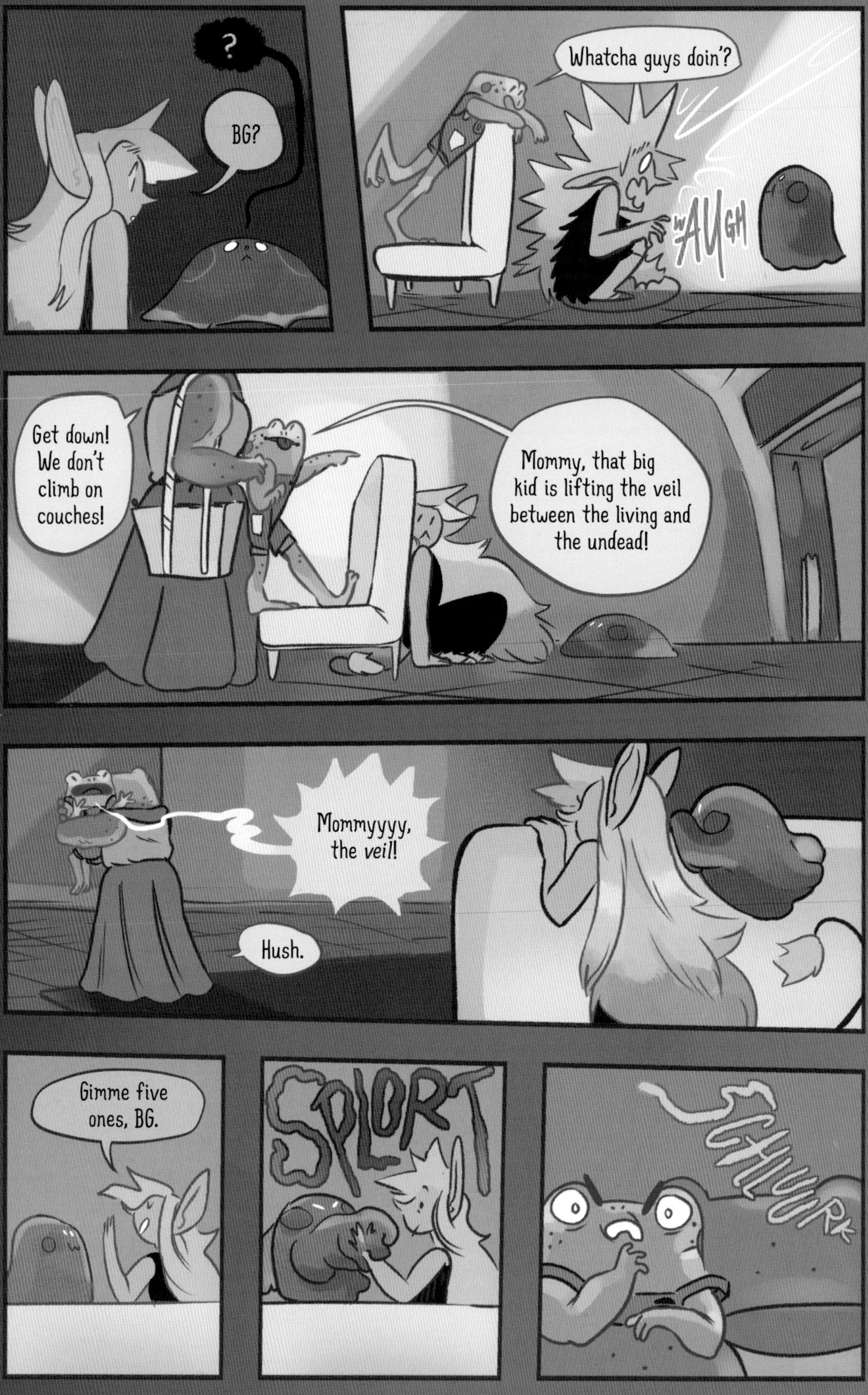

?
BG?
Whatcha guys doin'?
WAUGH
Get down! We don't climb on couches!
Mommy, that big kid is lifting the veil between the living and the undead!
Mommyyyy, the *veil*!
Hush.
Gimme five ones, BG.
SPLORT
SCHLURK

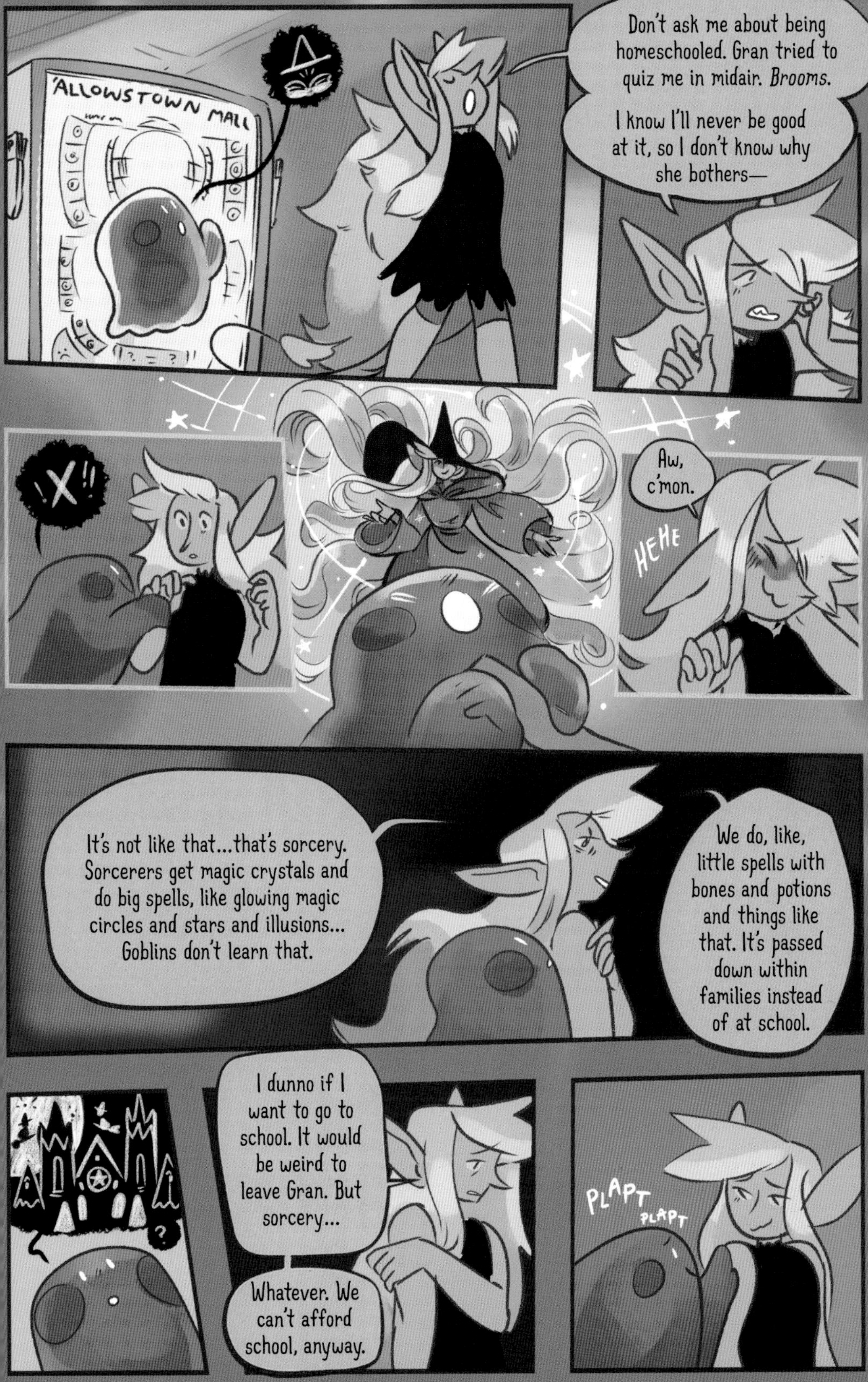
ALLOWSTOWN MALL
Don't ask me about being homeschooled. Gran tried to quiz me in midair. *Brooms.*
I know I'll never be good at it, so I don't know why she bothers—
!X!!
Aw, c'mon.
HEHE
It's not like that...that's sorcery. Sorcerers get magic crystals and do big spells, like glowing magic circles and stars and illusions... Goblins don't learn that.
We do, like, little spells with bones and potions and things like that. It's passed down within families instead of at school.
?
I dunno if I want to go to school. It would be weird to leave Gran. But sorcery...
Whatever. We can't afford school, anyway.
PLAPT PLAPT

Oh, sure!

I hope I get something good...

This is my only quarter.

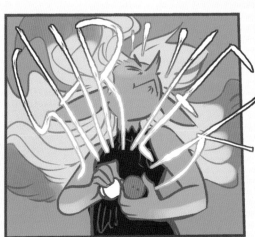

Just screams again? Why do I waste my money on this garbage?!

You got any money today, Blob Ghost?

Hmm...

Gotta do free stuff, then. Want to read some manga?

—STICKY—

I mean, do you want me to hold some manga open for you?

NOD!

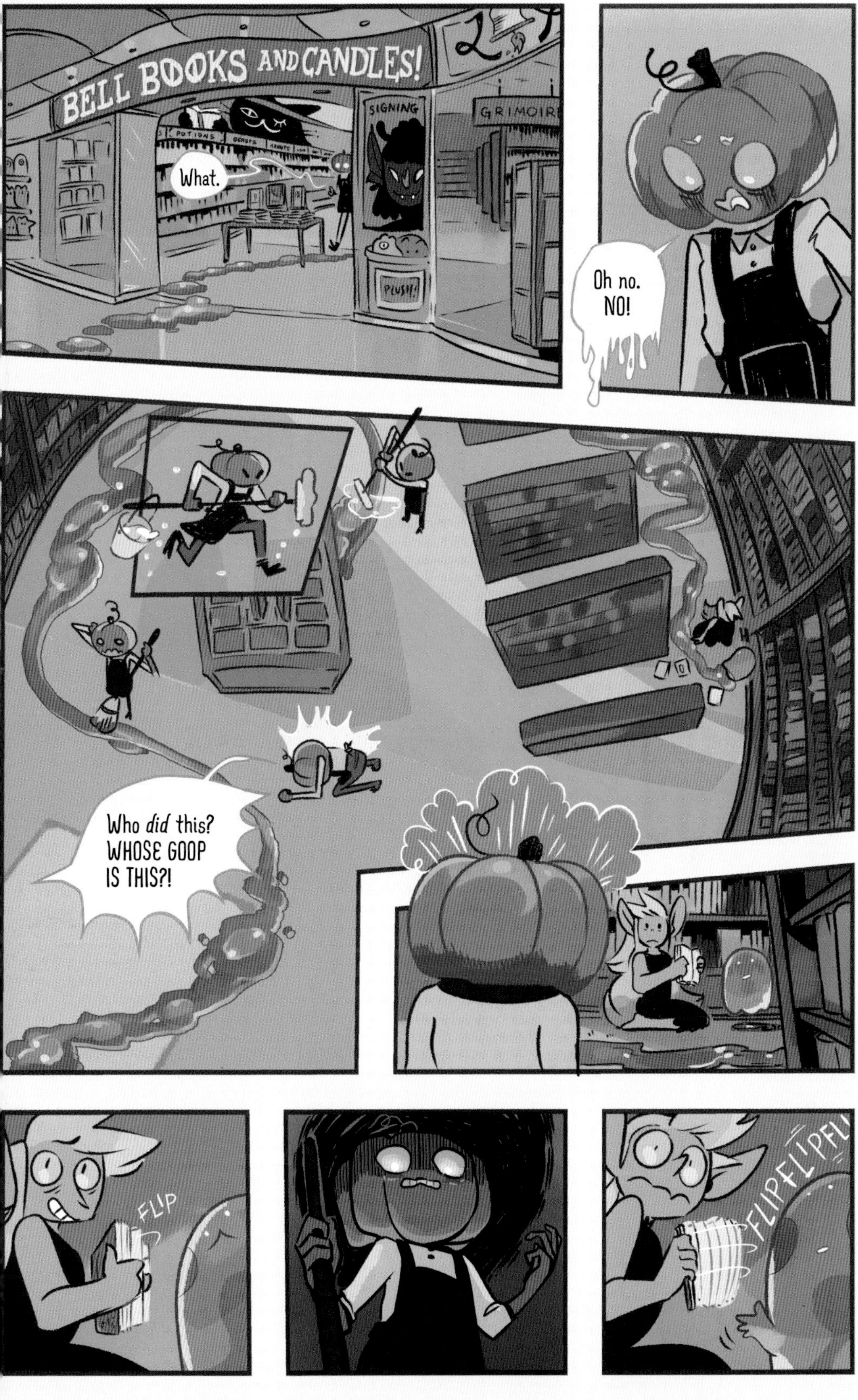
BELL BOOKS AND CANDLES!
SIGNING
GRIMOIRE
POTIONS
PLUSH!
What.
Oh no.
NO!
Who *did* this?
WHOSE GOOP
IS THIS?!
FLIP
FLIPFLIPFL

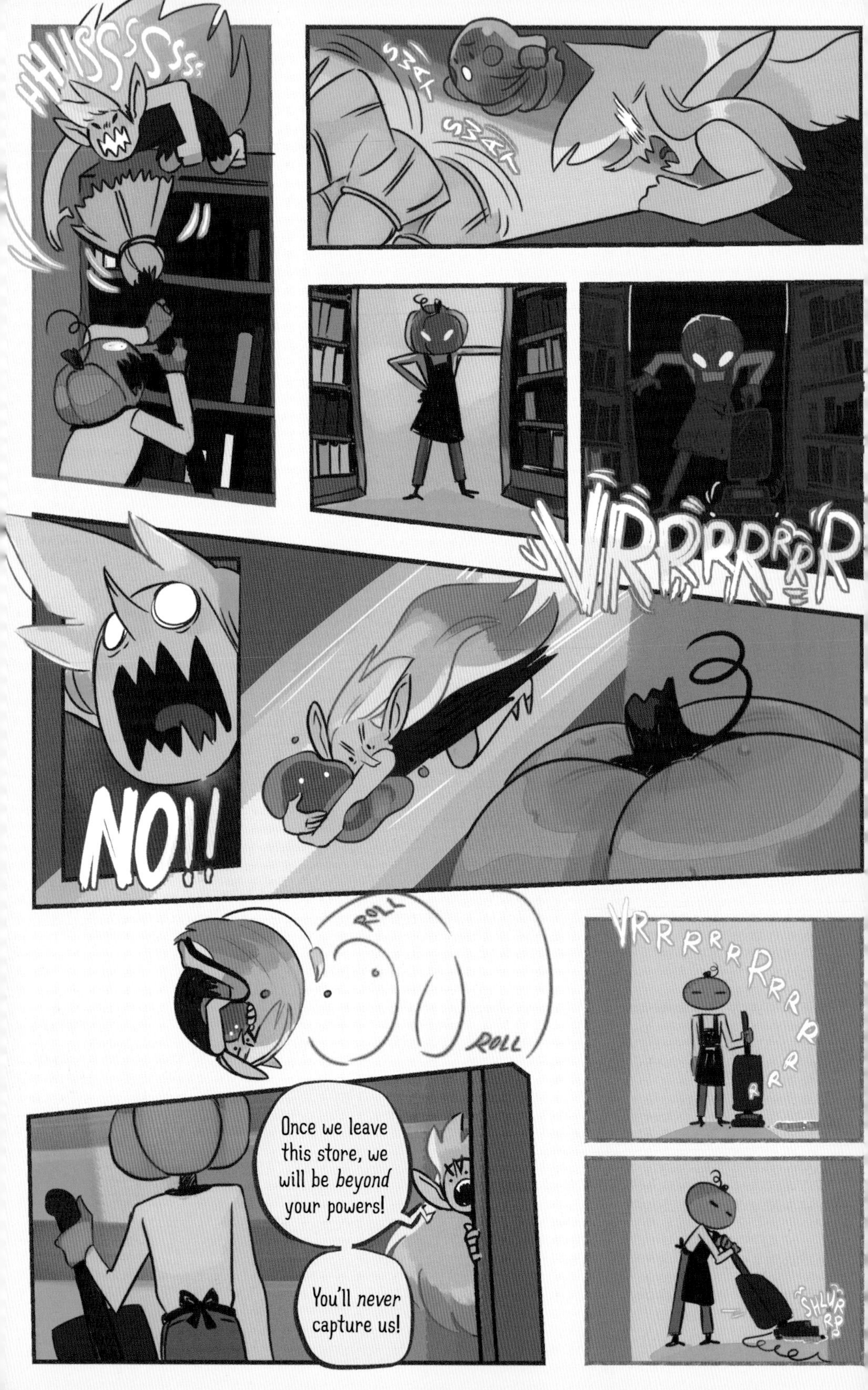

HHISSSSSsss
SSHAT
SSHAT
VRRRRRRRR
NO!!
ROLL
ROLL
VRRRRRRRRRRRRR
Once we leave this store, we will be *beyond* your powers!
You'll *never* capture us!
SHLURRP

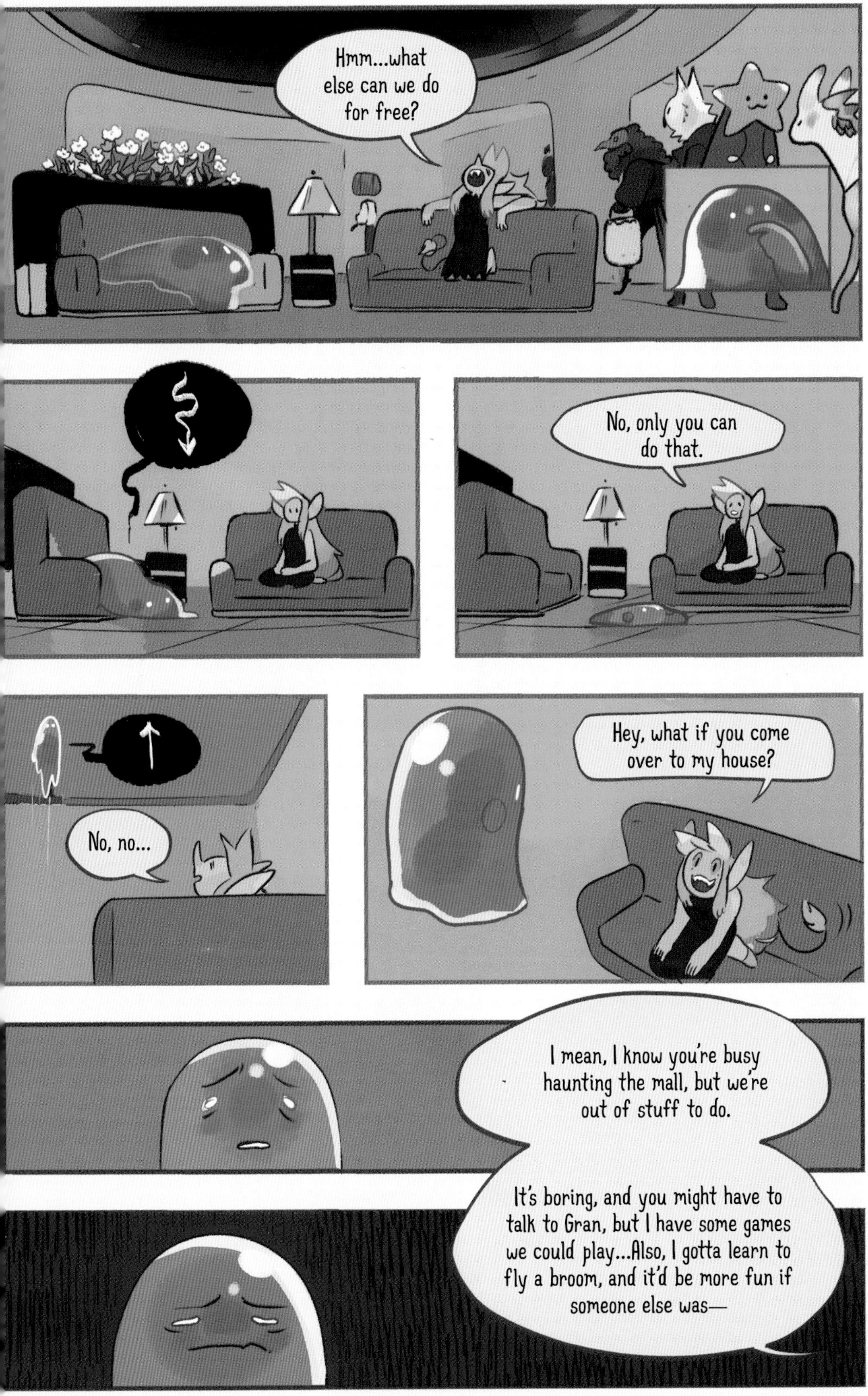
Hmm...what else can we do for free?
No, only you can do that.
No, no...
Hey, what if you come over to my house?
I mean, I know you're busy haunting the mall, but we're out of stuff to do.
It's boring, and you might have to talk to Gran, but I have some games we could play...Also, I gotta learn to fly a broom, and it'd be more fun if someone else was—

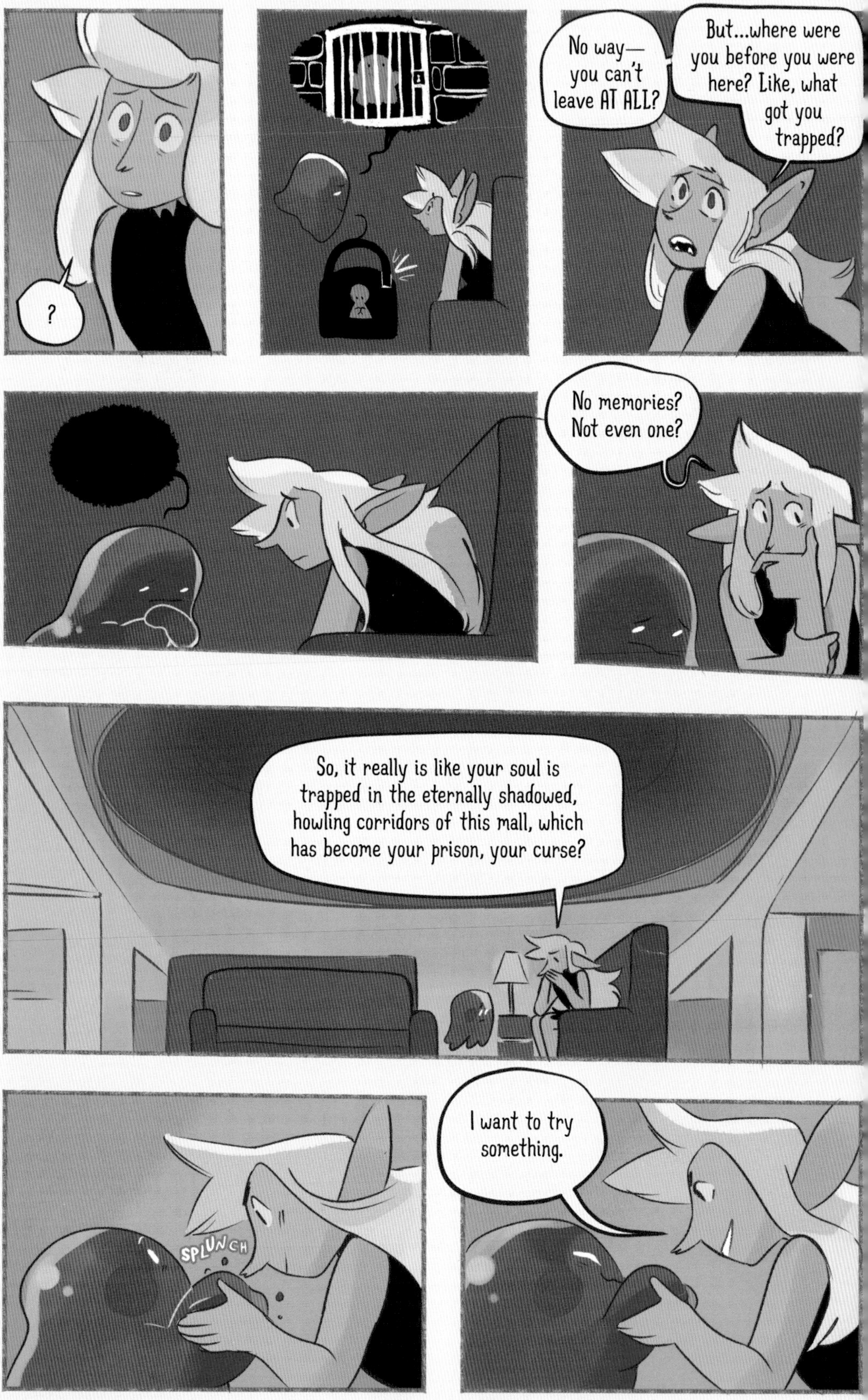
?
No way— you can't leave AT ALL?
But...where were you before you were here? Like, what got you trapped?
No memories? Not even one?
So, it really is like your soul is trapped in the eternally shadowed, howling corridors of this mall, which has become your prison, your curse?
SPLUNCH
I want to try something.

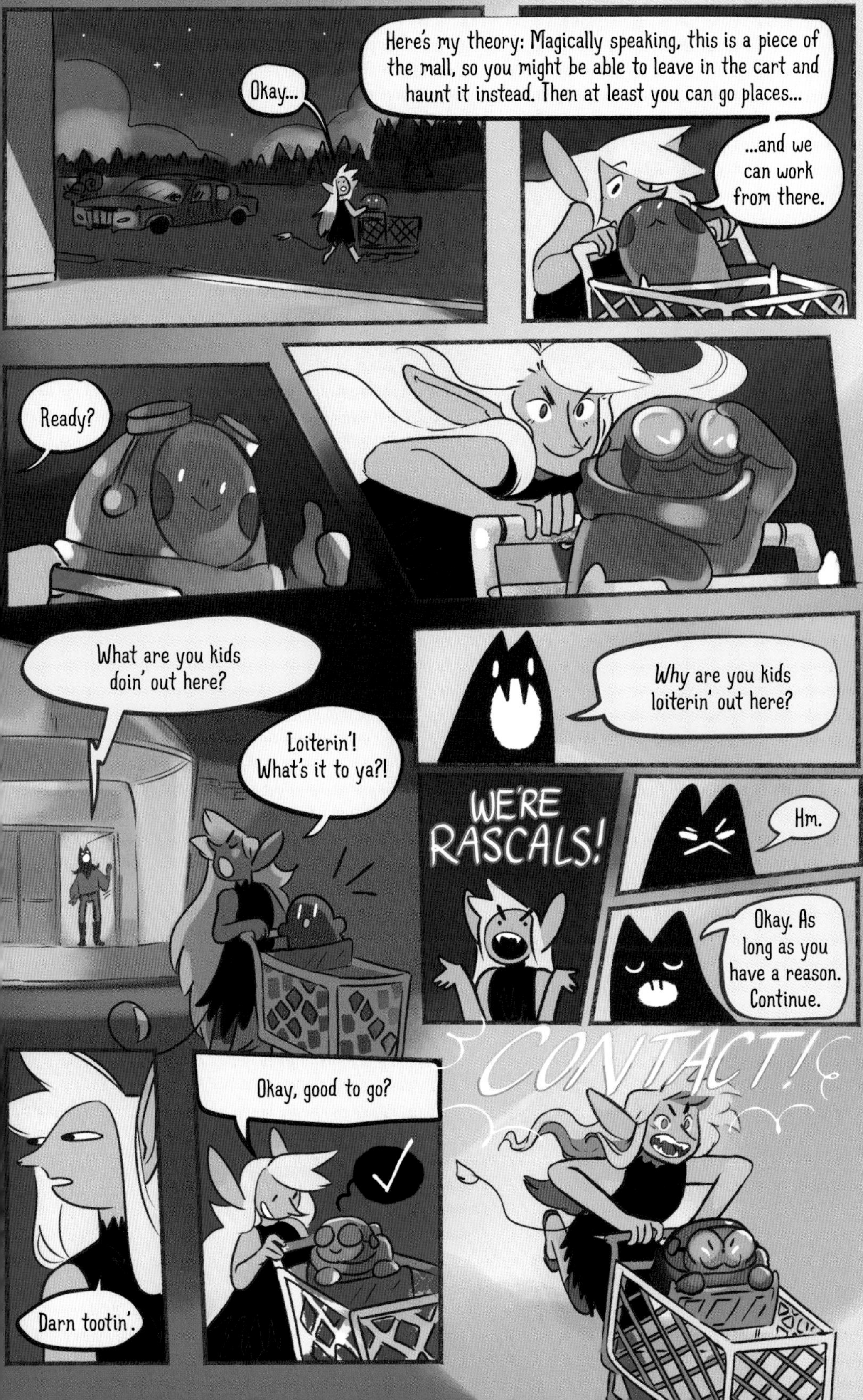
Okay...
Here's my theory: Magically speaking, this is a piece of the mall, so you might be able to leave in the cart and haunt it instead. Then at least you can go places...
...and we can work from there.
Ready?
What are you kids doin' out here?
Why are you kids loiterin' out here?
Loiterin'! What's it to ya?!
WE'RE RASCALS!
Hm.
Okay. As long as you have a reason. Continue.
Darn tootin'.
Okay, good to go?
CONTACT!

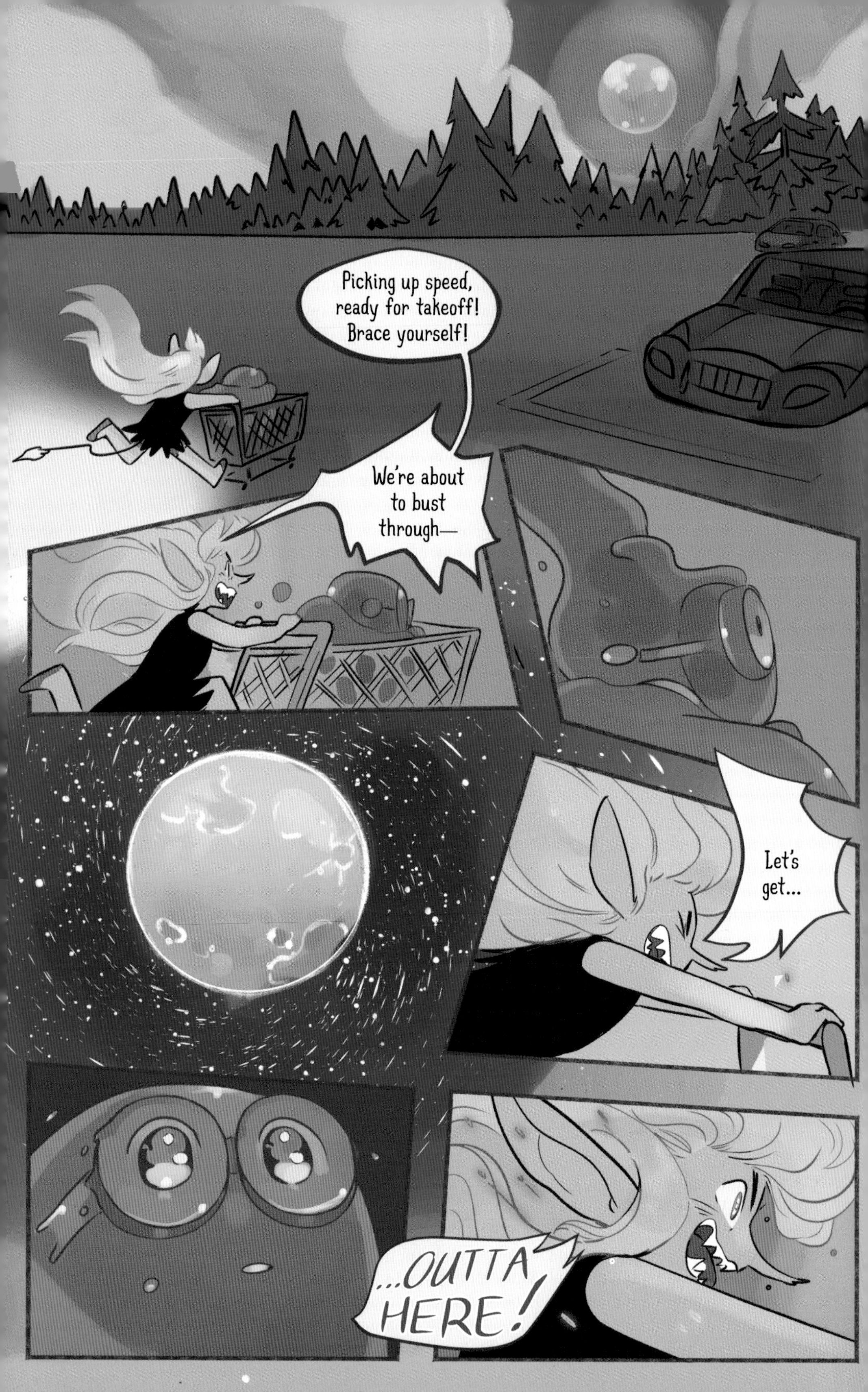

Picking up speed, ready for takeoff! Brace yourself!
We're about to bust through—
Let's get...
...OUTTA HERE!

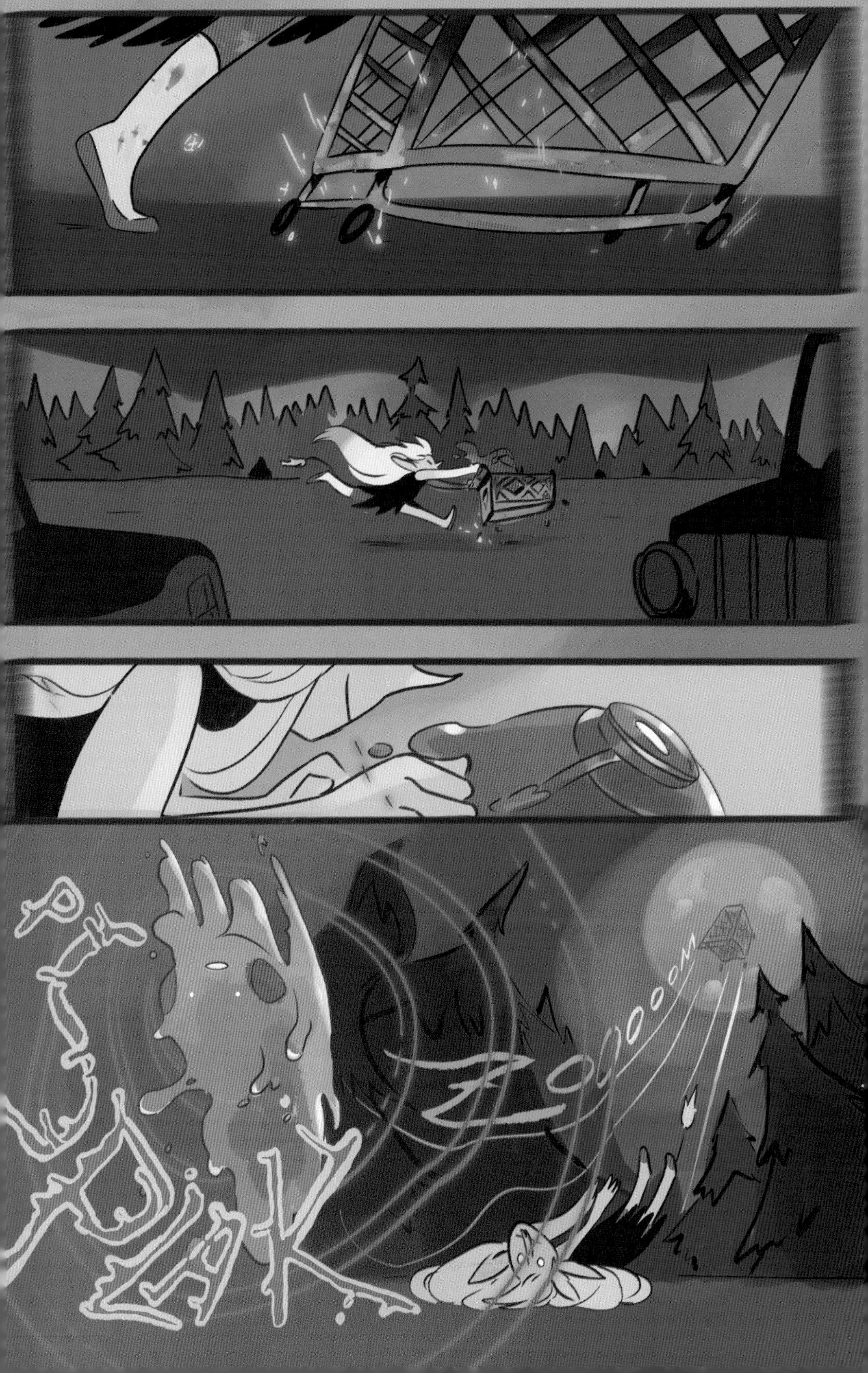

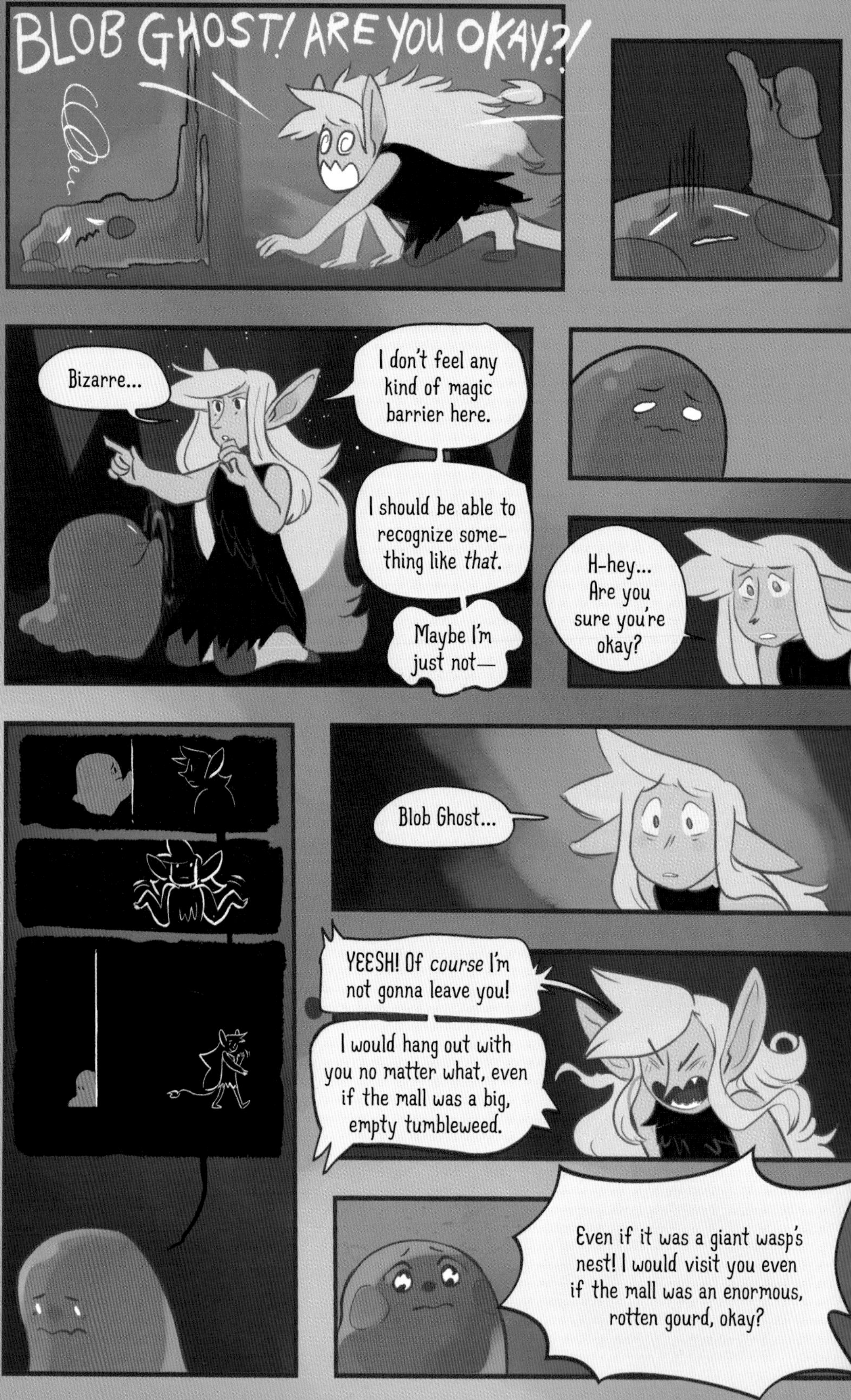
BLOB GHOST! ARE YOU OKAY?!
Bizarre...
I don't feel any kind of magic barrier here.
I should be able to recognize something like *that*.
Maybe I'm just not—
H-hey... Are you sure you're okay?
Blob Ghost...
YEESH! Of *course* I'm not gonna leave you!
I would hang out with you no matter what, even if the mall was a big, empty tumbleweed.
Even if it was a giant wasp's nest! I would visit you even if the mall was an enormous, rotten gourd, okay?

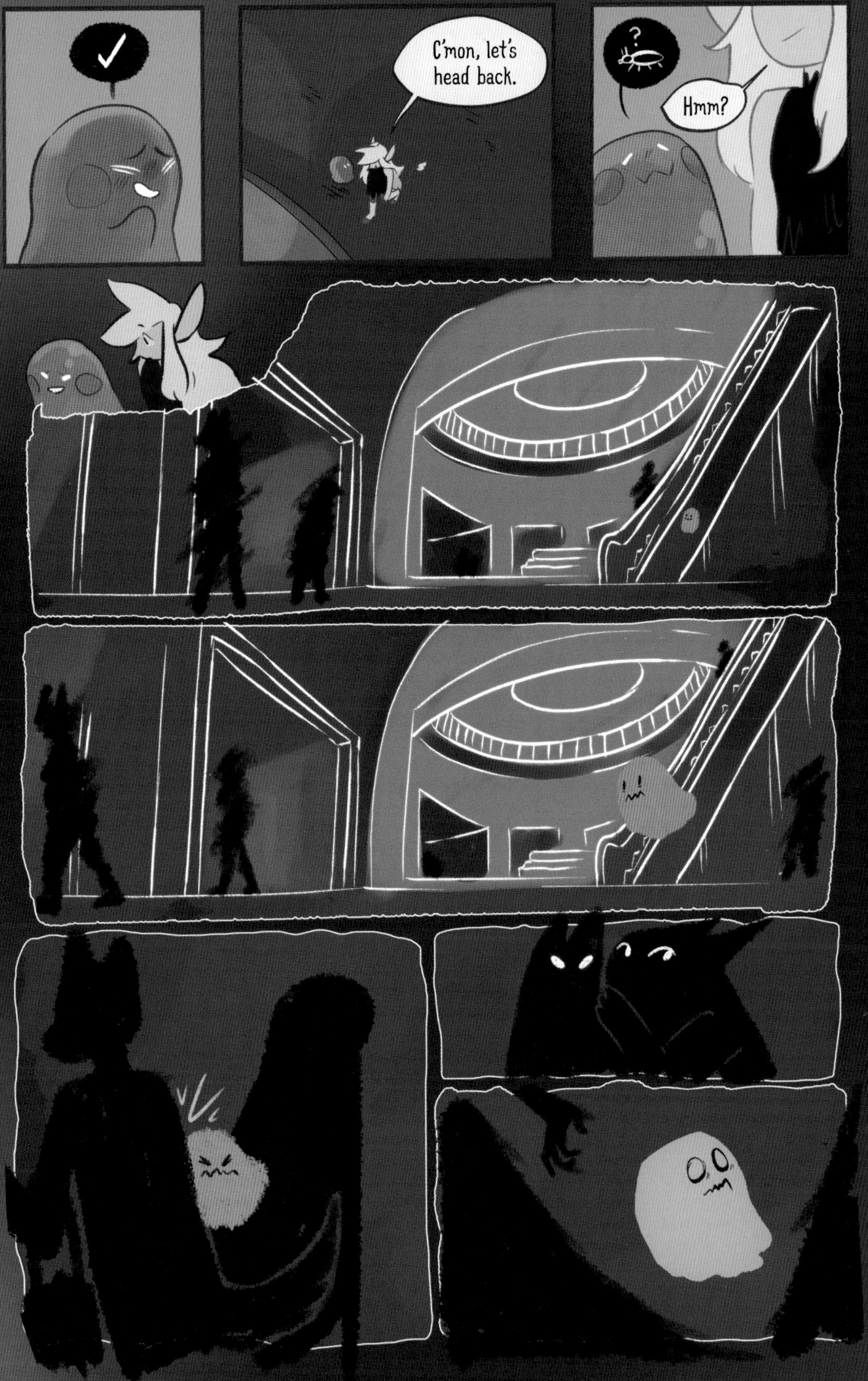
C'mon, let's head back.
Hmm?

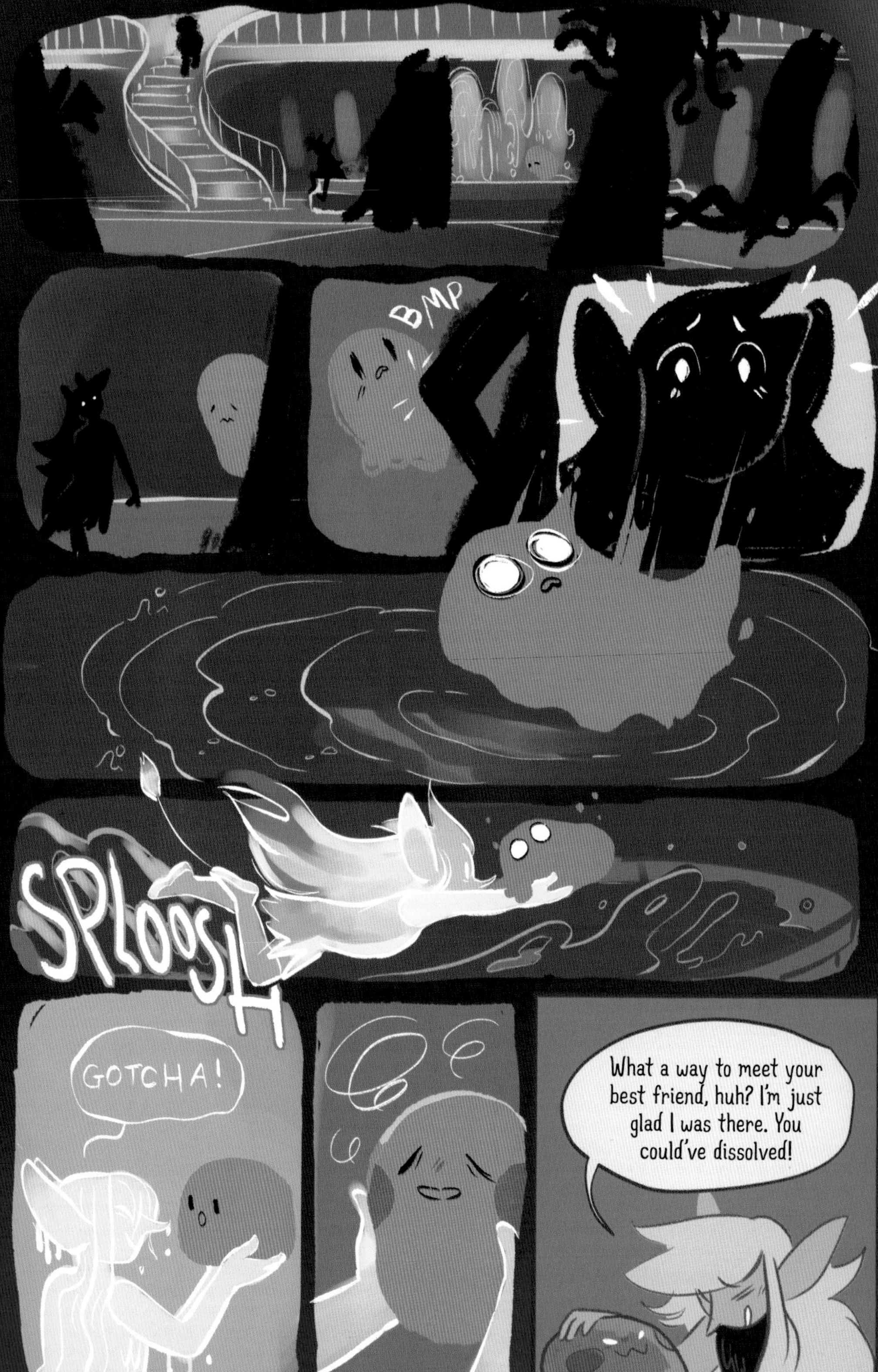
BMP
SPLOOSH
GOTCHA!
What a way to meet your best friend, huh? I'm just glad I was there. You could've dissolved!

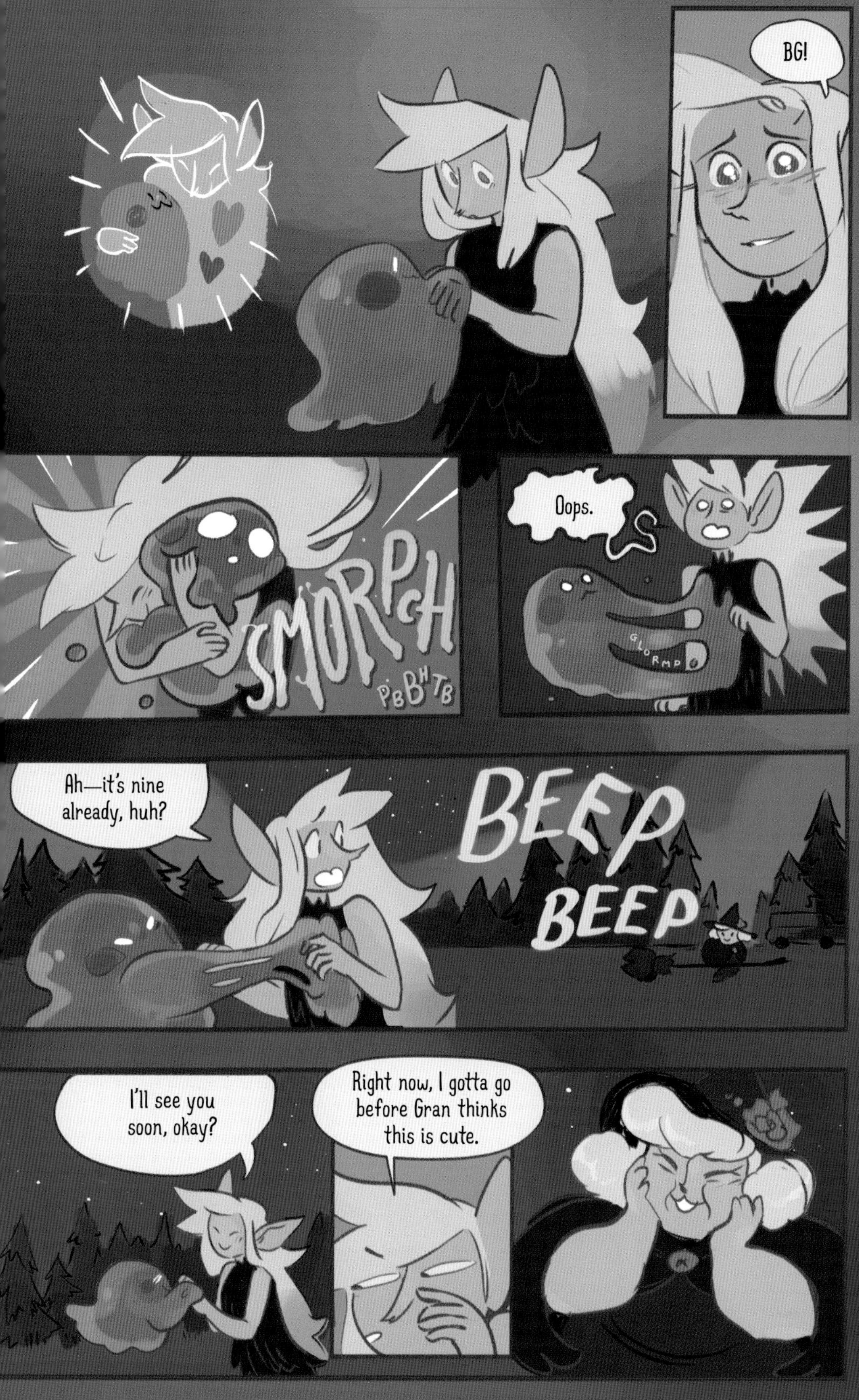
BG!
SMORPCH
PBBHTB
Oops.
GLORMP
Ah—it's nine already, huh?
BEEP
BEEP
I'll see you soon, okay?
Right now, I gotta go before Gran thinks this is cute.

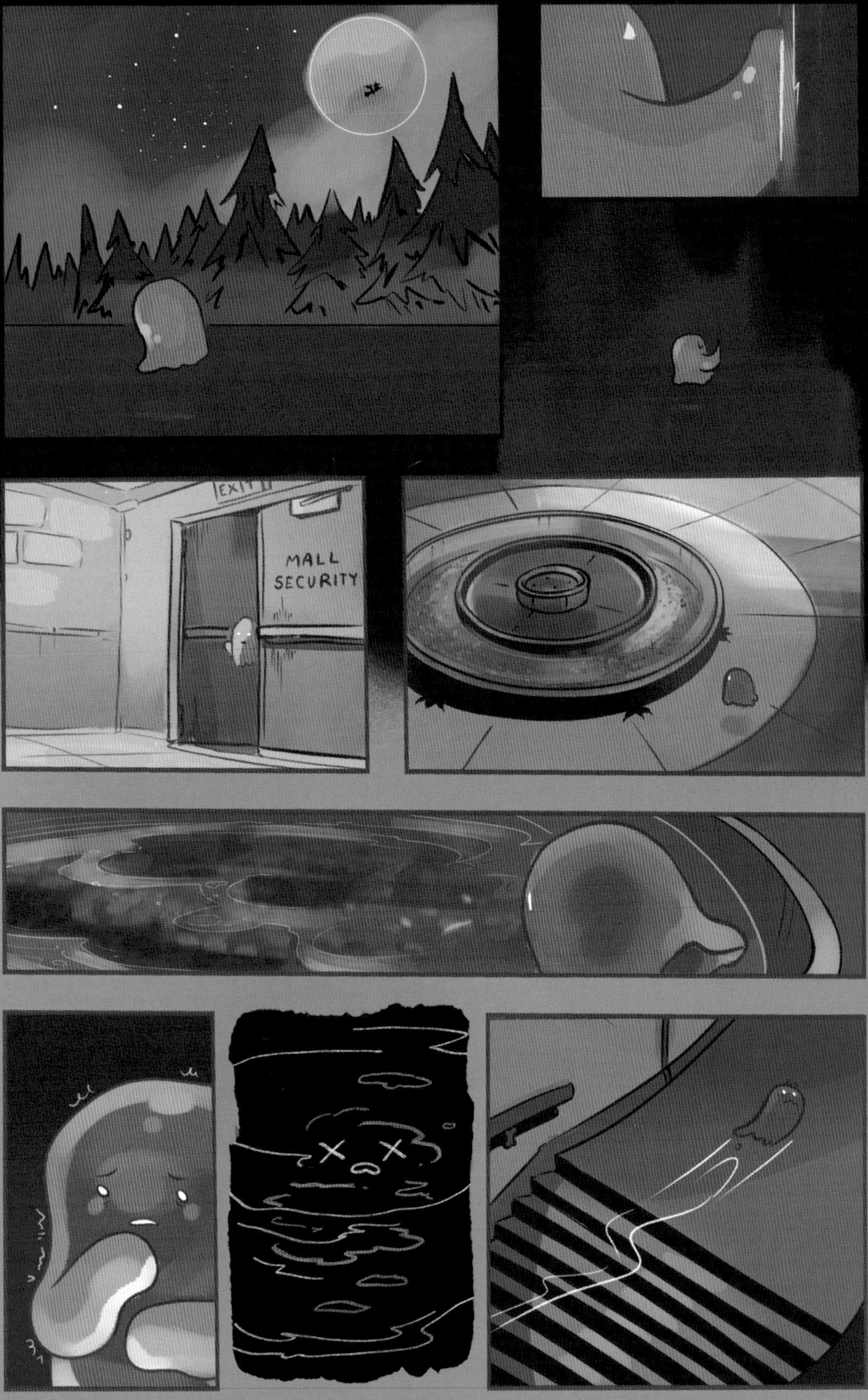
EXIT
MALL SECURITY

STORE
FRONT
FOR
RENT

MALL
OFFICE:
*018-88-8

SPACE UNDER
RENOVATION

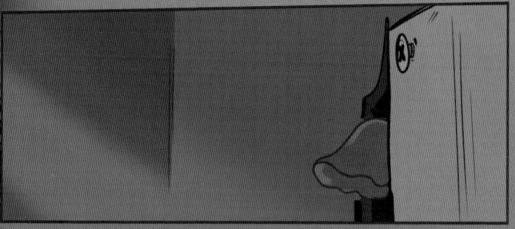

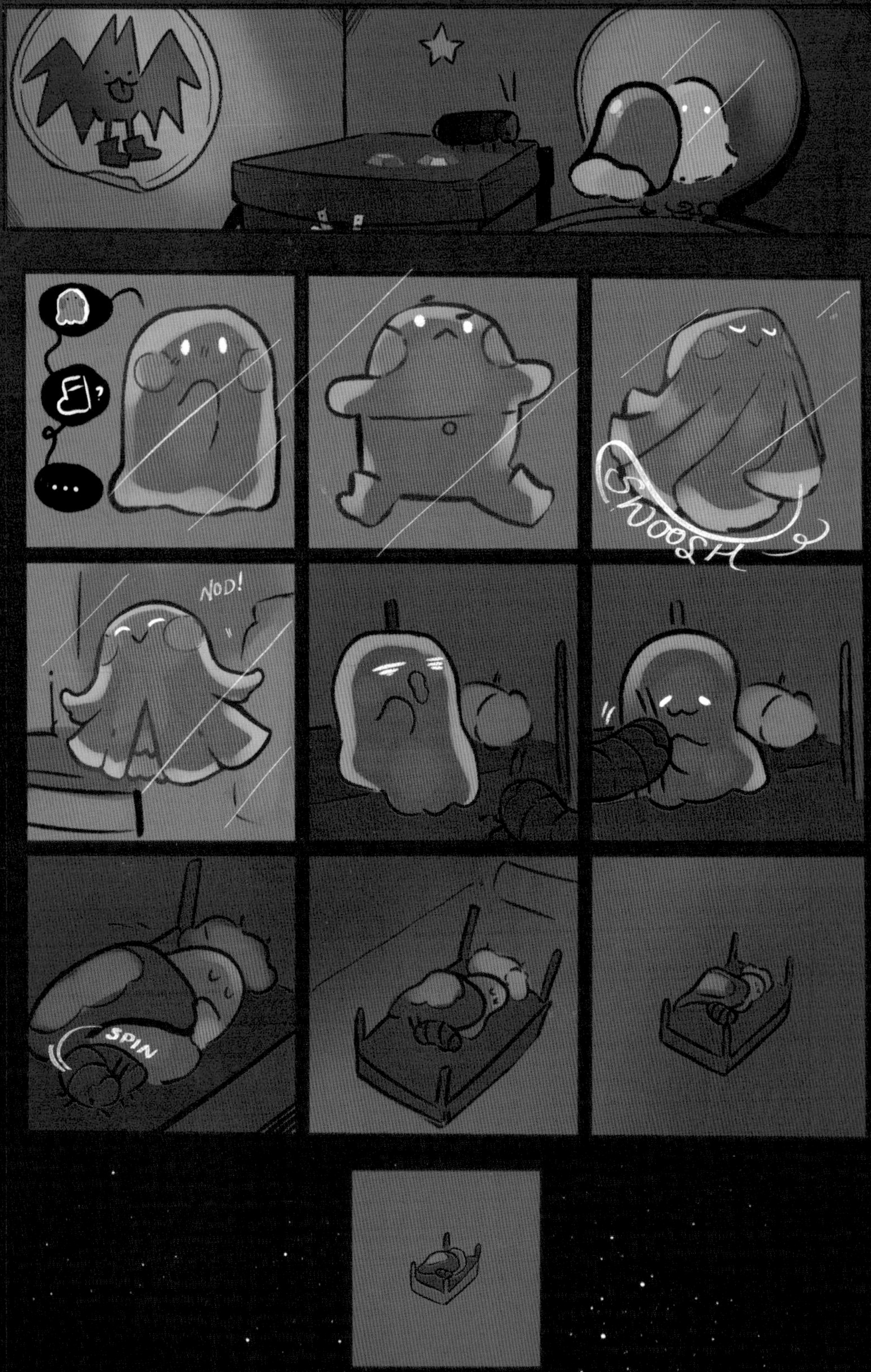

...
SWOOSH
NOD!
SPIN

Posts Past

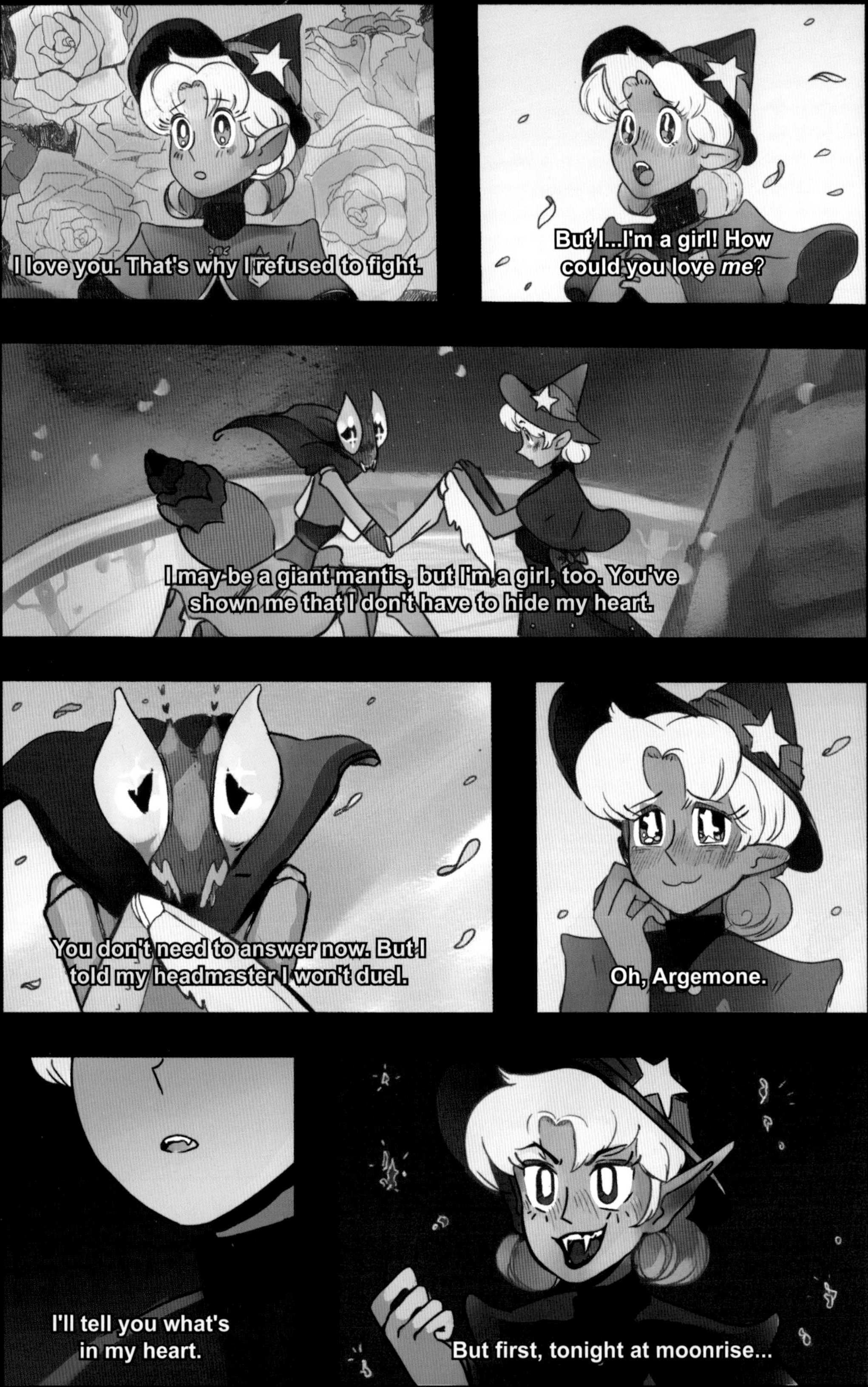
I love you. That's why I refused to fight.
But I...I'm a girl! How could you love *me*?
I may be a giant mantis, but I'm a girl, too. You've shown me that I don't have to hide my heart.
You don't need to answer now. But I told my headmaster I won't duel.
Oh, Argemone.
I'll tell you what's in my heart.
But first, tonight at moonrise...

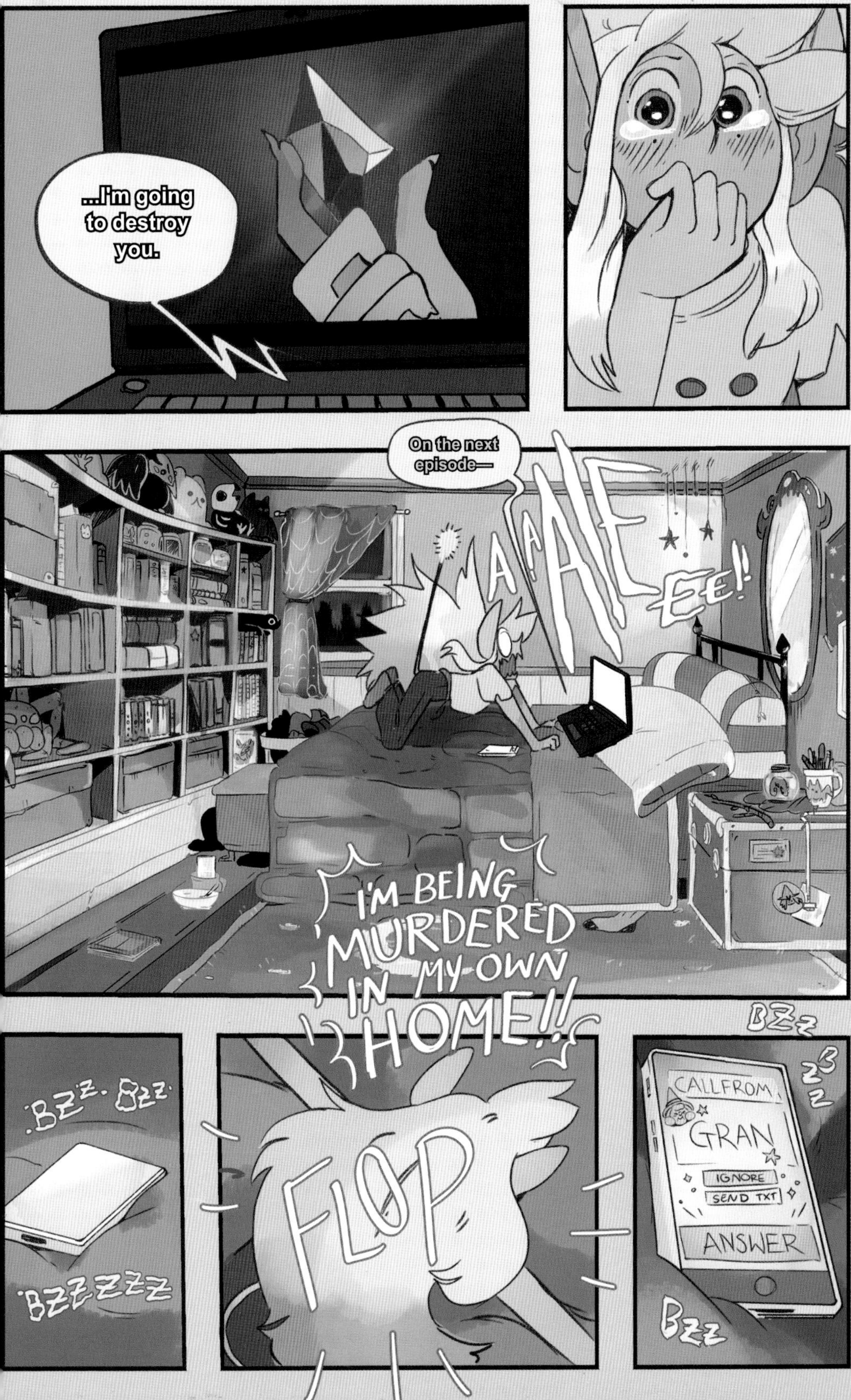
...I'm going to destroy you.
On the next episode—
AAAAEEE!!
I'M BEING MURDERED IN MY OWN HOME!!
BZZ. BZZ
BZZZZZZ
FLOP
BZZ
ZZZ
CALL FROM
GRAN
IGNORE
SEND TXT
ANSWER
BZZ

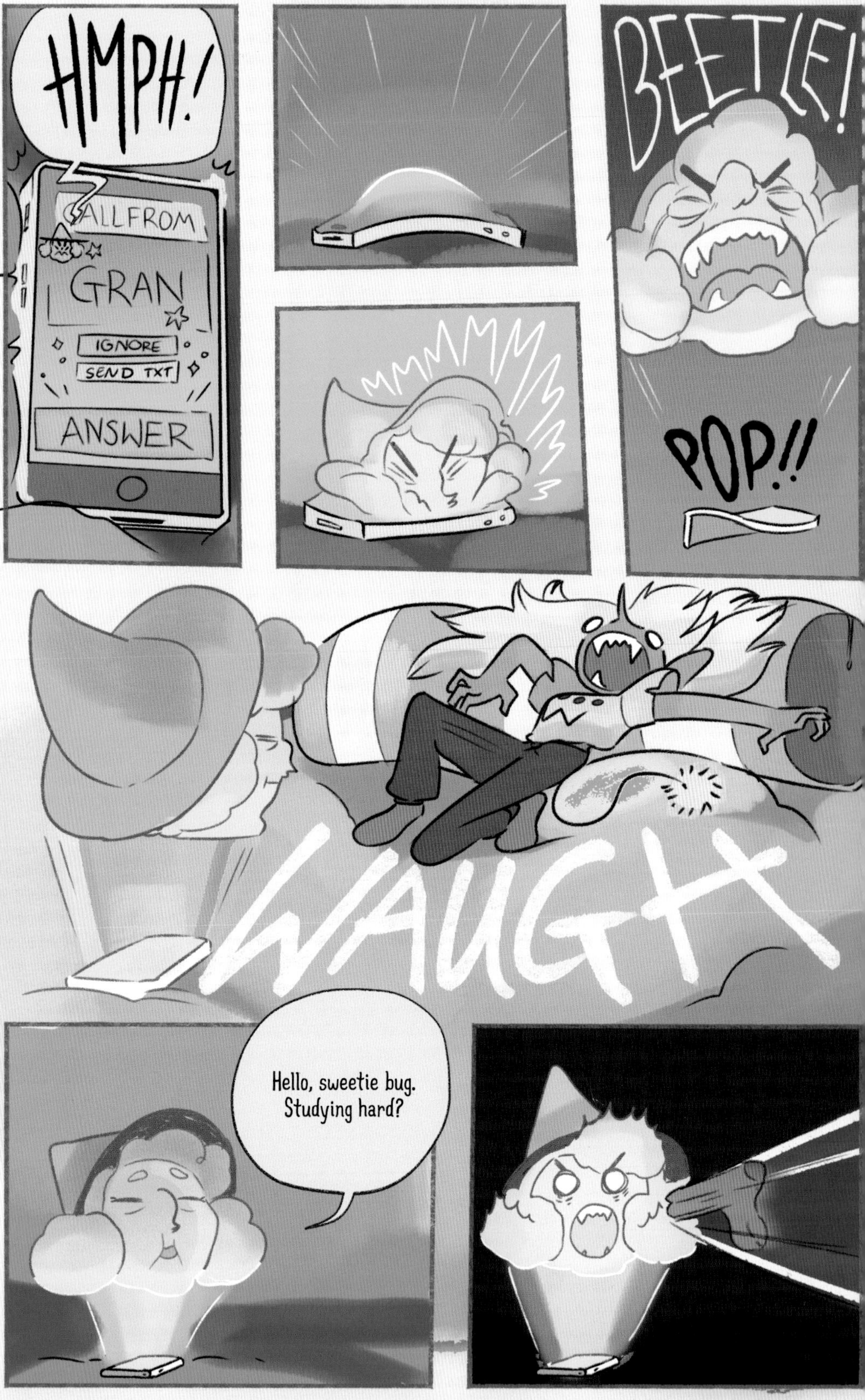
HMPH!
CALLFROM
GRAN
IGNORE
SEND TXT
ANSWER
MMMMMMM
BEETLE!
POP!!
WAUGH
Hello, sweetie bug. Studying hard?

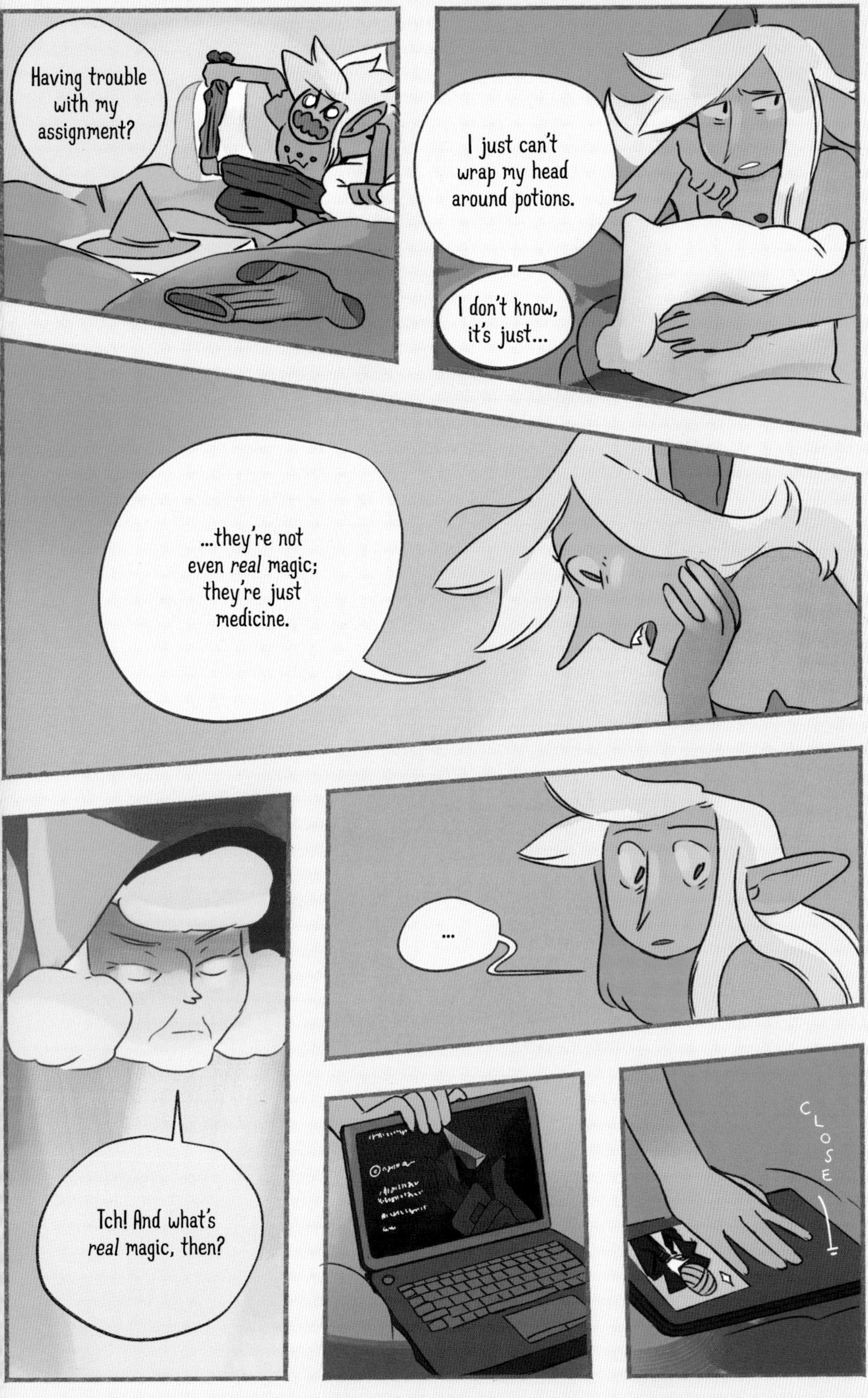
Having trouble with my assignment?
I just can't wrap my head around potions.
I don't know, it's just...
...they're not even *real* magic; they're just medicine.
Tch! And what's *real* magic, then?
...
CLOSE

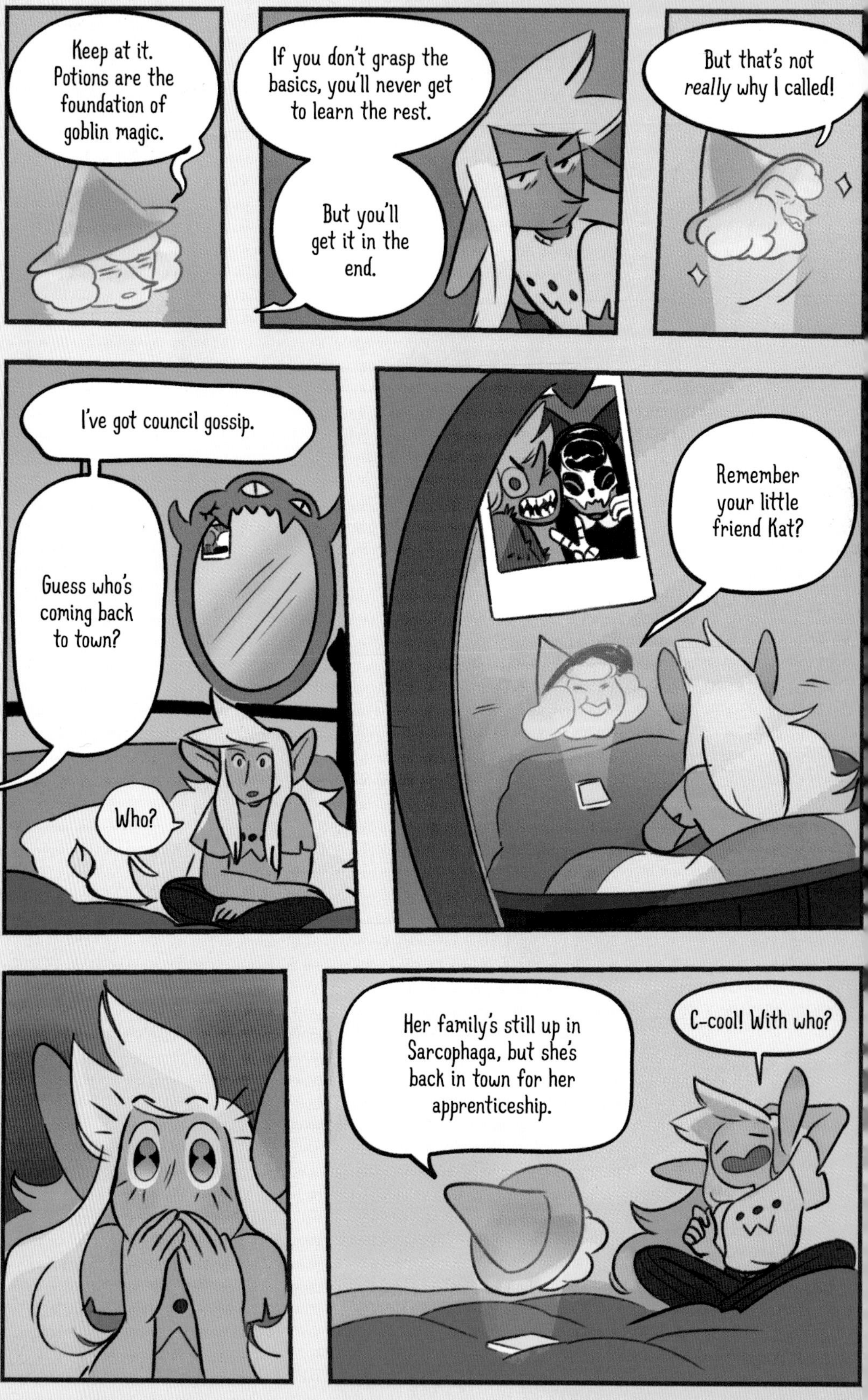
Keep at it. Potions are the foundation of goblin magic.
If you don't grasp the basics, you'll never get to learn the rest.
But you'll get it in the end.
But that's not *really* why I called!
I've got council gossip.
Guess who's coming back to town?
Who?
Remember your little friend Kat?
Her family's still up in Sarcophaga, but she's back in town for her apprenticeship.
C-cool! With who?

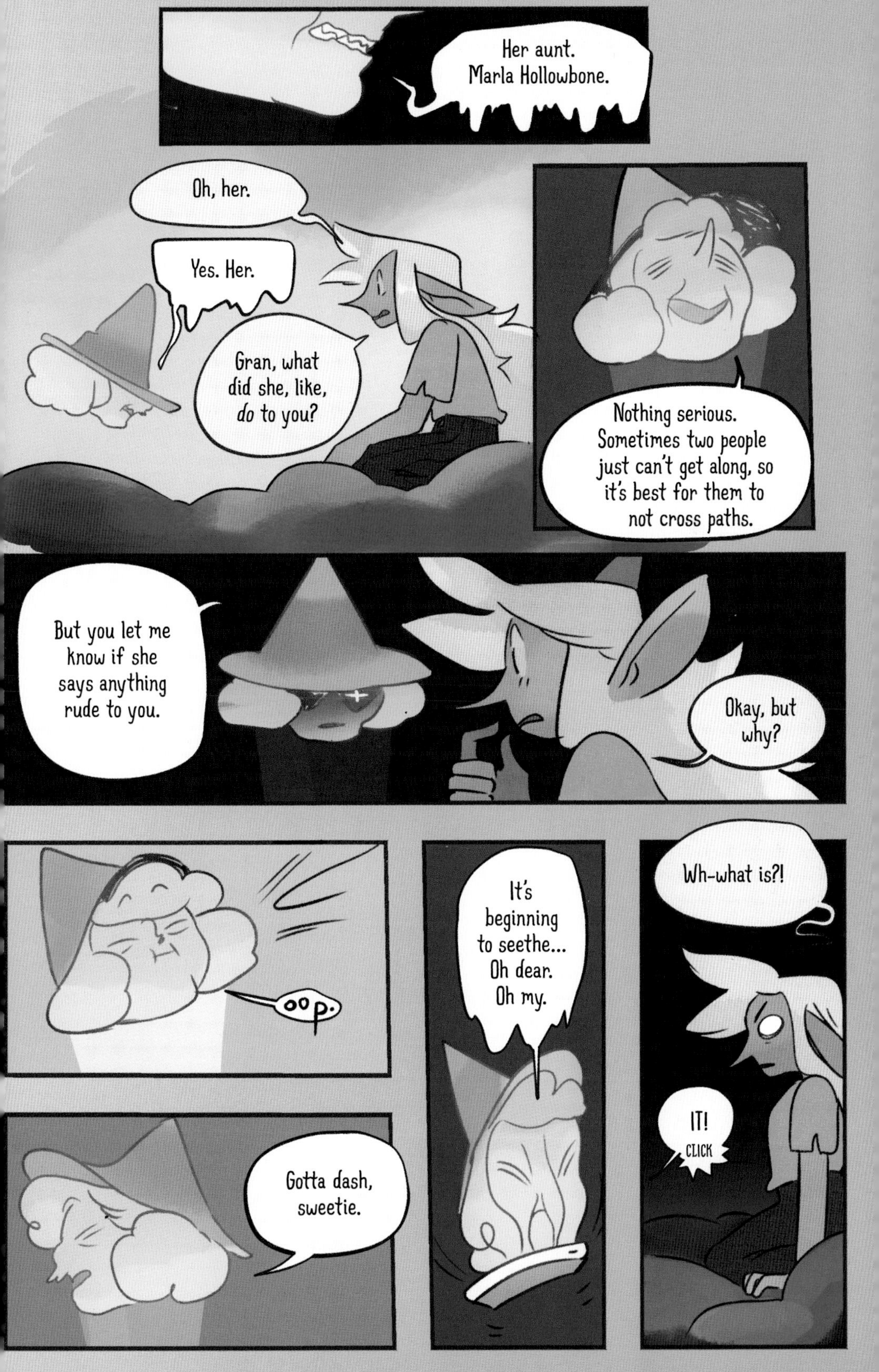
Her aunt. Marla Hollowbone.
Oh, her.
Yes. Her.
Gran, what did she, like, *do* to you?
Nothing serious. Sometimes two people just can't get along, so it's best for them to not cross paths.
But you let me know if she says anything rude to you.
Okay, but why?
oop.
Gotta dash, sweetie.
It's beginning to seethe... Oh dear. Oh my.
Wh-what is?!
IT!
CLICK

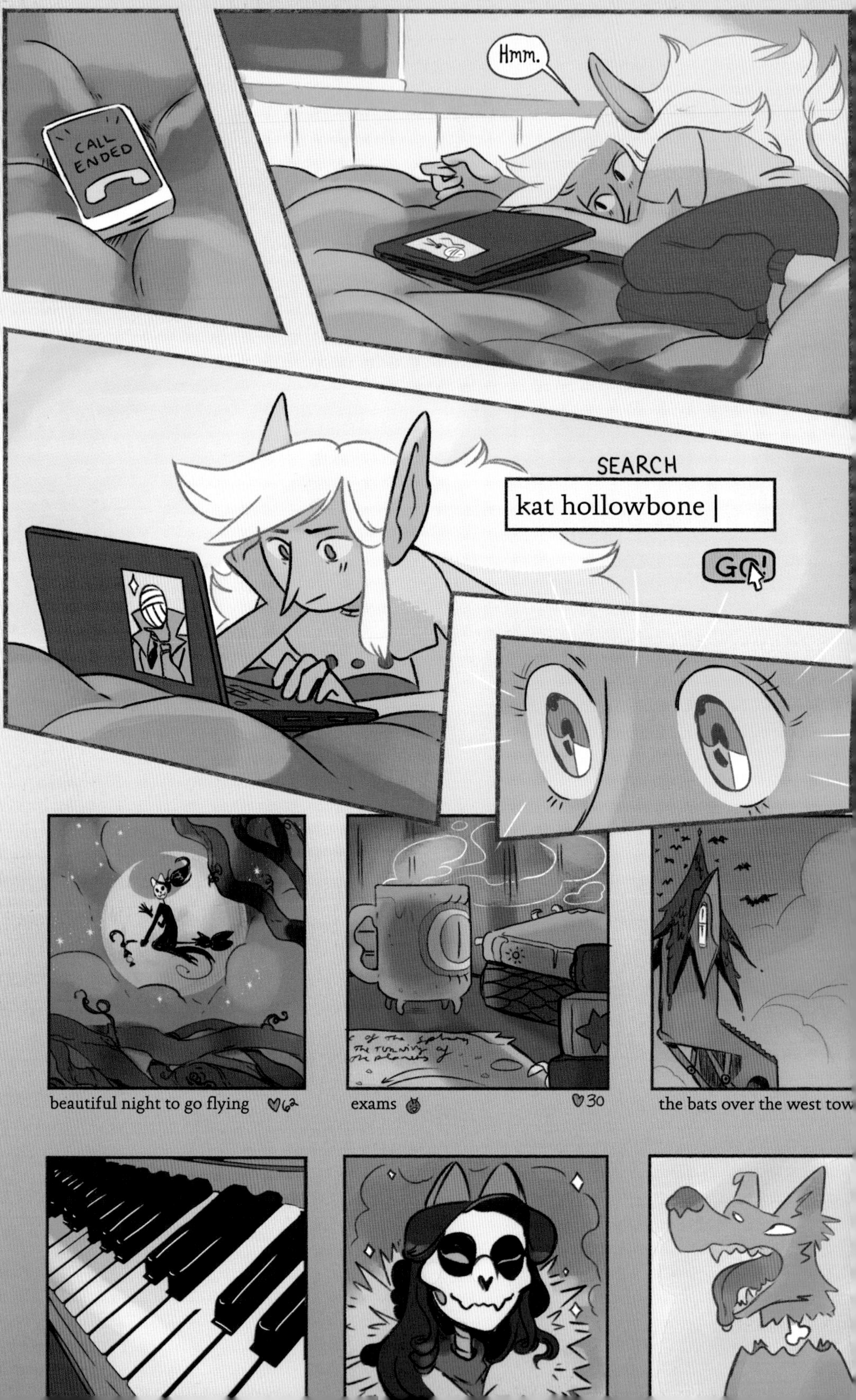
CALL ENDED
Hmm.
SEARCH
kat hollowbone |
GO!
beautiful night to go flying
62
exams
30
the bats over the west tow

KAT 🐾
SKELETON CAT &
SORCERESS IN TRAINING

FOLLOWERS
·2,103

OFFICIAL
SORCERY
APPRENTICE

♥300

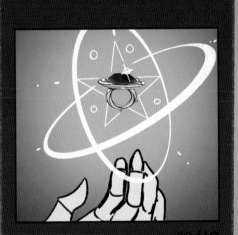

♥119

♥808

TWO THOUSAND FOLLOWERS?!?!?

She hasn't unfollowed me yet.
Good start, I guess.

Huh. Those
must be her
new friends.

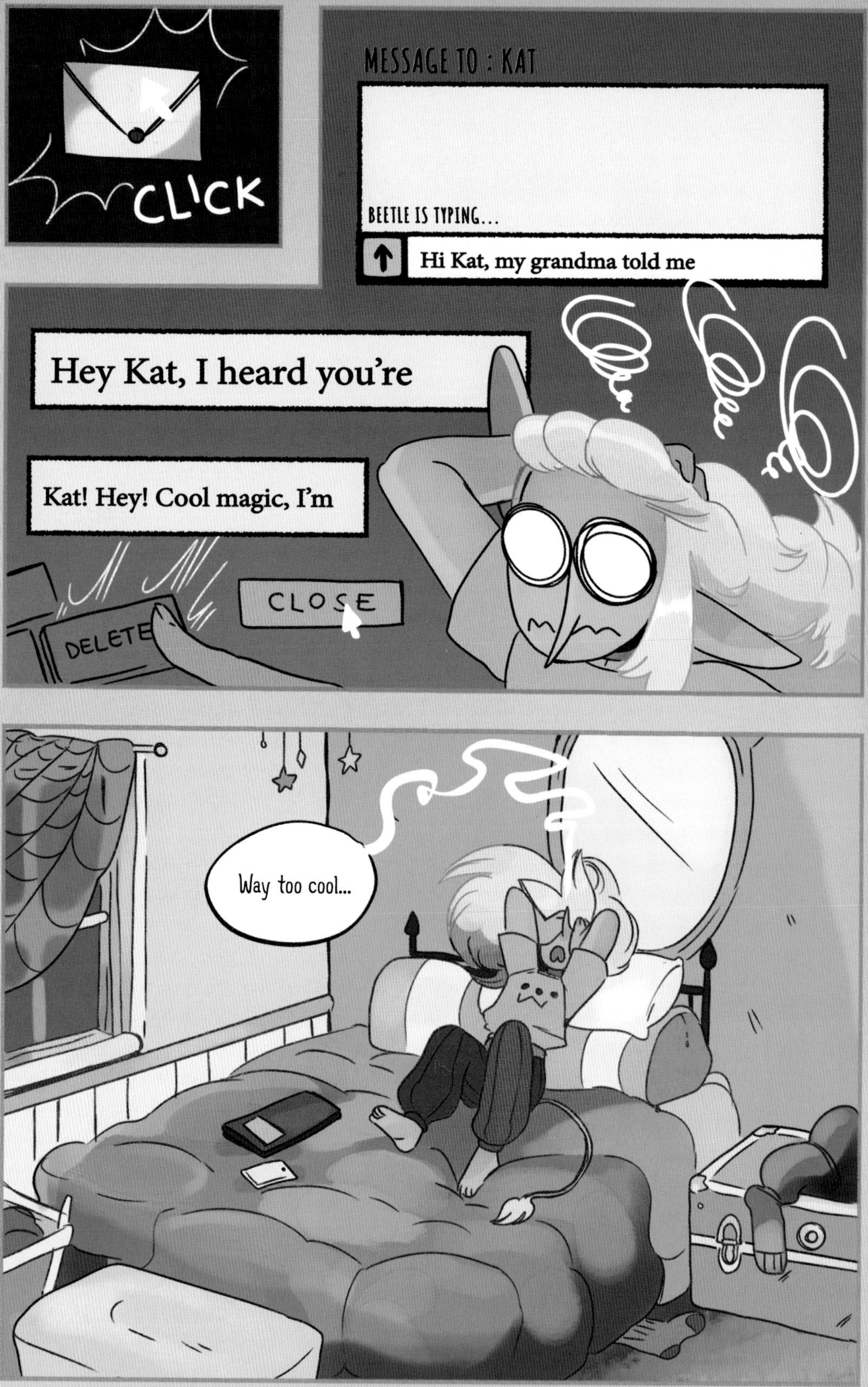
CLICK
MESSAGE TO : KAT
BEETLE IS TYPING...
Hi Kat, my grandma told me
Hey Kat, I heard you're
Kat! Hey! Cool magic, I'm
DELETE
CLOSE
Way too cool...

Kat Hollowbone

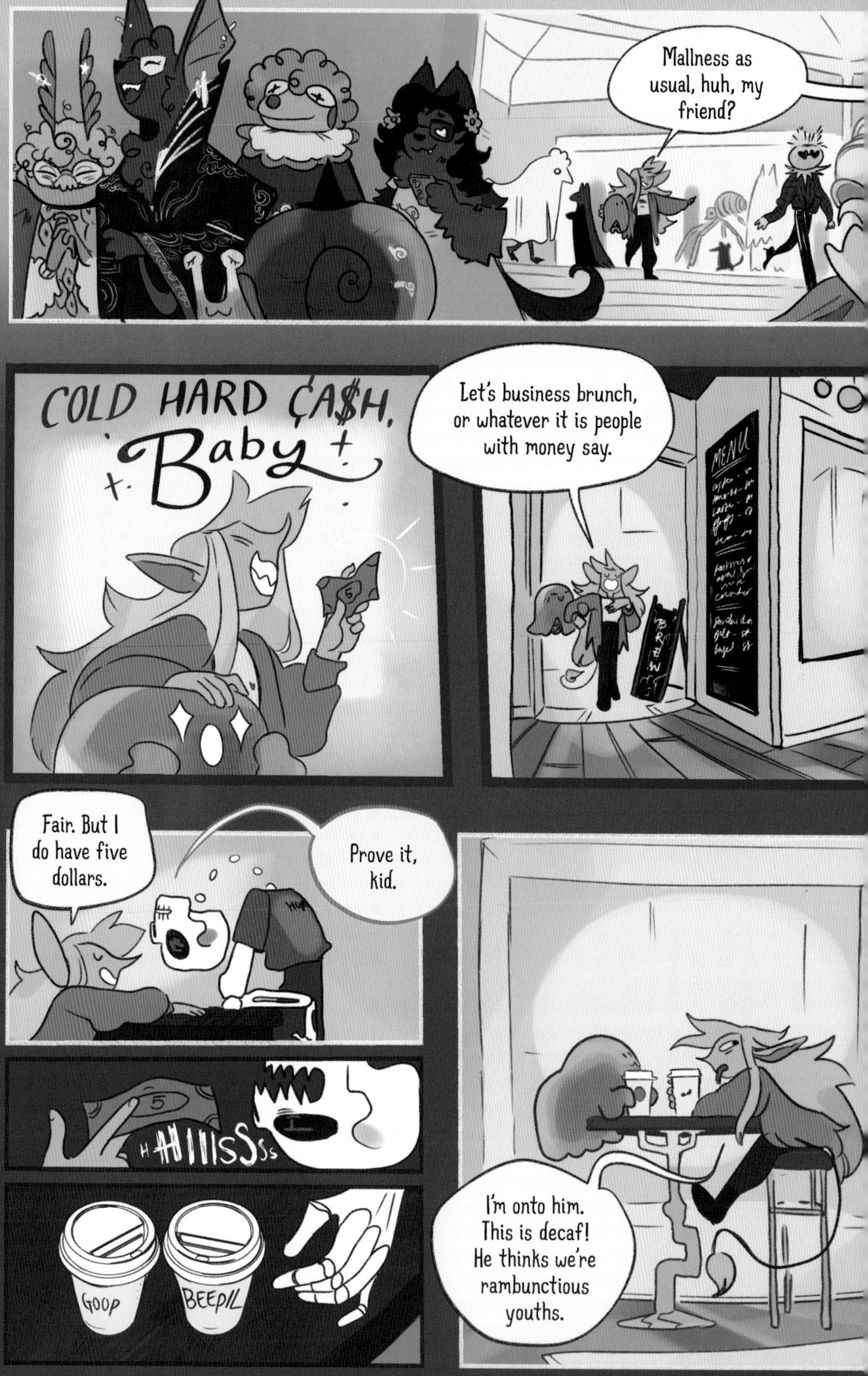
Mallness as usual, huh, my friend?
COLD HARD CA$H, Baby
Let's business brunch, or whatever it is people with money say.
MENU
Fair. But I do have five dollars.
Prove it, kid.
HHIIISSSs
GOOP
BEEPIL
I'm onto him. This is decaf! He thinks we're rambunctious youths.

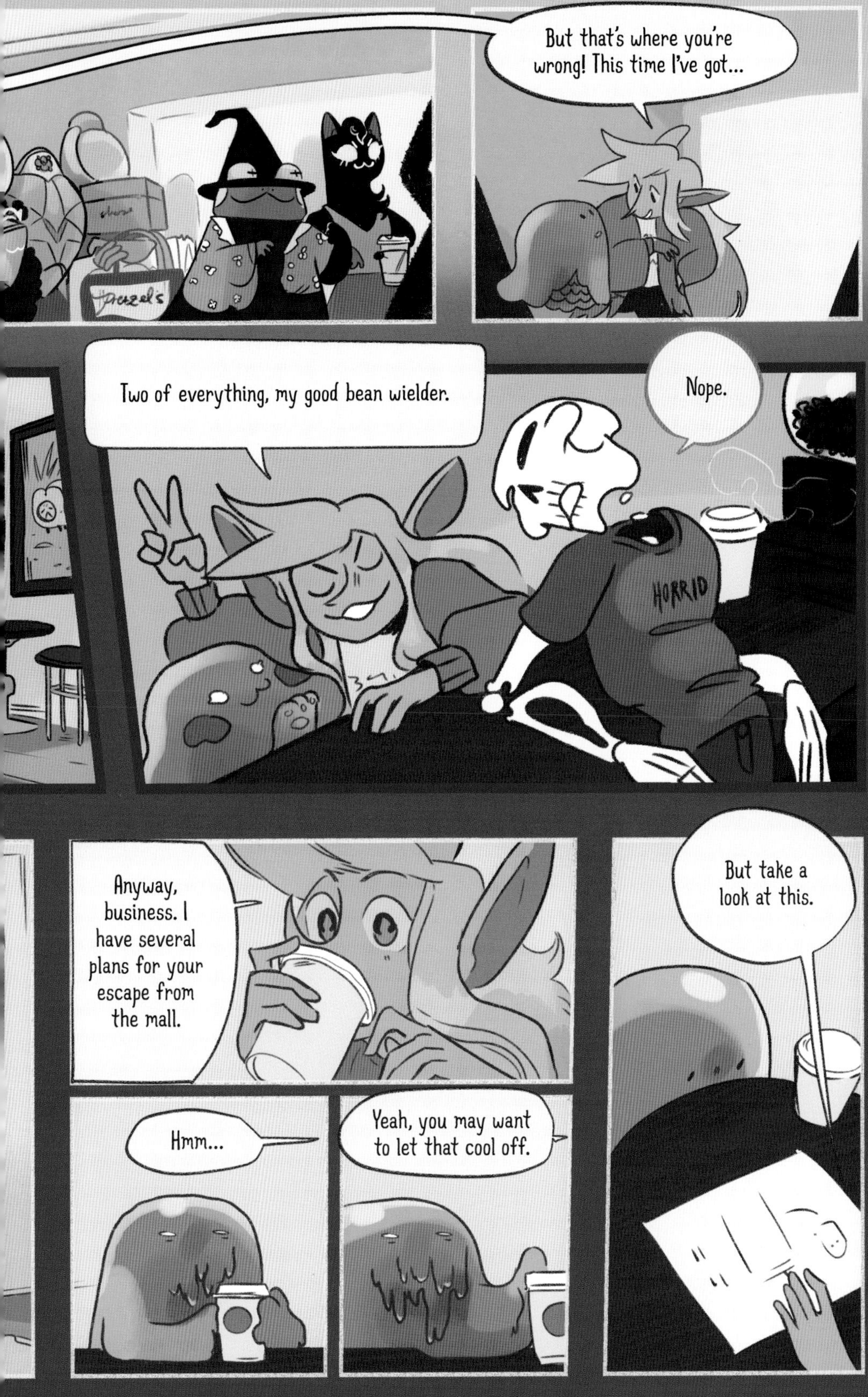
But that's where you're wrong! This time I've got...
Two of everything, my good bean wielder.
Nope.
HORRID
Anyway, business. I have several plans for your escape from the mall.
But take a look at this.
Hmm...
Yeah, you may want to let that cool off.

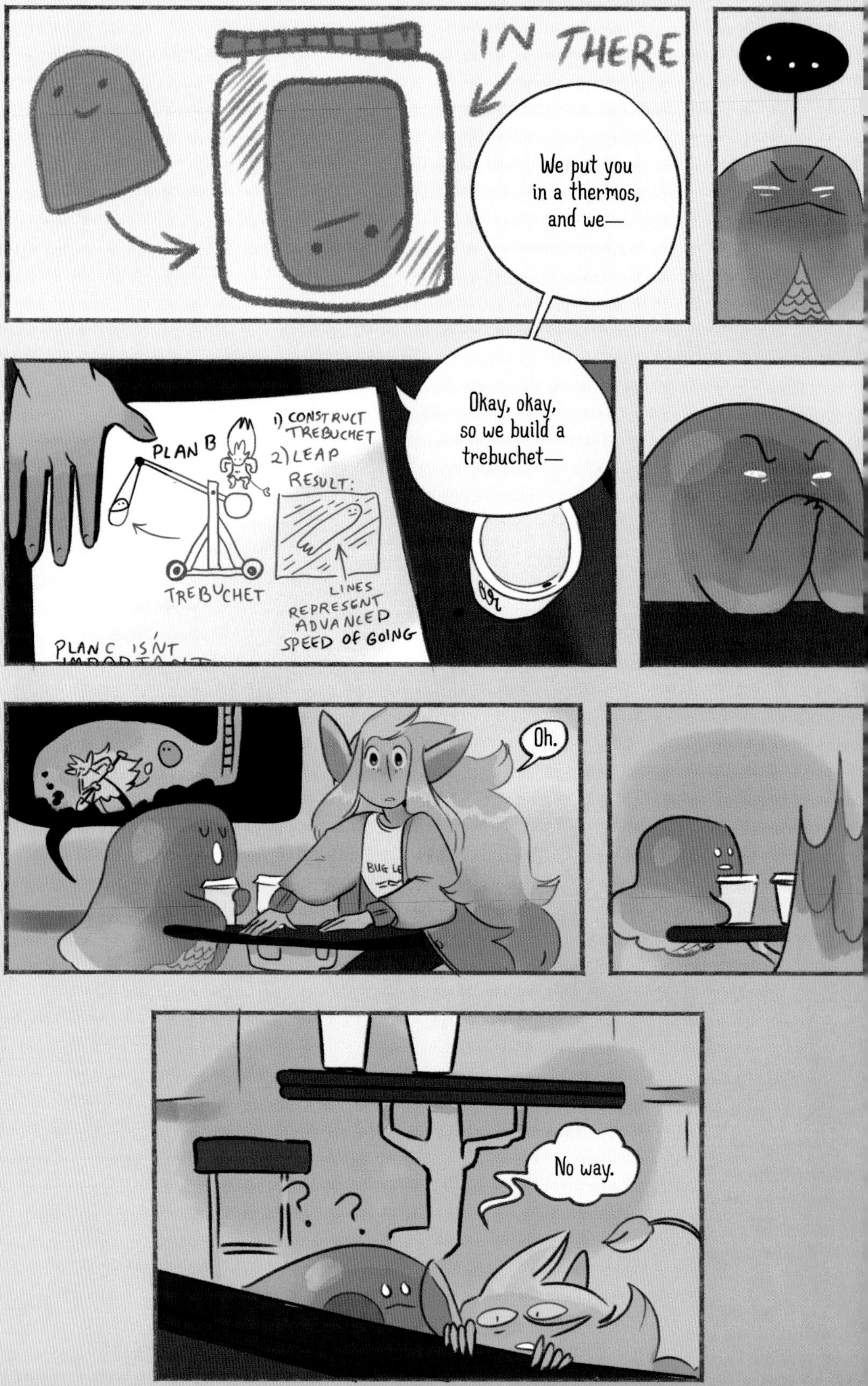
IN THERE
We put you in a thermos, and we—
...
Okay, okay, so we build a trebuchet—
PLAN B
1) CONSTRUCT TREBUCHET
2) LEAP
RESULT:
TREBUCHET
LINES REPRESENT ADVANCED SPEED OF GOING
PLAN C ISN'T
Oh.
BUG LE
No way.

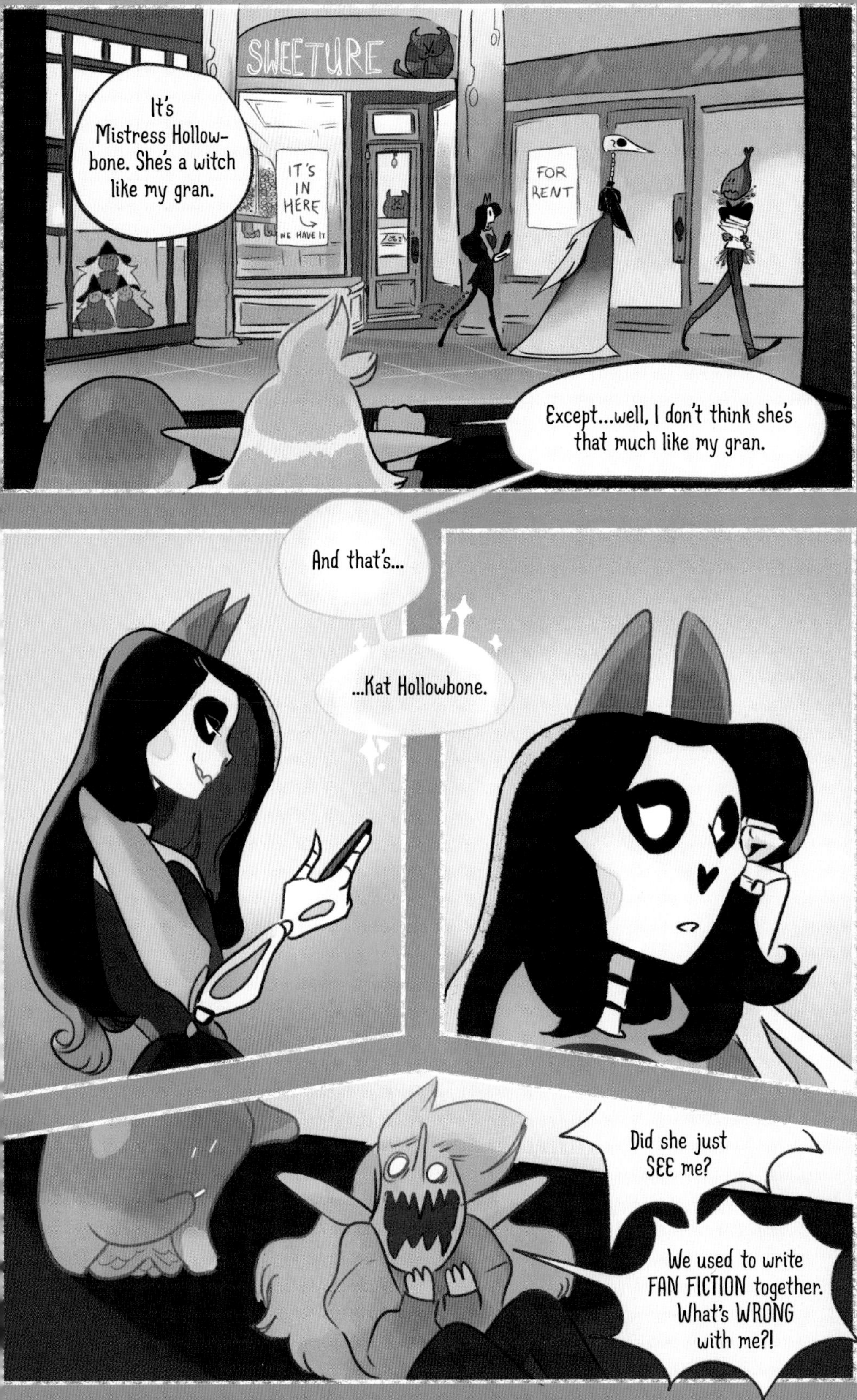
SWEETURE
IT'S IN HERE WE HAVE IT
FOR RENT
It's Mistress Hollow-bone. She's a witch like my gran.
Except...well, I don't think she's that much like my gran.
And that's...
...Kat Hollowbone.
Did she just SEE me?
We used to write FAN FICTION together. What's WRONG with me?!

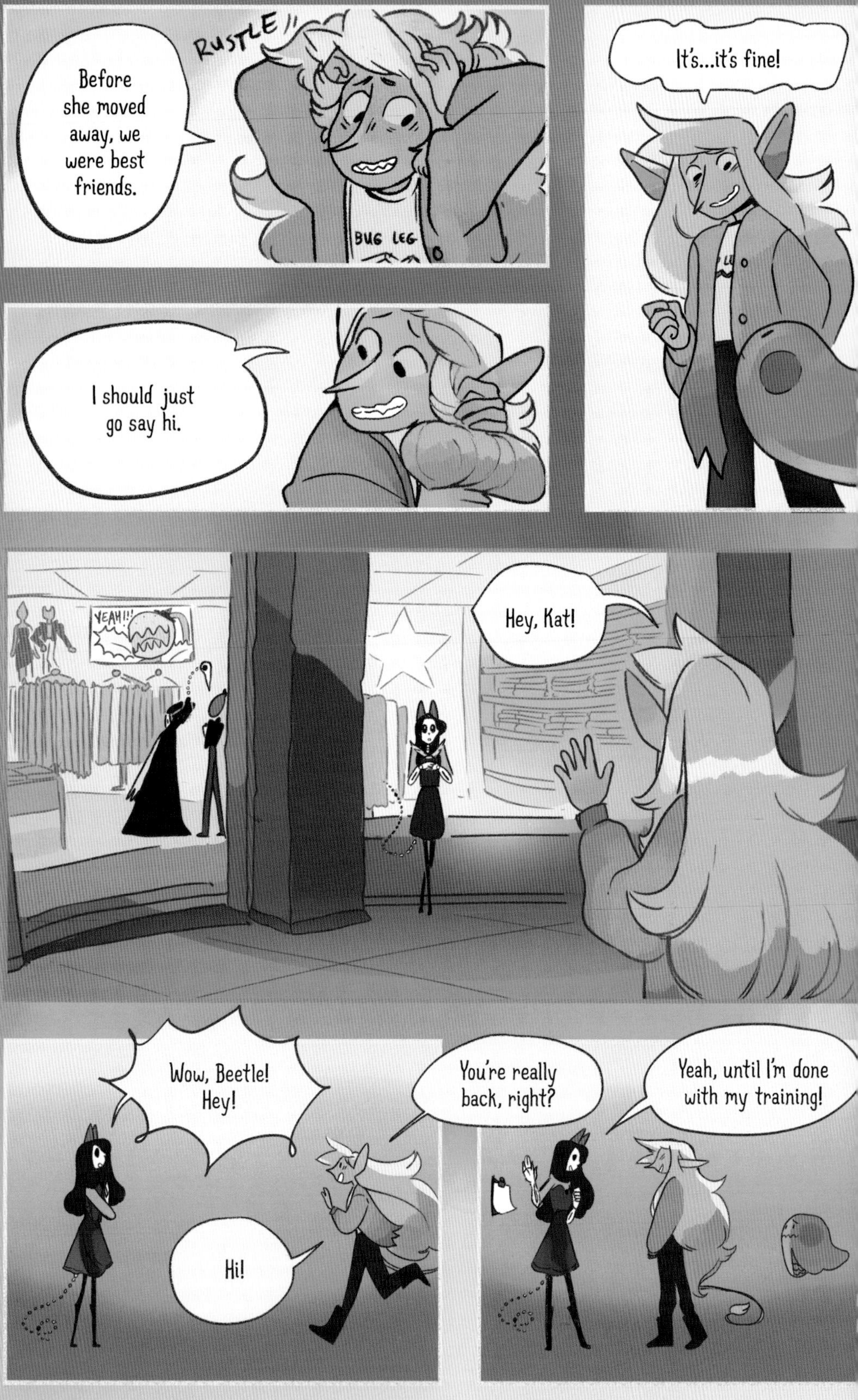
RUSTLE
Before she moved away, we were best friends.
BUG LEG
It's...it's fine!
I should just go say hi.
YEAH!!!
Hey, Kat!
Wow, Beetle! Hey!
Hi!
You're really back, right?
Yeah, until I'm done with my training!

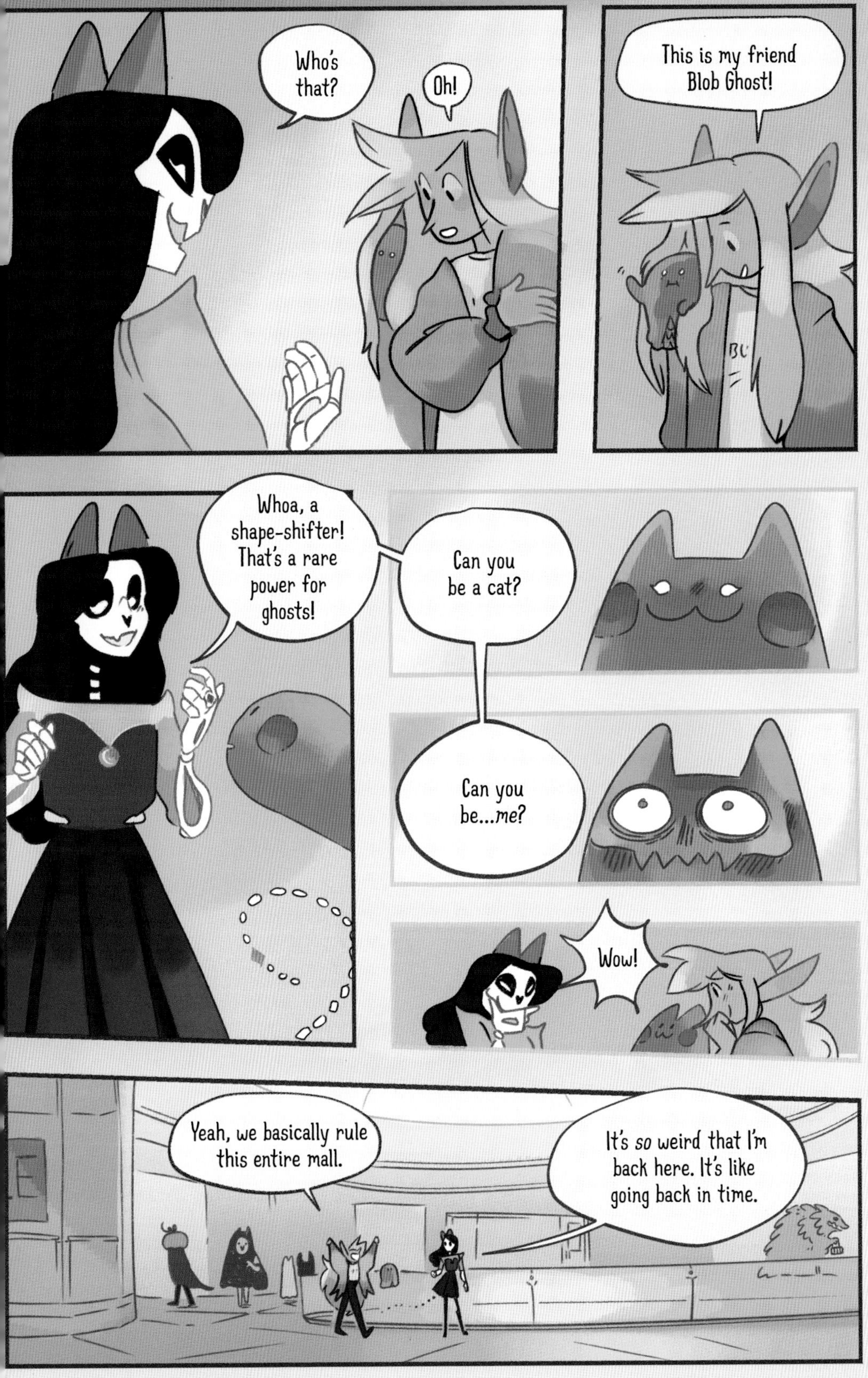
Who's that?
Oh!
This is my friend Blob Ghost!
Whoa, a shape-shifter! That's a rare power for ghosts!
Can you be a cat?
Can you be...*me*?
Wow!
Yeah, we basically rule this entire mall.
It's *so* weird that I'm back here. It's like going back in time.

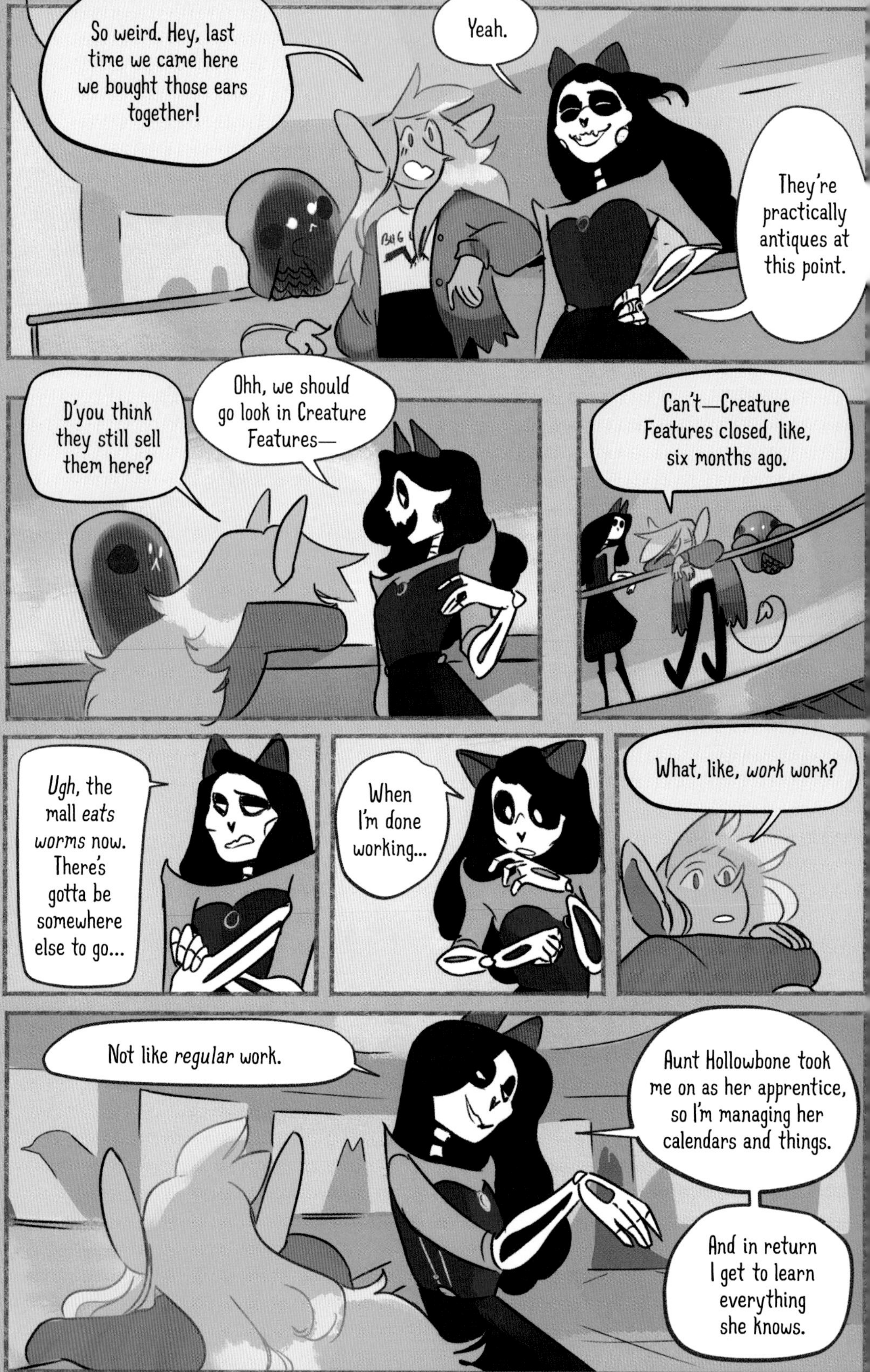
So weird. Hey, last time we came here we bought those ears together!
Yeah.
They're practically antiques at this point.
D'you think they still sell them here?
Ohh, we should go look in Creature Features—
Can't—Creature Features closed, like, six months ago.
Ugh, the mall *eats worms* now. There's gotta be somewhere else to go...
When I'm done working...
What, like, *work* work?
Not like *regular* work.
Aunt Hollowbone took me on as her apprentice, so I'm managing her calendars and things.
And in return I get to learn everything she knows.

And she knows...

...a lot.

SN AP!

HA HA!! UH!

SNAP!

BUG LE

-mmmmm-

GLE

Cool, so that's what you've been working on, huh?

Beetle, you were gonna be a witch, too, right?

Did you go to school yet?

Uhh...

...I'm just with my gran, but it's an all-apprenticship-style sort of thing.

Well, I'm sure you'll catch up soon! Lots of kids at school were way older than me. I'm on a bit of a fast track. I already got my crystal and everything.

See?

BUG LEG

That's. So.

Great.

For you!

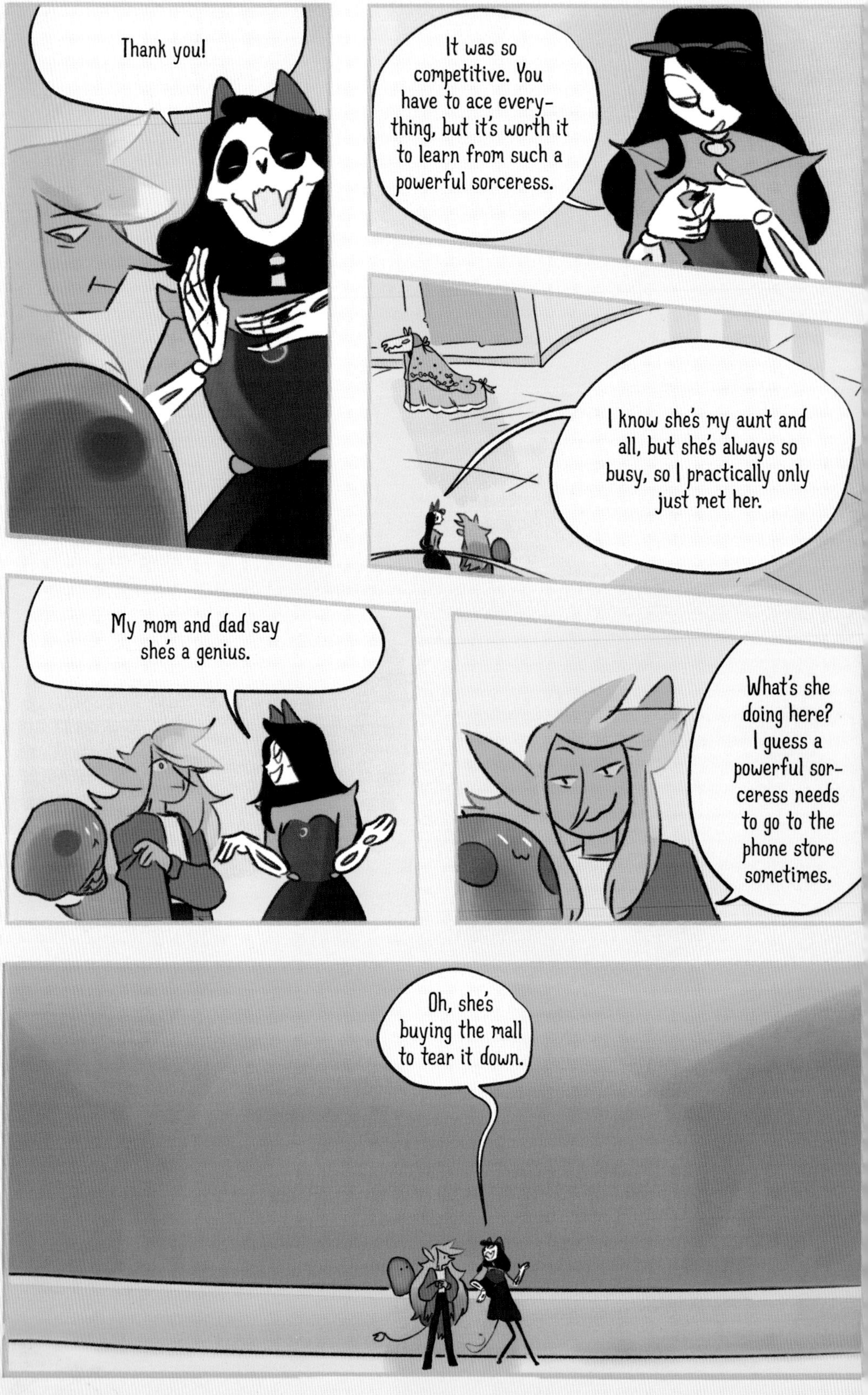
Thank you!
It was so competitive. You have to ace every-thing, but it's worth it to learn from such a powerful sorceress.
I know she's my aunt and all, but she's always so busy, so I practically only just met her.
My mom and dad say she's a genius.
What's she doing here? I guess a powerful sor-ceress needs to go to the phone store sometimes.
Oh, she's buying the mall to tear it down.

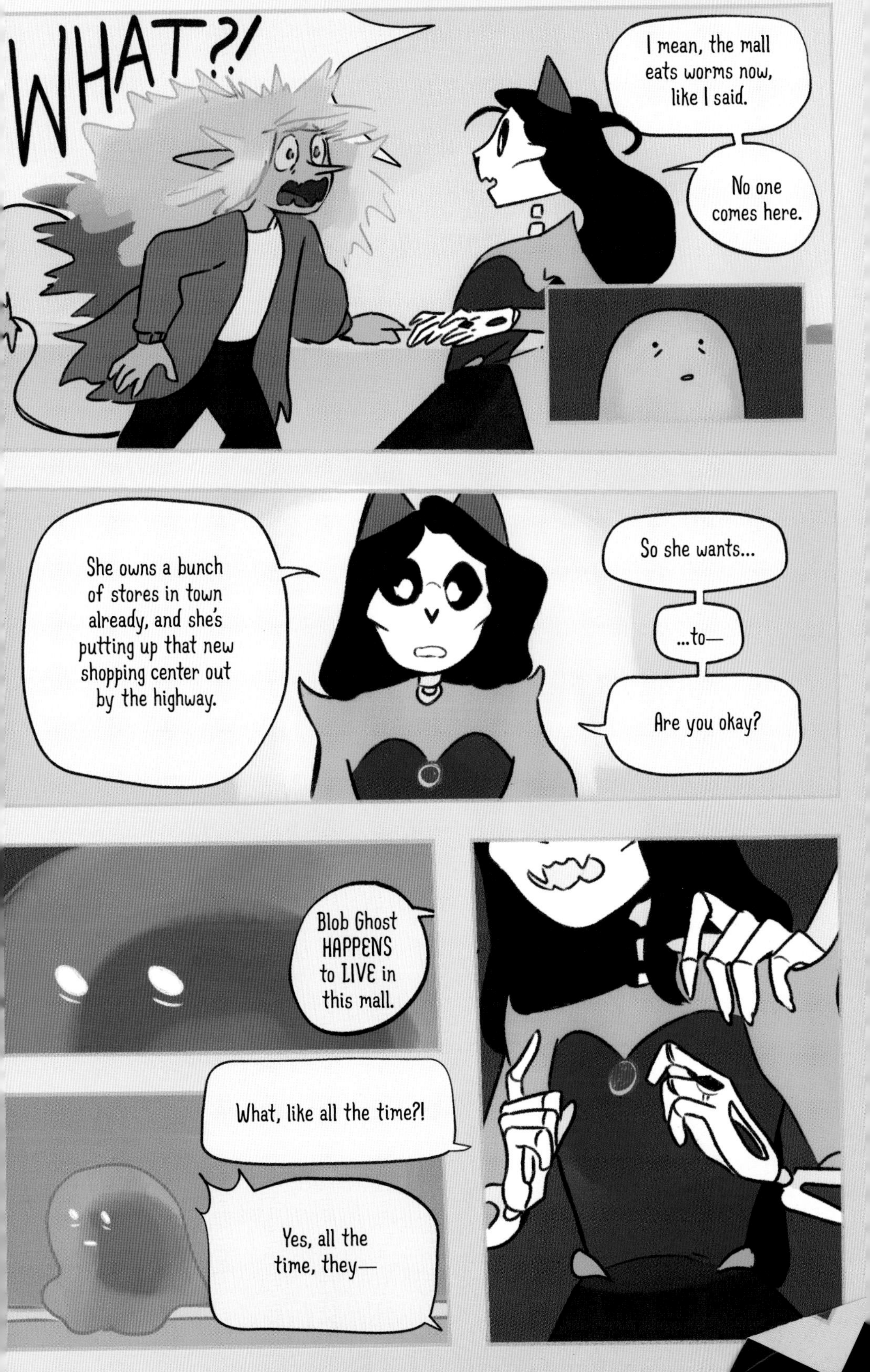
WHAT?!
I mean, the mall eats worms now, like I said.
No one comes here.
She owns a bunch of stores in town already, and she's putting up that new shopping center out by the highway.
So she wants...
...to—
Are you okay?
Blob Ghost HAPPENS to LIVE in this mall.
What, like all the time?!
Yes, all the time, they—

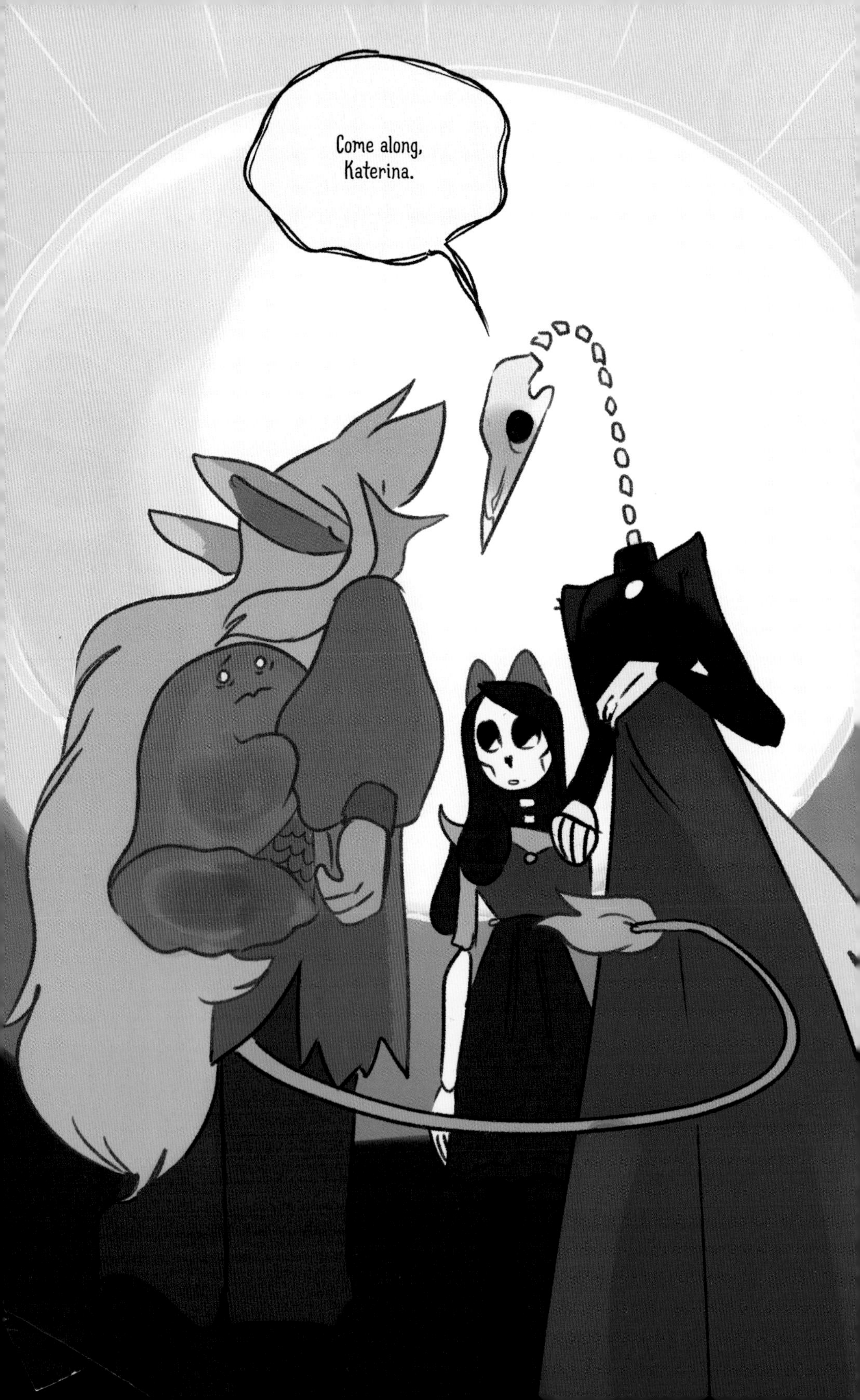
Come along, Katerina.

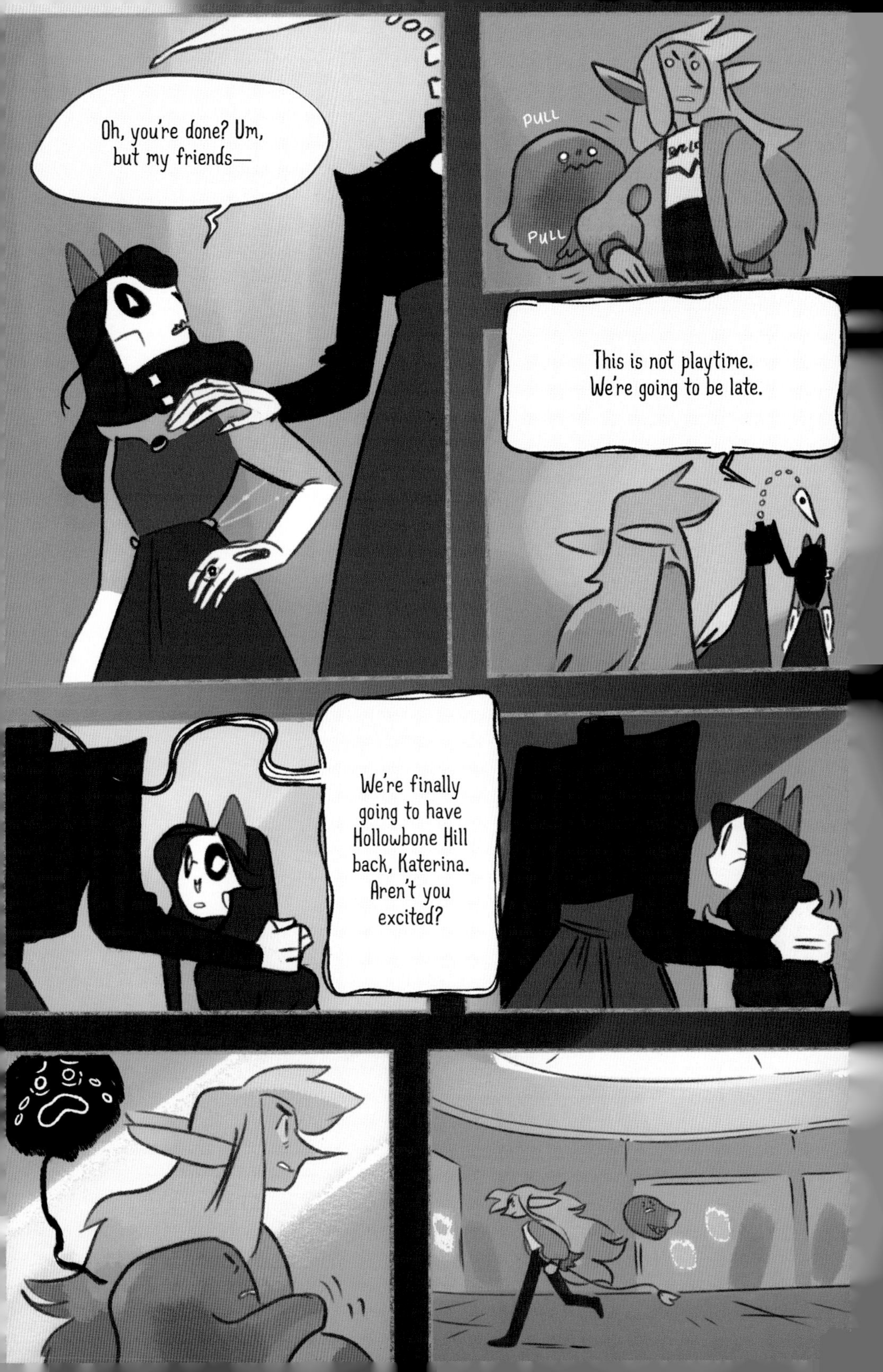

Oh, you're done? Um, but my friends—
PULL
PULL
This is not playtime. We're going to be late.
We're finally going to have Hollowbone Hill back, Katerina. Aren't you excited?

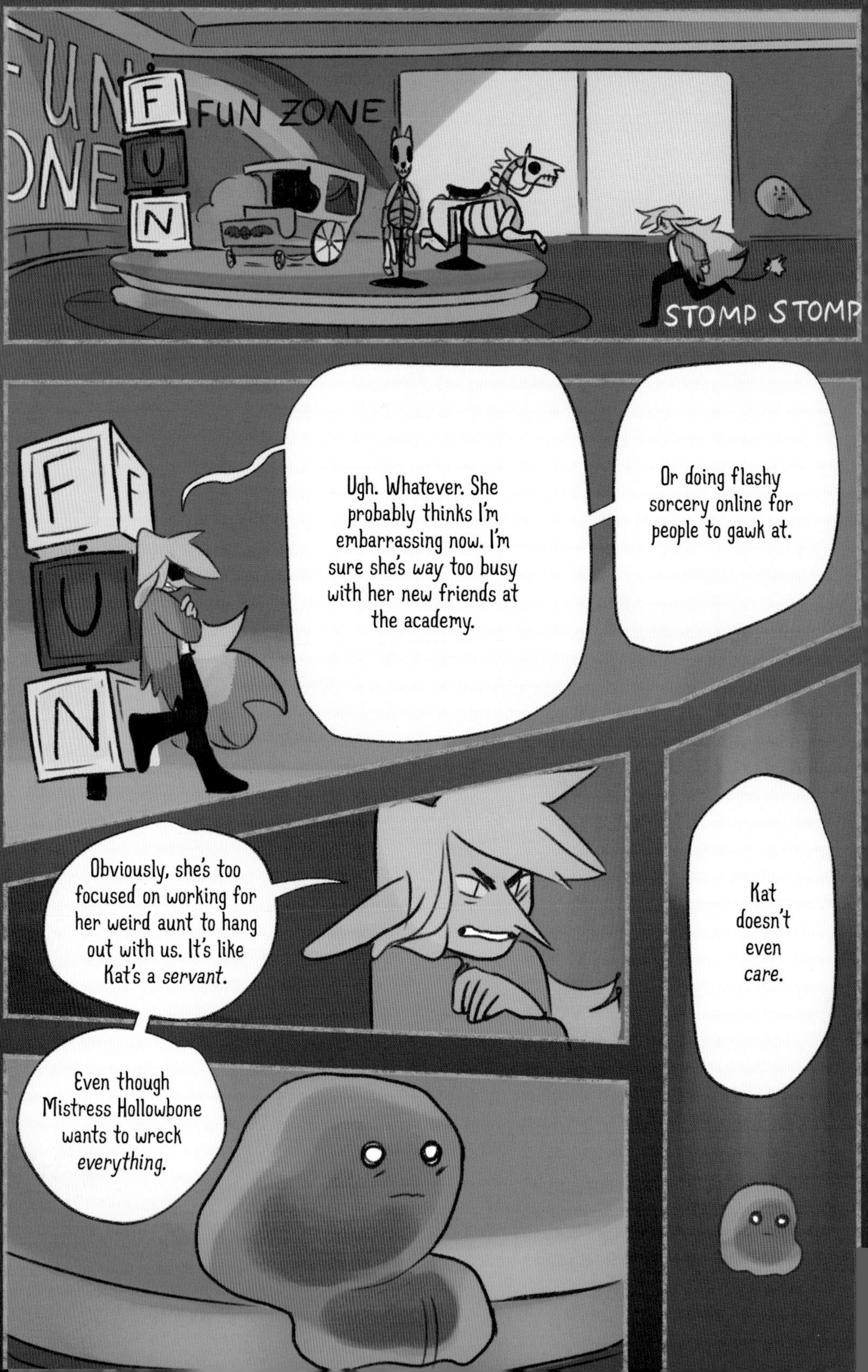
FUN ZONE
FUN
FUN ZONE
FUN
STOMP STOMP
Ugh. Whatever. She probably thinks I'm embarrassing now. I'm sure she's *way* too busy with her new friends at the academy.
Or doing flashy sorcery online for people to gawk at.
FUN
Obviously, she's too focused on working for her weird aunt to hang out with us. It's like Kat's a *servant*.
Even though Mistress Hollowbone wants to wreck *everything*.
Kat doesn't even *care*.

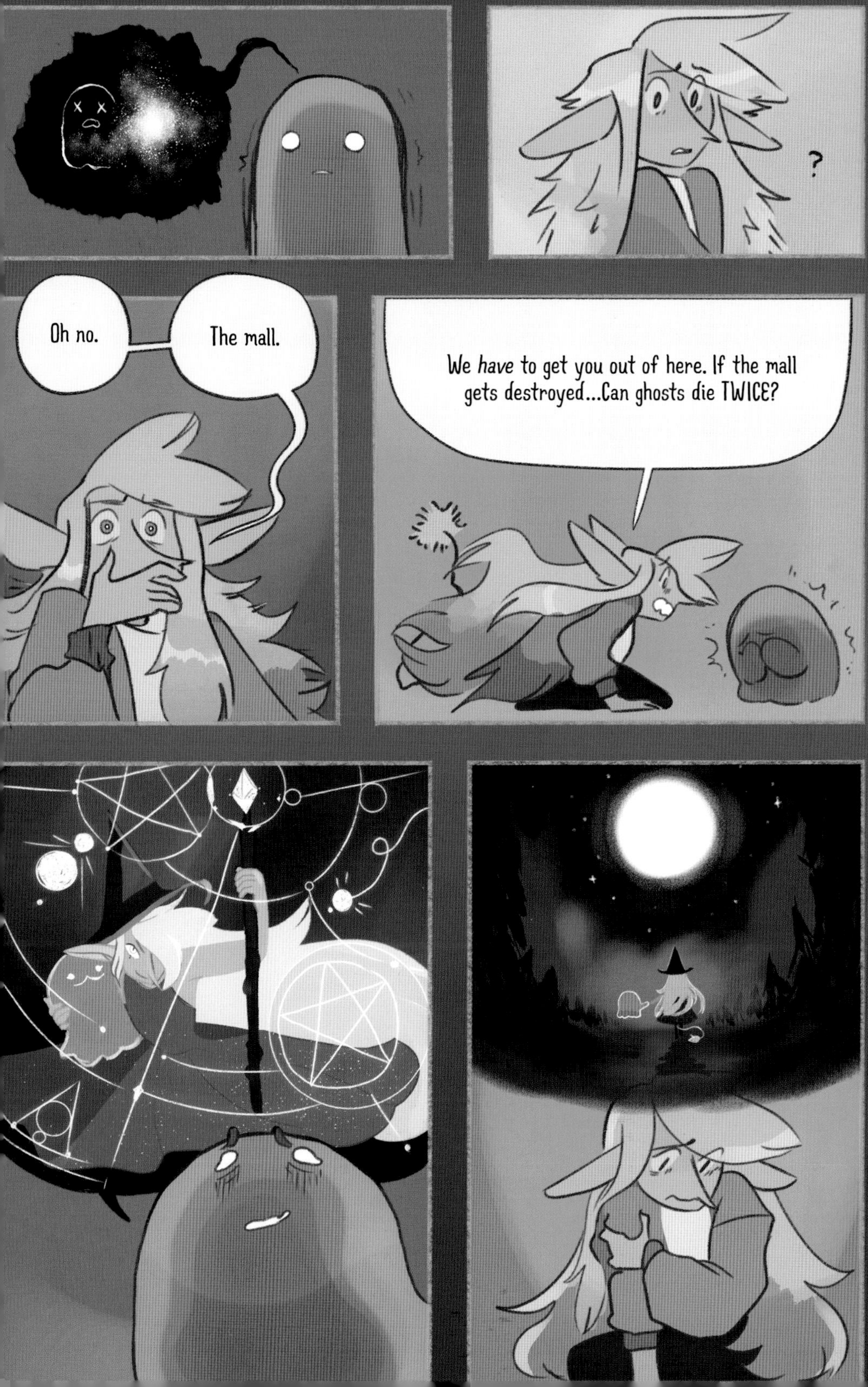
?
Oh no.
The mall.
We *have* to get you out of here. If the mall gets destroyed...Can ghosts die TWICE?

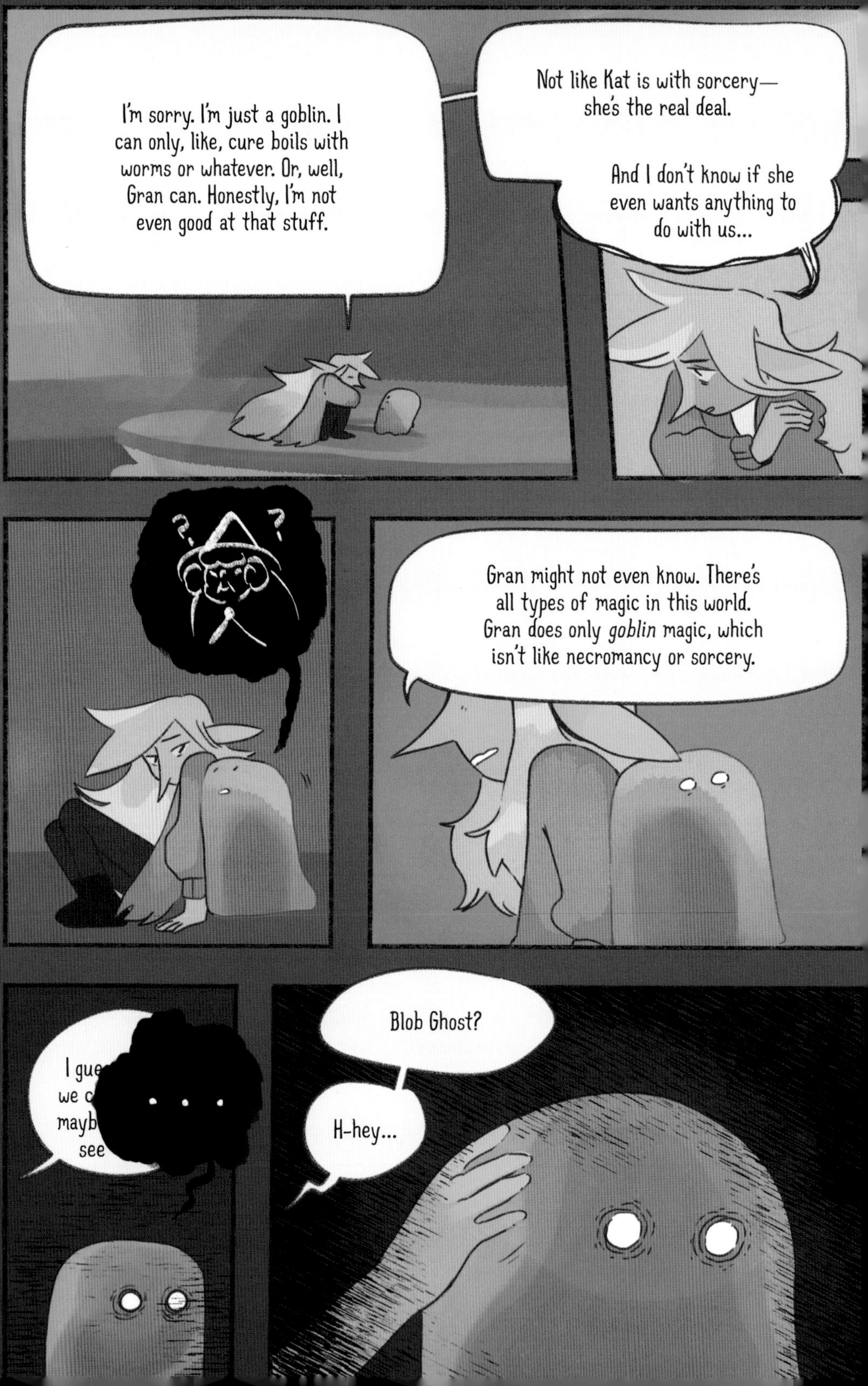

I'm sorry. I'm just a goblin. I can only, like, cure boils with worms or whatever. Or, well, Gran can. Honestly, I'm not even good at that stuff.
Not like Kat is with sorcery— she's the real deal.
And I don't know if she even wants anything to do with us...
? ?
Gran might not even know. There's all types of magic in this world. Gran does only *goblin* magic, which isn't like necromancy or sorcery.
. . .
Blob Ghost?
H-hey...

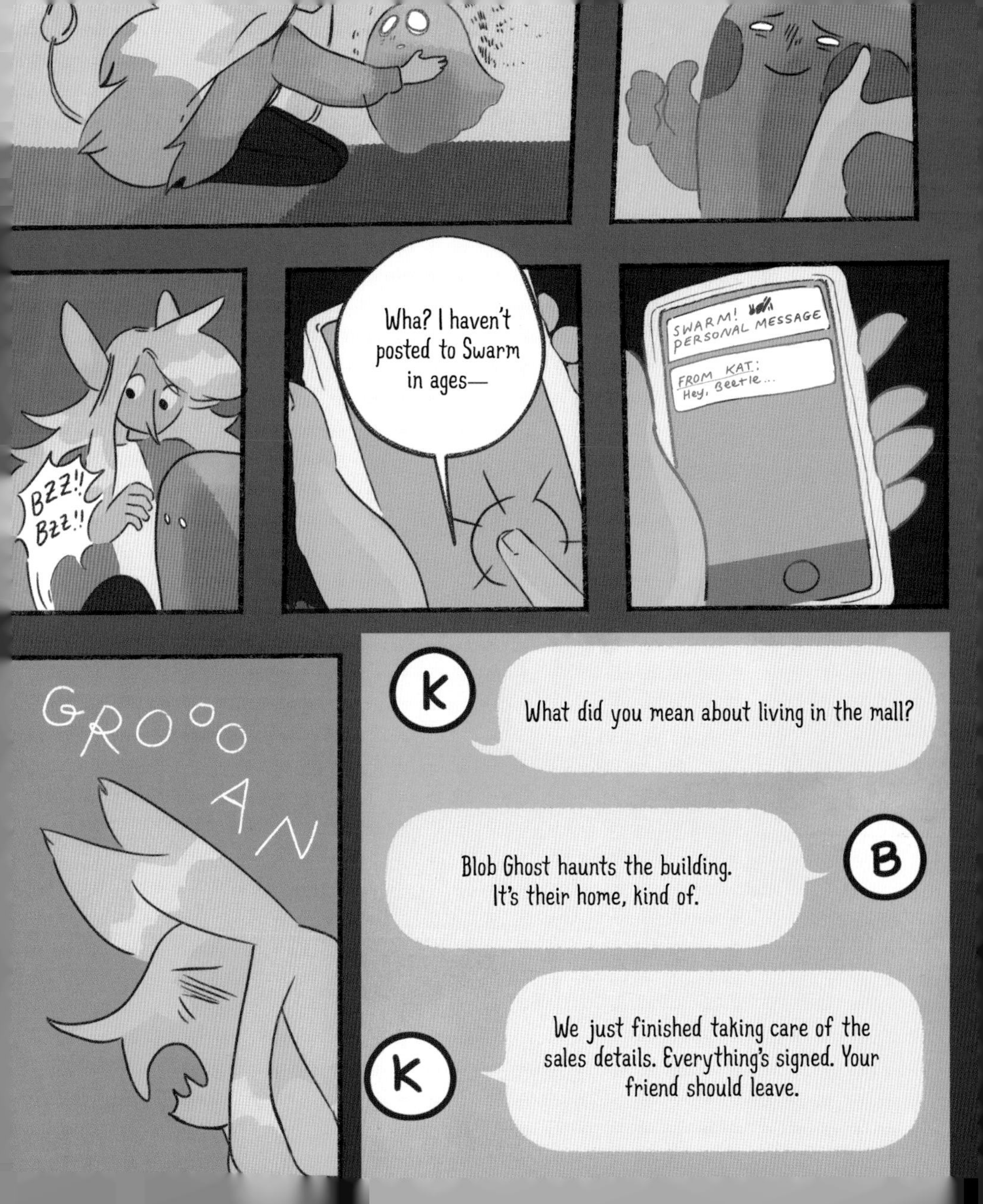
Wha? I haven't posted to Swarm in ages—
BZZ!! BZZ!!
SWARM! PERSONAL MESSAGE
FROM KAT: Hey, Beetle...
GROOOAN
K
What did you mean about living in the mall?
Blob Ghost haunts the building. It's their home, kind of.
B
K
We just finished taking care of the sales details. Everything's signed. Your friend should leave.

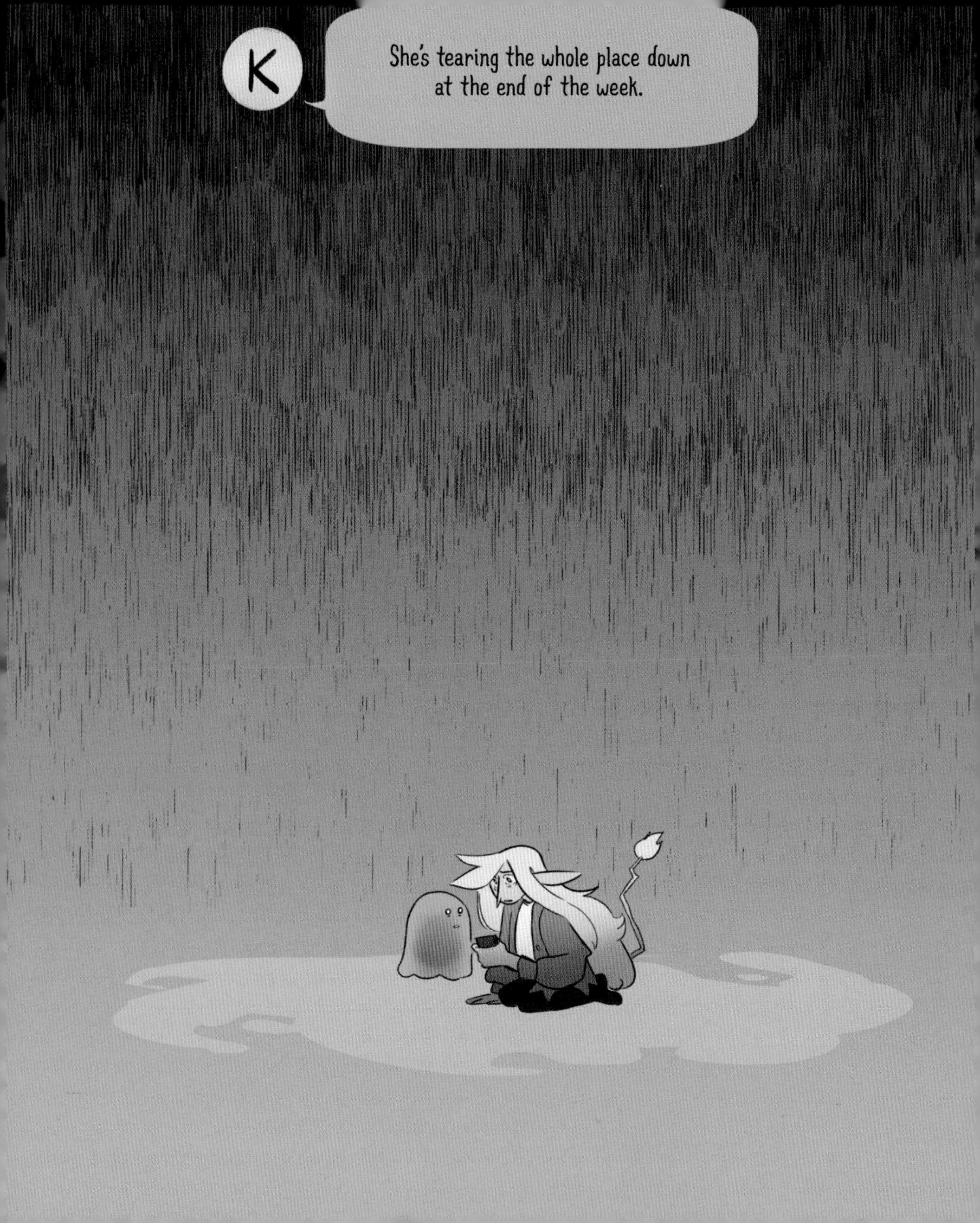
K
She's tearing the whole place down at the end of the week.

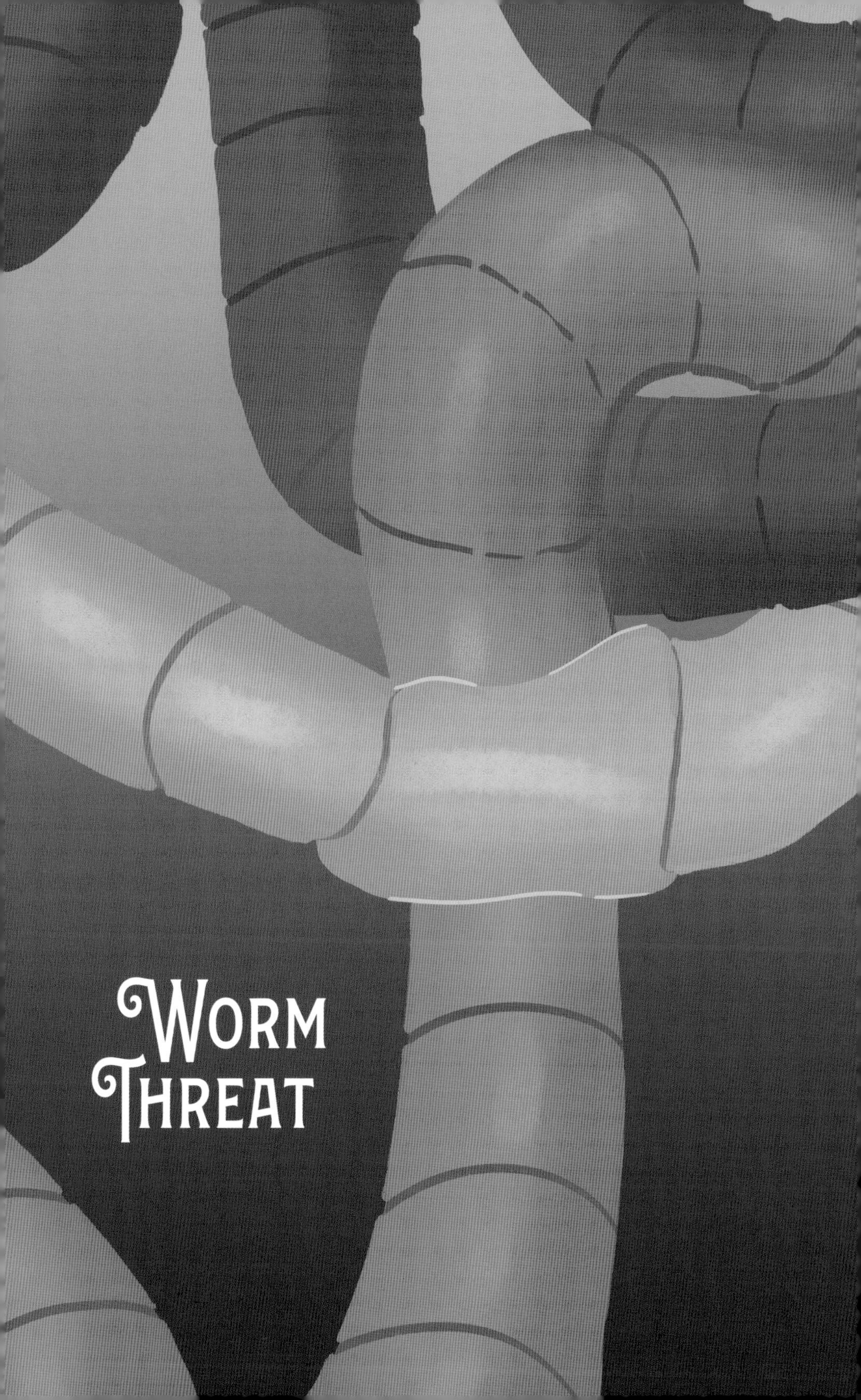

Worm Threat

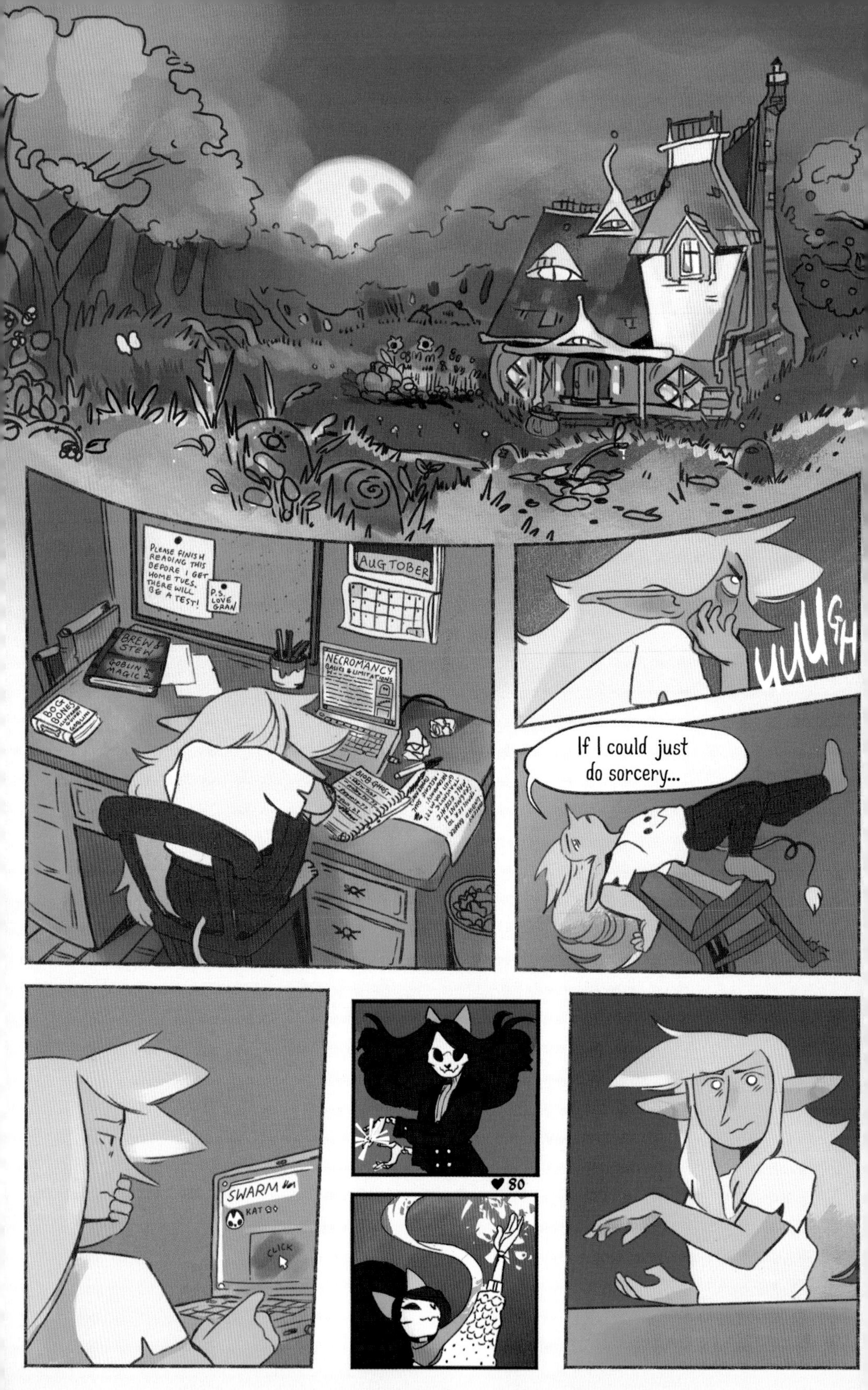
PLEASE FINISH READING THIS BEFORE I GET HOME TUES. THERE WILL BE A TEST!
P.S. LOVE GRAN
AUGTOBER
BREW & STEW
GOBLIN MAGIC 2
BOG BONES
NECROMANCY BASICS & LIMITATIONS
BLOB GHOST
UUUGH
If I could just do sorcery...
SWARM
KAT
CLICK
80

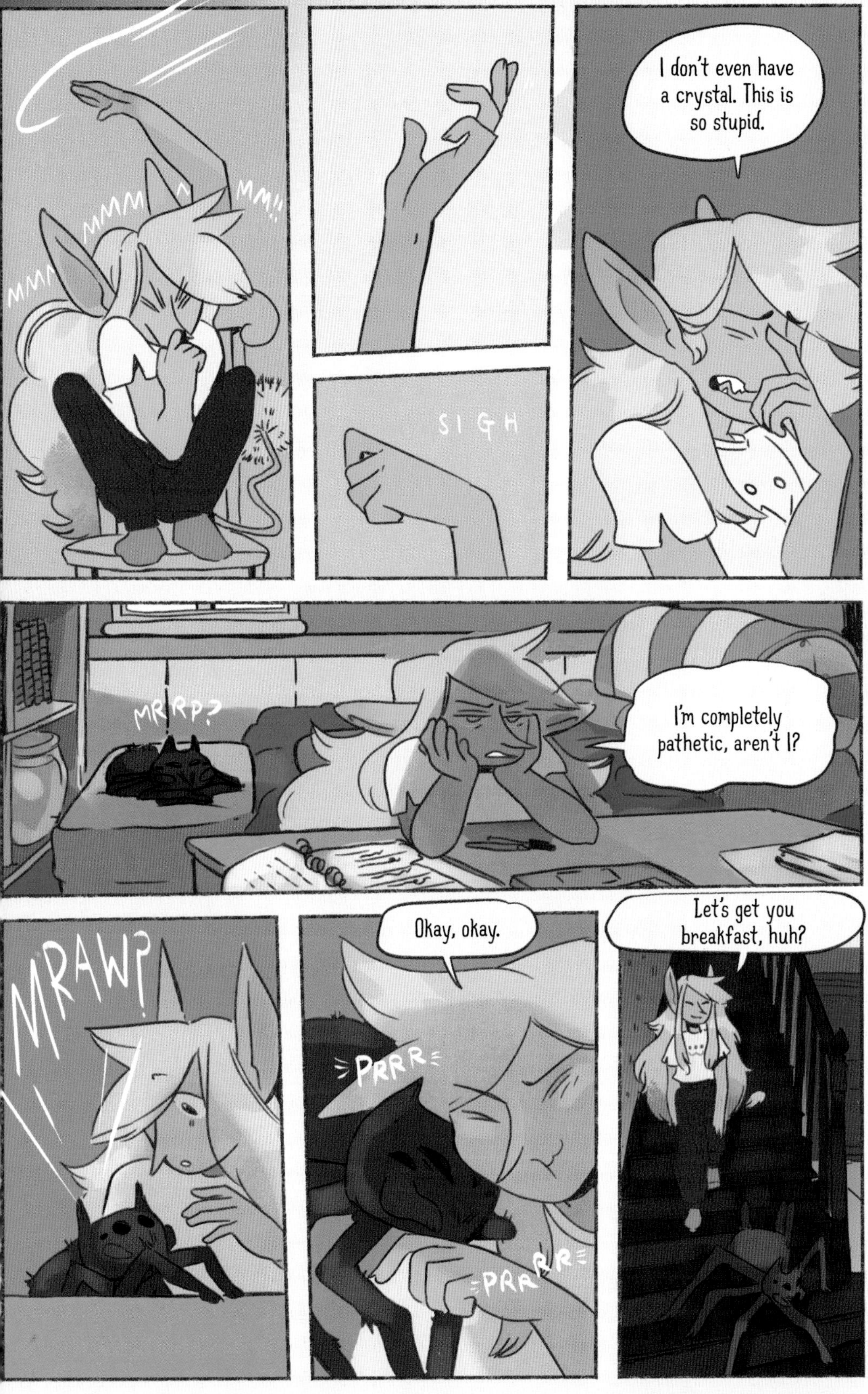
MMMMMMMM!!
SIGH
I don't even have a crystal. This is so stupid.
MRRP?
I'm completely pathetic, aren't I?
MRAW?!
Okay, okay.
PRRR
PRRRR
Let's get you breakfast, huh?

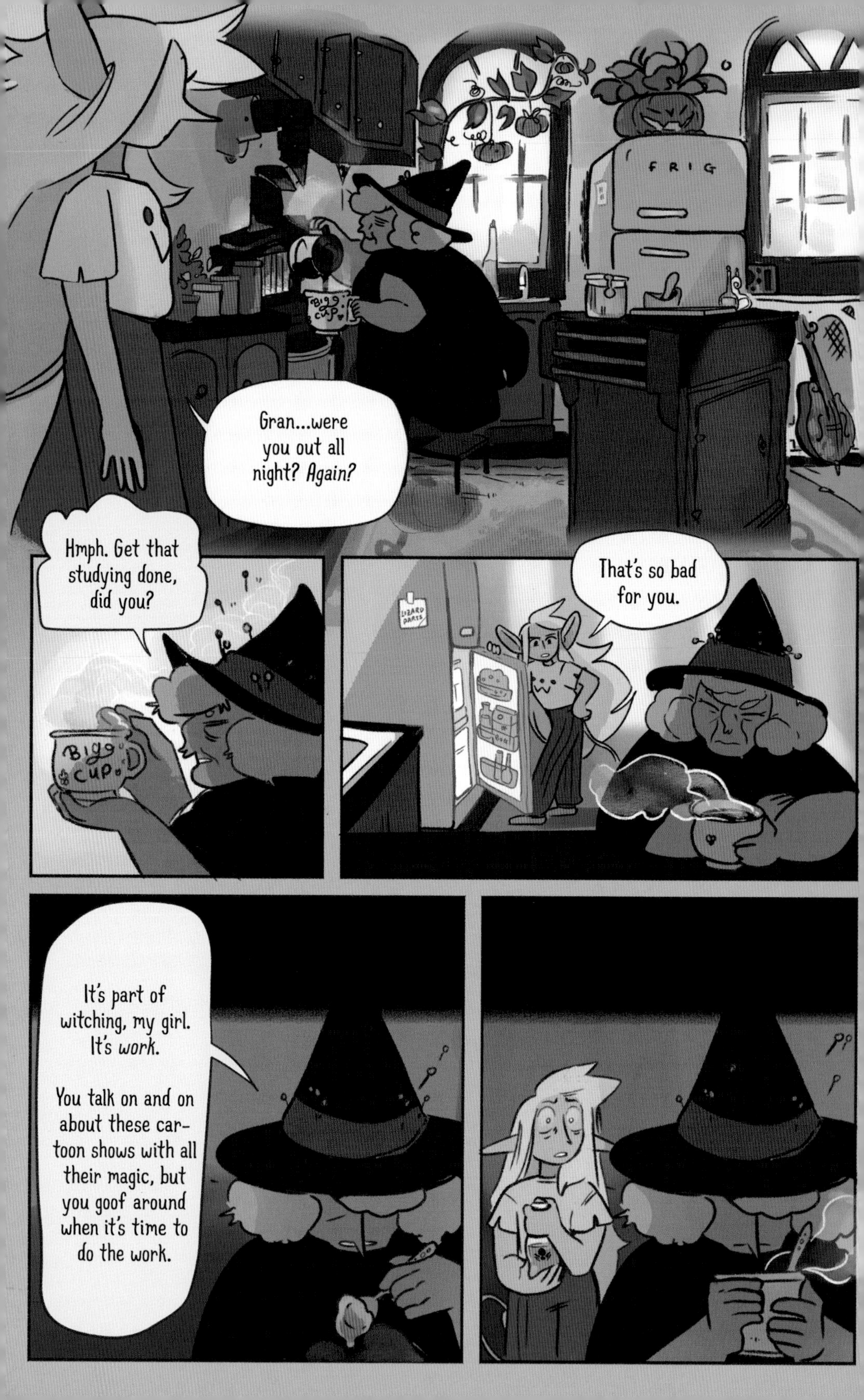
FRIG
Gran...were you out all night? Again?
Hmph. Get that studying done, did you?
That's so bad for you.
It's part of witching, my girl. It's *work*.
You talk on and on about these car-toon shows with all their magic, but you goof around when it's time to do the work.

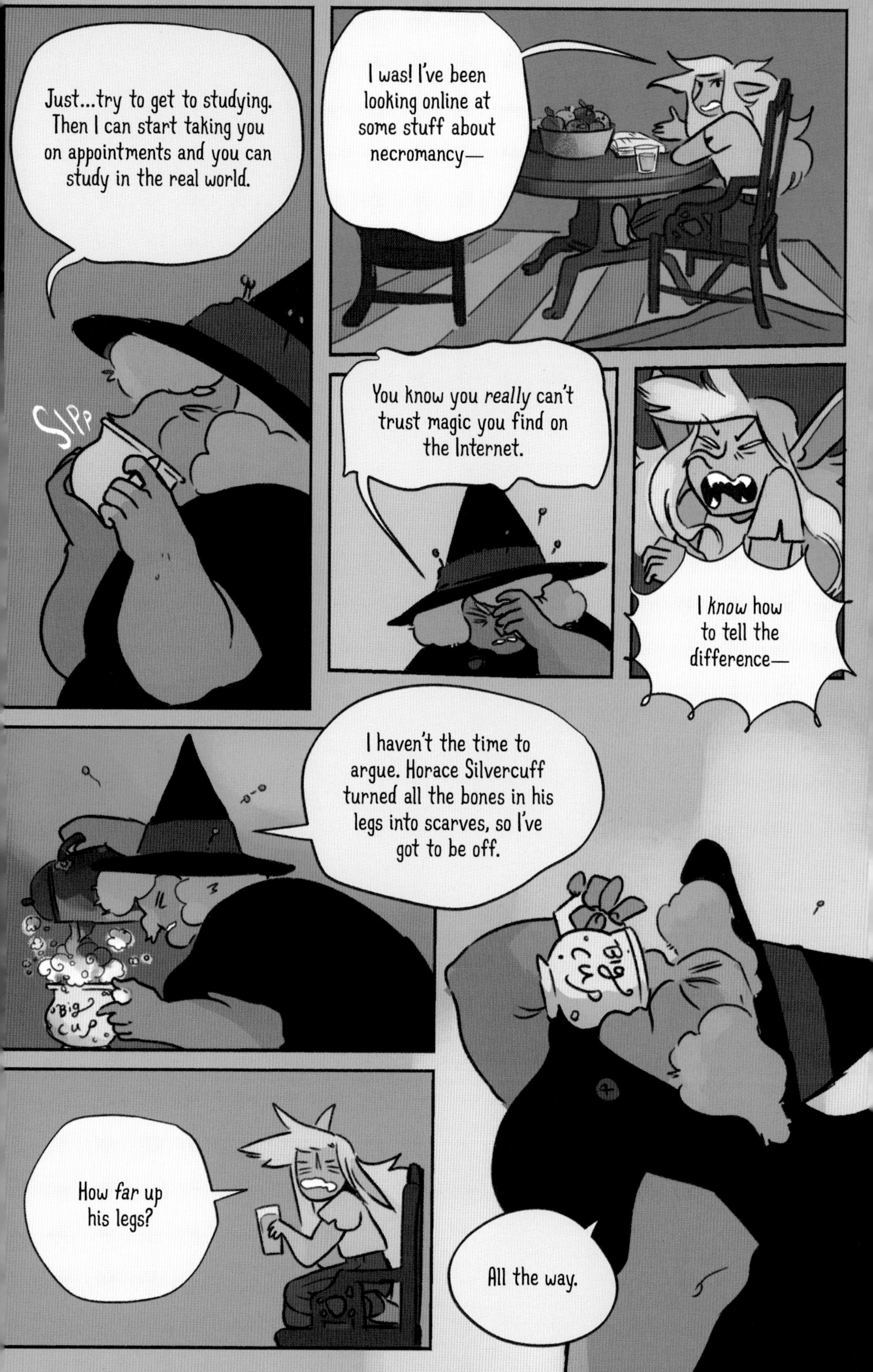
Just...try to get to studying. Then I can start taking you on appointments and you can study in the real world.
SIPP
I was! I've been looking online at some stuff about necromancy—
You know you *really* can't trust magic you find on the Internet.
I *know* how to tell the difference—
I haven't the time to argue. Horace Silvercuff turned all the bones in his legs into scarves, so I've got to be off.
Big cup
Big cup
How *far* up his legs?
All the way.

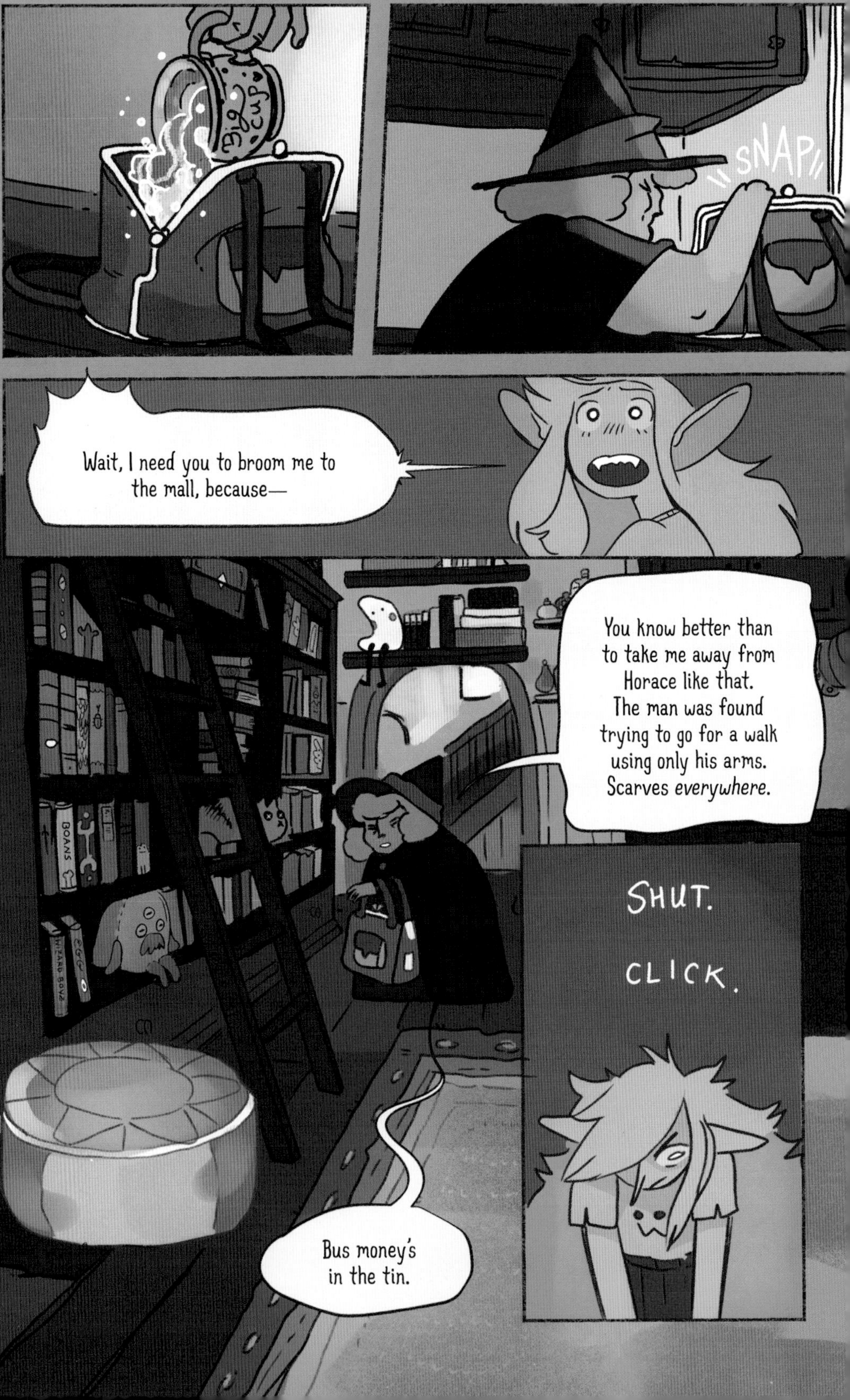
Big cup
SNAP
Wait, I need you to broom me to the mall, because—
You know better than to take me away from Horace like that. The man was found trying to go for a walk using only his arms. Scarves *everywhere*.
BOANS
WIZARD BOYZ
Bus money's in the tin.
SHUT.
CLICK.

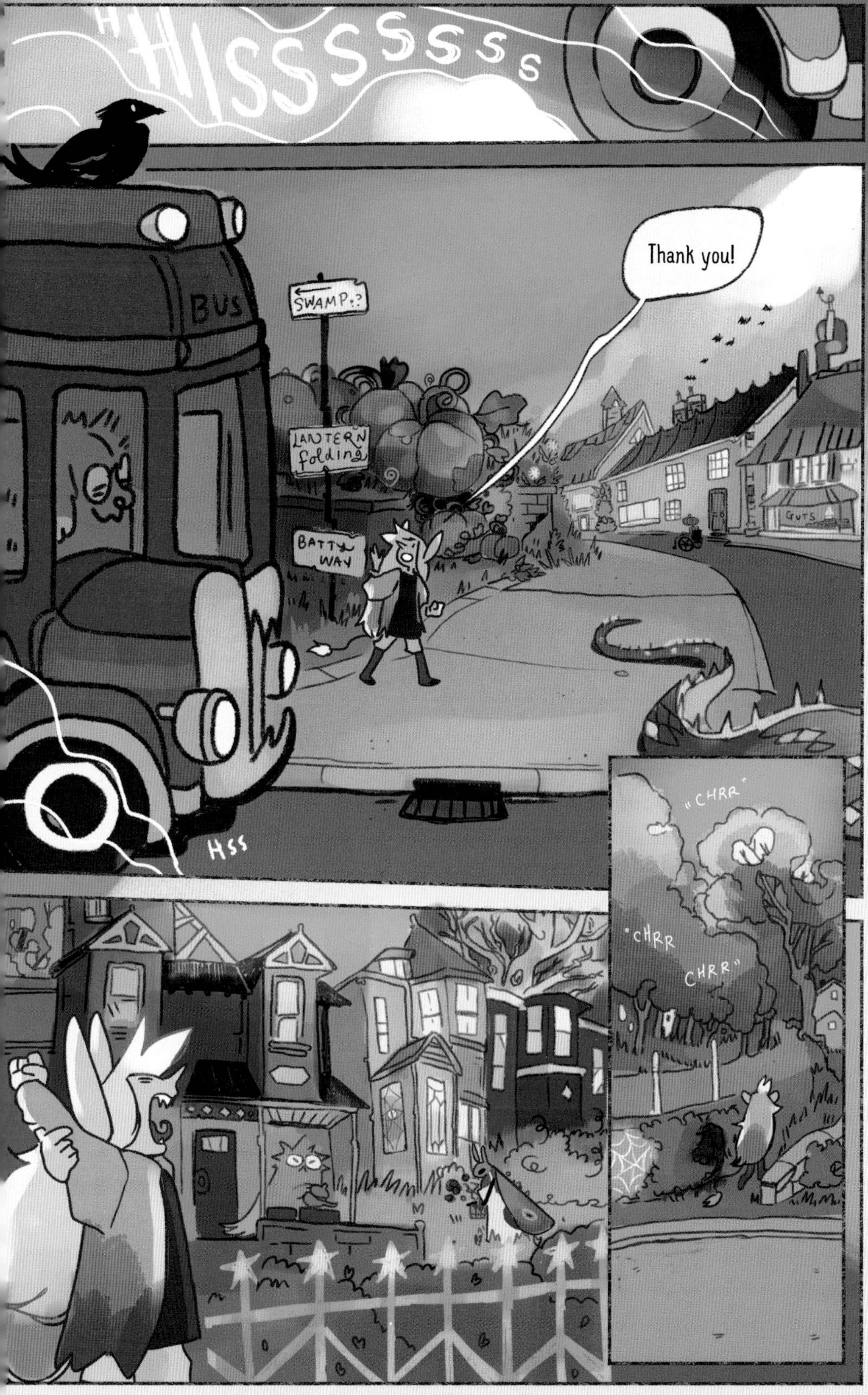

HHISSSSSSSs
BUS
SWAMP?
LANTERN folding
BATTY WAY
Thank you!
GUTS
Hss
"CHRR"
"CHRR
CHRR"

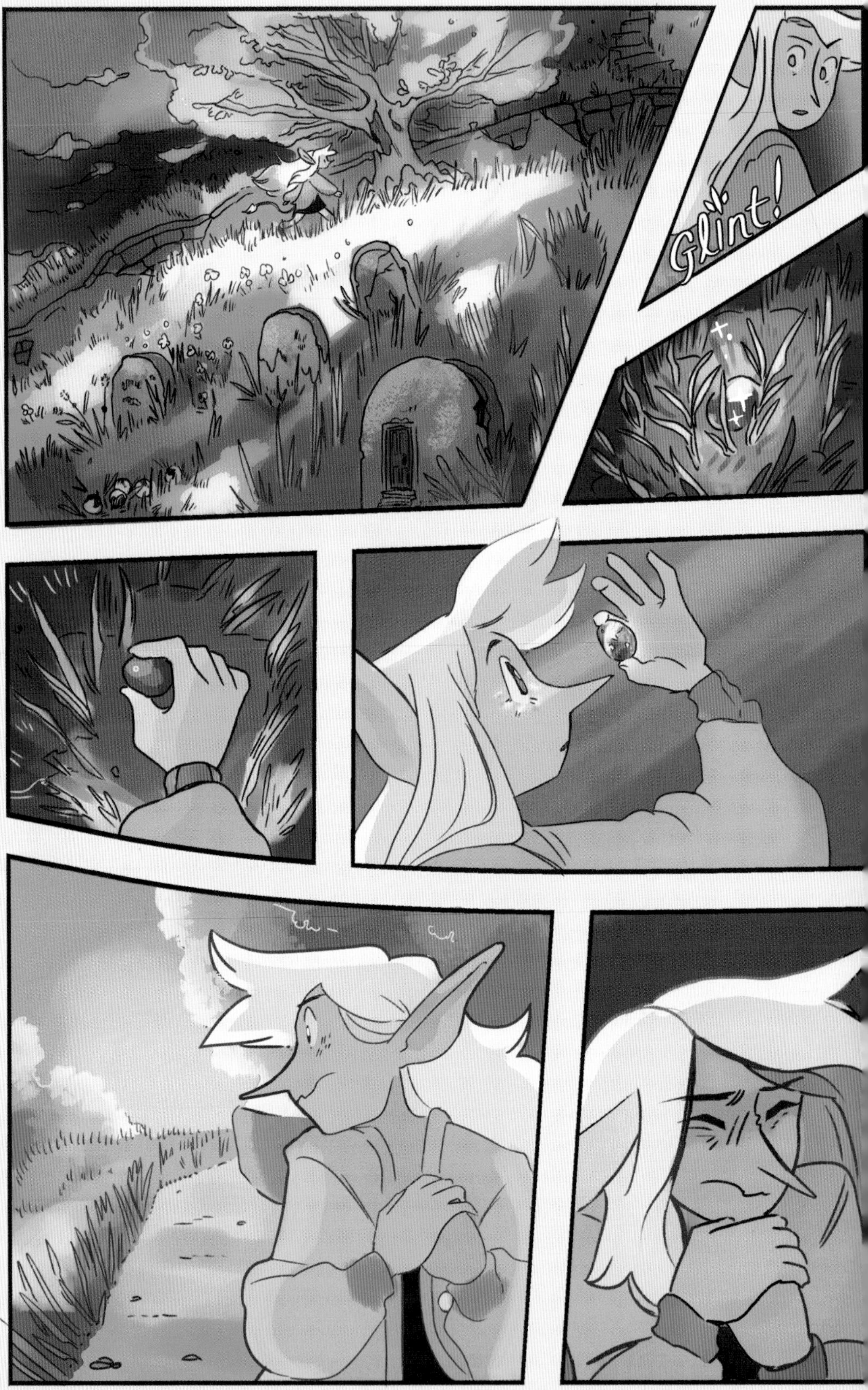
Glint!

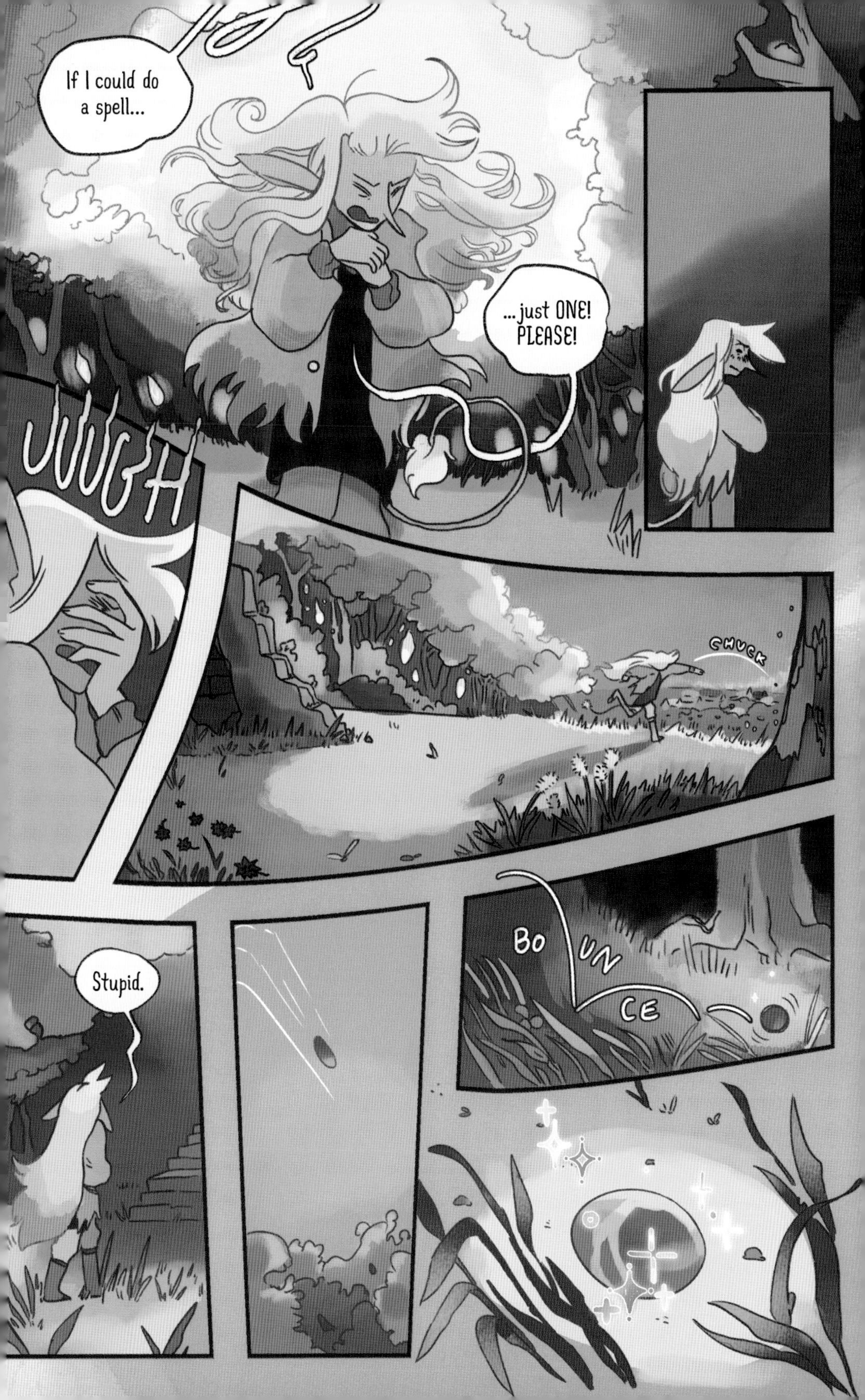
If I could do a spell...
...just ONE! PLEASE!
UUUGH
CHUCK
Stupid.
BO UN CE

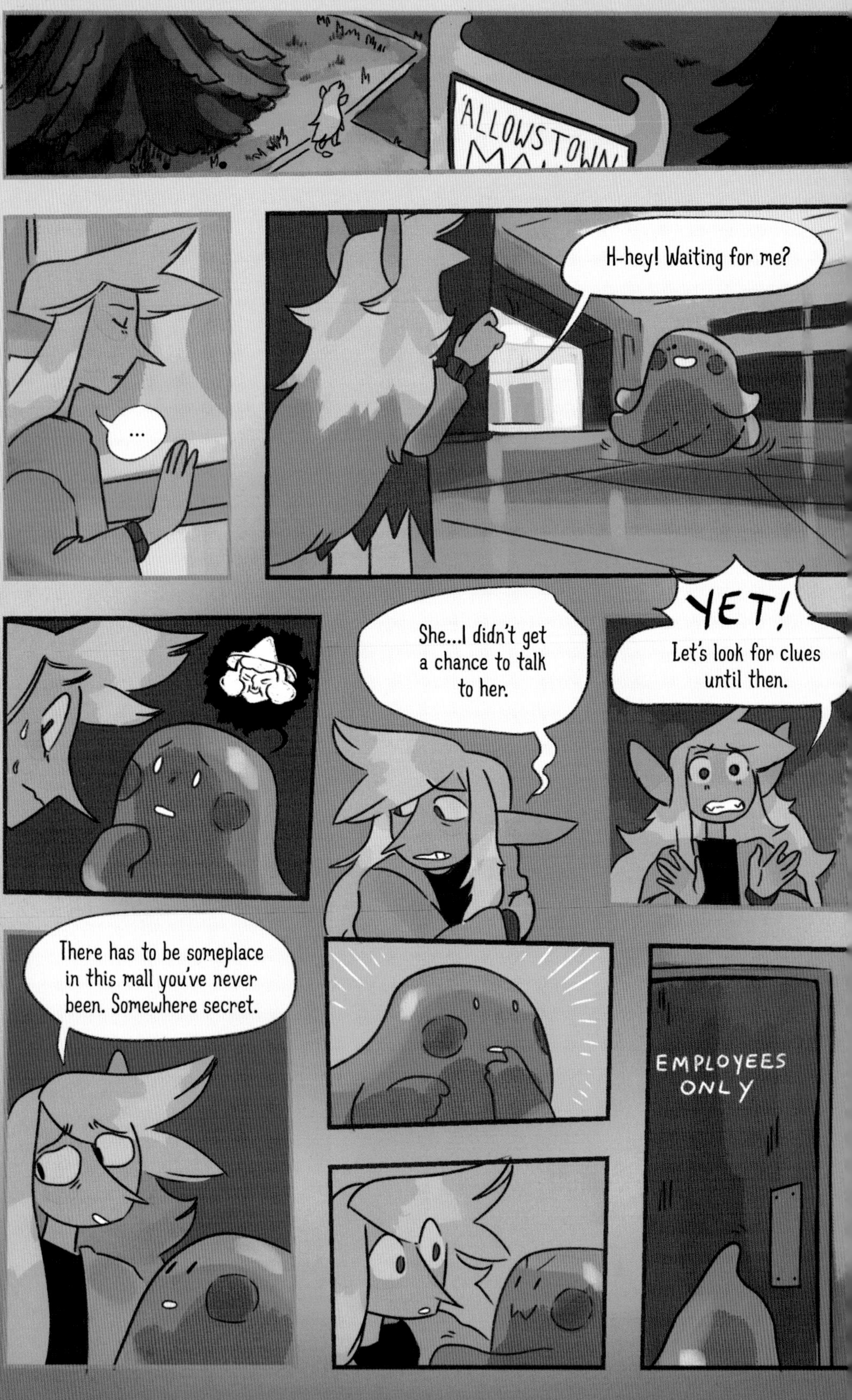

'ALLOWSTOWN MAL
...
H-hey! Waiting for me?
She...I didn't get a chance to talk to her.
YET!
Let's look for clues until then.
There has to be someplace in this mall you've never been. Somewhere secret.
EMPLOYEES ONLY

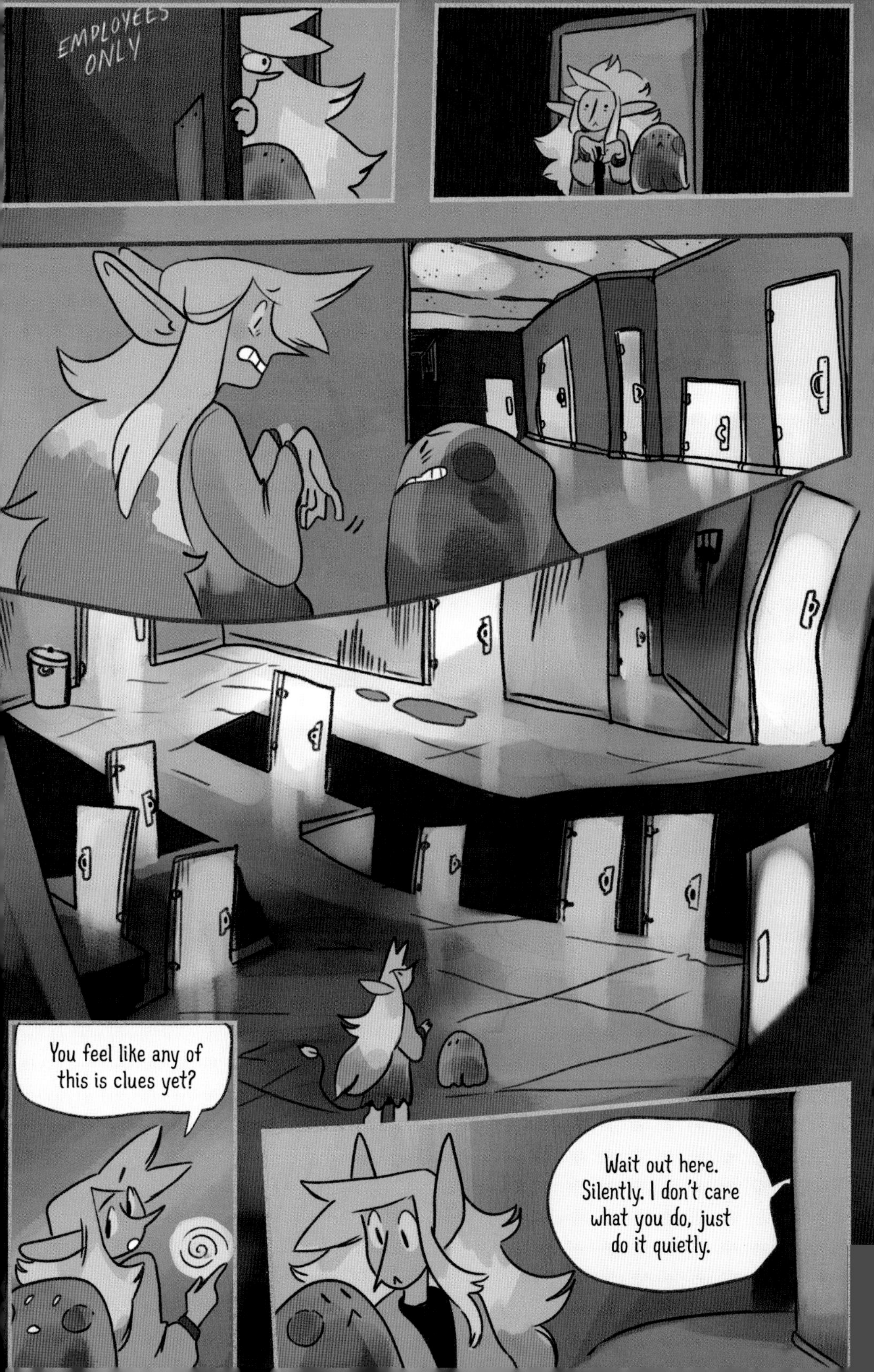
EMPLOYEES ONLY
You feel like any of this is clues yet?
Wait out here. Silently. I don't care what you do, just do it quietly.

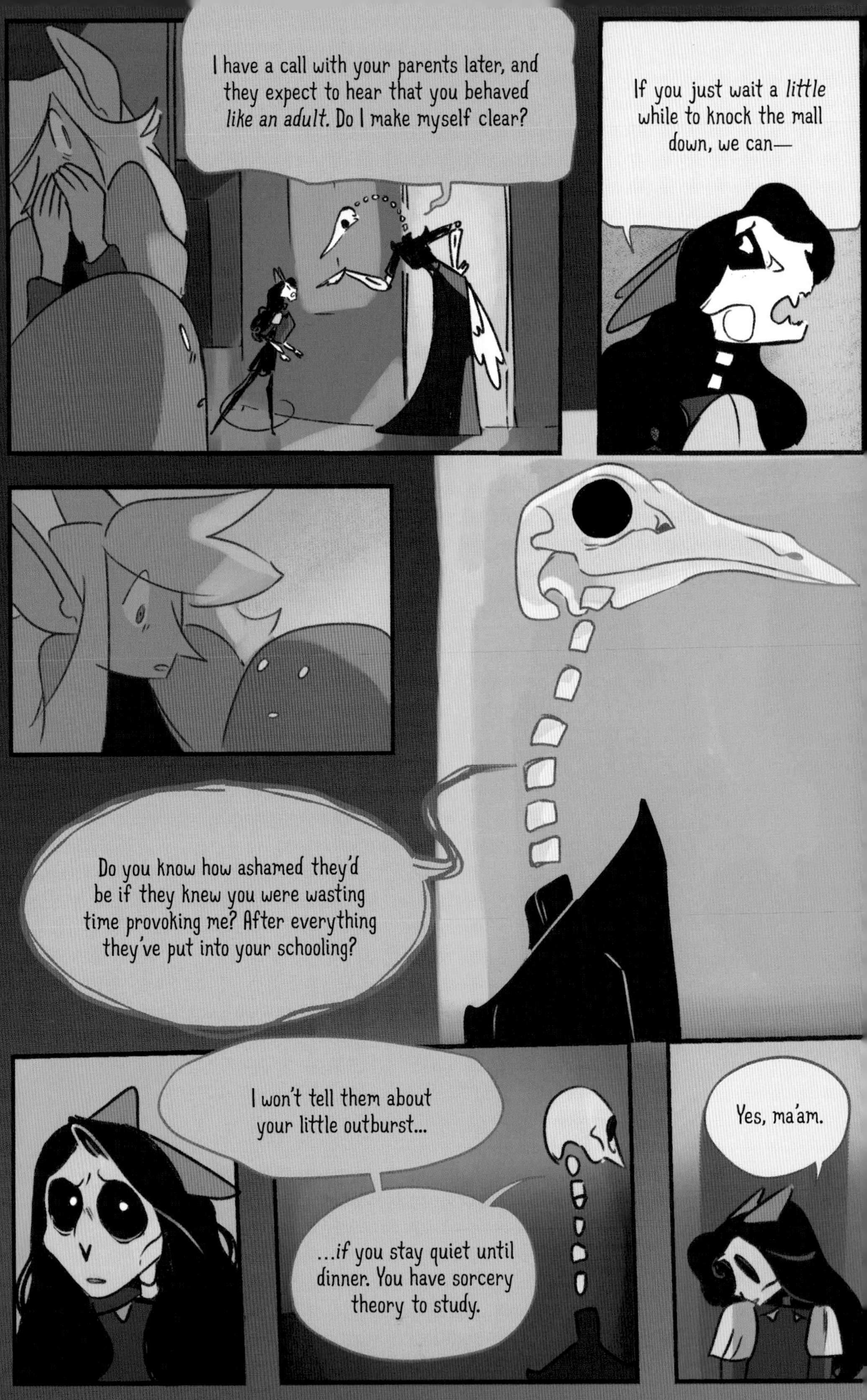
I have a call with your parents later, and they expect to hear that you behaved *like an adult*. Do I make myself clear?
If you just wait a *little* while to knock the mall down, we can—
Do you know how ashamed they'd be if they knew you were wasting time provoking me? After everything they've put into your schooling?
I won't tell them about your little outburst...
...*if* you stay quiet until dinner. You have sorcery theory to study.
Yes, ma'am.

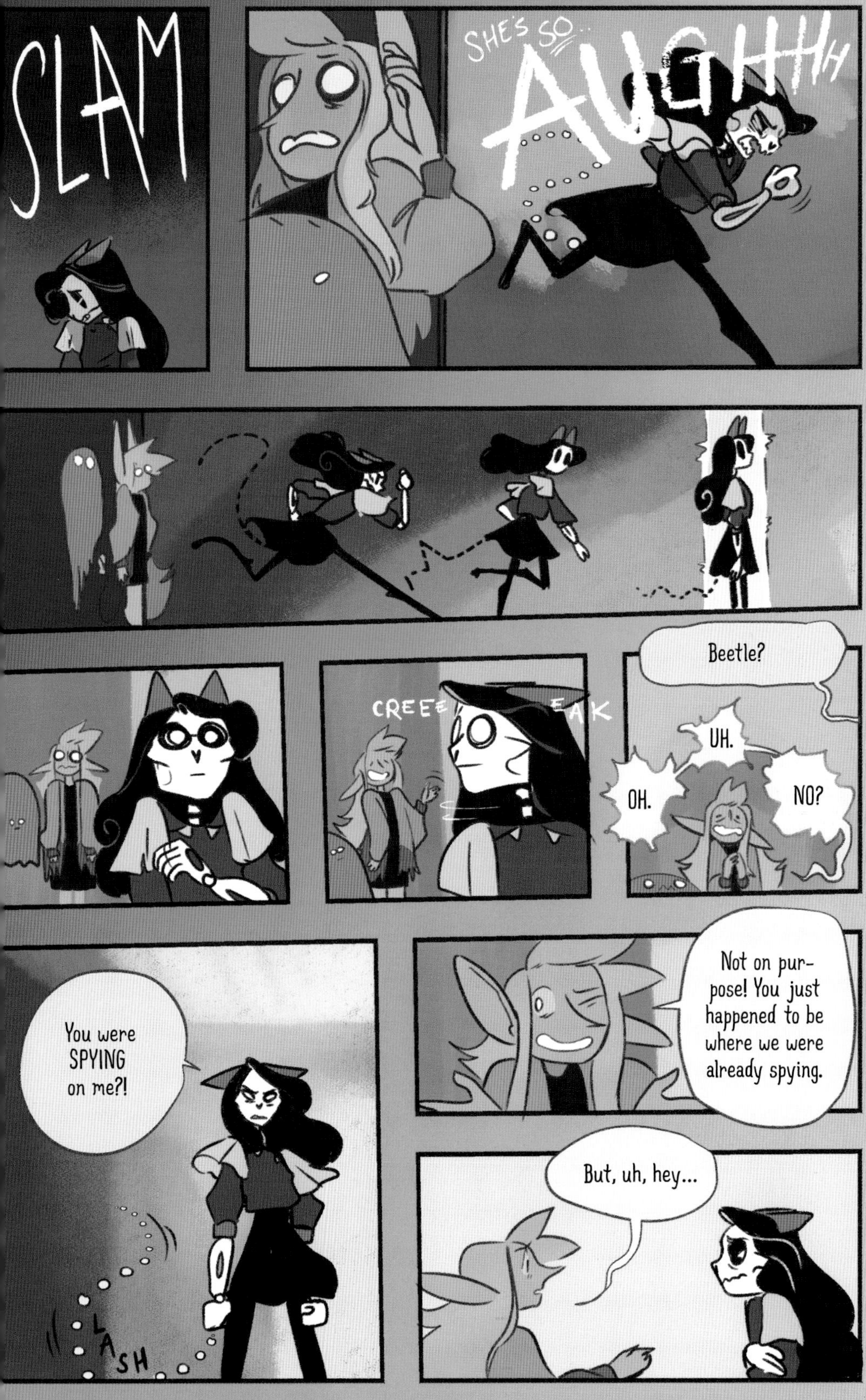
SLAM
SHE'S SO...
AUGHHH
Beetle?
UH.
OH.
NO?
CREEEEAK
You were SPYING on me?!
LASH
Not on purpose! You just happened to be where we were already spying.
But, uh, hey...

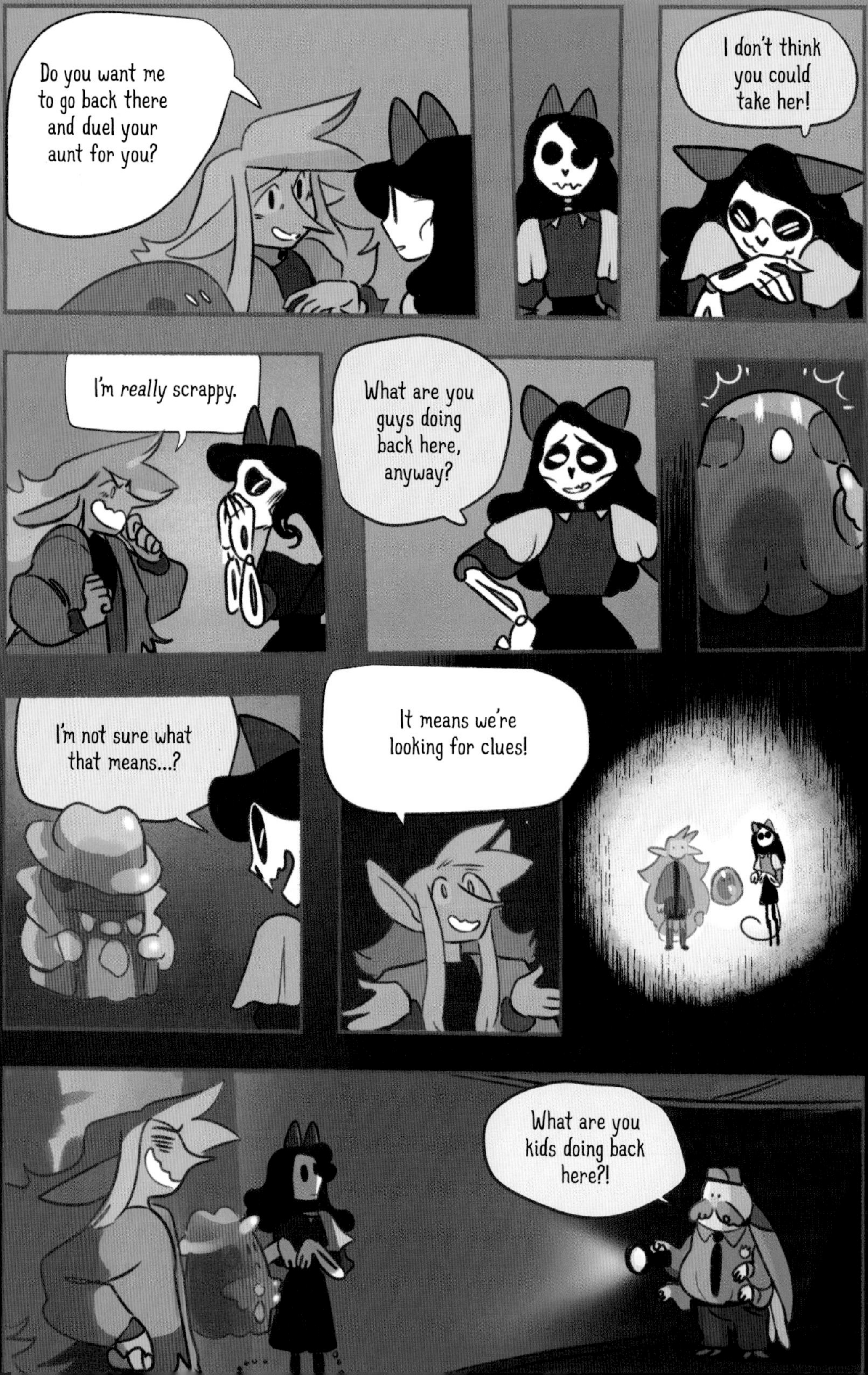
Do you want me to go back there and duel your aunt for you?
I don't think you could take her!
I'm *really* scrappy.
What are you guys doing back here, anyway?
I'm not sure what that means...?
It means we're looking for clues!
What are you kids doing back here?!

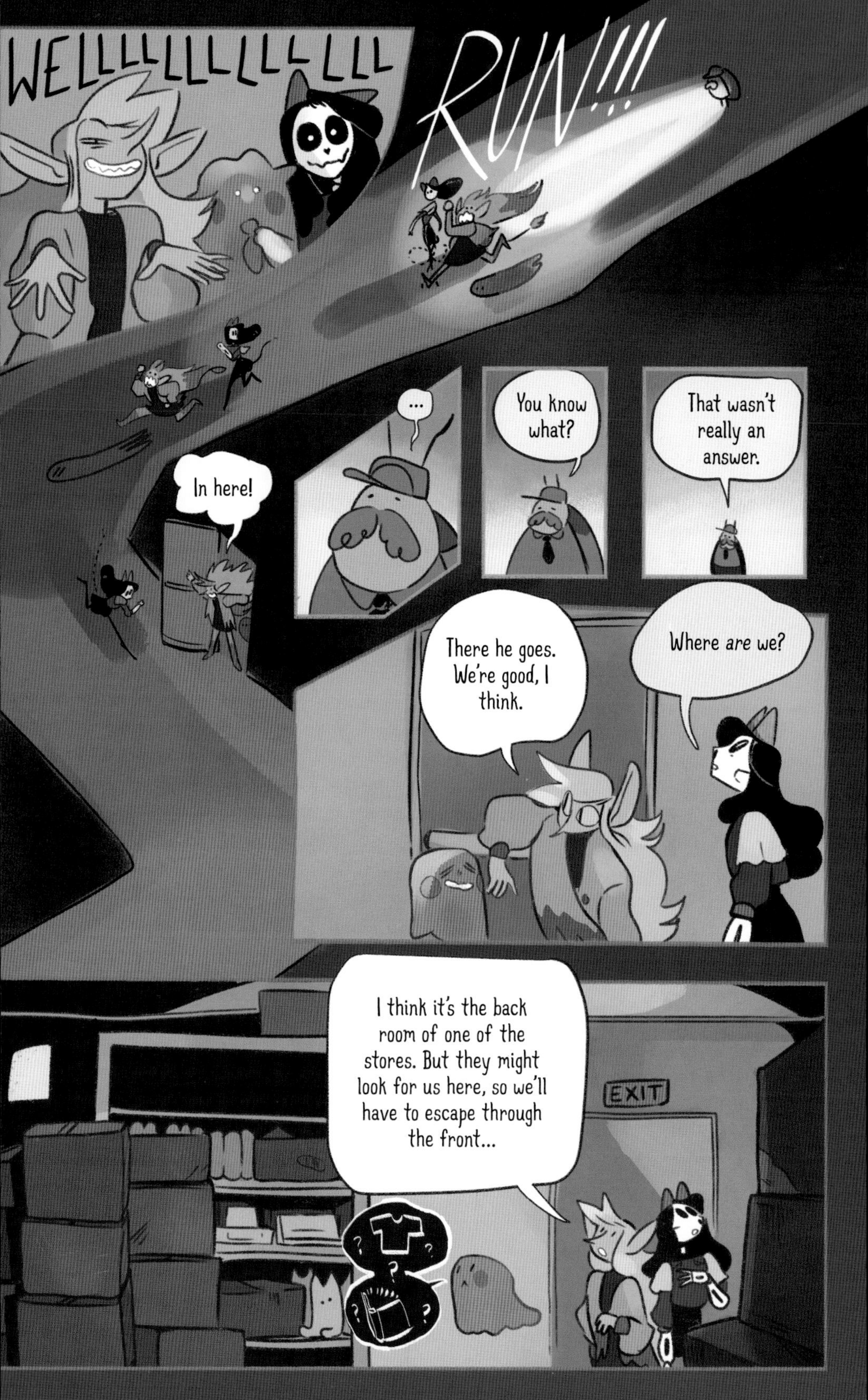
WELLLLLLLLLLLLL
RUN!!!
In here!
...
You know what?
That wasn't really an answer.
There he goes. We're good, I think.
Where are we?
I think it's the back room of one of the stores. But they might look for us here, so we'll have to escape through the front...
EXIT

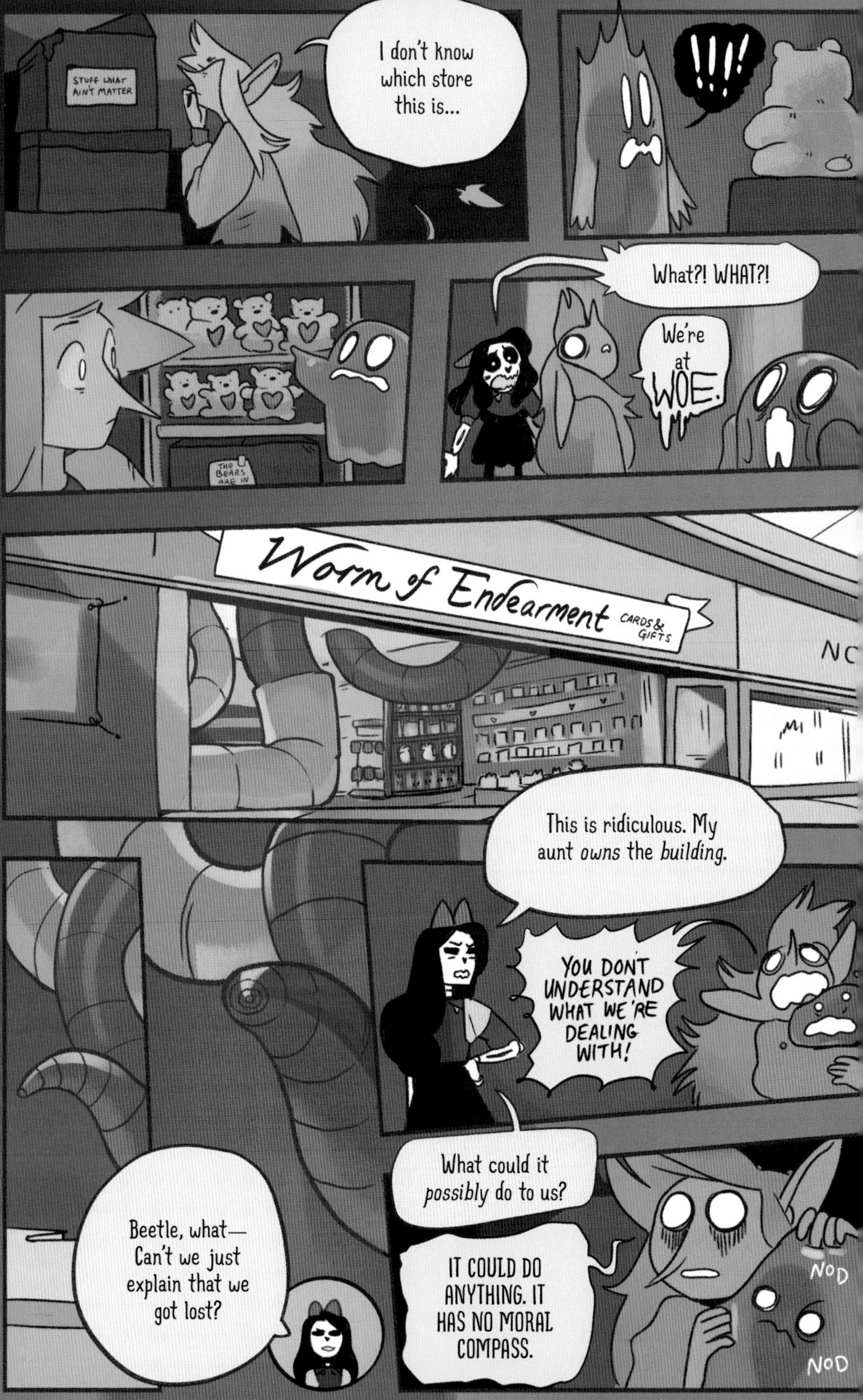
STUFF WHAT AIN'T MATTER
I don't know which store this is...
!!!!
THE BEARS ARE IN
What?! WHAT?!
We're at WOE.
Worm of Endearment
CARDS & GIFTS
This is ridiculous. My aunt *owns* the *building*.
YOU DON'T UNDERSTAND WHAT WE'RE DEALING WITH!
What could it *possibly* do to us?
Beetle, what— Can't we just explain that we got lost?
IT COULD DO ANYTHING. IT HAS NO MORAL COMPASS.
NOD
NOD

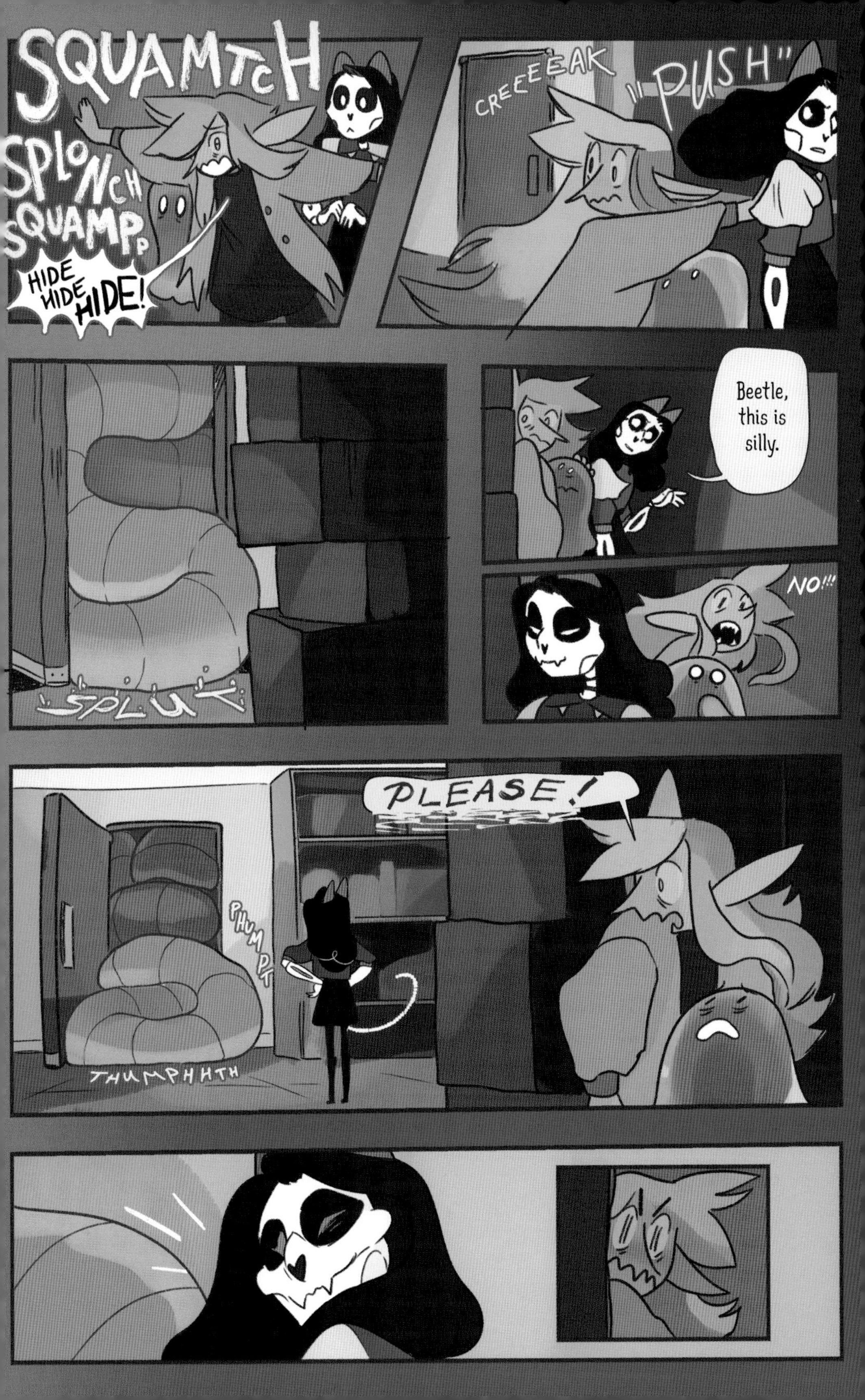
SQUAMTCH
SPLONCH
SQUAMPP
HIDE HIDE HIDE!
CREEEEAK
"PUSH"
SPLUT
Beetle, this is silly.
NO!!!
PLEASE!
PHUMPK
THUMPHHTH

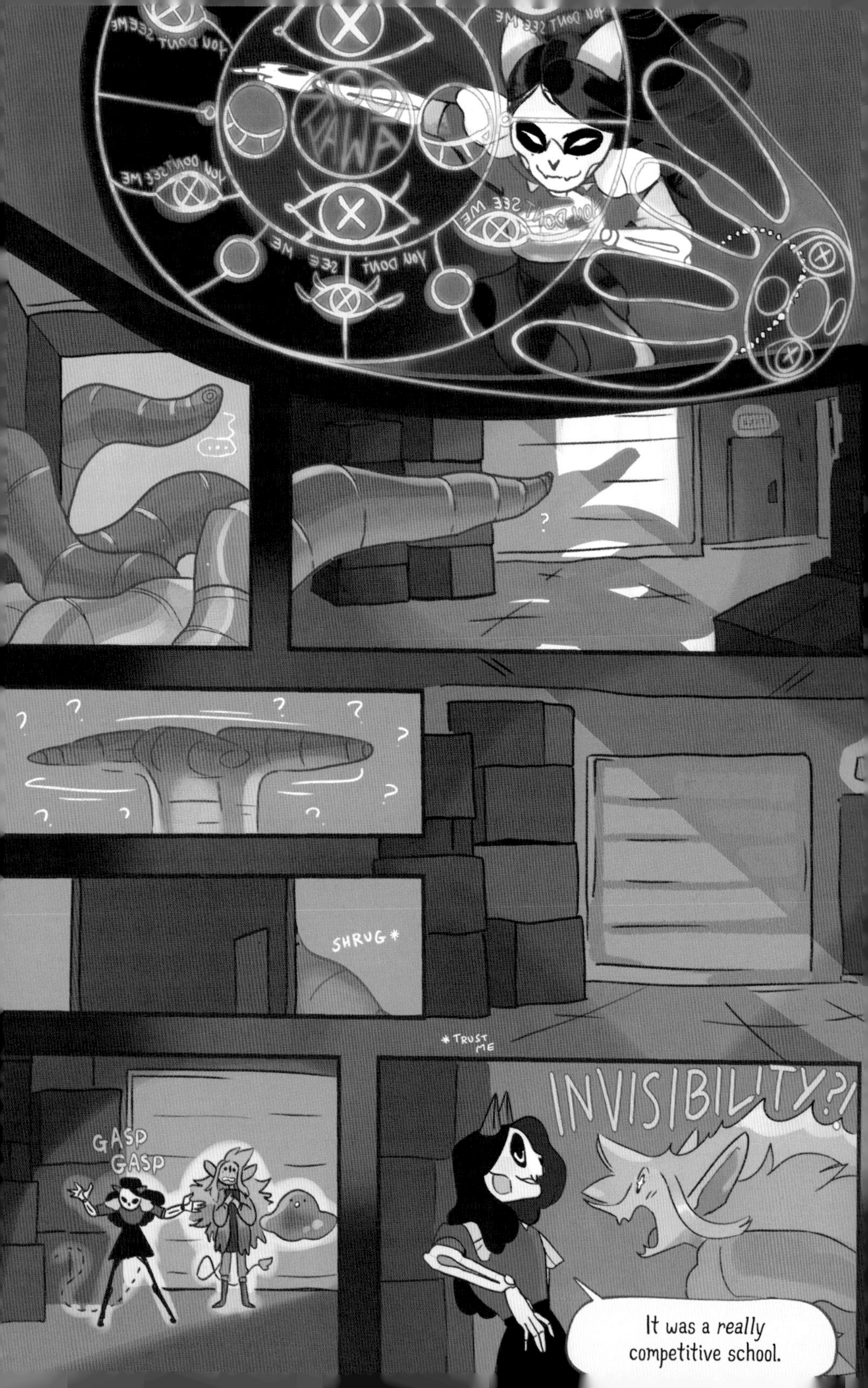
YOU DON'T SEE ME
AWAY
SHRUG*
*TRUST ME
GASP GASP
INVISIBILITY?!
It was a *really* competitive school.

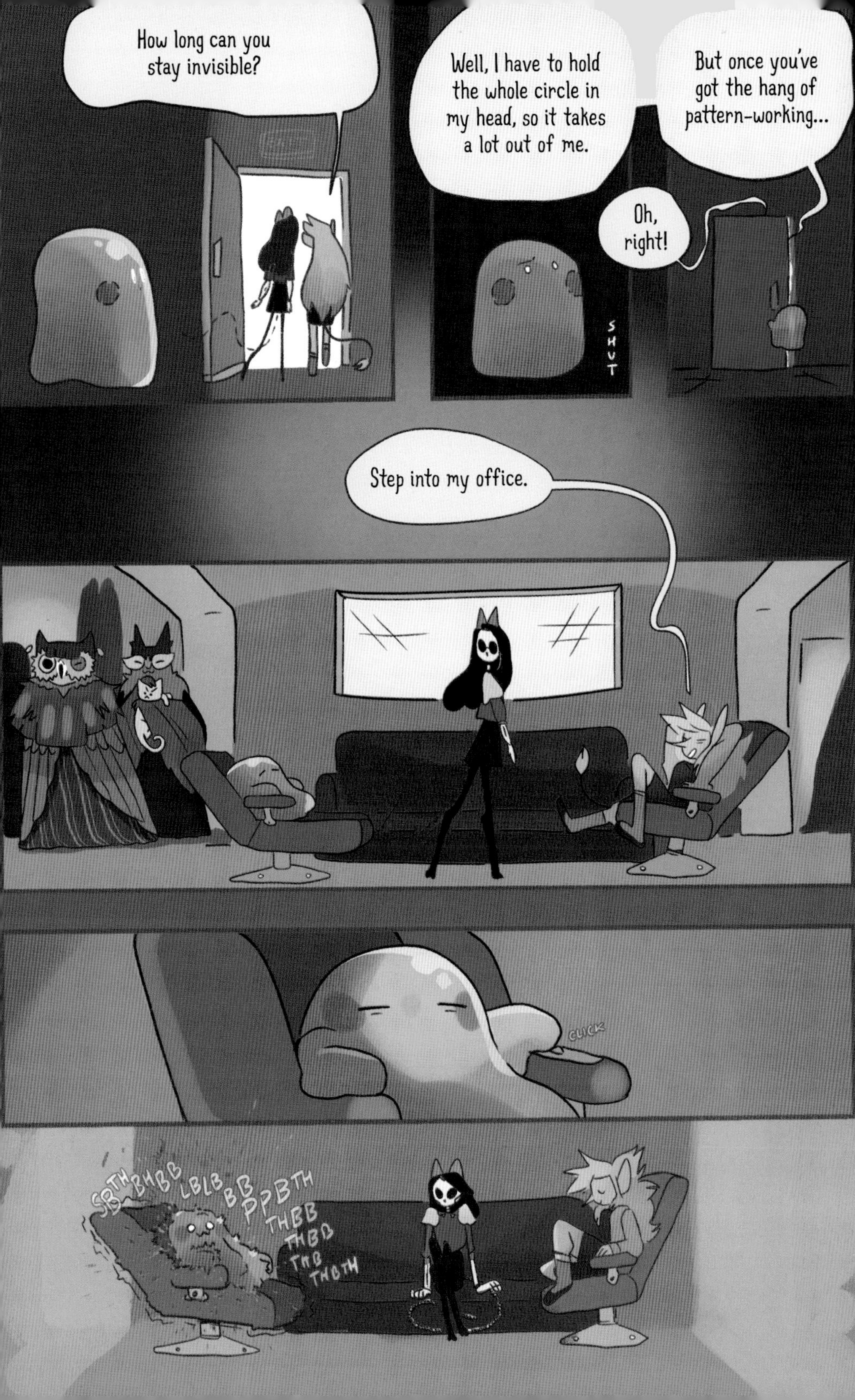
How long can you stay invisible?
Well, I have to hold the whole circle in my head, so it takes a lot out of me.
SHUT
But once you've got the hang of pattern-working...
Oh, right!
Step into my office.
CLICK
SBTH BHBB LBLB BB PPBTH THBB THBB THB THBTH

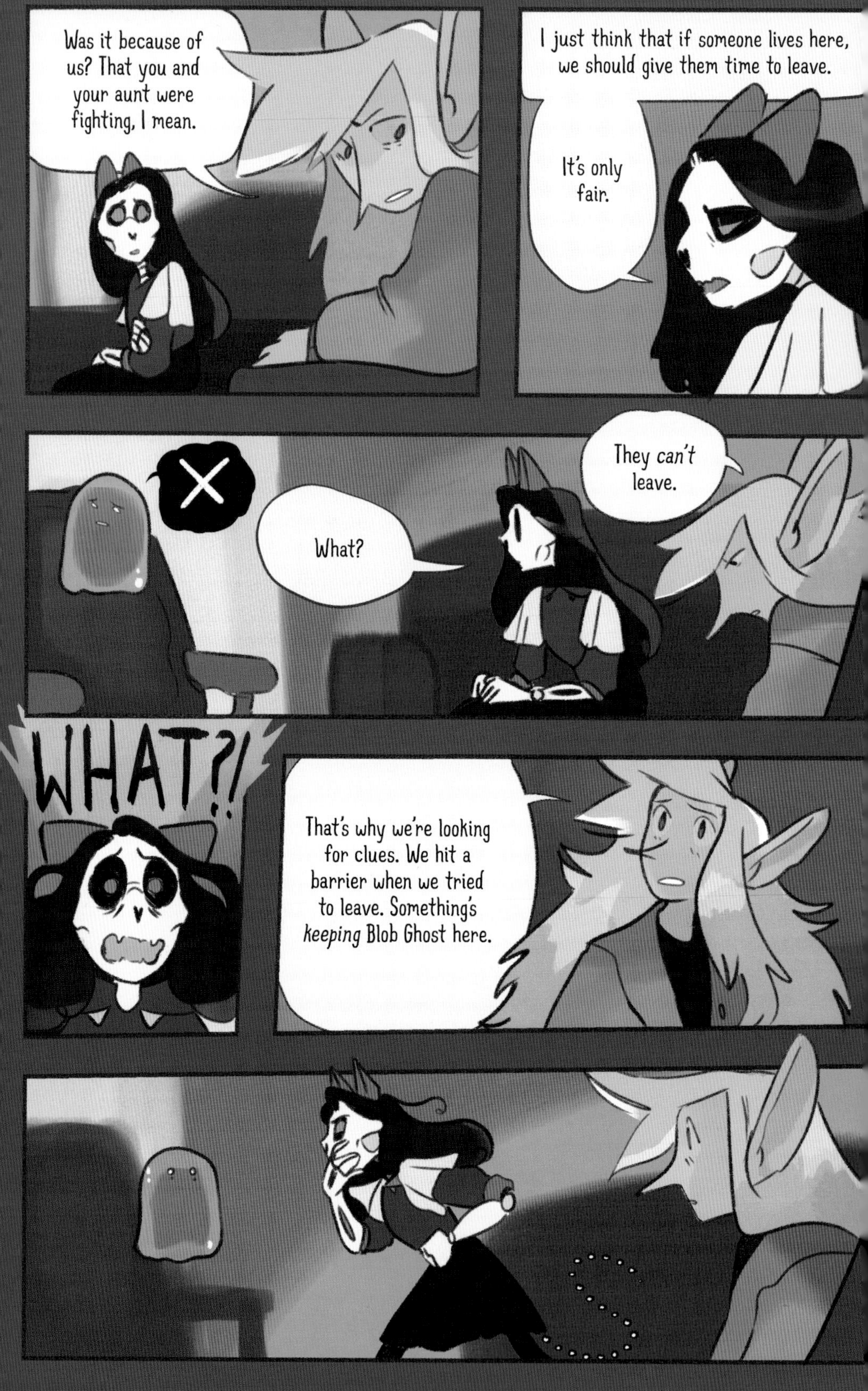
Was it because of us? That you and your aunt were fighting, I mean.
I just think that if someone lives here, we should give them time to leave.
It's only fair.
They *can't* leave.
What?
WHAT?!
That's why we're looking for clues. We hit a barrier when we tried to leave. Something's *keeping* Blob Ghost here.

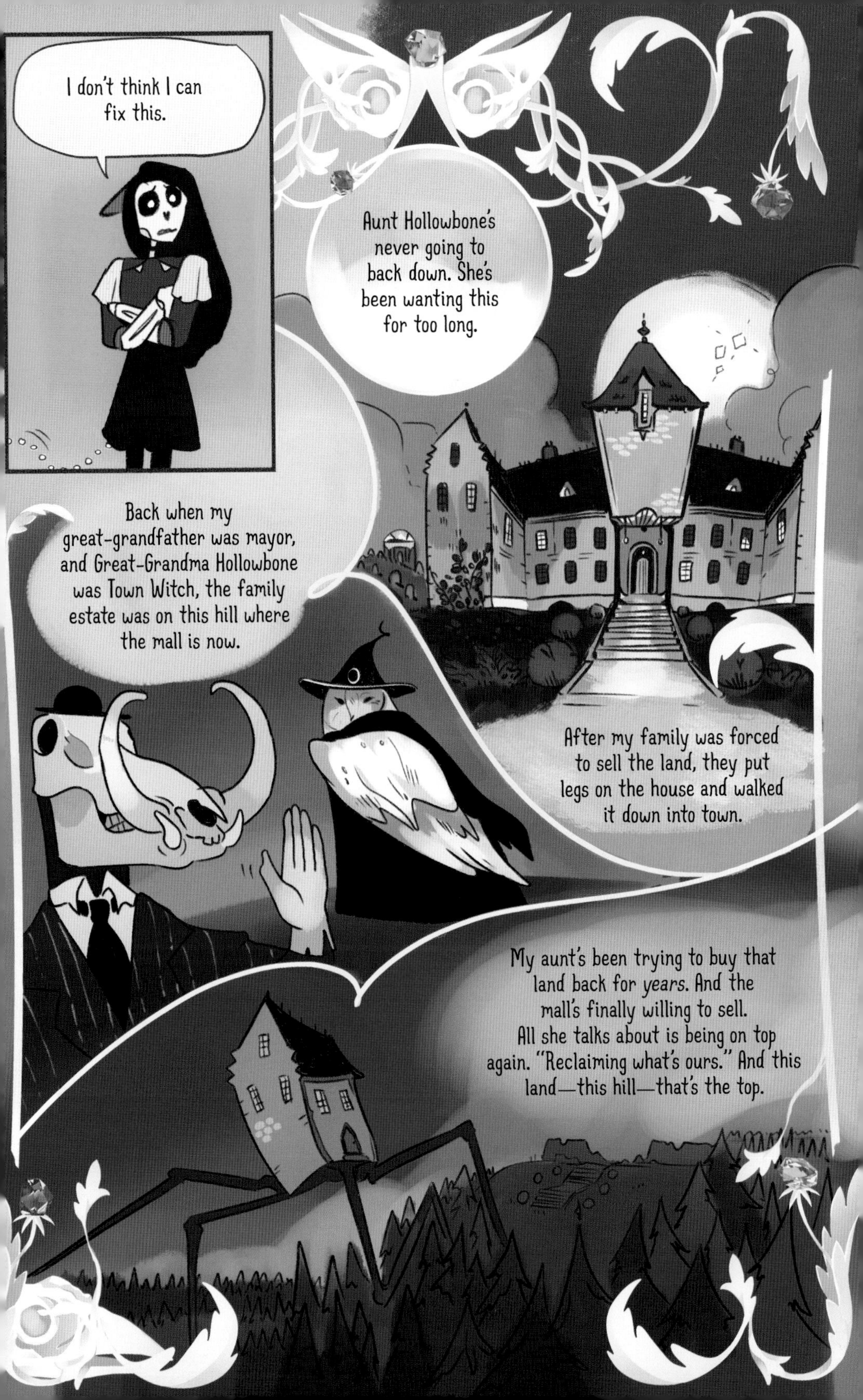
I don't think I can fix this.
Aunt Hollowbone's never going to back down. She's been wanting this for too long.
Back when my great-grandfather was mayor, and Great-Grandma Hollowbone was Town Witch, the family estate was on this hill where the mall is now.
After my family was forced to sell the land, they put legs on the house and walked it down into town.
My aunt's been trying to buy that land back for *years*. And the mall's finally willing to sell. All she talks about is being on top again. "Reclaiming what's ours." And this land—this hill—that's the top.

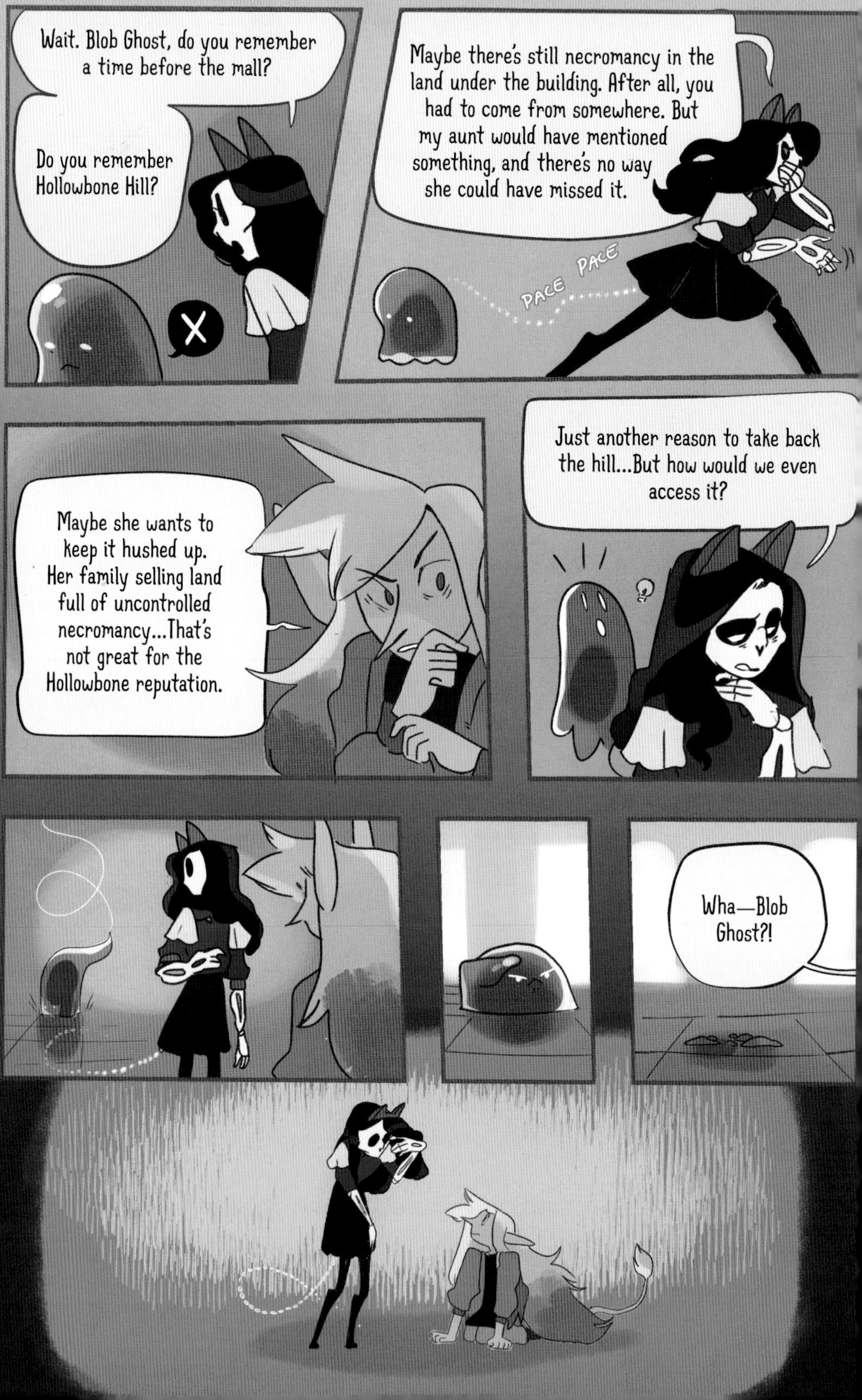

Wait. Blob Ghost, do you remember a time before the mall?
Do you remember Hollowbone Hill?
X
Maybe there's still necromancy in the land under the building. After all, you had to come from somewhere. But my aunt would have mentioned something, and there's no way she could have missed it.
PACE PACE
Maybe she wants to keep it hushed up. Her family selling land full of uncontrolled necromancy...That's not great for the Hollowbone reputation.
Just another reason to take back the hill...But how would we even access it?
Wha—Blob Ghost?!

THE UNDERMALL

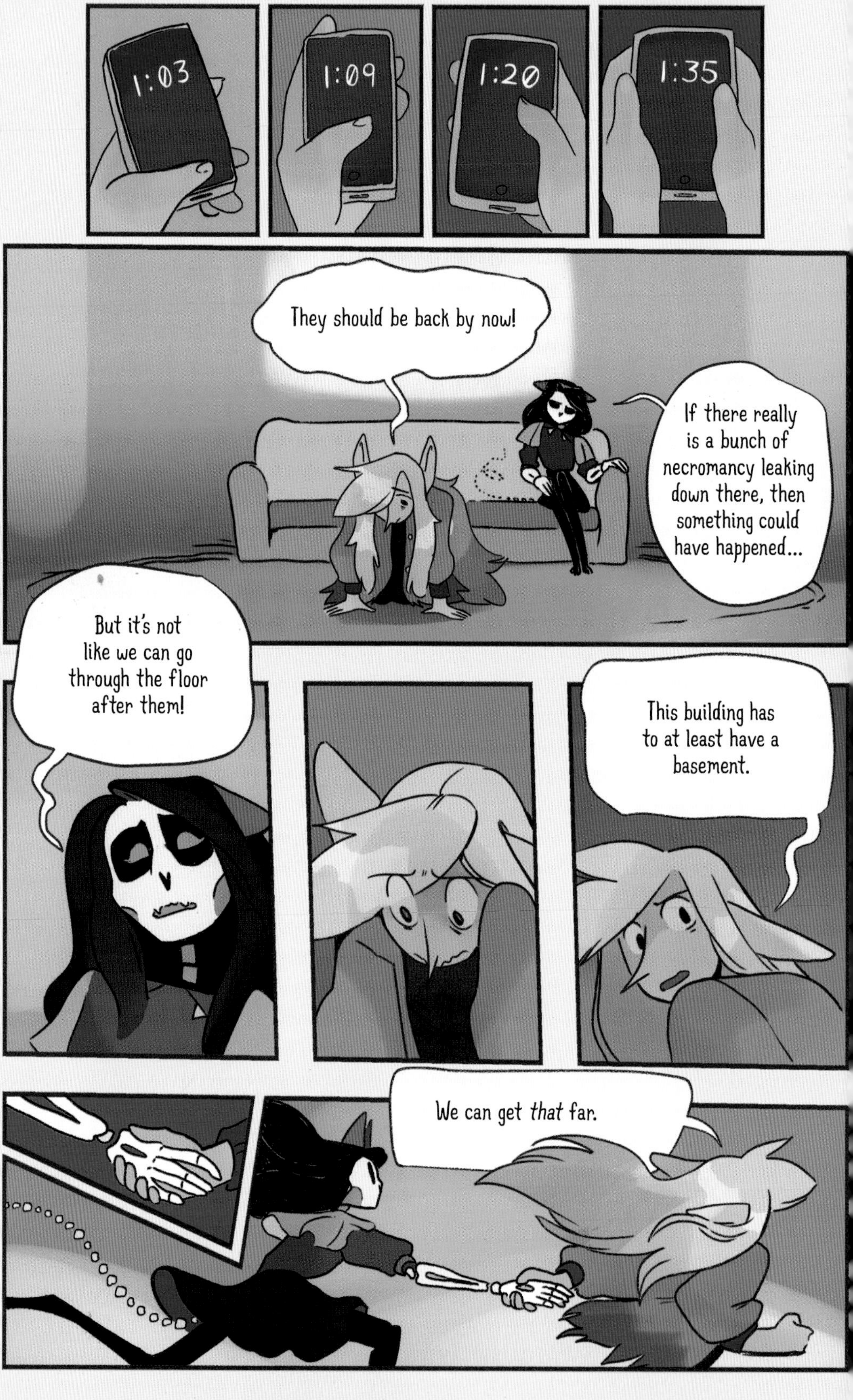
1:03
1:09
1:20
1:35
They should be back by now!
If there really is a bunch of necromancy leaking down there, then something could have happened...
But it's not like we can go through the floor after them!
This building has to at least have a basement.
We can get *that* far.

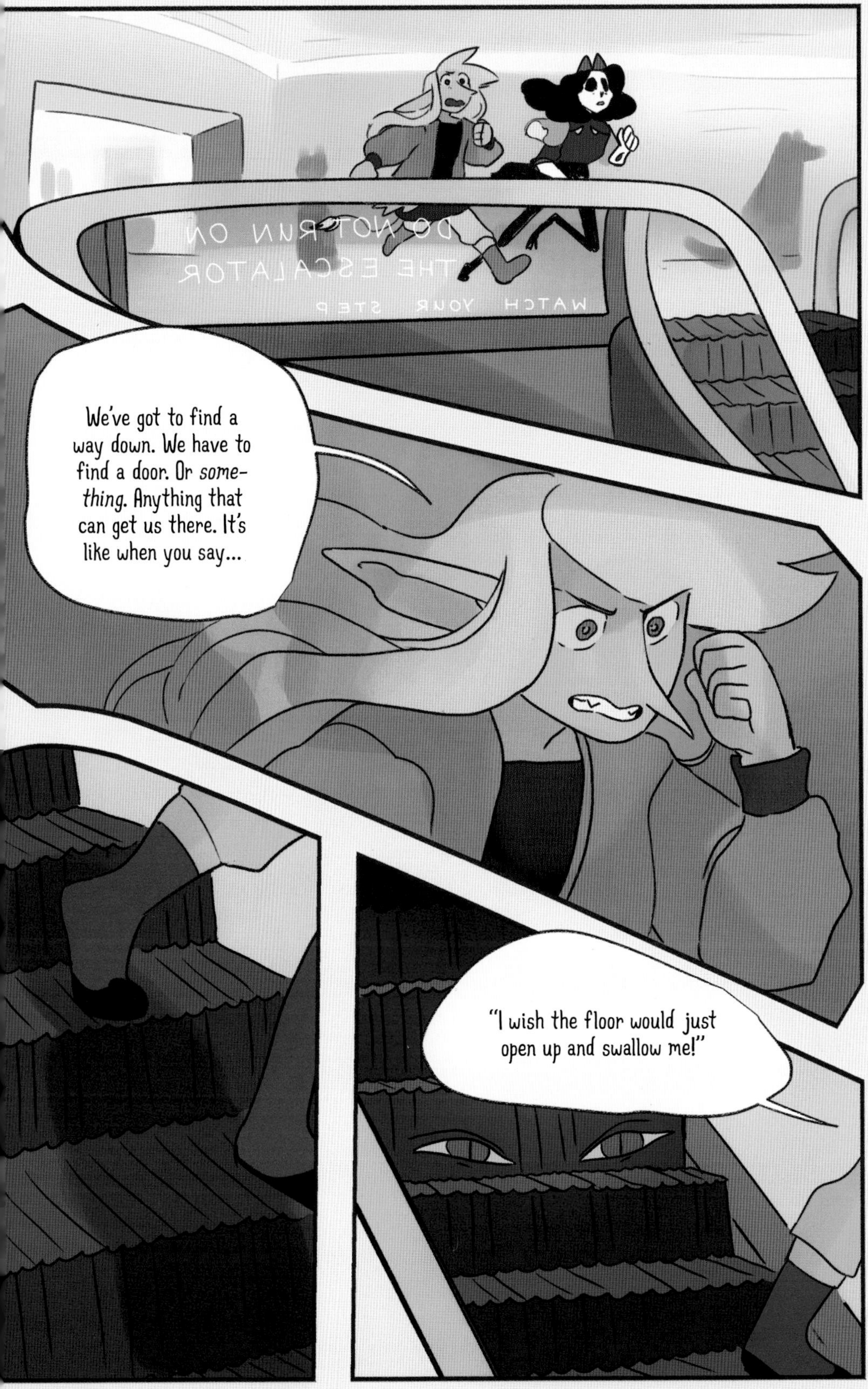
DO NOT RUN ON THE ESCALATOR
WATCH YOUR STEP
We've got to find a way down. We have to find a door. Or *something*. Anything that can get us there. It's like when you say...
"I wish the floor would just open up and swallow me!"

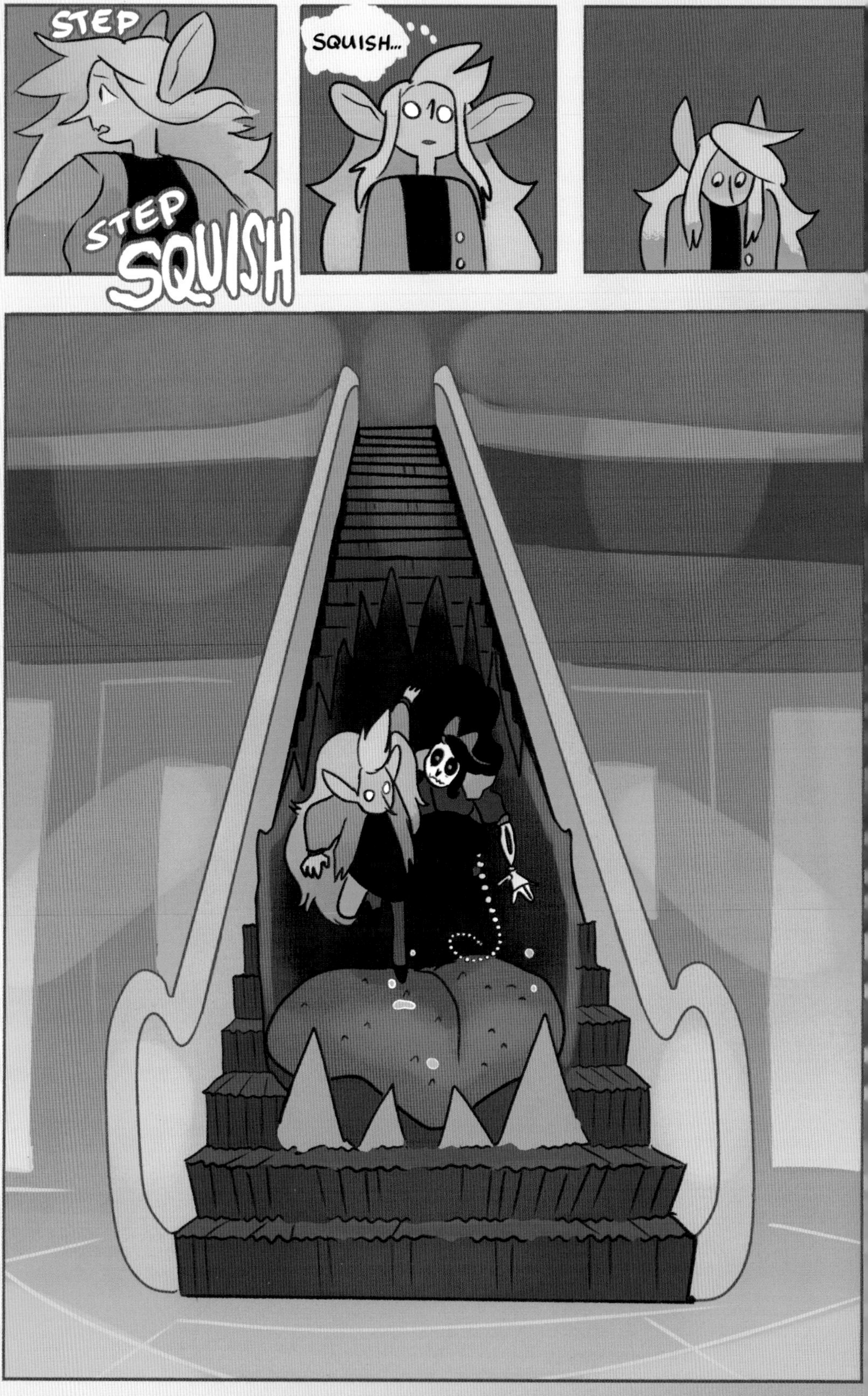
STEP
STEP
SQUISH
SQUISH...

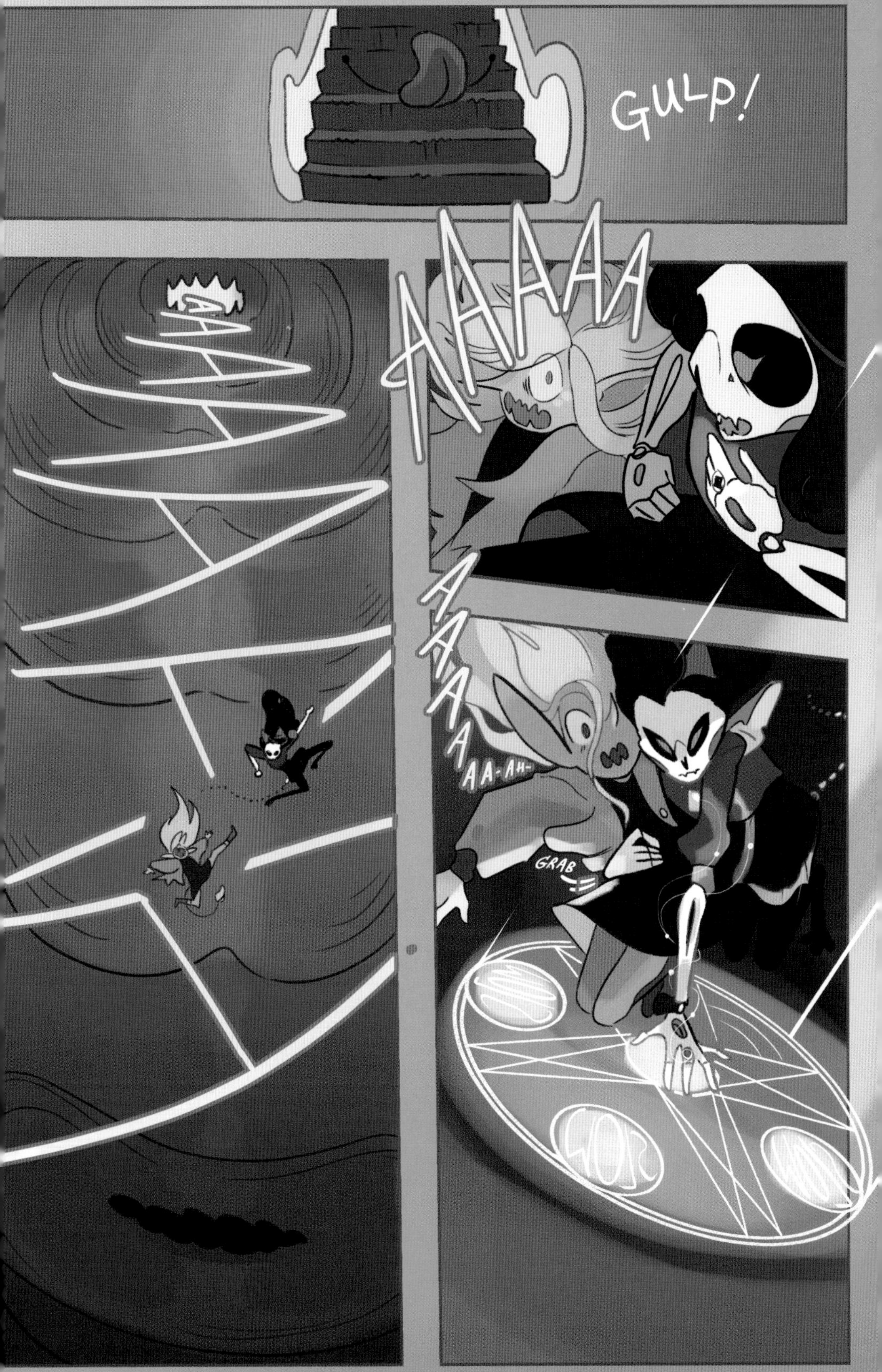
GULP!
AAAAAAAAAAAA
AAAAA
AAAAAAA-AH-
GRAB

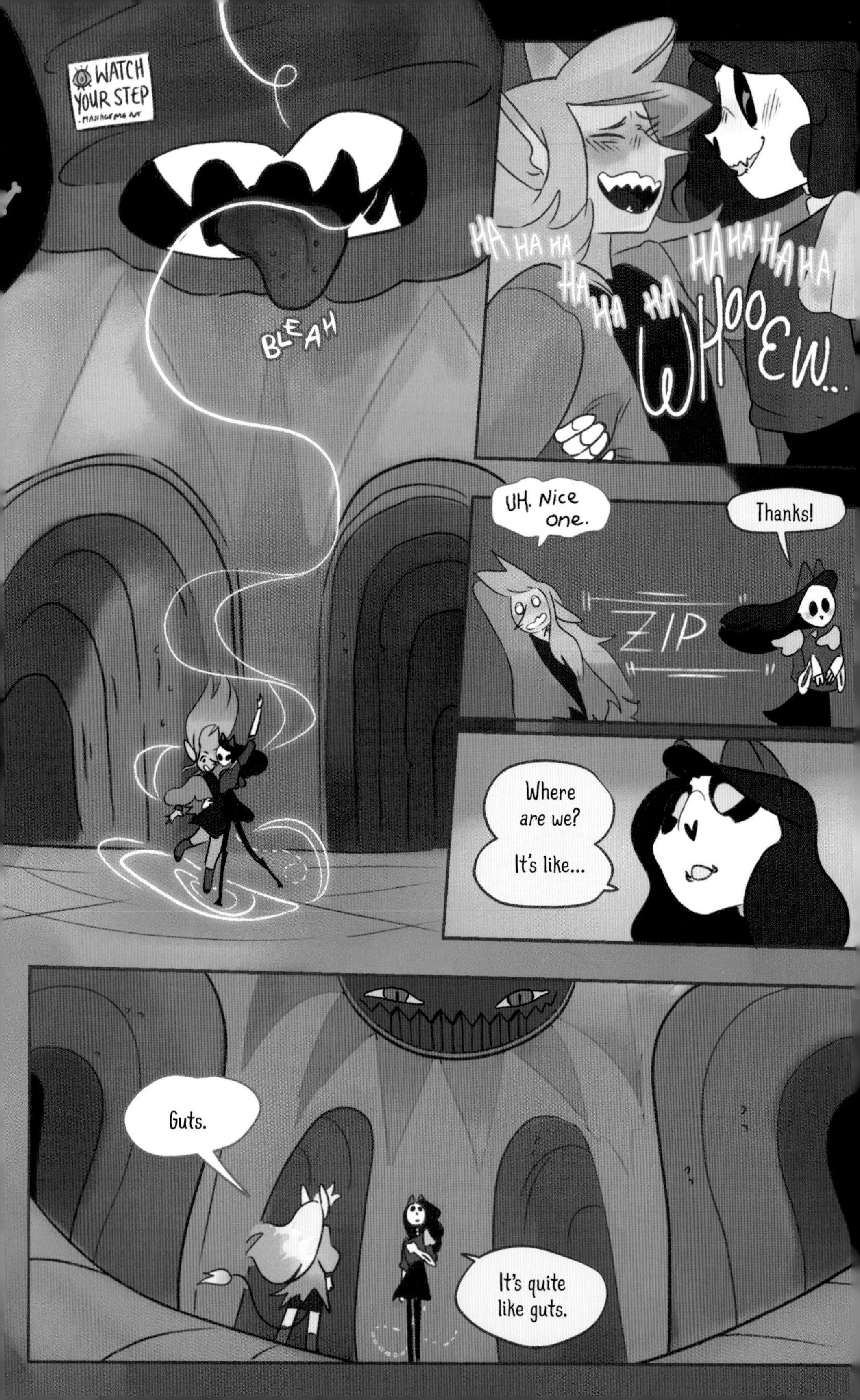
WATCH YOUR STEP
-MANAGEMENT
BLEAH
HA HA HA HA HA HA HA HA HA HA HA HA
WHOOEW...
UH. Nice one.
Thanks!
ZIP
Where are we?
It's like...
Guts.
It's quite like guts.

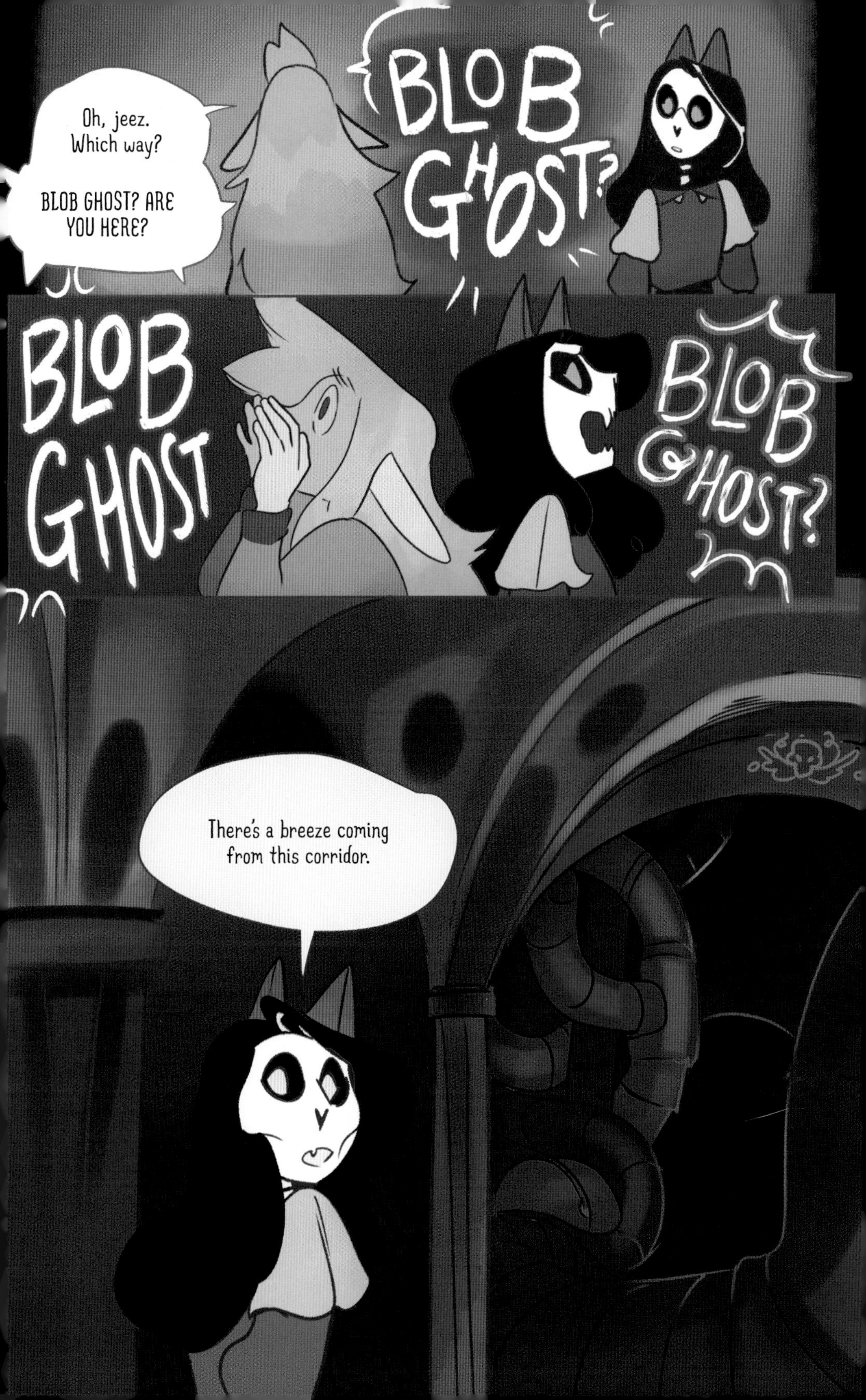

Oh, jeez. Which way?
BLOB GHOST? ARE YOU HERE?
BLOB GHOST?
BLOB GHOST
BLOB GHOST?
There's a breeze coming from this corridor.

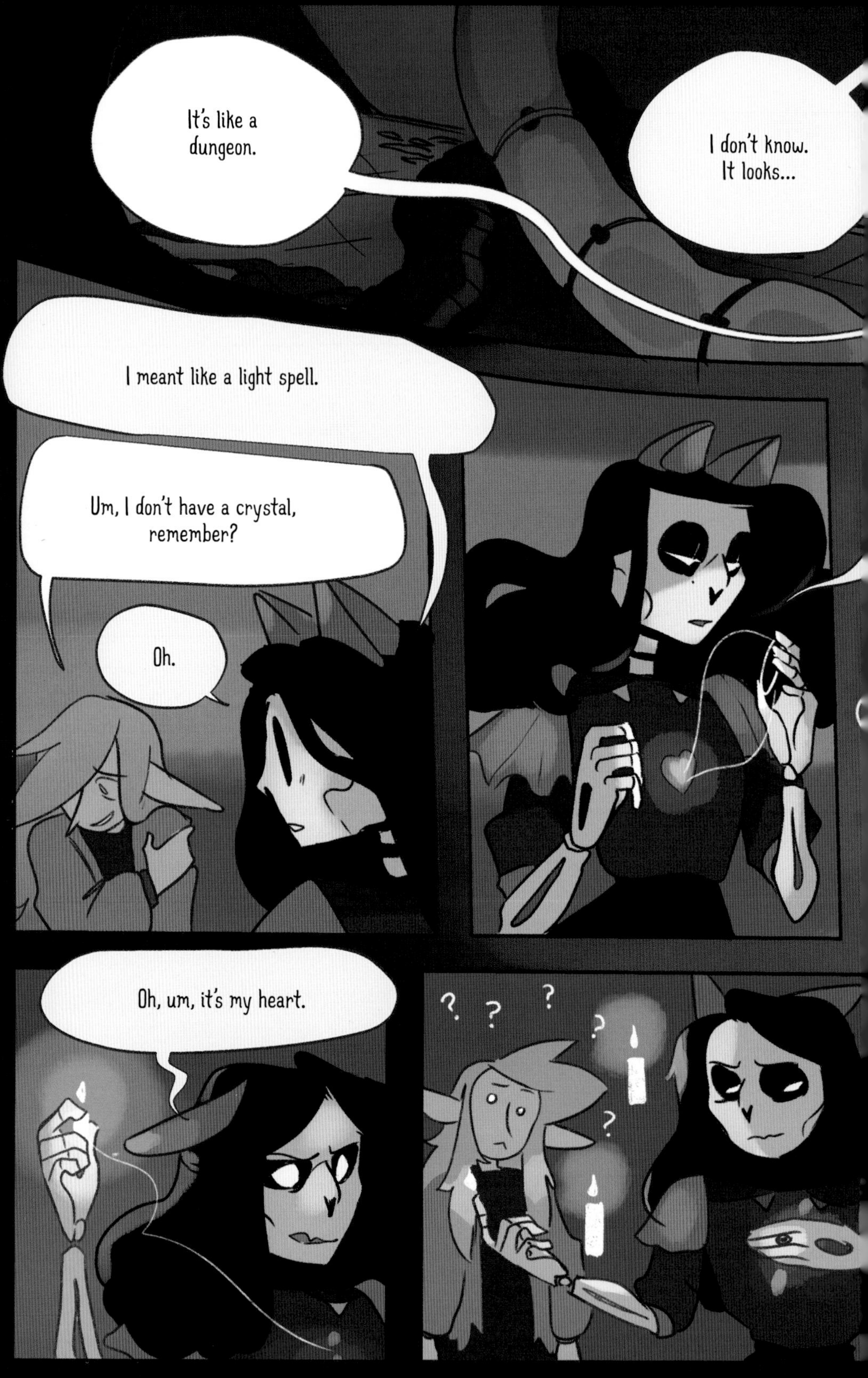
It's like a dungeon.
I don't know. It looks...
I meant like a light spell.
Um, I don't have a crystal, remember?
Oh.
Oh, um, it's my heart.
? ? ? ? ?

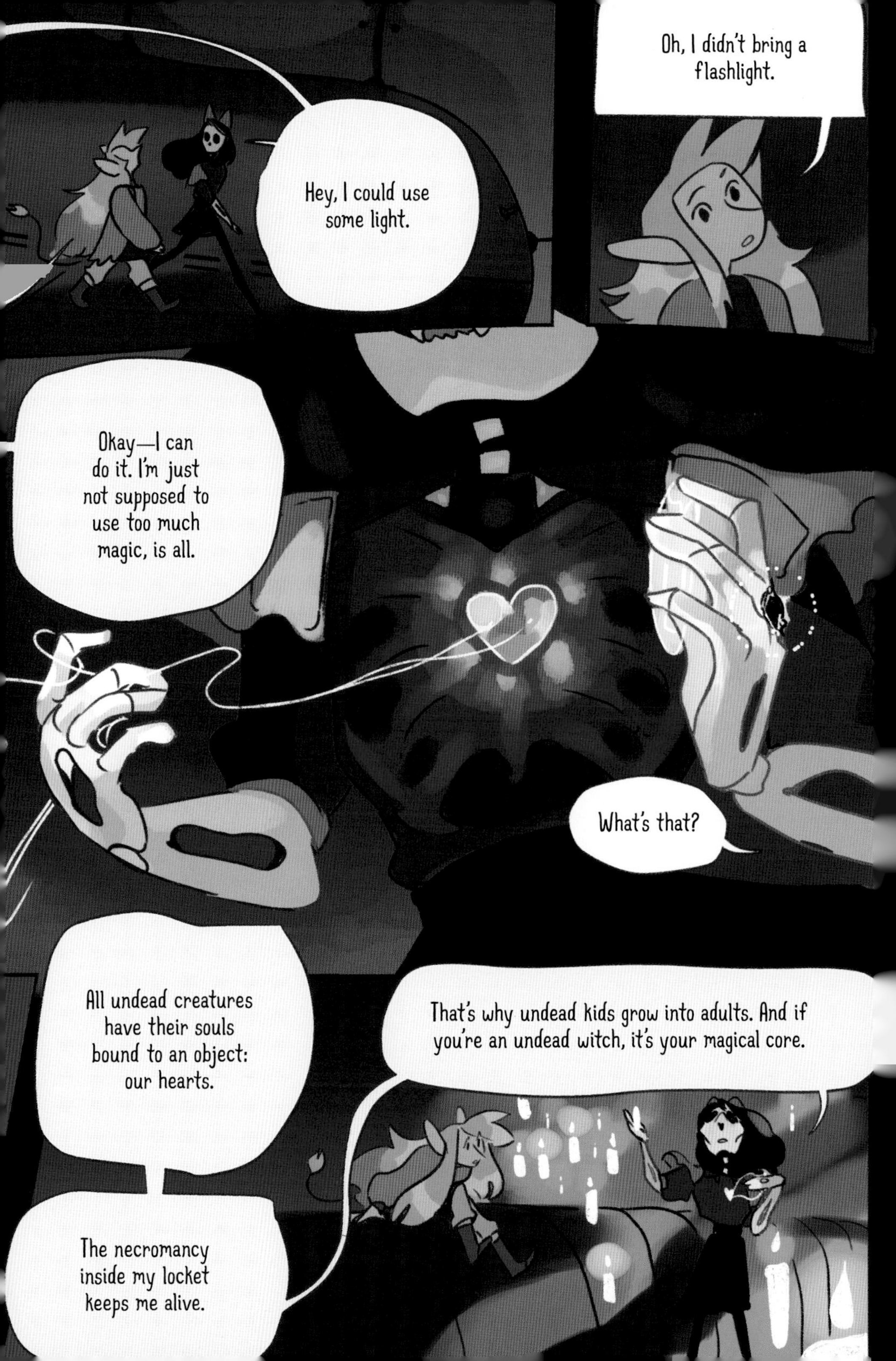
Hey, I could use some light.
Oh, I didn't bring a flashlight.
Okay—I can do it. I'm just not supposed to use too much magic, is all.
What's that?
All undead creatures have their souls bound to an object: our hearts.
The necromancy inside my locket keeps me alive.
That's why undead kids grow into adults. And if you're an undead witch, it's your magical core.

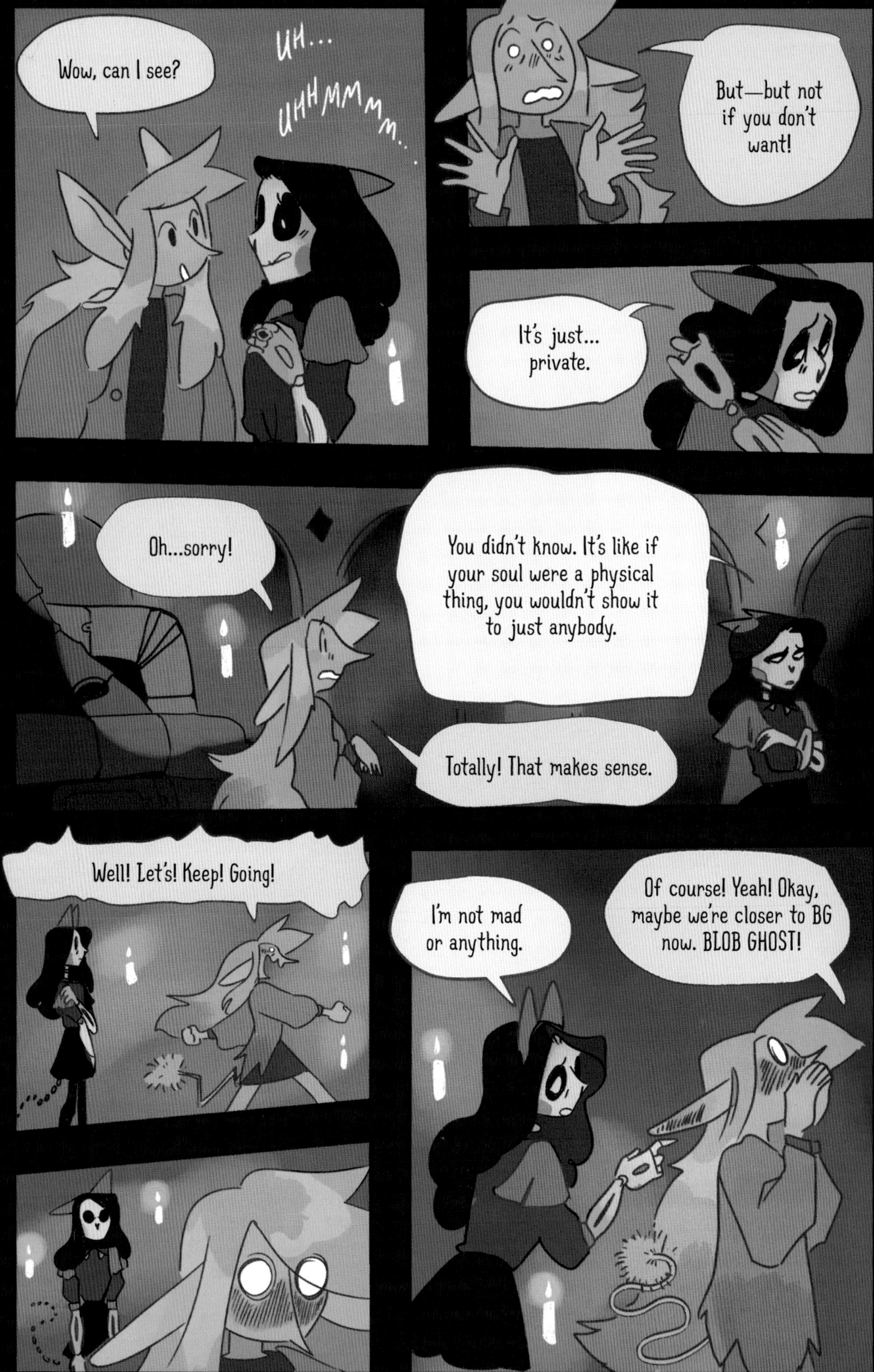
Wow, can I see?
UH... UHHMMMMM...
But—but not if you don't want!
It's just... private.
Oh...sorry!
You didn't know. It's like if your soul were a physical thing, you wouldn't show it to just anybody.
Totally! That makes sense.
Well! Let's! Keep! Going!
I'm not mad or anything.
Of course! Yeah! Okay, maybe we're closer to BG now. BLOB GHOST!

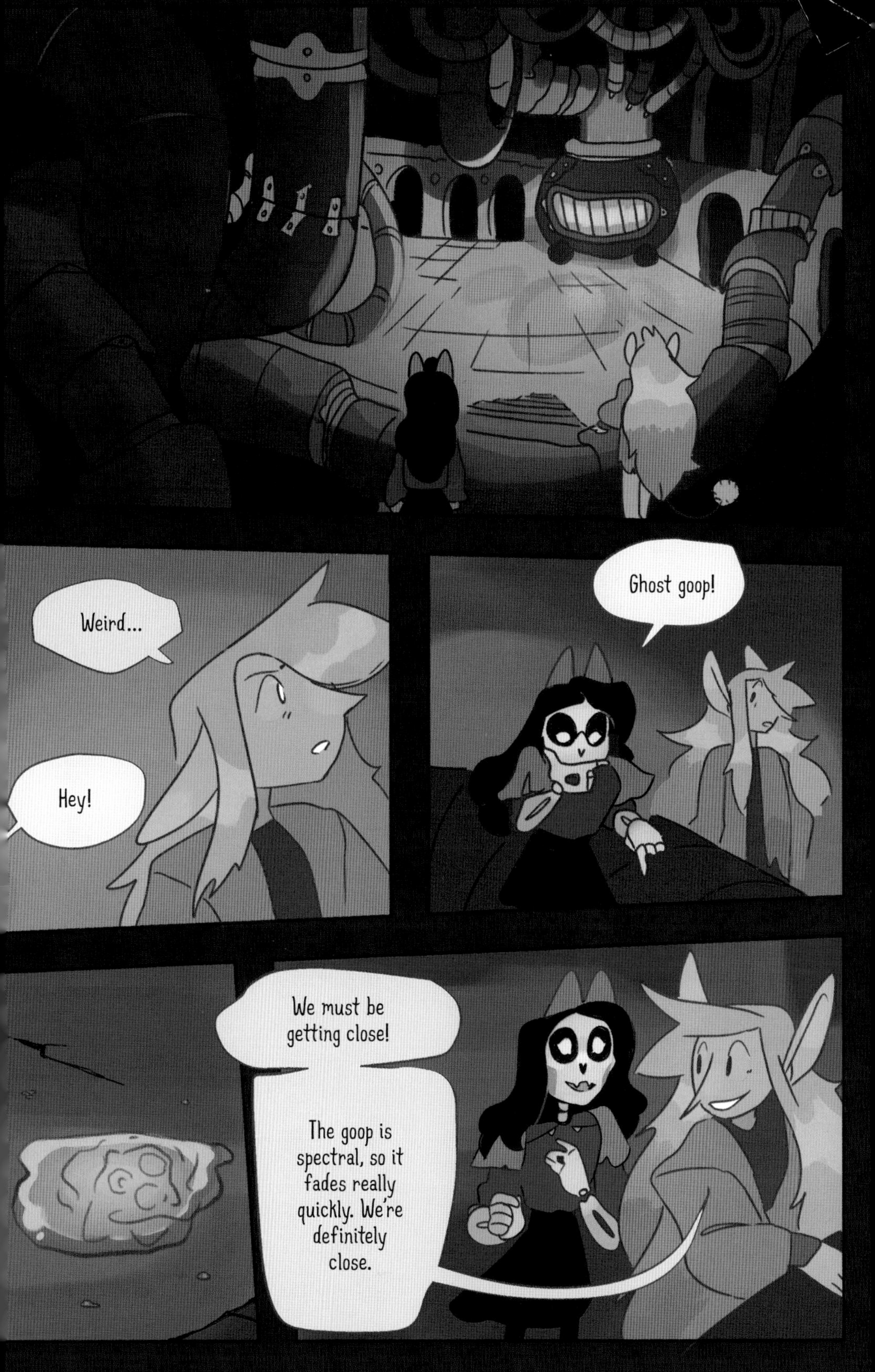
Weird...
Hey!
Ghost goop!
We must be getting close!
The goop is spectral, so it fades really quickly. We're definitely close.

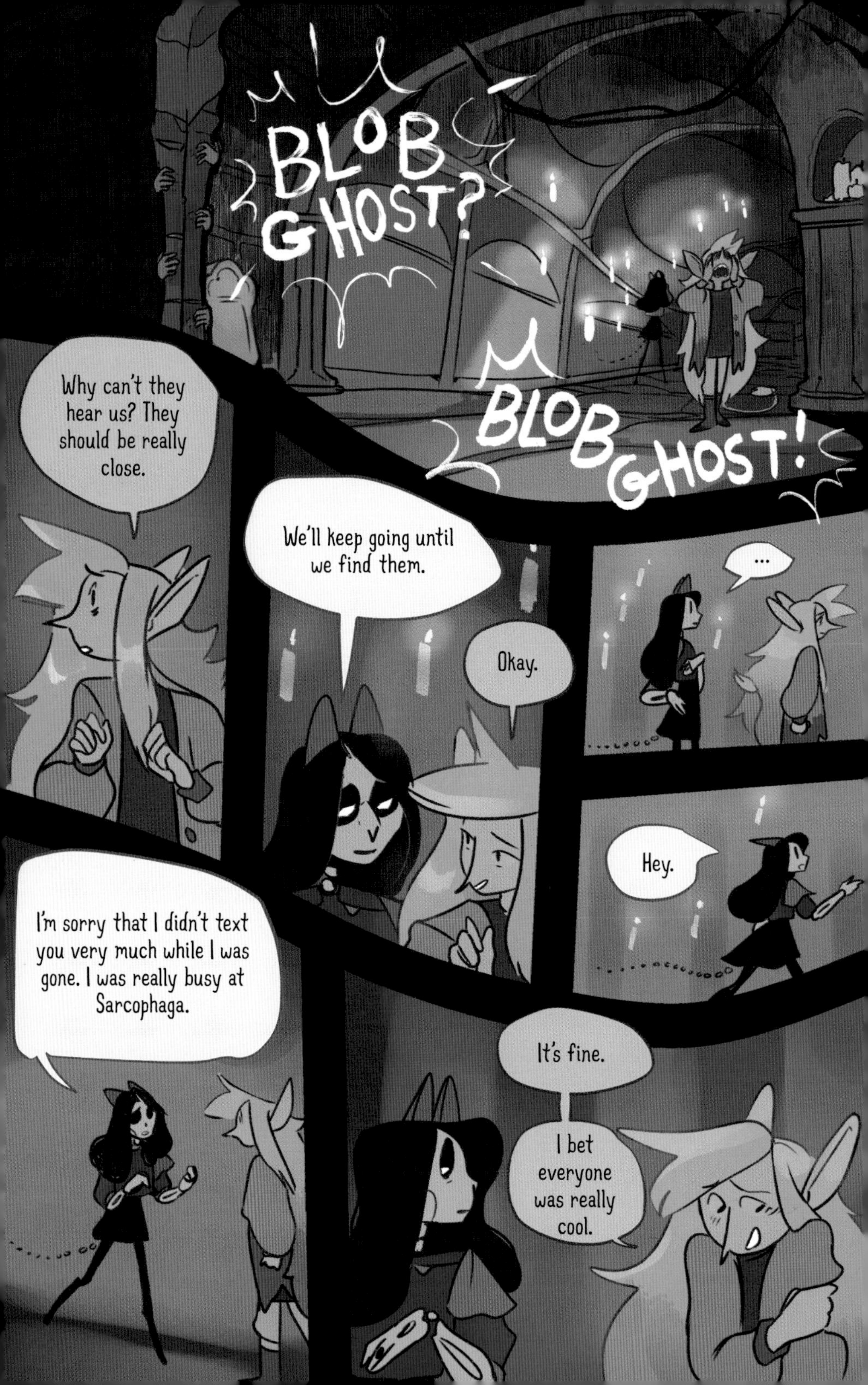

BLOB GHOST?
BLOB GHOST!
Why can't they hear us? They should be really close.
We'll keep going until we find them.
Okay.
...
Hey.
I'm sorry that I didn't text you very much while I was gone. I was really busy at Sarcophaga.
It's fine.
I bet everyone was really cool.

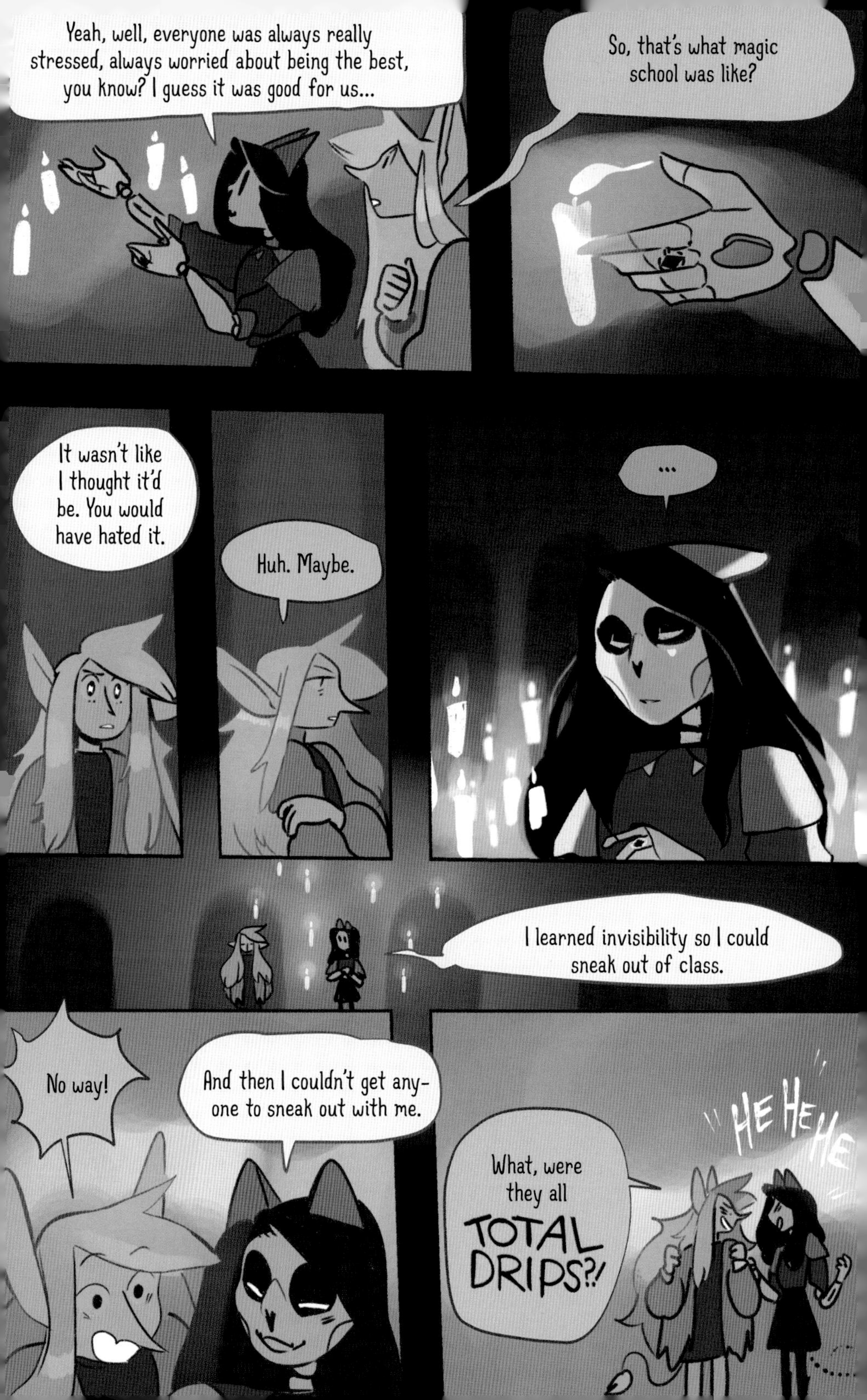

Yeah, well, everyone was always really stressed, always worried about being the best, you know? I guess it was good for us...
So, that's what magic school was like?
It wasn't like I thought it'd be. You would have hated it.
Huh. Maybe.
...
I learned invisibility so I could sneak out of class.
No way!
And then I couldn't get any-one to sneak out with me.
What, were they all TOTAL DRIPS?!
HE HE HE HE

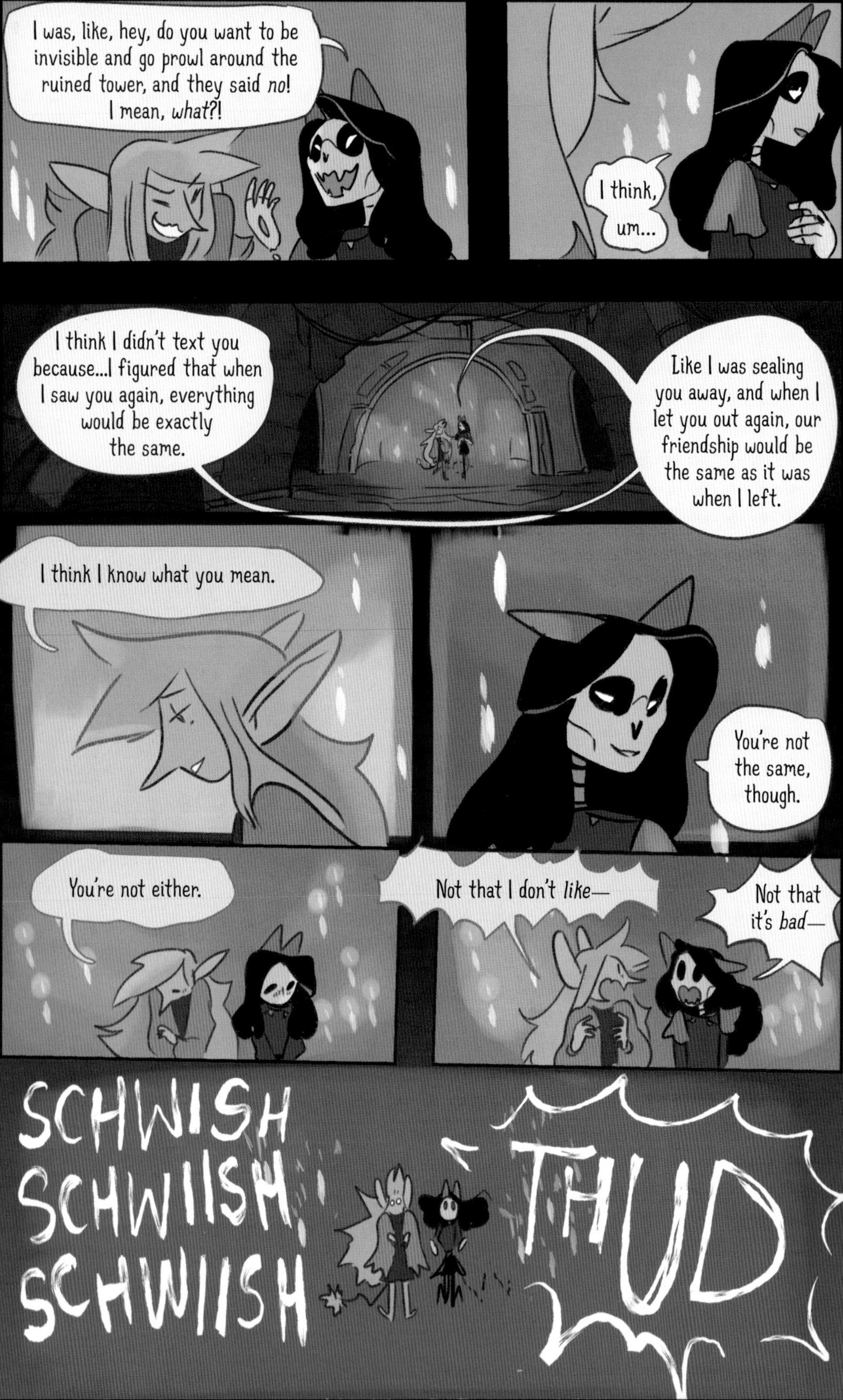
I was, like, hey, do you want to be invisible and go prowl around the ruined tower, and they said *no*! I mean, *what*?!
I think, um...
I think I didn't text you because...I figured that when I saw you again, everything would be exactly the same.
Like I was sealing you away, and when I let you out again, our friendship would be the same as it was when I left.
I think I know what you mean.
You're not the same, though.
You're not either.
Not that I don't *like*—
Not that it's *bad*—
SCHWISH
SCHWIISH
SCHWIISH
THUD

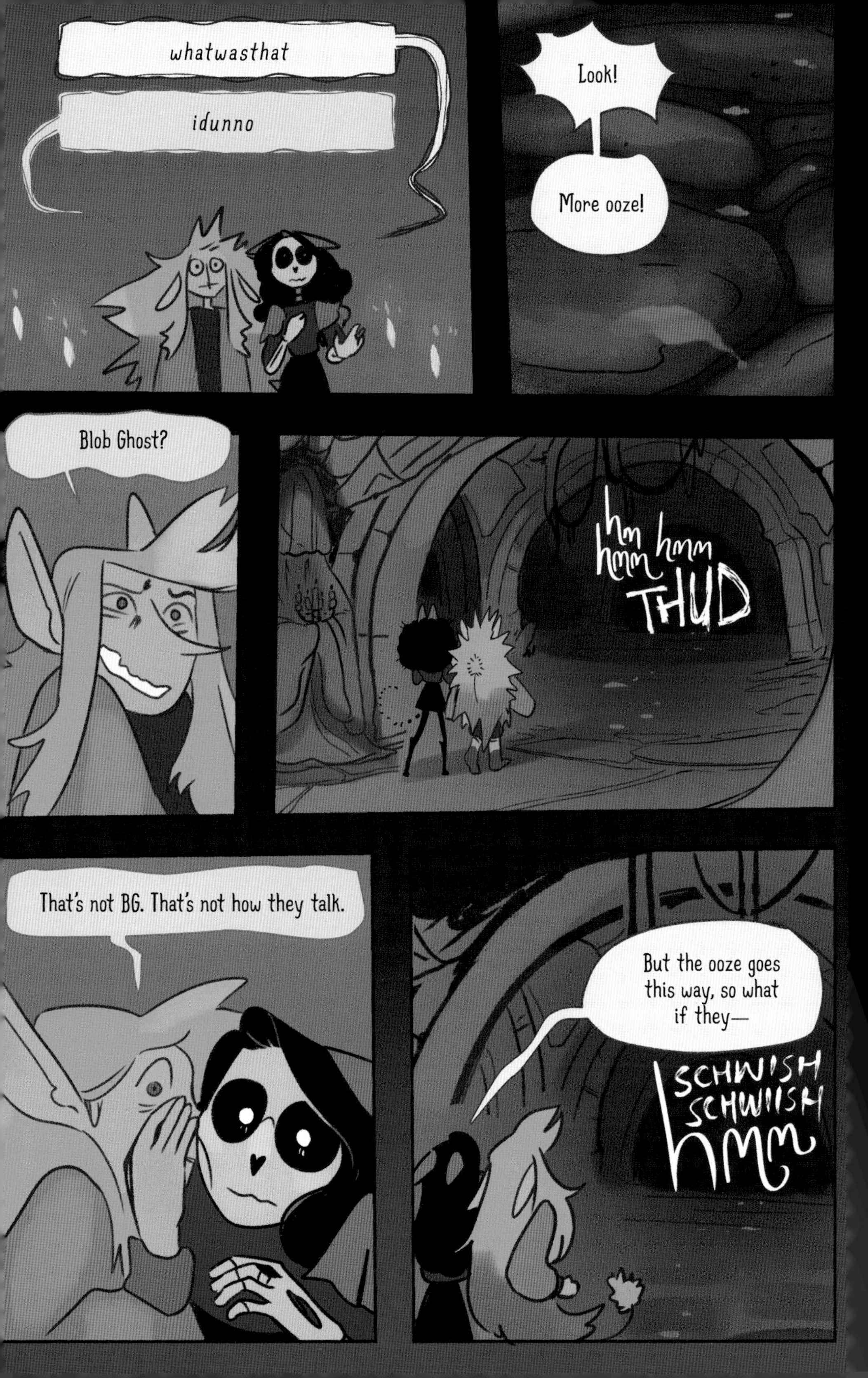
whatwasthat
idunno
Look!
More ooze!
Blob Ghost?
hm hmm hmm
THUD
That's not BG. That's not how they talk.
But the ooze goes this way, so what if they—
SCHWISH SCHWIISH
hmm

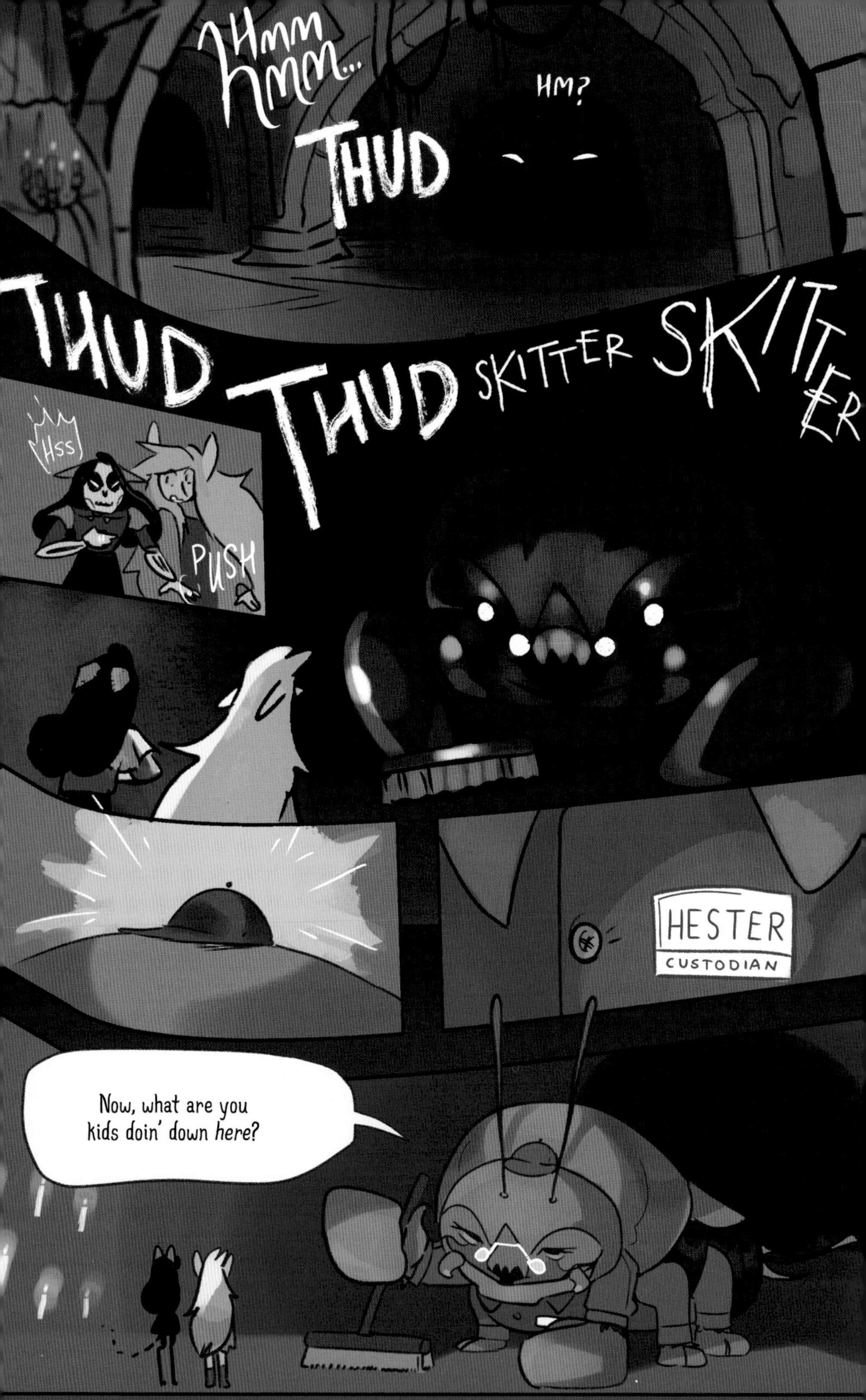

Hmm hmm...
HM?
THUD
THUD
THUD
SKITTER
SKITTER
HSS
PUSH
HESTER
CUSTODIAN
Now, what are you kids doin' down here?

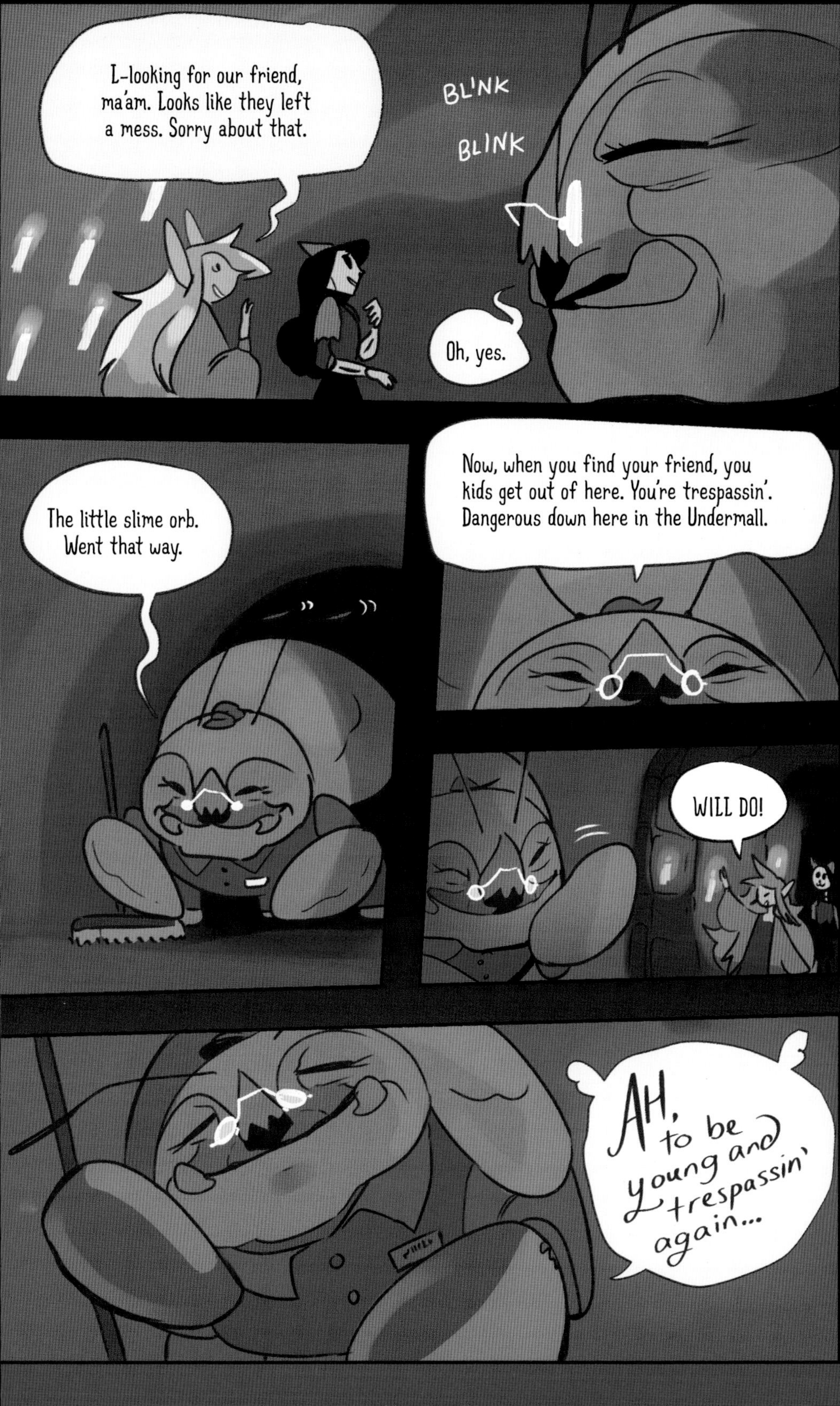
L-looking for our friend, ma'am. Looks like they left a mess. Sorry about that.
BLINK
BLINK
Oh, yes.
The little slime orb. Went that way.
Now, when you find your friend, you kids get out of here. You're trespassin'. Dangerous down here in the Undermall.
WILL DO!
AH, to be young and trespassin' again...

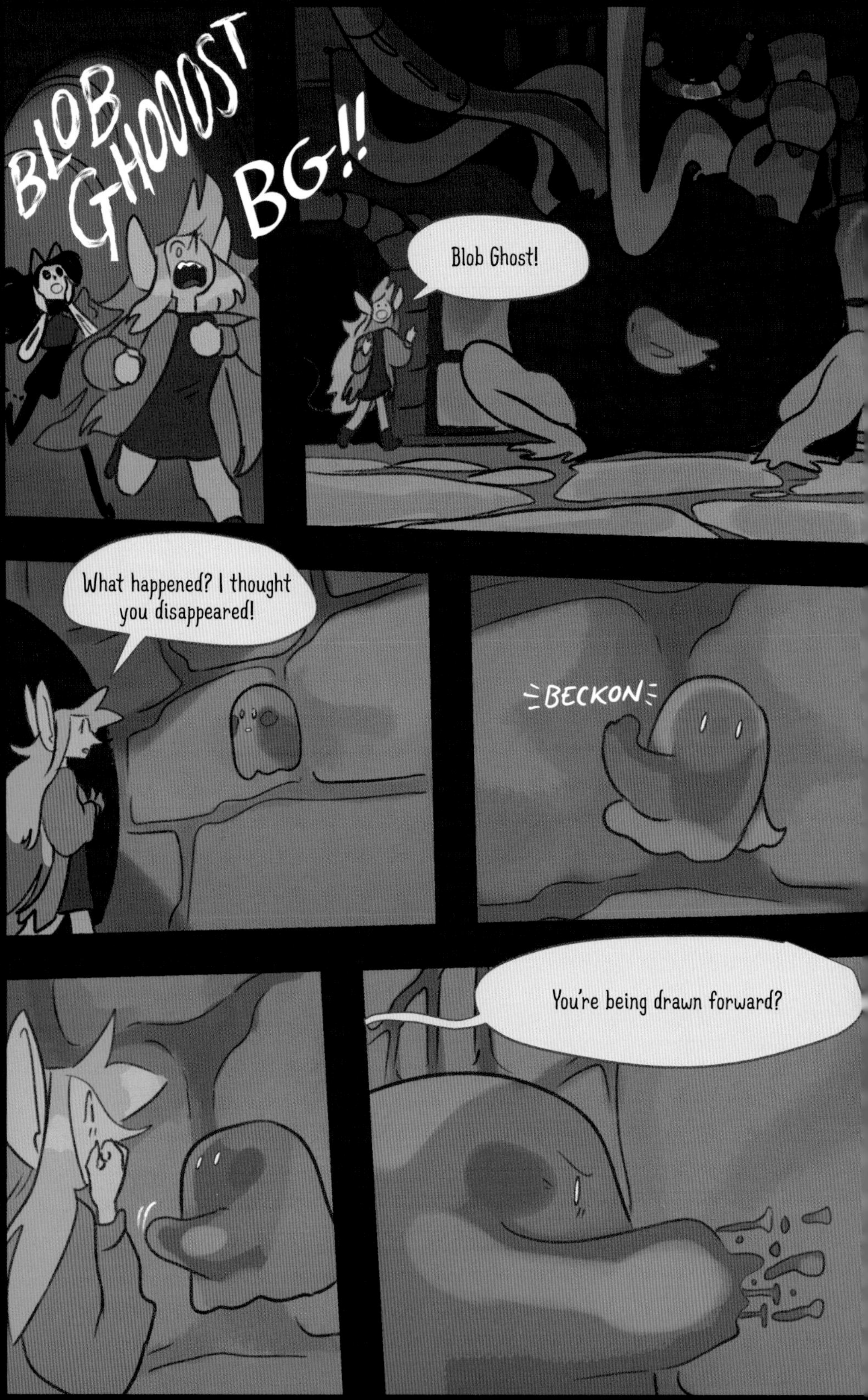
BLOB GHOOOST
BG!!
Blob Ghost!
What happened? I thought you disappeared!
BECKON
You're being drawn forward?

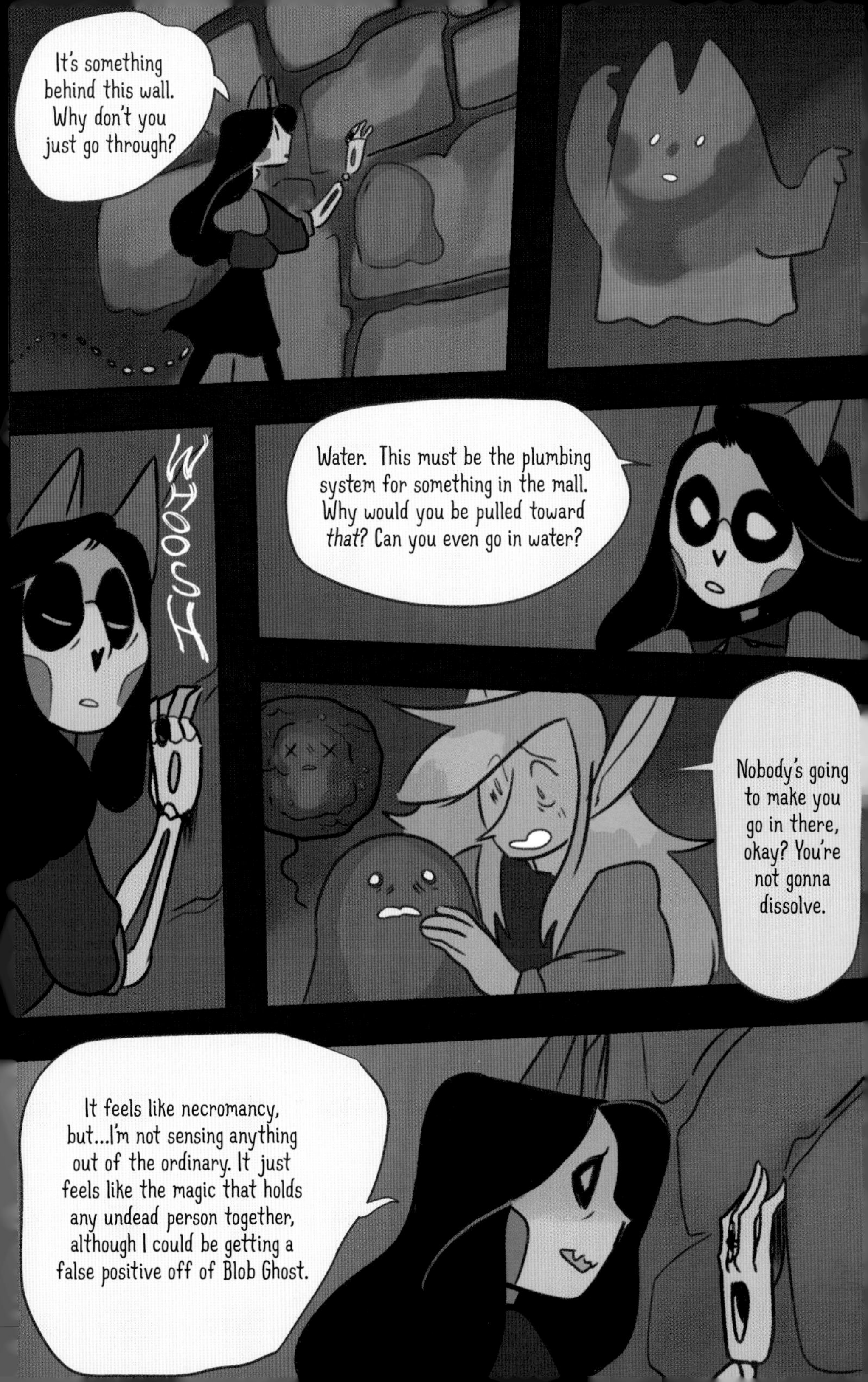
It's something behind this wall. Why don't you just go through?
WHOOSH
Water. This must be the plumbing system for something in the mall. Why would you be pulled toward *that*? Can you even go in water?
Nobody's going to make you go in there, okay? You're not gonna dissolve.
It feels like necromancy, but...I'm not sensing anything out of the ordinary. It just feels like the magic that holds any undead person together, although I could be getting a false positive off of Blob Ghost.

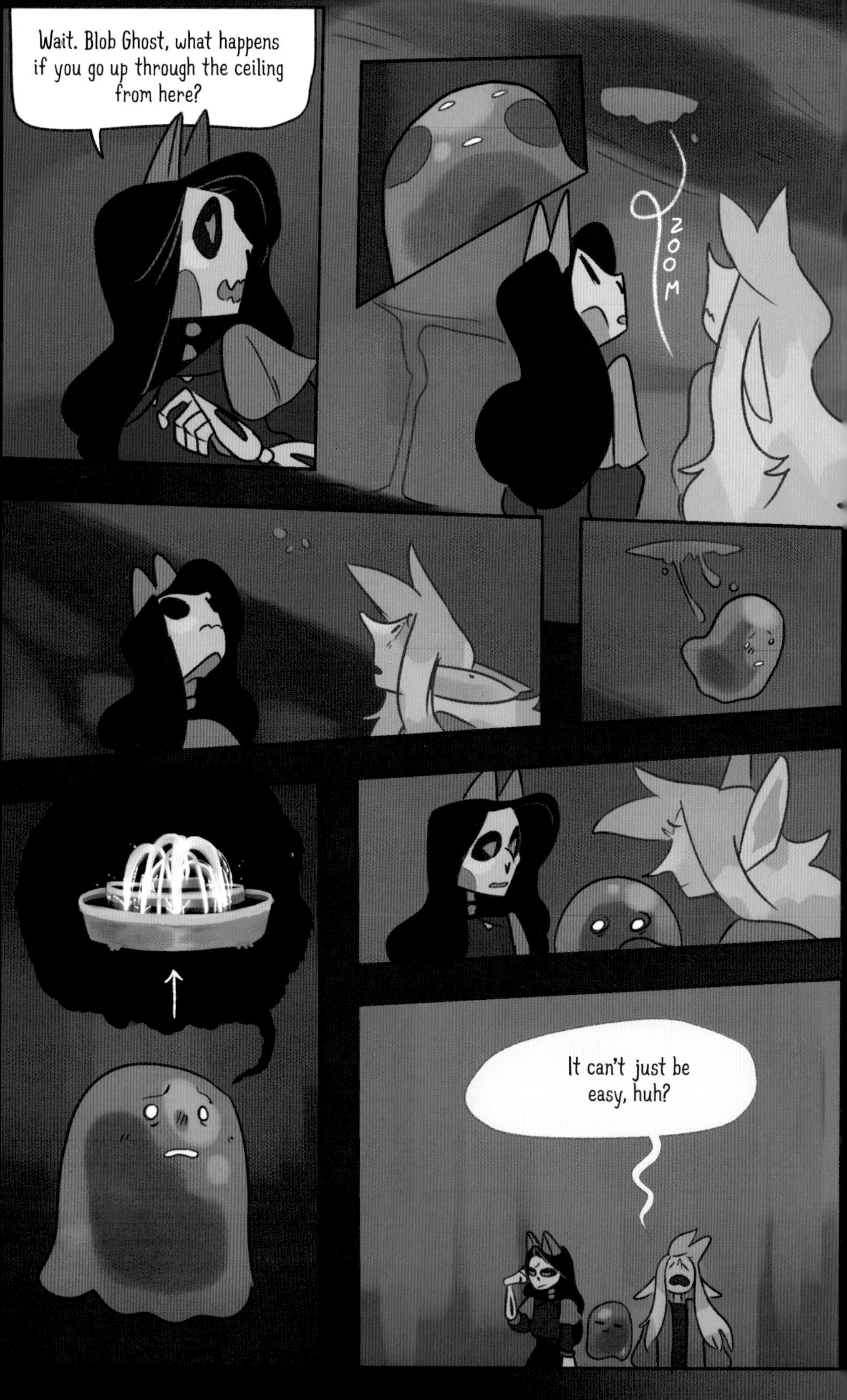
Wait. Blob Ghost, what happens if you go up through the ceiling from here?
ZOOM
It can't just be easy, huh?

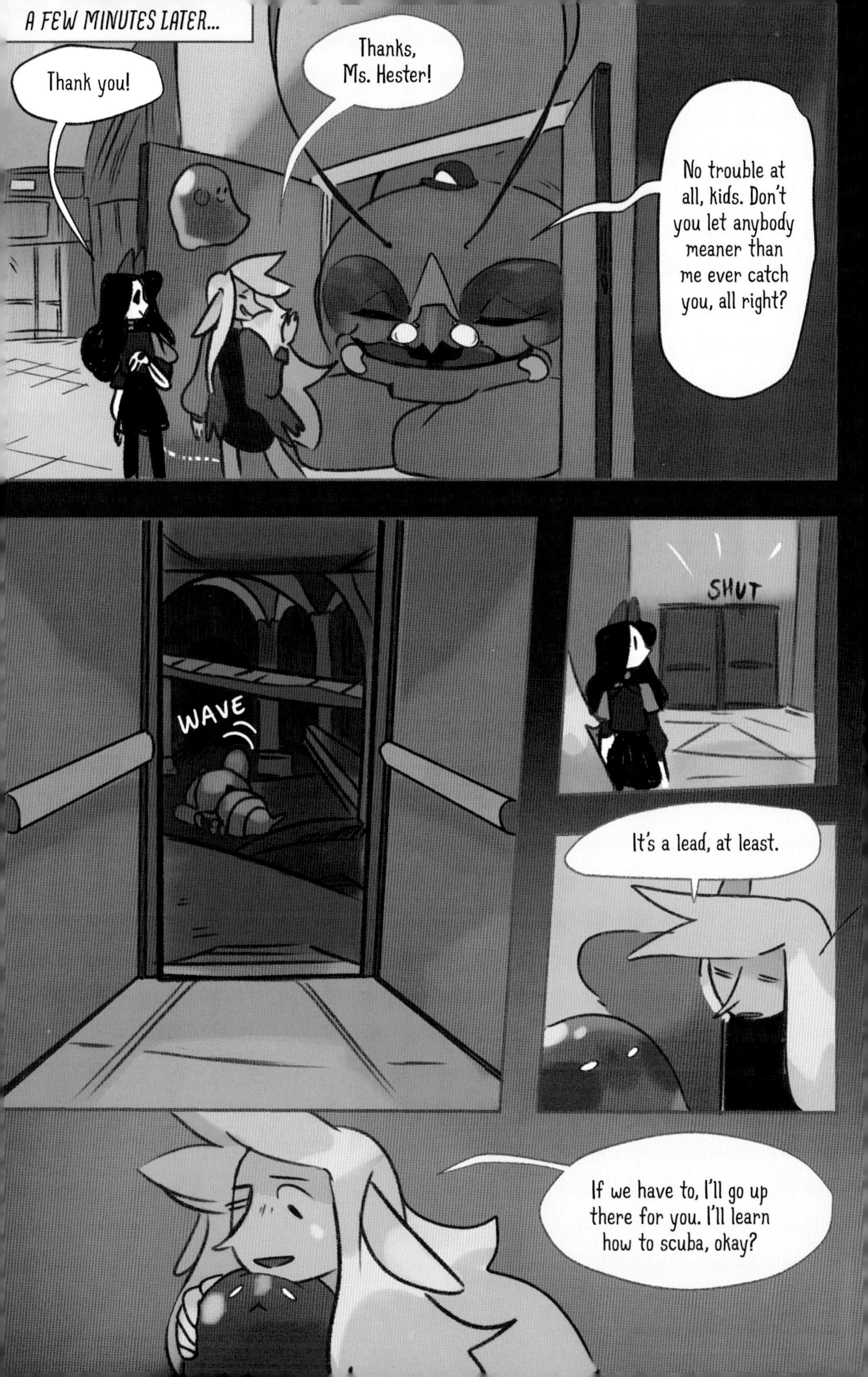
A FEW MINUTES LATER...
Thank you!
Thanks, Ms. Hester!
No trouble at all, kids. Don't you let anybody meaner than me ever catch you, all right?
WAVE
SHUT
It's a lead, at least.
If we have to, I'll go up there for you. I'll learn how to scuba, okay?

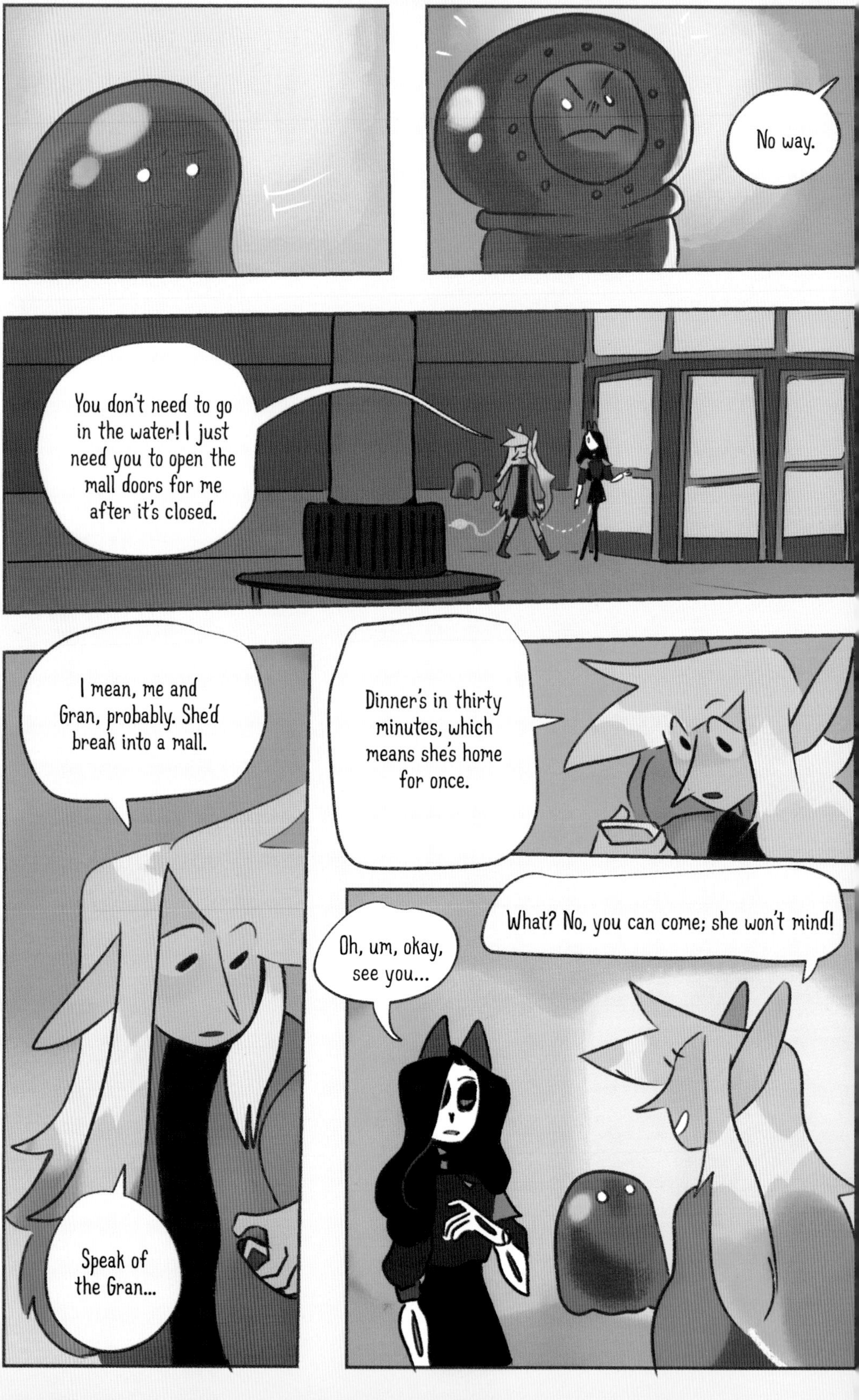
No way.
You don't need to go in the water! I just need you to open the mall doors for me after it's closed.
I mean, me and Gran, probably. She'd break into a mall.
Dinner's in thirty minutes, which means she's home for once.
Speak of the Gran...
Oh, um, okay, see you...
What? No, you can come; she won't mind!

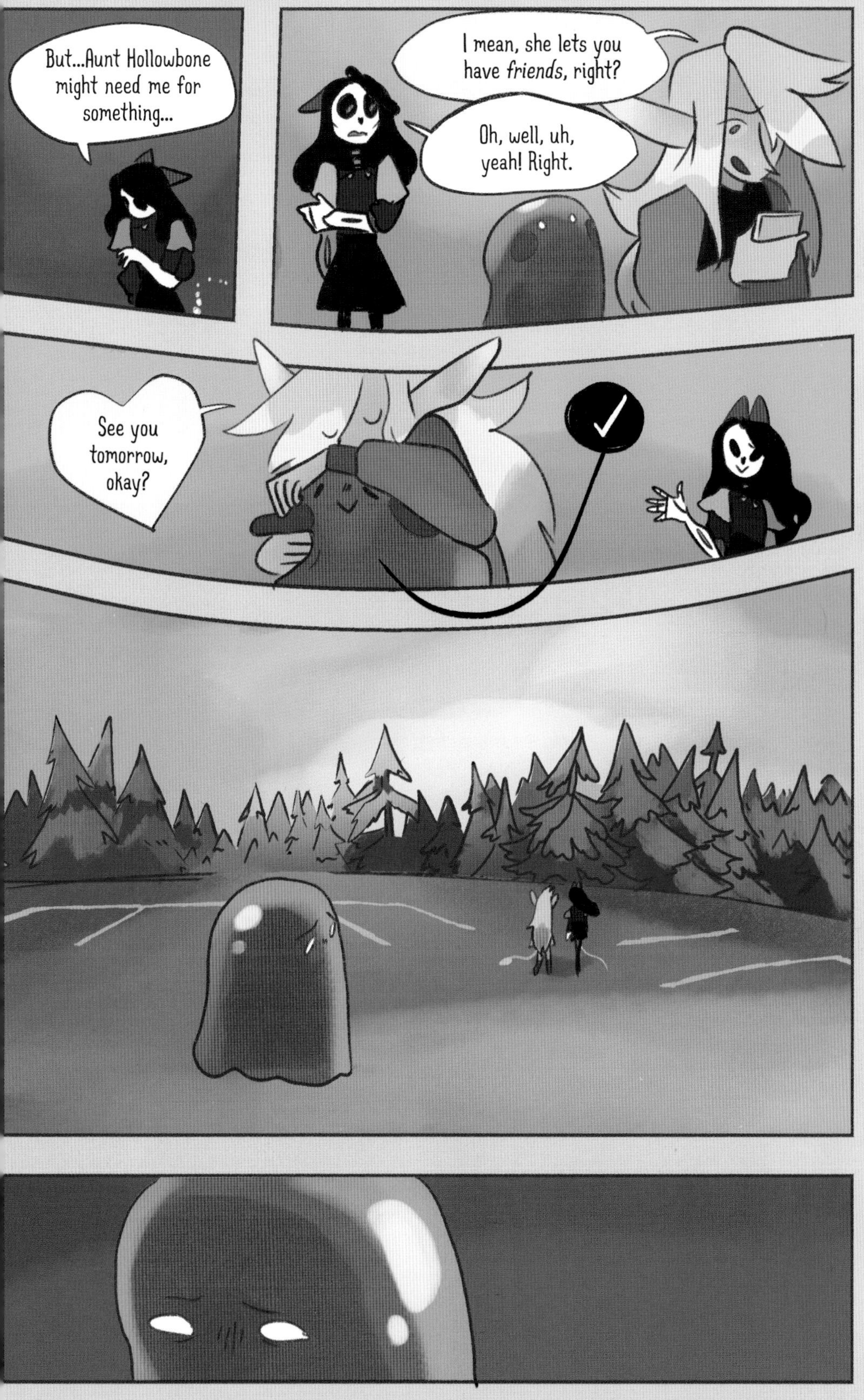
But...Aunt Hollowbone might need me for something...
I mean, she lets you have *friends*, right?
Oh, well, uh, yeah! Right.
See you tomorrow, okay?

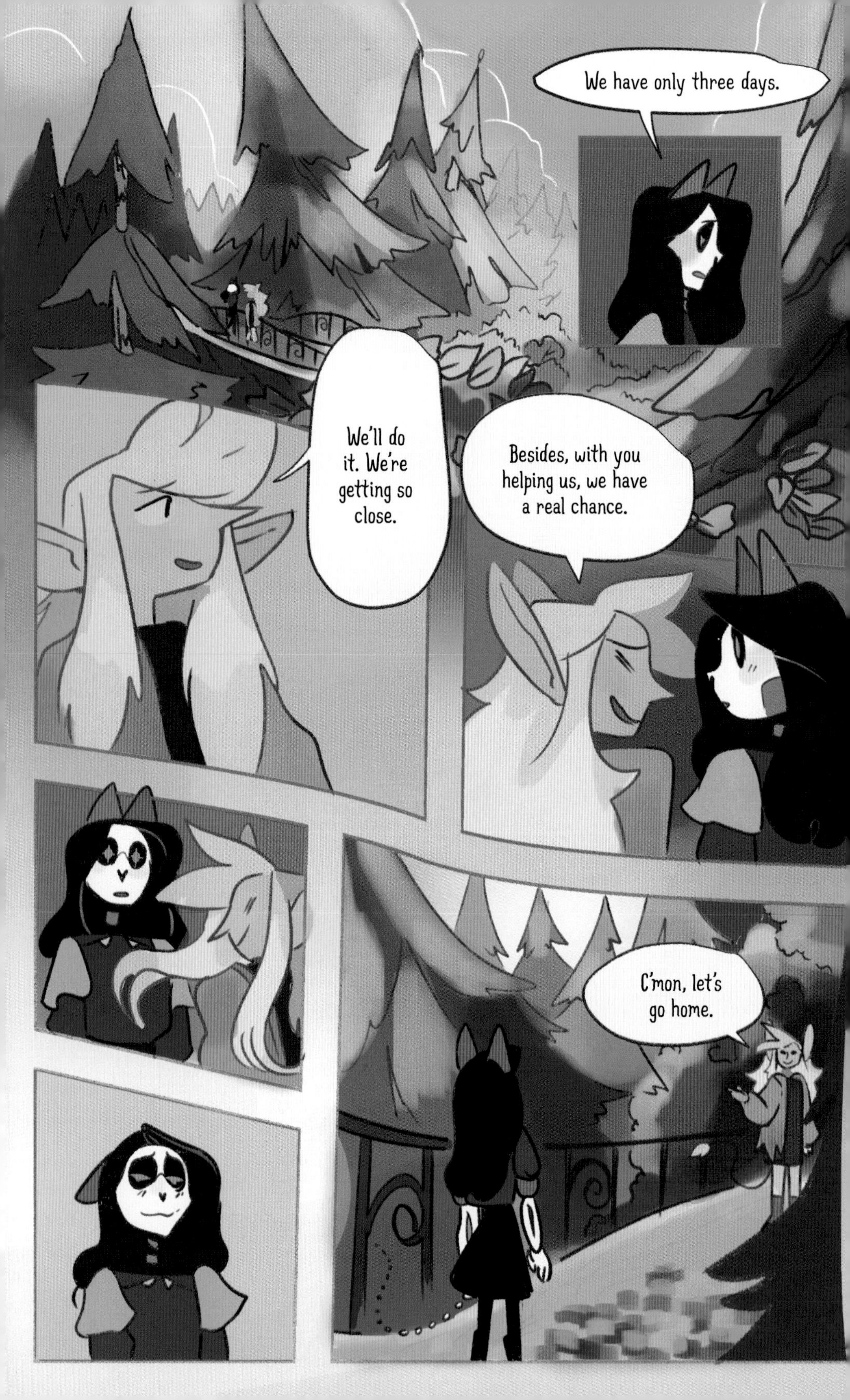
We have only three days.
We'll do it. We're getting so close.
Besides, with you helping us, we have a real chance.
C'mon, let's go home.

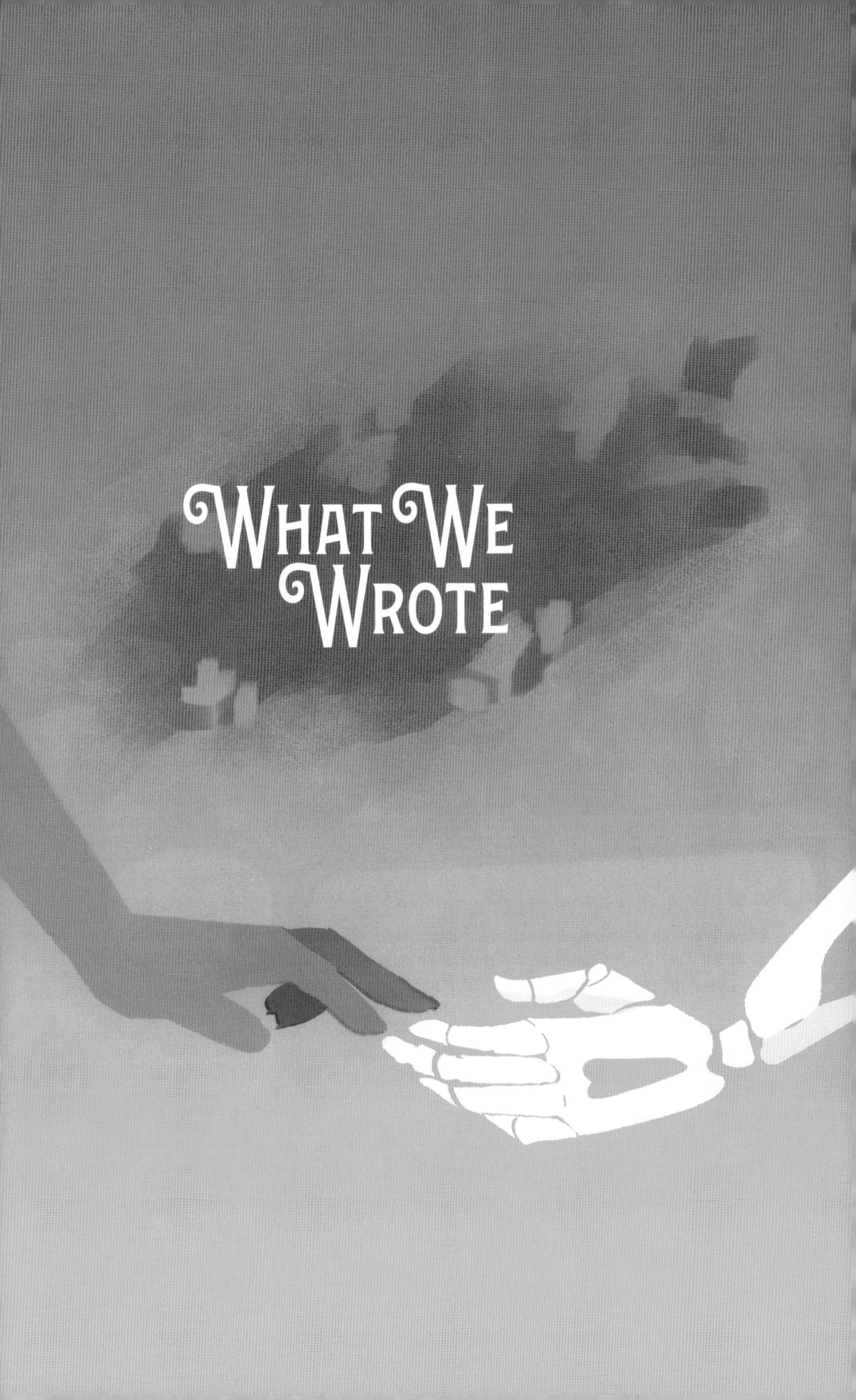
WHAT WE
WROTE

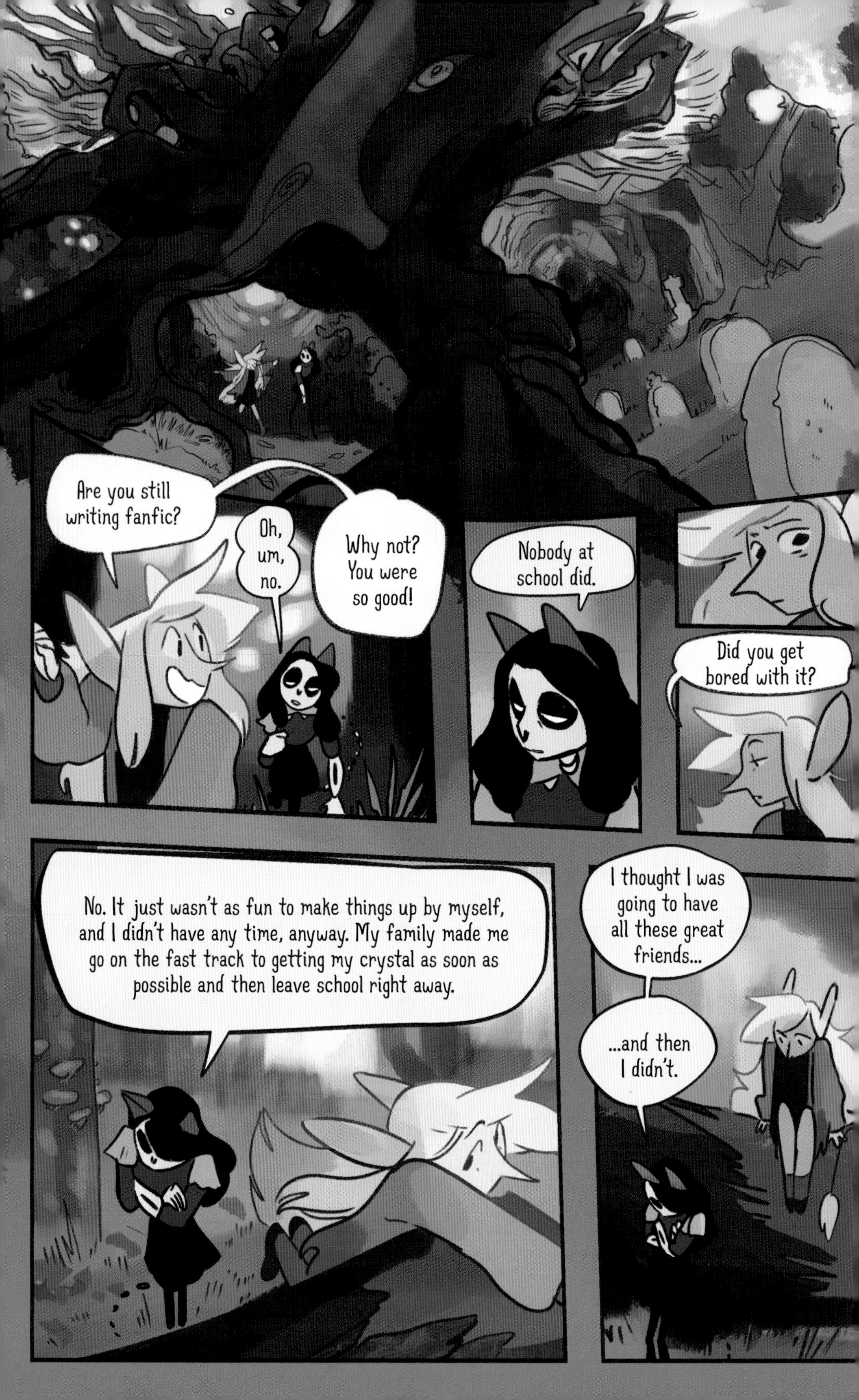
Are you still writing fanfic?
Oh, um, no.
Why not? You were so good!
Nobody at school did.
Did you get bored with it?
No. It just wasn't as fun to make things up by myself, and I didn't have any time, anyway. My family made me go on the fast track to getting my crystal as soon as possible and then leave school right away.
I thought I was going to have all these great friends...
...and then I didn't.

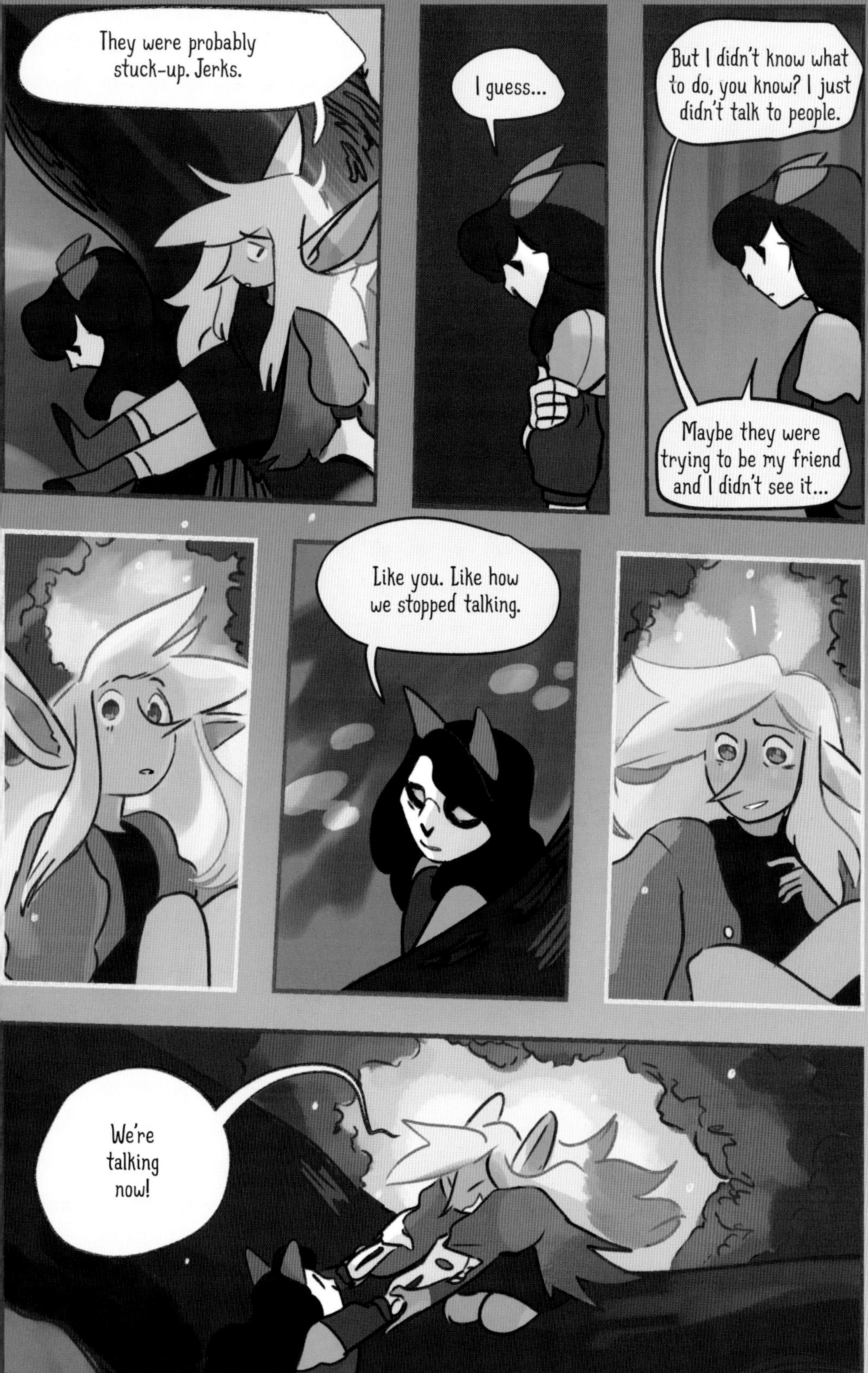
They were probably stuck-up. Jerks.
I guess...
But I didn't know what to do, you know? I just didn't talk to people.
Maybe they were trying to be my friend and I didn't see it...
Like you. Like how we stopped talking.
We're talking now!

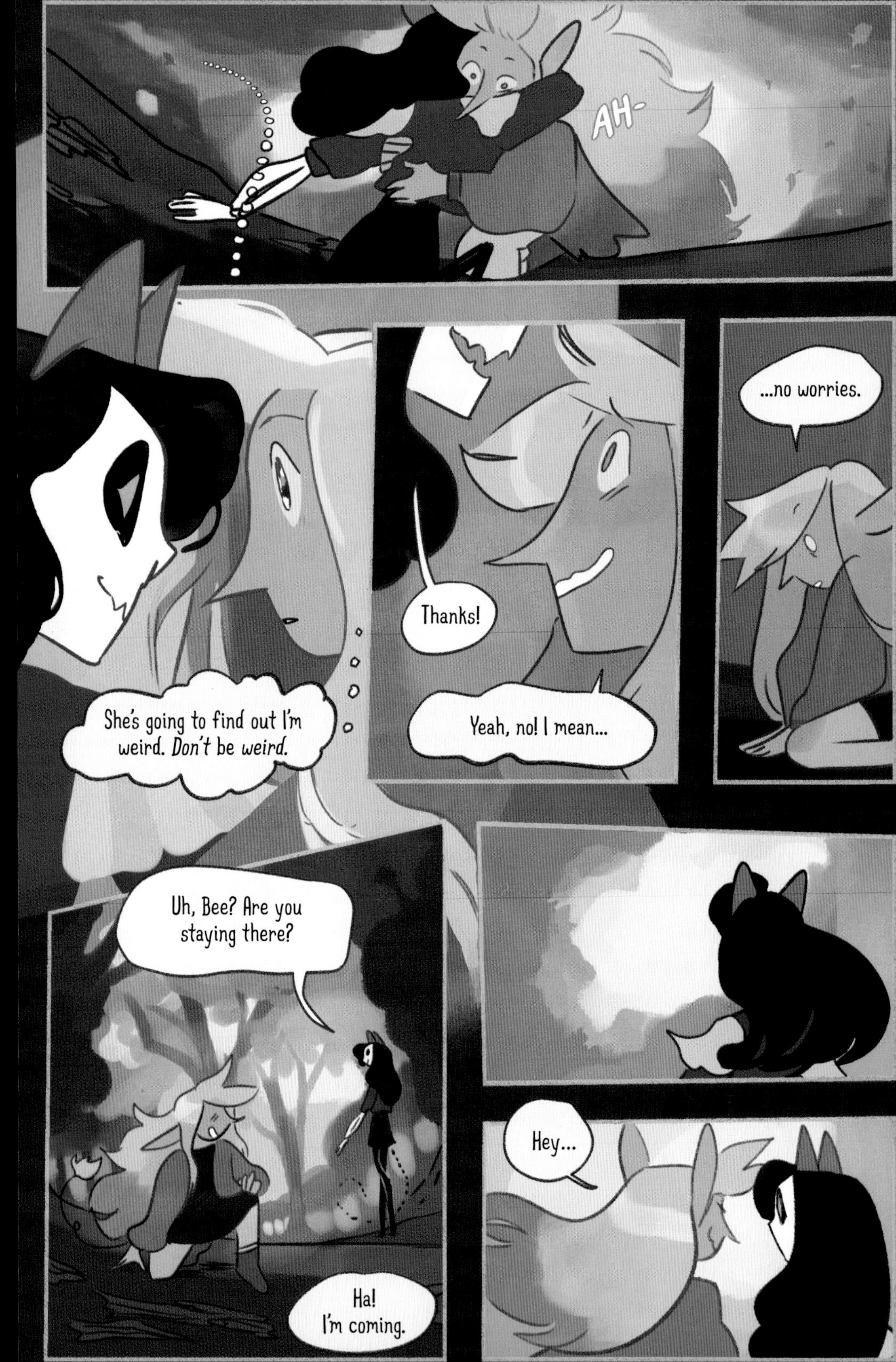
AH-
She's going to find out I'm weird. *Don't* be *weird.*
Thanks!
Yeah, no! I mean...
...no worries.
Uh, Bee? Are you staying there?
Ha! I'm coming.
Hey...

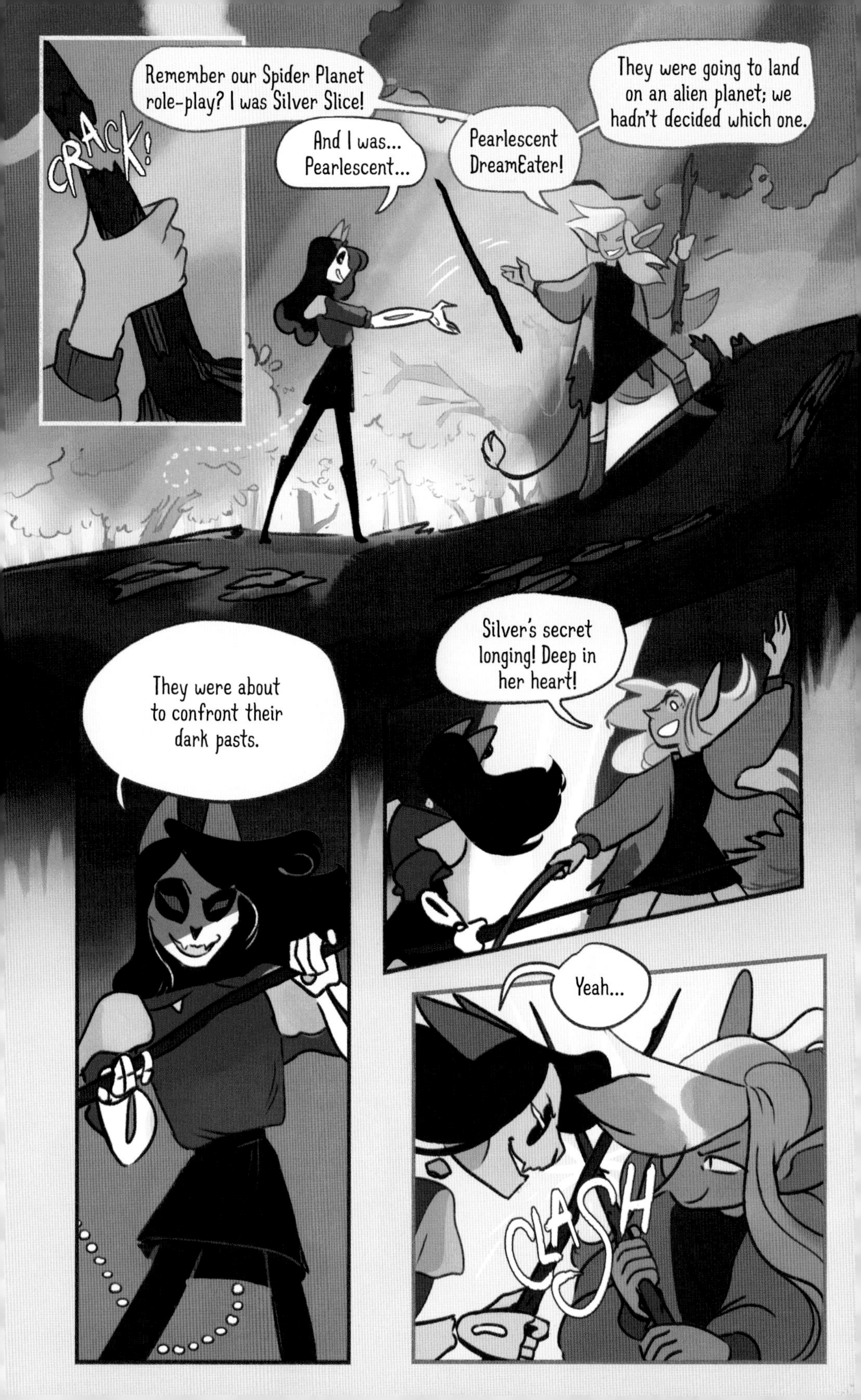
CRACK!
Remember our Spider Planet role-play? I was Silver Slice!
They were going to land on an alien planet; we hadn't decided which one.
And I was... Pearlescent...
Pearlescent DreamEater!
They were about to confront their dark pasts.
Silver's secret longing! Deep in her heart!
Yeah...
CLASH

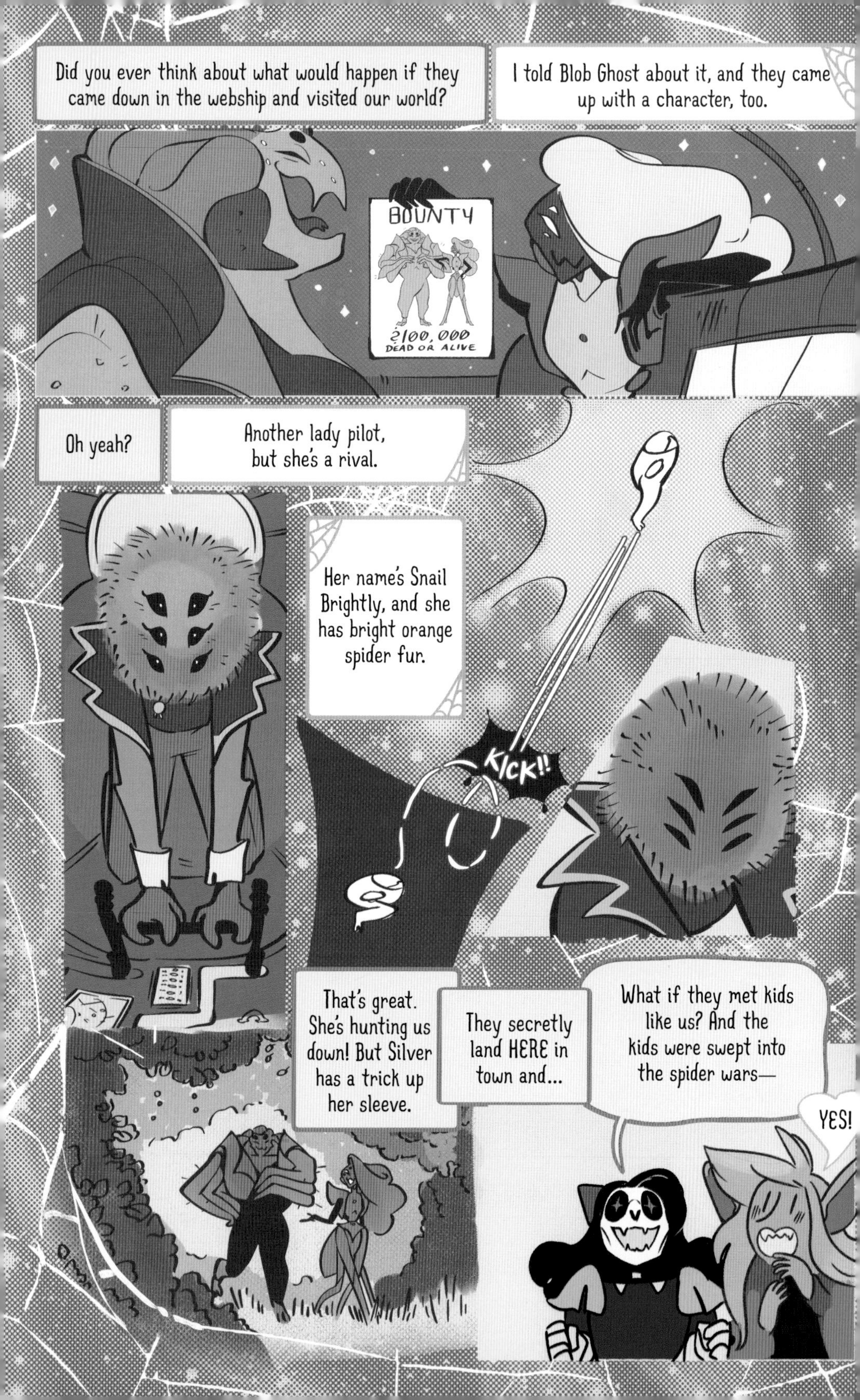
Did you ever think about what would happen if they came down in the webship and visited our world?
I told Blob Ghost about it, and they came up with a character, too.
BOUNTY
$100,000
DEAD OR ALIVE
Oh yeah?
Another lady pilot, but she's a rival.
Her name's Snail Brightly, and she has bright orange spider fur.
KICK!!
That's great. She's hunting us down! But Silver has a trick up her sleeve.
They secretly land HERE in town and...
What if they met kids like us? And the kids were swept into the spider wars—
YES!

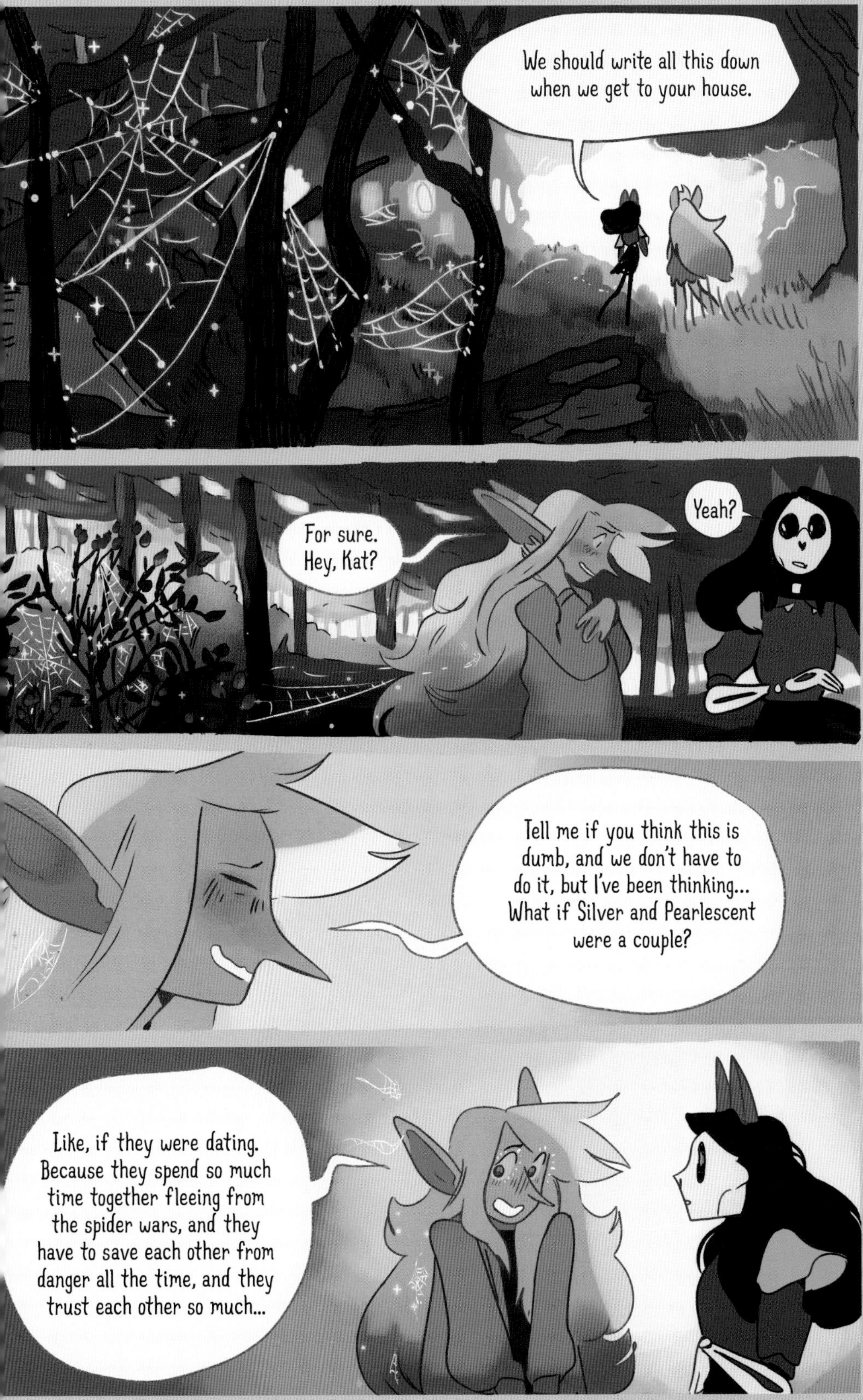

We should write all this down when we get to your house.
For sure. Hey, Kat?
Yeah?
Tell me if you think this is dumb, and we don't have to do it, but I've been thinking... What if Silver and Pearlescent were a couple?
Like, if they were dating. Because they spend so much time together fleeing from the spider wars, and they have to save each other from danger all the time, and they trust each other so much...

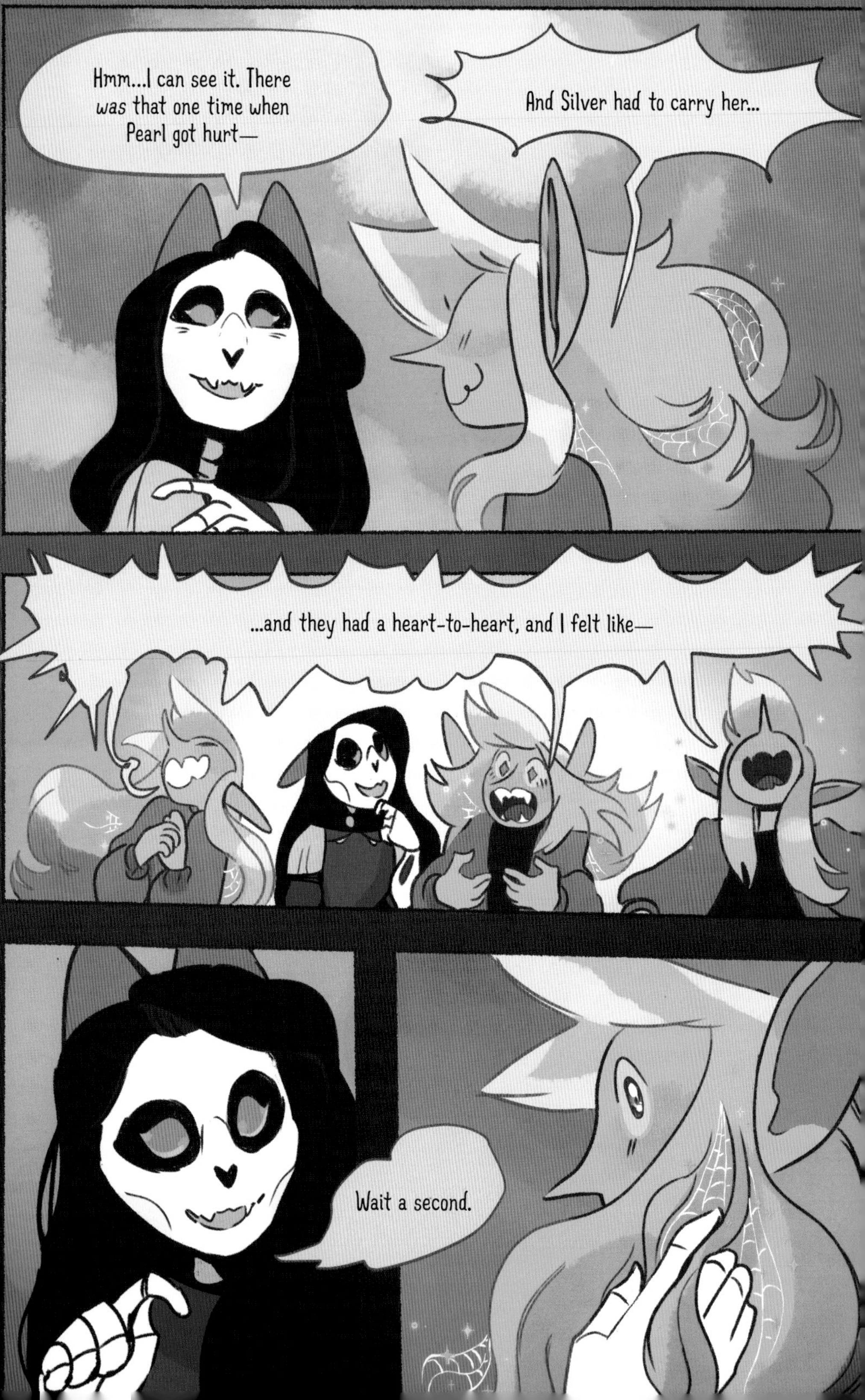
Hmm...I can see it. There *was* that one time when Pearl got hurt—
And Silver had to carry her...
...and they had a heart-to-heart, and I felt like—
Wait a second.

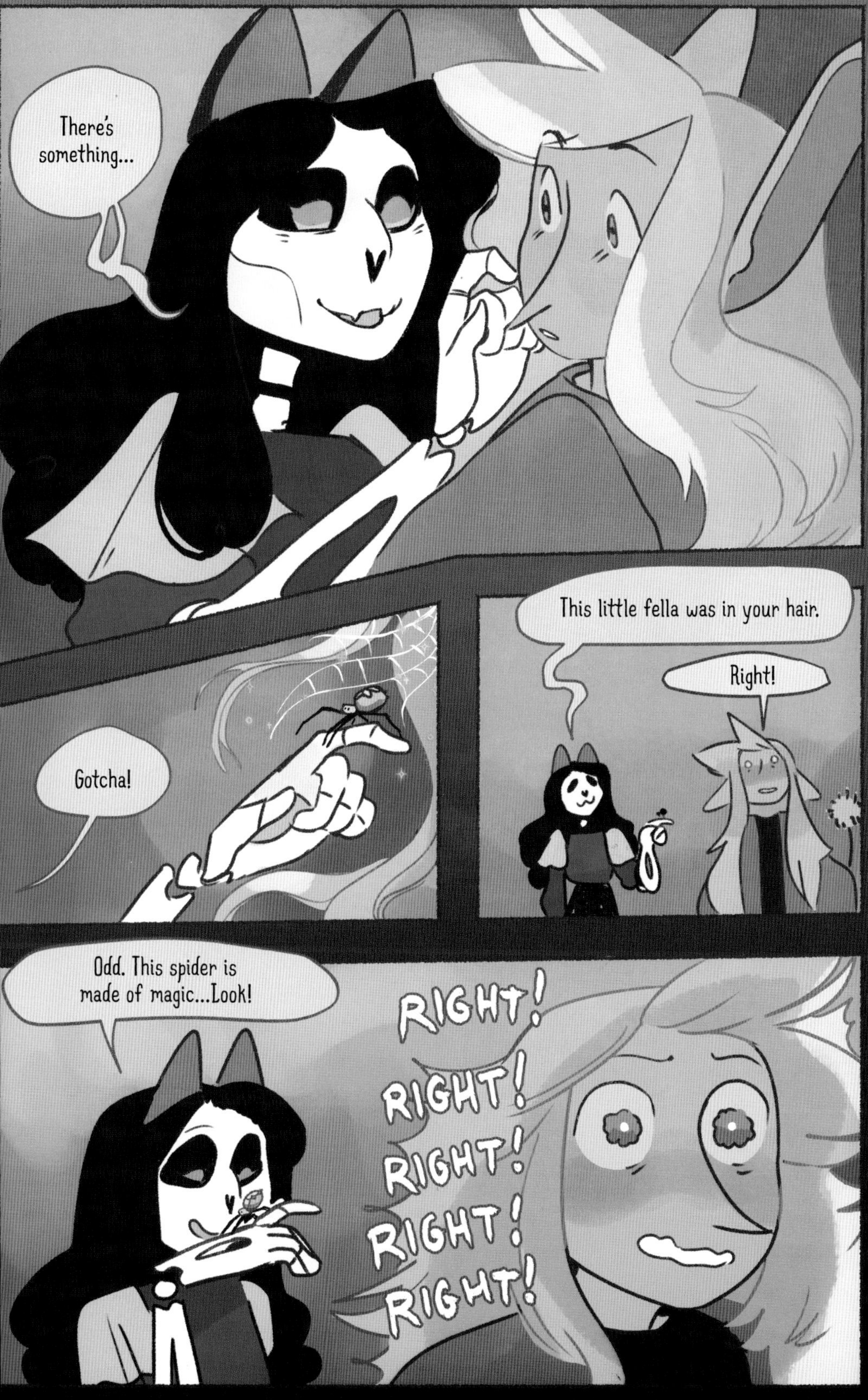
There's something...
Gotcha!
This little fella was in your hair.
Right!
Odd. This spider is made of magic...Look!
RIGHT!
RIGHT!
RIGHT!
RIGHT!
RIGHT!

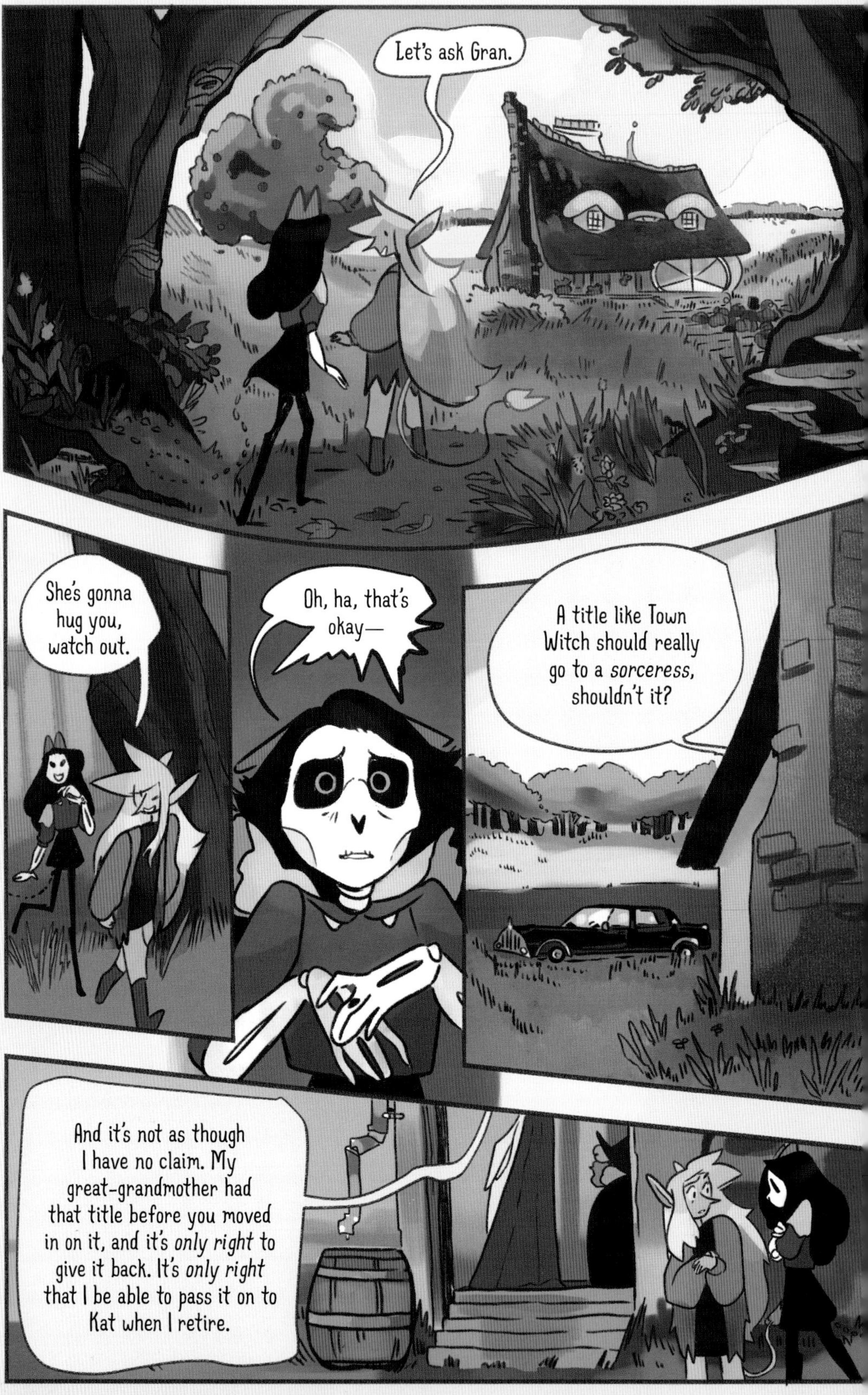
Let's ask Gran.
She's gonna hug you, watch out.
Oh, ha, that's okay—
A title like Town Witch should really go to a *sorceress*, shouldn't it?
And it's not as though I have no claim. My great-grandmother had that title before you moved in on it, and it's *only right* to give it back. It's *only right* that I be able to pass it on to Kat when I retire.

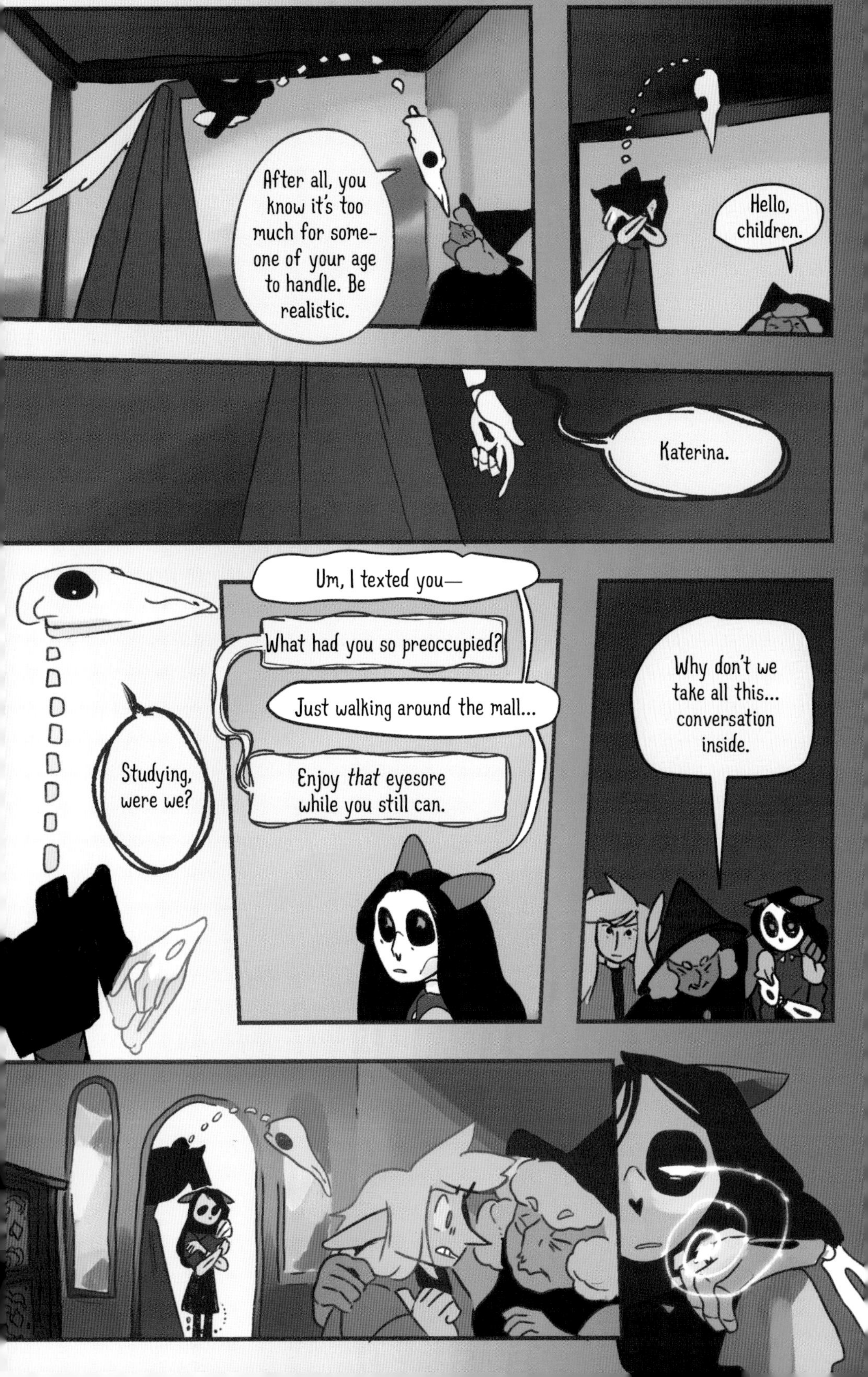
After all, you know it's too much for someone of your age to handle. Be realistic.
Hello, children.
Katerina.
Studying, were we?
Um, I texted you—
What had you so preoccupied?
Just walking around the mall...
Enjoy *that* eyesore while you still can.
Why don't we take all this... conversation inside.

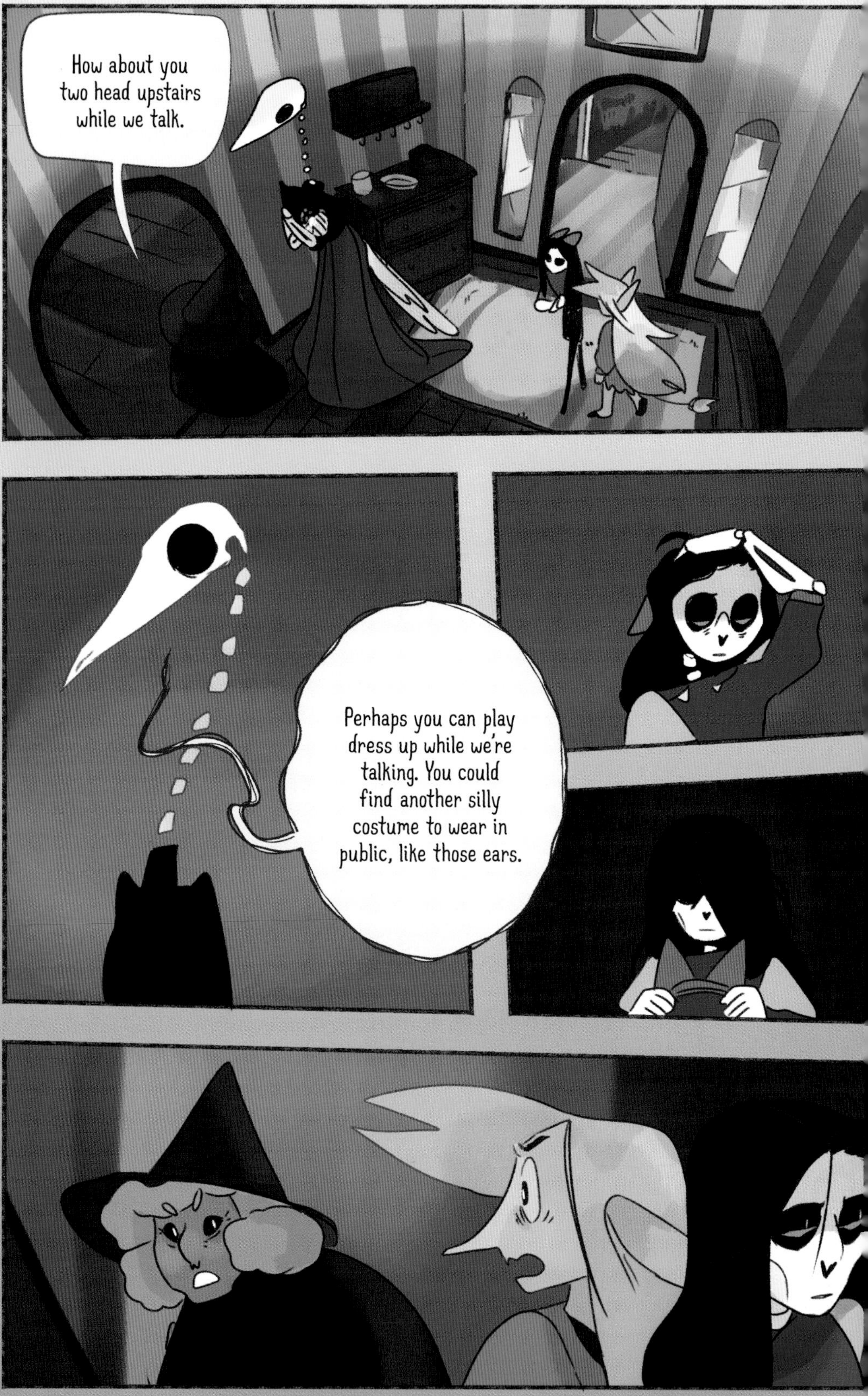
How about you two head upstairs while we talk.
Perhaps you can play dress up while we're talking. You could find another silly costume to wear in public, like those ears.

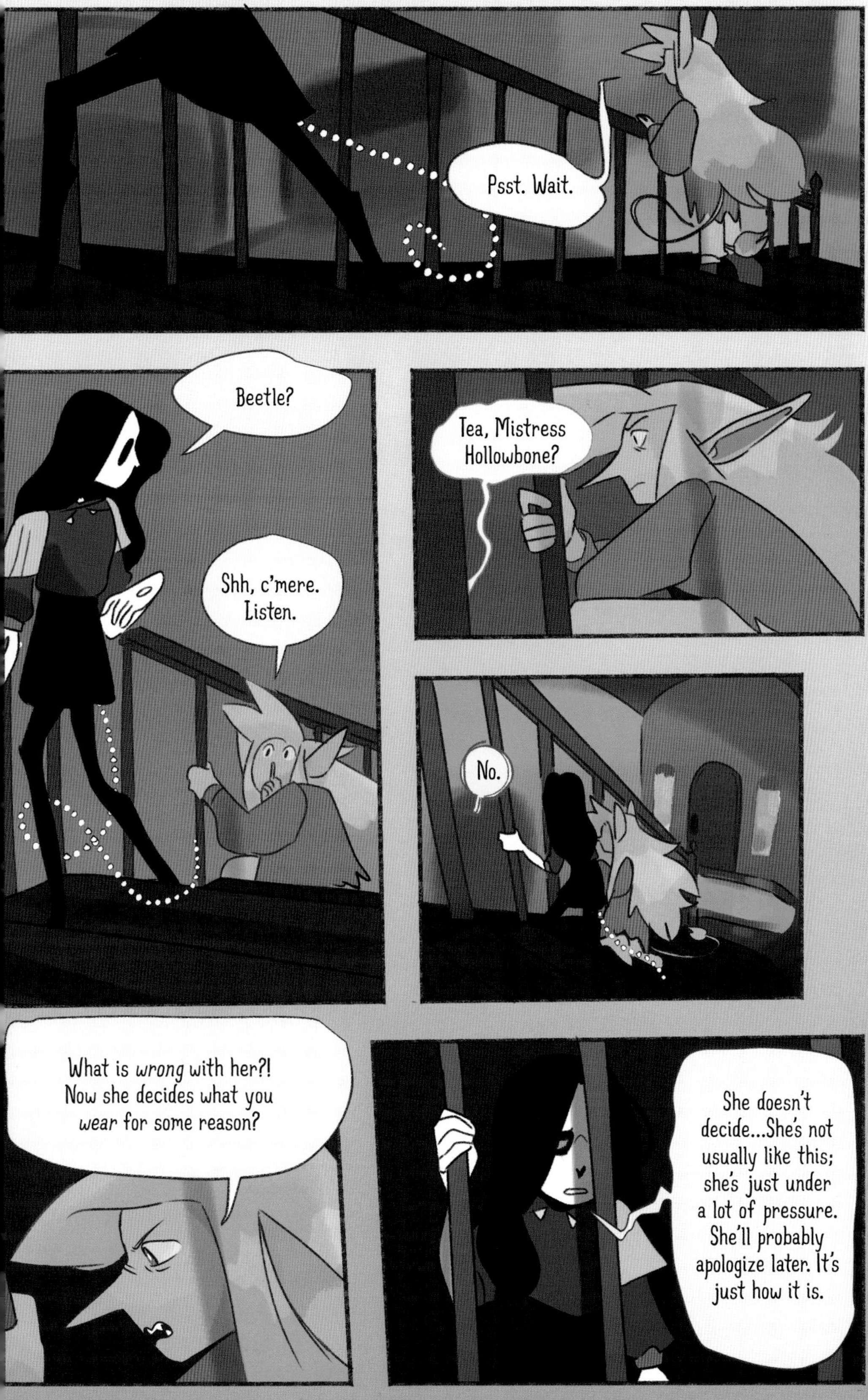
Psst. Wait.
Beetle?
Shh, c'mere. Listen.
Tea, Mistress Hollowbone?
No.
What is *wrong* with her?! Now she decides what you *wear* for some reason?
She doesn't decide...She's not usually like this; she's just under a lot of pressure. She'll probably apologize later. It's just how it is.

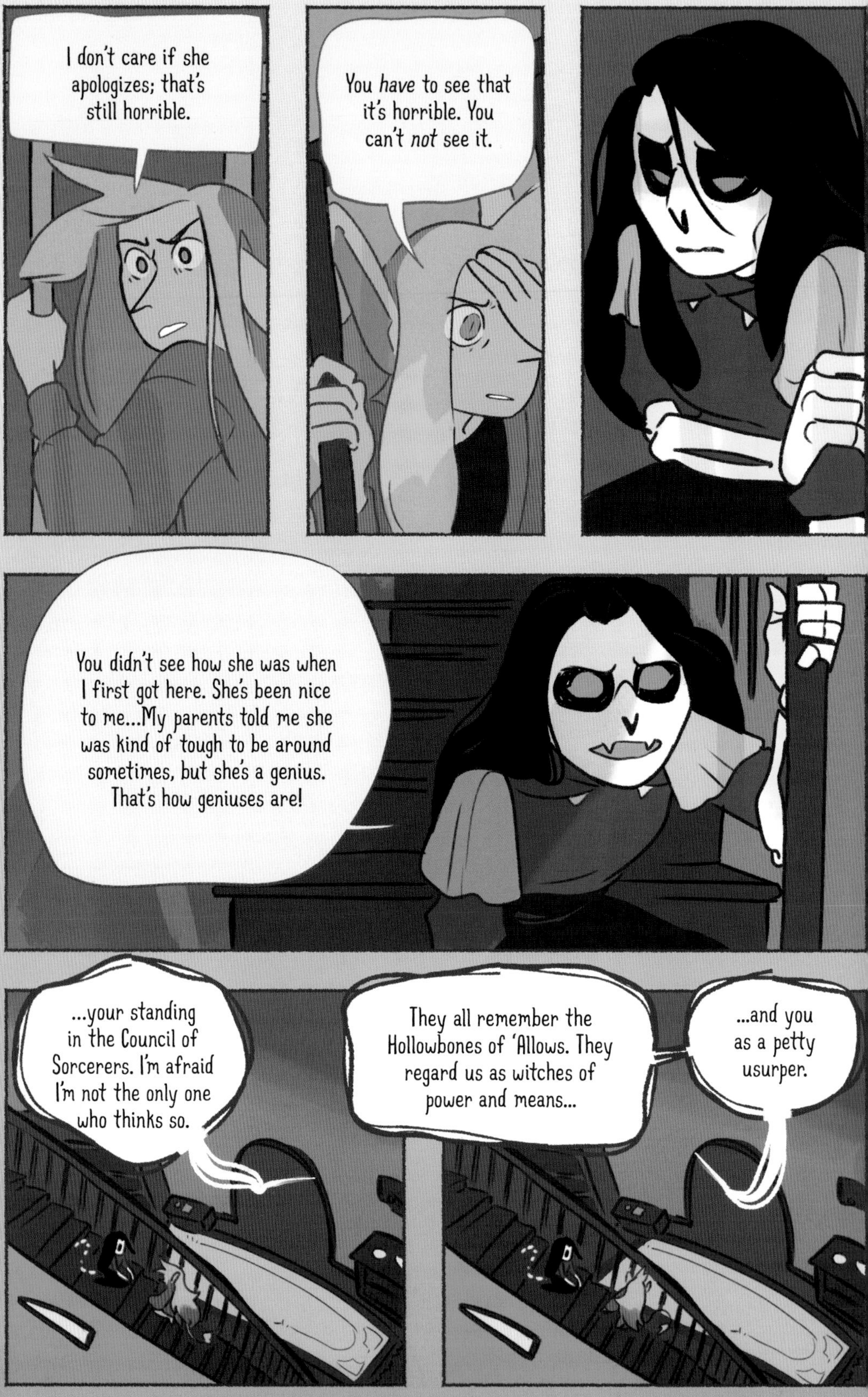

I don't care if she apologizes; that's still horrible.
You *have* to see that it's horrible. You can't *not* see it.
You didn't see how she was when I first got here. She's been nice to me...My parents told me she was kind of tough to be around sometimes, but she's a genius. That's how geniuses are!
...your standing in the Council of Sorcerers. I'm afraid I'm not the only one who thinks so.
They all remember the Hollowbones of 'Allows. They regard us as witches of power and means...
...and you as a petty usurper.

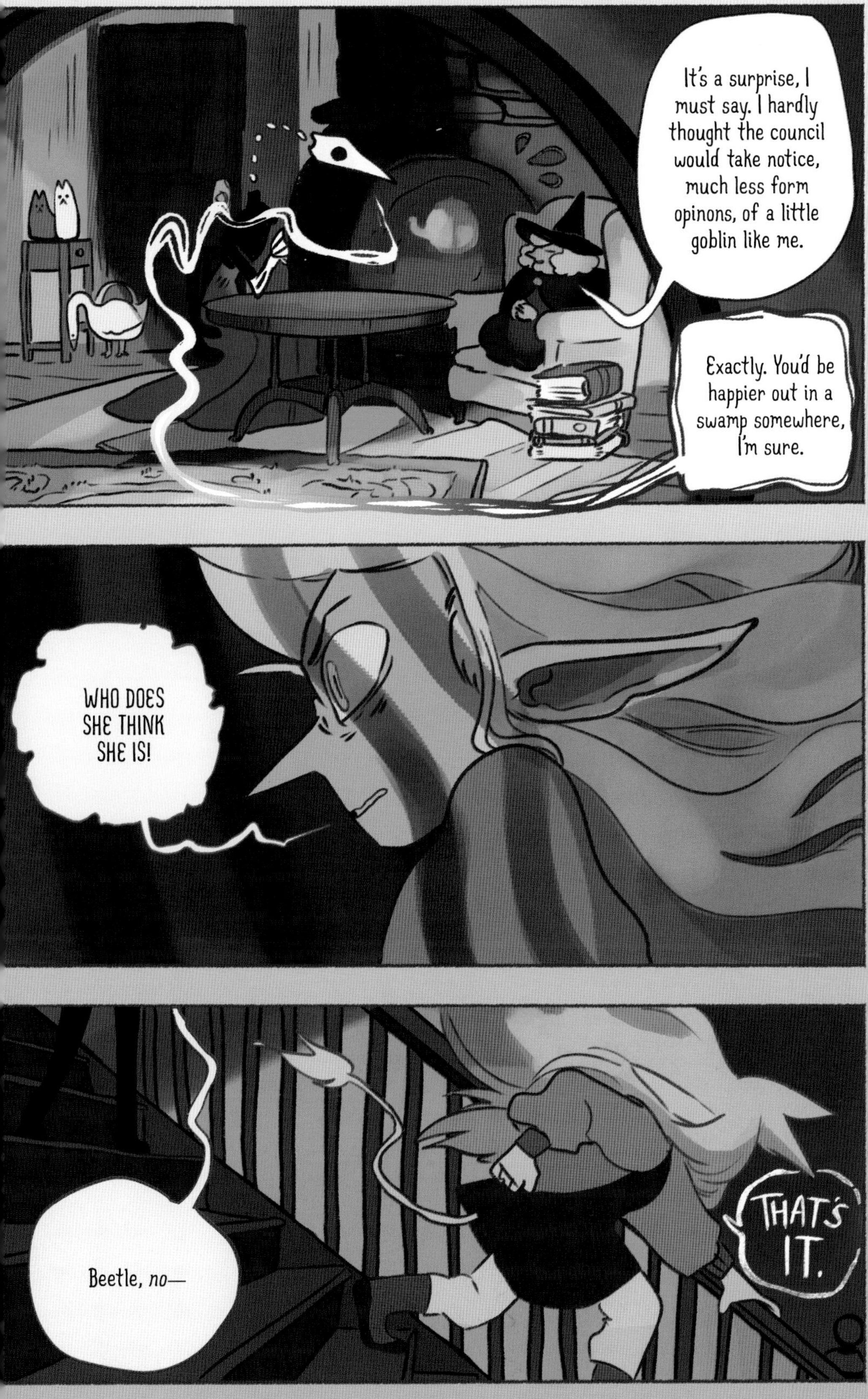
It's a surprise, I must say. I hardly thought the council would take notice, much less form opinons, of a little goblin like me.
Exactly. You'd be happier out in a swamp somewhere, I'm sure.
WHO DOES SHE THINK SHE IS!
THAT'S IT.
Beetle, *no*—

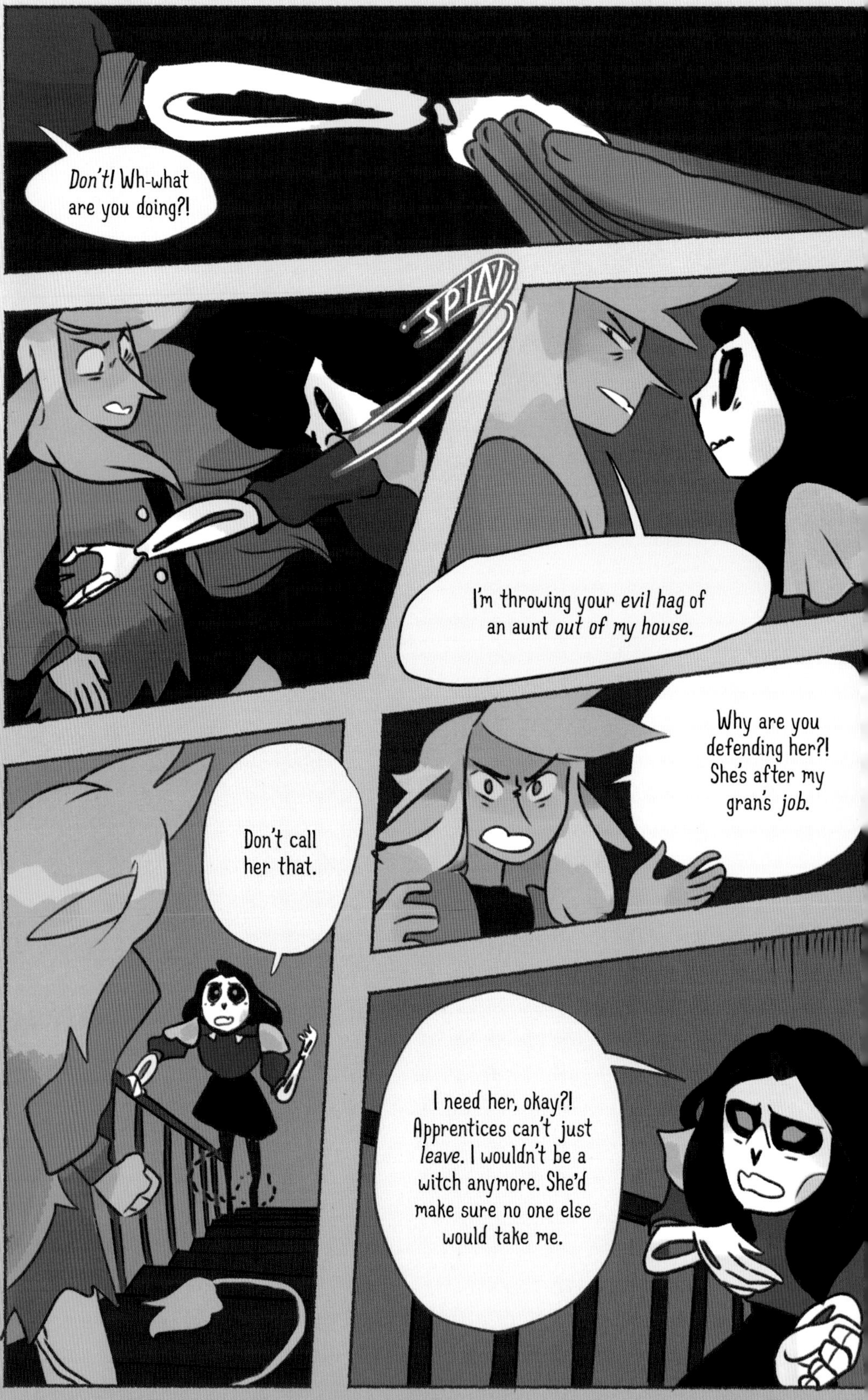
Don't! Wh-what are you doing?!
SPIN
I'm throwing your evil hag of an aunt out of my house.
Don't call her that.
Why are you defending her?! She's after my gran's job.
I need her, okay?! Apprentices can't just leave. I wouldn't be a witch anymore. She'd make sure no one else would take me.

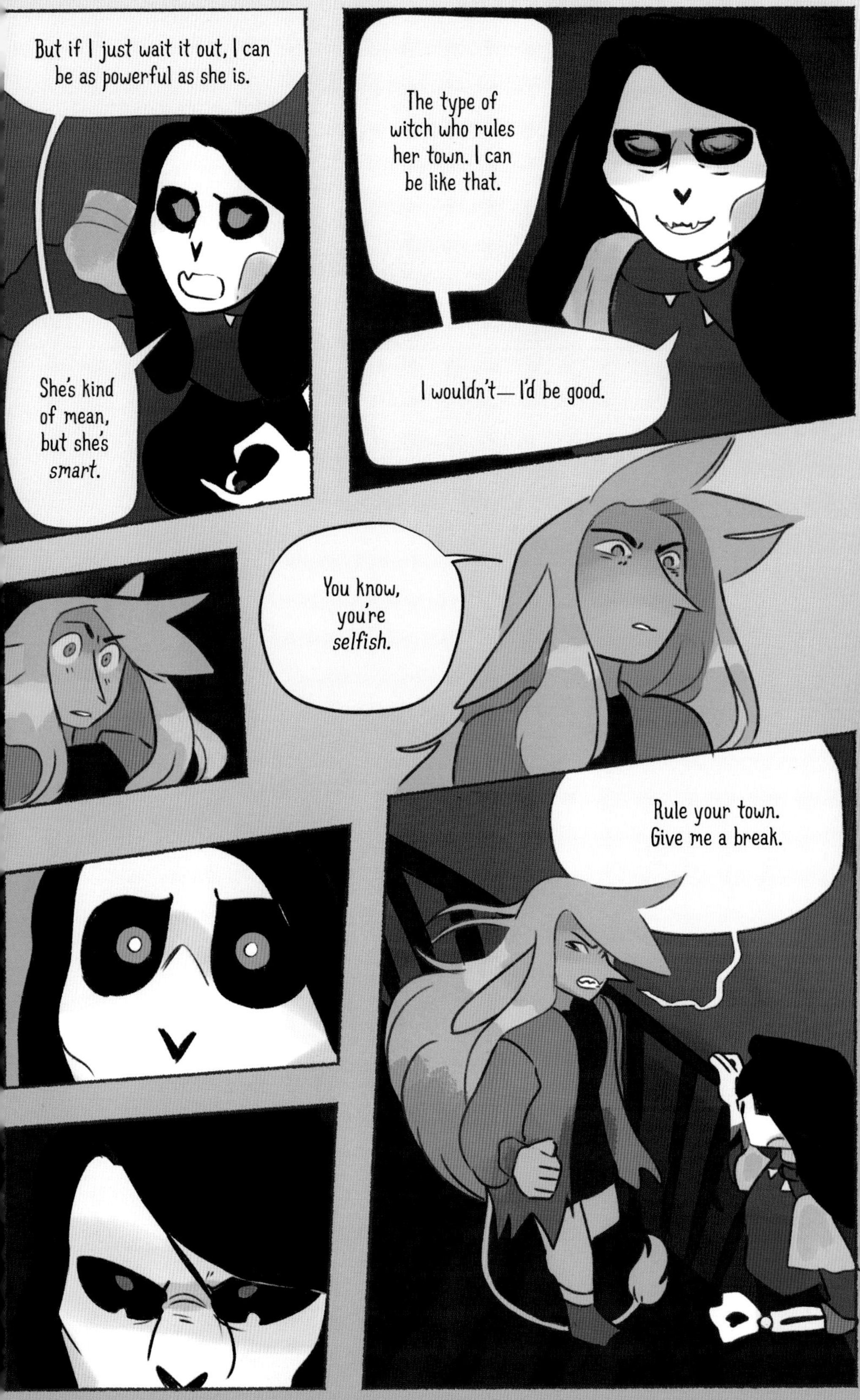
But if I just wait it out, I can be as powerful as she is.
She's kind of mean, but she's *smart*.
The type of witch who rules her town. I can be like that.
I wouldn't— I'd be good.
You know, you're *selfish*.
Rule your town. Give me a break.

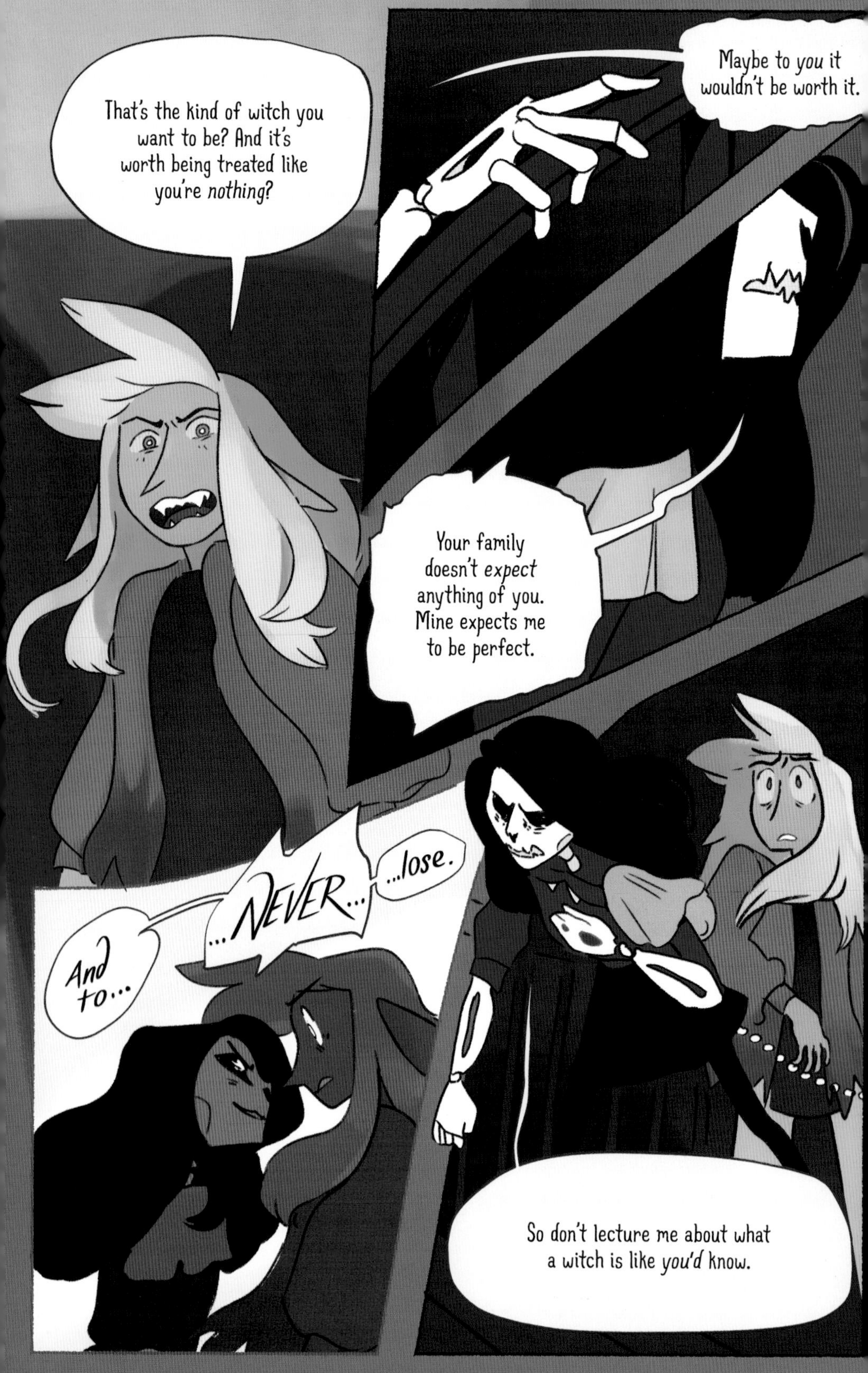
That's the kind of witch you want to be? And it's worth being treated like you're *nothing*?
Maybe to *you* it wouldn't be worth it.
Your family doesn't *expect* anything of you. Mine expects me to be perfect.
And to...
...NEVER...
...lose.
So don't lecture me about what a witch is like *you'd* know.

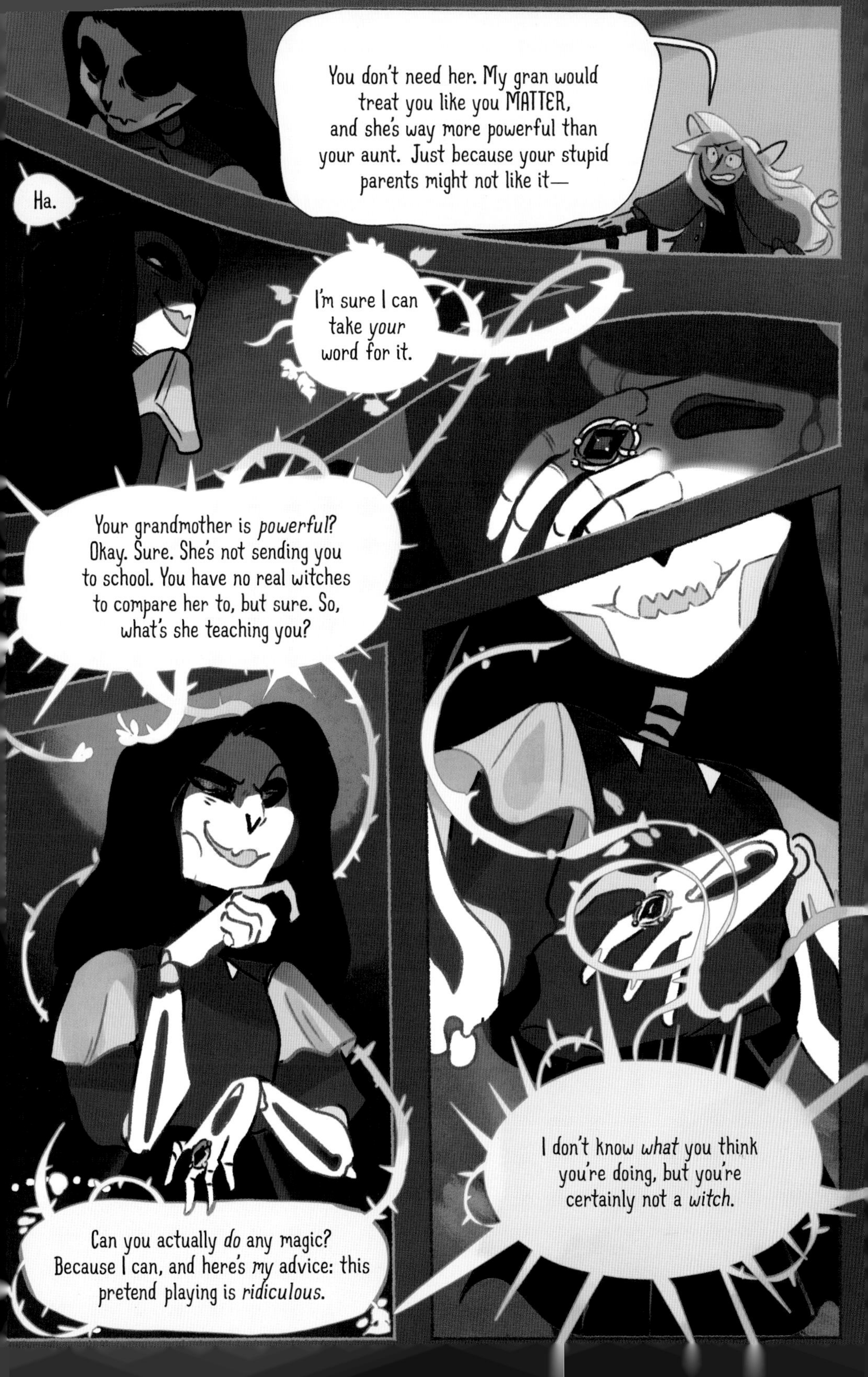
You don't need her. My gran would treat you like you MATTER, and she's way more powerful than your aunt. Just because your stupid parents might not like it—
Ha.
I'm sure I can take *your* word for it.
Your grandmother is *powerful*? Okay. Sure. She's not sending you to school. You have no real witches to compare her to, but sure. So, what's she teaching you?
Can you actually *do* any magic? Because I can, and here's *my* advice: this pretend playing is *ridiculous*.
I don't know *what* you think you're doing, but you're certainly not a *witch*.

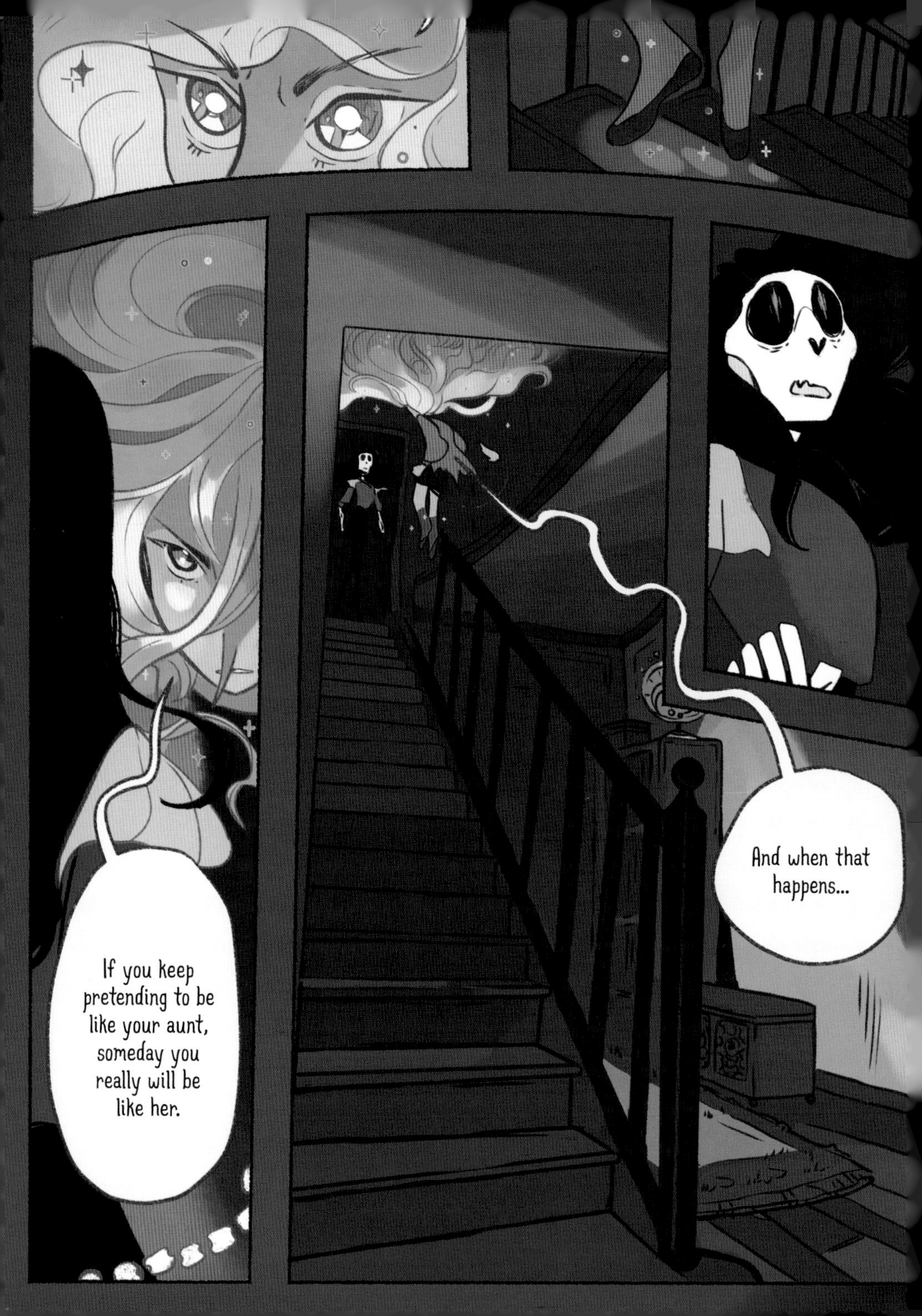
If you keep pretending to be like your aunt, someday you really will be like her.
And when that happens...

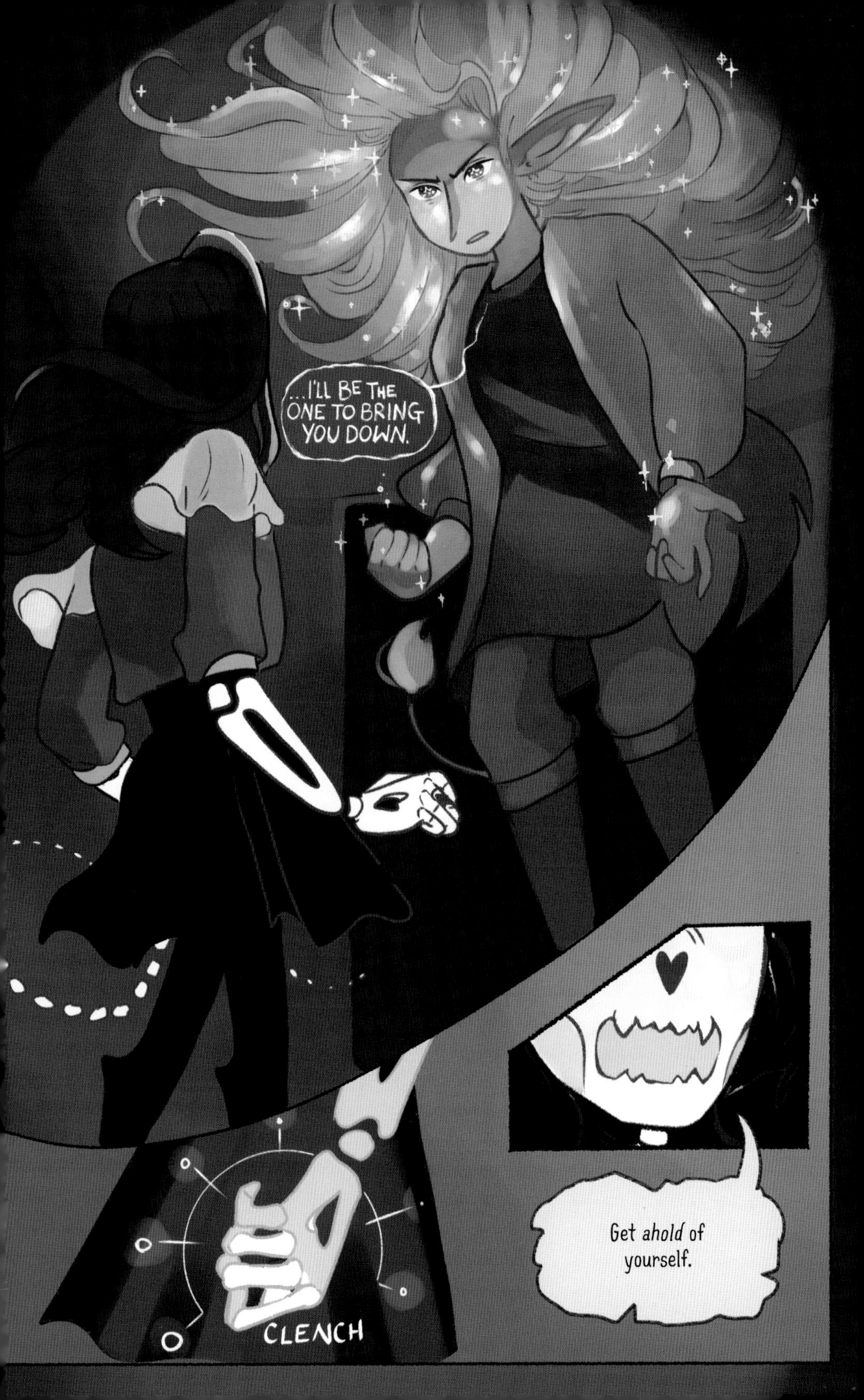
...I'LL BE THE ONE TO BRING YOU DOWN.
CLENCH
Get ahold of yourself.

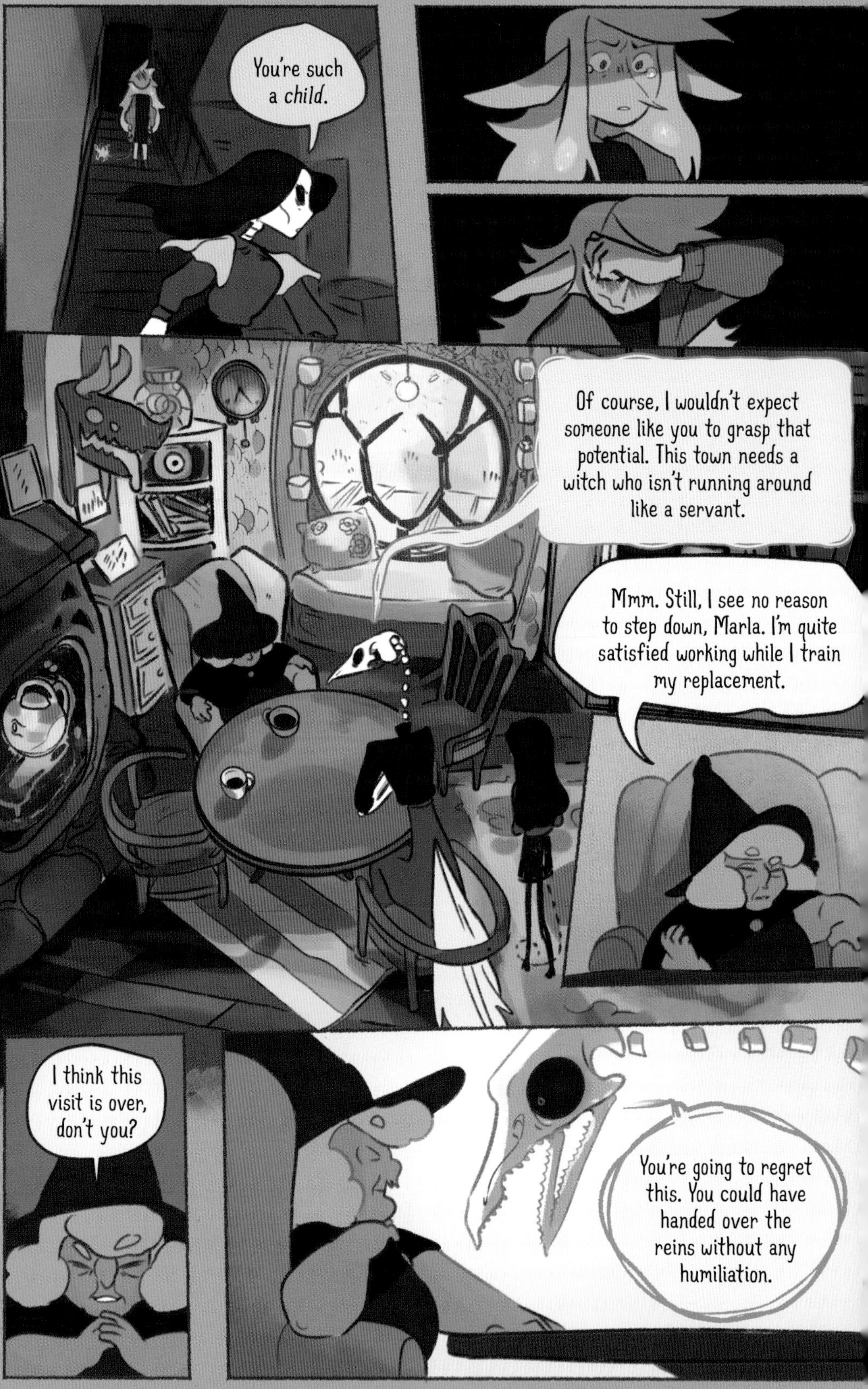
You're such a *child*.
Of course, I wouldn't expect someone like you to grasp that potential. This town needs a witch who isn't running around like a servant.
Mmm. Still, I see no reason to step down, Marla. I'm quite satisfied working while I train my replacement.
I think this visit is over, don't you?
You're going to regret this. You could have handed over the reins without any humiliation.

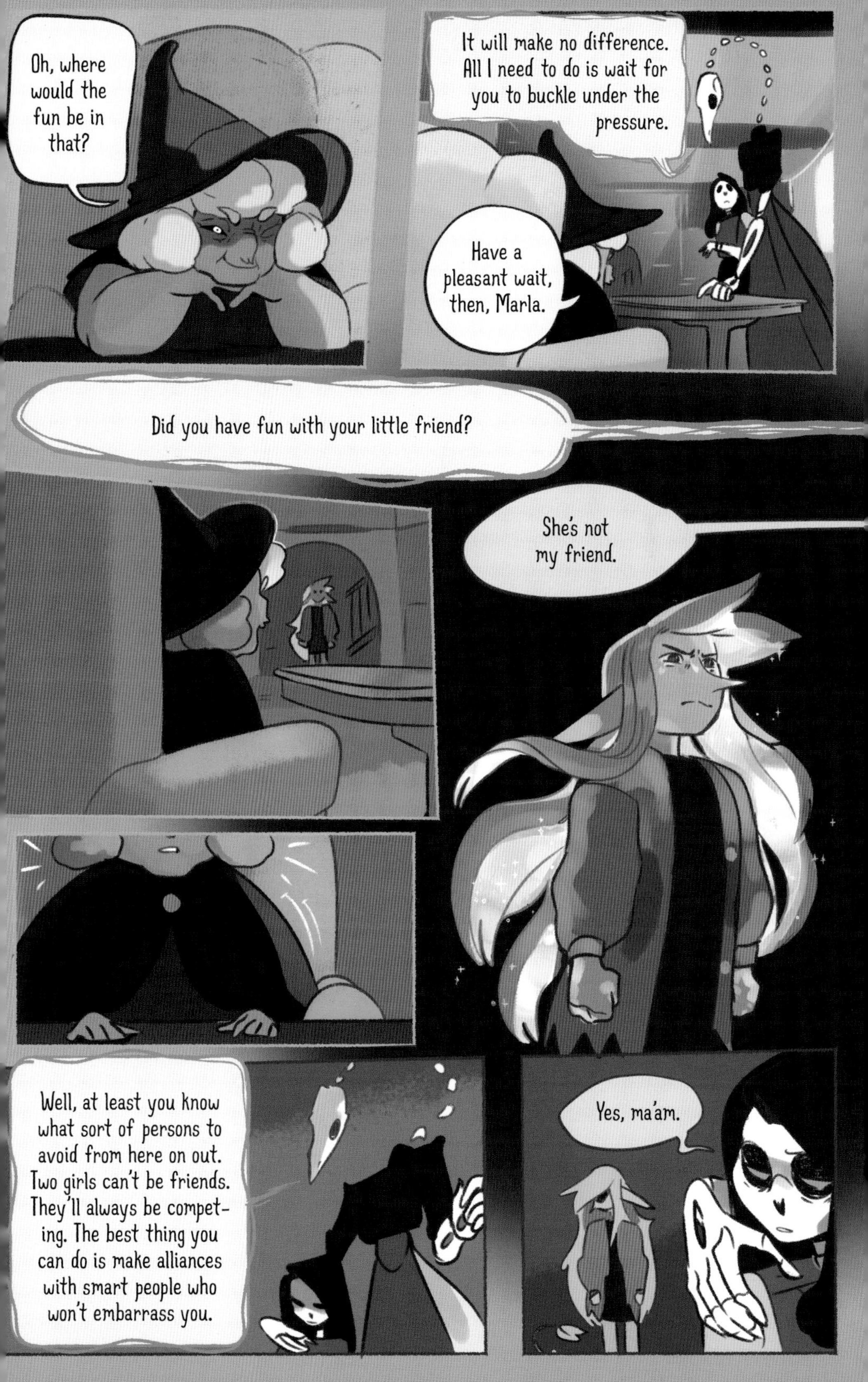

Oh, where would the fun be in that?
It will make no difference. All I need to do is wait for you to buckle under the pressure.
Have a pleasant wait, then, Marla.
Did you have fun with your little friend?
She's not my friend.
Well, at least you know what sort of persons to avoid from here on out. Two girls can't be friends. They'll always be competing. The best thing you can do is make alliances with smart people who won't embarrass you.
Yes, ma'am.

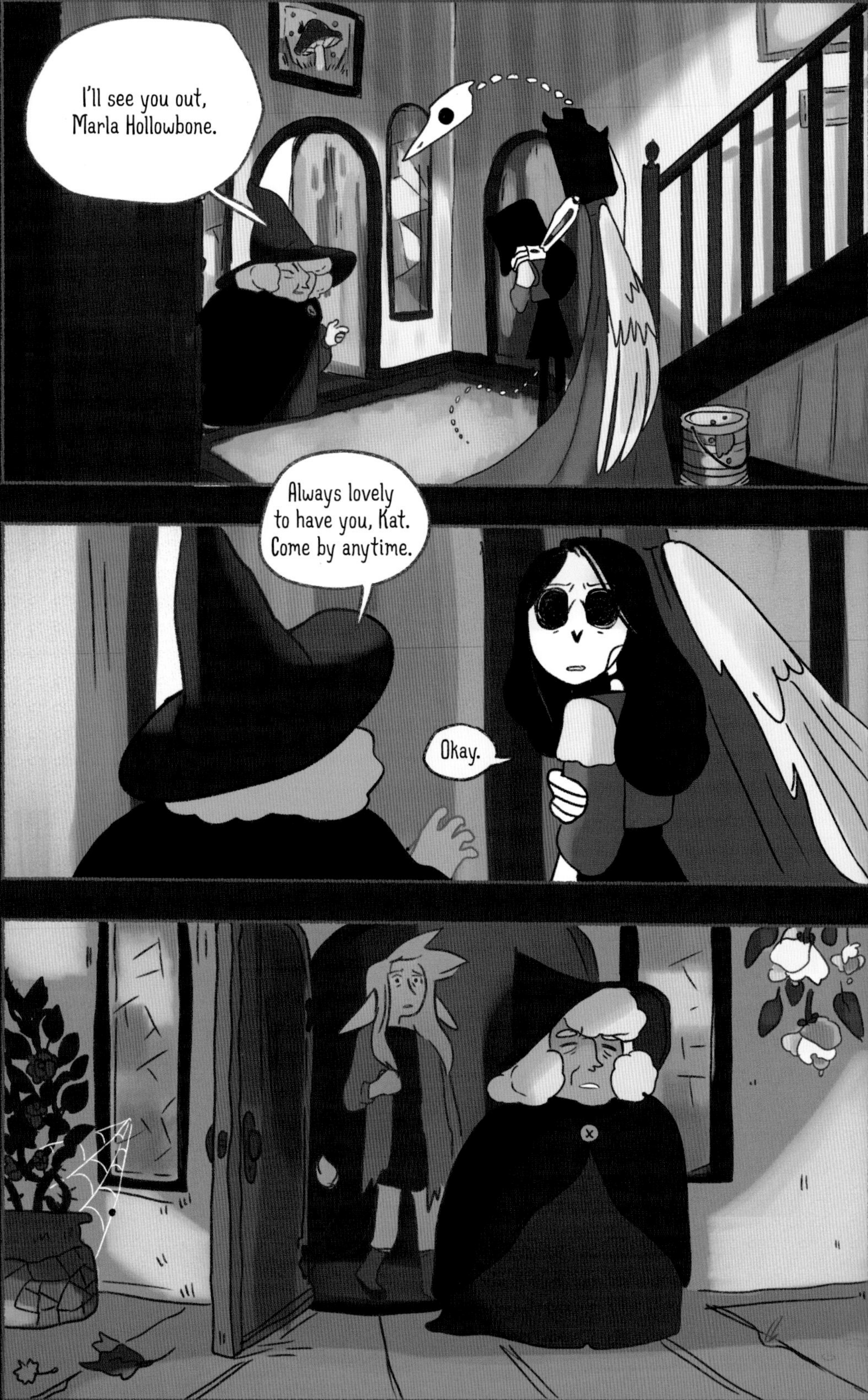
I'll see you out,
Marla Hollowbone.
Always lovely
to have you, Kat.
Come by anytime.
Okay.

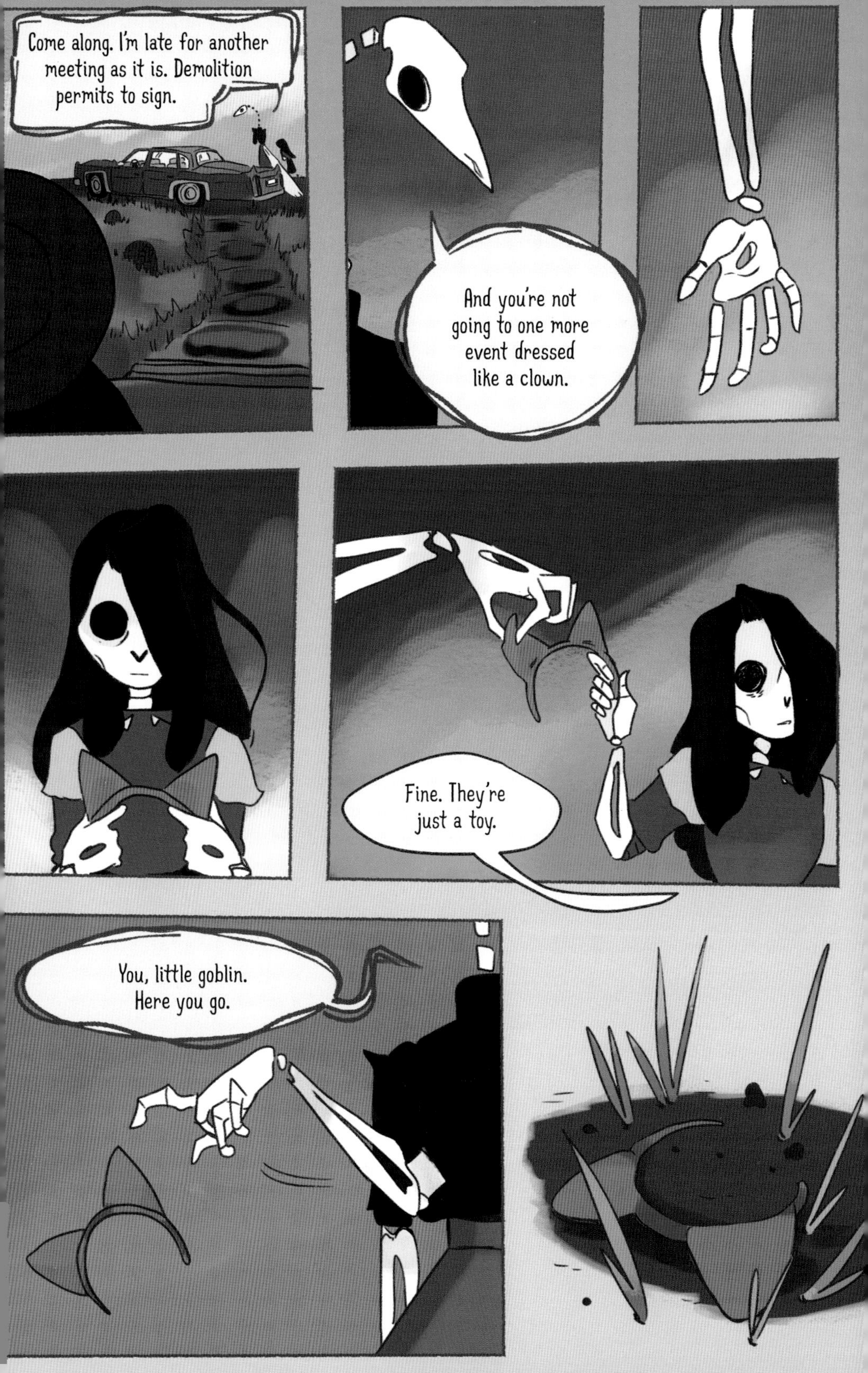
Come along. I'm late for another meeting as it is. Demolition permits to sign.
And you're not going to one more event dressed like a clown.
Fine. They're just a toy.
You, little goblin. Here you go.

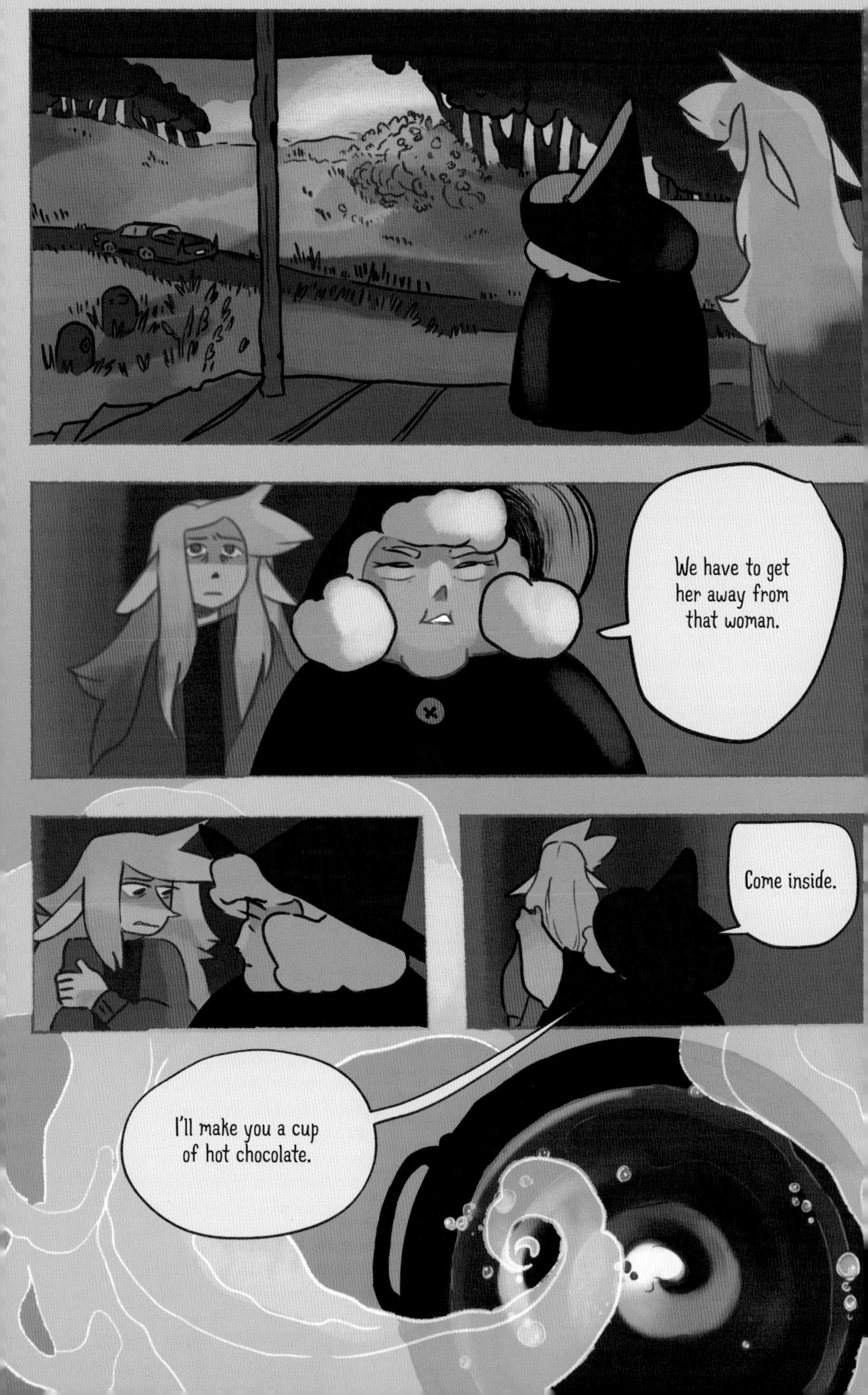
We have to get her away from that woman.
Come inside.
I'll make you a cup of hot chocolate.

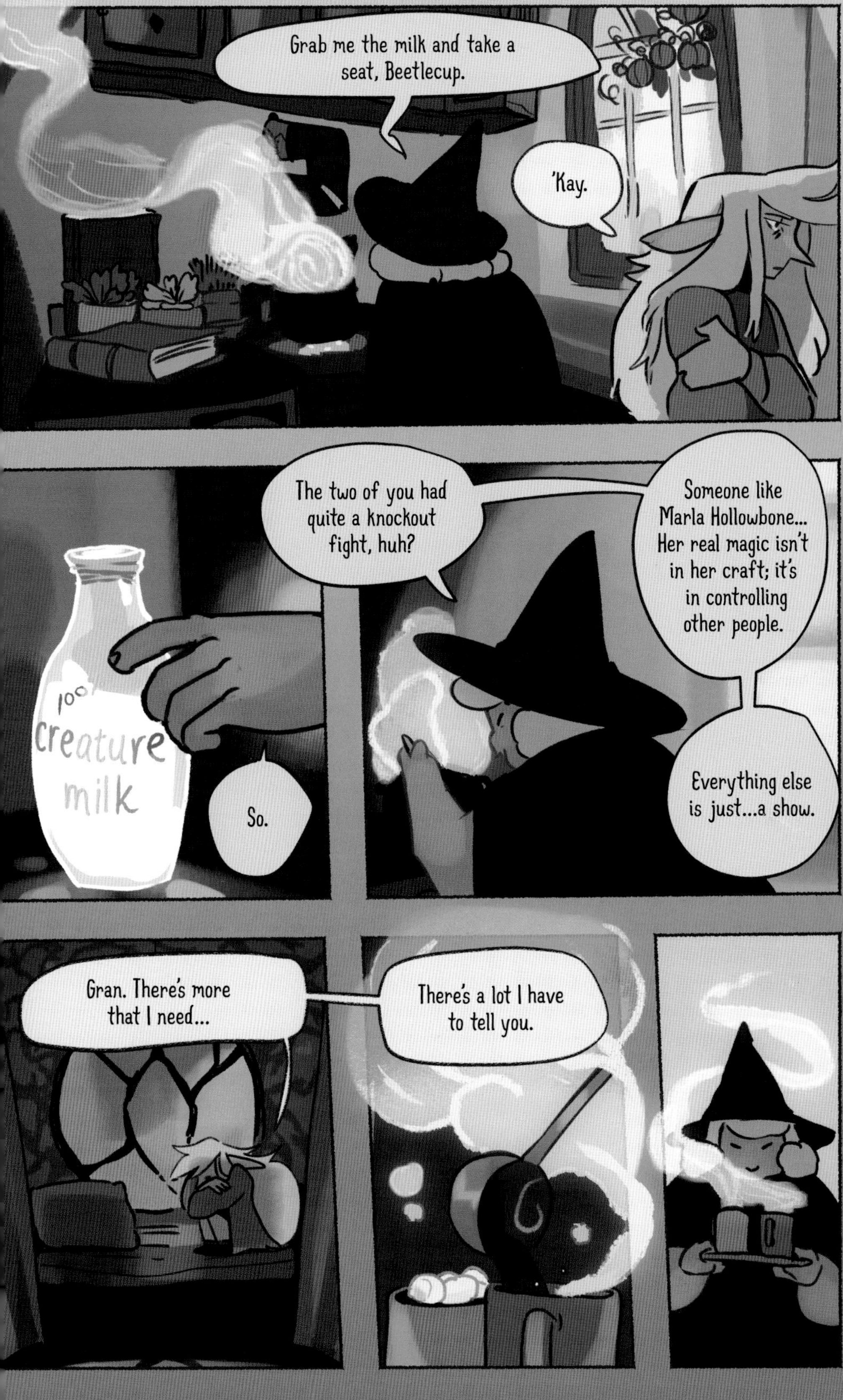
Grab me the milk and take a seat, Beetlecup.
'Kay.
The two of you had quite a knockout fight, huh?
Someone like Marla Hollowbone... Her real magic isn't in her craft; it's in controlling other people.
100
creature milk
So.
Everything else is just...a show.
Gran. There's more that I need...
There's a lot I have to tell you.

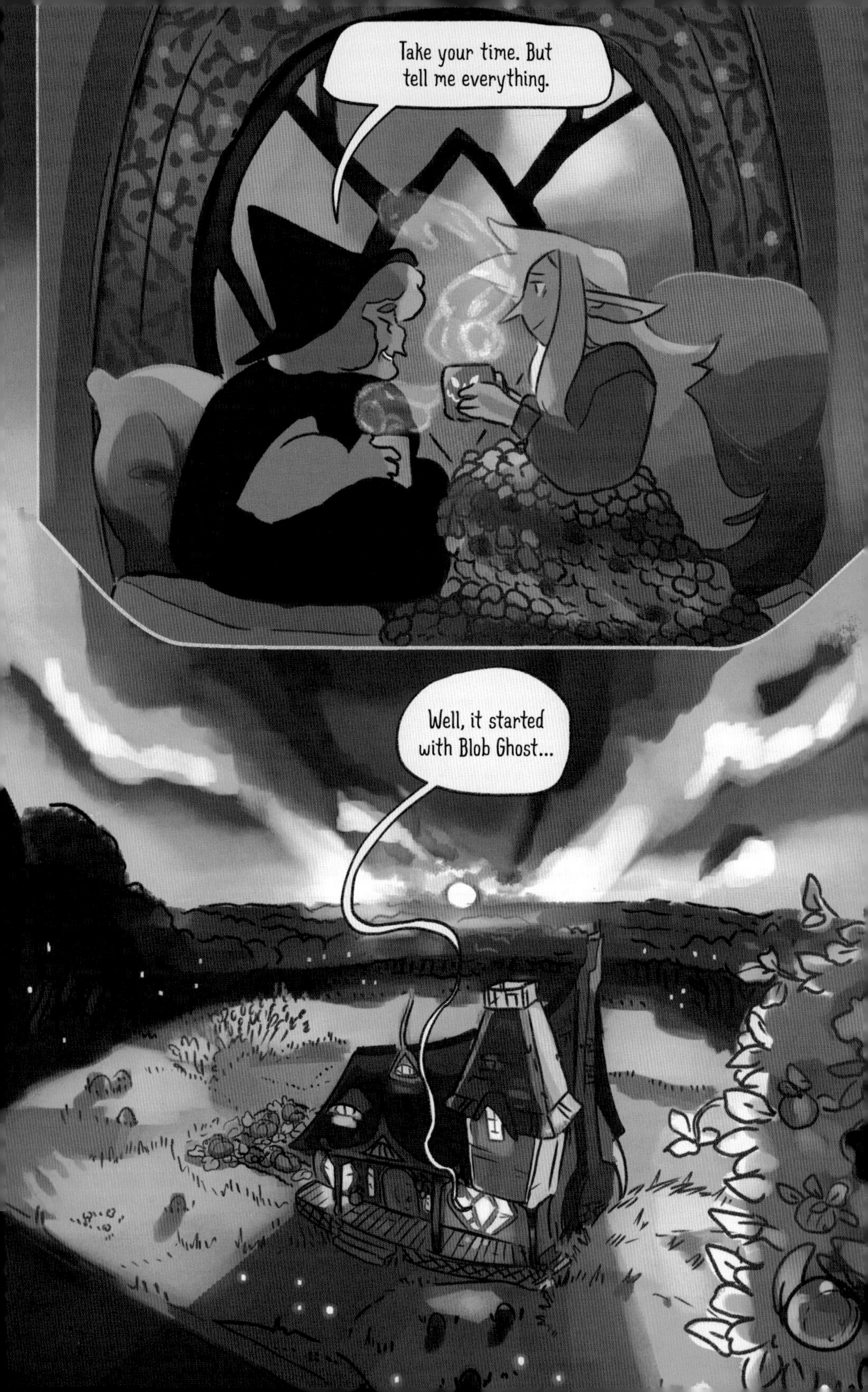
Take your time. But tell me everything.
Well, it started with Blob Ghost...

THE JAR

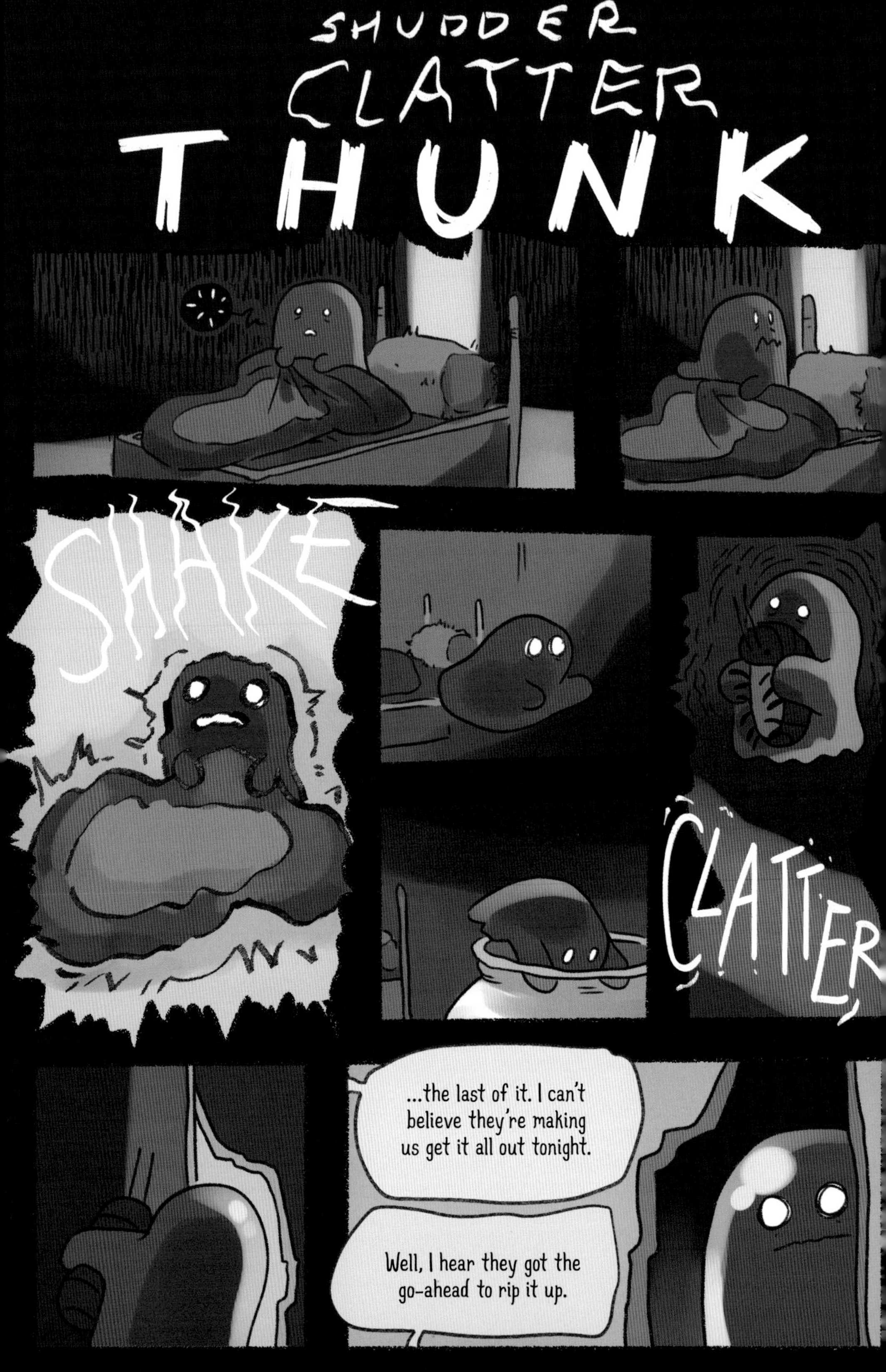
SHUDDER
CLATTER
THUNK
SHAKE
CLATTER
...the last of it. I can't believe they're making us get it all out tonight.
Well, I hear they got the go-ahead to rip it up.

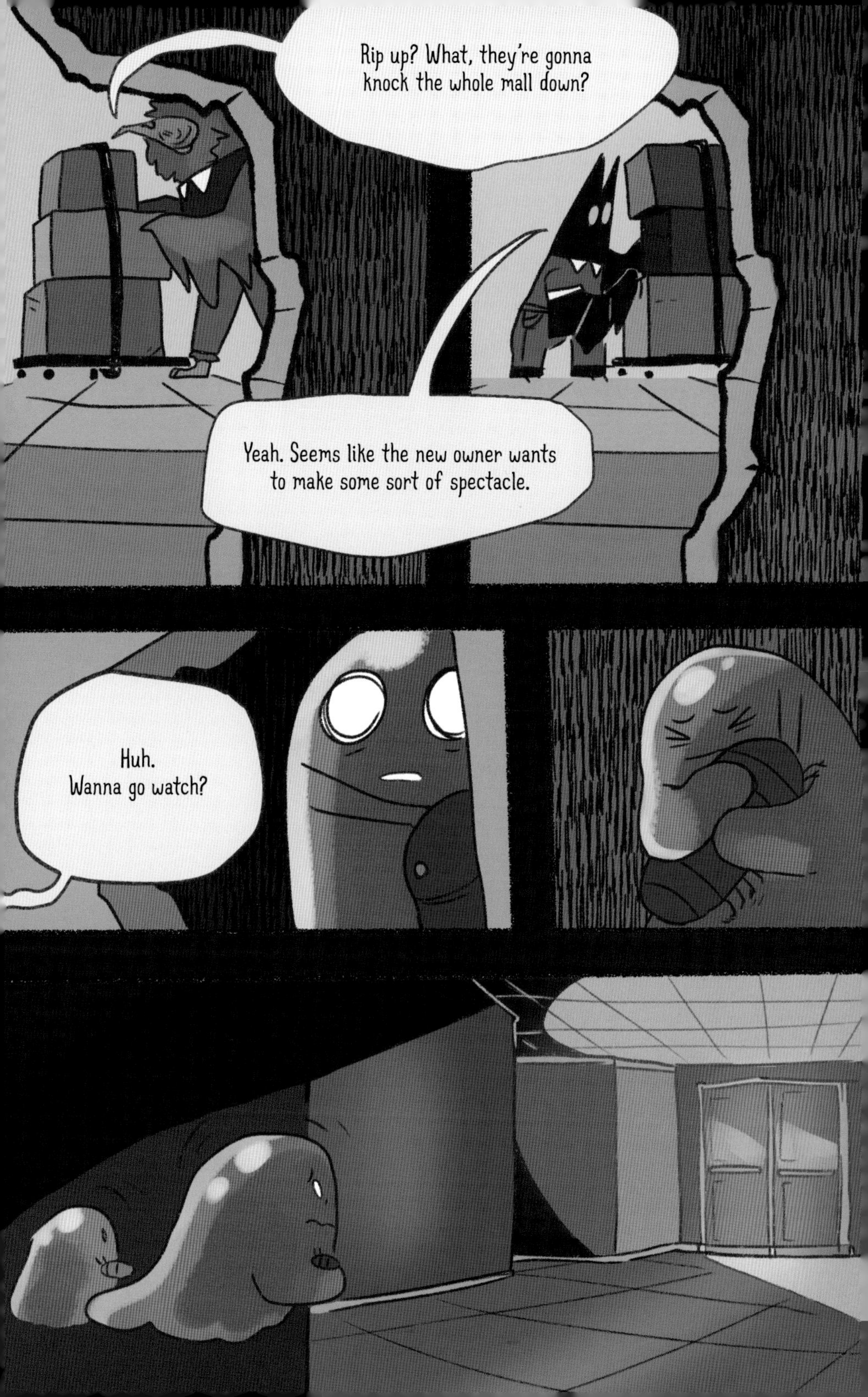
Rip up? What, they're gonna knock the whole mall down?
Yeah. Seems like the new owner wants to make some sort of spectacle.
Huh. Wanna go watch?

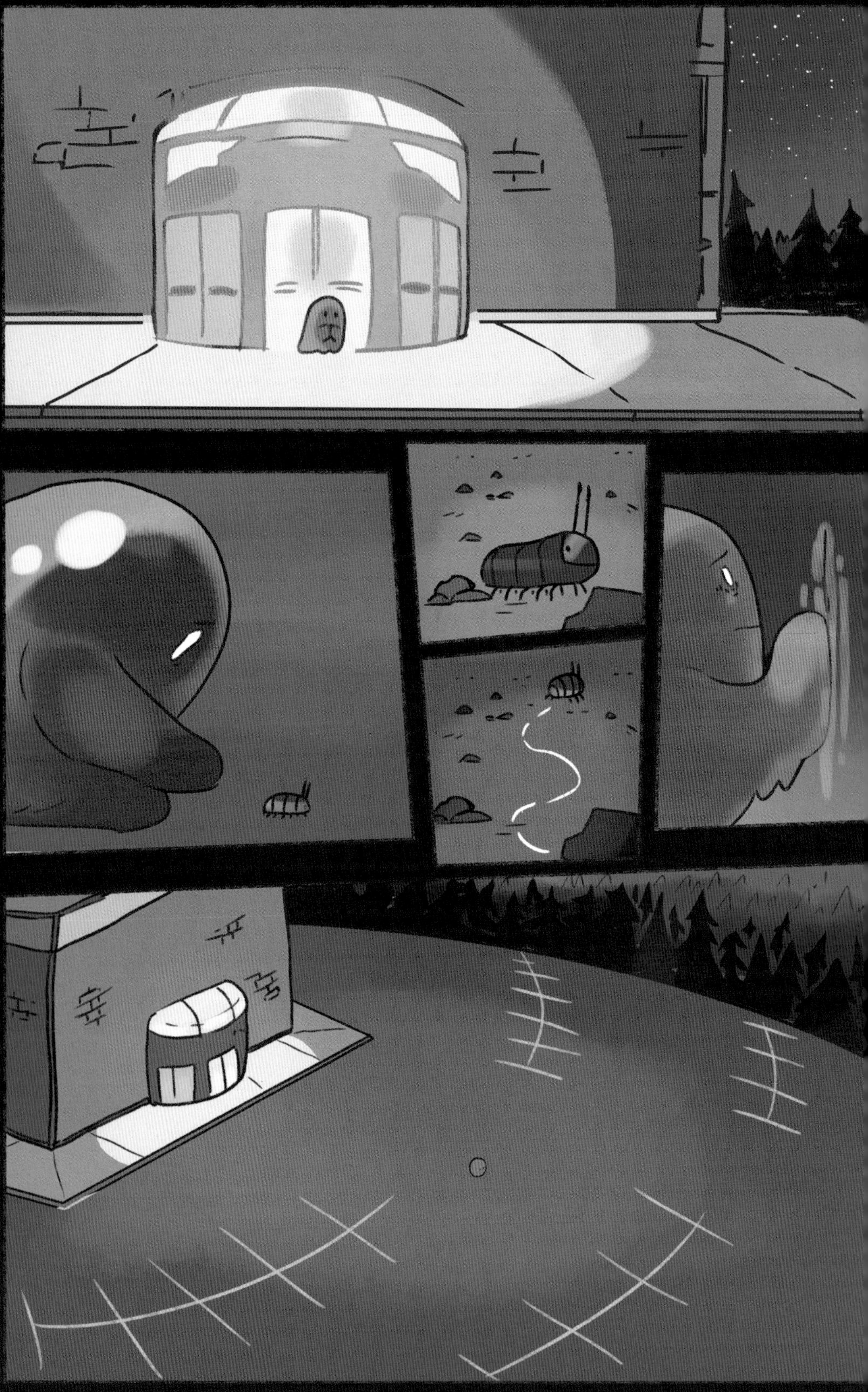

SORCERY

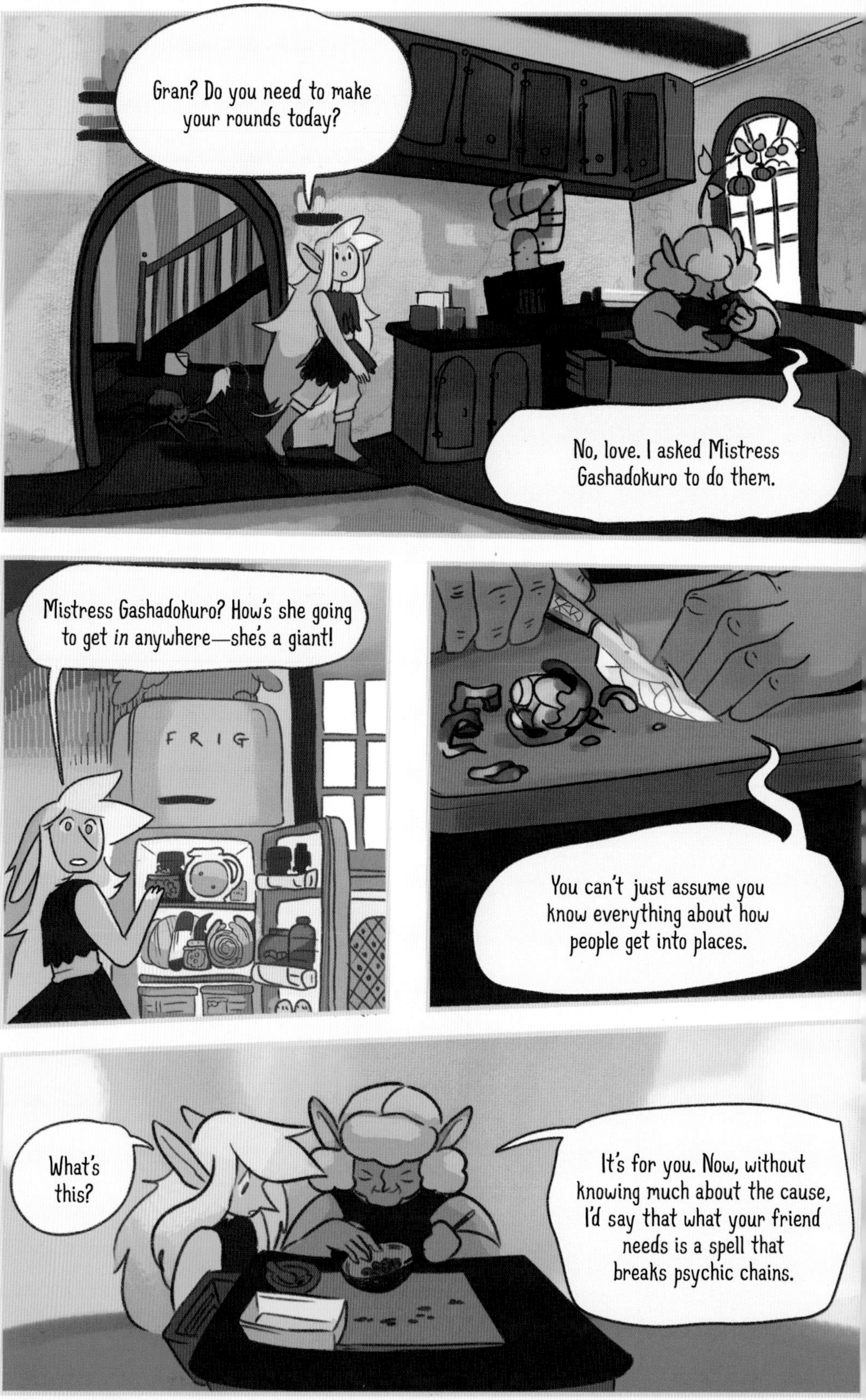
Gran? Do you need to make your rounds today?
No, love. I asked Mistress Gashadokuro to do them.
Mistress Gashadokuro? How's she going to get *in* anywhere—she's a giant!
FRIG
You can't just assume you know everything about how people get into places.
What's this?
It's for you. Now, without knowing much about the cause, I'd say that what your friend needs is a spell that breaks psychic chains.

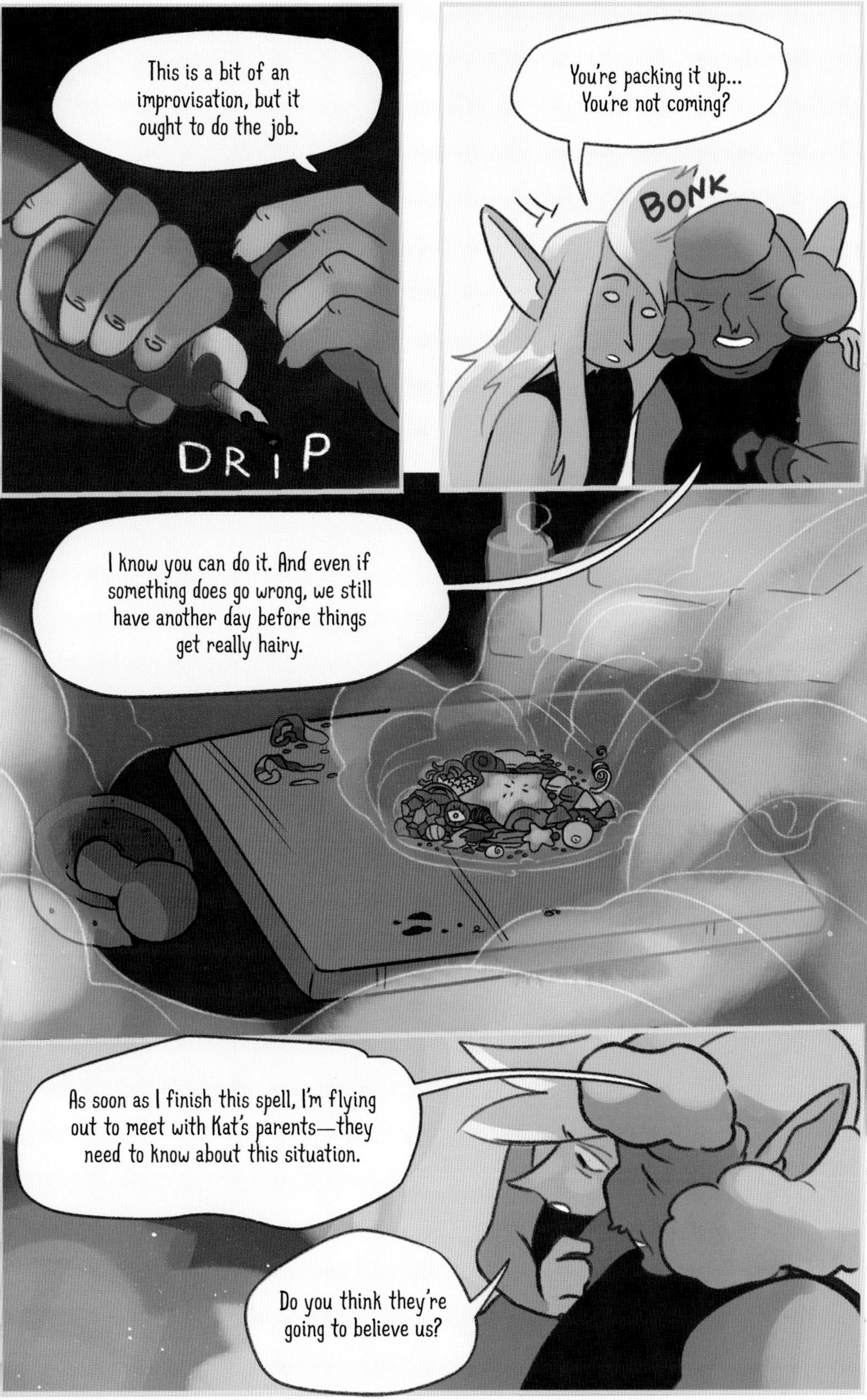
This is a bit of an improvisation, but it ought to do the job.
DRIP
You're packing it up... You're not coming?
BONK
I know you can do it. And even if something does go wrong, we still have another day before things get really hairy.
As soon as I finish this spell, I'm flying out to meet with Kat's parents—they need to know about this situation.
Do you think they're going to believe us?

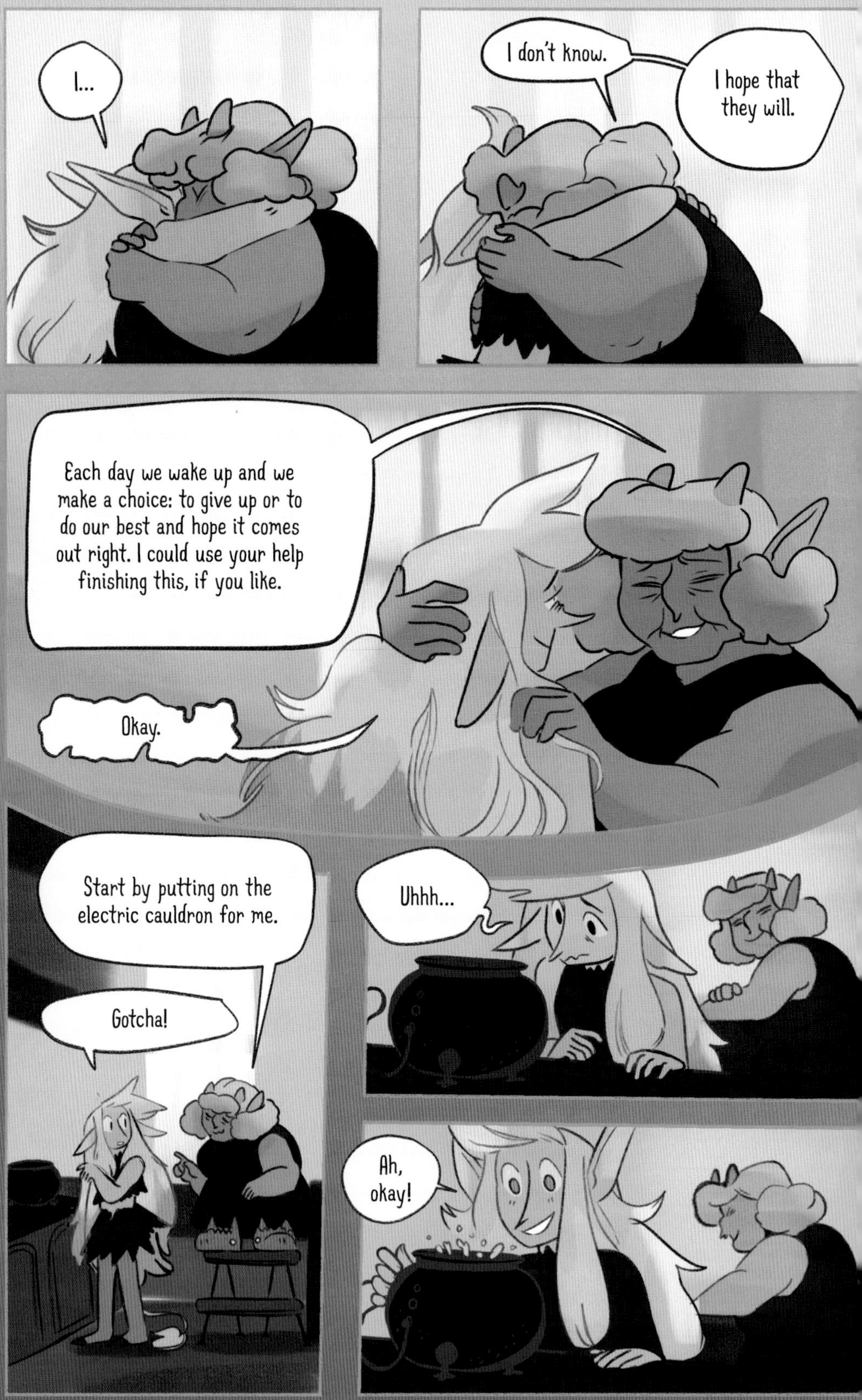
I...
I don't know.
I hope that they will.
Each day we wake up and we make a choice: to give up or to do our best and hope it comes out right. I could use your help finishing this, if you like.
Okay.
Start by putting on the electric cauldron for me.
Gotcha!
Uhhh...
Ah, okay!

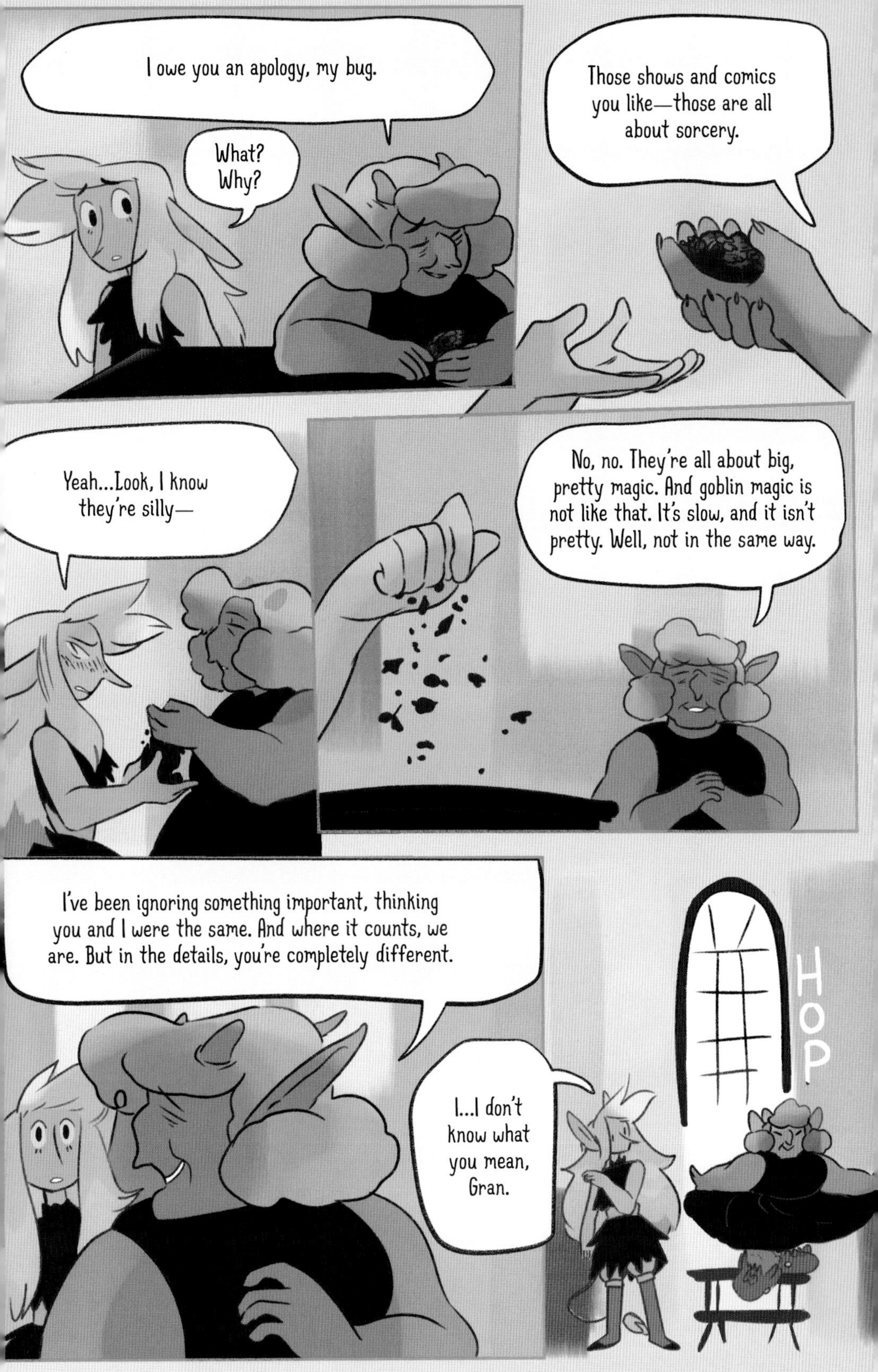
I owe you an apology, my bug.
What? Why?
Those shows and comics you like—those are all about sorcery.
Yeah...Look, I know they're silly—
No, no. They're all about big, pretty magic. And goblin magic is not like that. It's slow, and it isn't pretty. Well, not in the same way.
I've been ignoring something important, thinking you and I were the same. And where it counts, we are. But in the details, you're completely different.
I...I don't know what you mean, Gran.
HOP

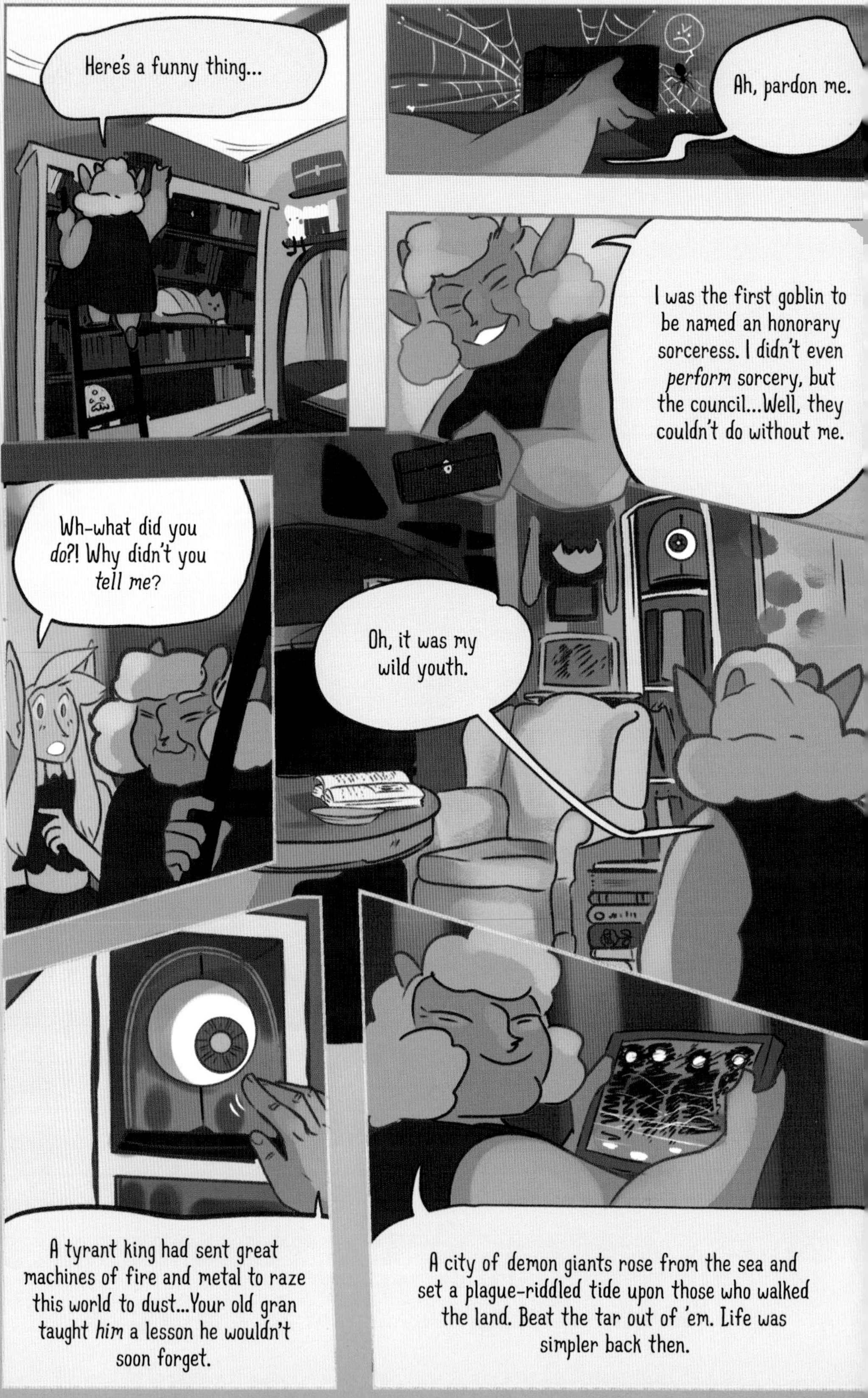

Here's a funny thing...
Ah, pardon me.
I was the first goblin to be named an honorary sorceress. I didn't even *perform* sorcery, but the council...Well, they couldn't do without me.
Wh-what did you *do*?! Why didn't you *tell me*?
Oh, it was my wild youth.
A tyrant king had sent great machines of fire and metal to raze this world to dust...Your old gran taught *him* a lesson he wouldn't soon forget.
A city of demon giants rose from the sea and set a plague-riddled tide upon those who walked the land. Beat the tar out of 'em. Life was simpler back then.

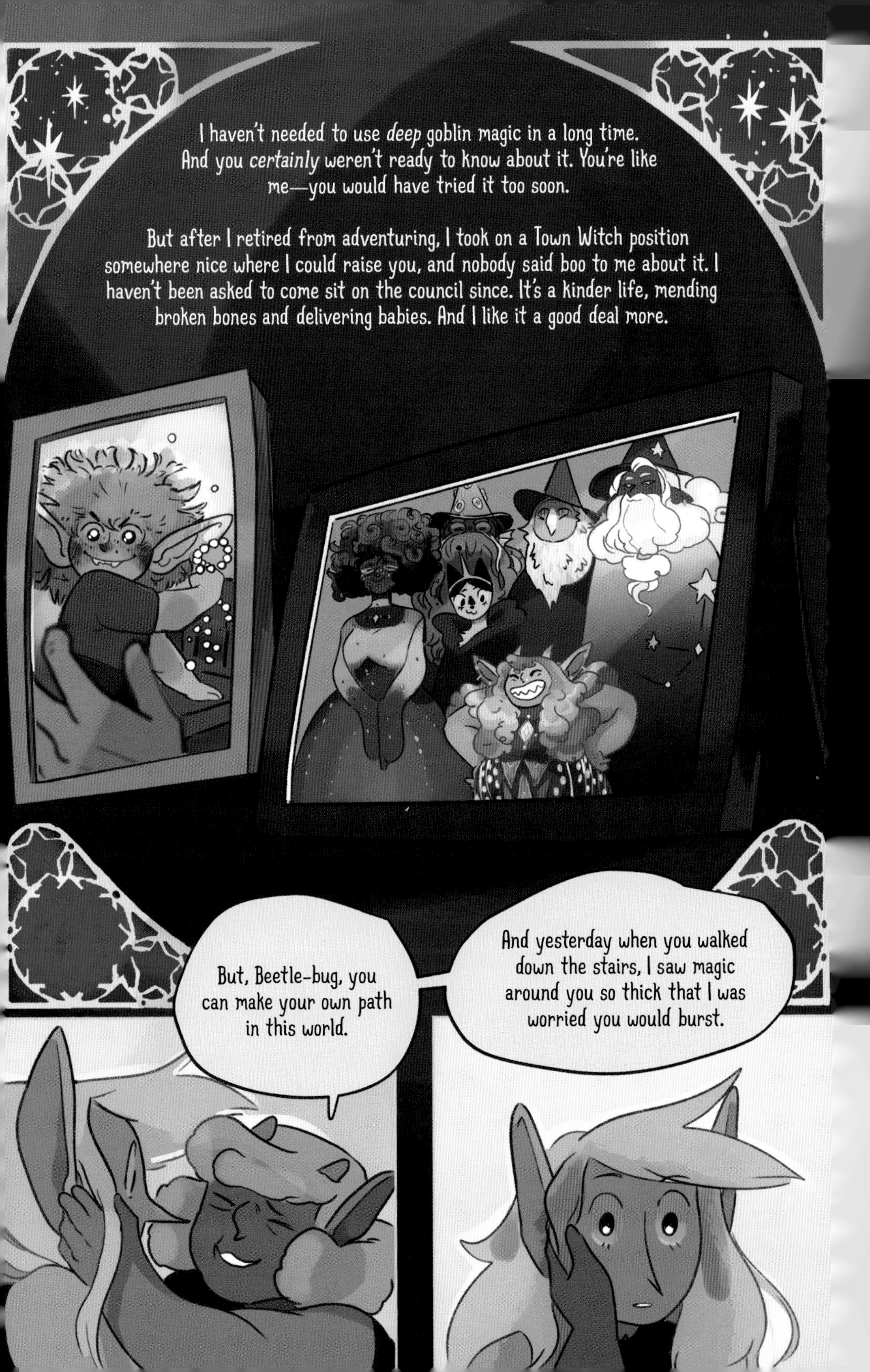
I haven't needed to use *deep* goblin magic in a long time. And you *certainly* weren't ready to know about it. You're like me—you would have tried it too soon.
But after I retired from adventuring, I took on a Town Witch position somewhere nice where I could raise you, and nobody said boo to me about it. I haven't been asked to come sit on the council since. It's a kinder life, mending broken bones and delivering babies. And I like it a good deal more.
But, Beetle-bug, you can make your own path in this world.
And yesterday when you walked down the stairs, I saw magic around you so thick that I was worried you would burst.

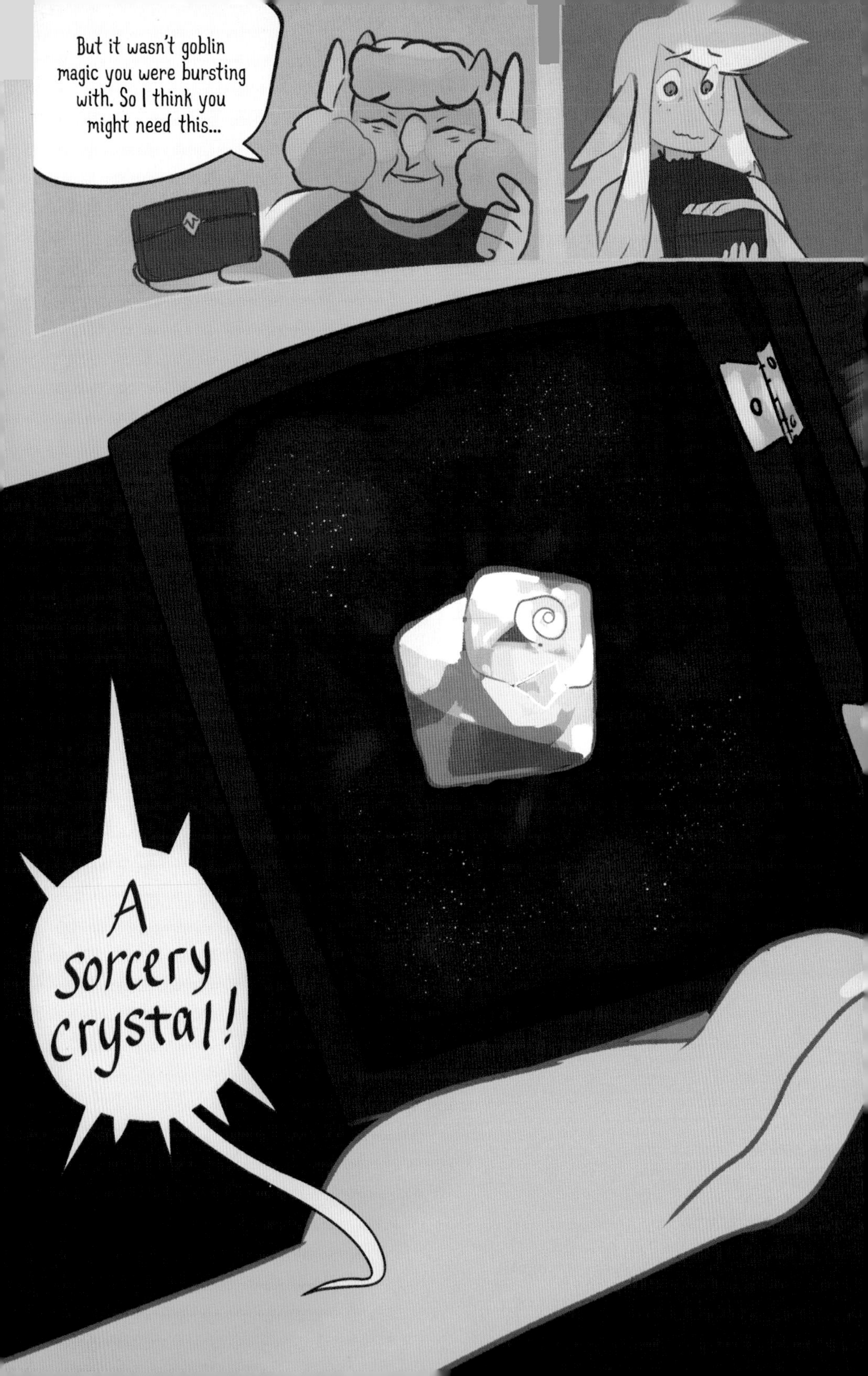
But it wasn't goblin magic you were bursting with. So I think you might need this...
A sorcery crystal!

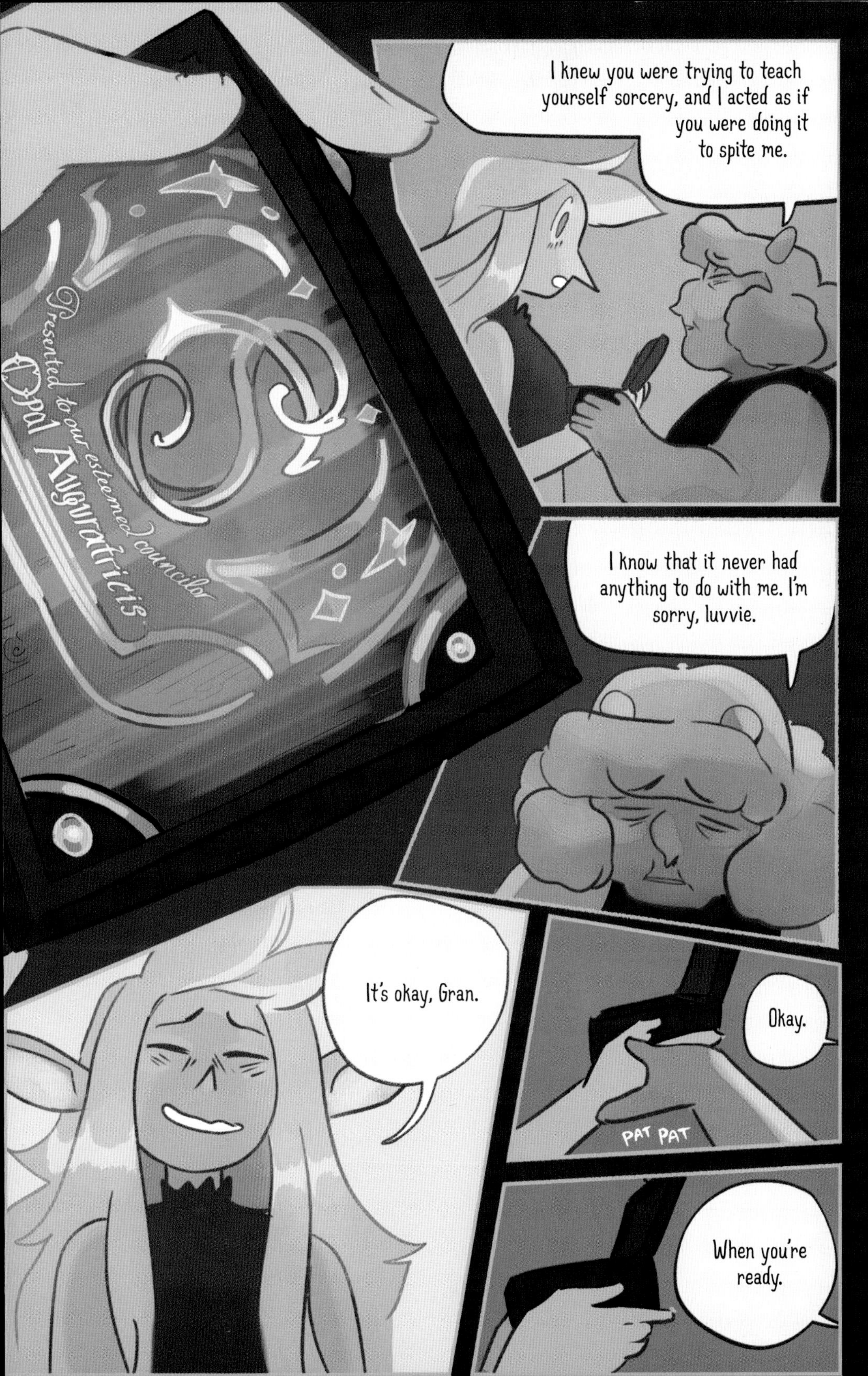
Presented to our esteemed councilor
Opal Augurätricis
I knew you were trying to teach yourself sorcery, and I acted as if you were doing it to spite me.
I know that it never had anything to do with me. I'm sorry, luvvie.
It's okay, Gran.
Okay.
PAT PAT
When you're ready.

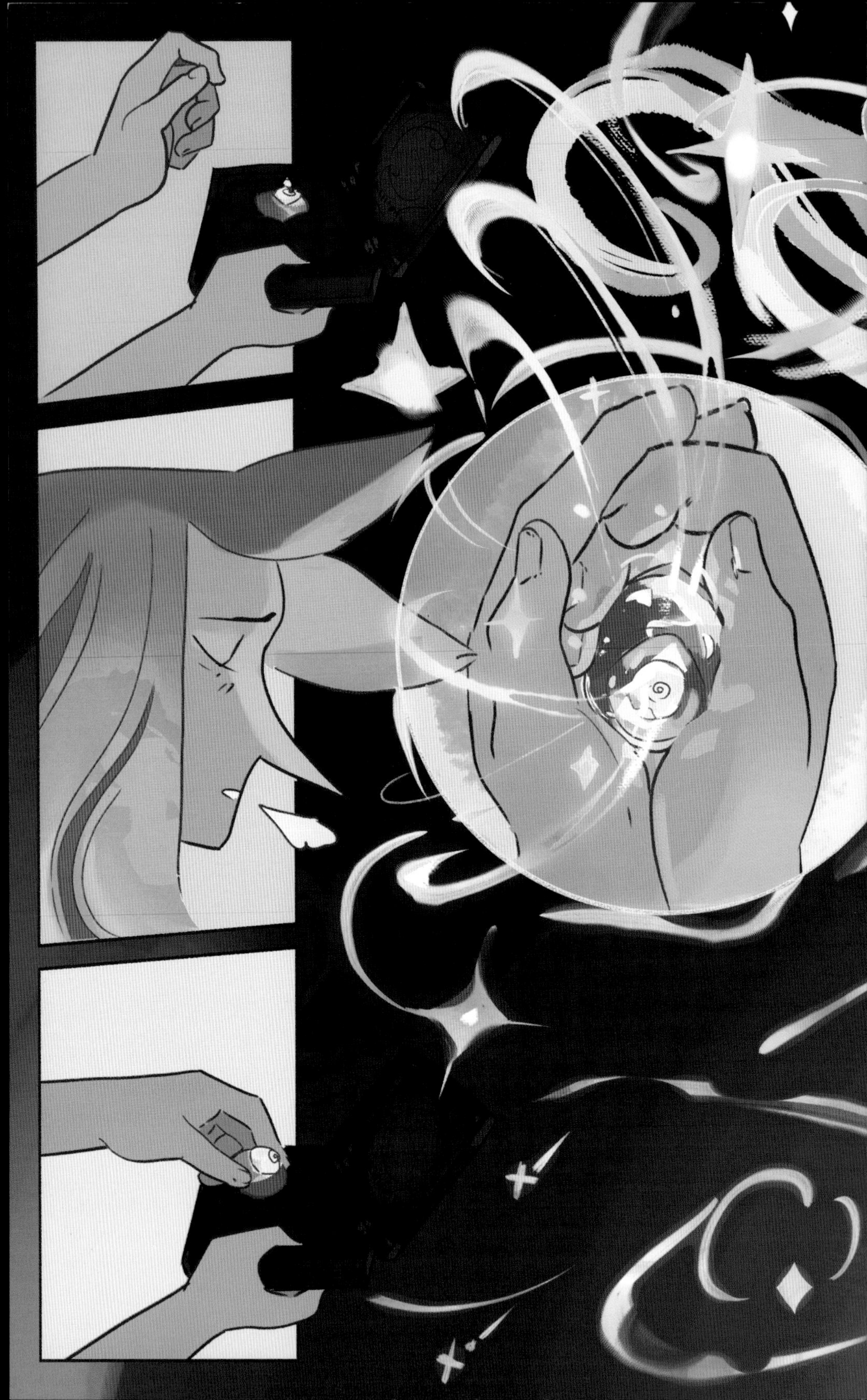

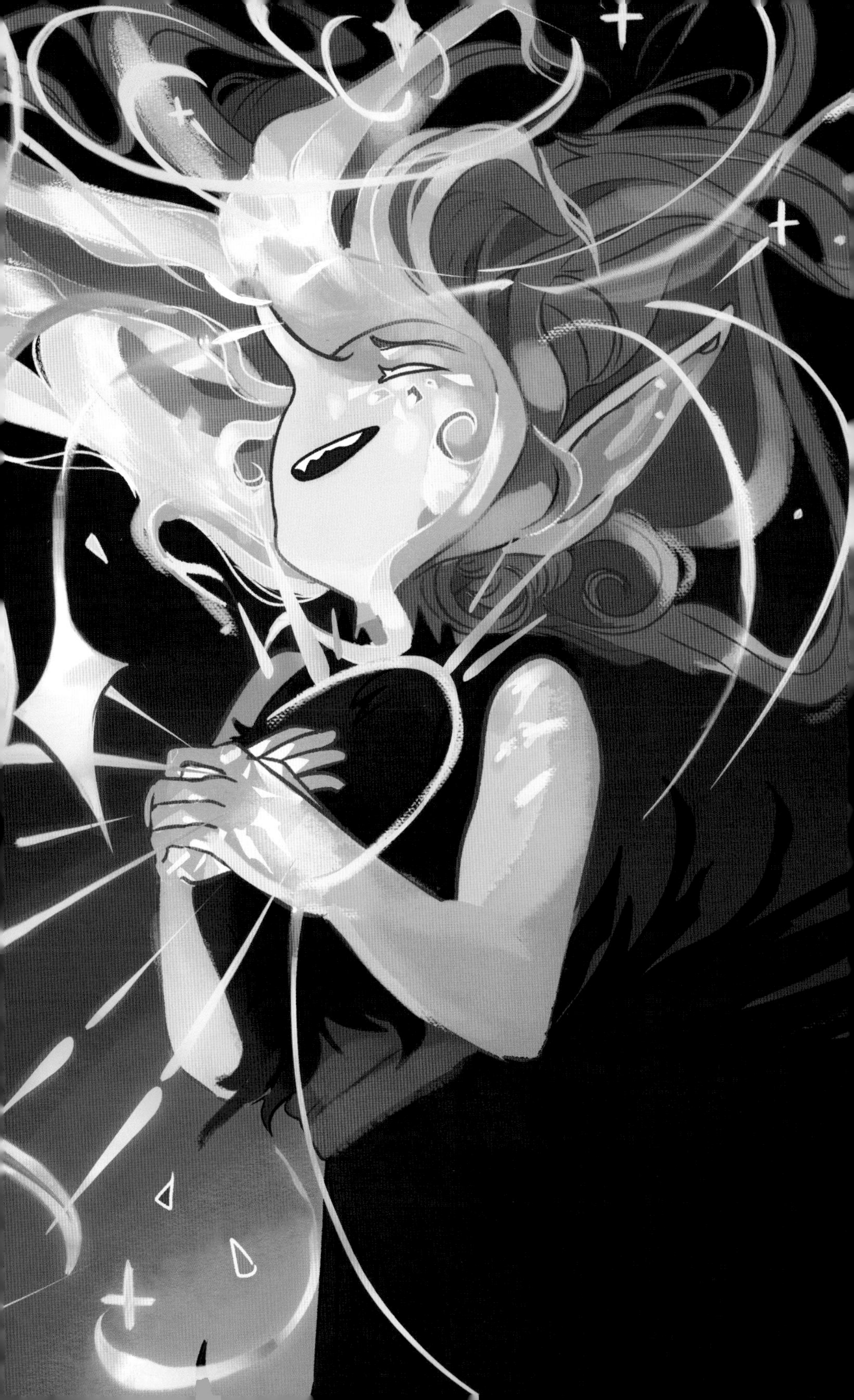

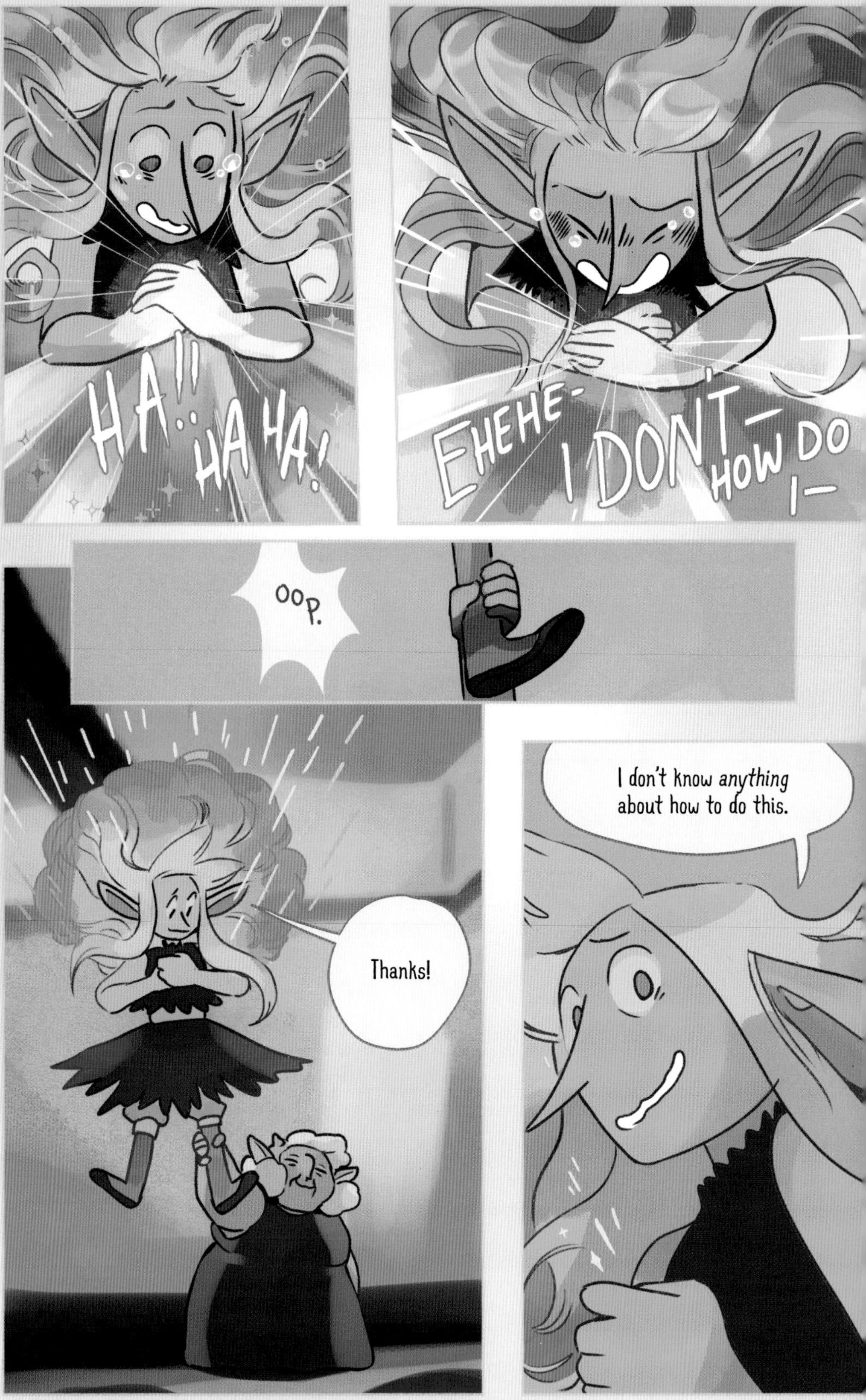
HA!! HA HA HA!
EHEHE- I DON'T- HOW DO I-
OOP.
Thanks!
I don't know *anything* about how to do this.

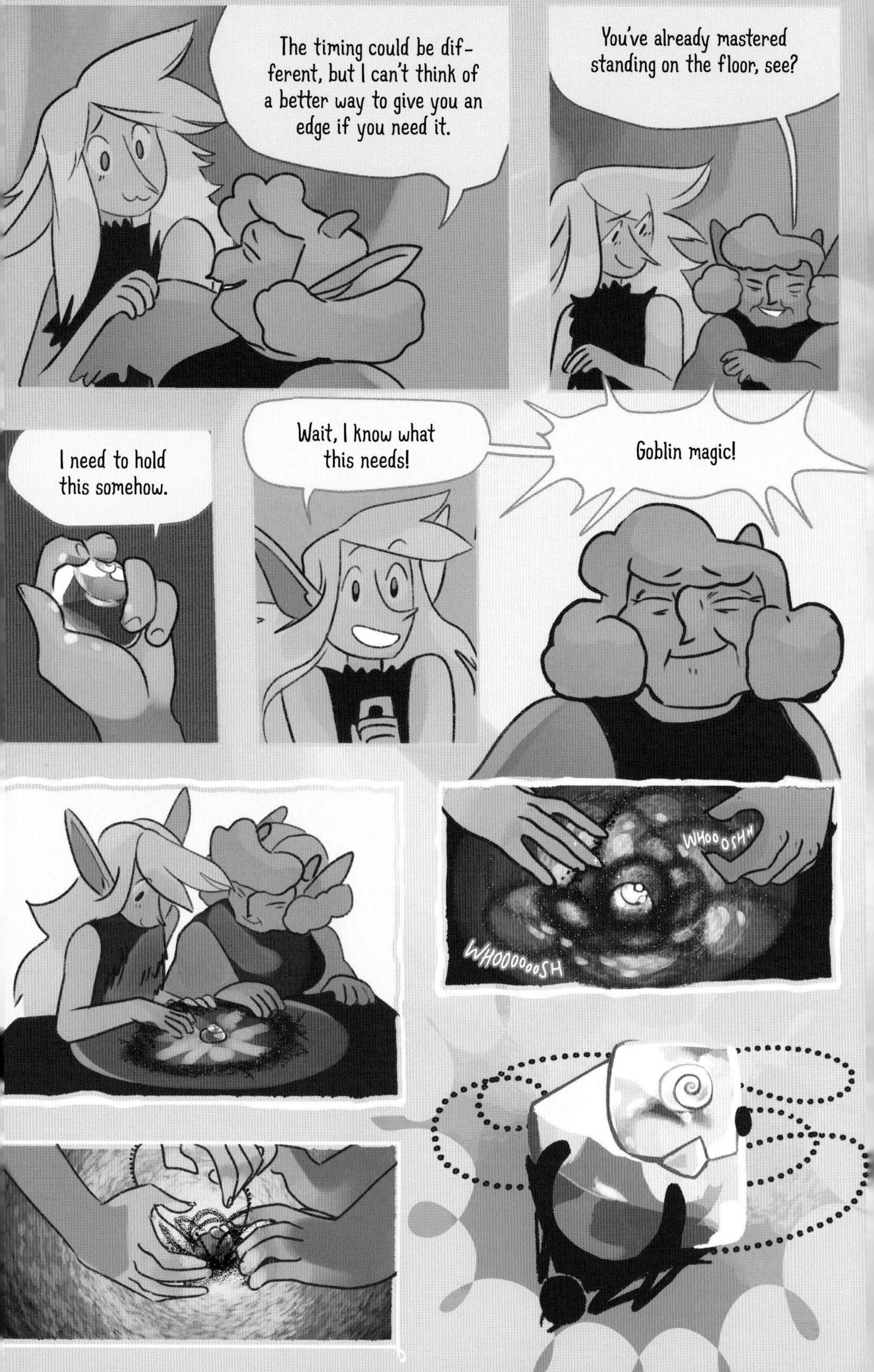

The timing could be dif-ferent, but I can't think of a better way to give you an edge if you need it.
You've already mastered standing on the floor, see?
I need to hold this somehow.
Wait, I know what this needs!
Goblin magic!
WHOOOSHH
WHOOOOOOSH

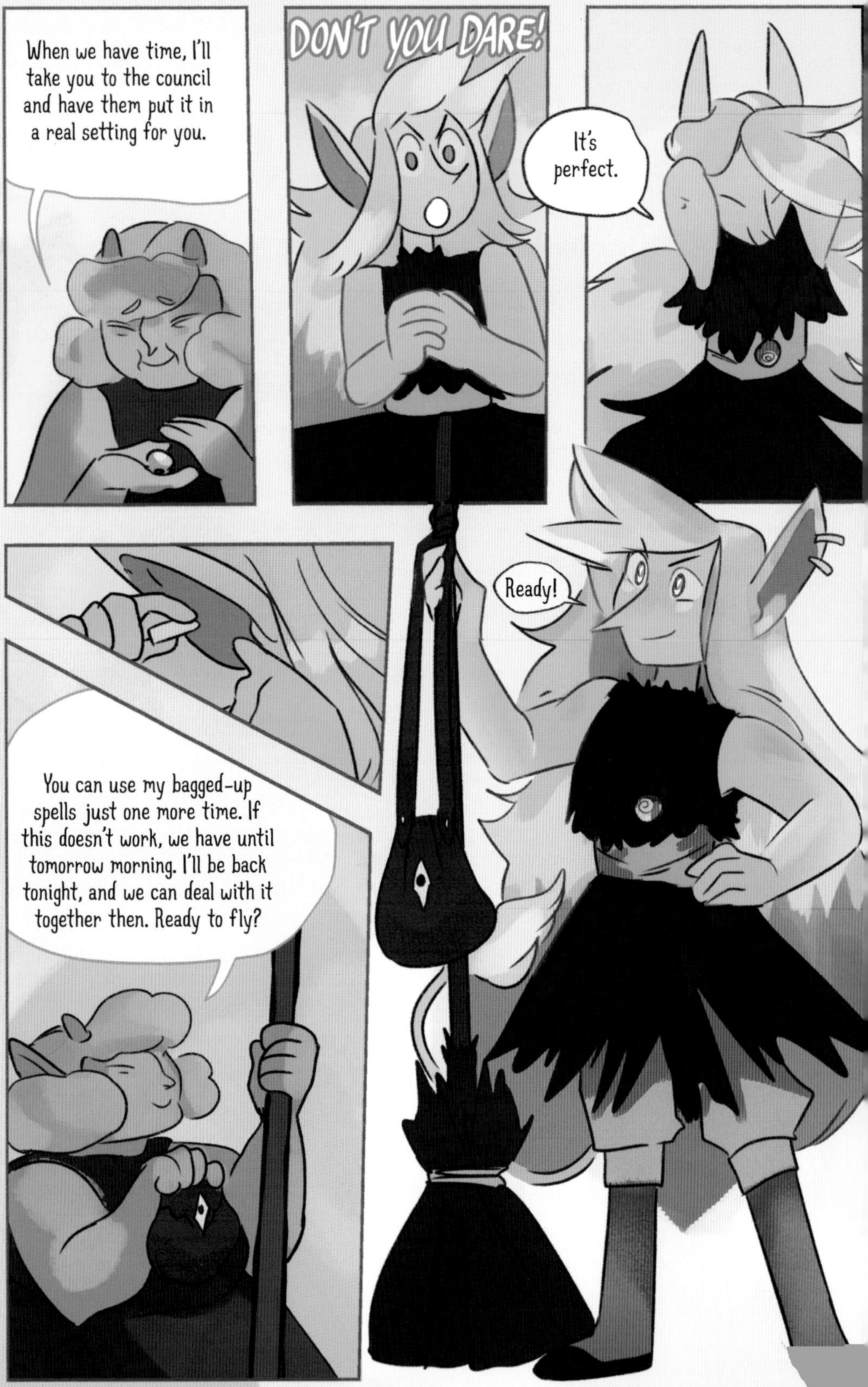
When we have time, I'll take you to the council and have them put it in a real setting for you.
DON'T YOU DARE!
It's perfect.
Ready!
You can use my bagged-up spells just one more time. If this doesn't work, we have until tomorrow morning. I'll be back tonight, and we can deal with it together then. Ready to fly?

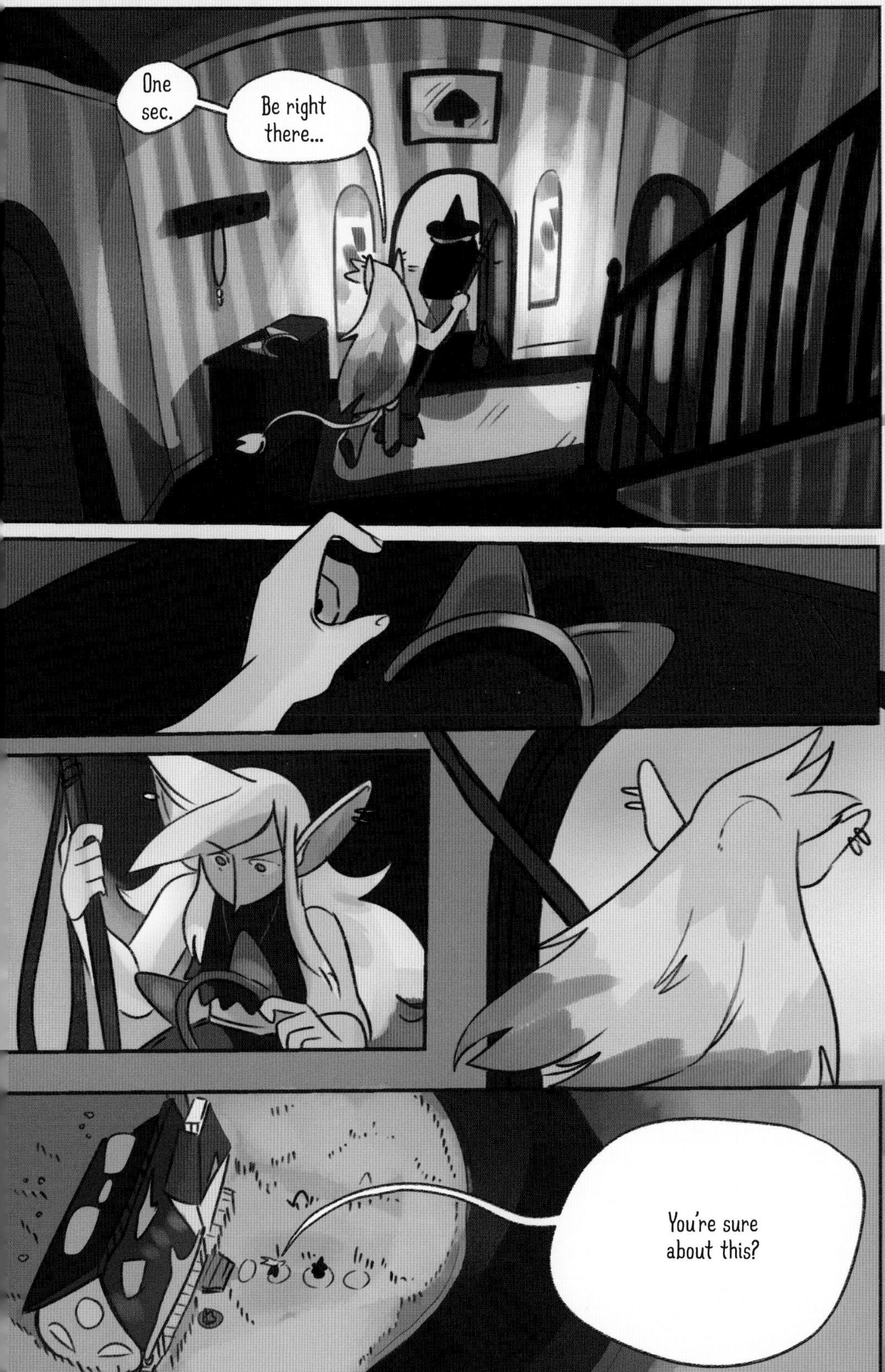
One sec.
Be right there...
You're sure about this?

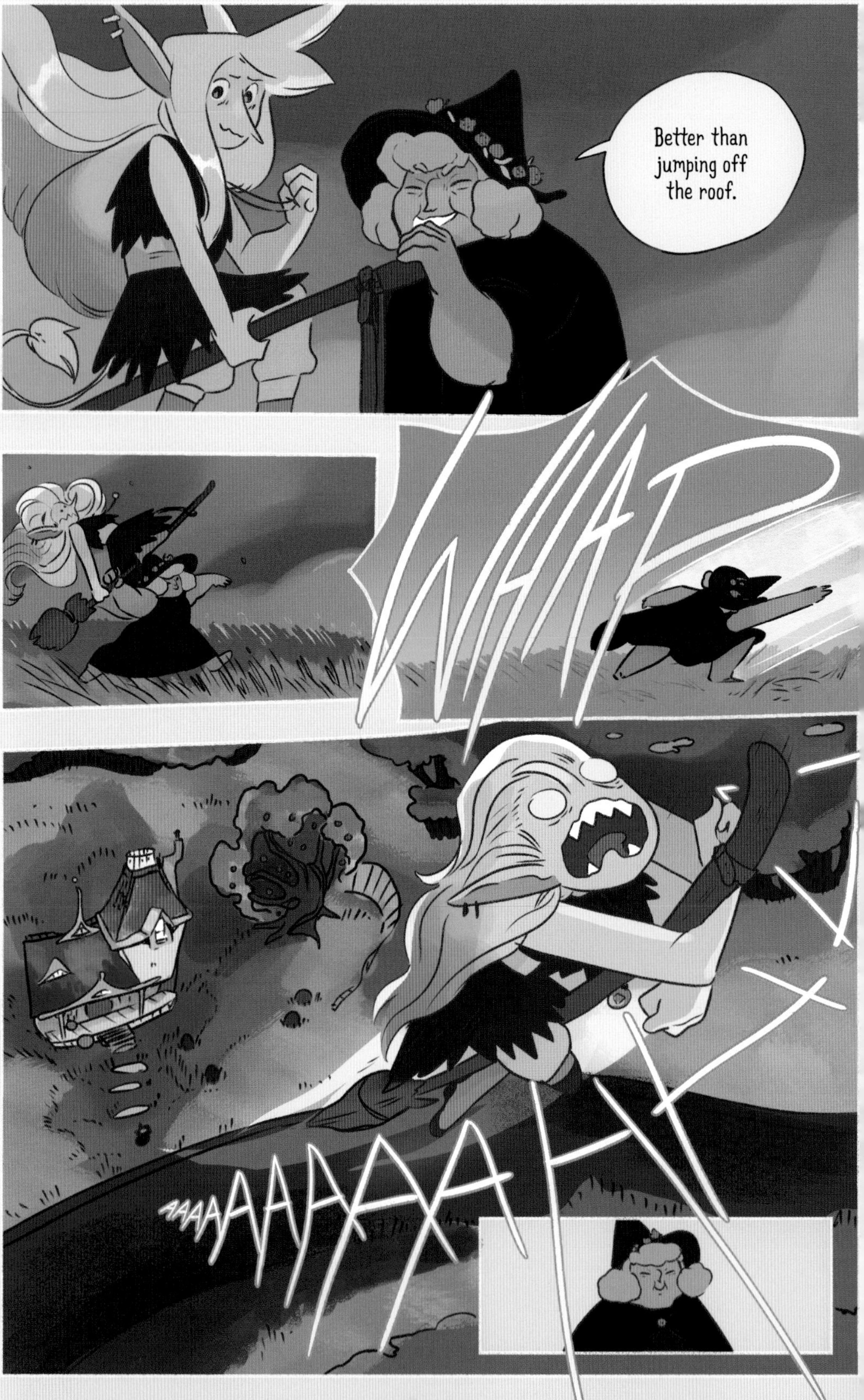
Better than jumping off the roof.
WHAT?
AAAAAAAAAAH

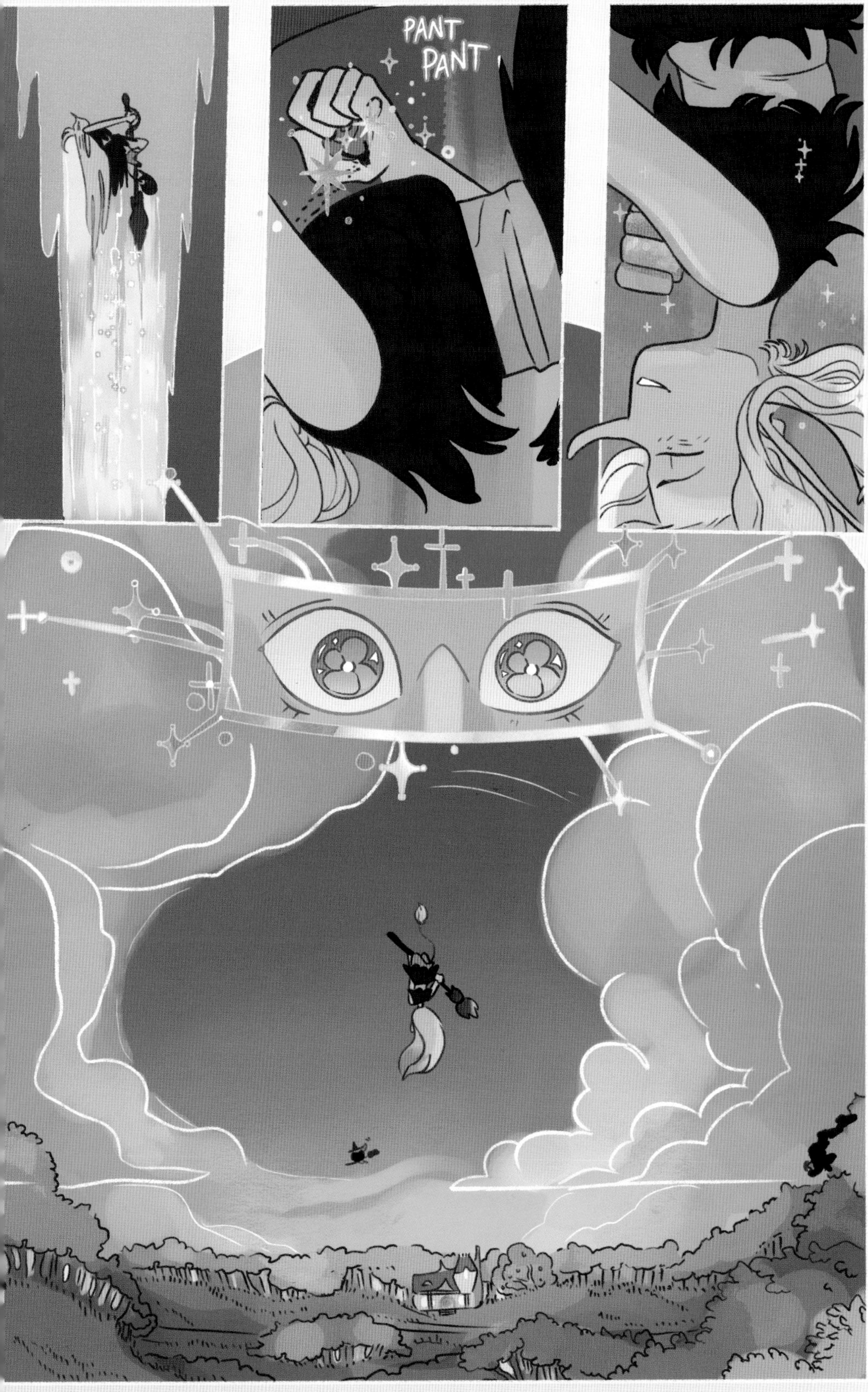
PANT
PANT

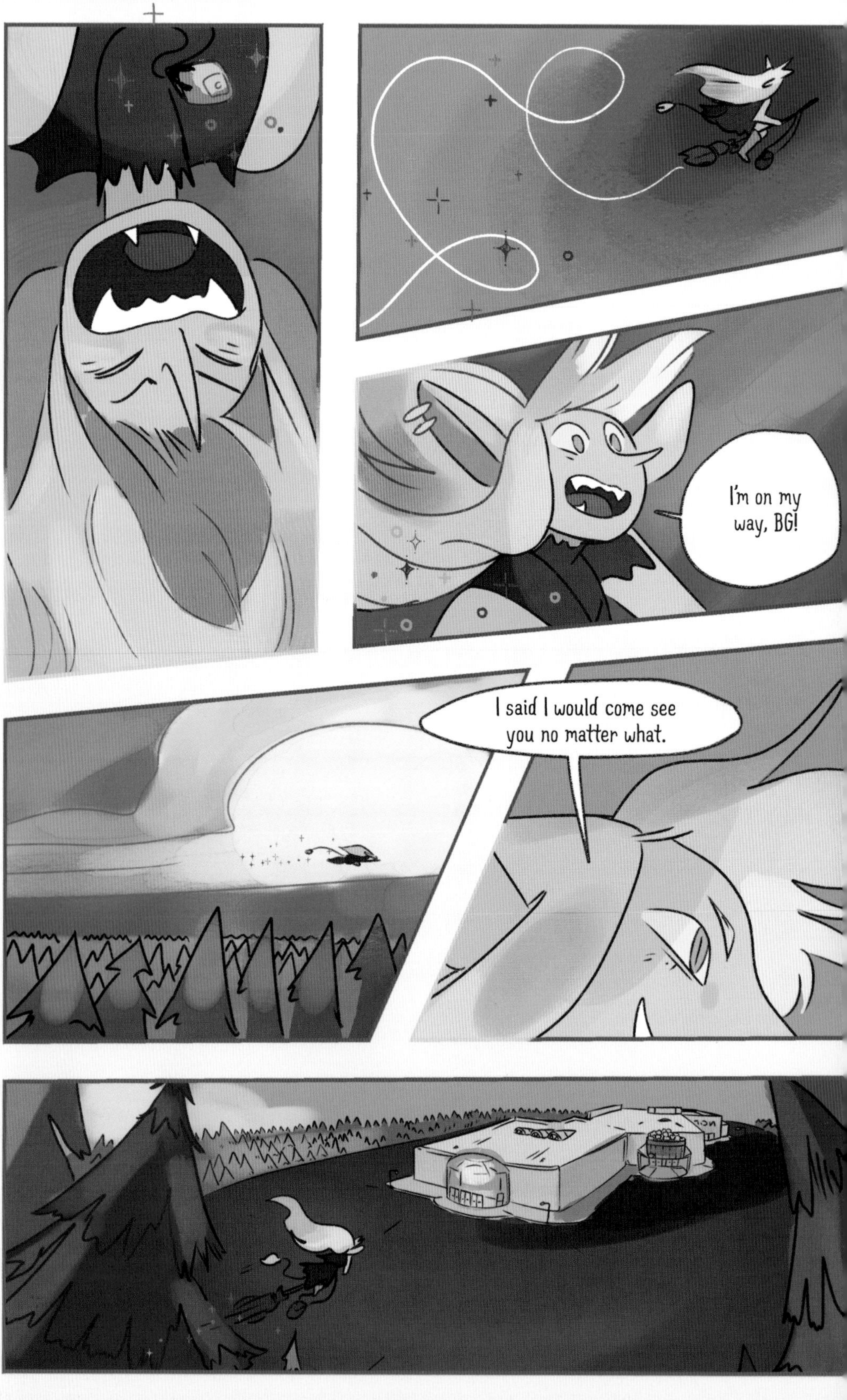
I'm on my way, BG!
I said I would come see you no matter what.

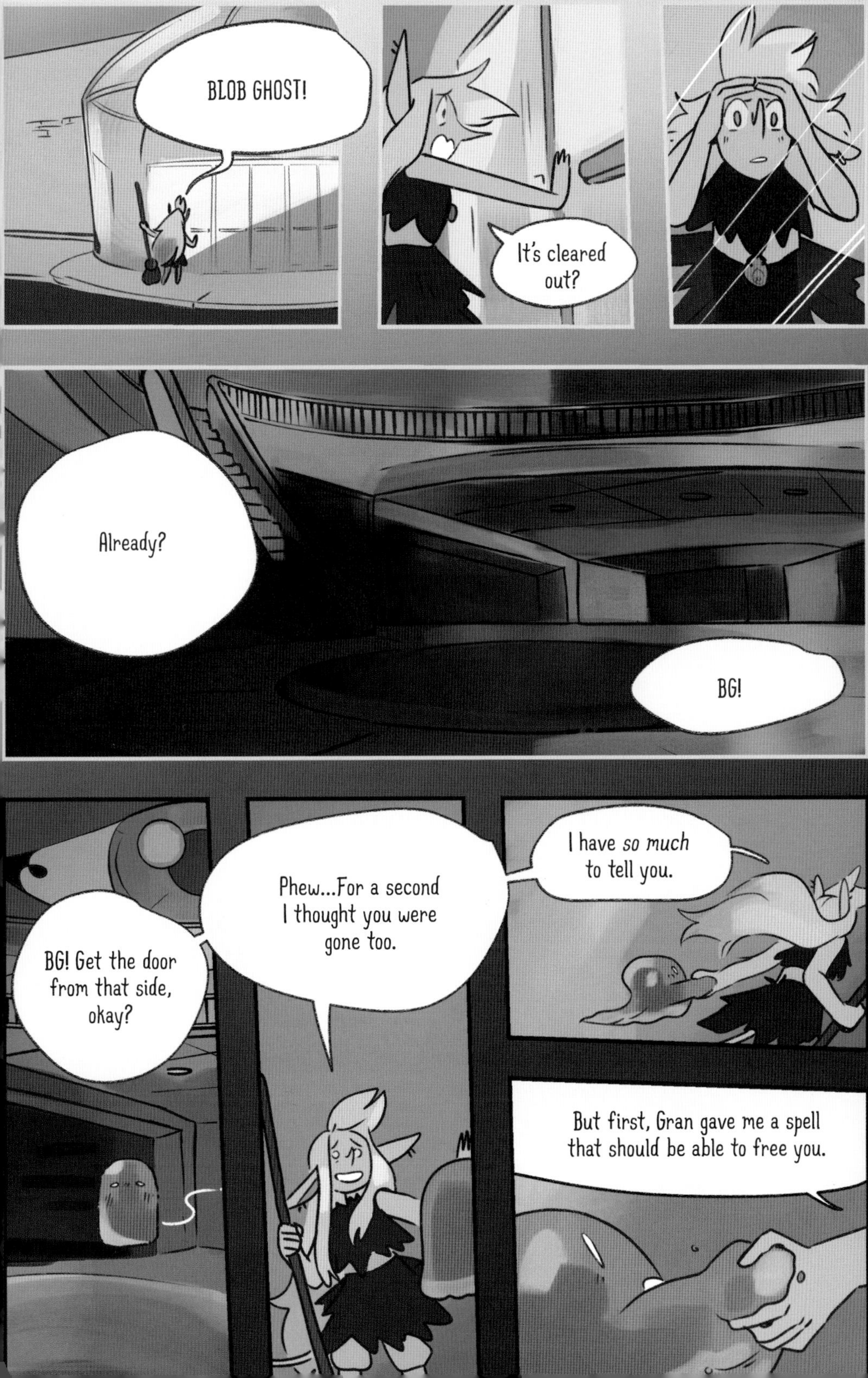
BLOB GHOST!
It's cleared out?
Already?
BG!
BG! Get the door from that side, okay?
Phew...For a second I thought you were gone too.
I have *so much* to tell you.
But first, Gran gave me a spell that should be able to free you.

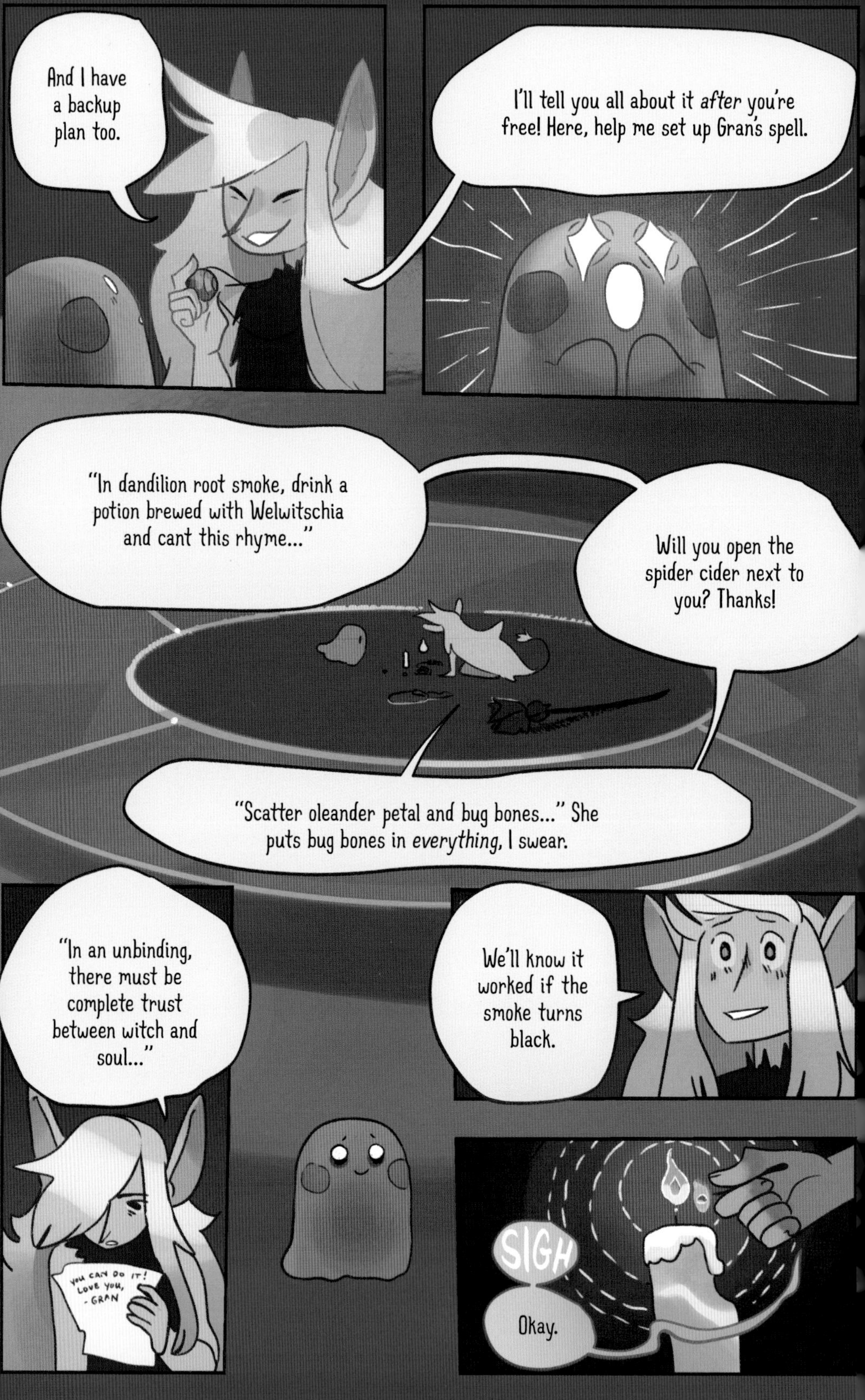
And I have a backup plan too.
I'll tell you all about it *after* you're free! Here, help me set up Gran's spell.
"In dandilion root smoke, drink a potion brewed with Welwitschia and cant this rhyme..."
Will you open the spider cider next to you? Thanks!
"Scatter oleander petal and bug bones..." She puts bug bones in *everything*, I swear.
"In an unbinding, there must be complete trust between witch and soul..."
YOU CAN DO IT! LOVE YOU, - GRAN
We'll know it worked if the smoke turns black.
SIGH
Okay.

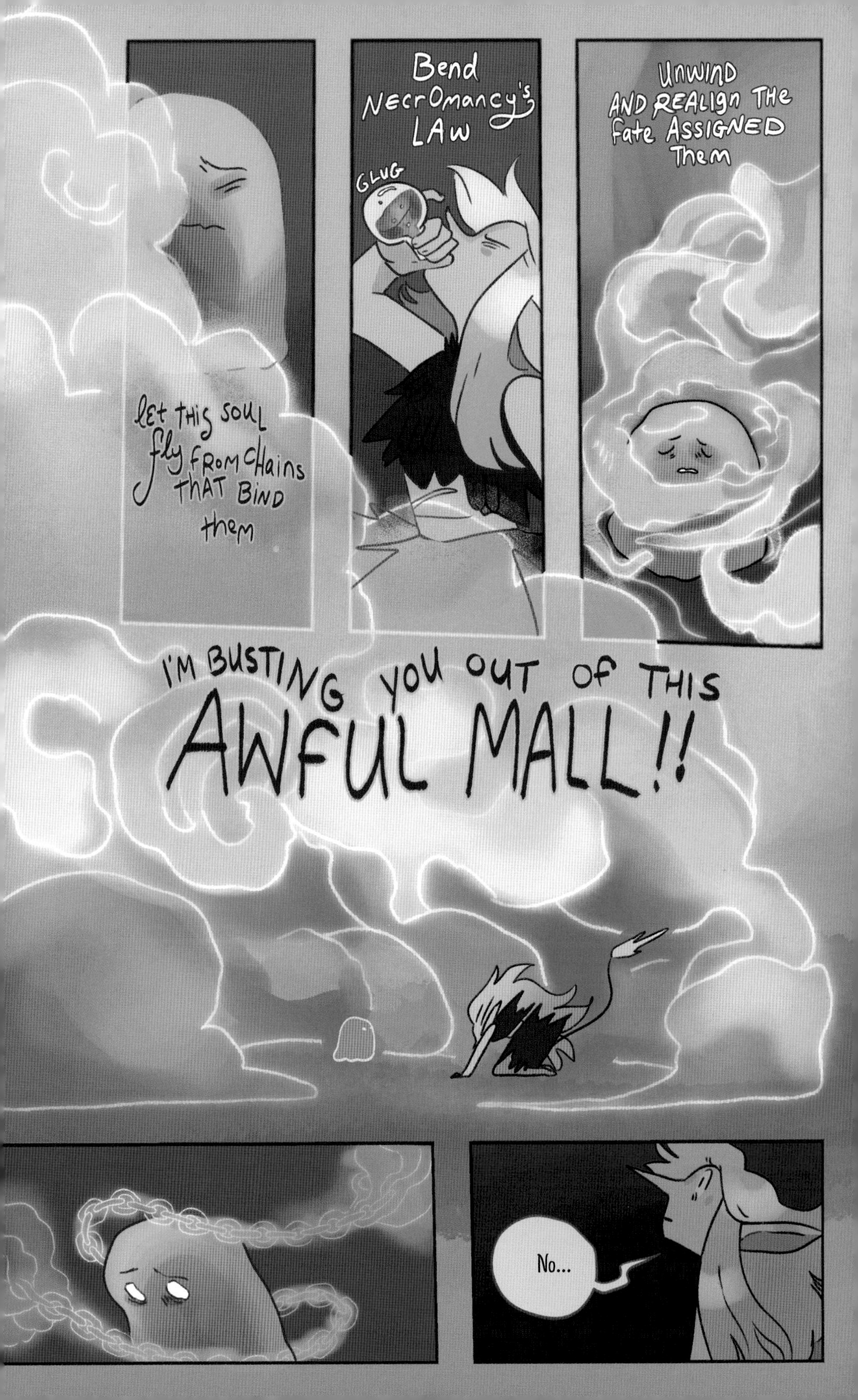
Let this soul fly from chains that bind them
Bend Necromancy's LAW
GLUG
Unwind and realign the fate assigned them
I'M BUSTING YOU OUT OF THIS
AWFUL MALL!!
No...

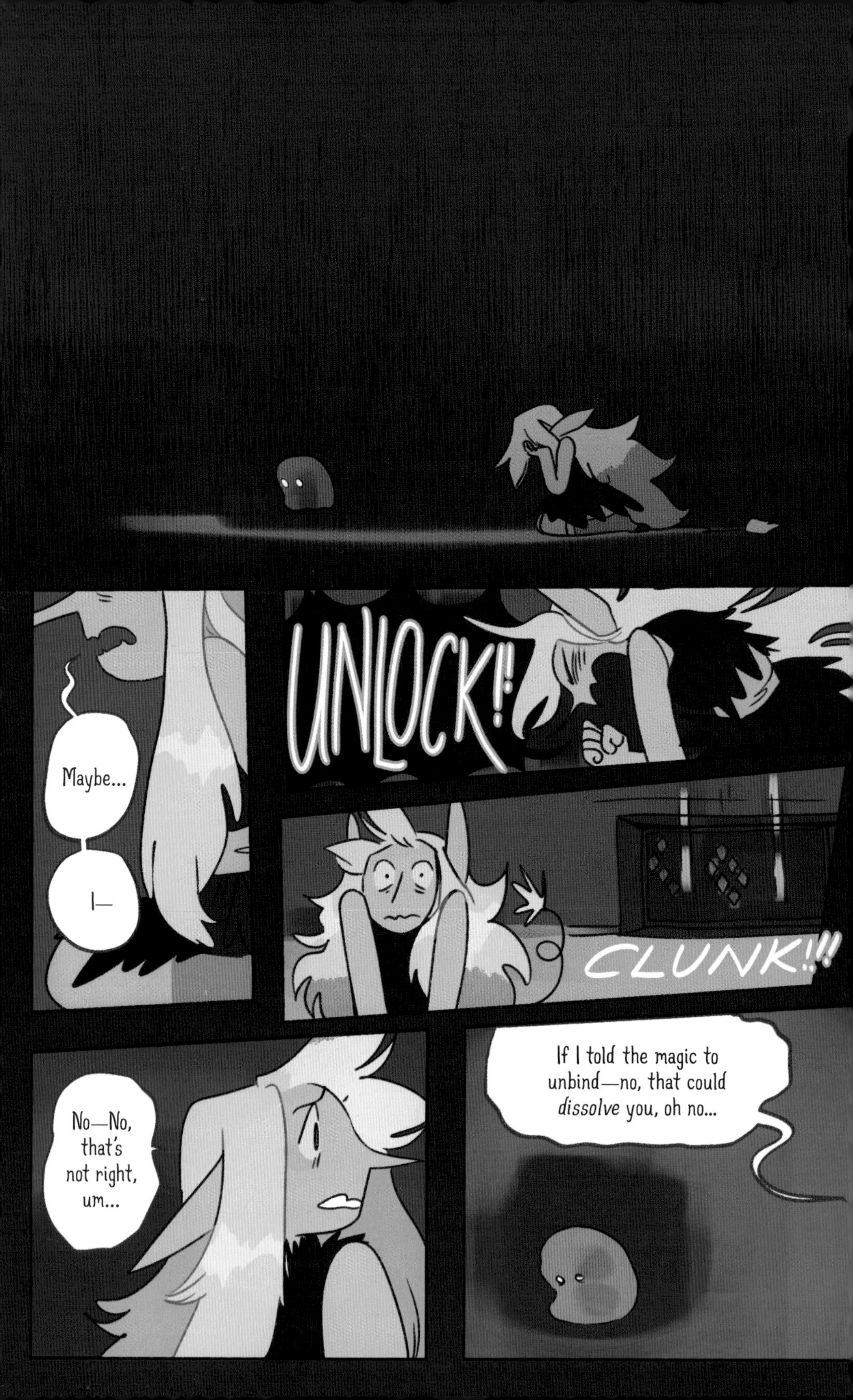
Maybe...
I—
UNLOCK!!
CLUNK!!!
No—No, that's not right, um...
If I told the magic to unbind—no, that could *dissolve* you, oh no...

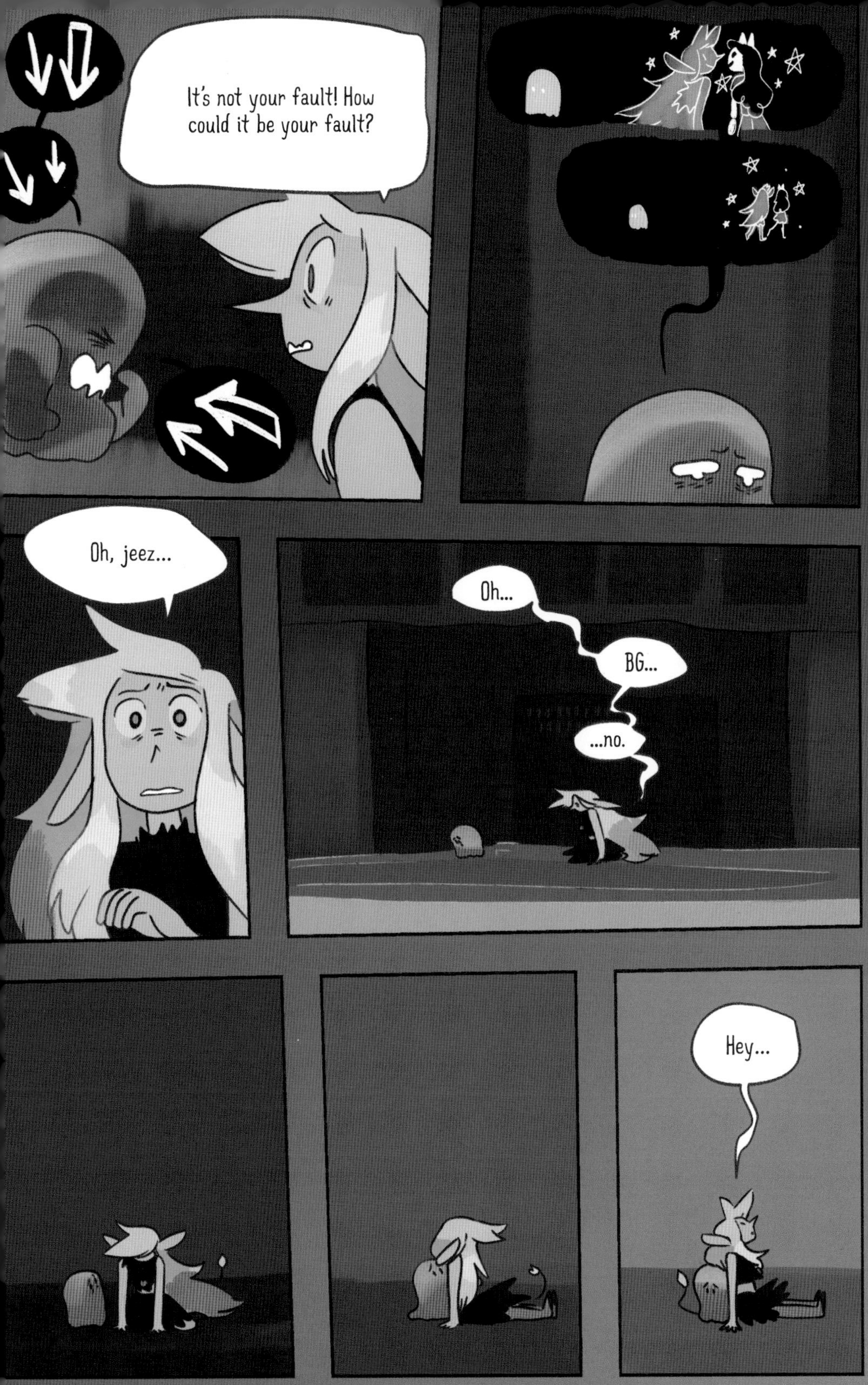
It's not your fault! How could it be your fault?
Oh, jeez...
Oh...
BG...
...no.
Hey...

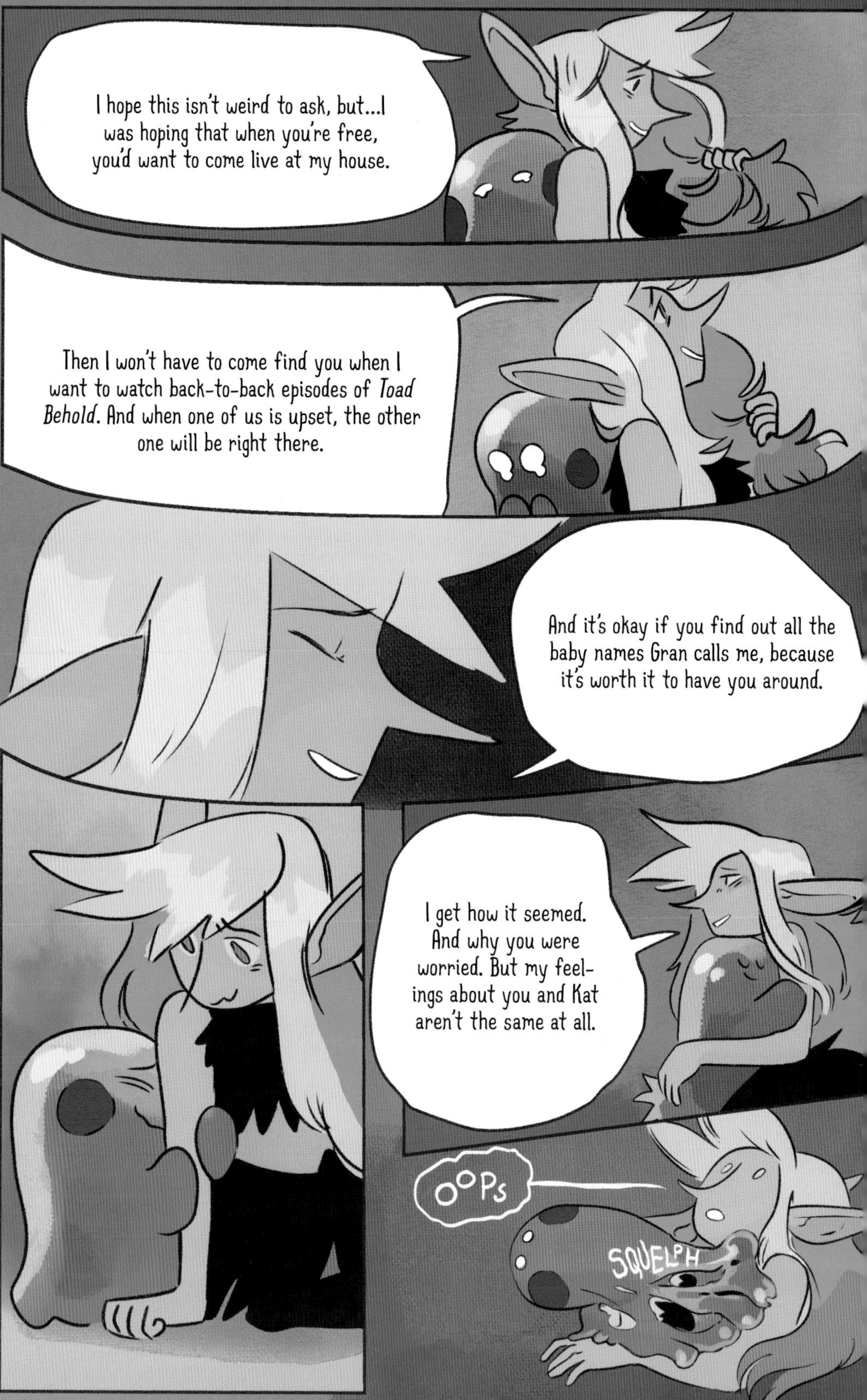

I hope this isn't weird to ask, but...I was hoping that when you're free, you'd want to come live at my house.
Then I won't have to come find you when I want to watch back-to-back episodes of *Toad Behold*. And when one of us is upset, the other one will be right there.
And it's okay if you find out all the baby names Gran calls me, because it's worth it to have you around.
I get how it seemed. And why you were worried. But my feel-ings about you and Kat aren't the same at all.
OOPS
SQUELPH

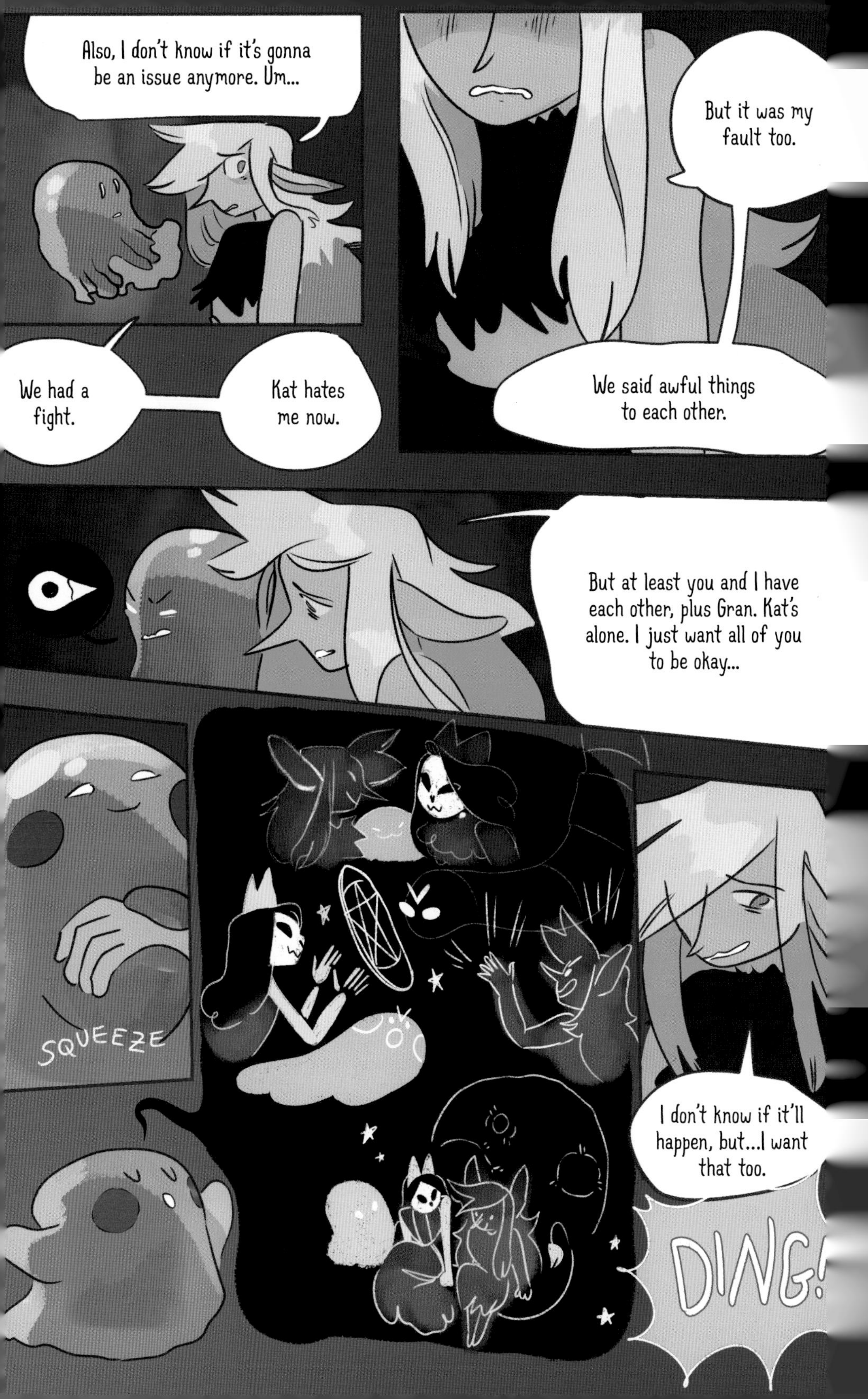

Also, I don't know if it's gonna be an issue anymore. Um...
But it was my fault too.
We had a fight.
Kat hates me now.
We said awful things to each other.
But at least you and I have each other, plus Gran. Kat's alone. I just want all of you to be okay...
SQUEEZE
I don't know if it'll happen, but...I want that too.
DING!

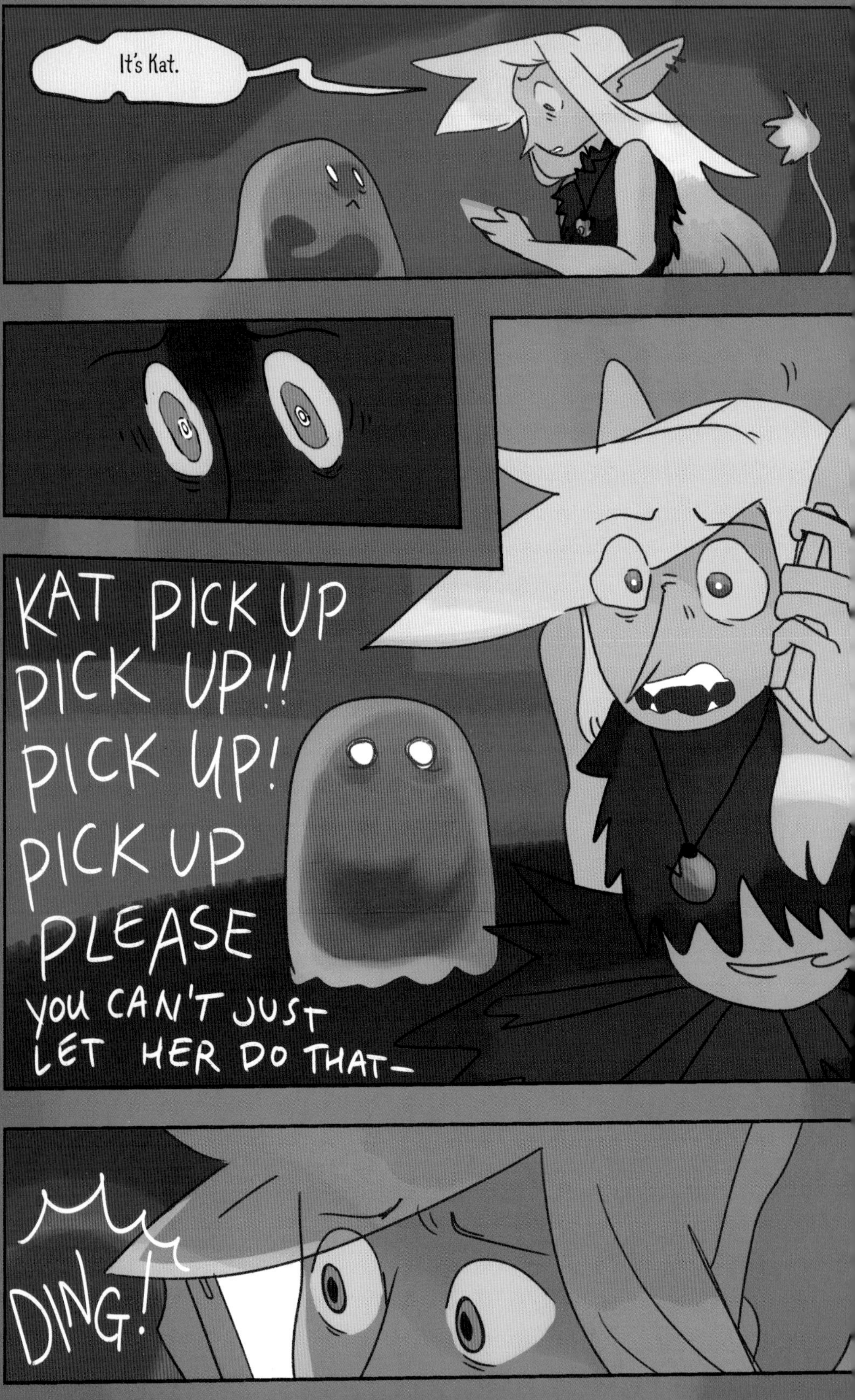
It's Kat.
KAT PICK UP
PICK UP!!
PICK UP!
PICK UP
PLEASE
YOU CAN'T JUST
LET HER DO THAT—
DING!

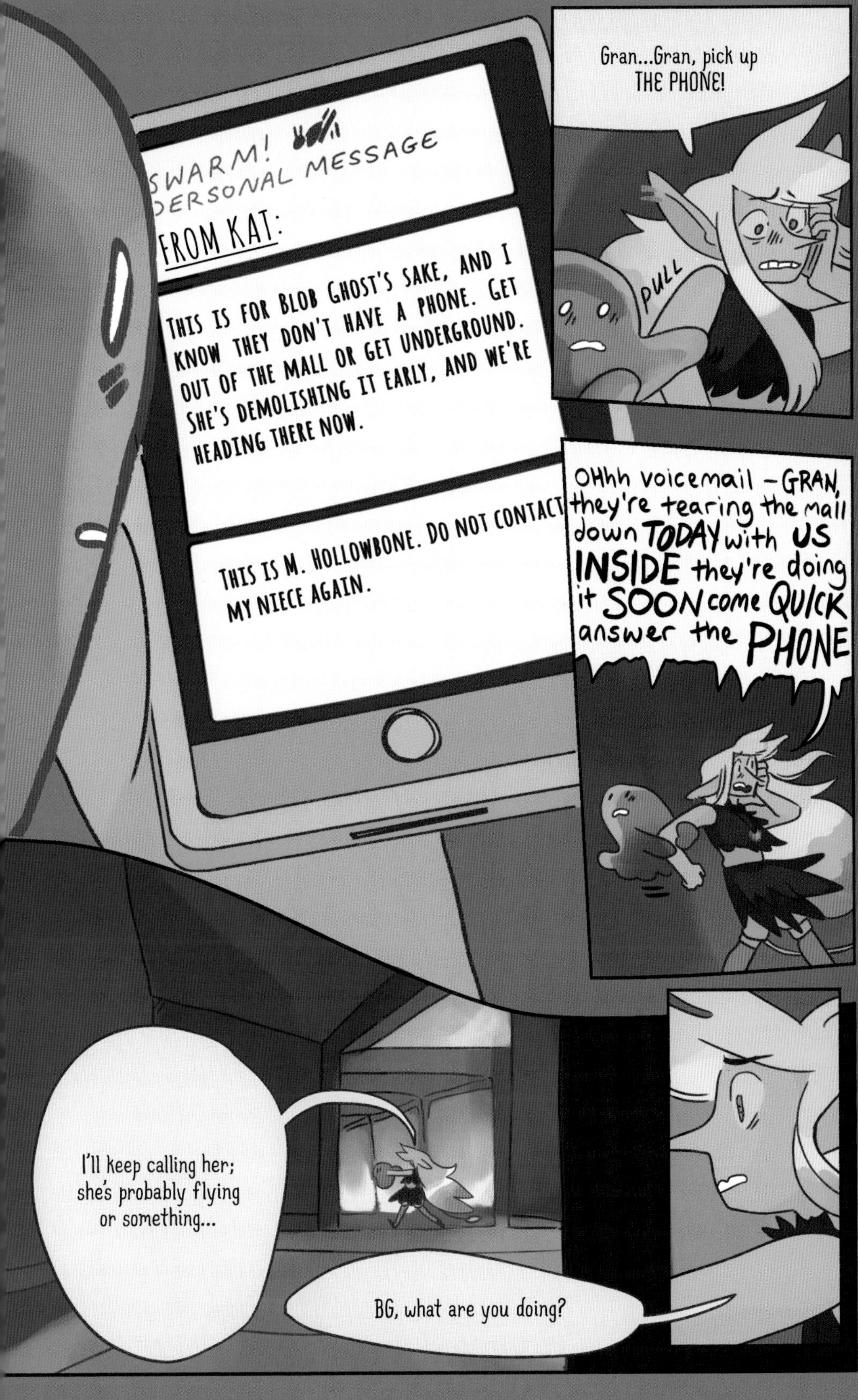
SWARM! PERSONAL MESSAGE
FROM KAT:
THIS IS FOR BLOB GHOST'S SAKE, AND I KNOW THEY DON'T HAVE A PHONE. GET OUT OF THE MALL OR GET UNDERGROUND. SHE'S DEMOLISHING IT EARLY, AND WE'RE HEADING THERE NOW.
THIS IS M. HOLLOWBONE. DO NOT CONTACT MY NIECE AGAIN.
Gran...Gran, pick up THE PHONE!
PULL
OHhh voicemail –GRAN, they're tearing the mall down TODAY with US INSIDE they're doing it SOON come QUICK answer the PHONE
I'll keep calling her; she's probably flying or something...
BG, what are you doing?

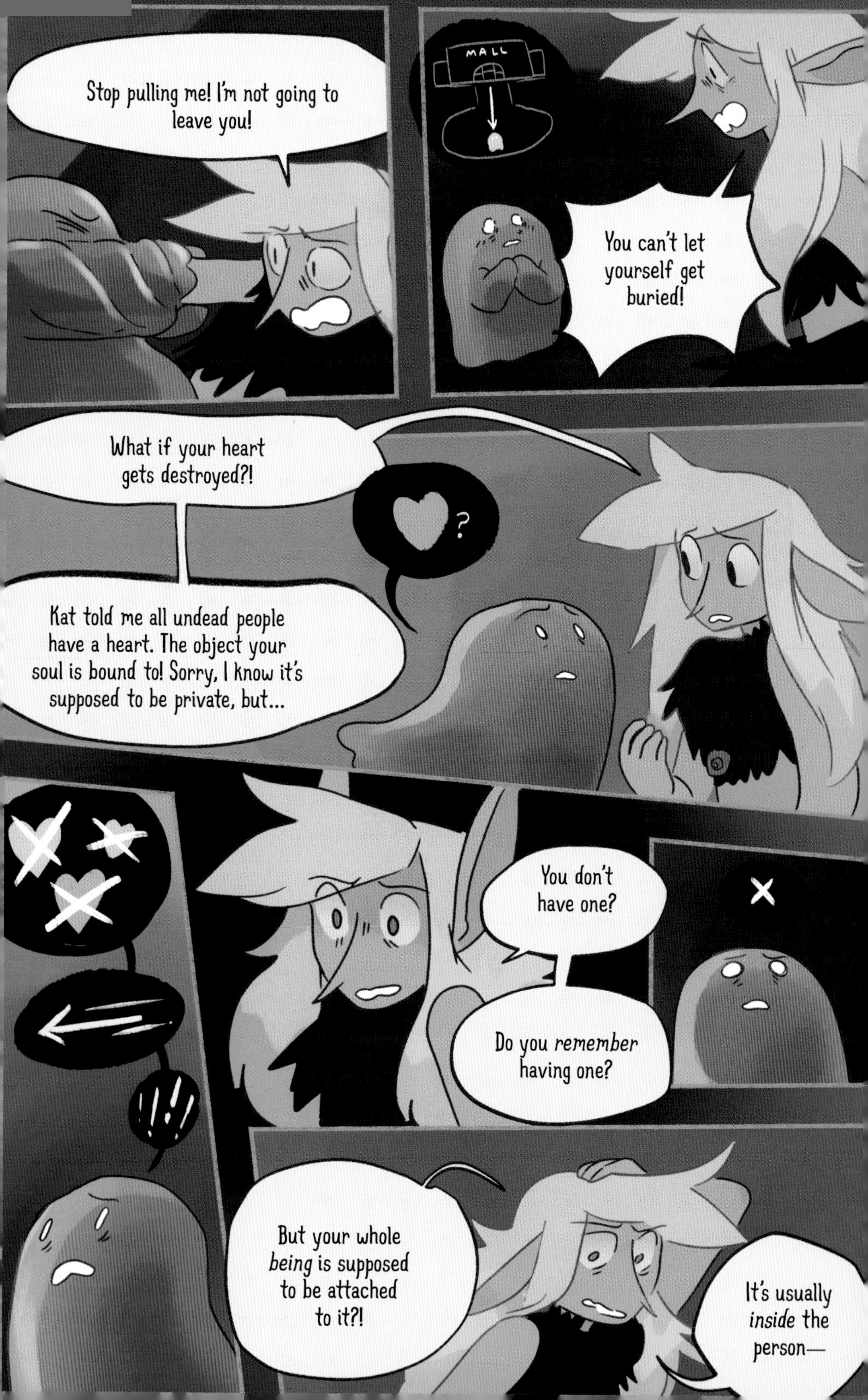
Stop pulling me! I'm not going to leave you!
MALL
You can't let yourself get buried!
What if your heart gets destroyed?!
Kat told me all undead people have a heart. The object your soul is bound to! Sorry, I know it's supposed to be private, but...
?
You don't have one?
Do you *remember* having one?
!!!
But your whole *being* is supposed to be attached to it?!
It's usually *inside* the person—

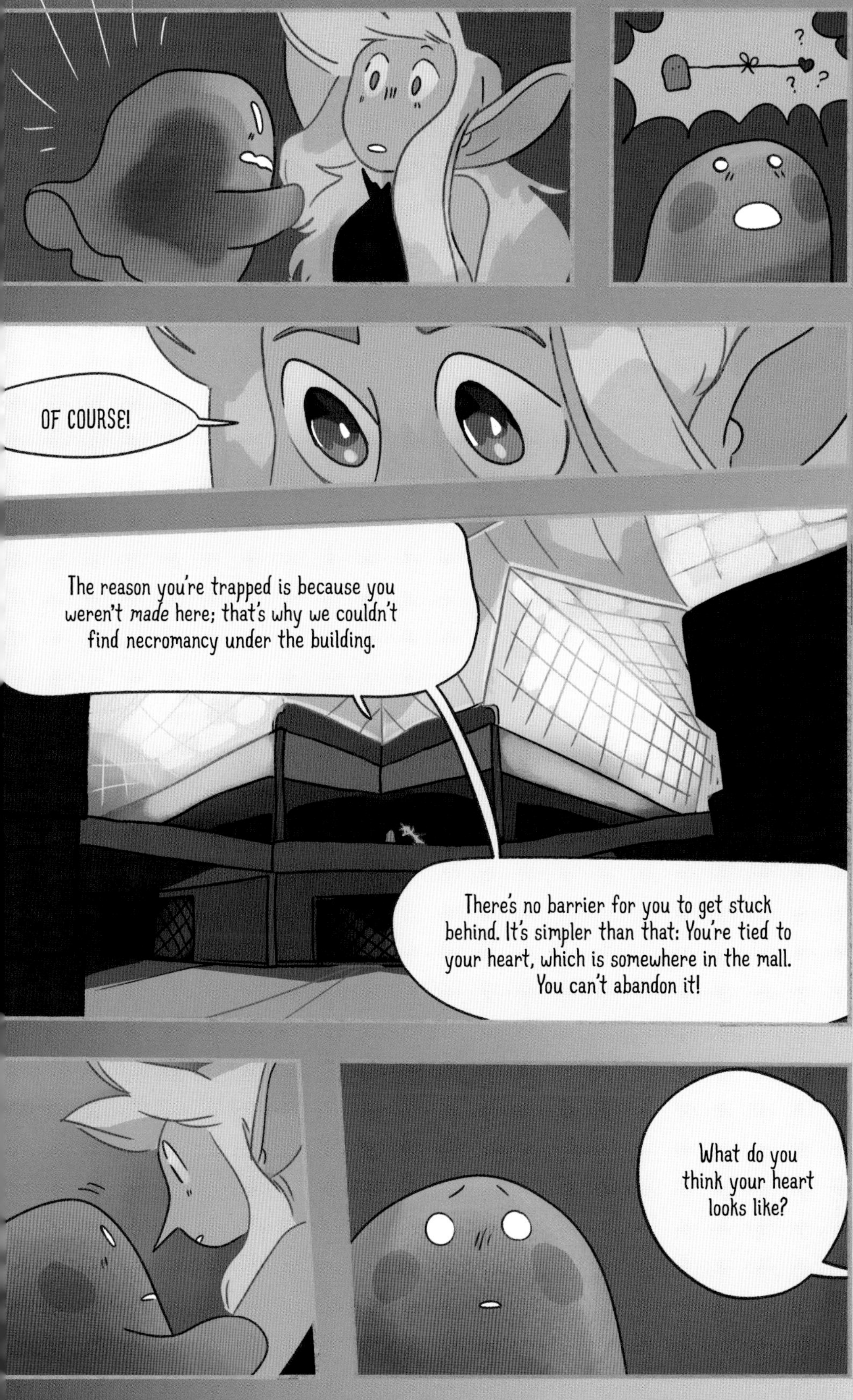
OF COURSE!
The reason you're trapped is because you weren't *made* here; that's why we couldn't find necromancy under the building.
There's no barrier for you to get stuck behind. It's simpler than that: You're tied to your heart, which is somewhere in the mall. You can't abandon it!
What do you think your heart looks like?

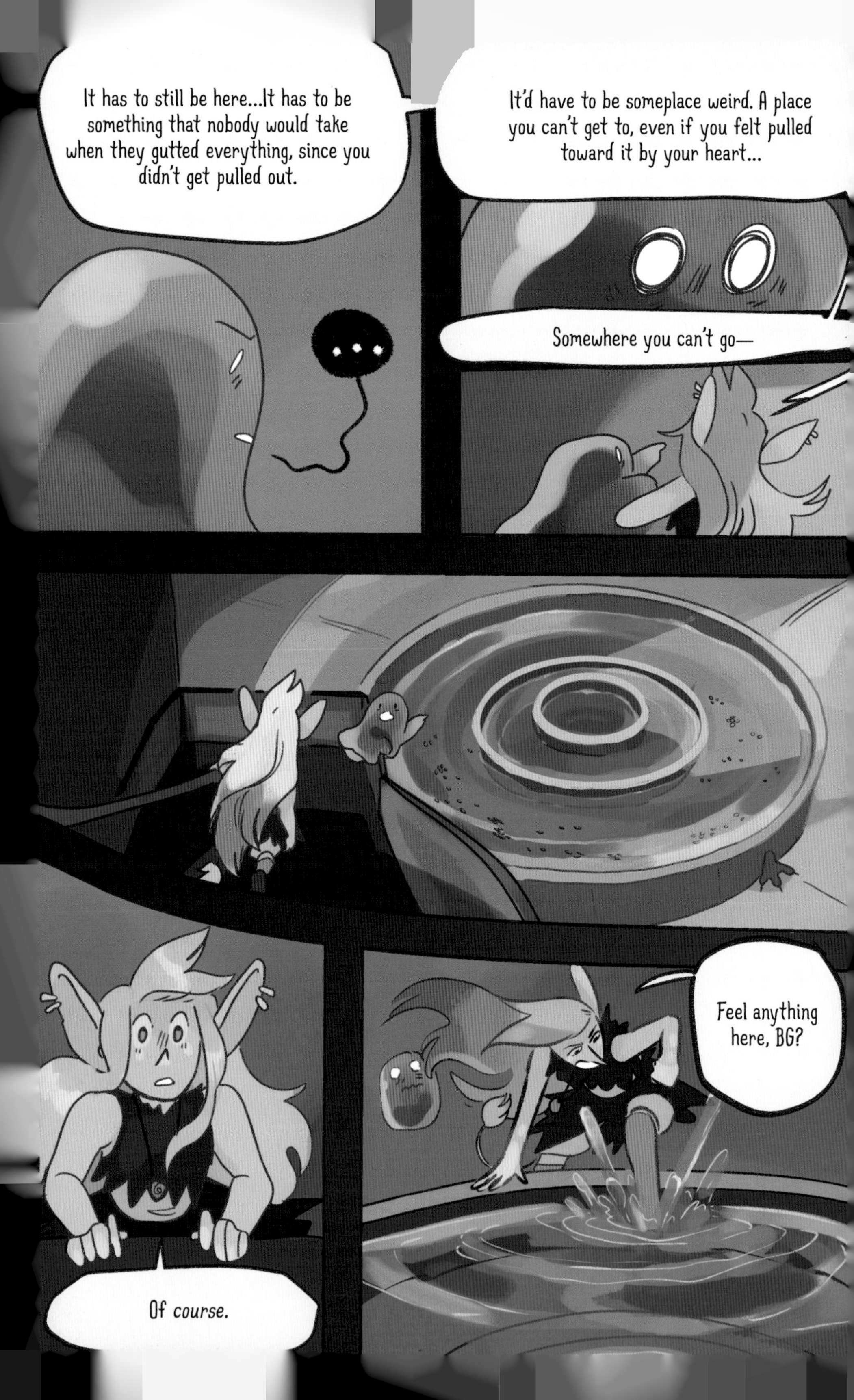
It has to still be here...It has to be something that nobody would take when they gutted everything, since you didn't get pulled out.
It'd have to be someplace weird. A place you can't get to, even if you felt pulled toward it by your heart...
Somewhere you can't go—
Feel anything here, BG?
Of course.

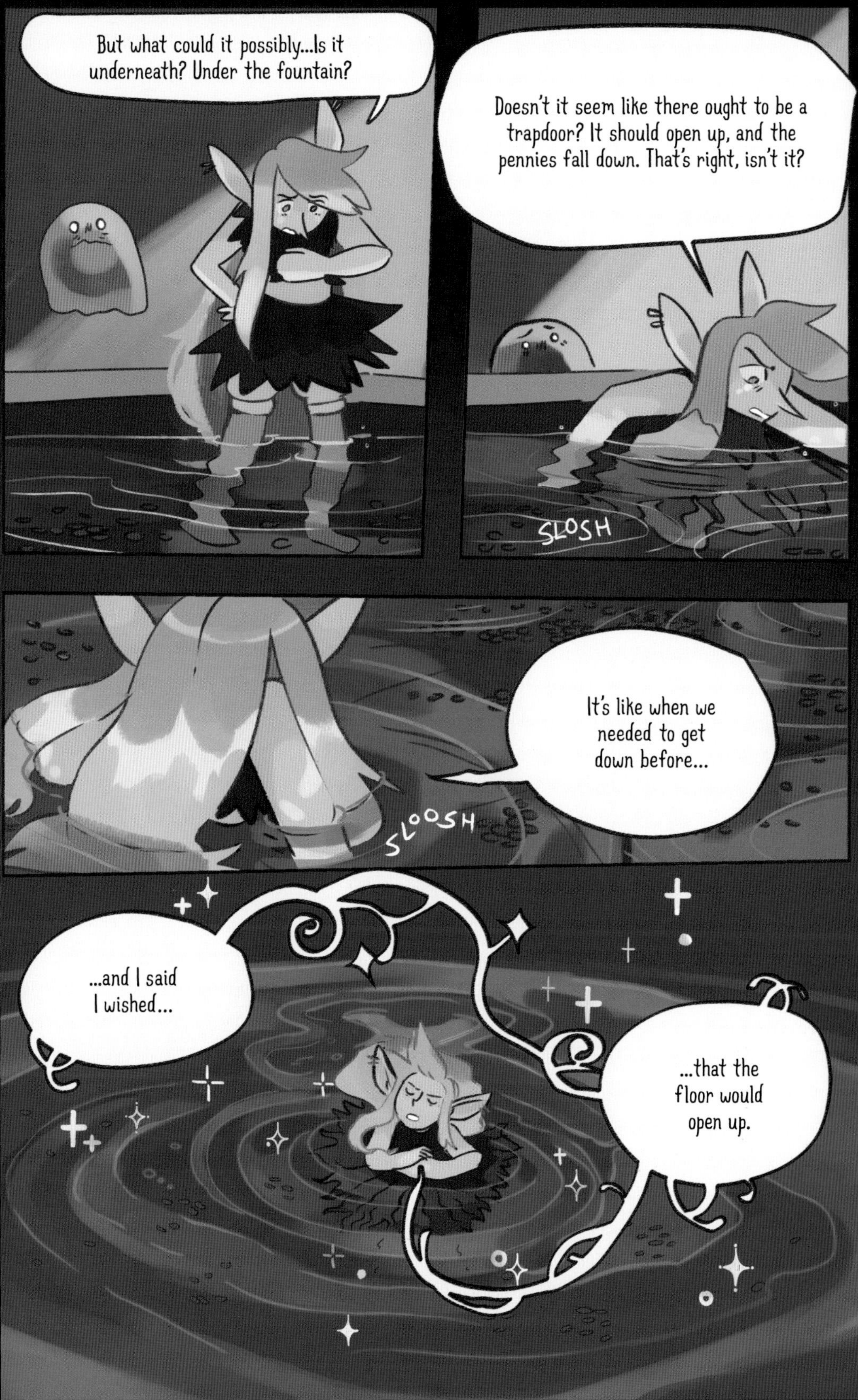
But what could it possibly...Is it underneath? Under the fountain?
Doesn't it seem like there ought to be a trapdoor? It should open up, and the pennies fall down. That's right, isn't it?
SLOSH
It's like when we needed to get down before...
SLOOSH
...and I said I wished...
...that the floor would open up.

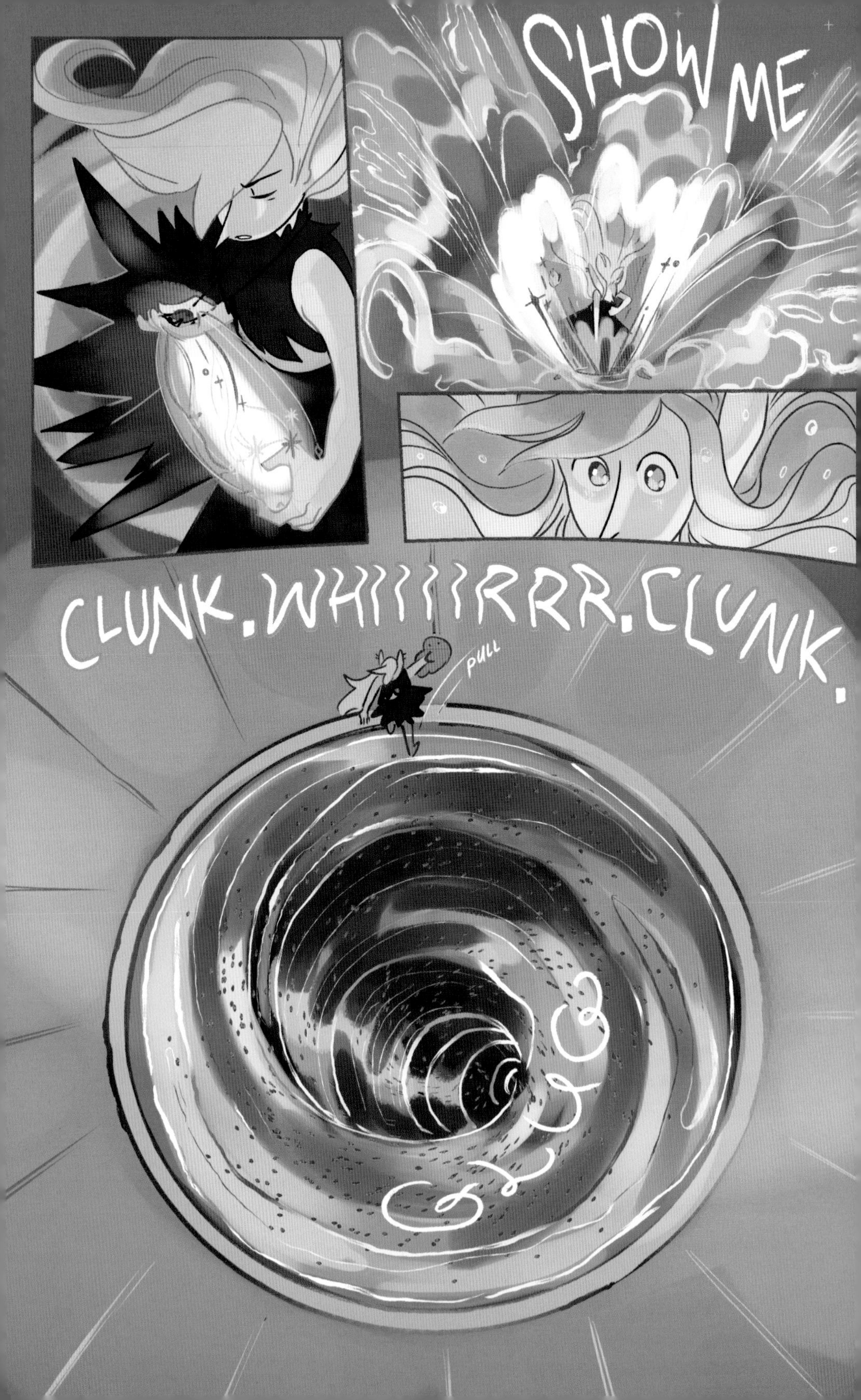
SHOW ME
CLUNK. WHIIIIRRR. CLUNK.
PULL

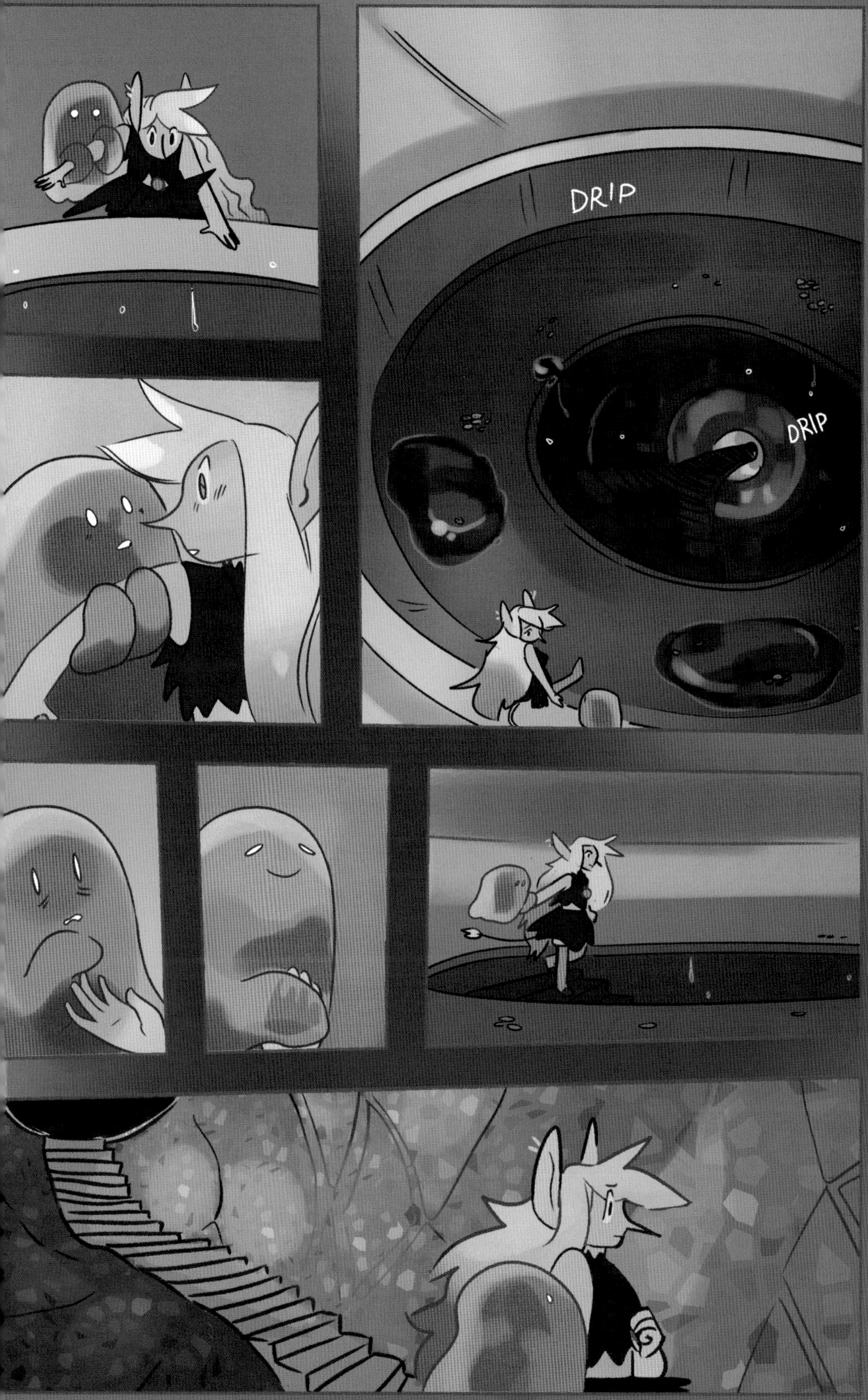
DRIP
DRIP

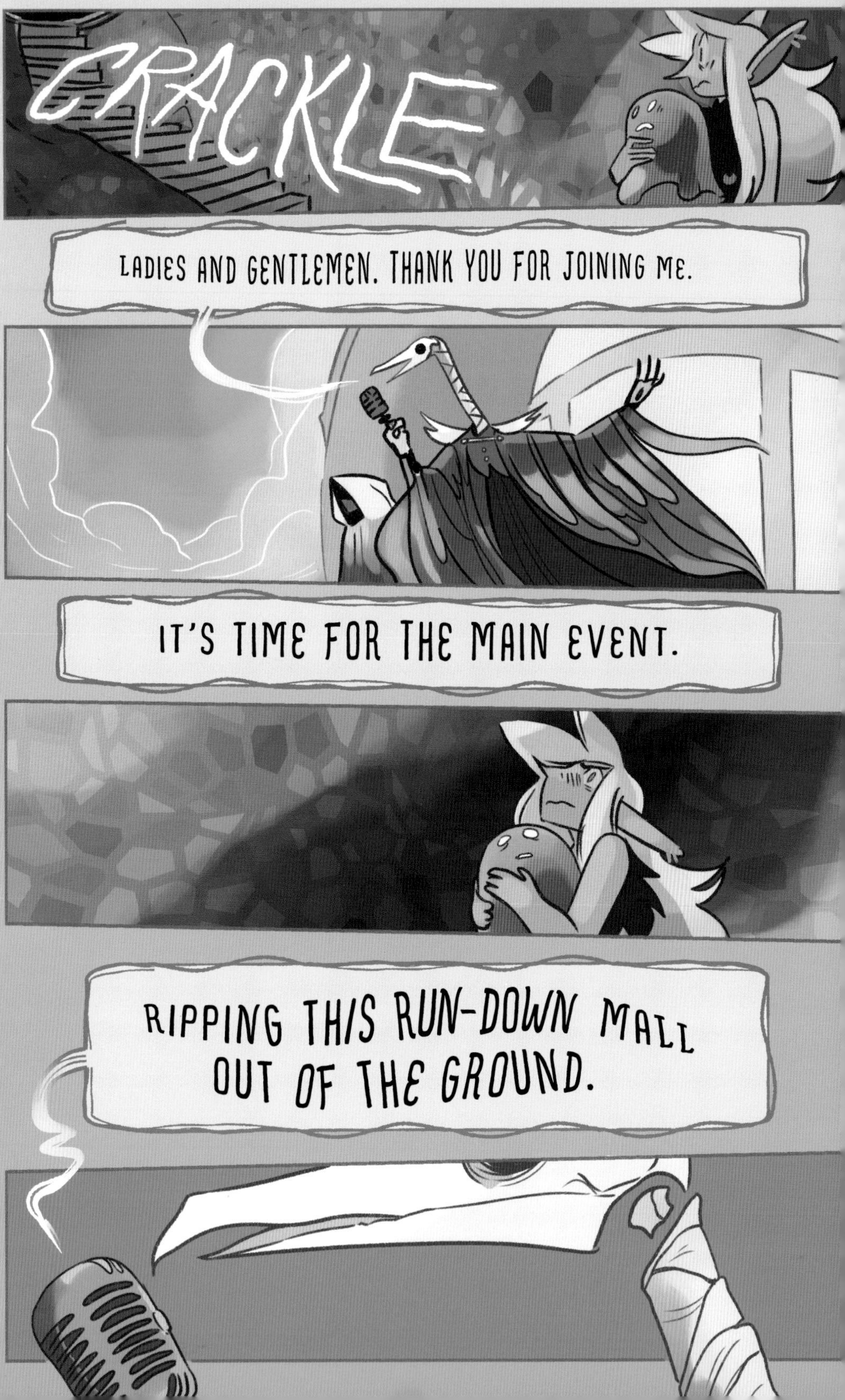
CRACKLE
LADIES AND GENTLEMEN. THANK YOU FOR JOINING ME.
IT'S TIME FOR THE MAIN EVENT.
RIPPING THIS RUN-DOWN MALL OUT OF THE GROUND.

THE HAUNTED HEART

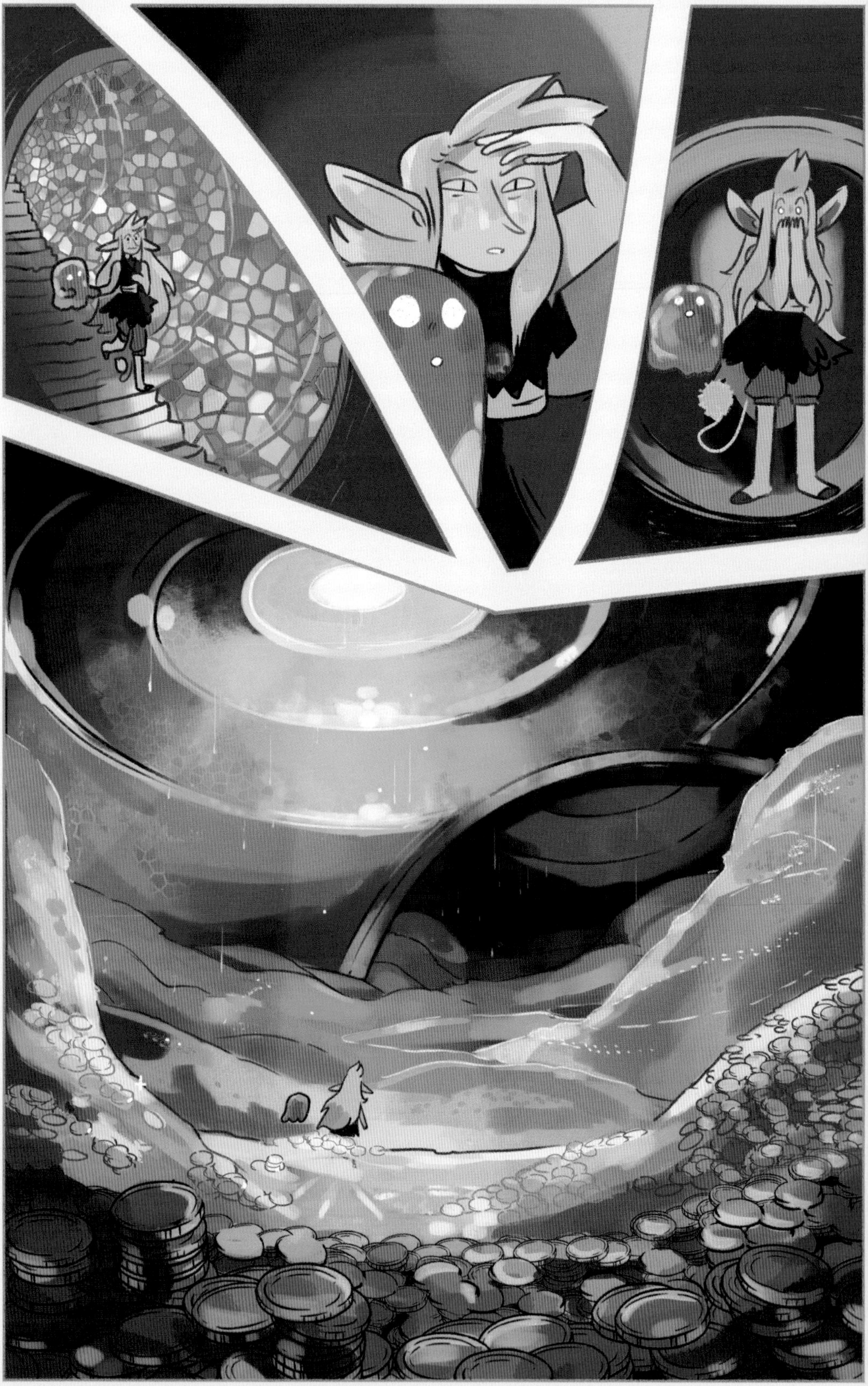

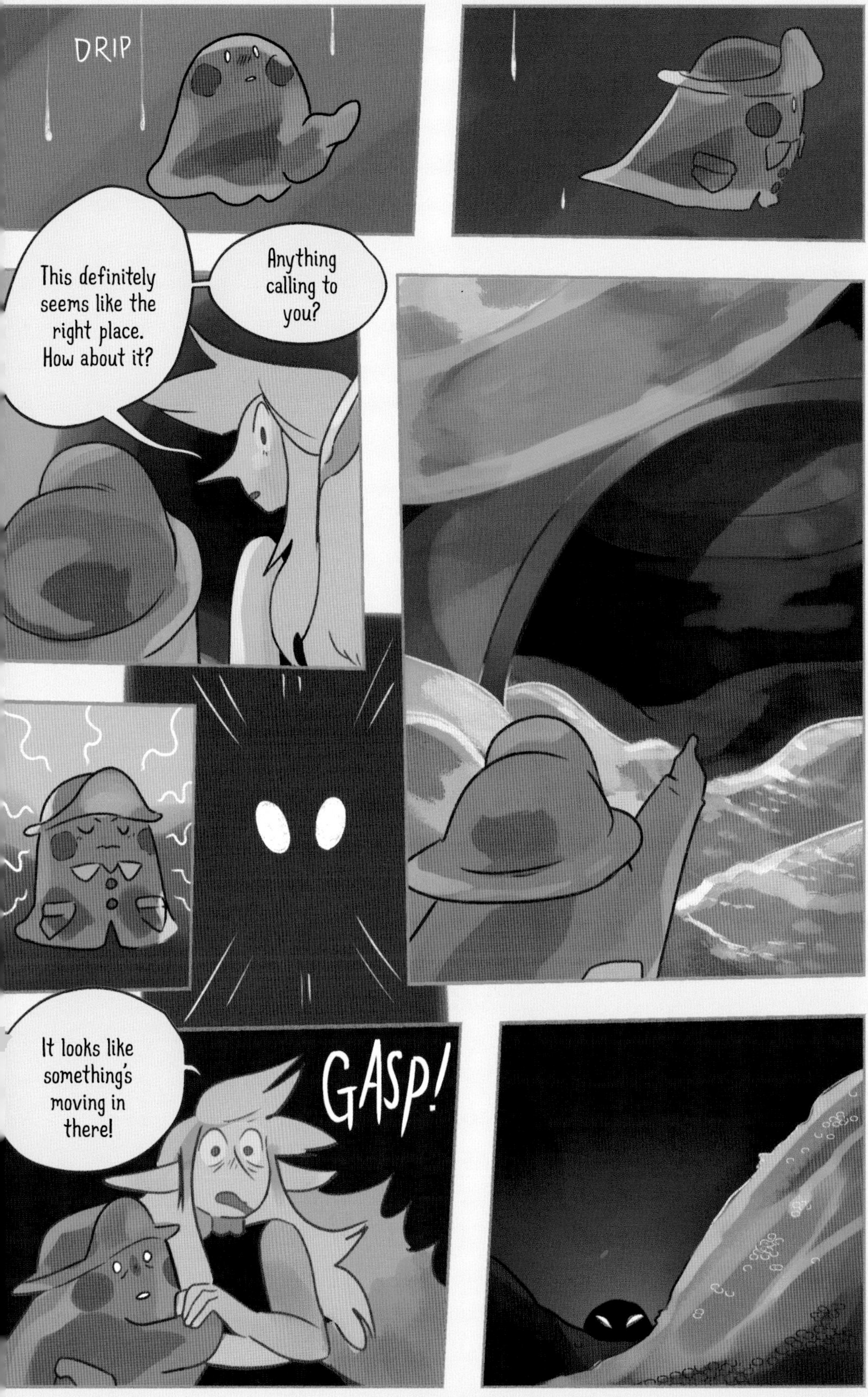
DRIP
This definitely seems like the right place. How about it?
Anything calling to you?
It looks like something's moving in there!
GASP!

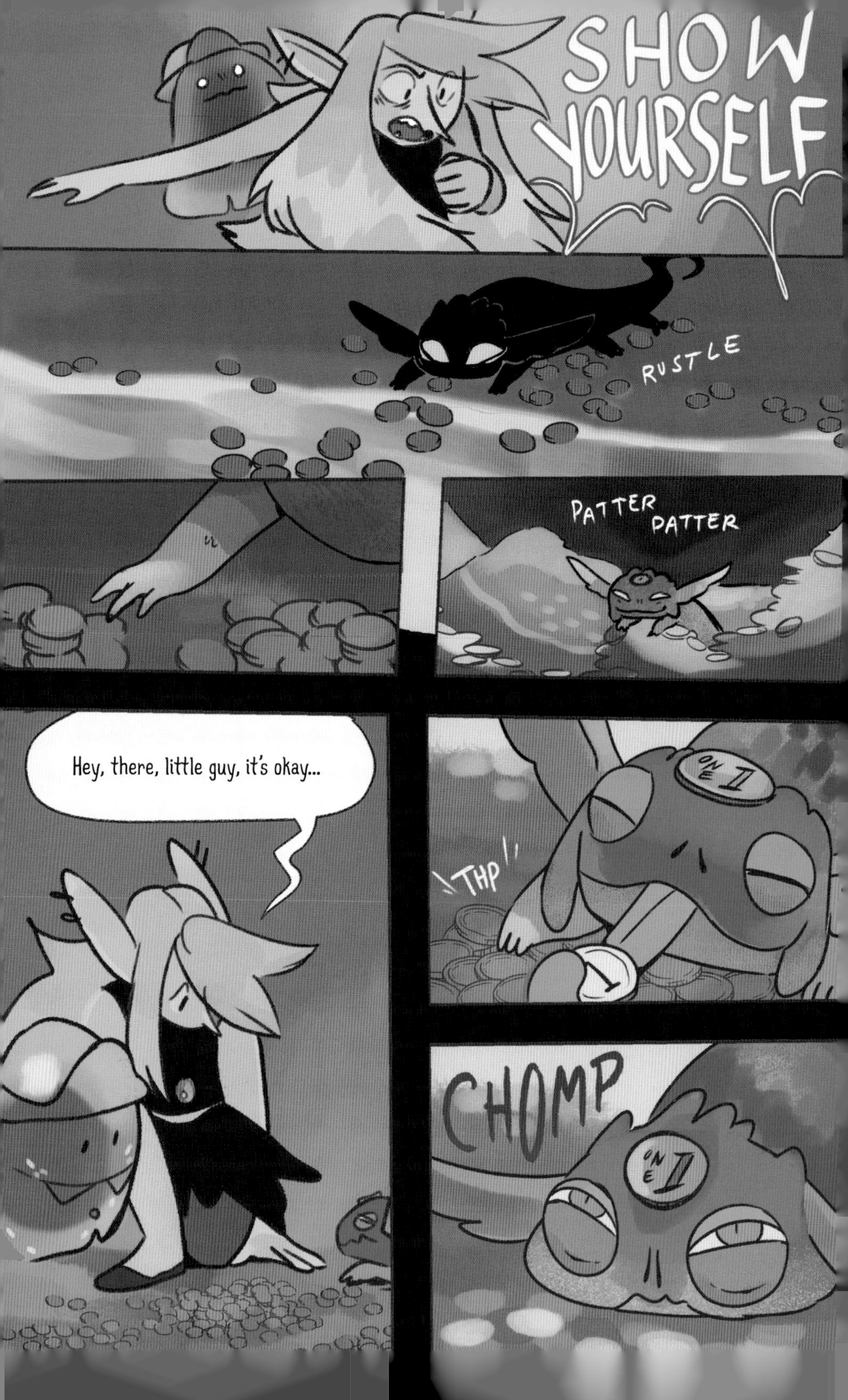
SHOW YOURSELF
RUSTLE
PATTER PATTER
Hey, there, little guy, it's okay...
THP
CHOMP

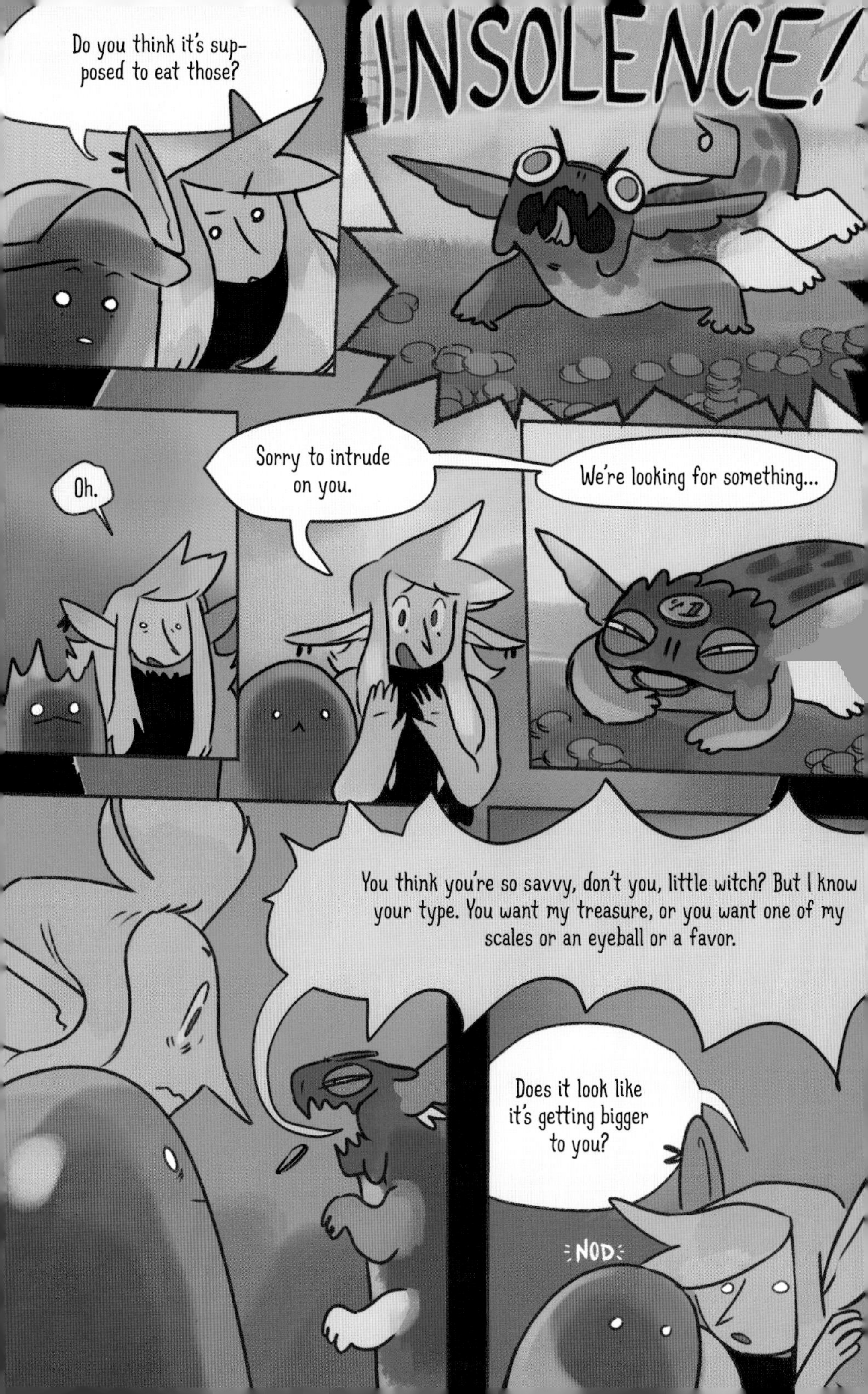

Do you think it's sup-posed to eat those?
INSOLENCE!
Oh.
Sorry to intrude on you.
We're looking for something...
You think you're so savvy, don't you, little witch? But I know your type. You want my treasure, or you want one of my scales or an eyeball or a favor.
Does it look like it's getting bigger to you?
NOD

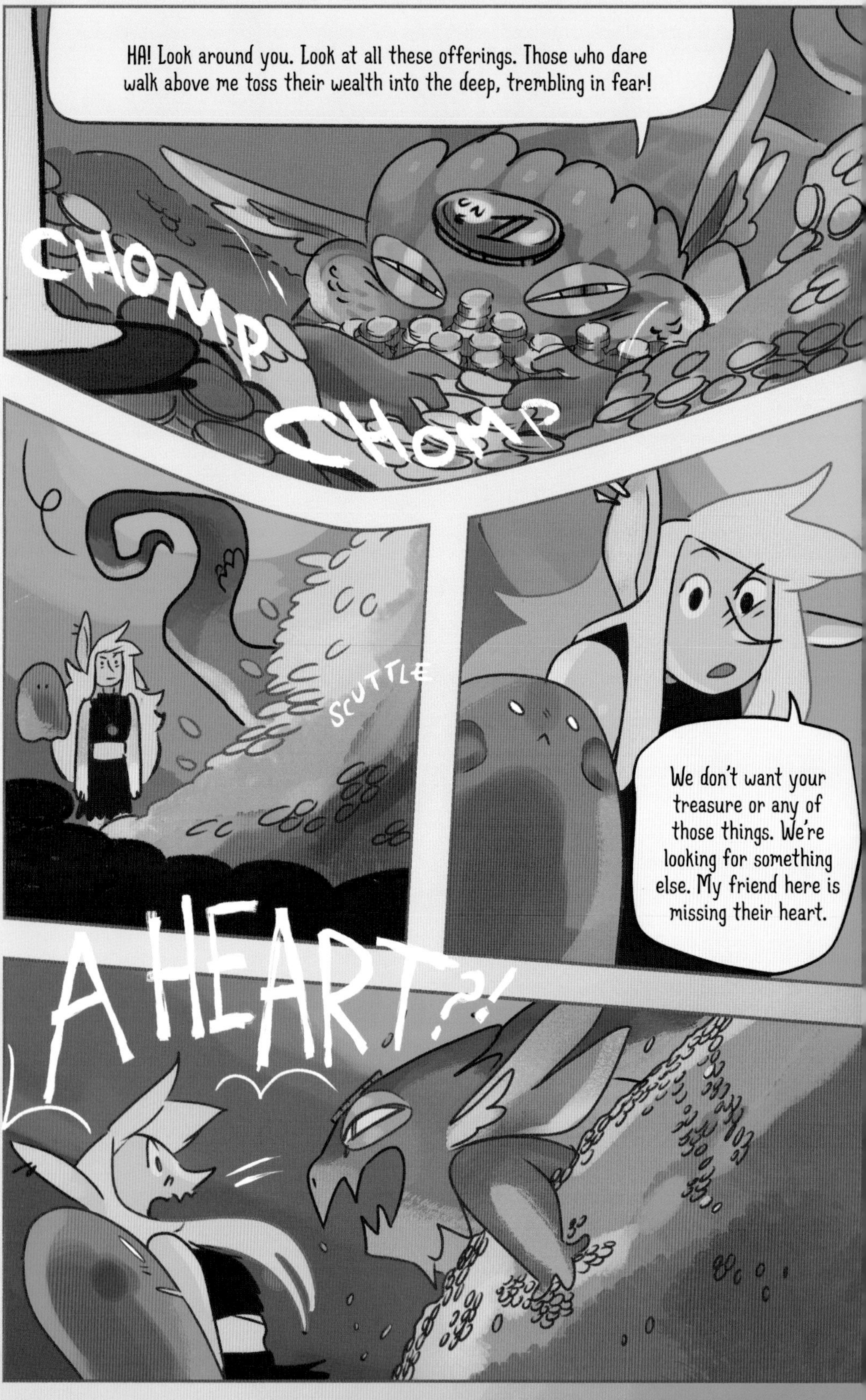
HA! Look around you. Look at all these offerings. Those who dare walk above me toss their wealth into the deep, trembling in fear!
CHOMP
CHOMP
SCUTTLE
We don't want your treasure or any of those things. We're looking for something else. My friend here is missing their heart.
A HEART?!

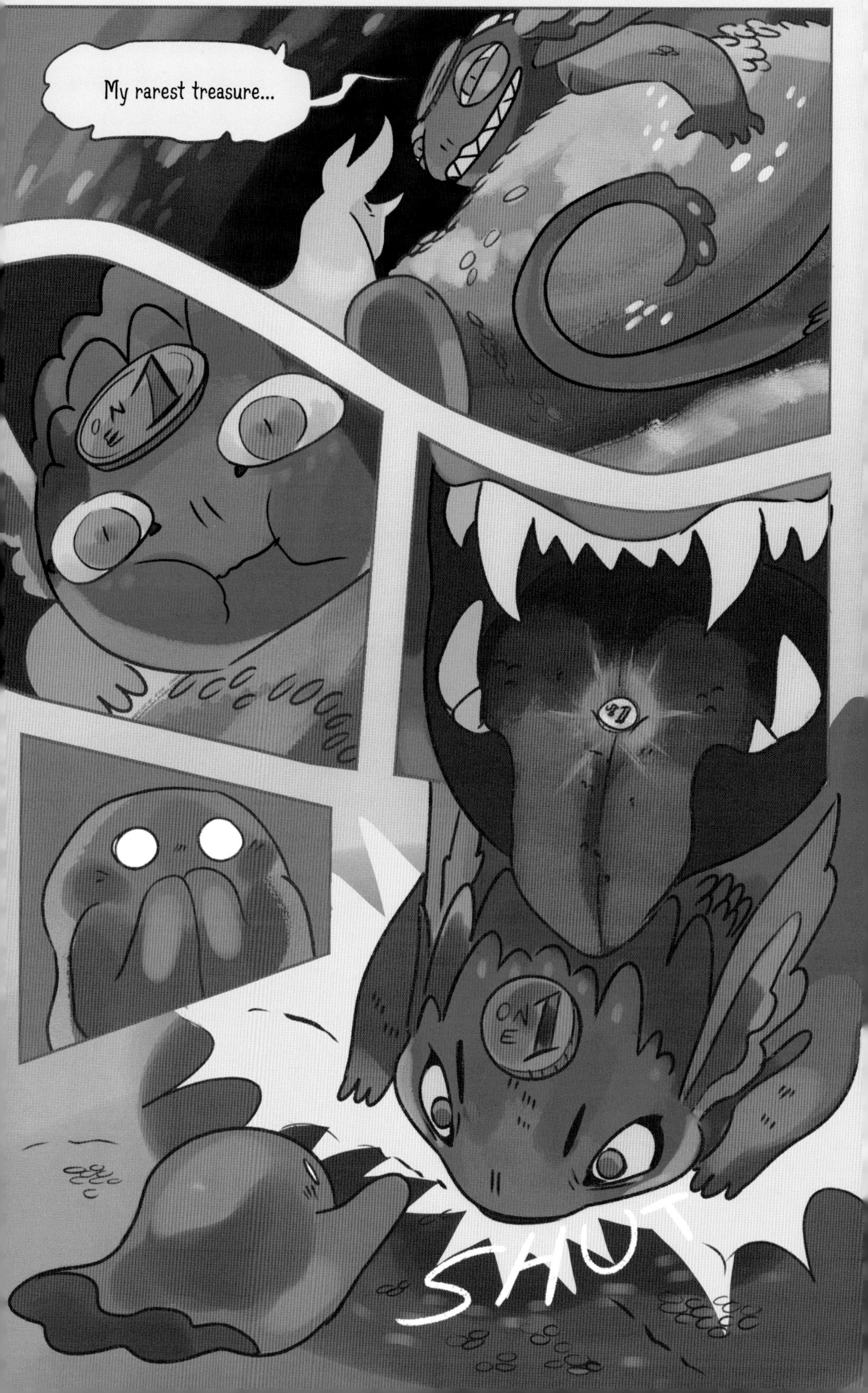
My rarest treasure...
ONE 1
SHUT

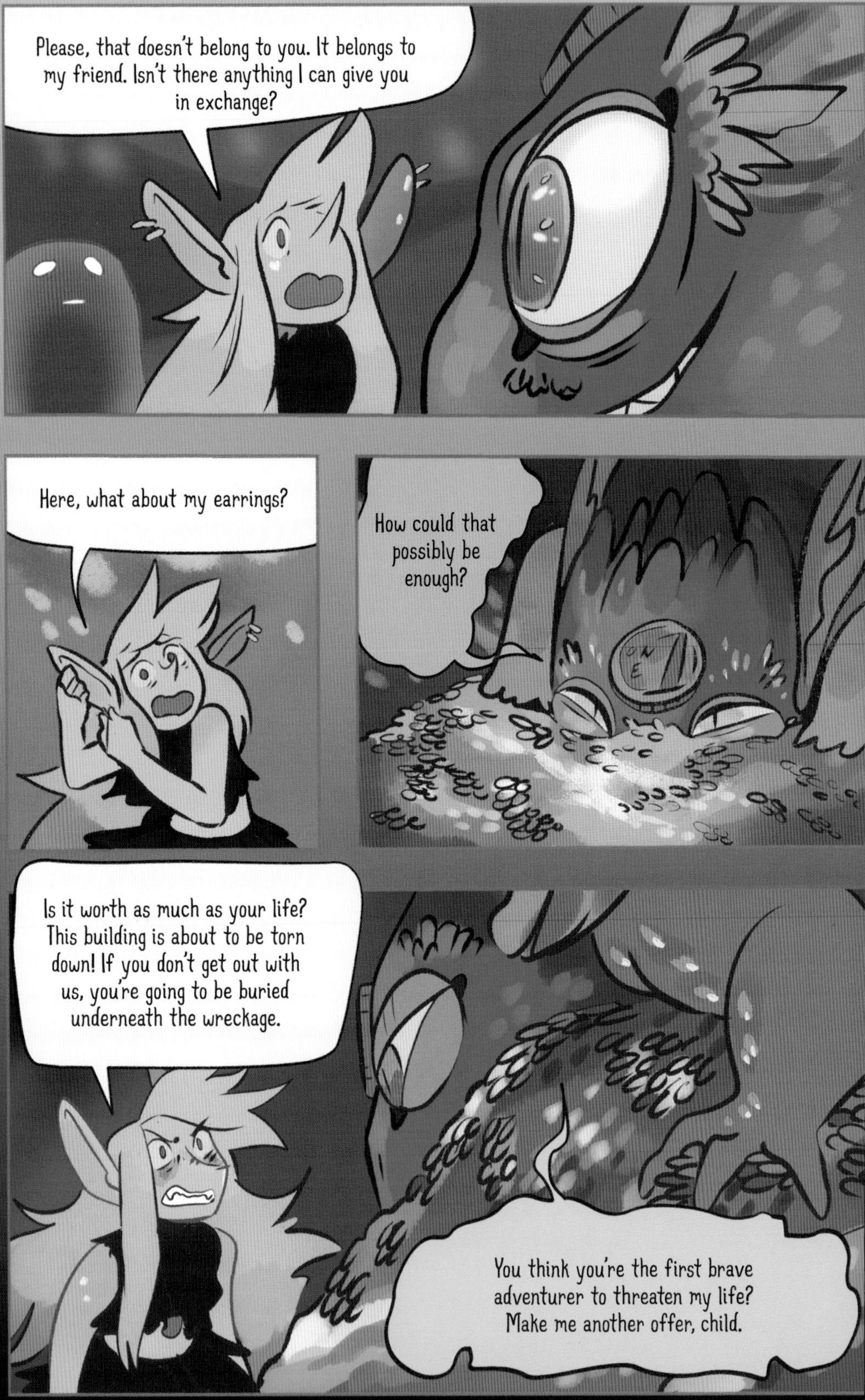
Please, that doesn't belong to you. It belongs to my friend. Isn't there anything I can give you in exchange?
Here, what about my earrings?
How could that possibly be enough?
Is it worth as much as your life? This building is about to be torn down! If you don't get out with us, you're going to be buried underneath the wreckage.
You think you're the first brave adventurer to threaten my life? Make me another offer, child.

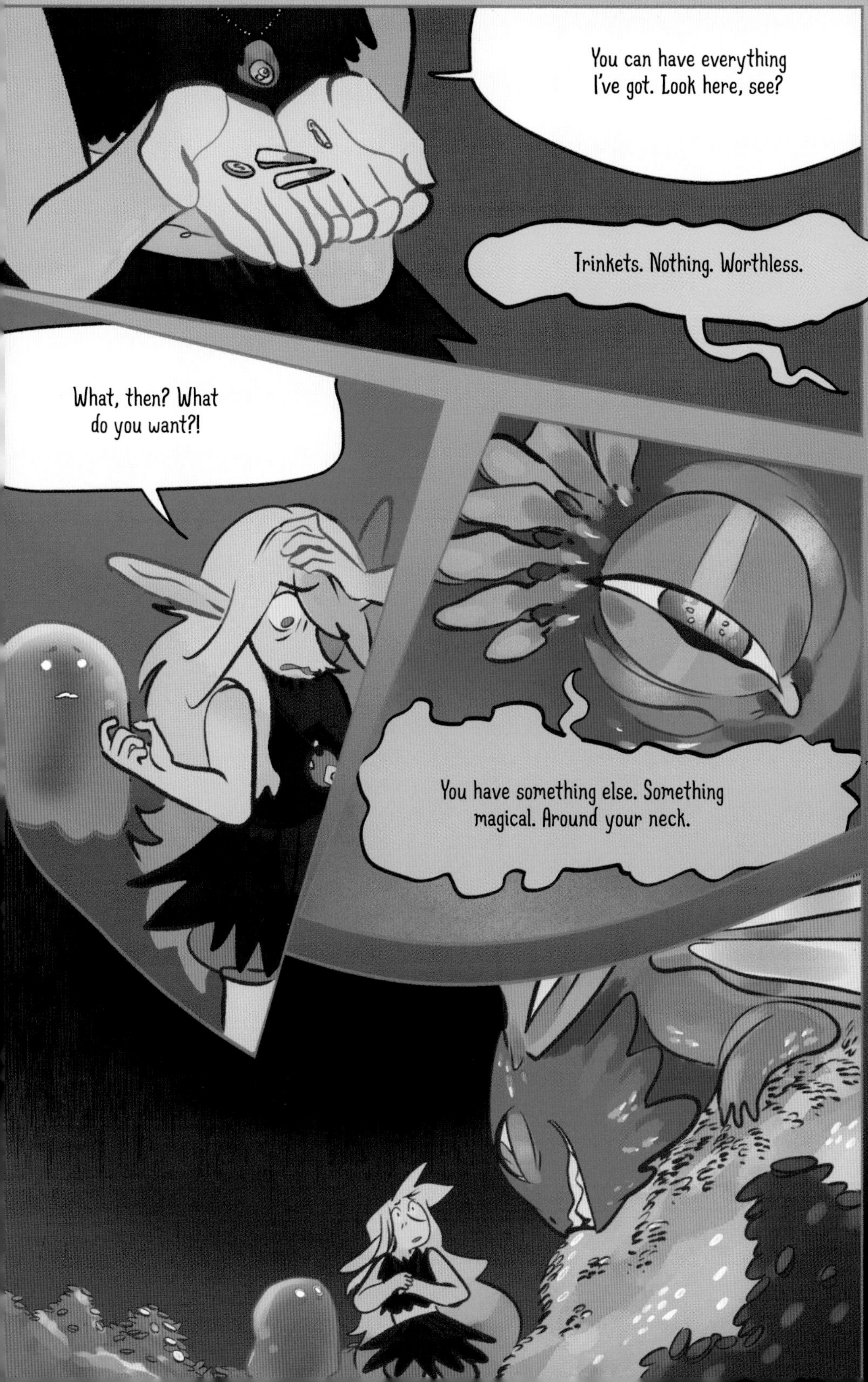
You can have everything I've got. Look here, see?
Trinkets. Nothing. Worthless.
What, then? What do you want?!
You have something else. Something magical. Around your neck.

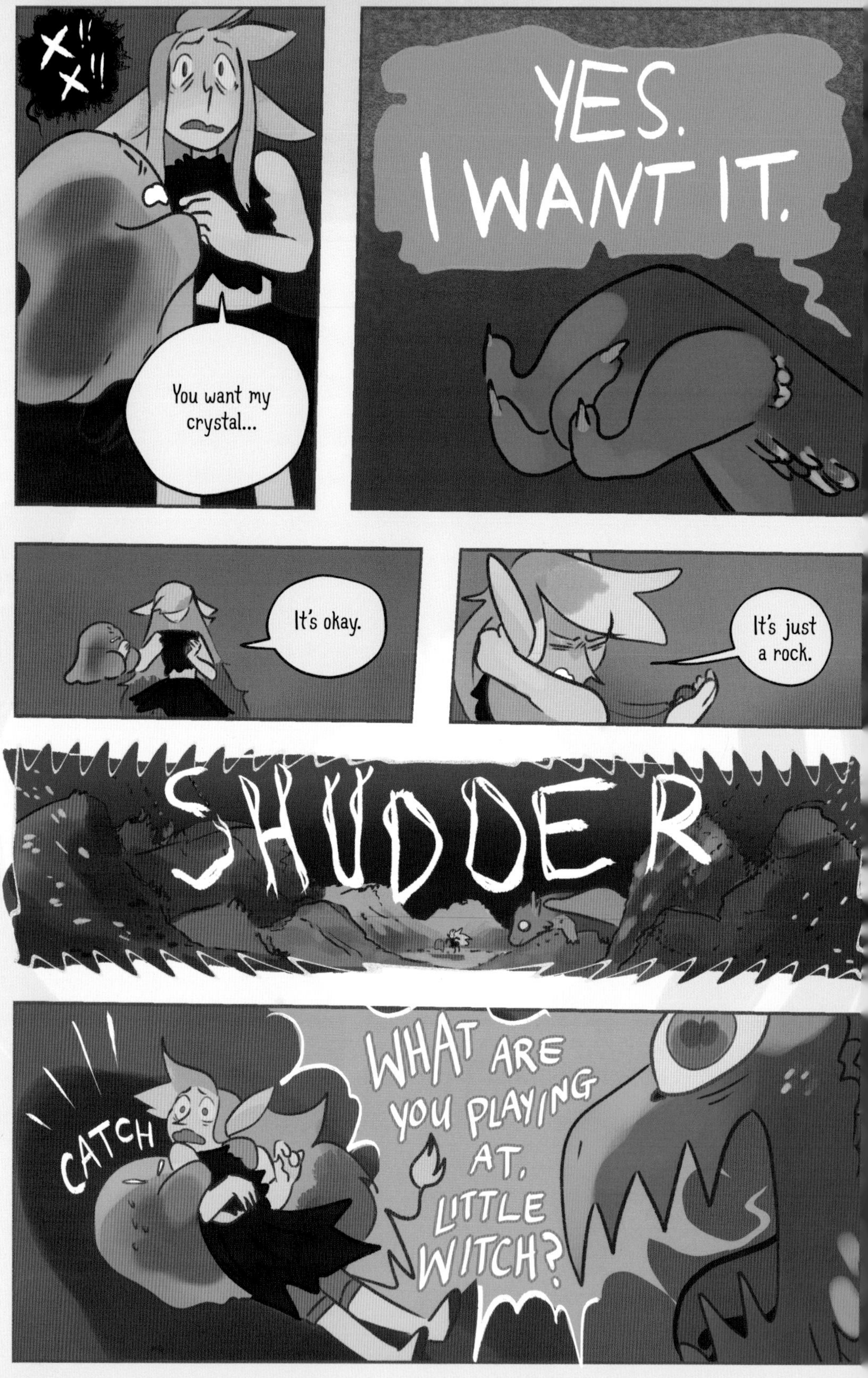
X!!
X!!
You want my crystal...
YES. I WANT IT.
It's okay.
It's just a rock.
SHUDDER
CATCH
WHAT ARE YOU PLAYING AT, LITTLE WITCH?

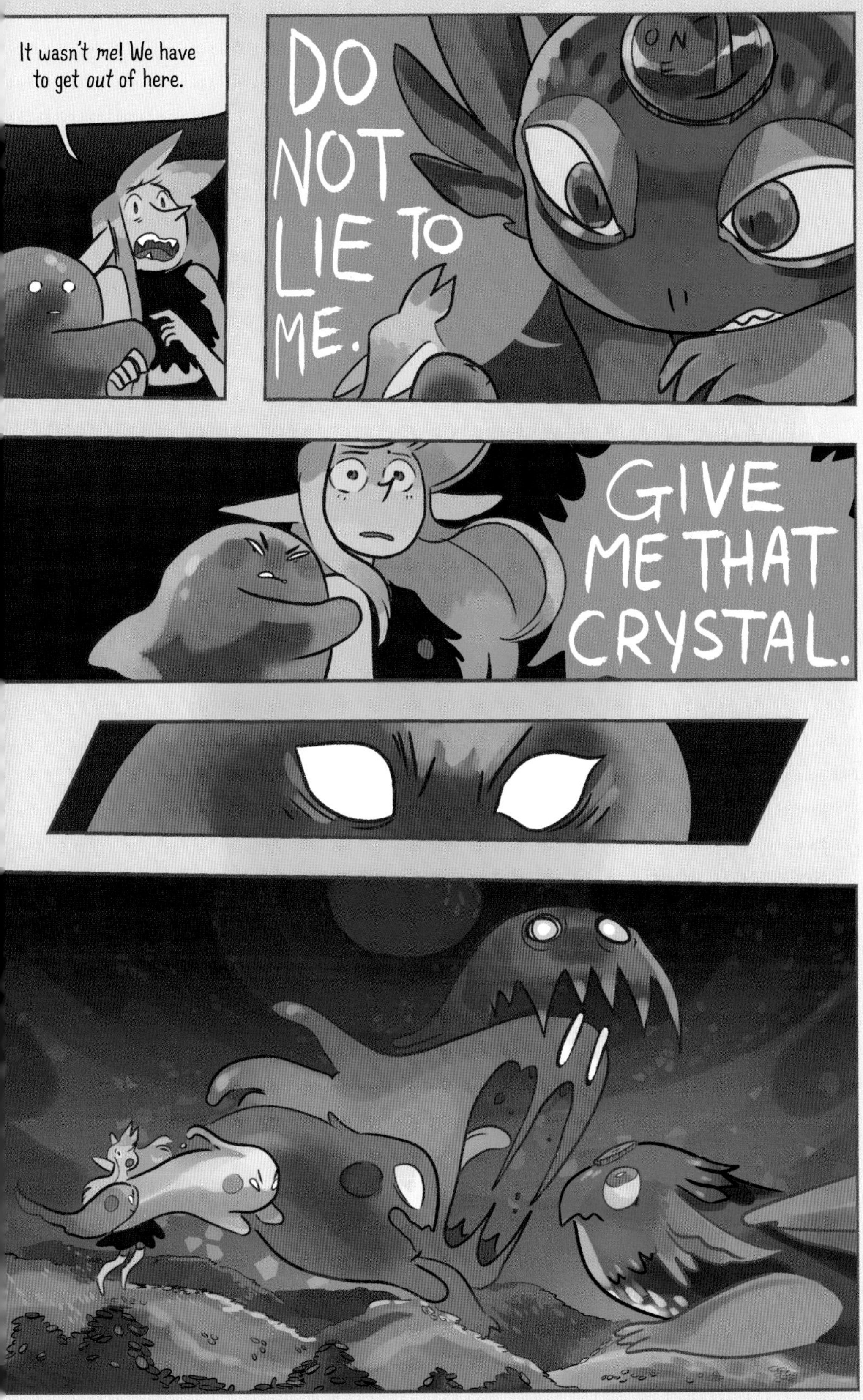
It wasn't *me*! We have to get *out* of here.
DO NOT LIE TO ME.
GIVE ME THAT CRYSTAL.

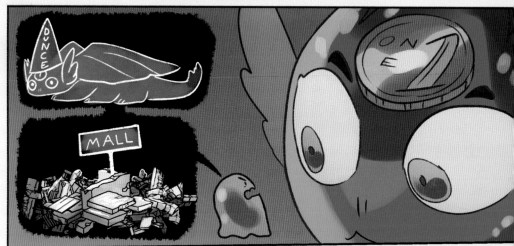

Explain this, witch.

They're saying that the whole building is about to be demolished.

You *have* to give us that coin so we can all leave, or the three of us are going to be crushed down here.

It seems that you are some kind of beast. Make a dragon's promise with me. Is she telling the truth?

NOD

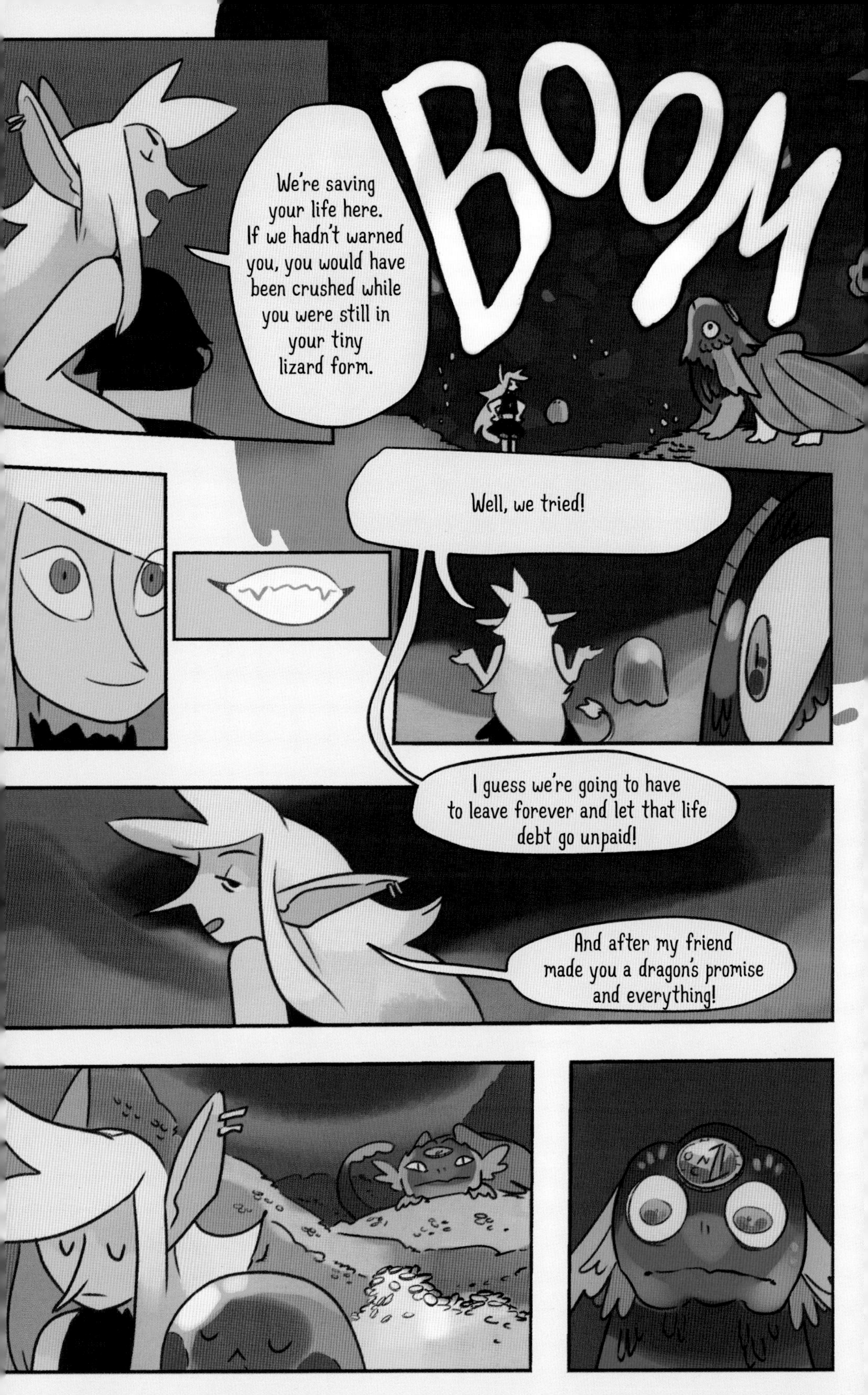
We're saving your life here. If we hadn't warned you, you would have been crushed while you were still in your tiny lizard form.
BOOM
Well, we tried!
I guess we're going to have to leave forever and let that life debt go unpaid!
And after my friend made you a dragon's promise and everything!

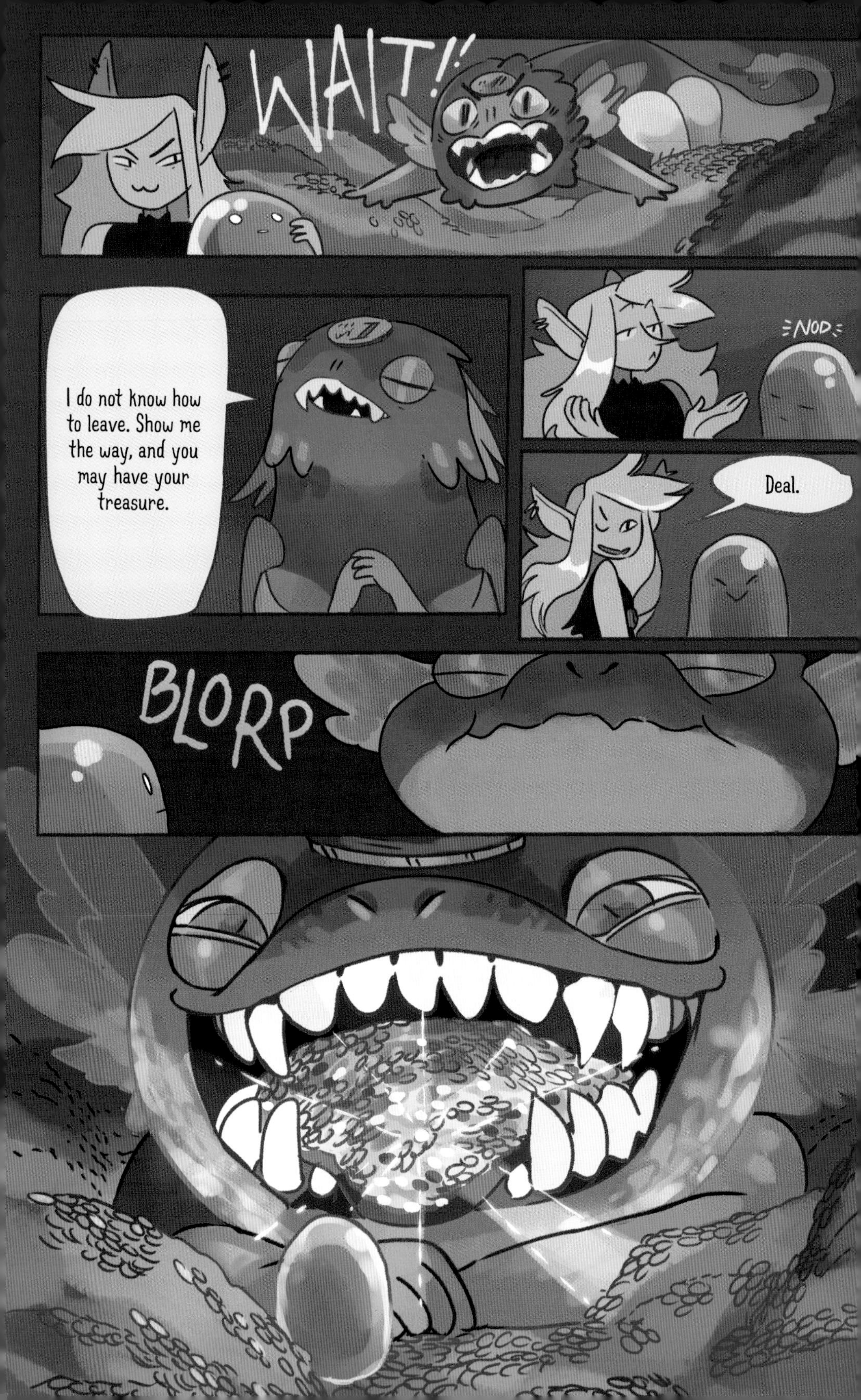
WAIT!!
I do not know how to leave. Show me the way, and you may have your treasure.
NOD
Deal.
BLORP

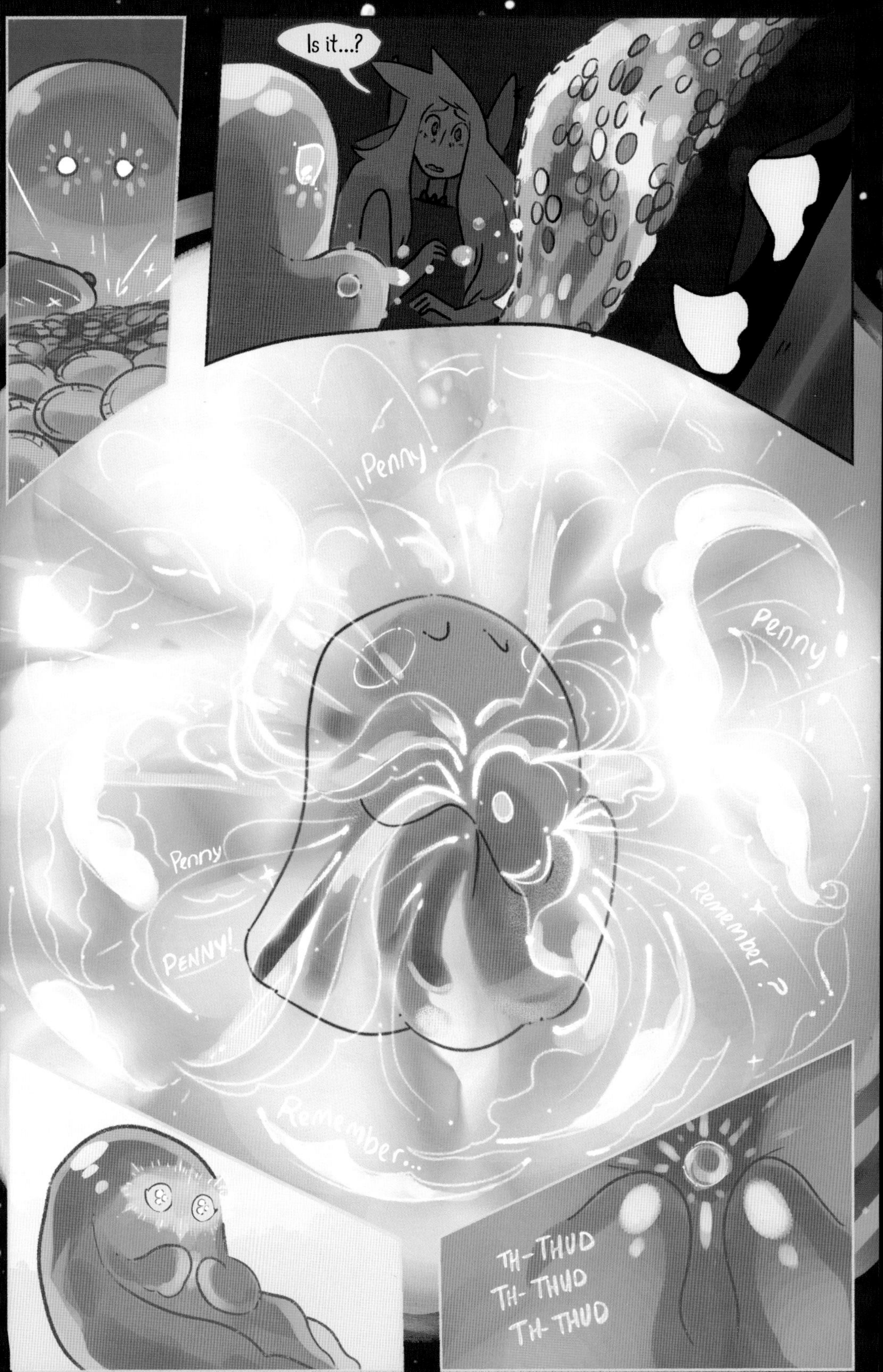

Is it...?
Penny
Penny
Penny
PENNY!
Remember?
Remember...
TH-THUD
TH-THUD
TH-THUD

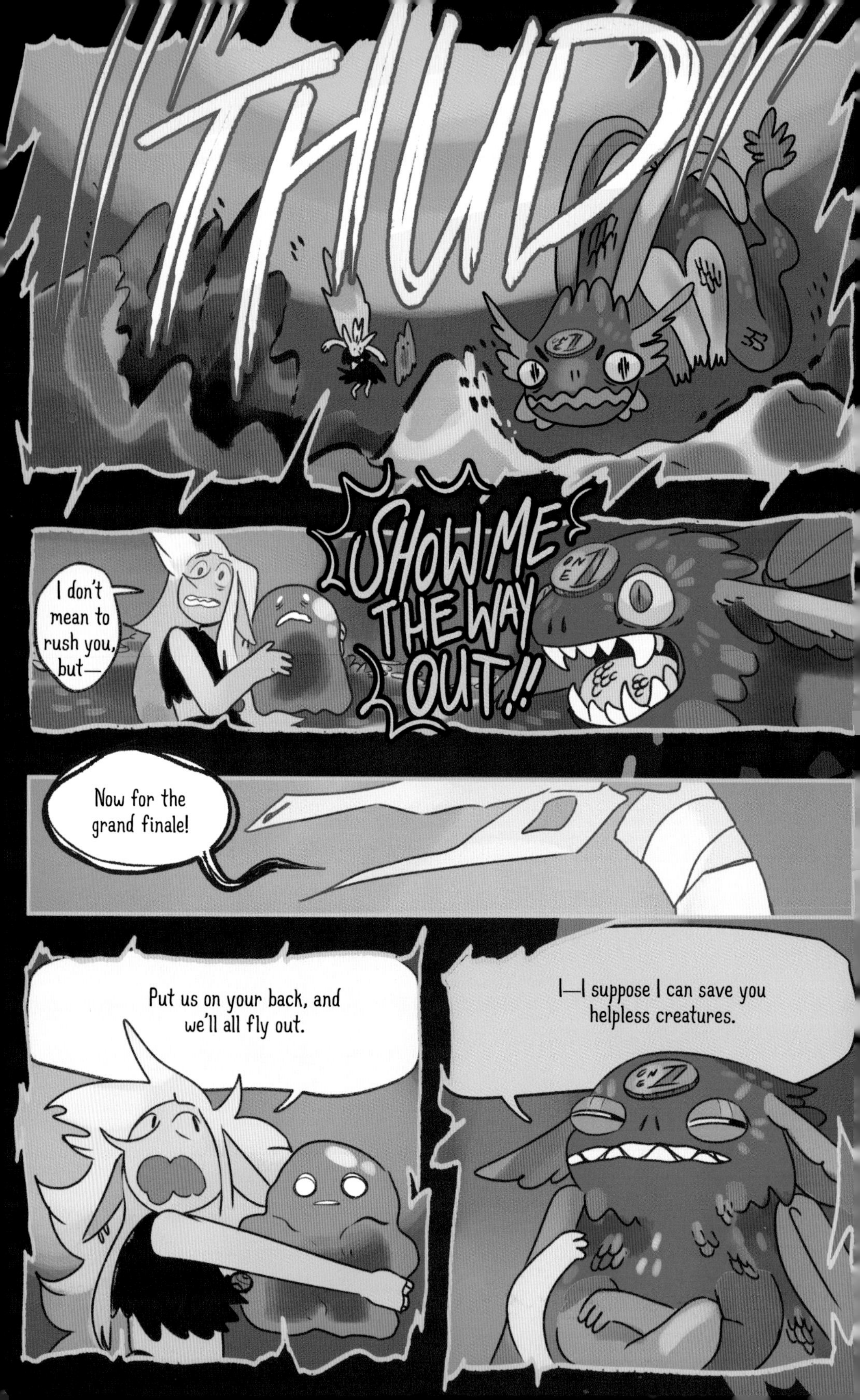
THUD!!
I don't mean to rush you, but—
SHOW ME THE WAY OUT!!
Now for the grand finale!
Put us on your back, and we'll all fly out.
I—I suppose I can save you helpless creatures.

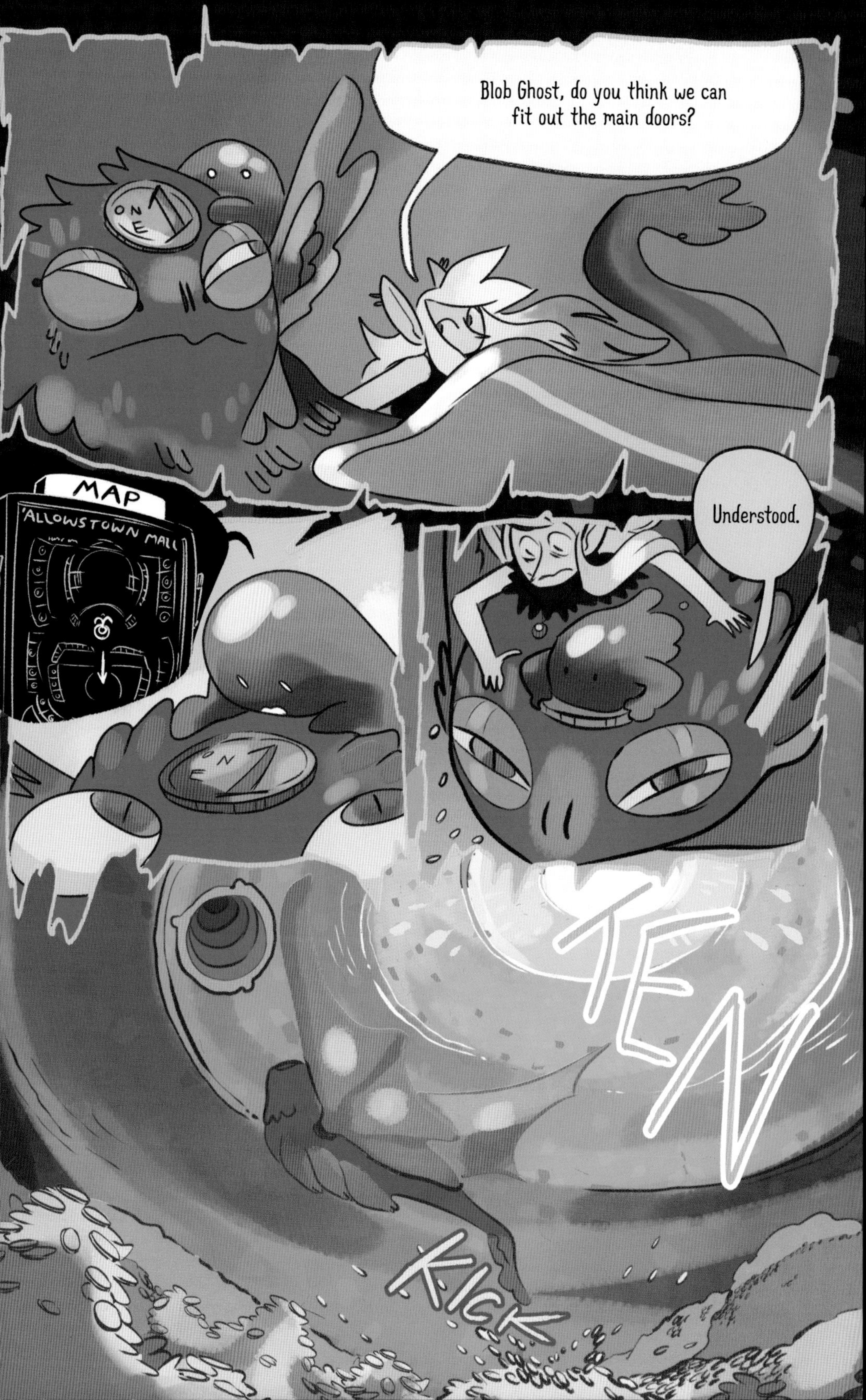
Blob Ghost, do you think we can fit out the main doors?
Understood.
MAP
'ALLOWSTOWN MALL
TEN
KICK

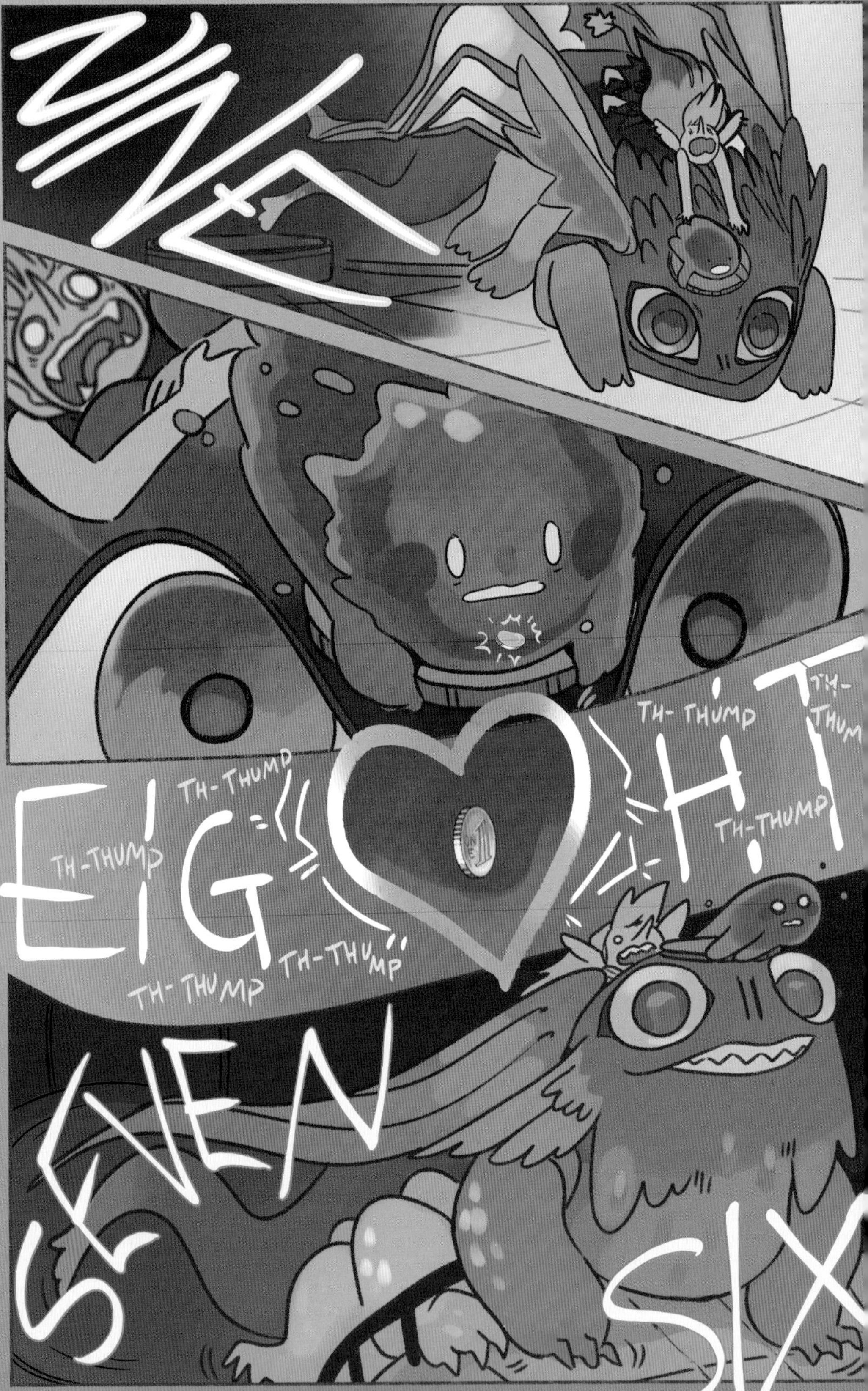
NINE
TH-THUMP
TH-THUMP
EIGHT
TH-THUMP
TH-THUMP
TH-THUMP
TH-THUMP
TH-THUMP
TH-THUM
SEVEN
SIX

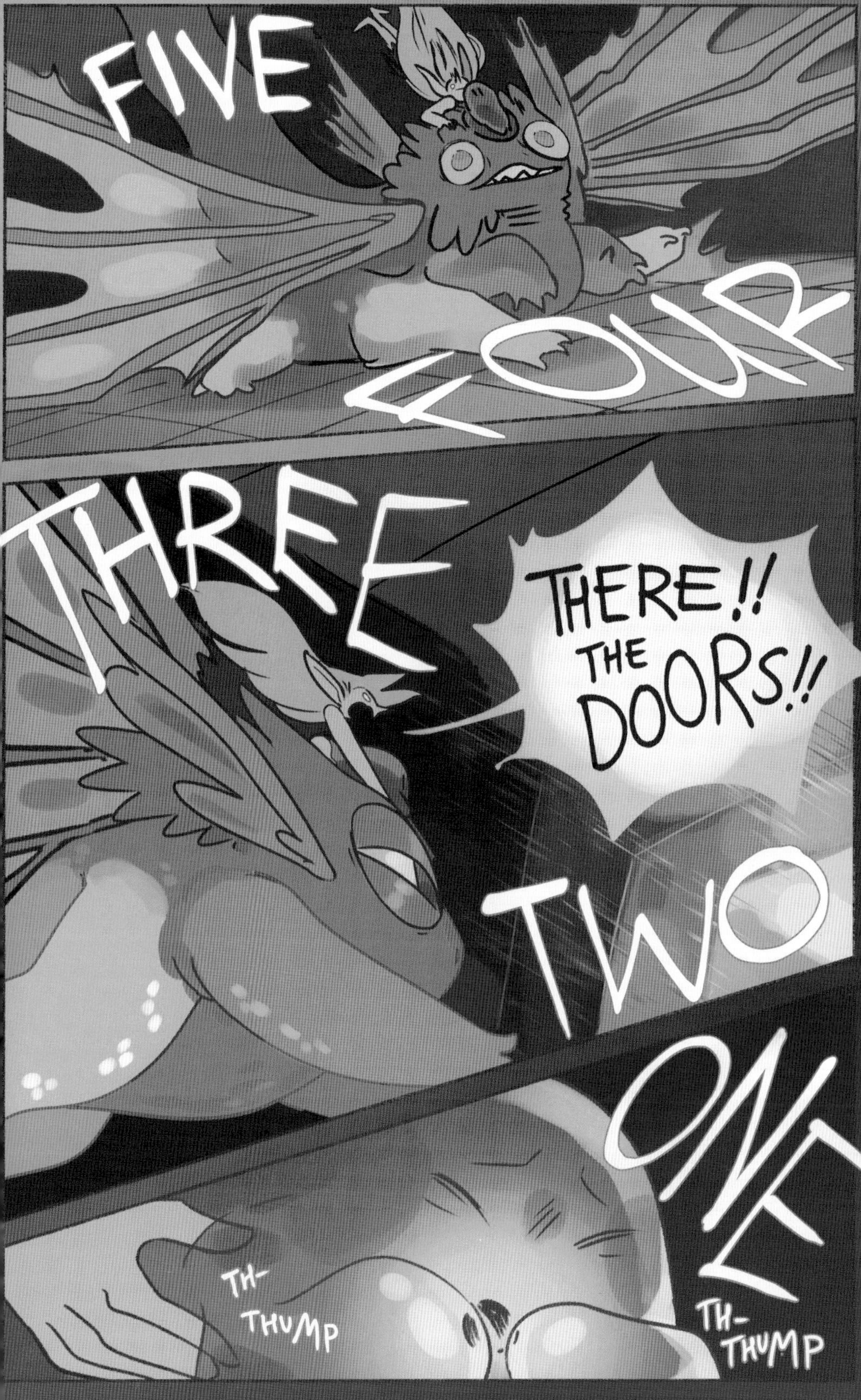
FIVE
FOUR
THREE
THERE!! THE DOORS!!
TWO
ONE
TH- THUMP
TH- THUMP

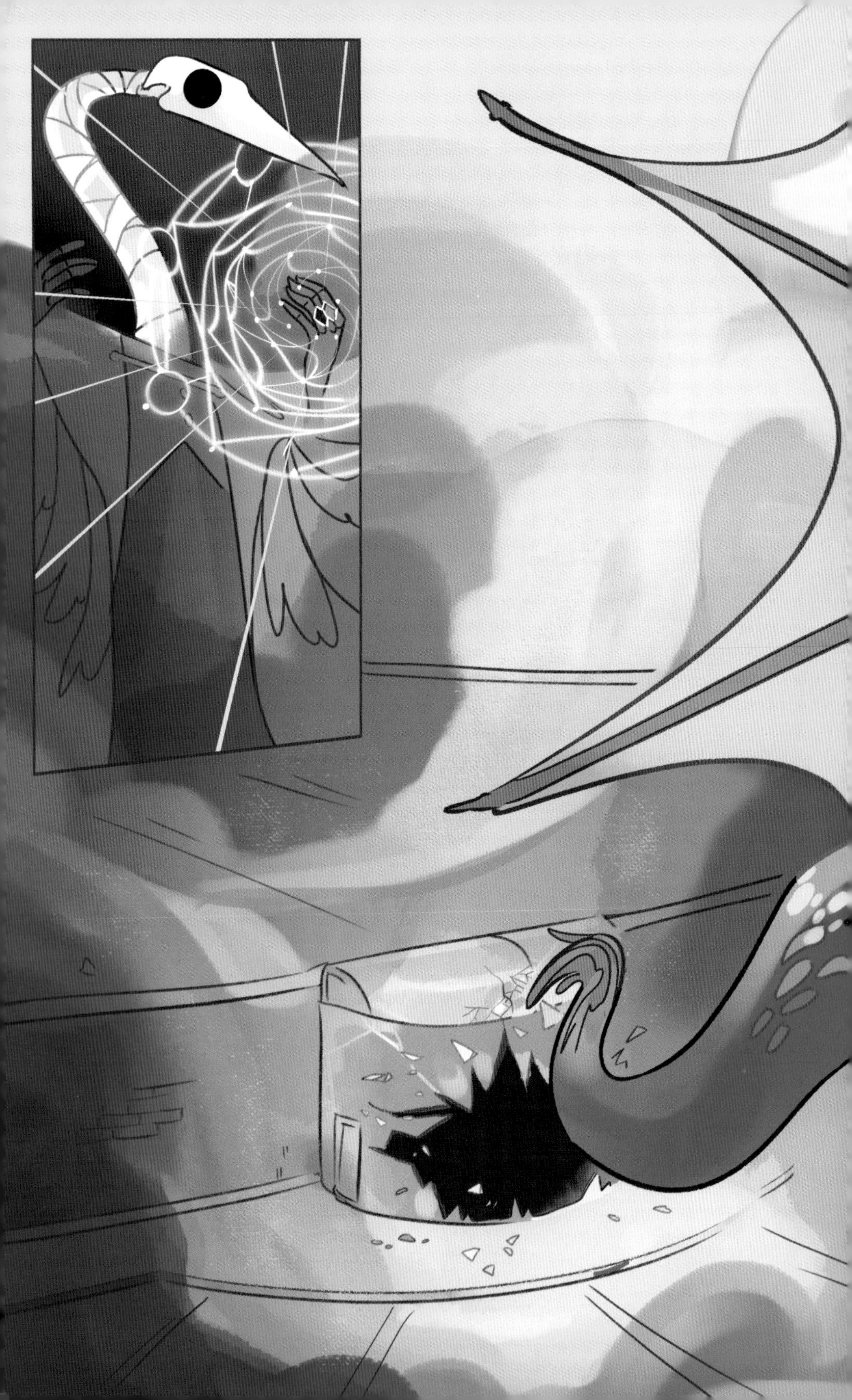

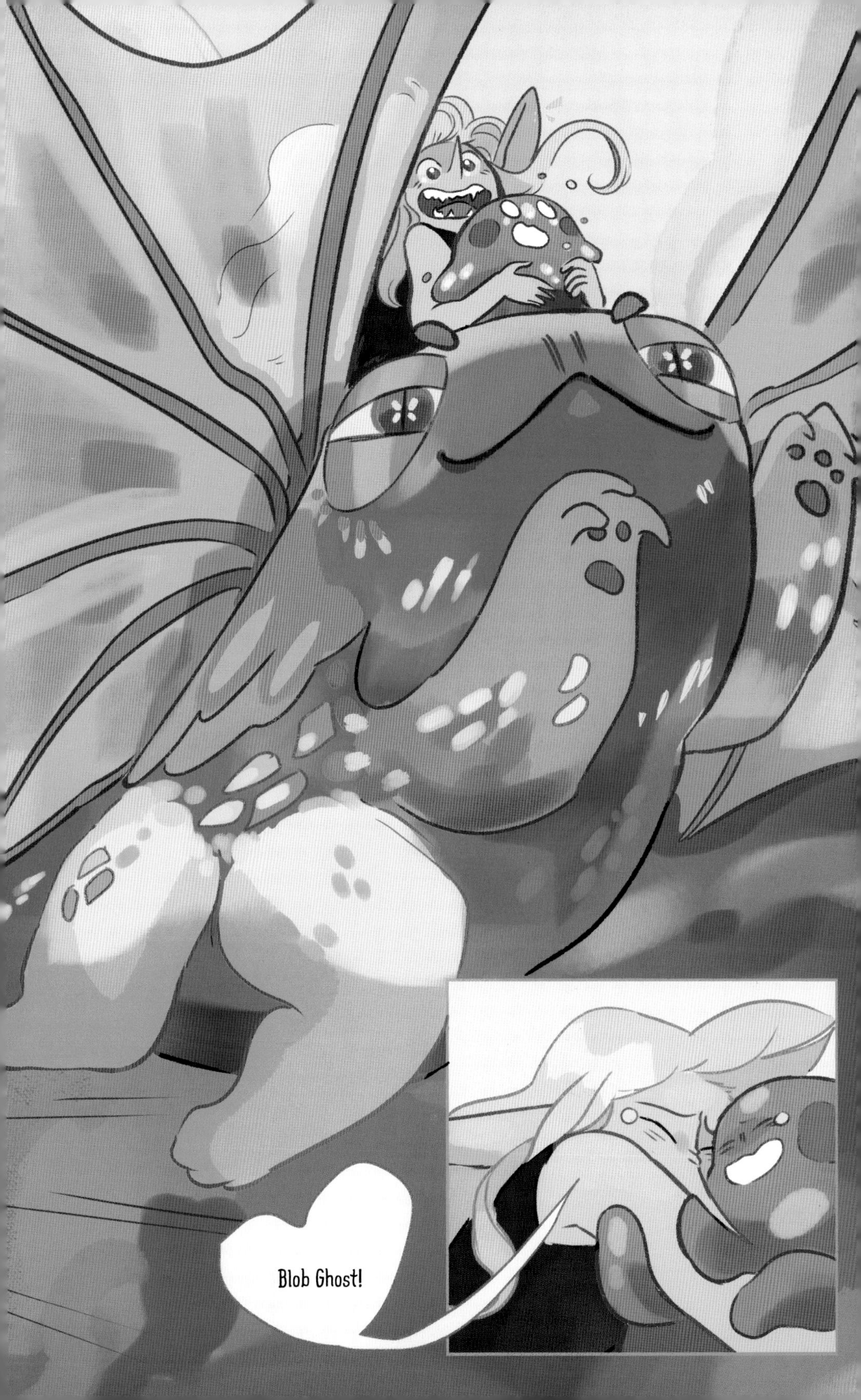
Blob Ghost!

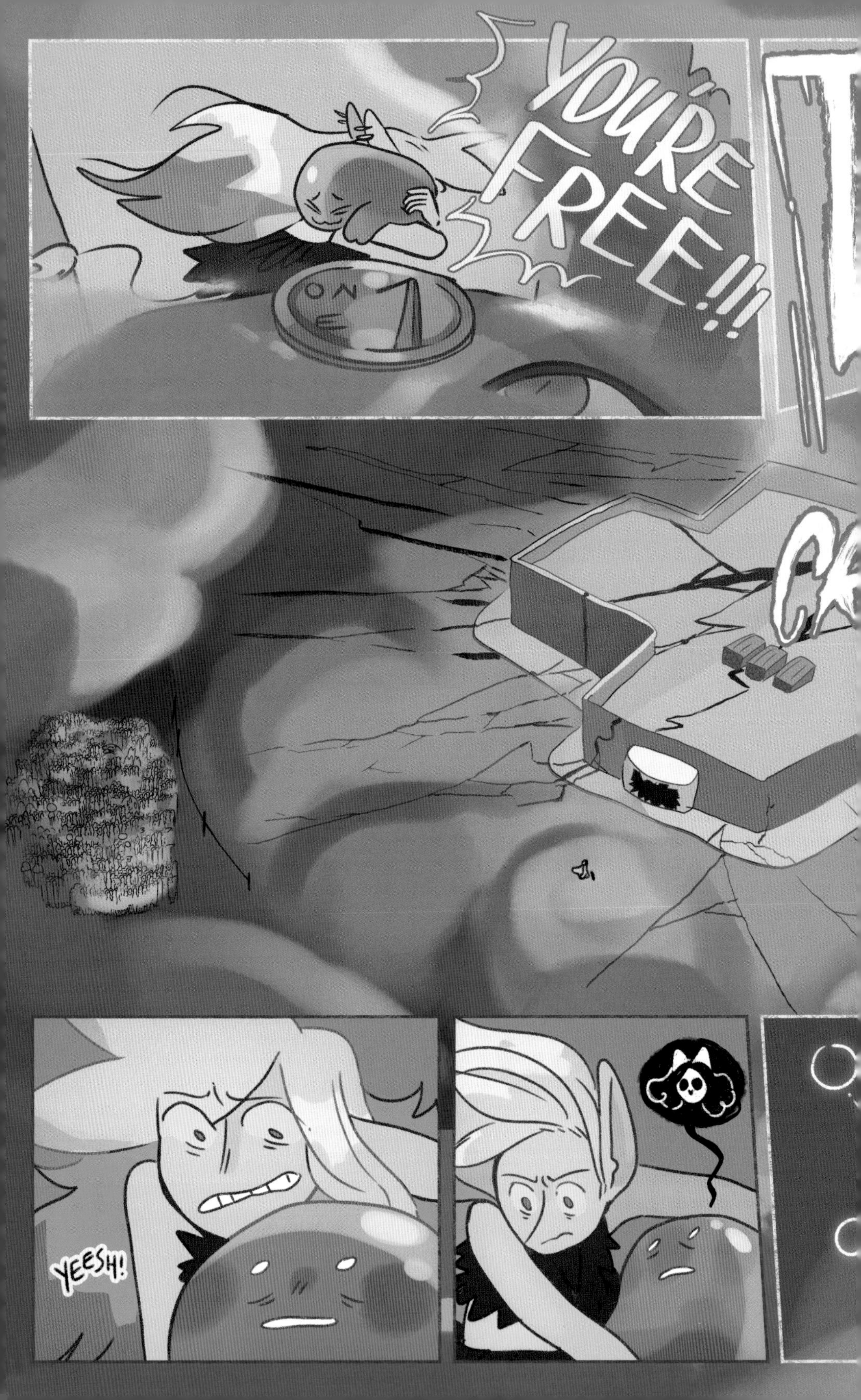
YOU'RE FREE!!!
YEESH!

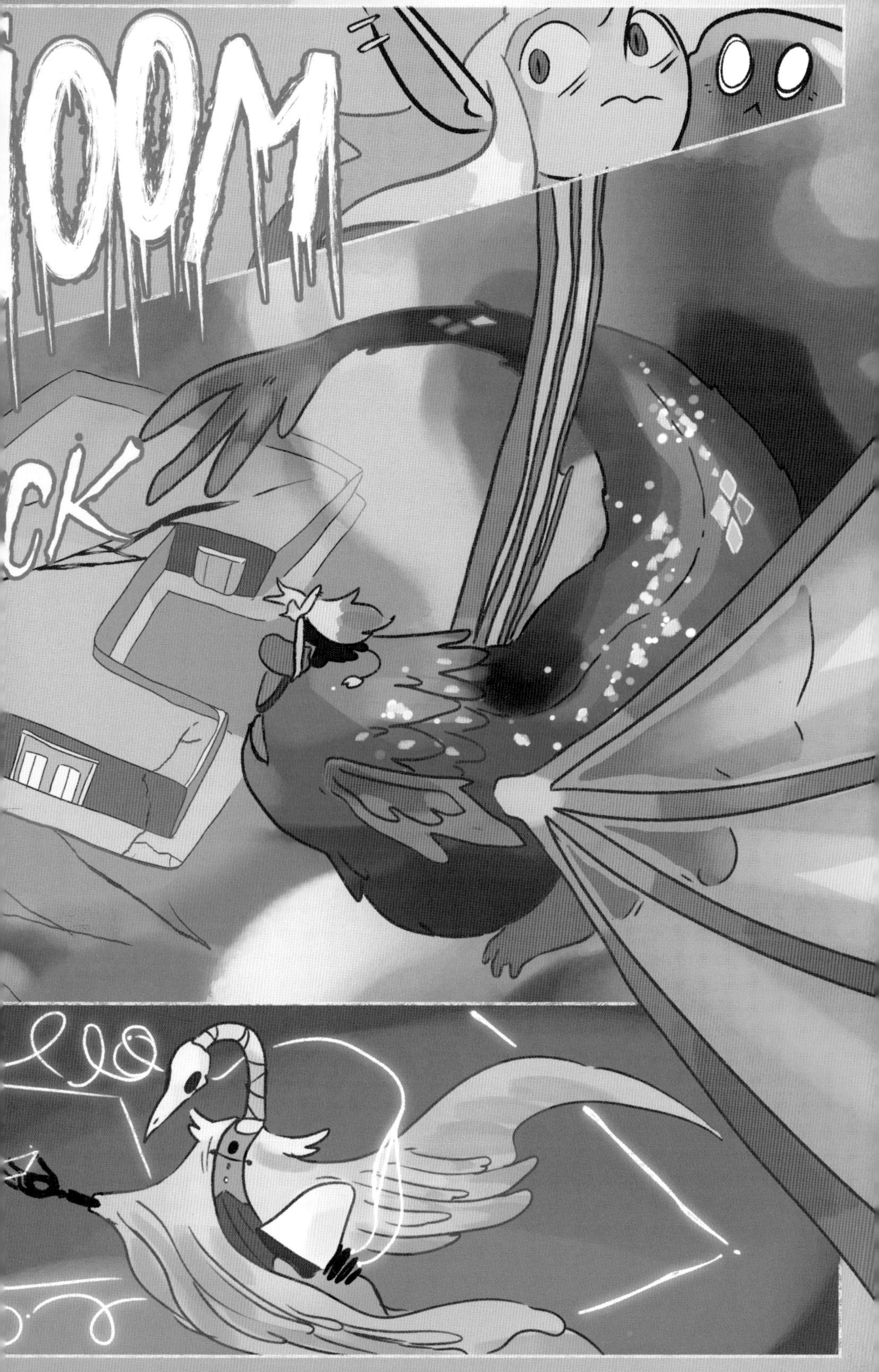

OOM
CK!

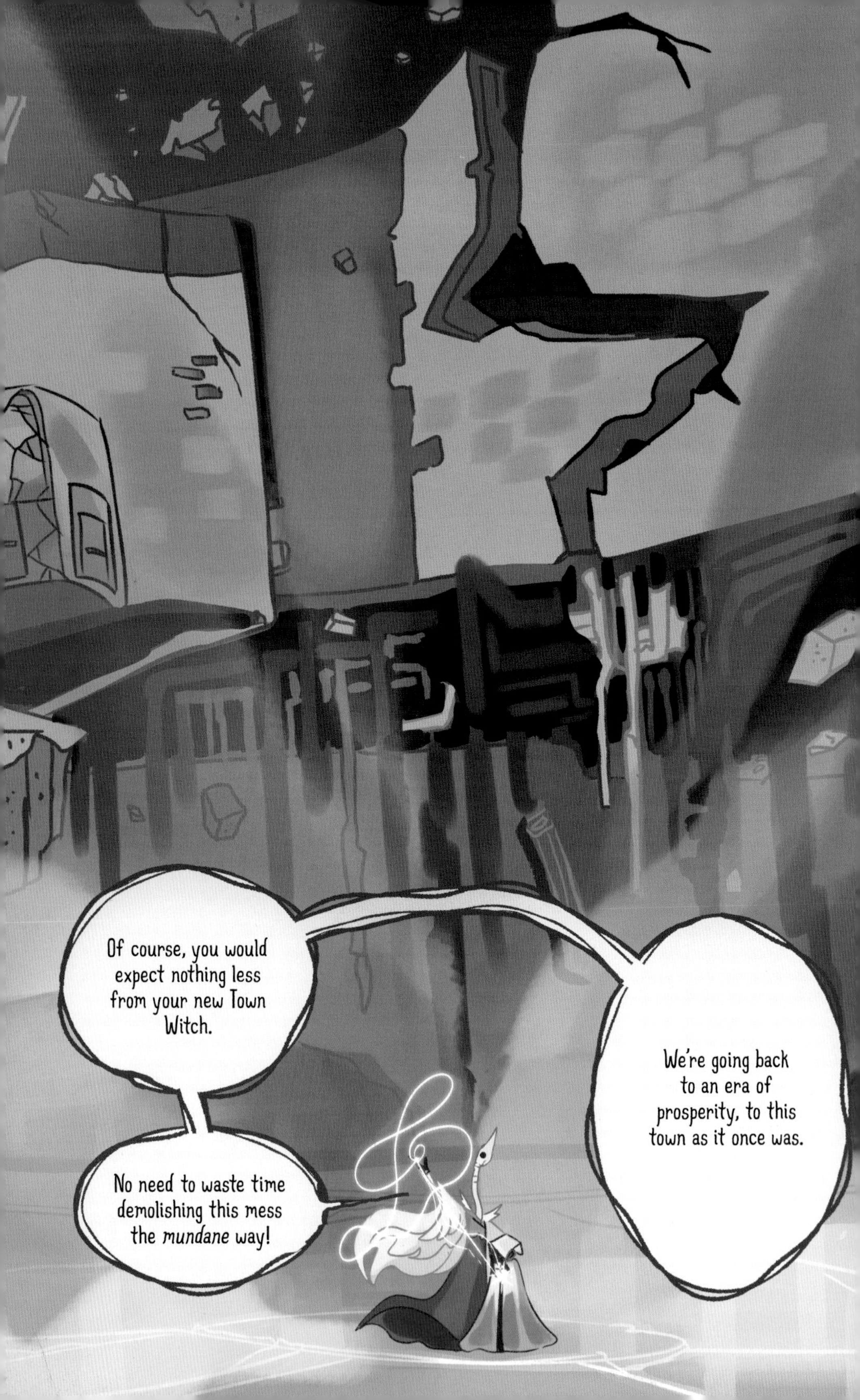
Of course, you would expect nothing less from your new Town Witch.
We're going back to an era of prosperity, to this town as it once was.
No need to waste time demolishing this mess the *mundane* way!

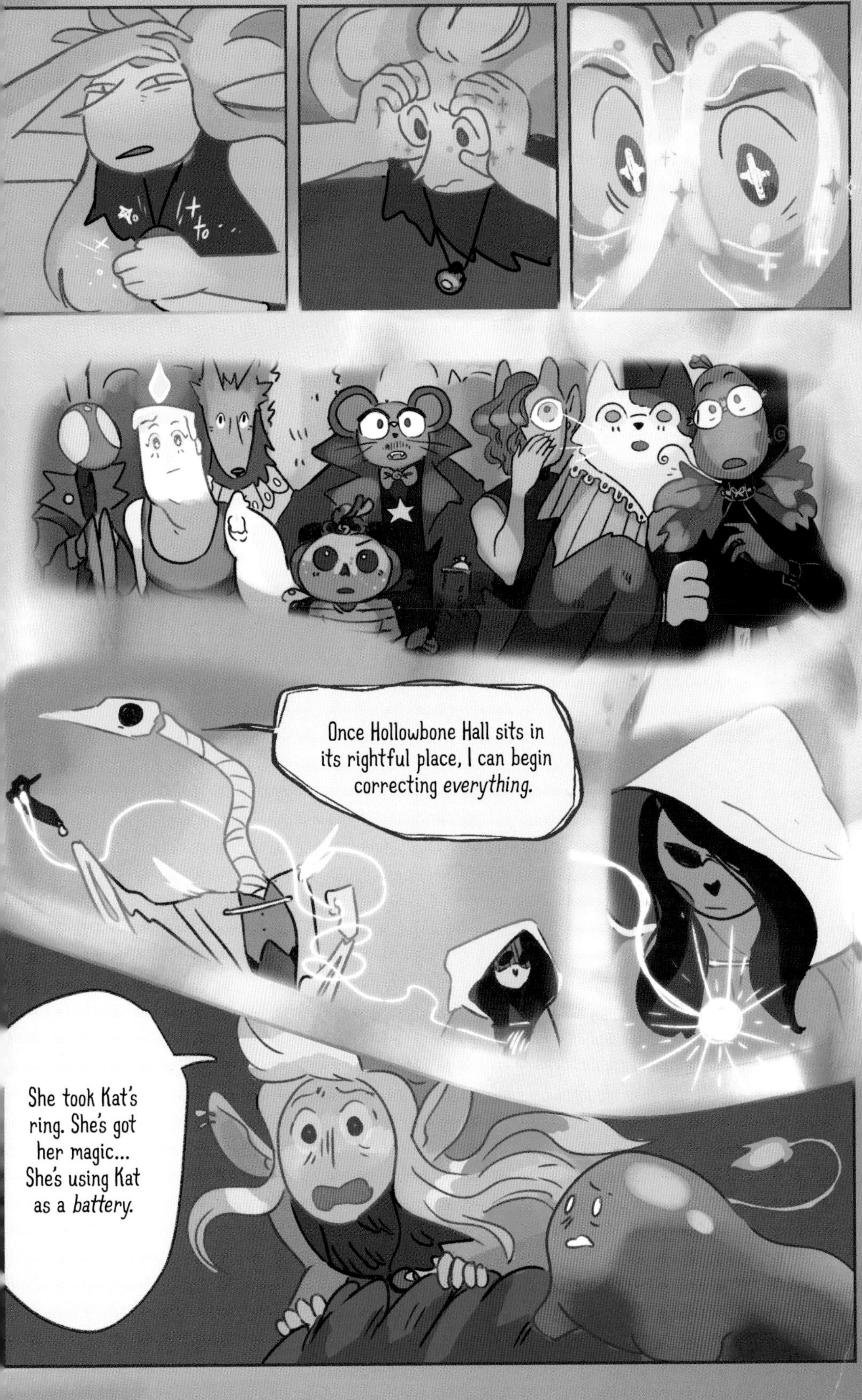
Once Hollowbone Hall sits in its rightful place, I can begin correcting *everything*.
She took Kat's ring. She's got her magic... She's using Kat as a *battery*.

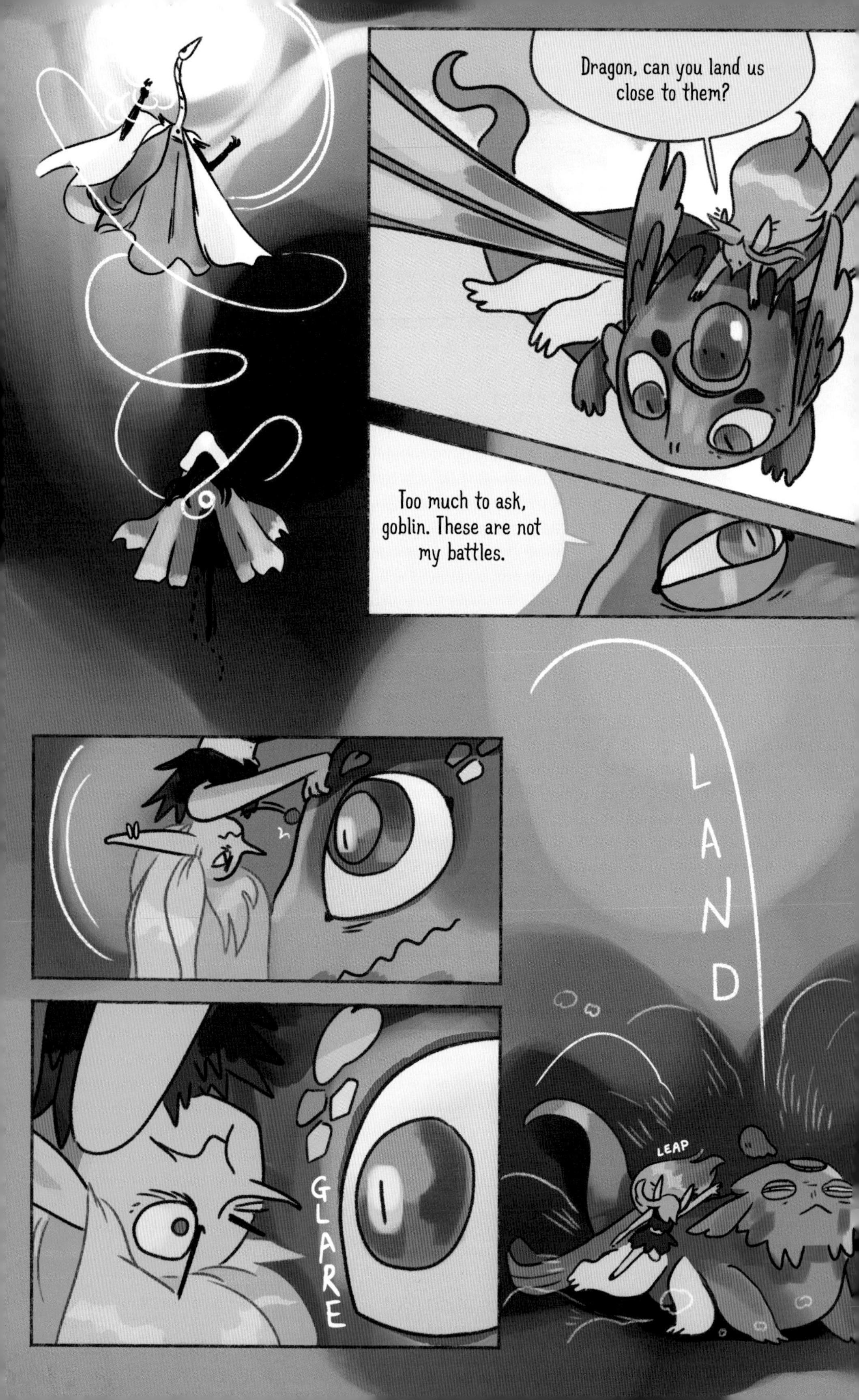
Dragon, can you land us close to them?
Too much to ask, goblin. These are not my battles.
LAND
LEAP
GLARE

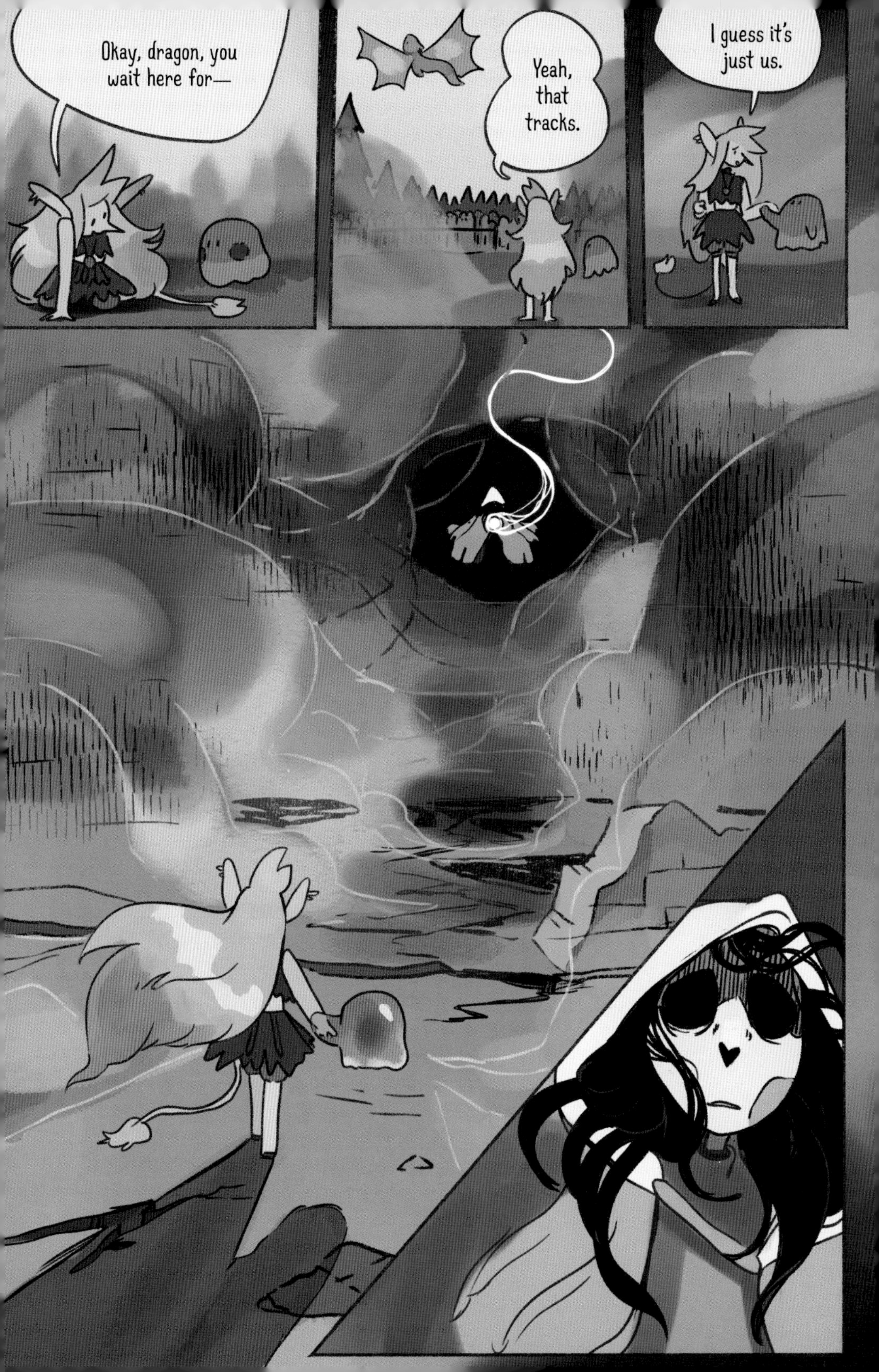
Okay, dragon, you wait here for—
Yeah, that tracks.
I guess it's just us.

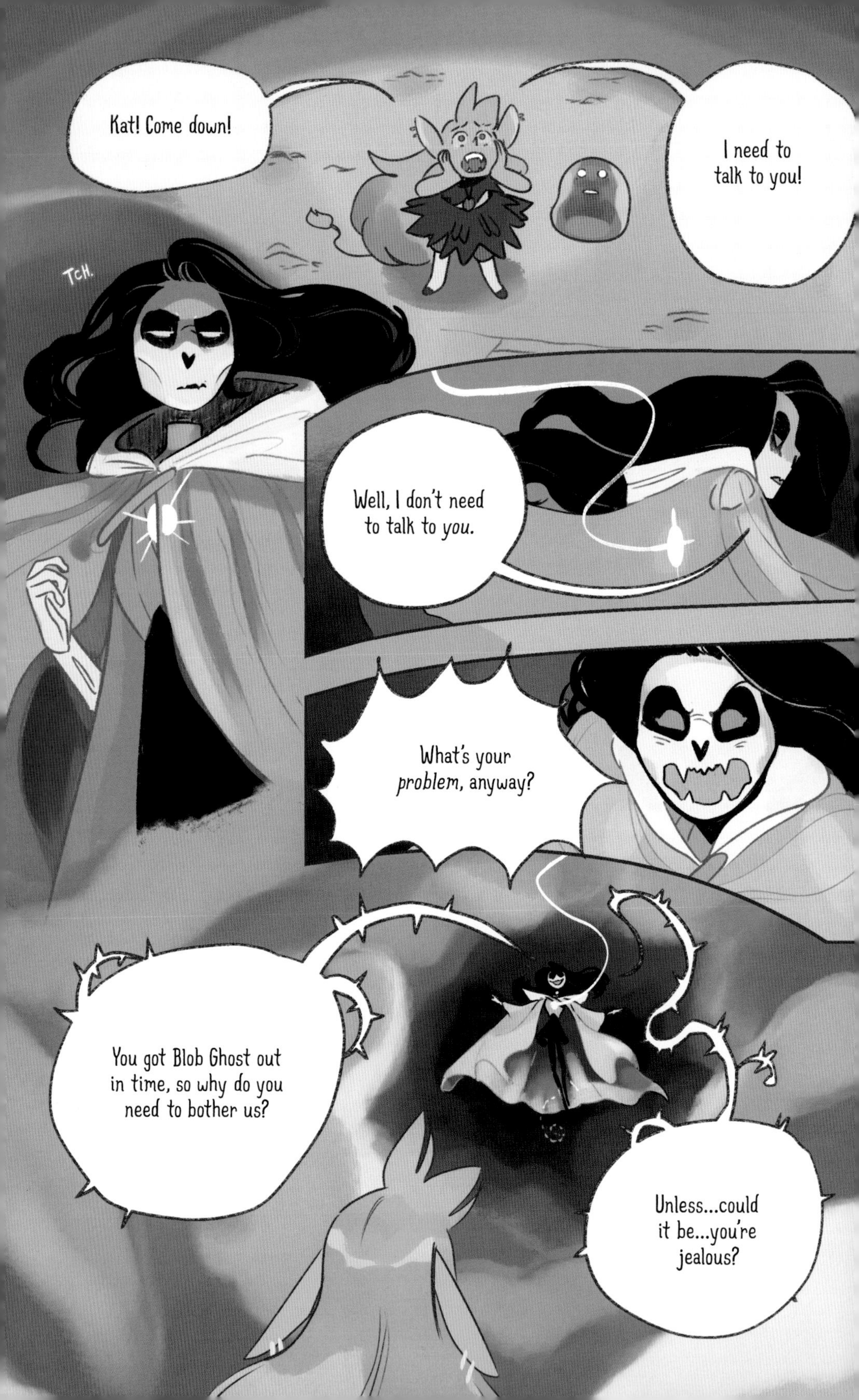
Kat! Come down!
I need to talk to you!
TCH.
Well, I don't need to talk to *you*.
What's your *problem*, anyway?
You got Blob Ghost out in time, so why do you need to bother us?
Unless...could it be...you're jealous?

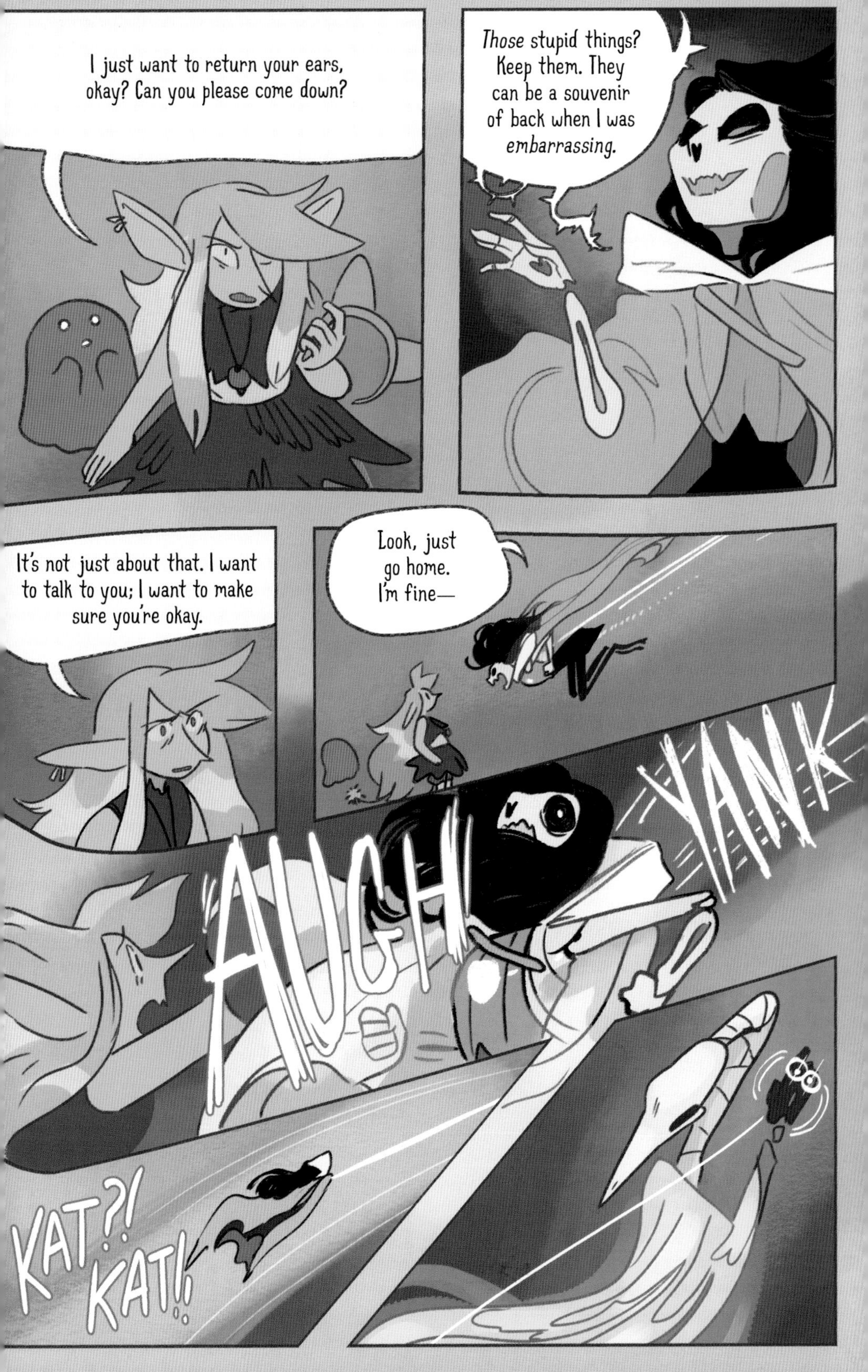
I just want to return your ears, okay? Can you please come down?
Those stupid things? Keep them. They can be a souvenir of back when I was *embarrassing*.
It's not just about that. I want to talk to you; I want to make sure you're okay.
Look, just go home. I'm fine—
YANK
AUGH
KAT?!
KAT!!

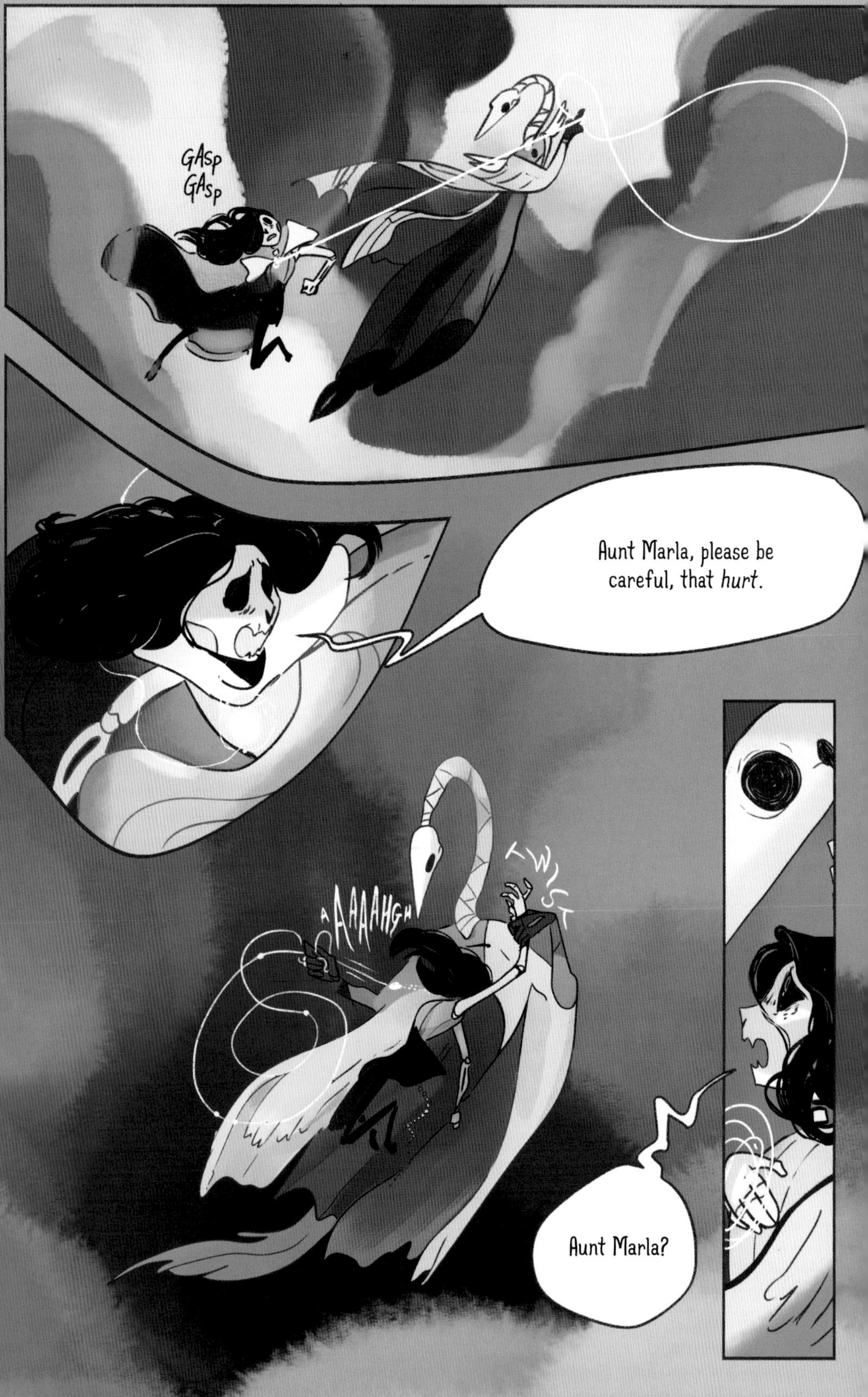
GASP
GASP
Aunt Marla, please be careful, that *hurt*.
AAAAAHGH
TWIST
Aunt Marla?

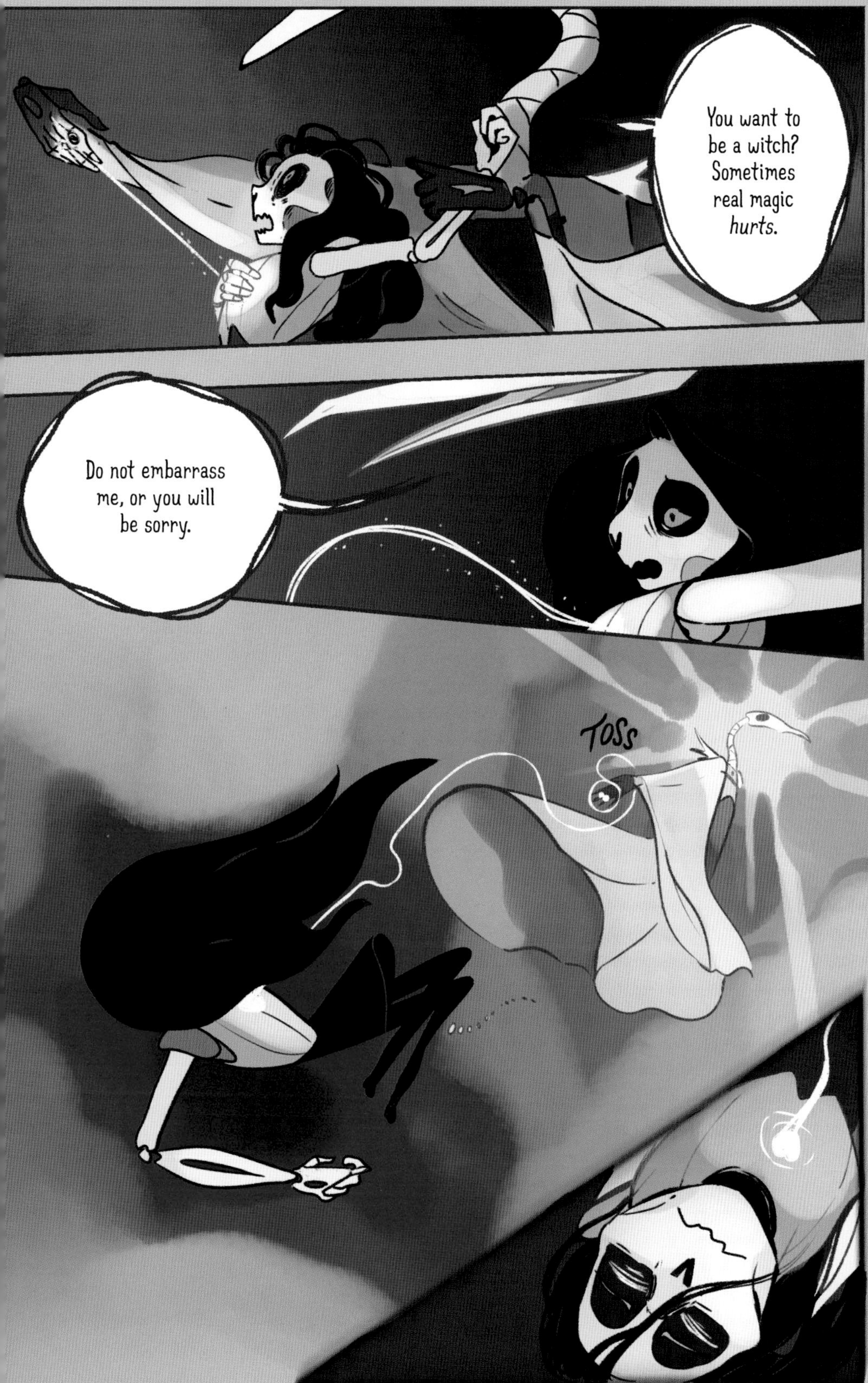
You want to be a witch? Sometimes real magic *hurts.*
Do not embarrass me, or you will be sorry.
TOSS

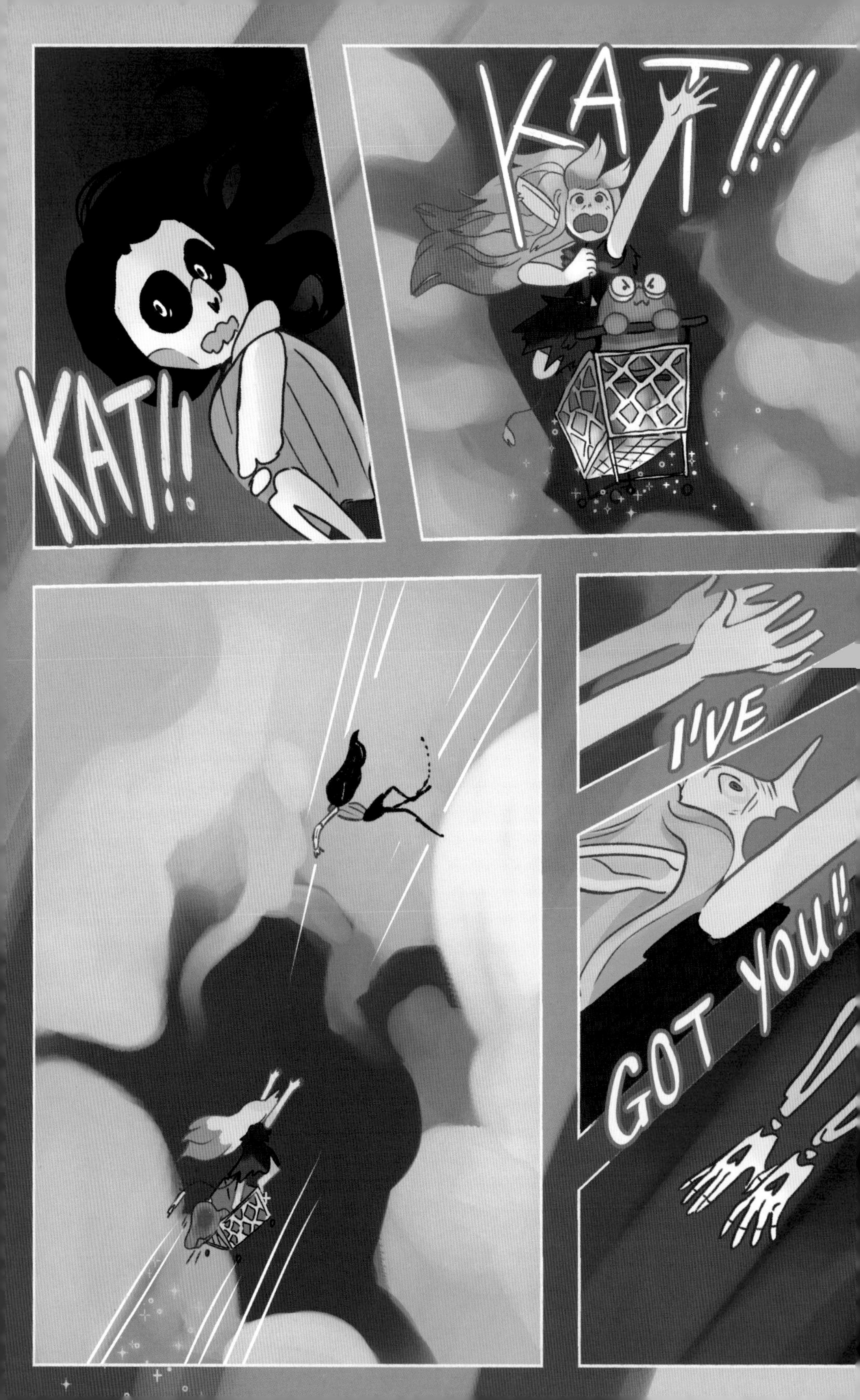
KAT!!
KAT!!!
I'VE
GOT YOU!!

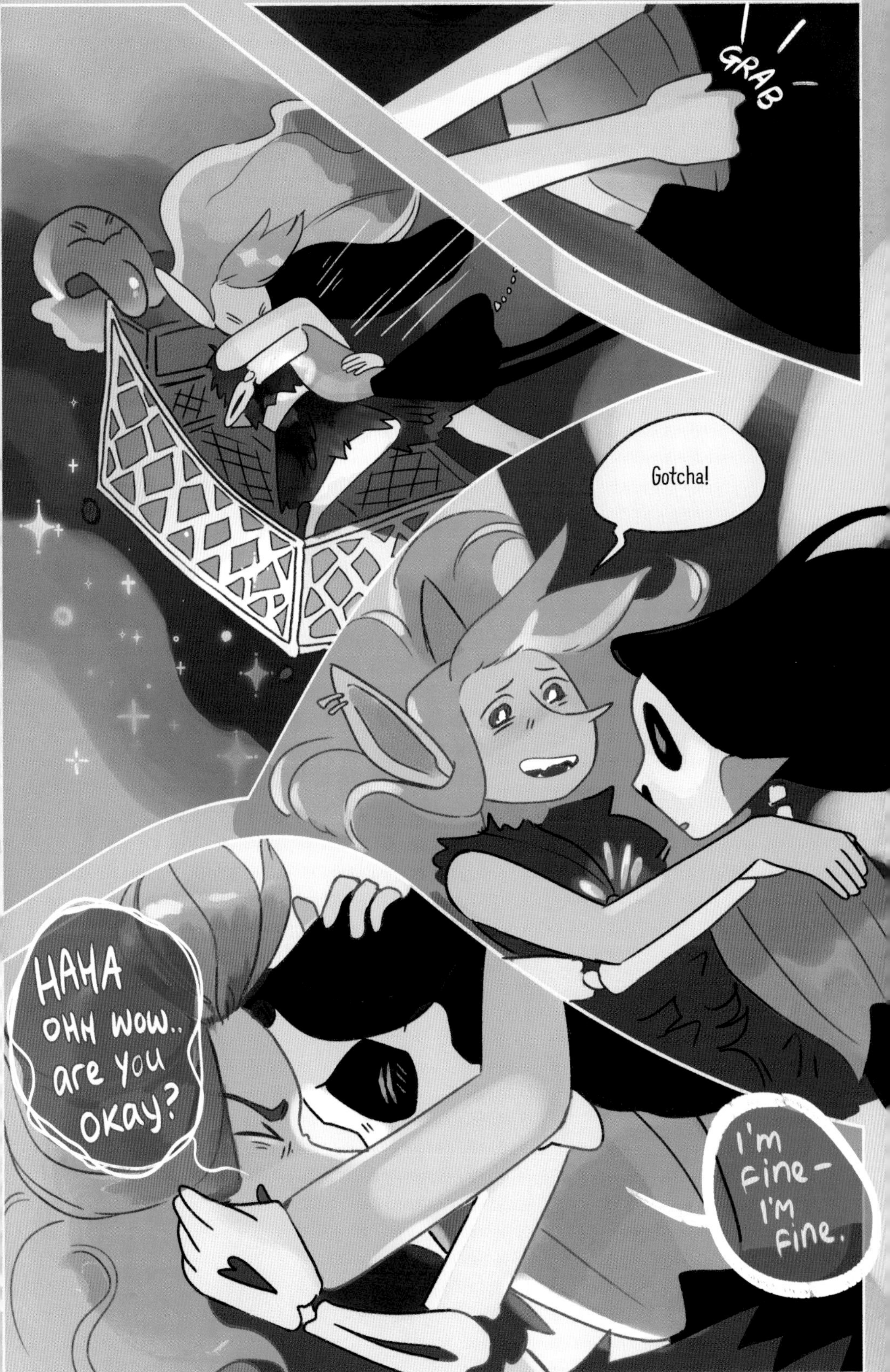
GRAB
Gotcha!
HAHA OHH WOW.. are you okay?
I'm fine- I'm fine.

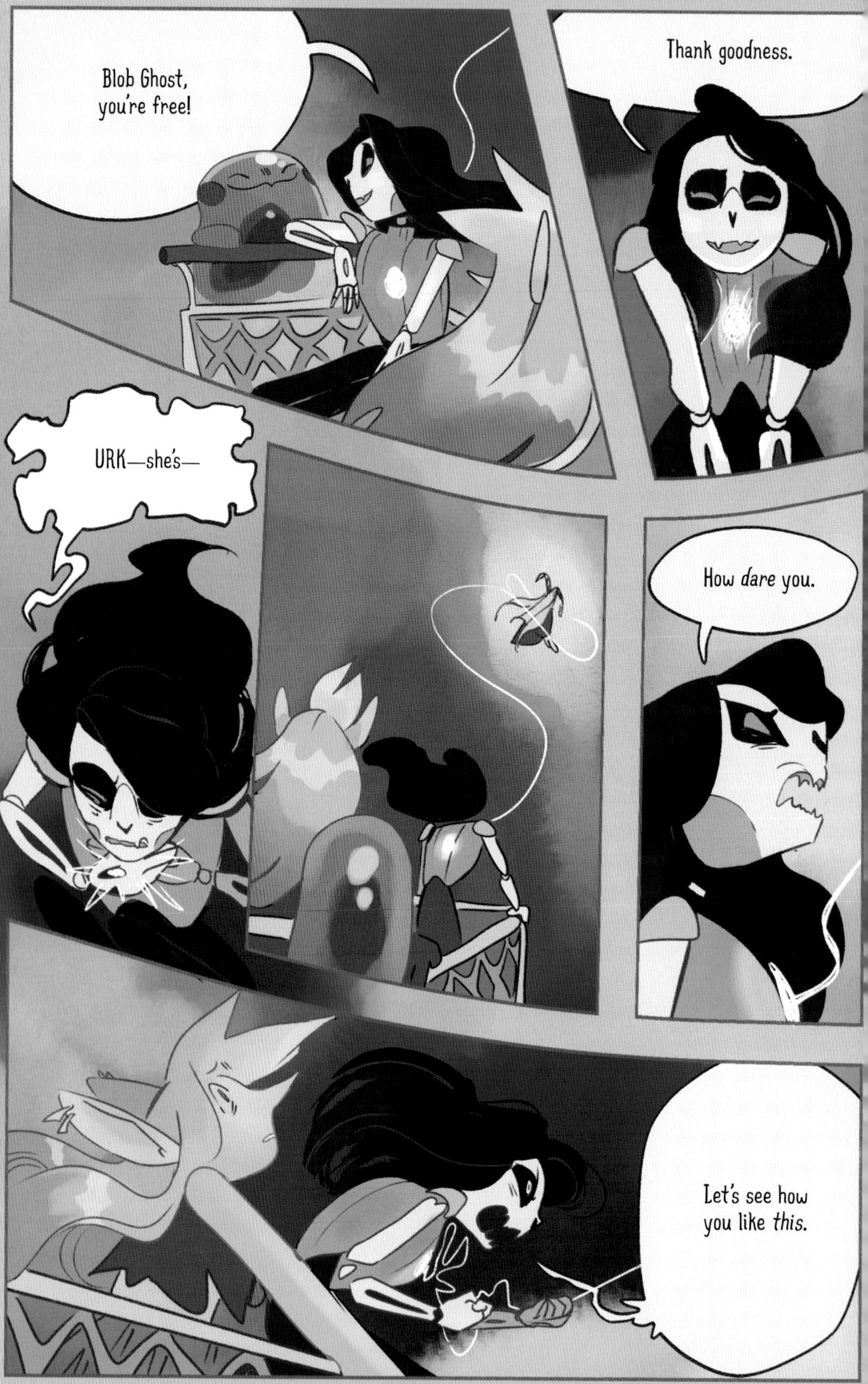
Blob Ghost, you're free!
Thank goodness.
URK—she's—
How *dare* you.
Let's see how you like *this*.

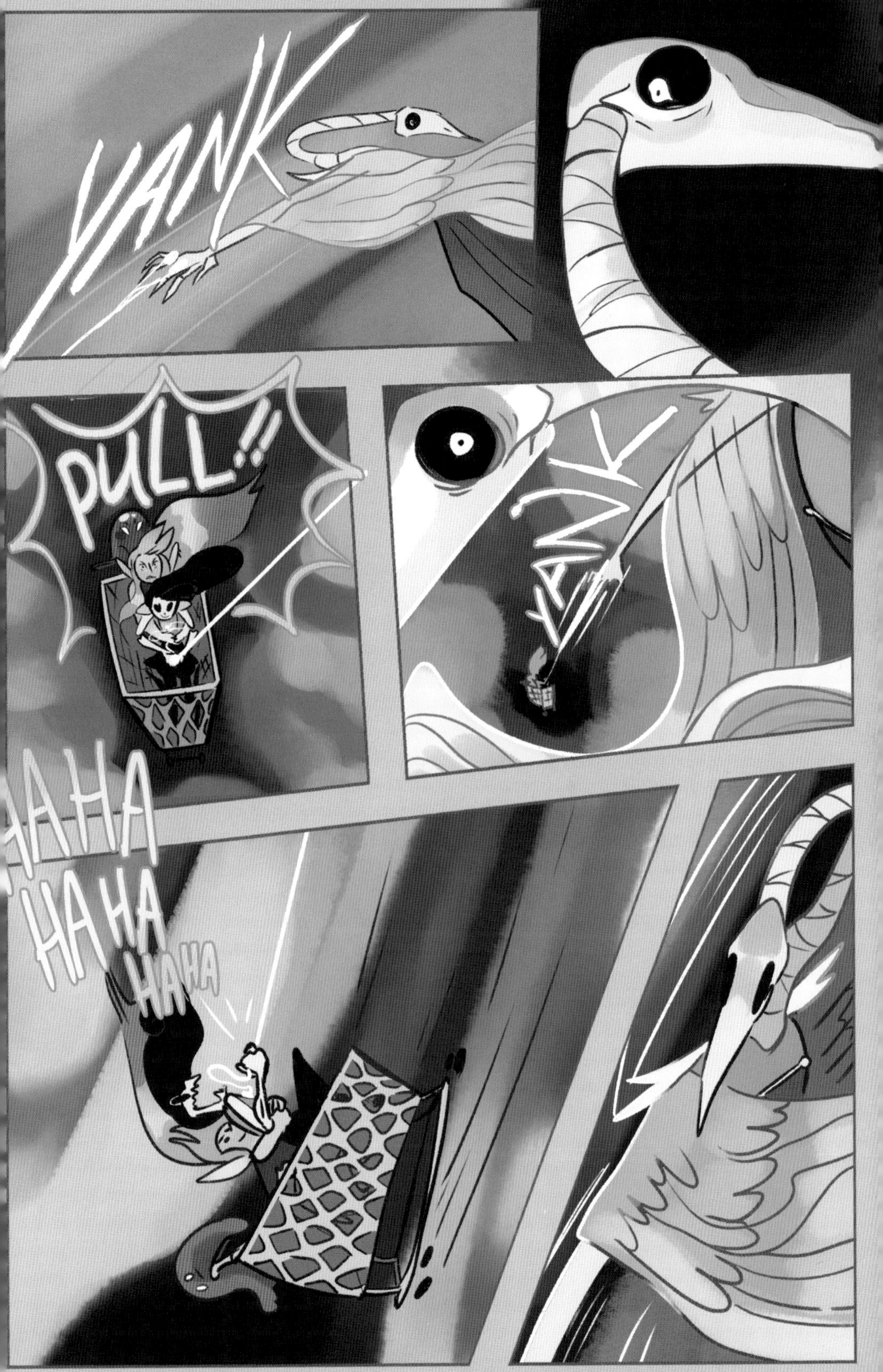

YANK
PULL!!
YANK
HAHA
HAHA
HAHA

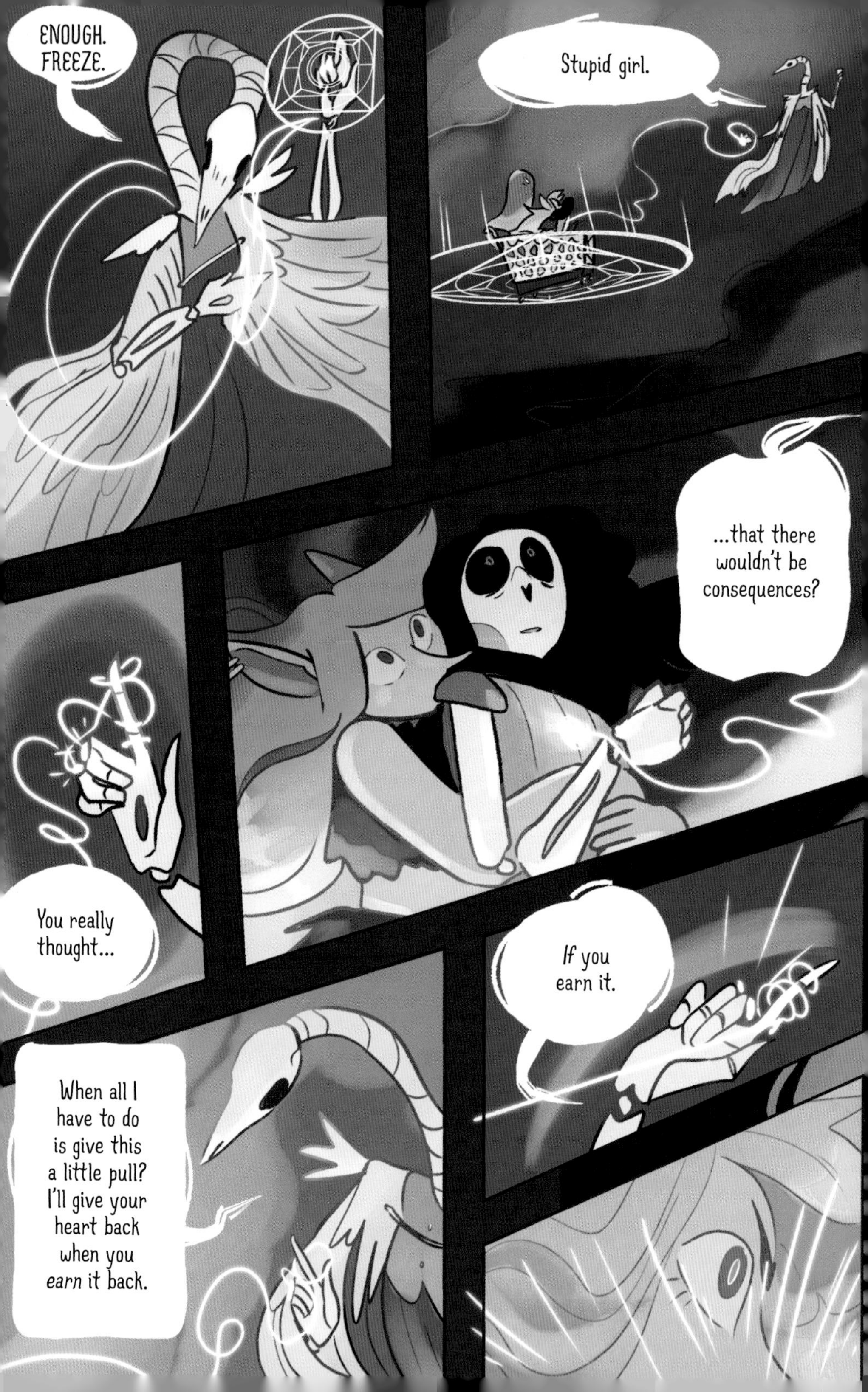
ENOUGH. FREEZE.
Stupid girl.
You really thought...
...that there wouldn't be consequences?
When all I have to do is give this a little pull? I'll give your heart back when you *earn* it back.
If you earn it.

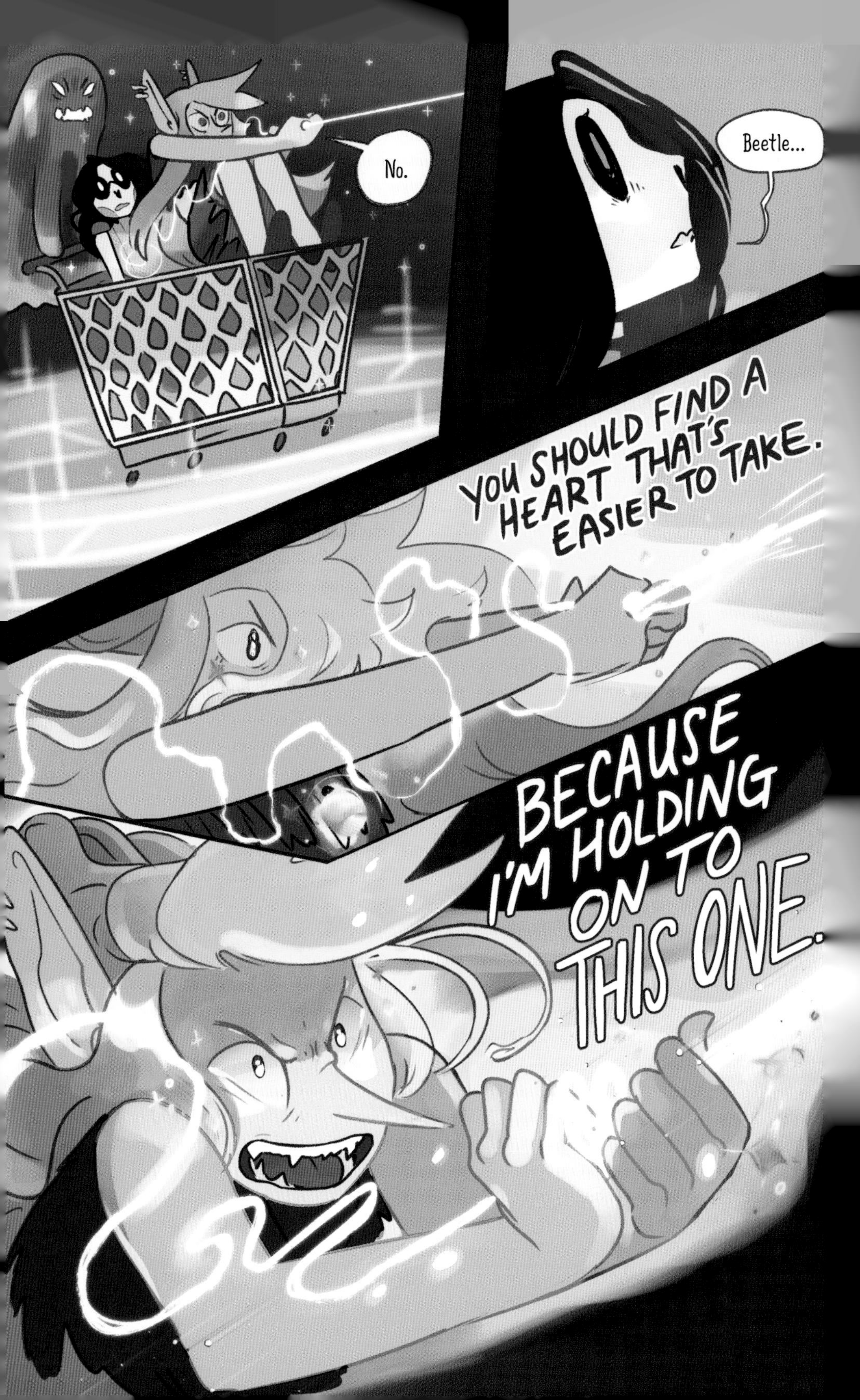
No.
Beetle...
YOU SHOULD FIND A HEART THAT'S EASIER TO TAKE.
BECAUSE I'M HOLDING ON TO THIS ONE.

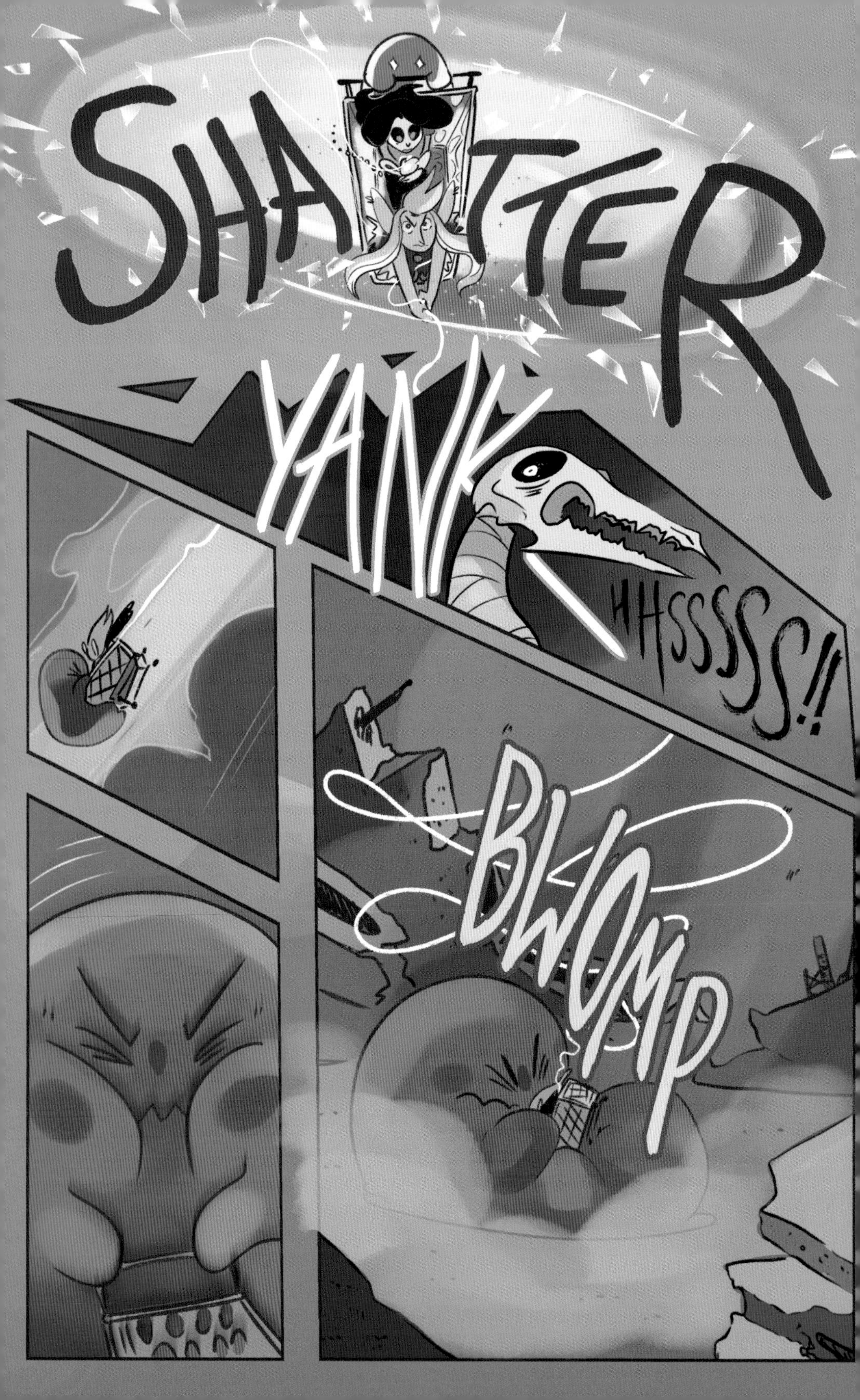
SHATTER
YANK
HHSSSSSS!!
BWOMP

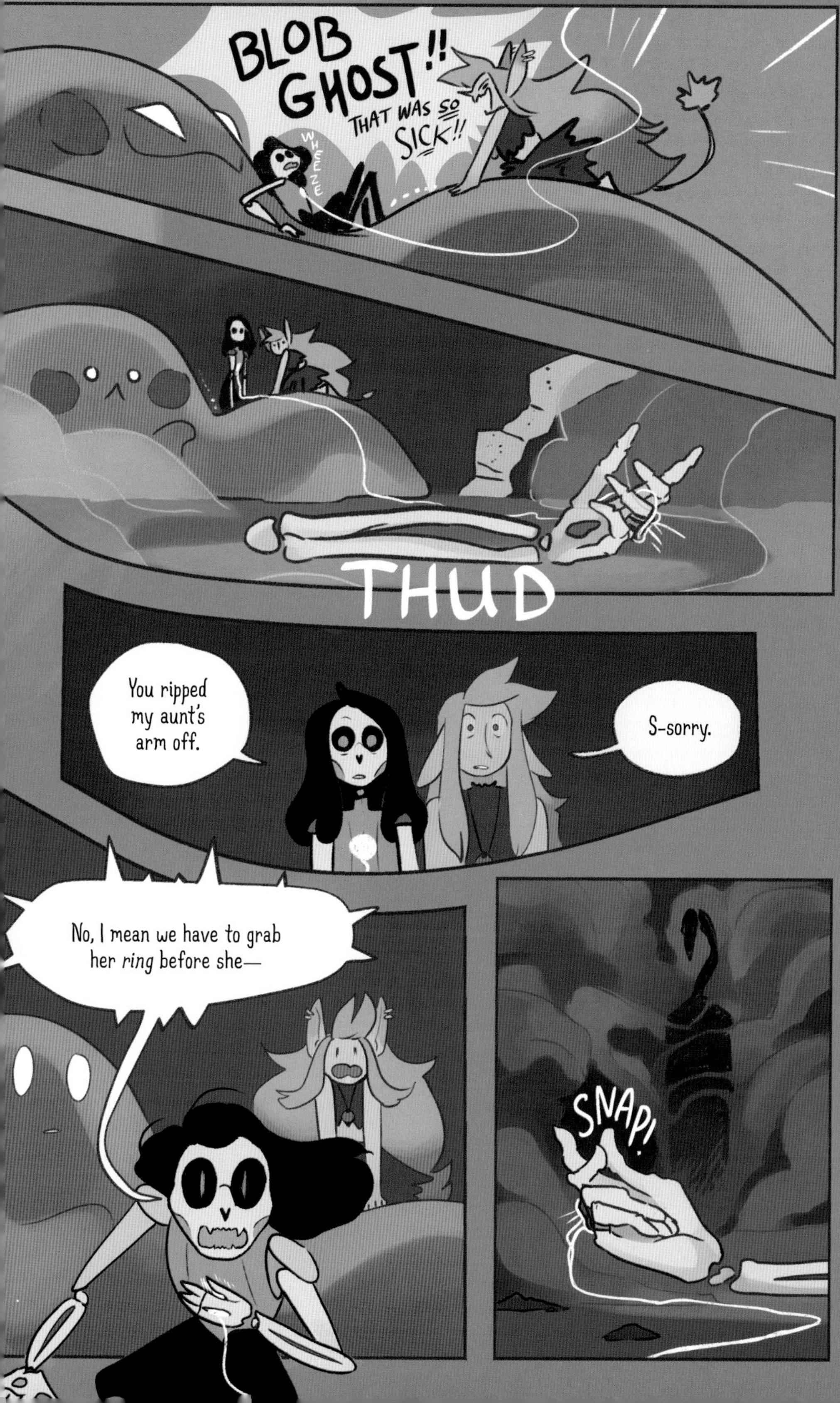
BLOB GHOST!!
THAT WAS SO SICK!!
WHEEZE
THUD
You ripped my aunt's arm off.
S-sorry.
No, I mean we have to grab her *ring* before she—
SNAP!

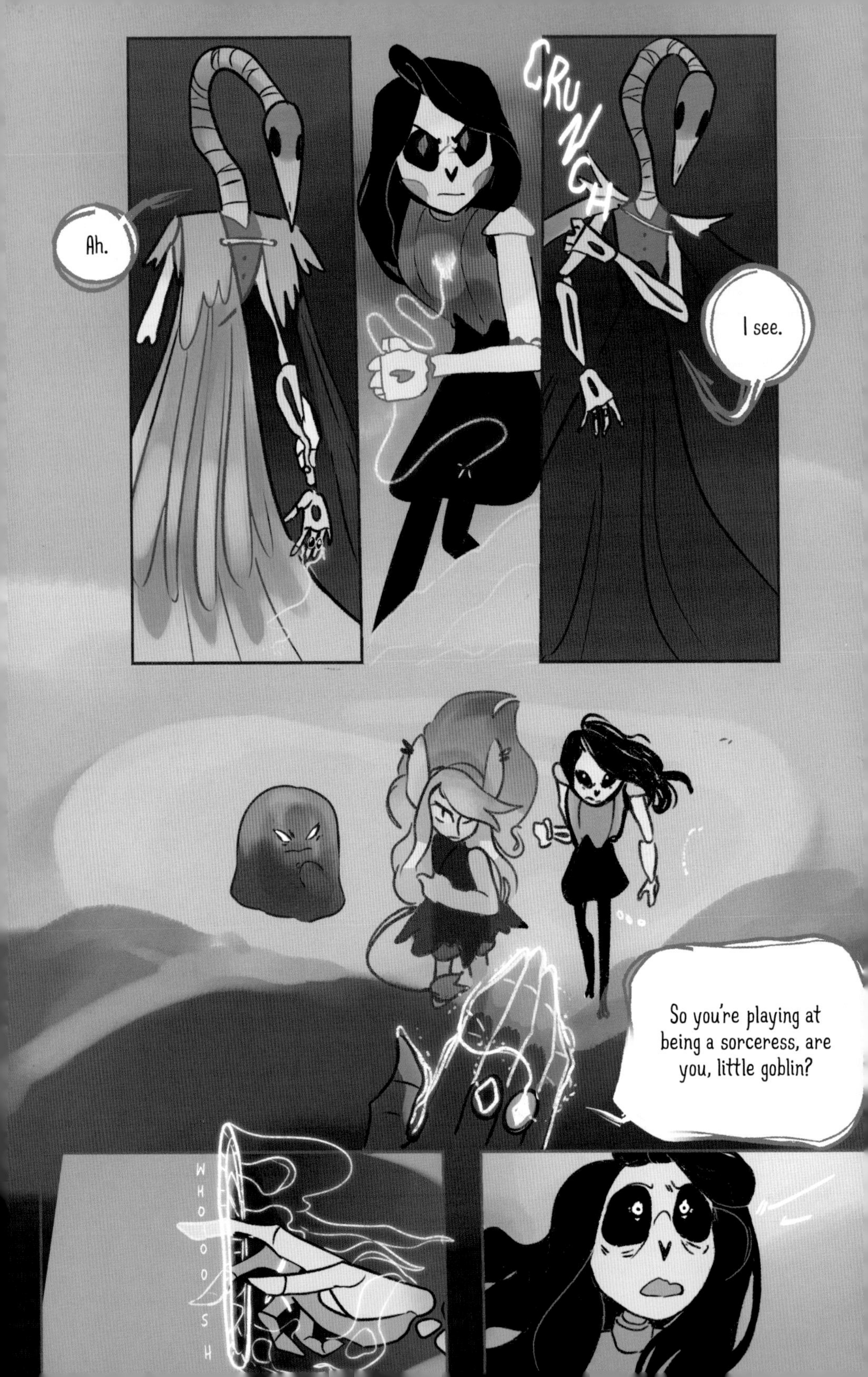
Ah.
CRUNCH
I see.
So you're playing at being a sorceress, are you, little goblin?
WHOOOOSH

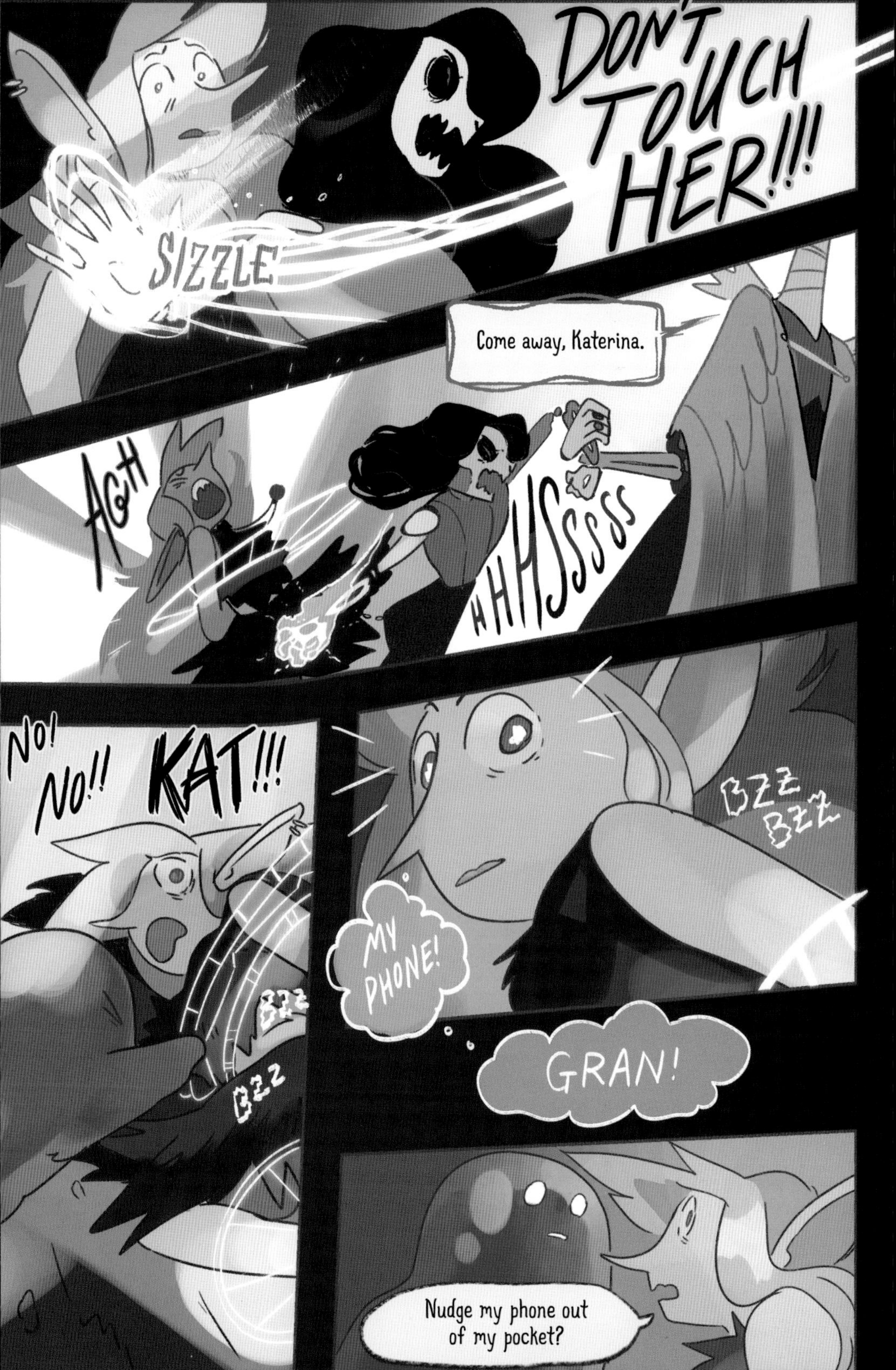
DON'T TOUCH HER!!!
SIZZLE
Come away, Katerina.
AGH
AHHSSSSSS
No! No!! KAT!!!
BZZ BZZ
MY PHONE!
BZZ
BZZ
GRAN!
Nudge my phone out of my pocket?

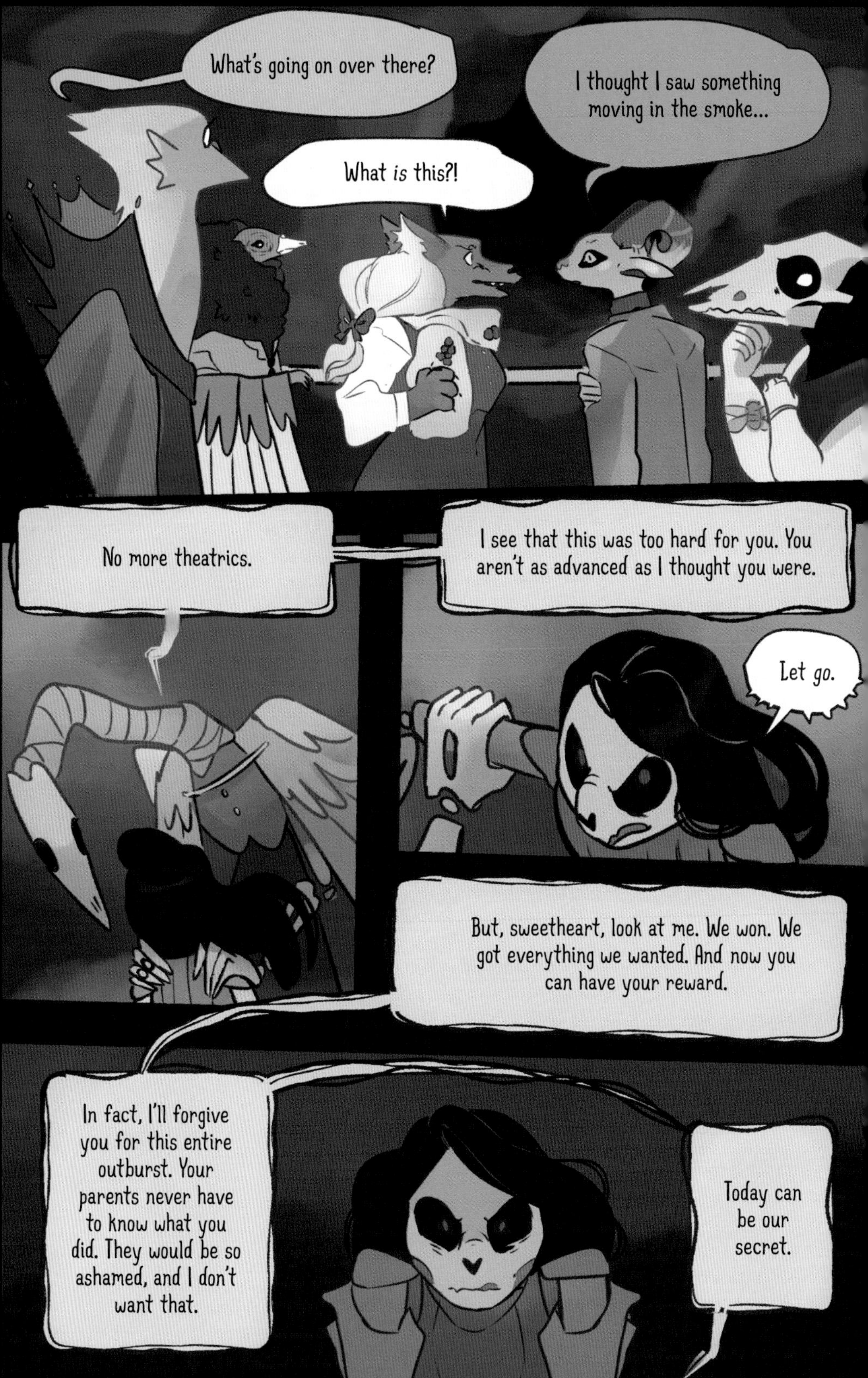
What's going on over there?
I thought I saw something moving in the smoke...
What *is* this?!
No more theatrics.
I see that this was too hard for you. You aren't as advanced as I thought you were.
Let *go.*
But, sweetheart, look at me. We won. We got everything we wanted. And now you can have your reward.
In fact, I'll forgive you for this entire outburst. Your parents never have to know what you did. They would be so ashamed, and I don't want that.
Today can be our secret.

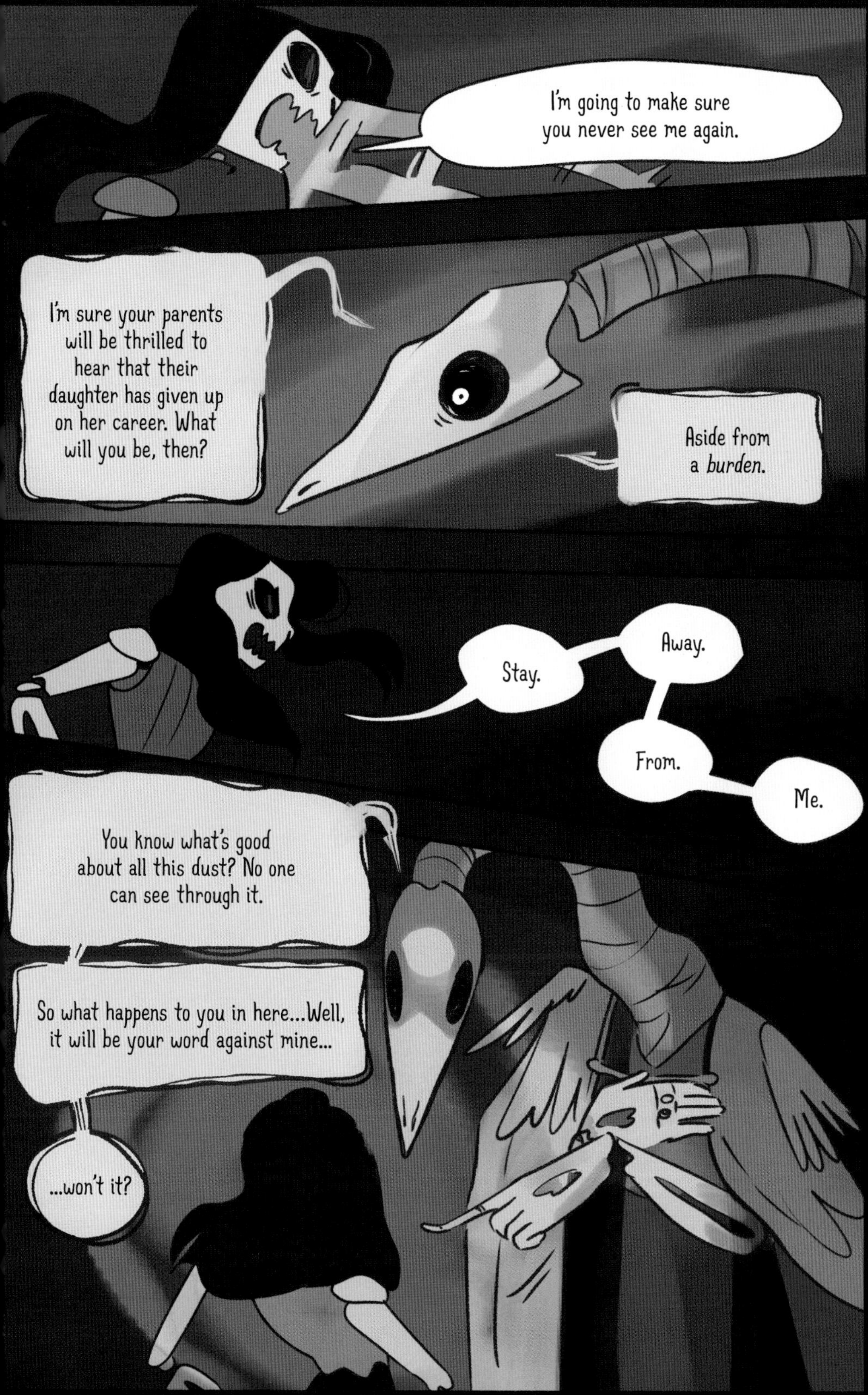
I'm going to make sure you never see me again.
I'm sure your parents will be thrilled to hear that their daughter has given up on her career. What will you be, then?
Aside from a *burden.*
Stay.
Away.
From.
Me.
You know what's good about all this dust? No one can see through it.
So what happens to you in here...Well, it will be your word against mine...
...won't it?

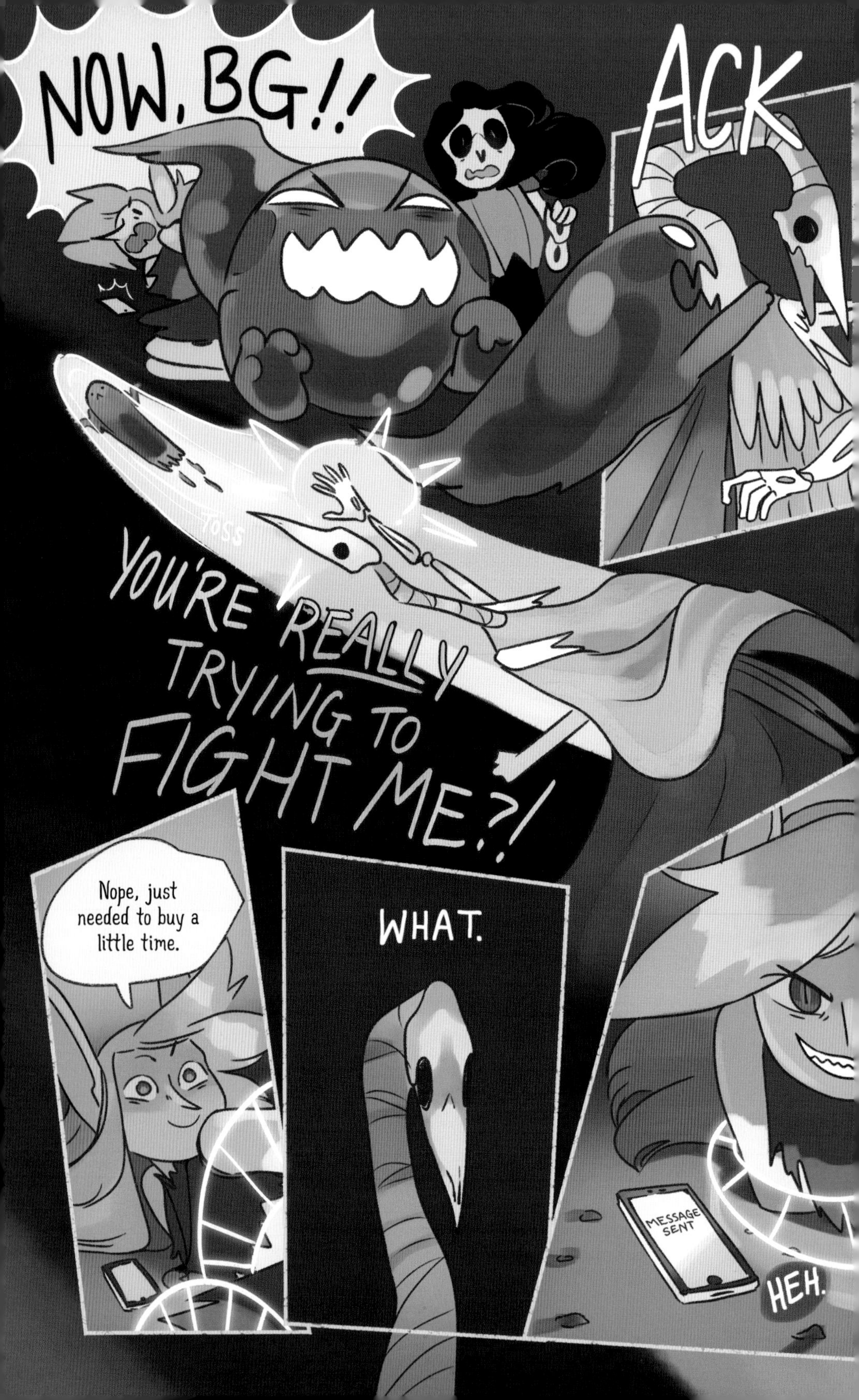
NOW, BG!!
ACK
TOSS
YOU'RE REALLY TRYING TO FIGHT ME?!
Nope, just needed to buy a little time.
WHAT.
MESSAGE SENT
HEH.

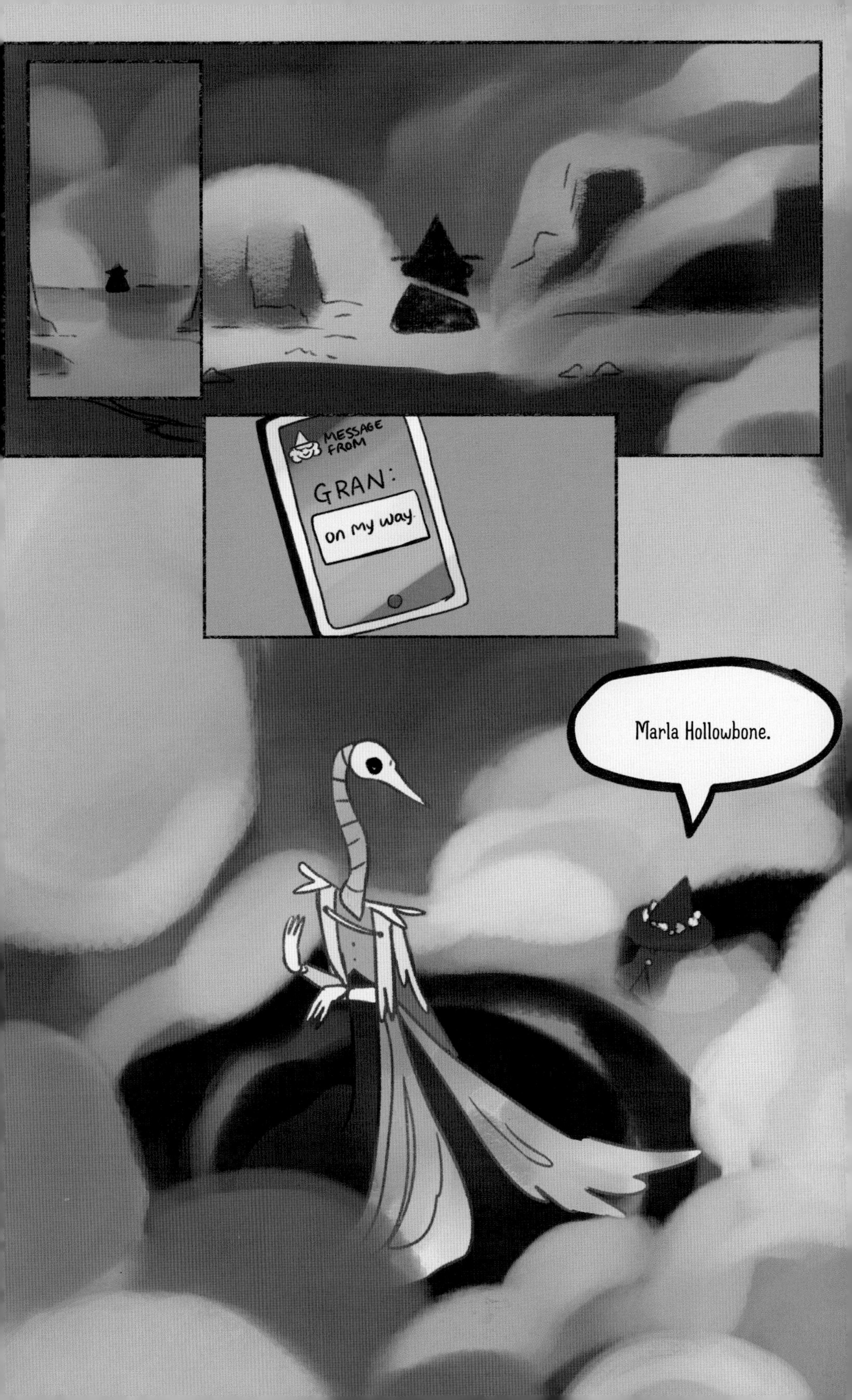
MESSAGE FROM
GRAN:
on my way.
Marla Hollowbone.

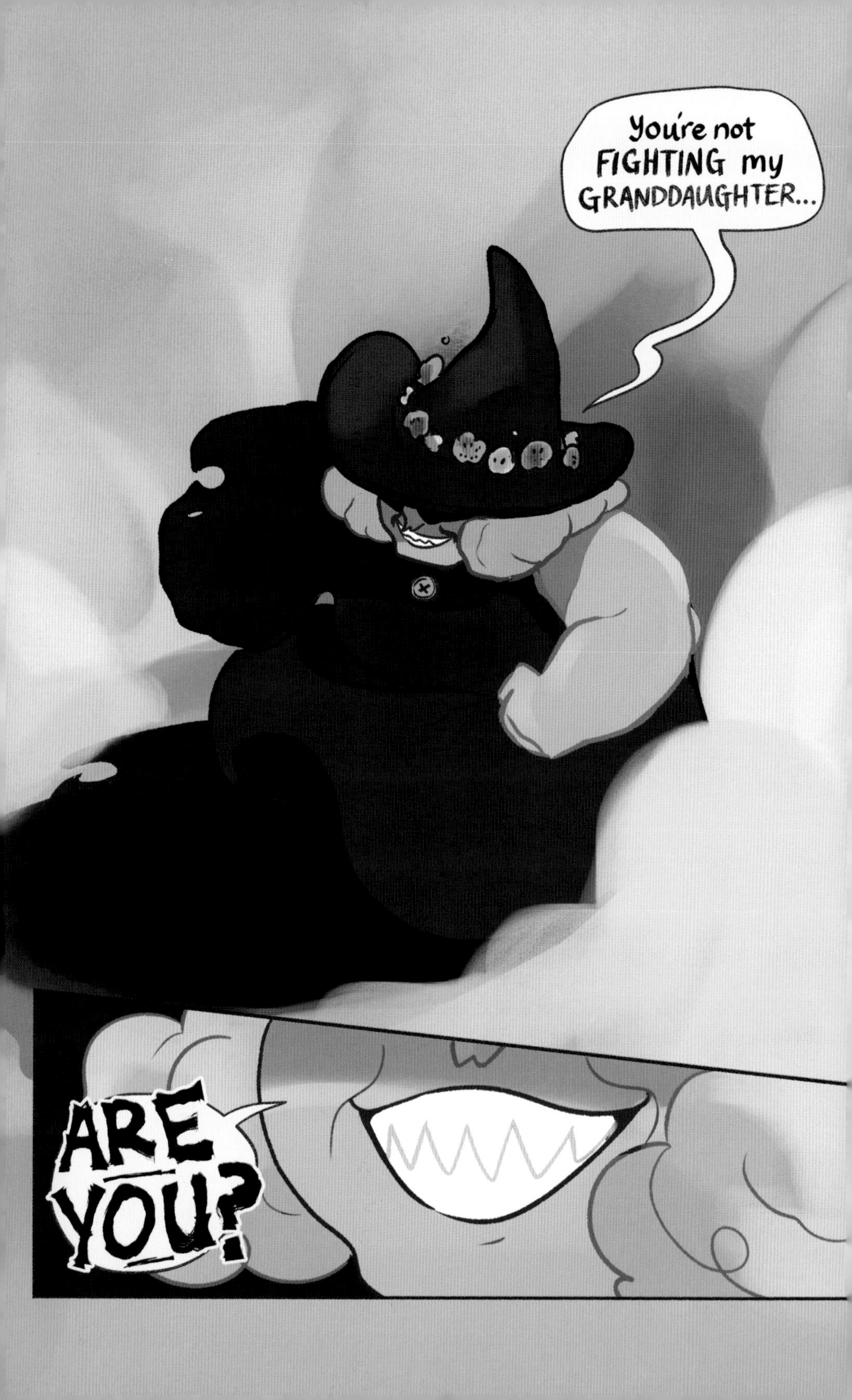
You're not FIGHTING my GRANDDAUGHTER...
ARE YOU?

GOBLIN MAGIC

Run, kids!
CRACK
GOOD LUCK!

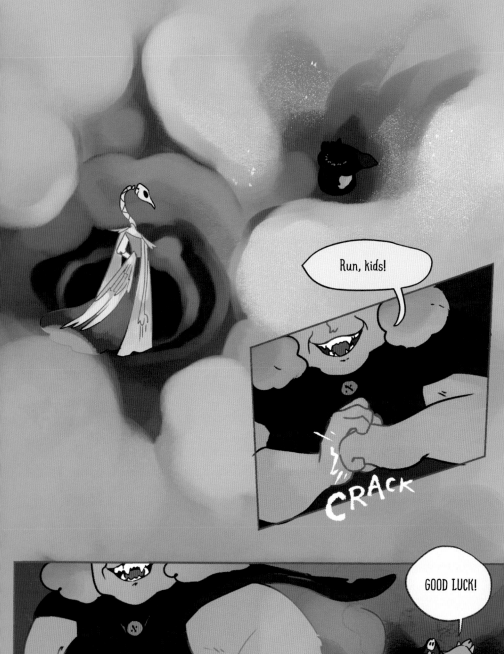

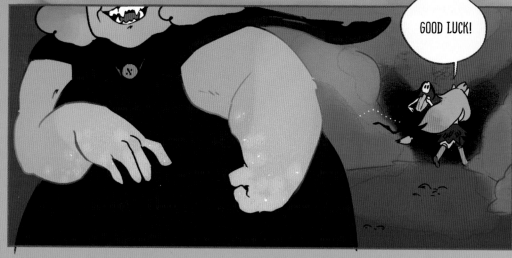

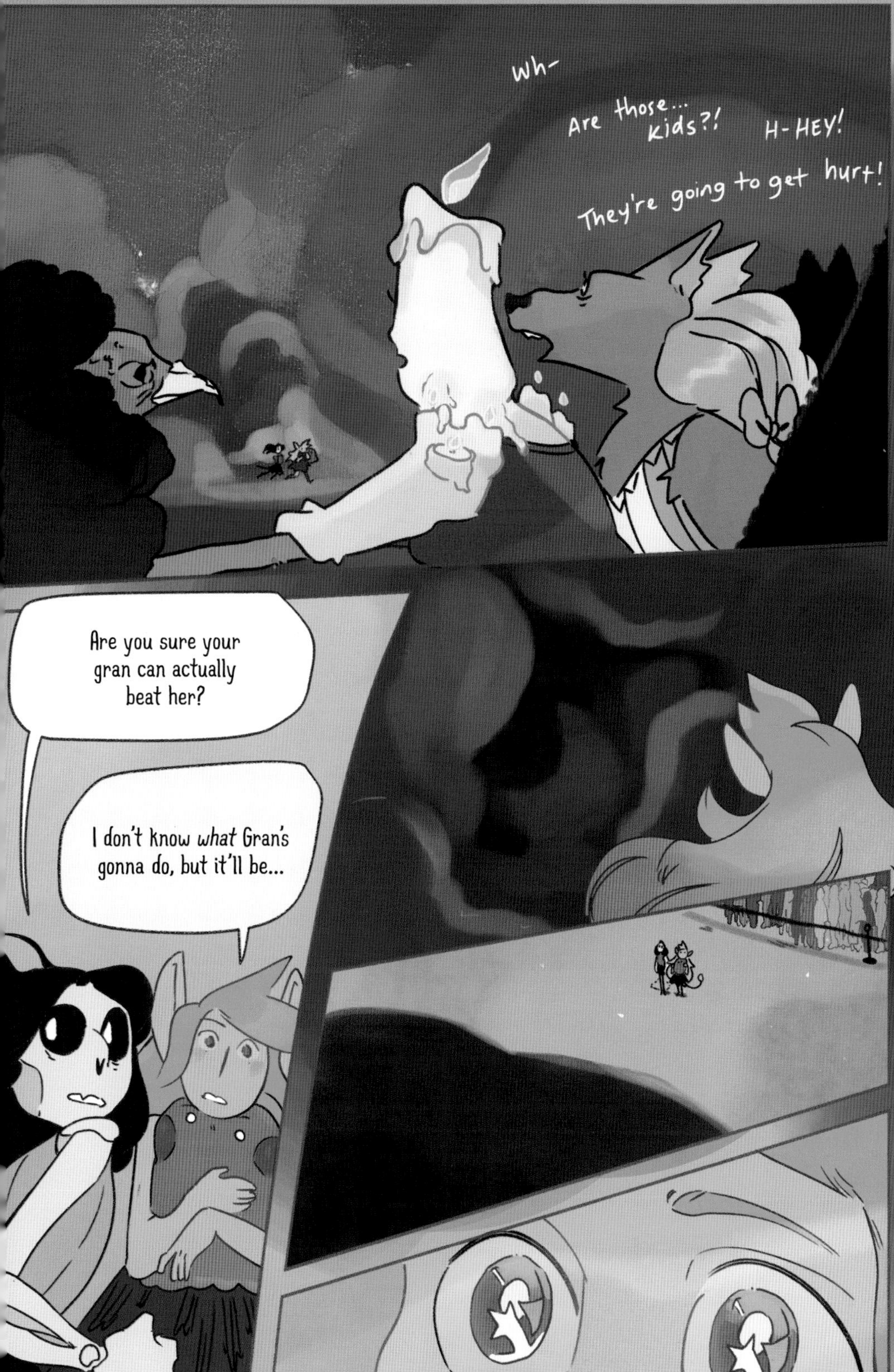
Wh-
Are those... kids?!
H-HEY!
They're going to get hurt!
Are you sure your gran can actually beat her?
I don't know *what* Gran's gonna do, but it'll be...

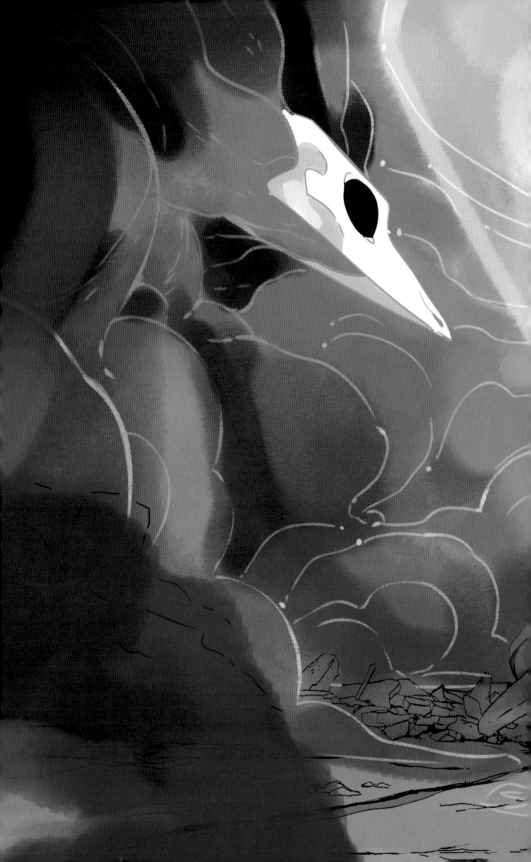

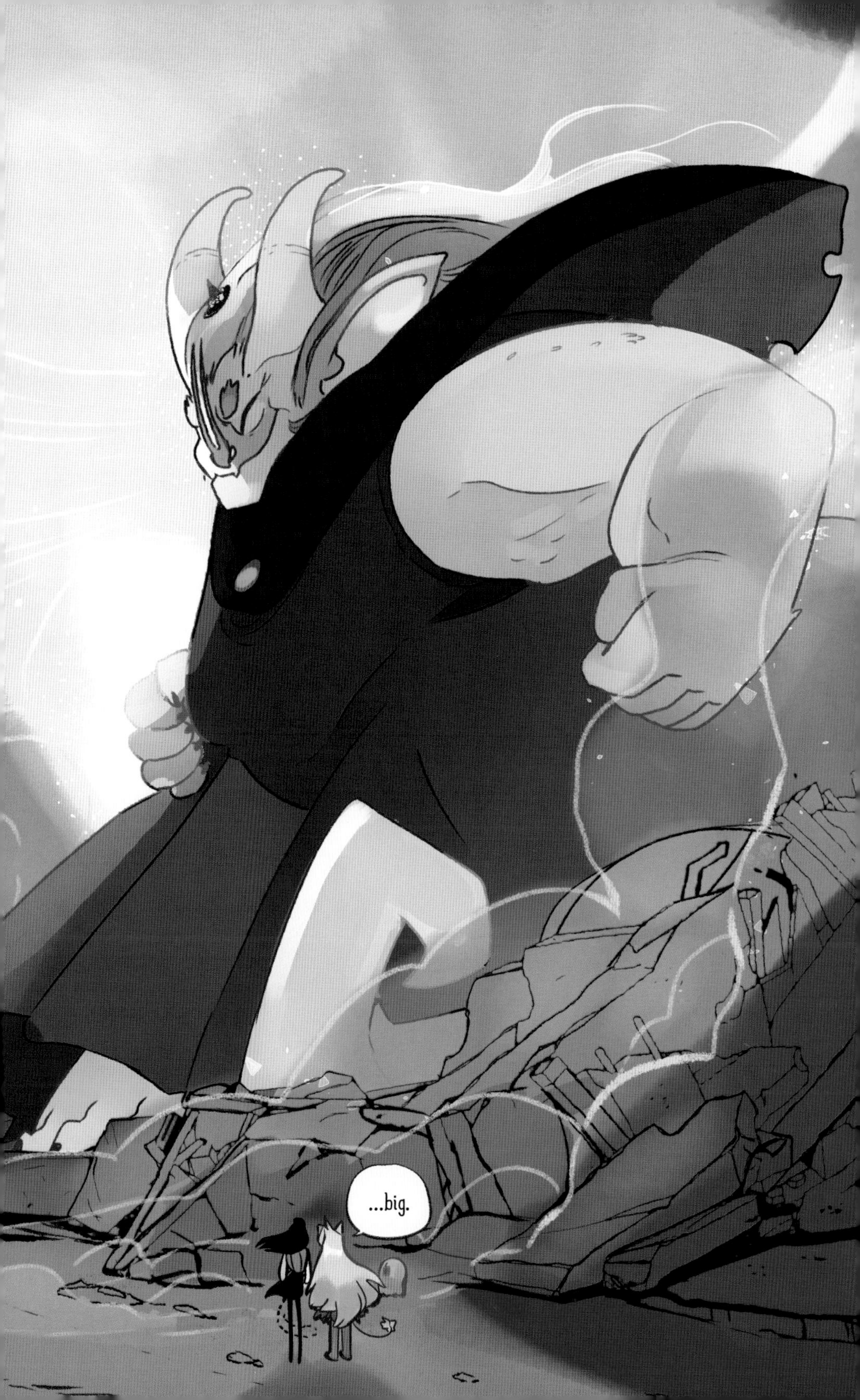
...big.

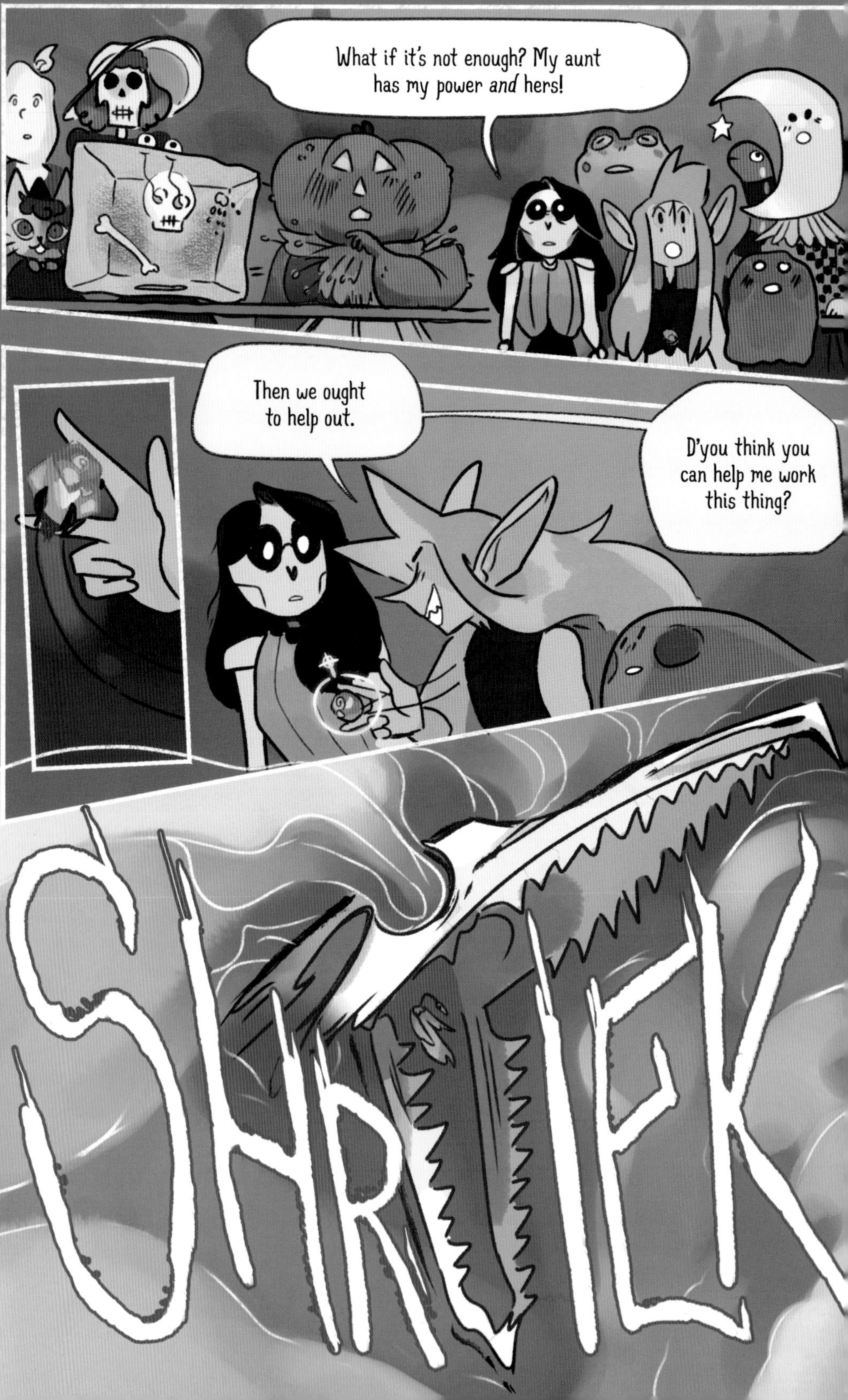
What if it's not enough? My aunt has my power *and* hers!
Then we ought to help out.
D'you think you can help me work this thing?
SHRIEK

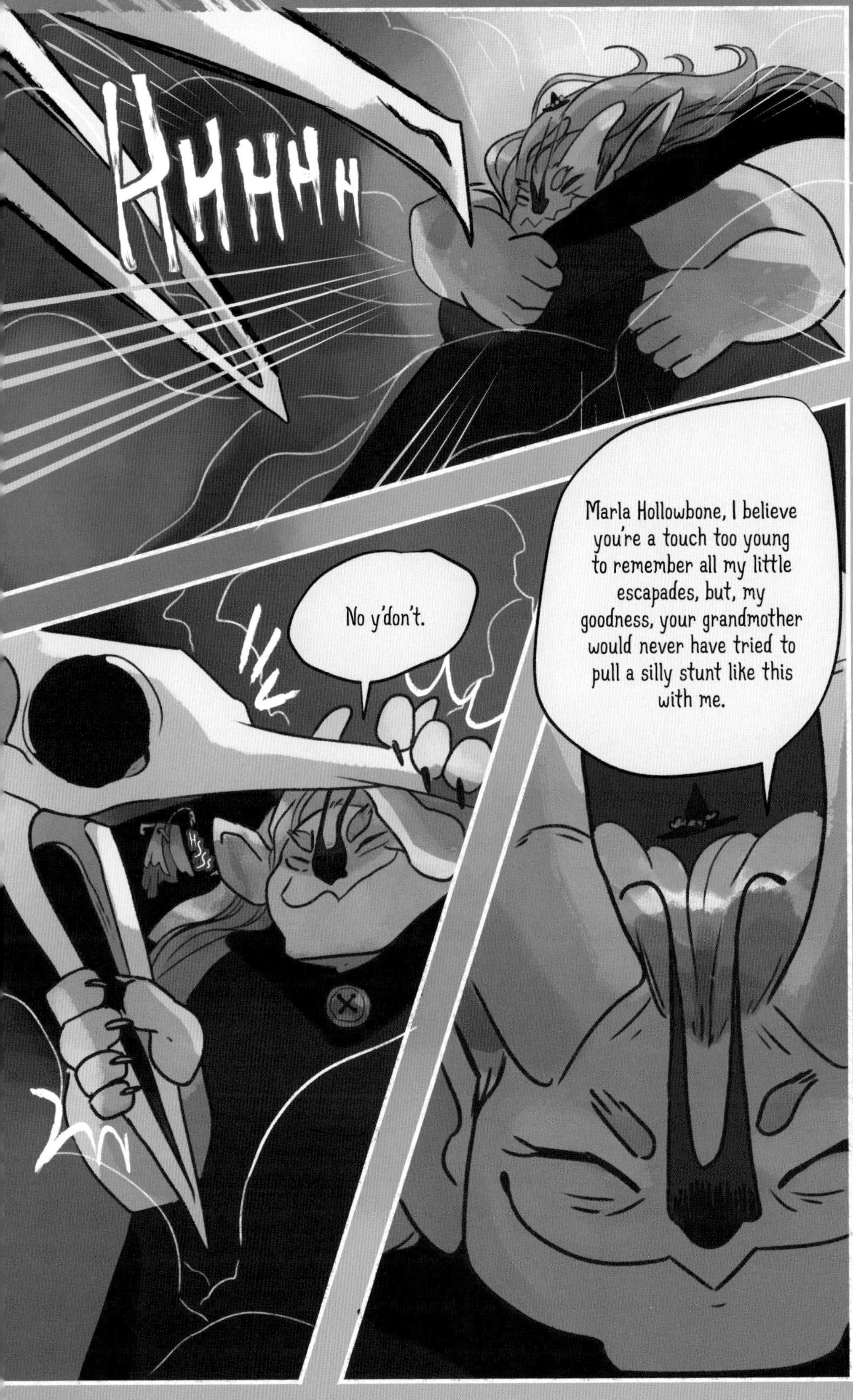
No y'don't.
Marla Hollowbone, I believe you're a touch too young to remember all my little escapades, but, my goodness, your grandmother would never have tried to pull a silly stunt like this with me.

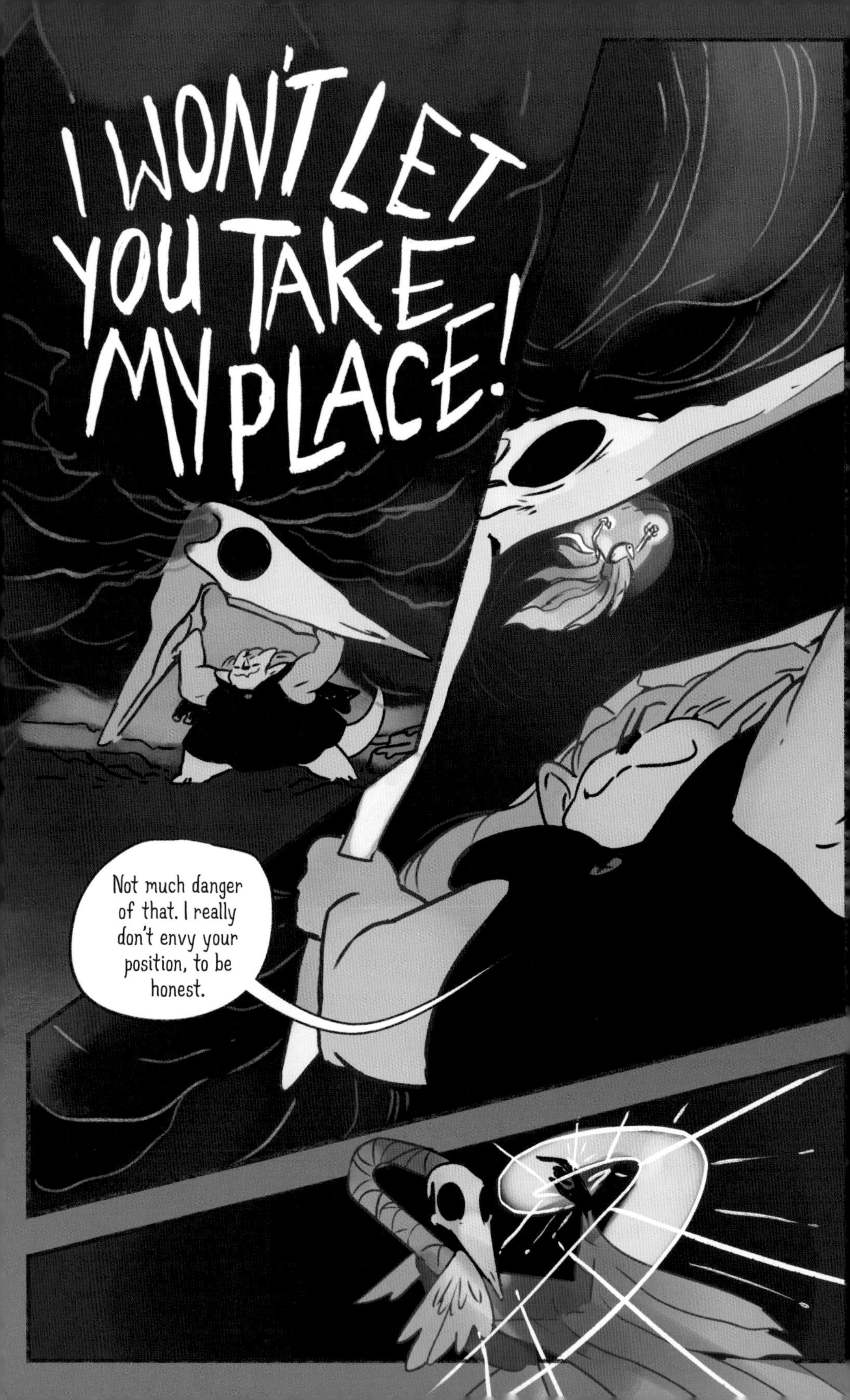
I WON'T LET YOU TAKE MY PLACE!
Not much danger of that. I really don't envy your position, to be honest.

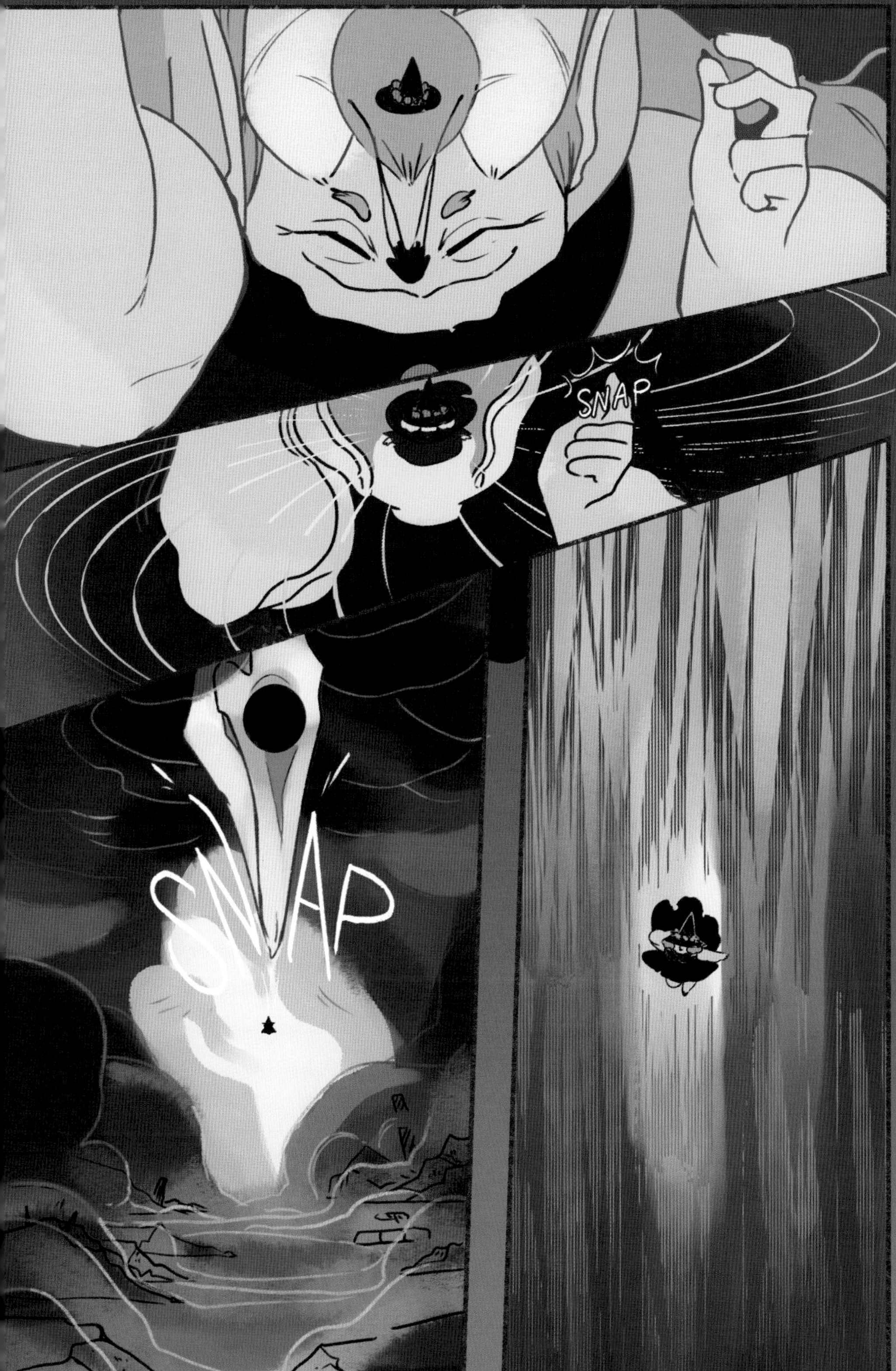
SNAP
SNAP

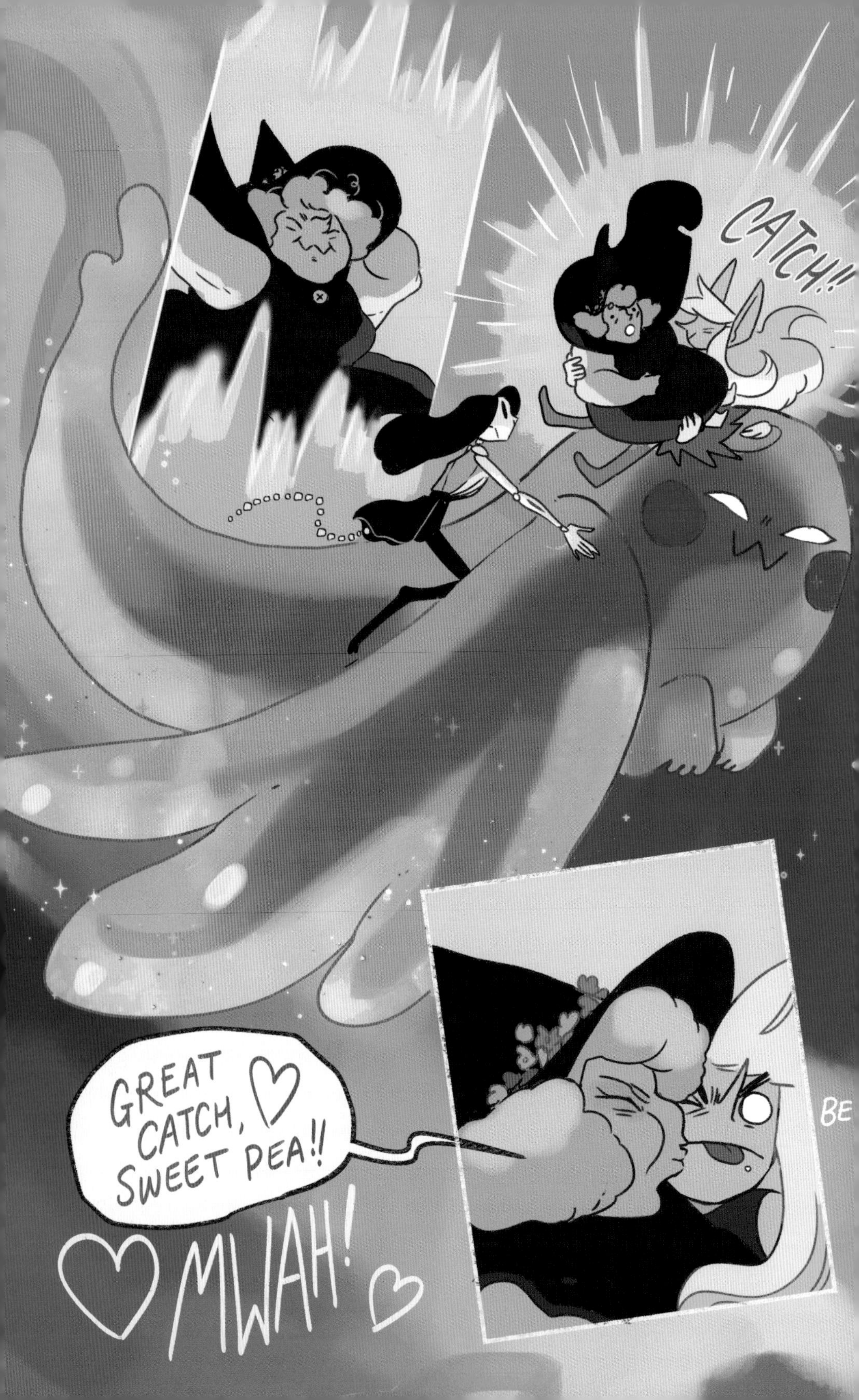
CATCH!!
GREAT CATCH, ♡ SWEET PEA!!
BE
♡ MWAH! ♡

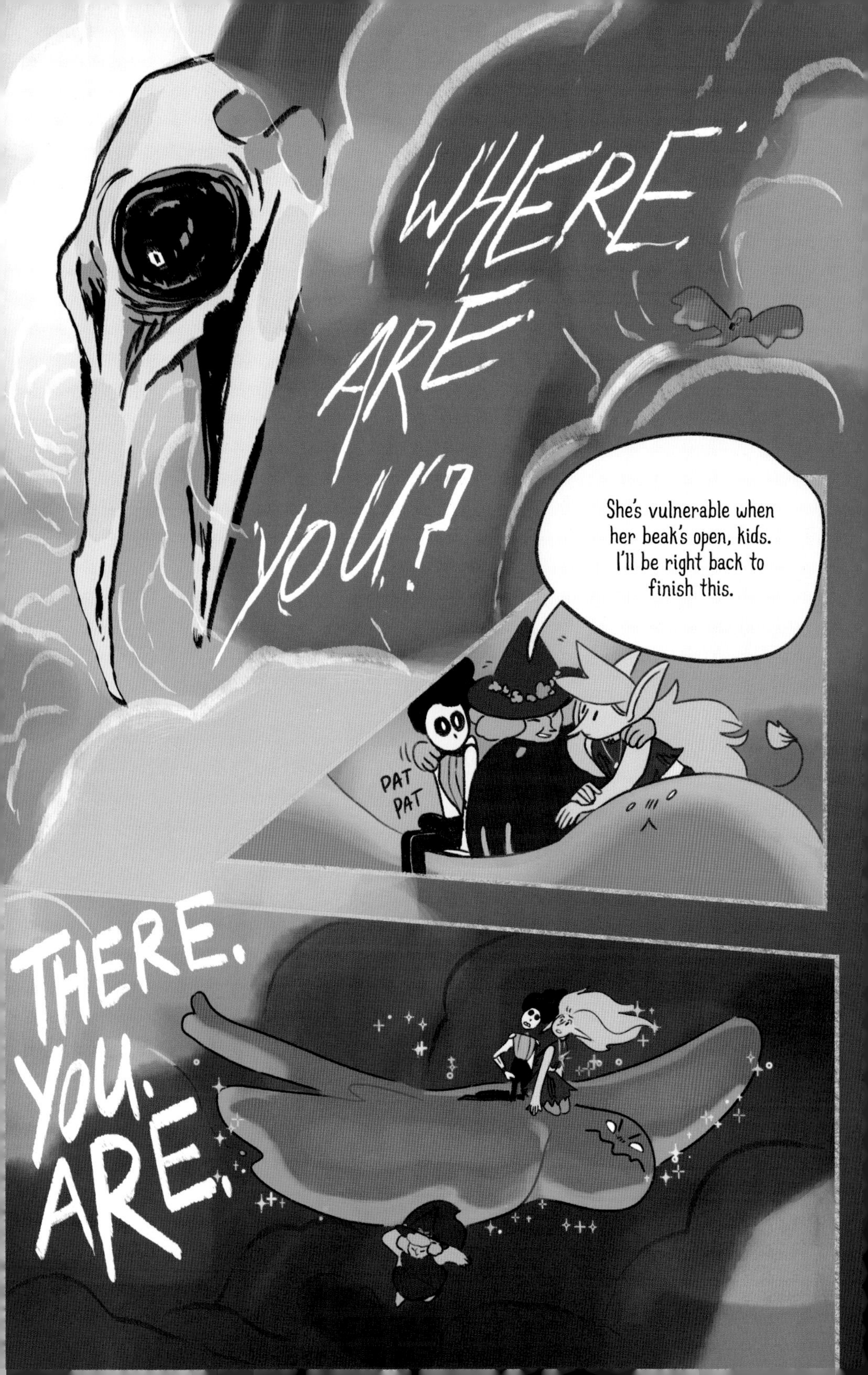
WHERE ARE YOU?
She's vulnerable when her beak's open, kids. I'll be right back to finish this.
PAT PAT
THERE. YOU. ARE.

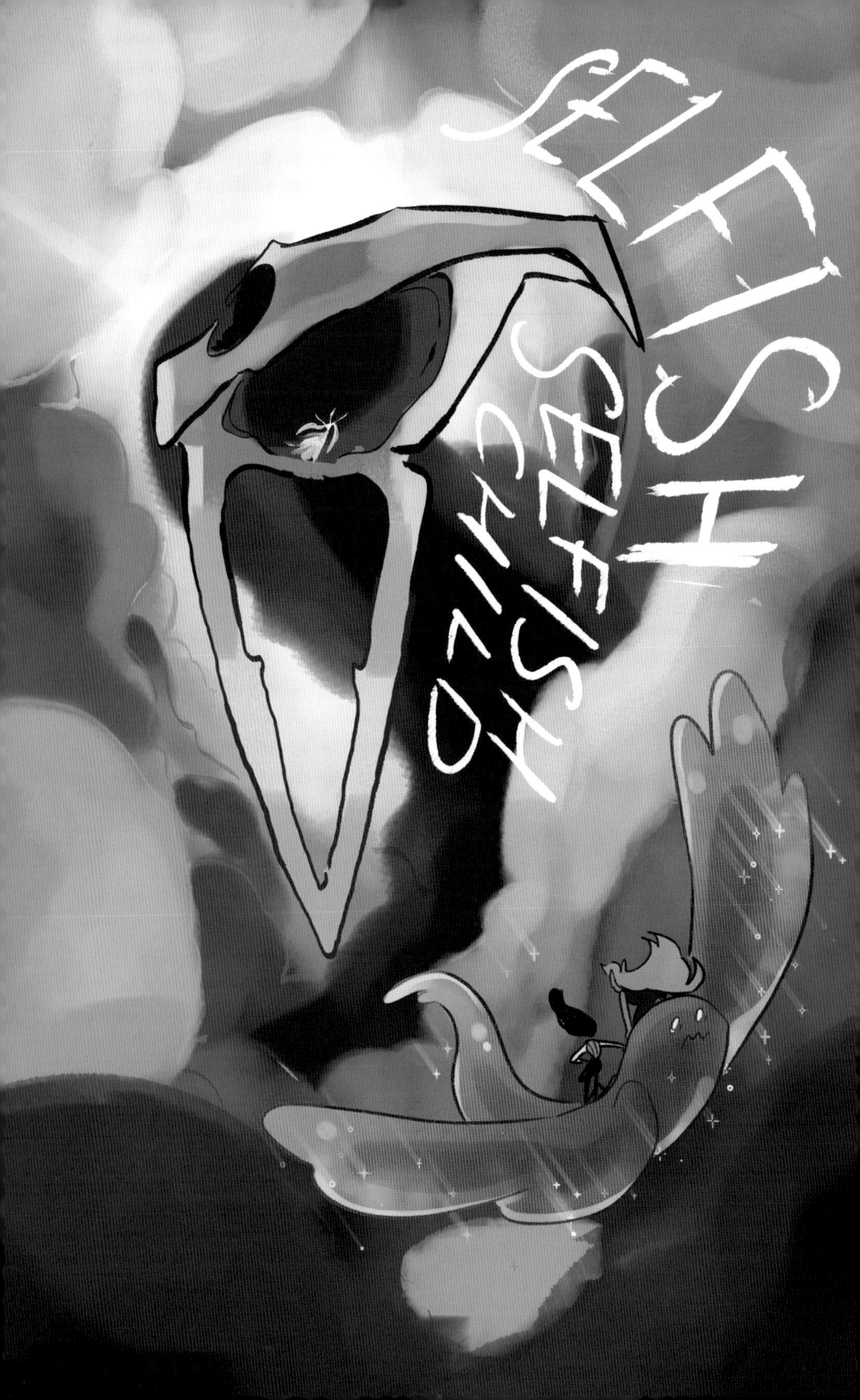
SELFISH
SELFISH
CHILD

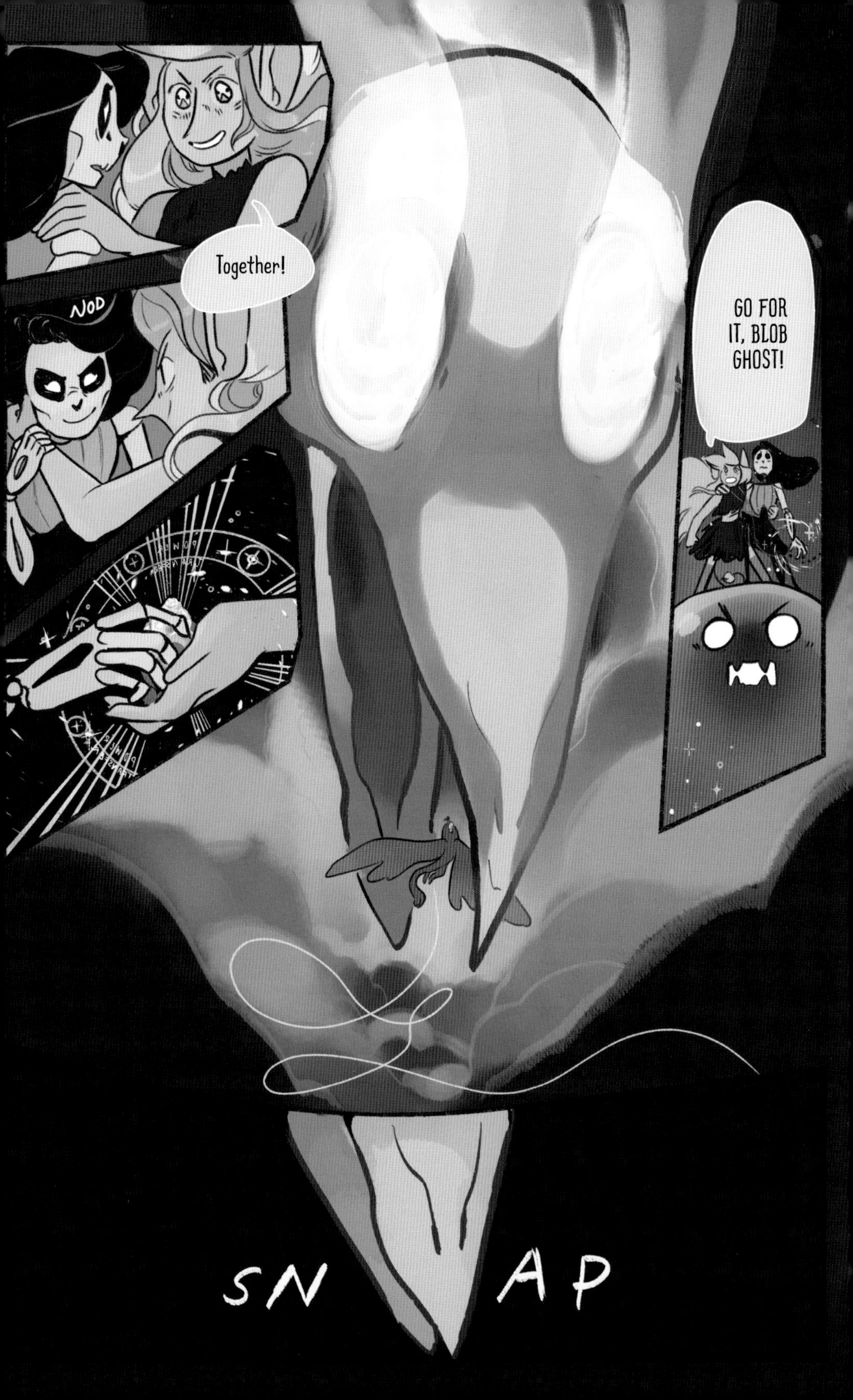

Together!
NOD
GO FOR IT, BLOB GHOST!
SN AP

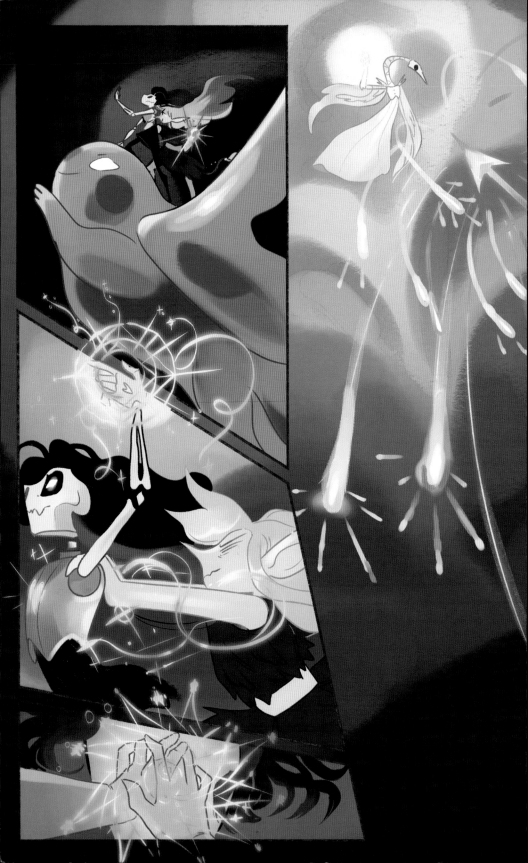

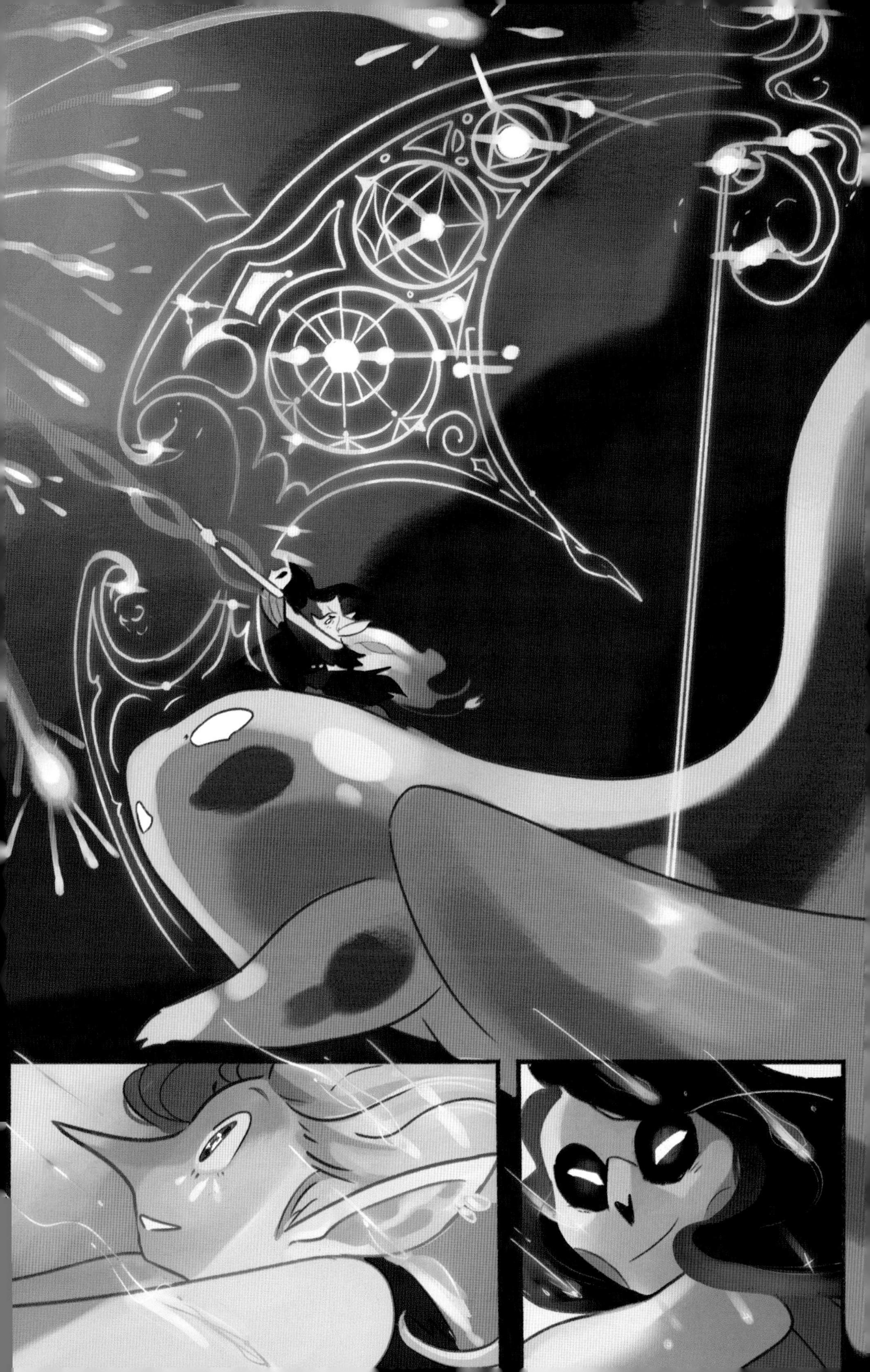

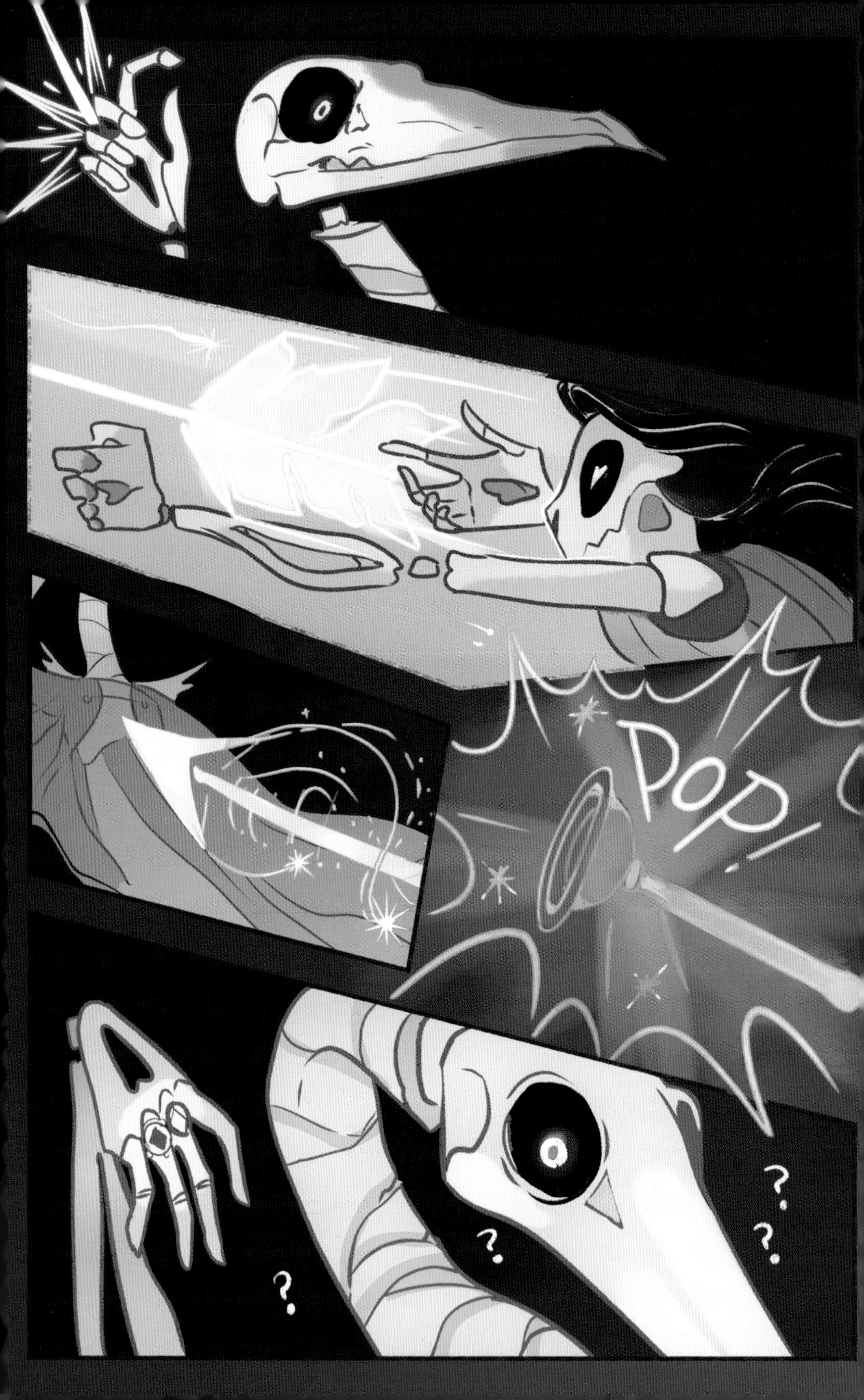
POP!!
?
?
?
?
?

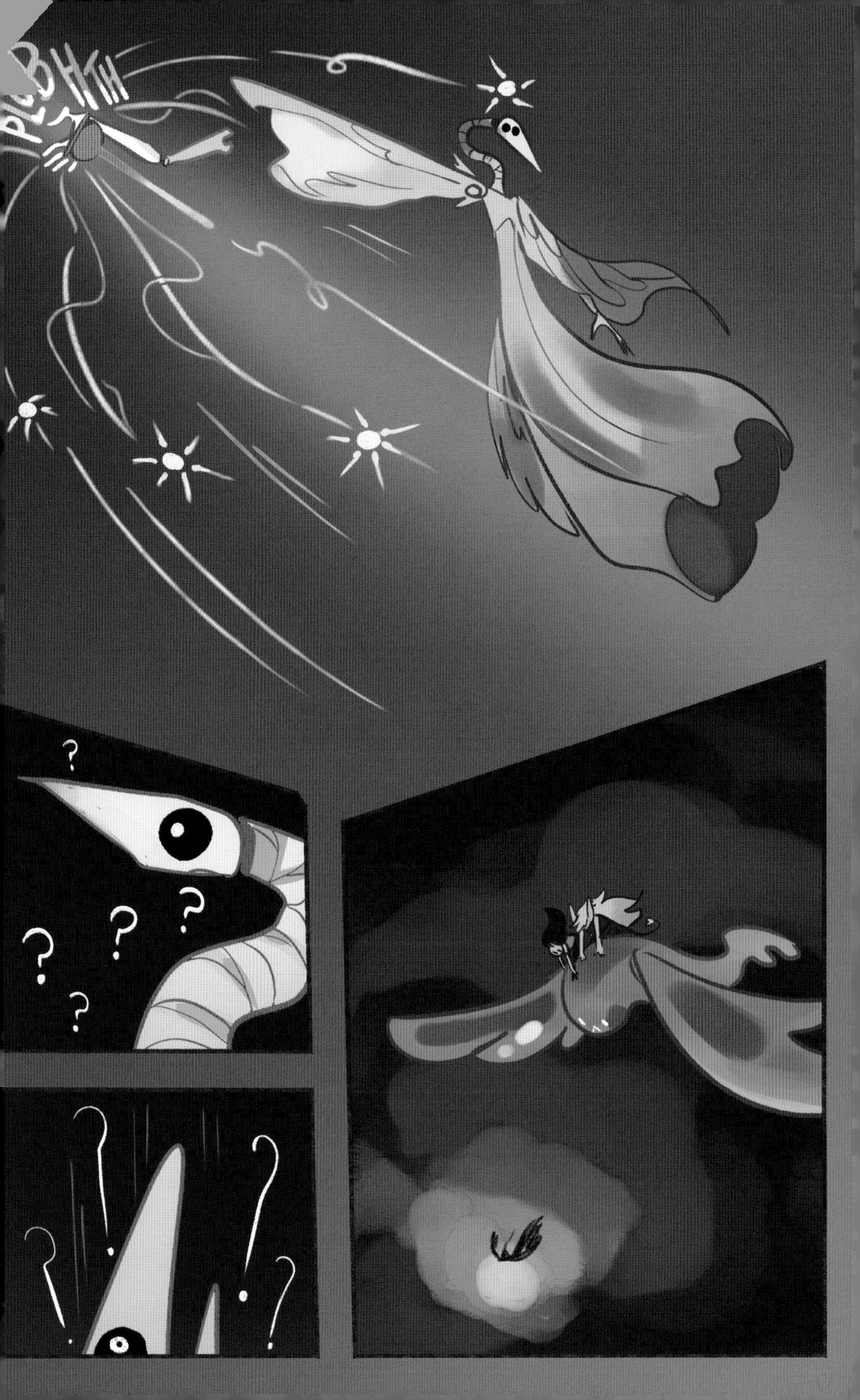

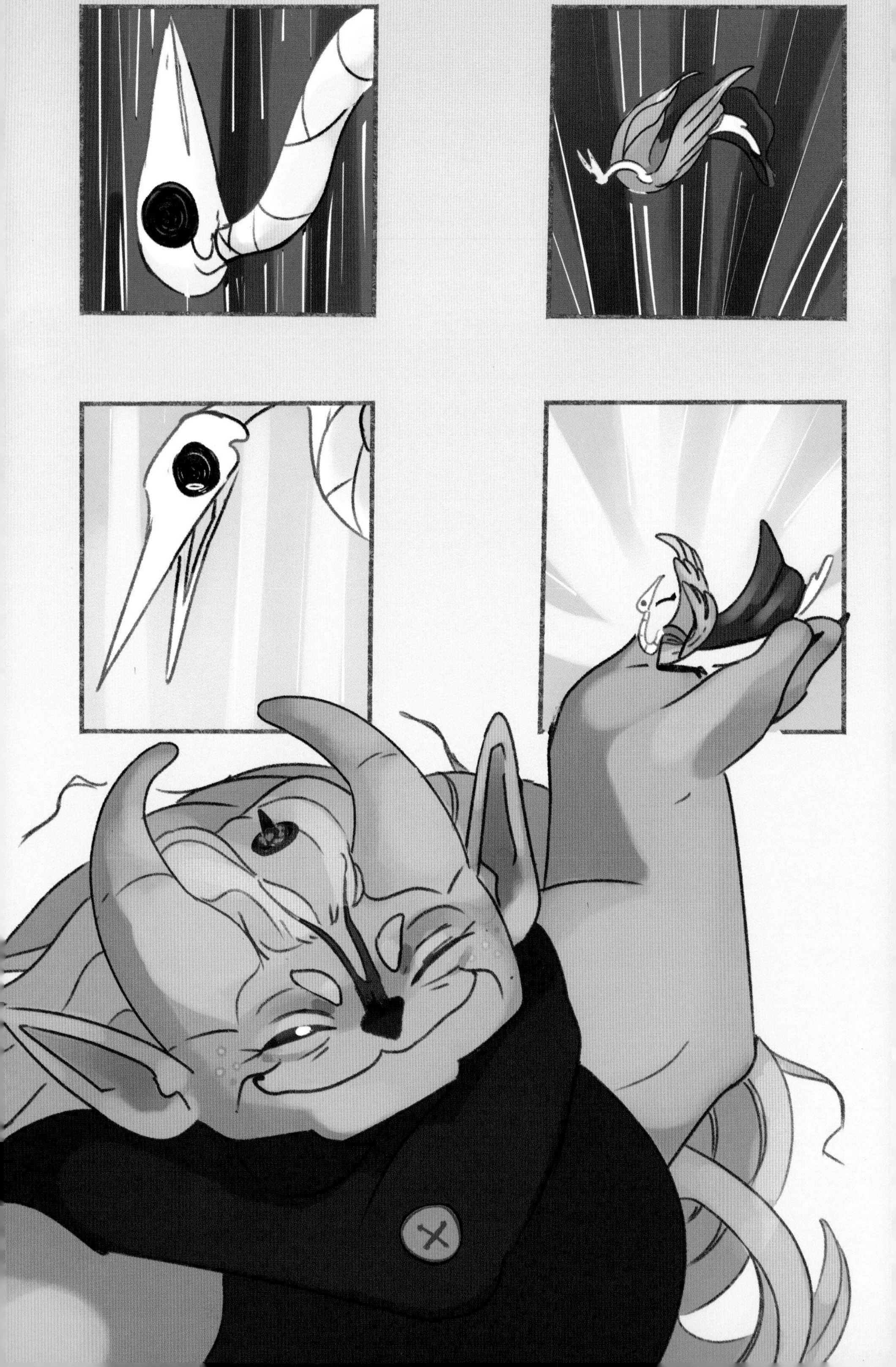

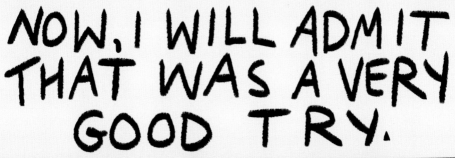

NOW, I WILL ADMIT THAT WAS A VERY GOOD TRY.

THE COUNCIL WILL HEAR ABOUT THIS!

That's them now, as a matter of fact.

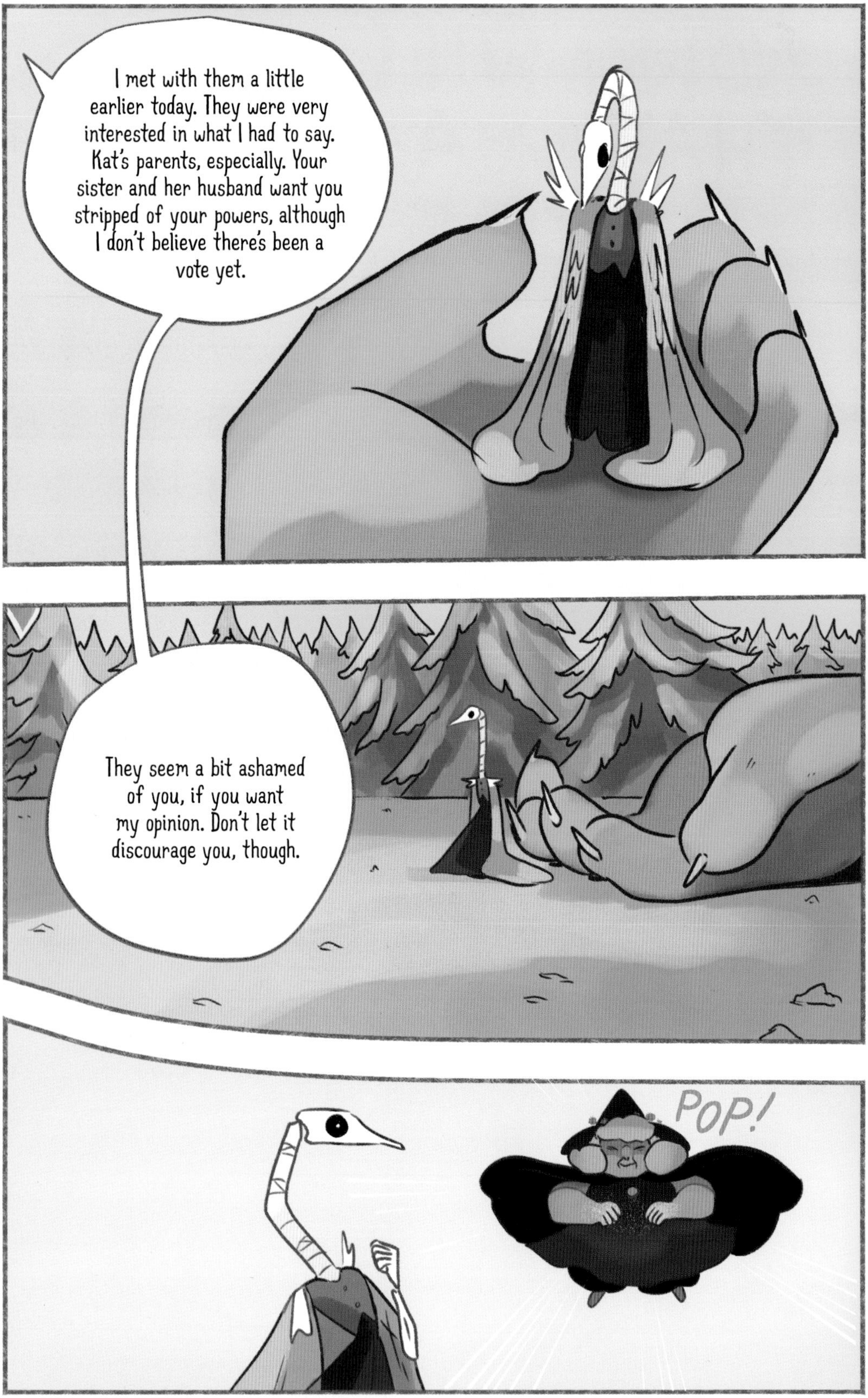
I met with them a little earlier today. They were very interested in what I had to say. Kat's parents, especially. Your sister and her husband want you stripped of your powers, although I don't believe there's been a vote yet.
They seem a bit ashamed of you, if you want my opinion. Don't let it discourage you, though.
POP!

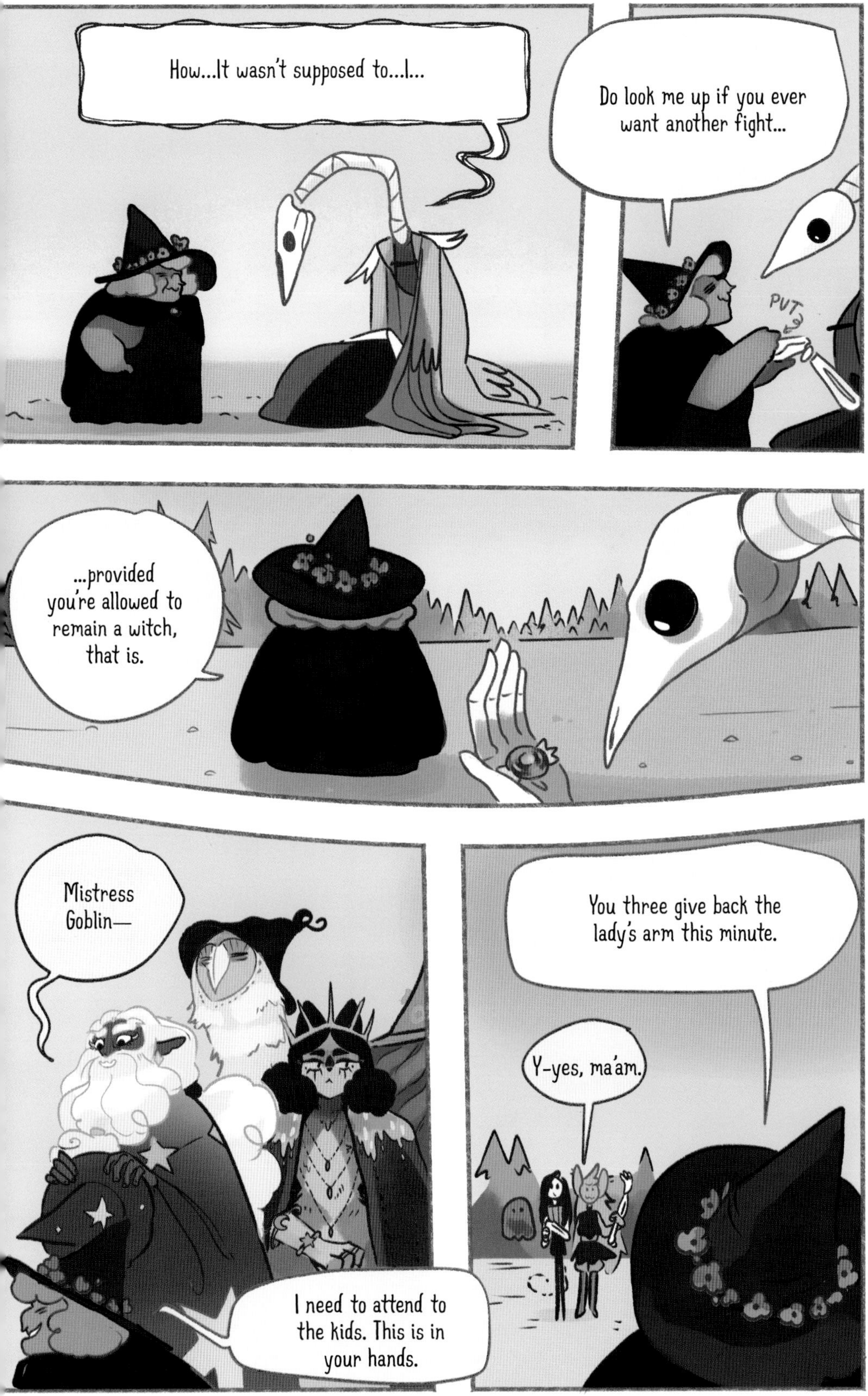
How...It wasn't supposed to...I...
Do look me up if you ever want another fight...
PUT
...provided you're allowed to remain a witch, that is.
Mistress Goblin—
I need to attend to the kids. This is in your hands.
You three give back the lady's arm this minute.
Y-yes, ma'am.

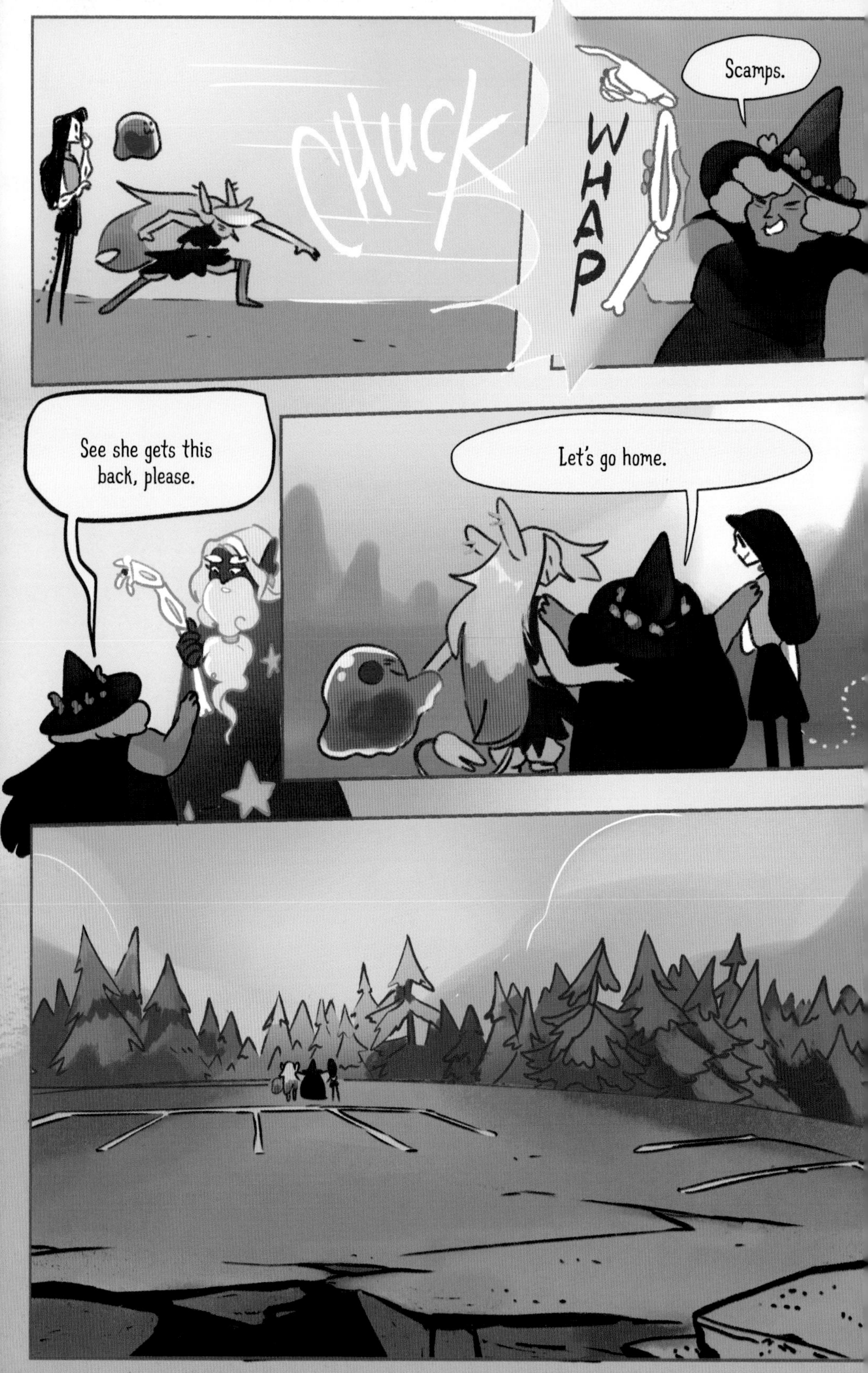
CHUCK
WHAP
Scamps.
See she gets this back, please.
Let's go home.

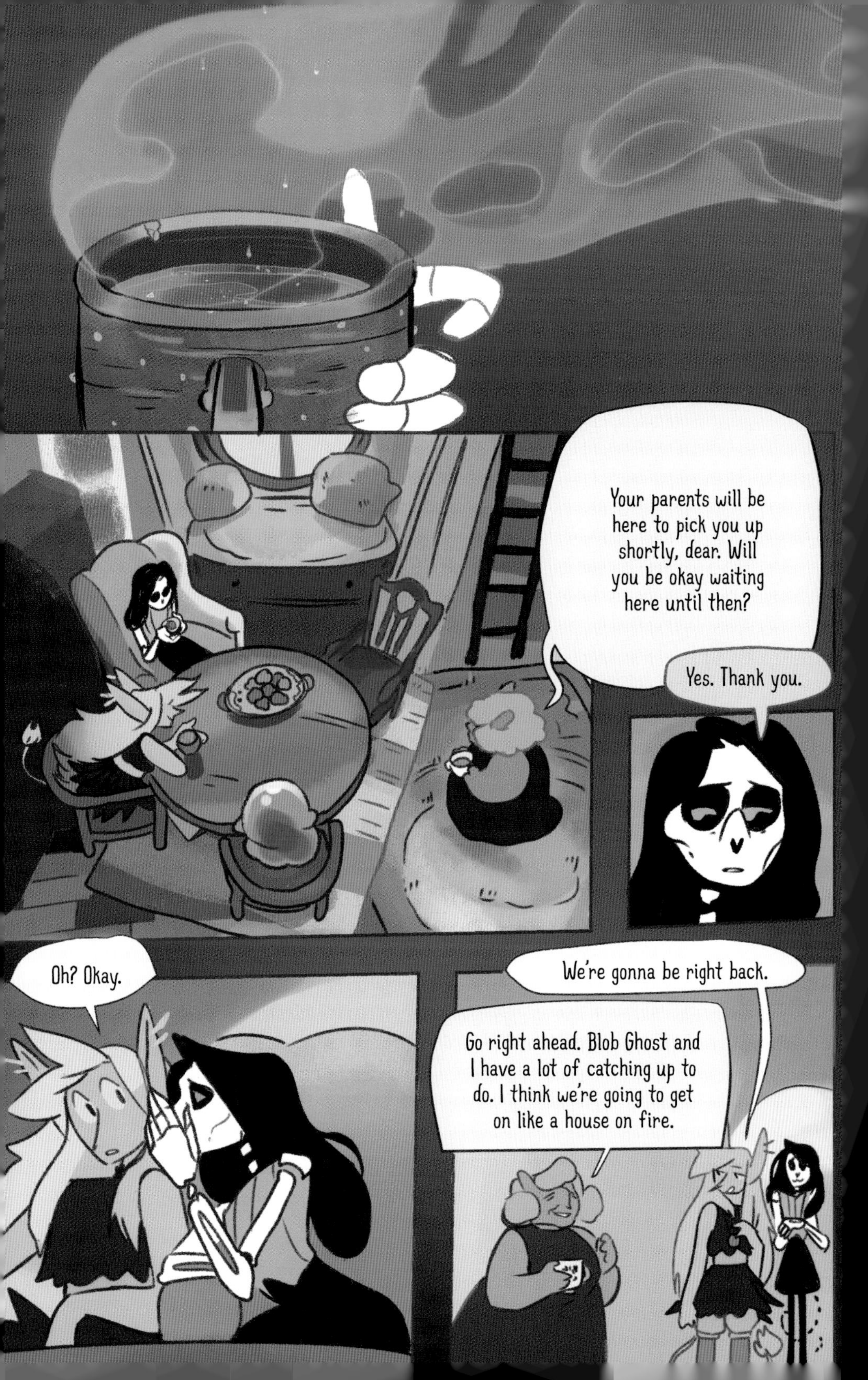
Your parents will be here to pick you up shortly, dear. Will you be okay waiting here until then?
Yes. Thank you.
Oh? Okay.
We're gonna be right back.
Go right ahead. Blob Ghost and I have a lot of catching up to do. I think we're going to get on like a house on fire.

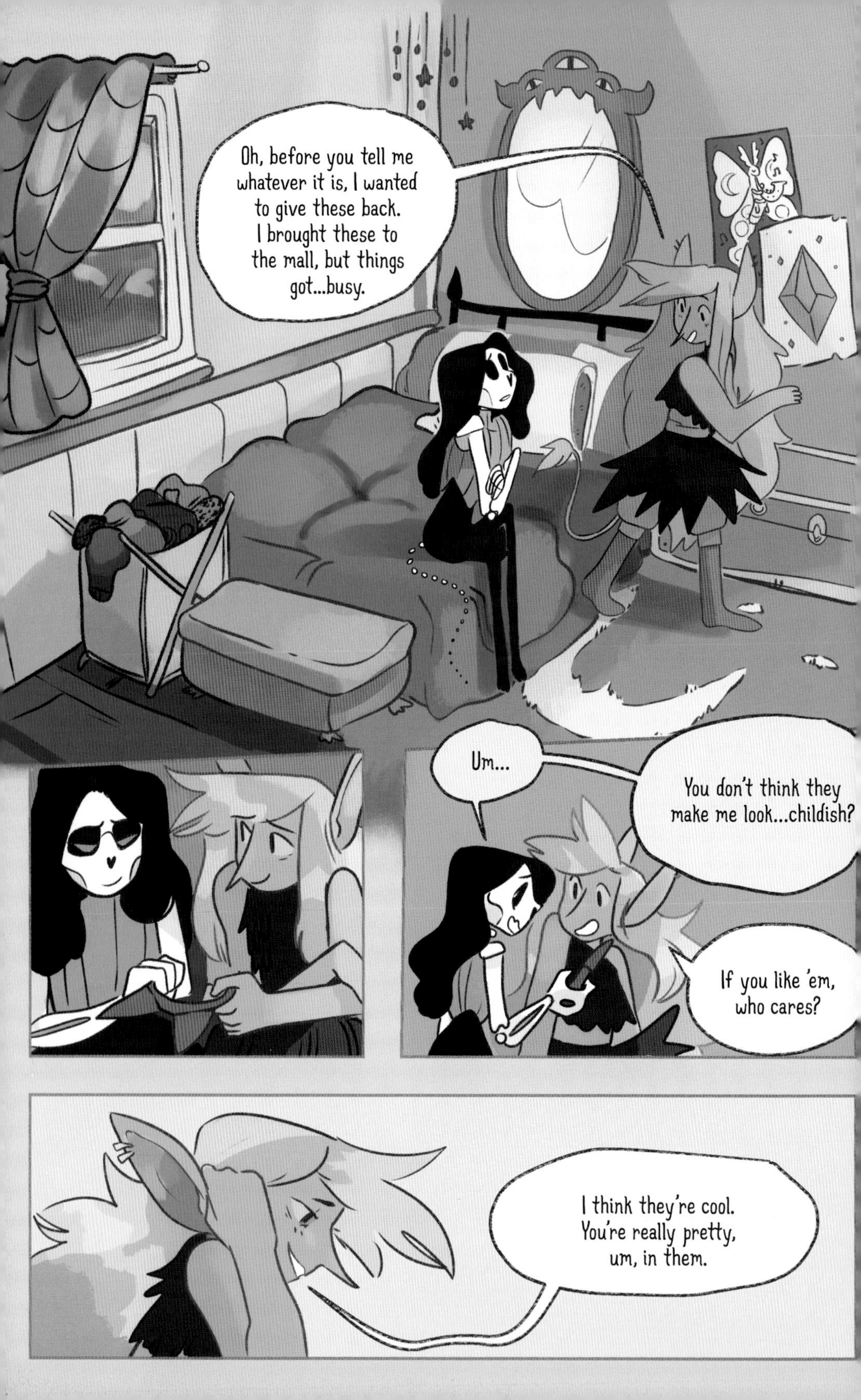
Oh, before you tell me whatever it is, I wanted to give these back. I brought these to the mall, but things got...busy.
Um...
You don't think they make me look...childish?
If you like 'em, who cares?
I think they're cool. You're really pretty, um, in them.

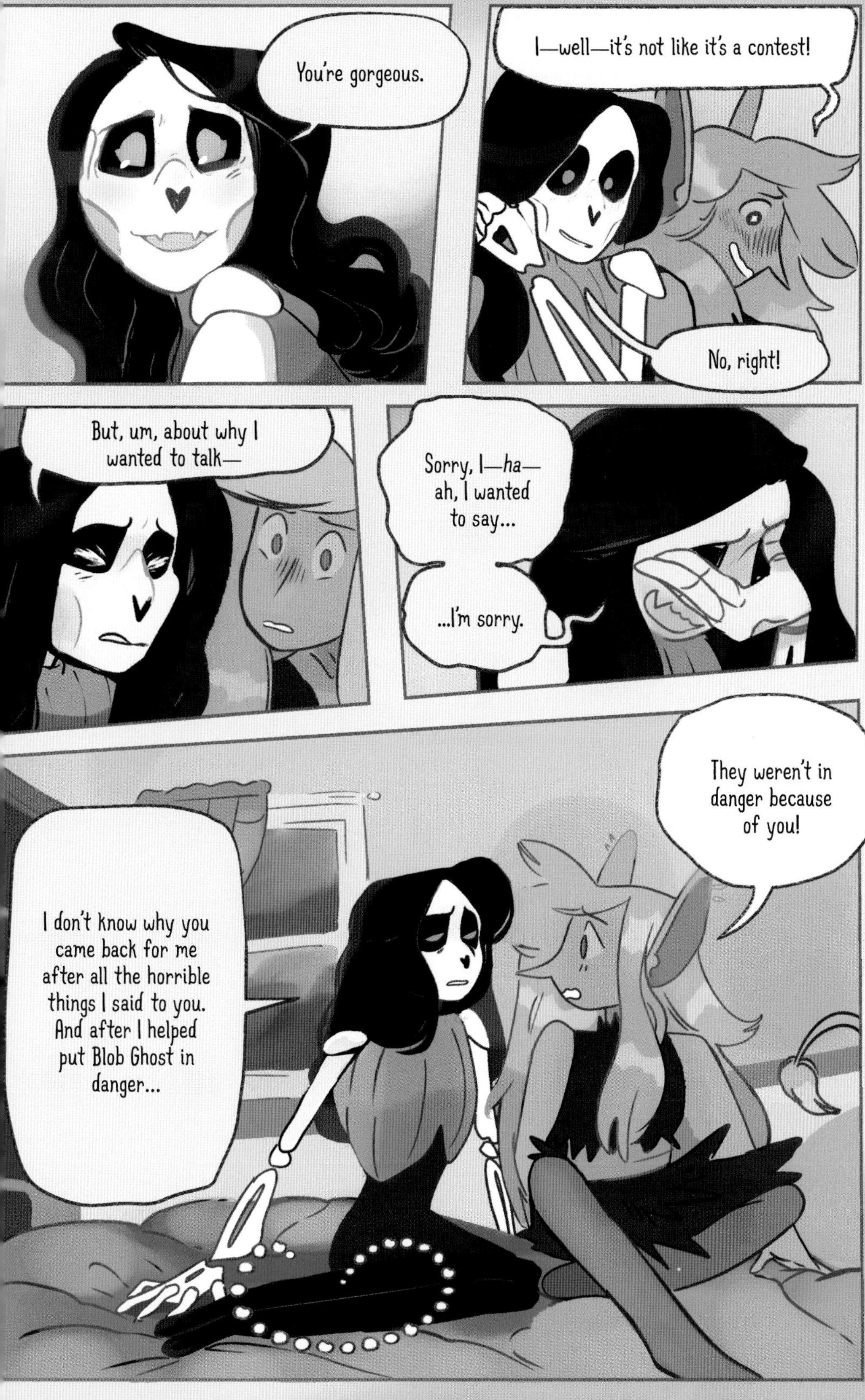
You're gorgeous.
I—well—it's not like it's a contest!
No, right!
But, um, about why I wanted to talk—
Sorry, I—*ha*—ah, I wanted to say...
...I'm sorry.
I don't know why you came back for me after all the horrible things I said to you. And after I helped put Blob Ghost in danger...
They weren't in danger because of you!

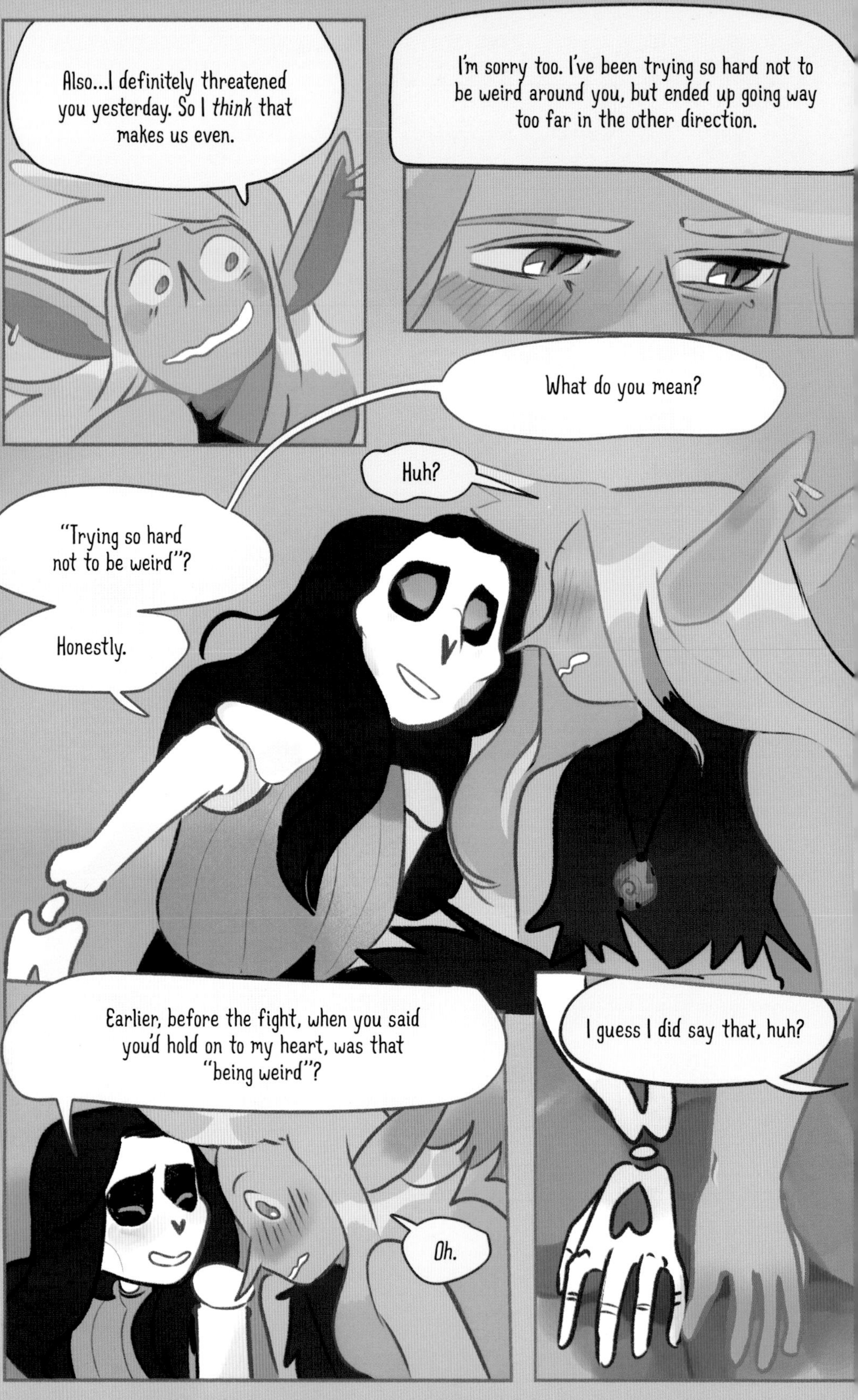
Also...I definitely threatened you yesterday. So I *think* that makes us even.
I'm sorry too. I've been trying so hard not to be weird around you, but ended up going way too far in the other direction.
What do you mean?
Huh?
"Trying so hard not to be weird"?
Honestly.
Earlier, before the fight, when you said you'd hold on to my heart, was that "being weird"?
Oh.
I guess I did say that, huh?

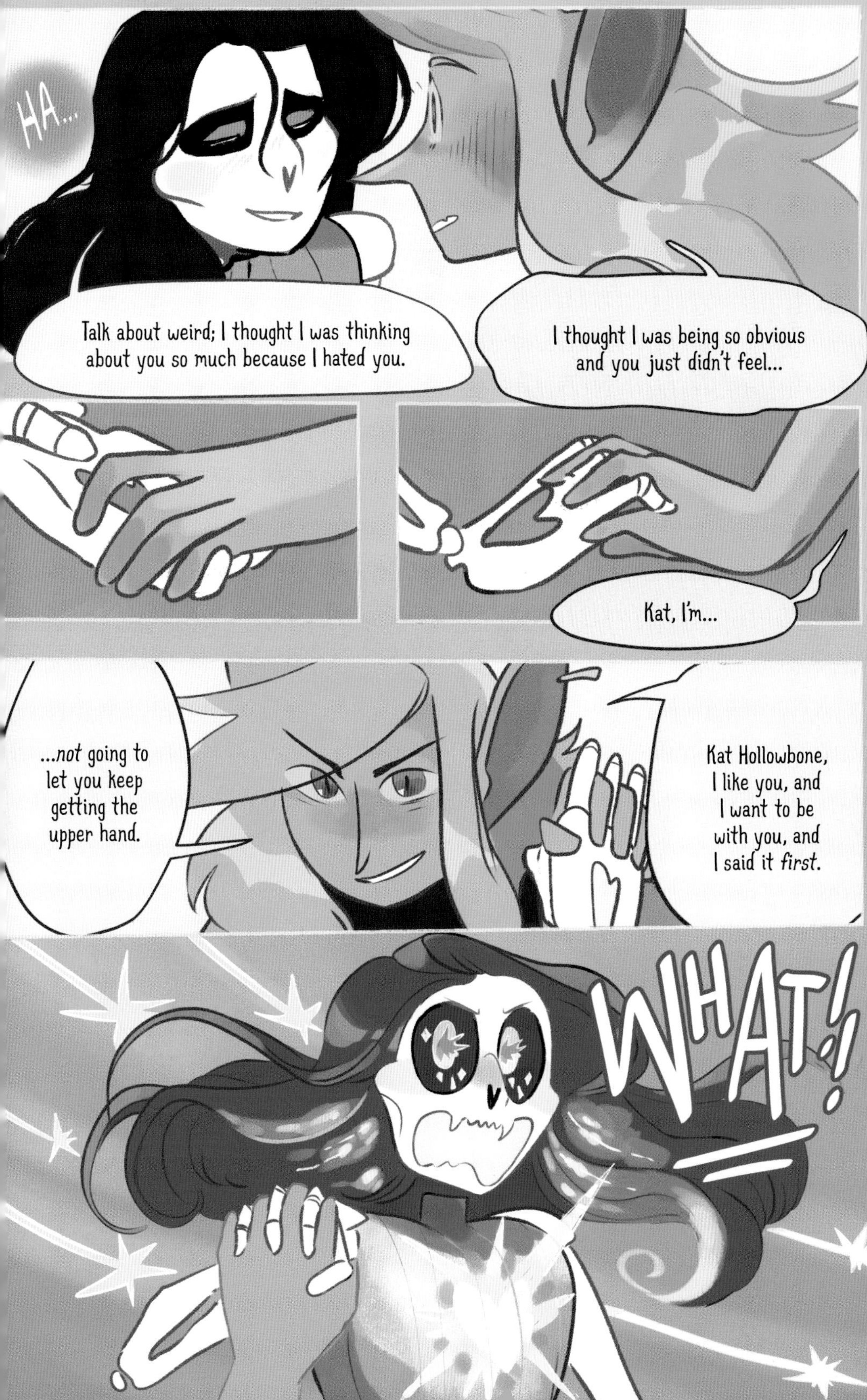
HA...
Talk about weird; I thought I was thinking about you so much because I hated you.
I thought I was being so obvious and you just didn't feel...
Kat, I'm...
...*not* going to let you keep getting the upper hand.
Kat Hollowbone, I like you, and I want to be with you, and I said it *first*.
WHAT!?

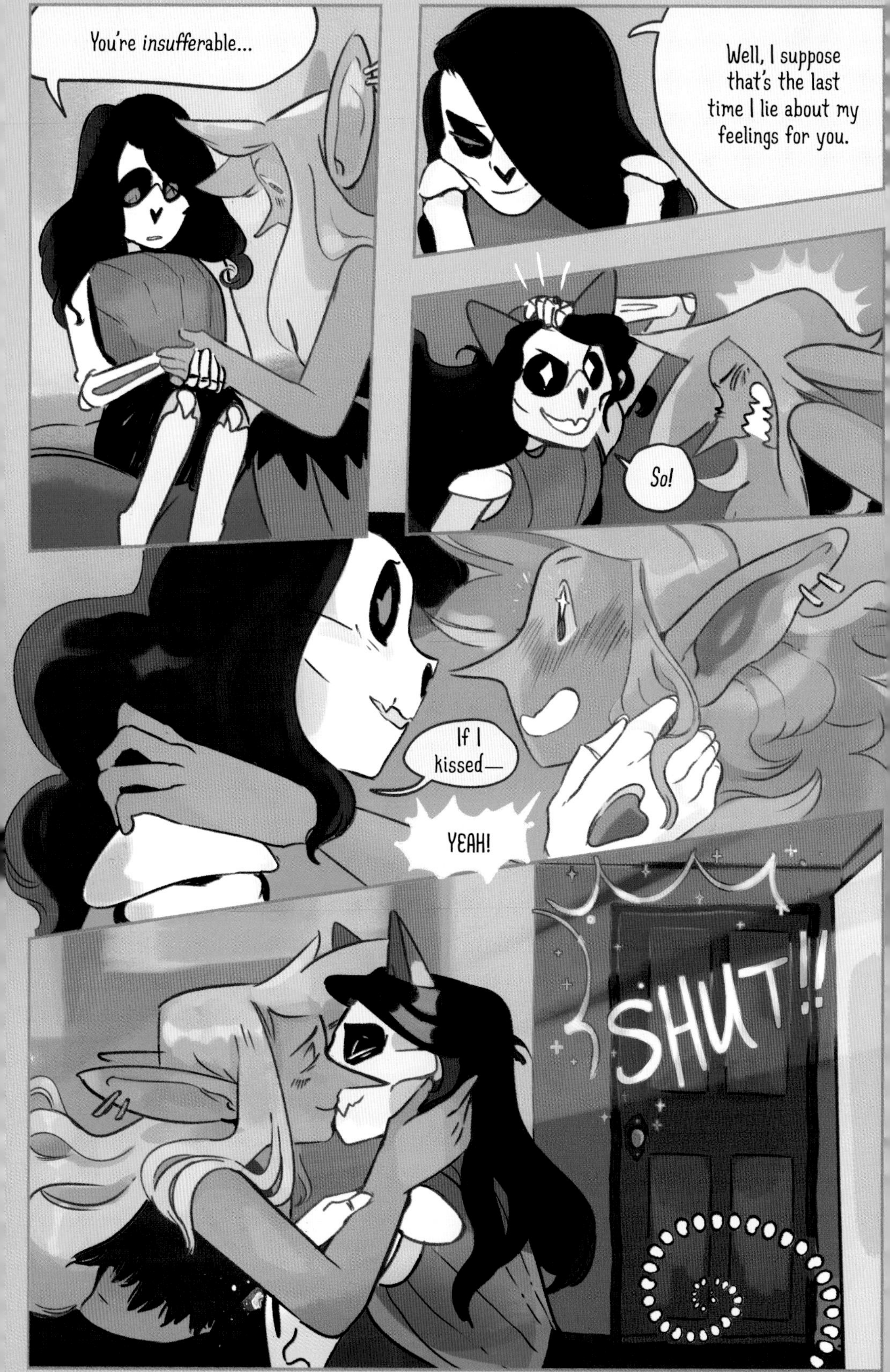
You're *insufferable*...
Well, I suppose that's the last time I lie about my feelings for you.
So!
If I kissed—
YEAH!
SHUT!!

PENNY

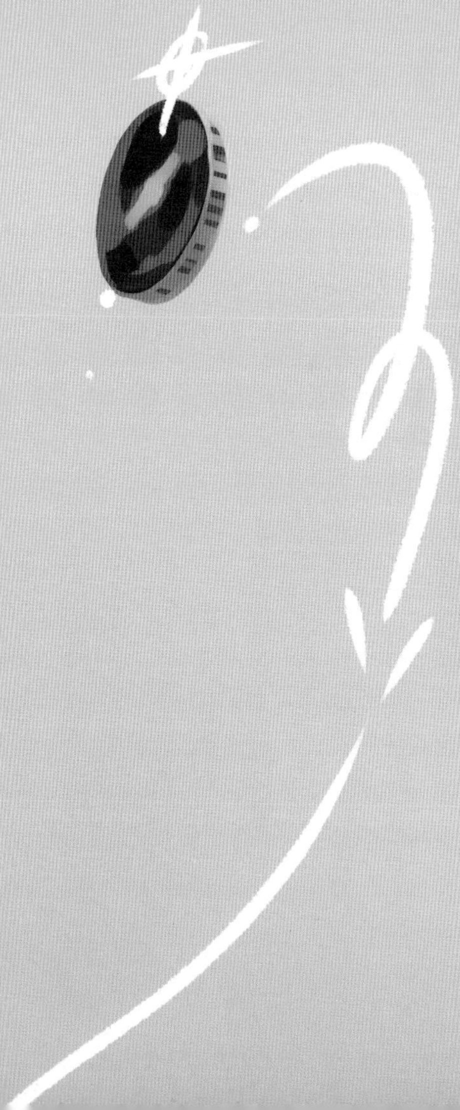

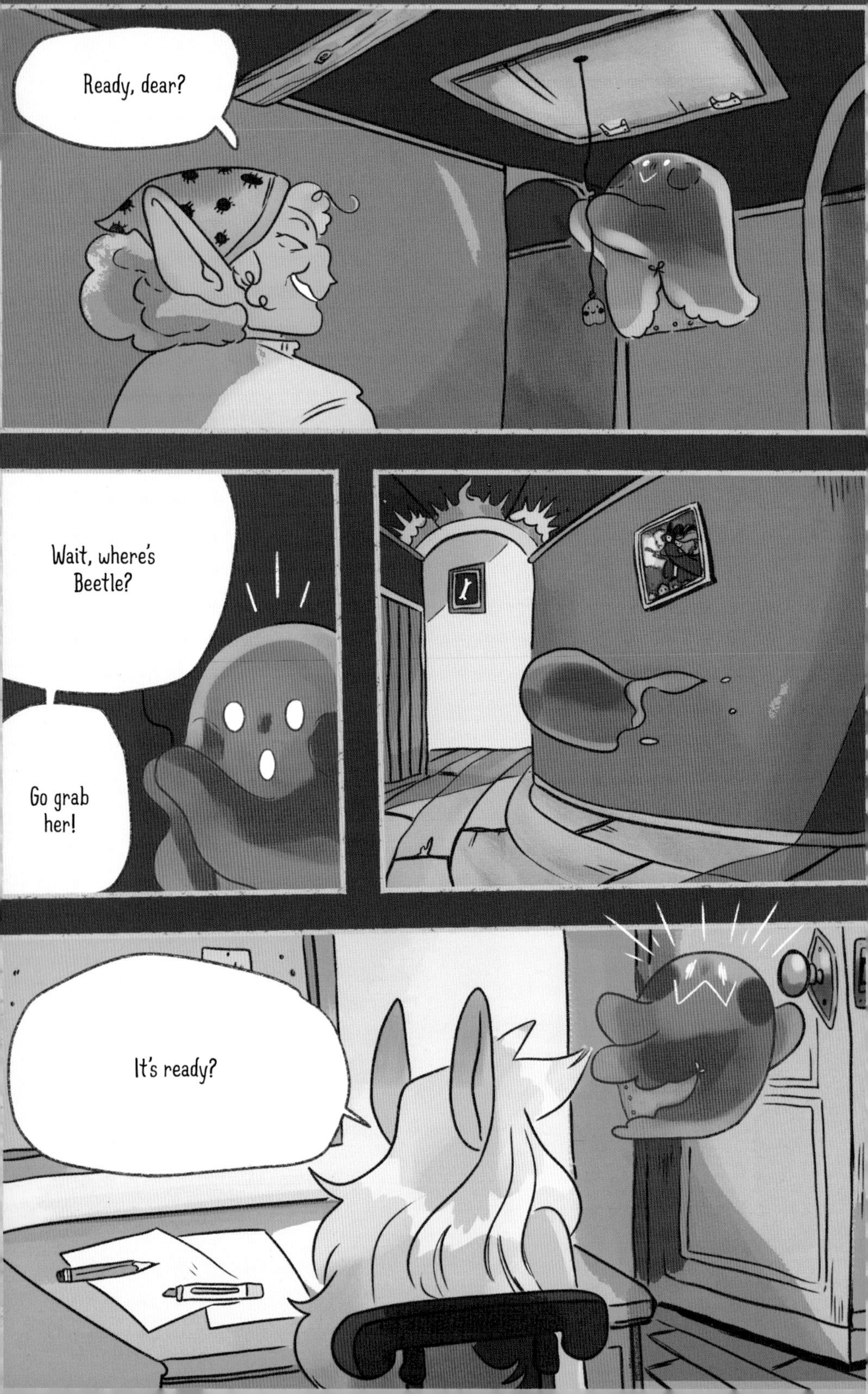
Ready, dear?
Wait, where's Beetle?
Go grab her!
It's ready?

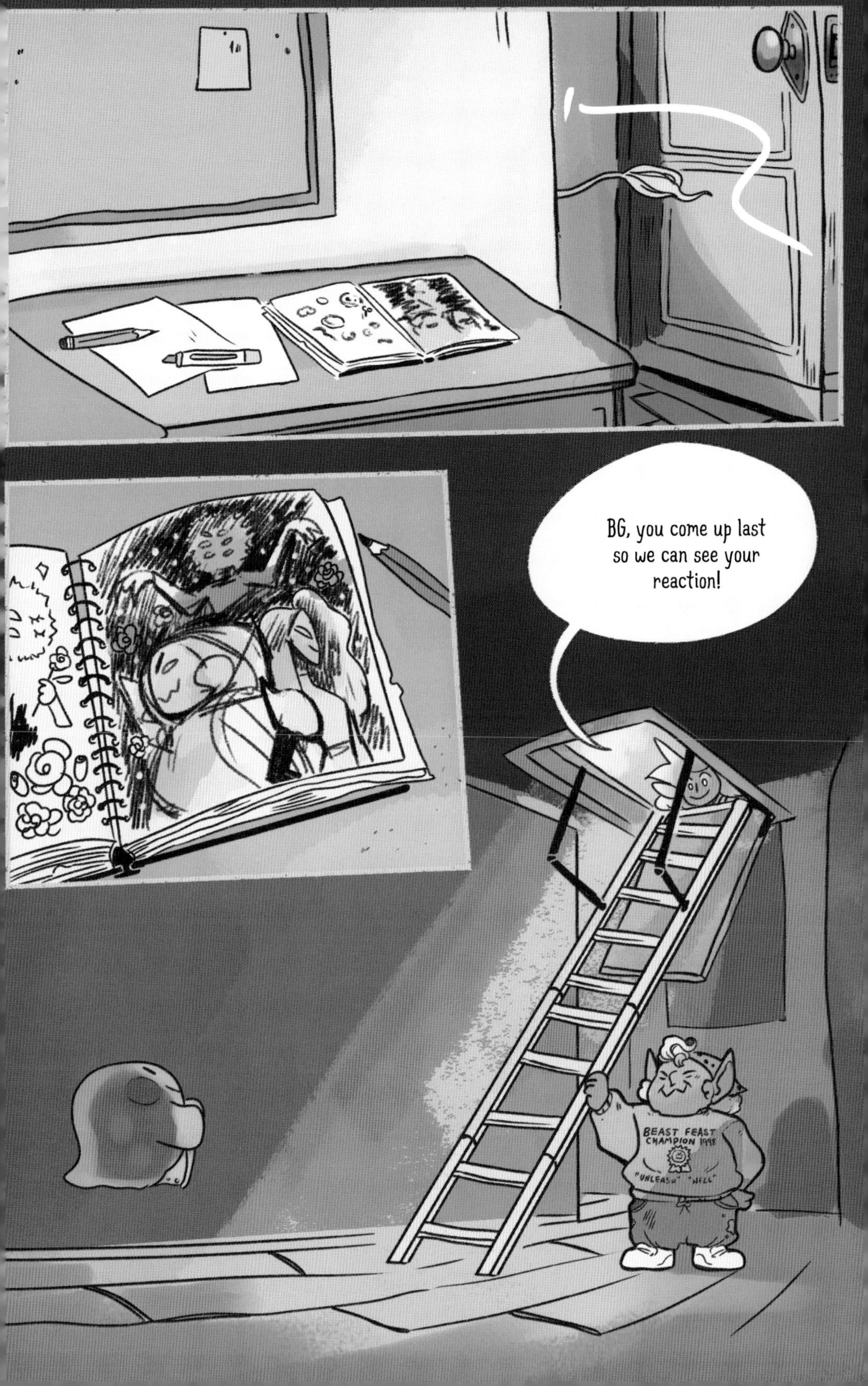
BG, you come up last so we can see your reaction!
BEAST FEAST CHAMPION 1998
"UNLEASH" "HELL"

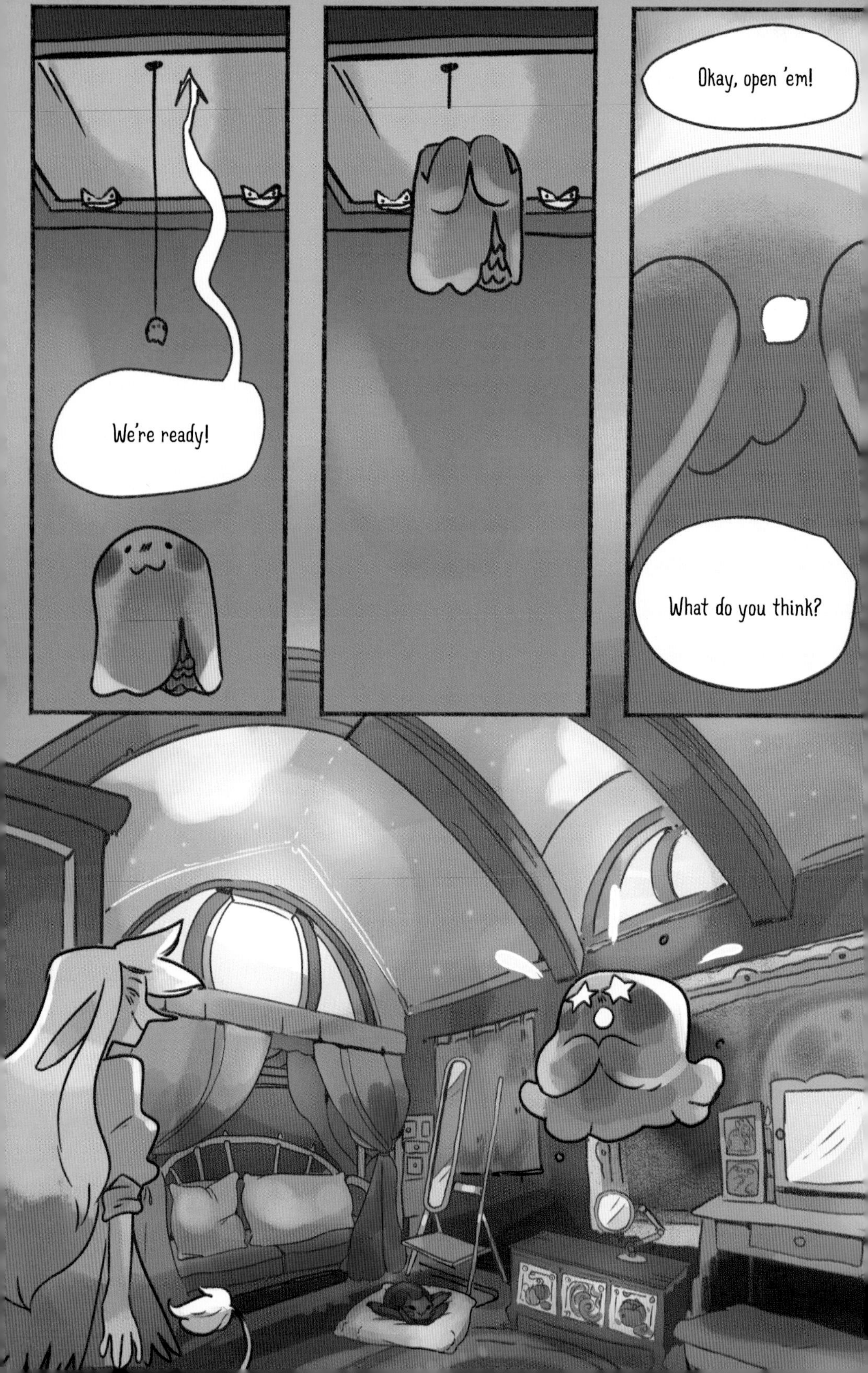
We're ready!
Okay, open 'em!
What do you think?

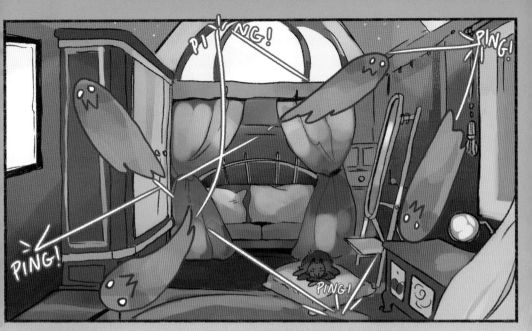

Looks like they hate it.

Your new class-mate is going to be here any minute, you know.

Are you going to teach us today?

That's Thursday. Today, you're with—

RATTLE

RATTLE

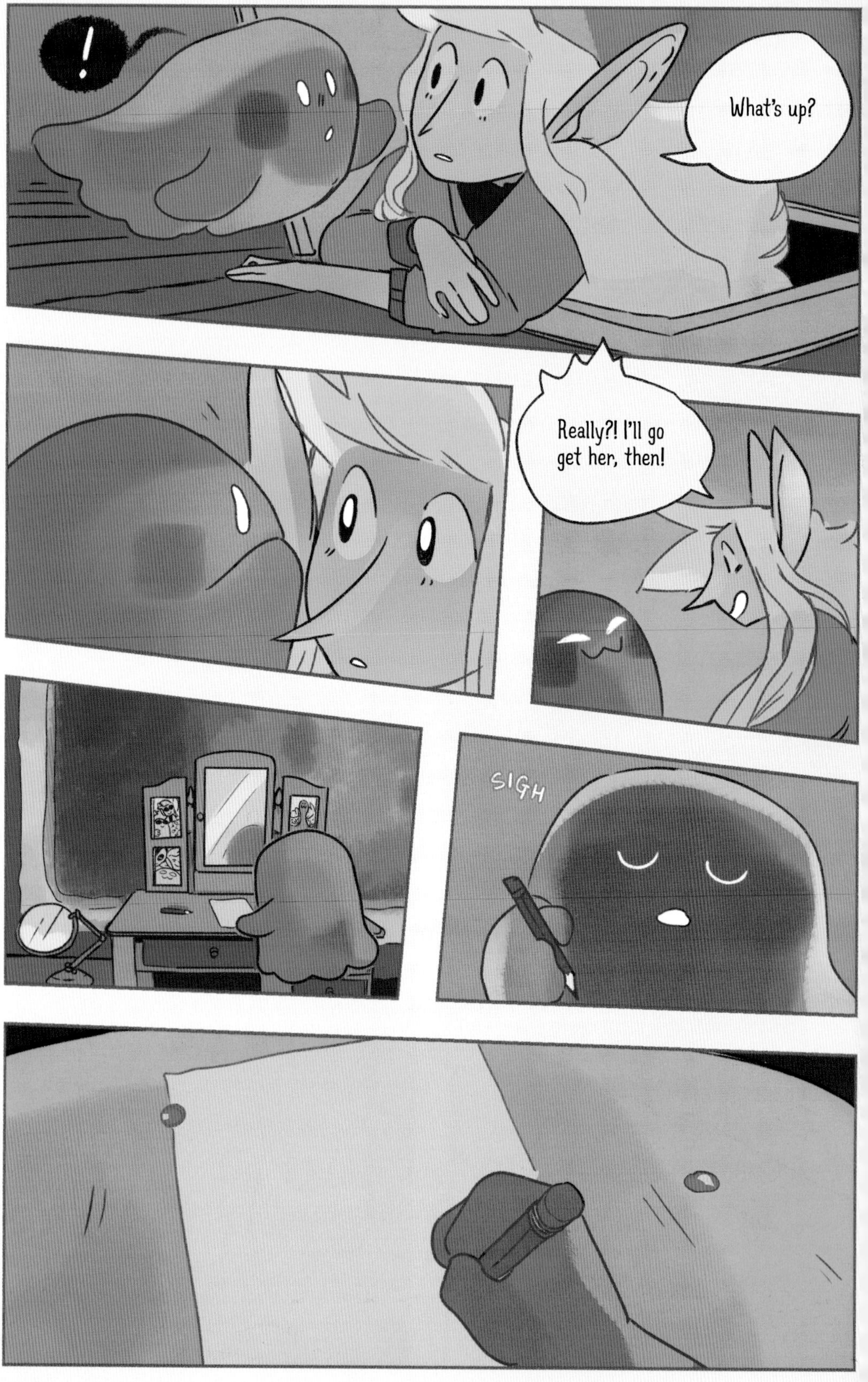
!
What's up?
Really?! I'll go get her, then!
SIGH

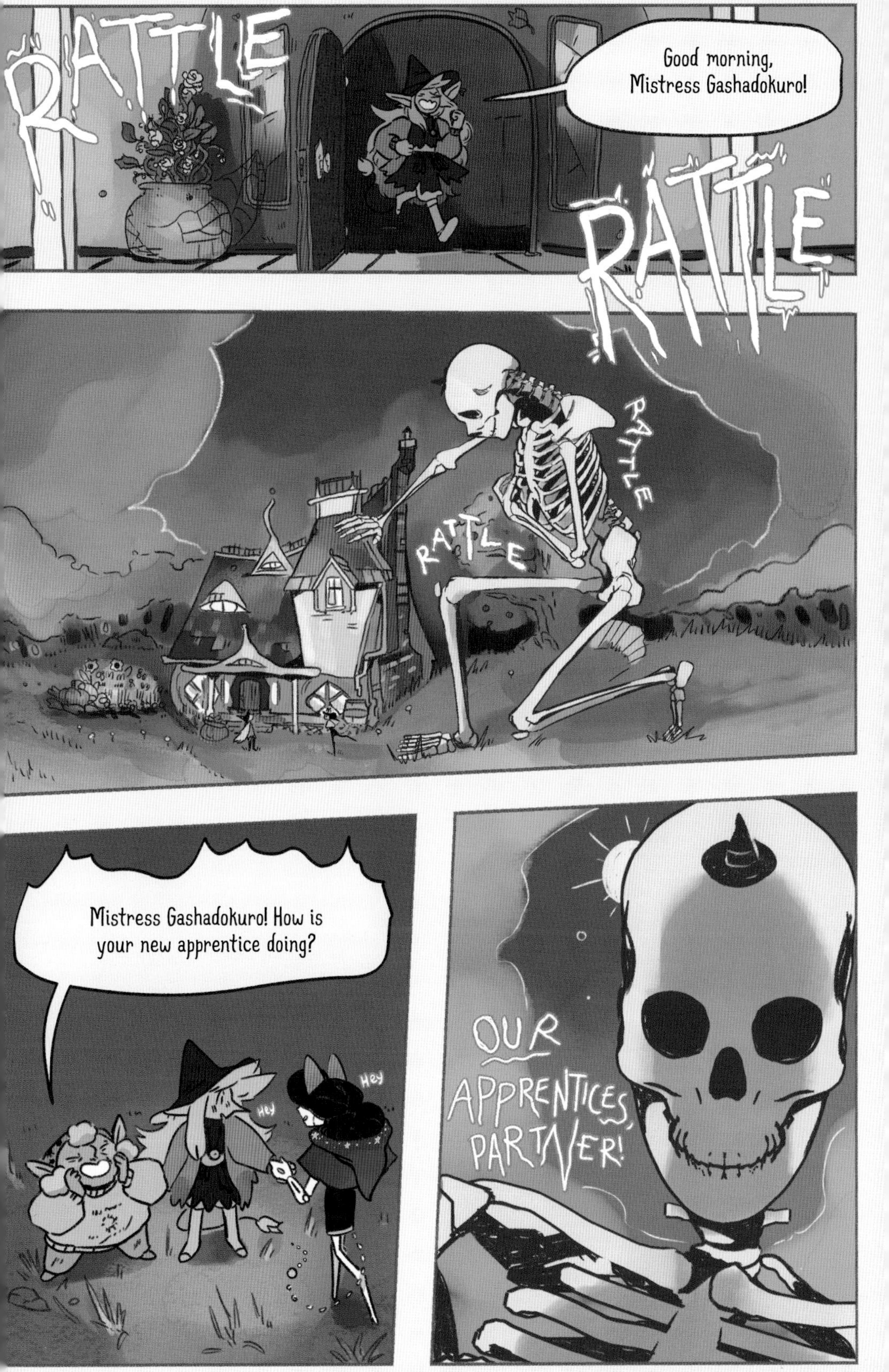
RATTLE
Good morning, Mistress Gashadokuro!
RATTLE
RATTLE
RATTLE
Mistress Gashadokuro! How is your new apprentice doing?
Hey
Hey
OUR APPRENTICES, PARTNER!

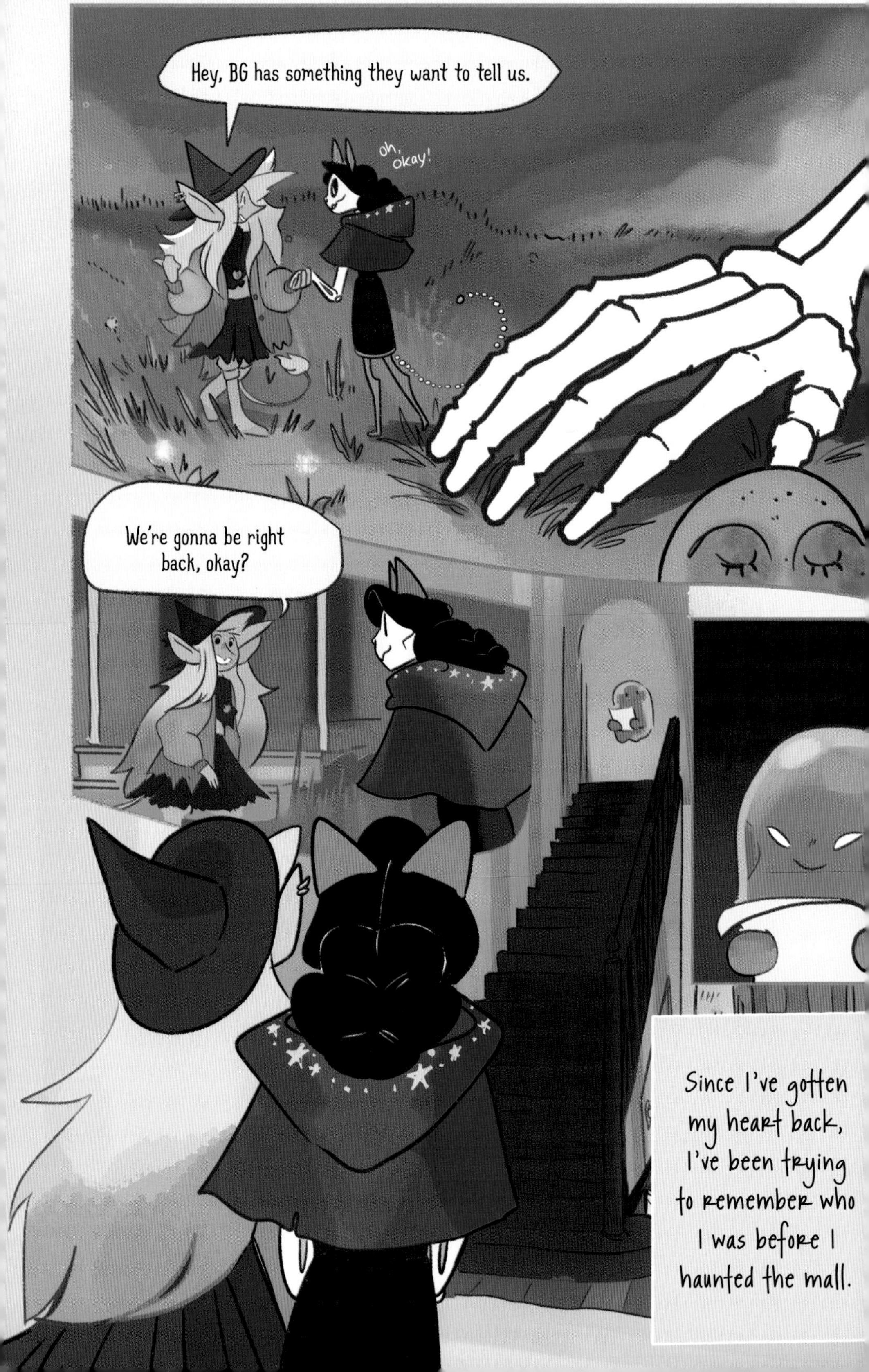
Hey, BG has something they want to tell us.
Oh, okay!
We're gonna be right back, okay?
Since I've gotten my heart back, I've been trying to remember who I was before I haunted the mall.

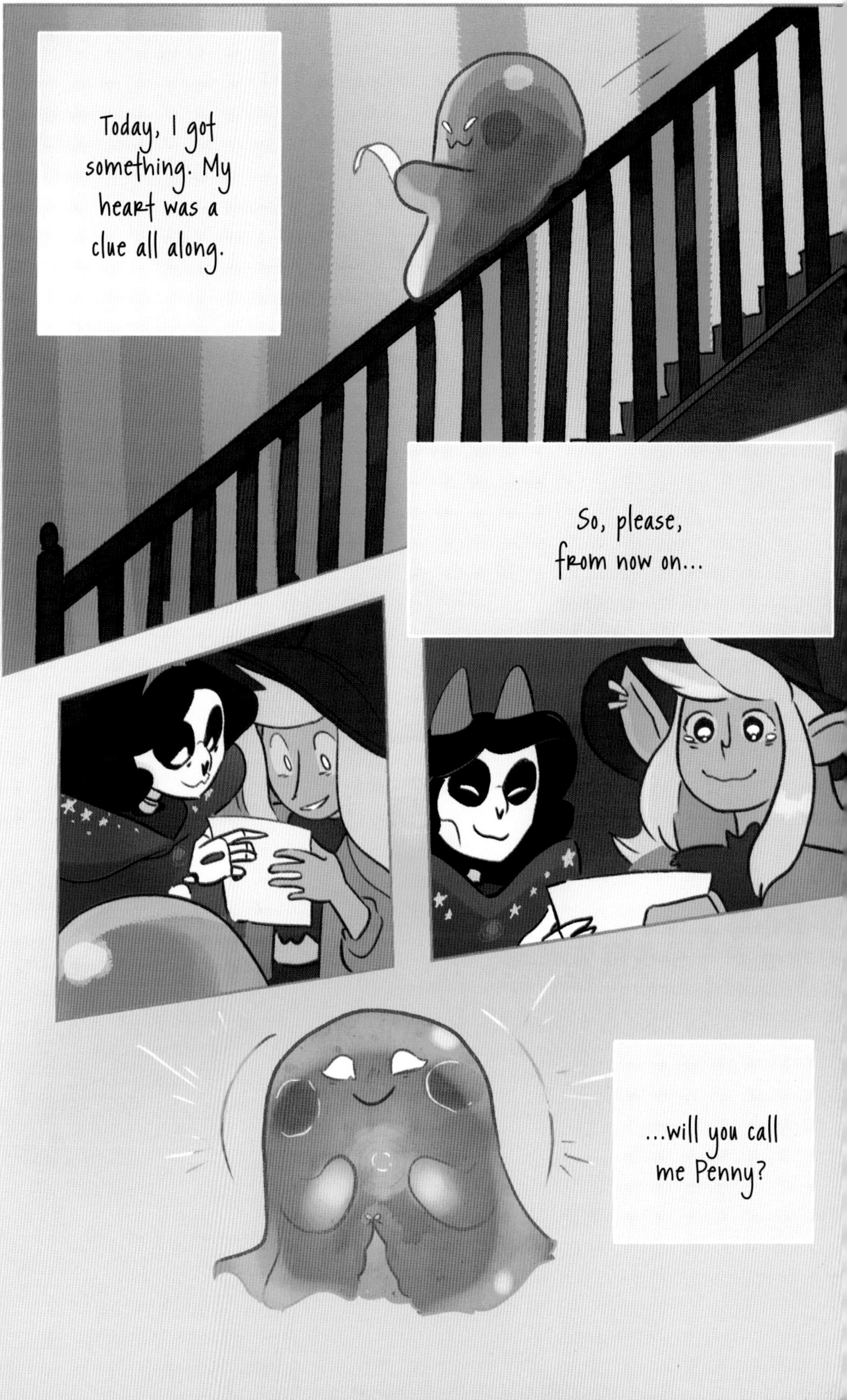
Today, I got something. My heart was a clue all along.
So, please, from now on...
...will you call me Penny?

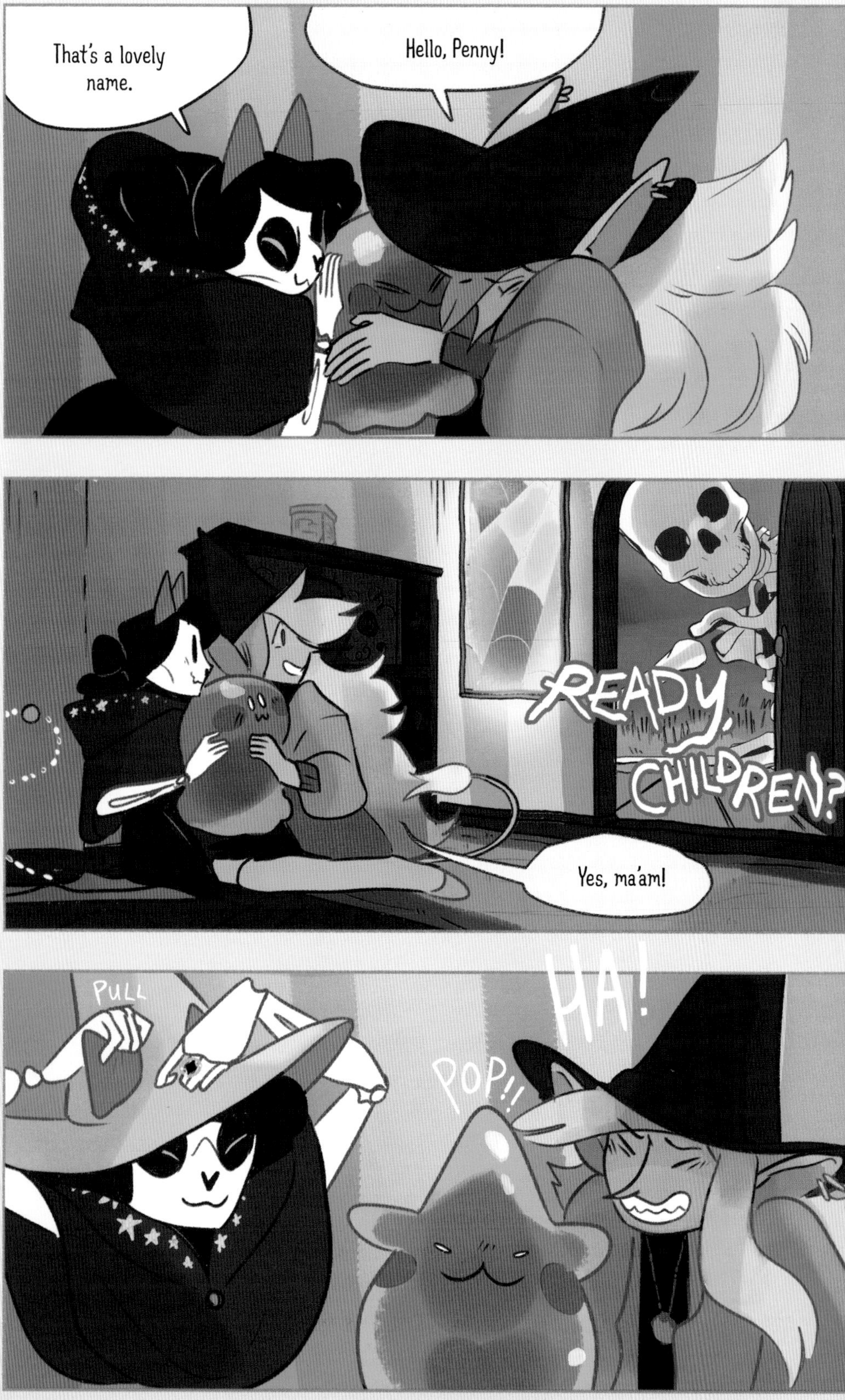
That's a lovely name.
Hello, Penny!
READY, CHILDREN?
Yes, ma'am!
PULL
HA!
POP!!

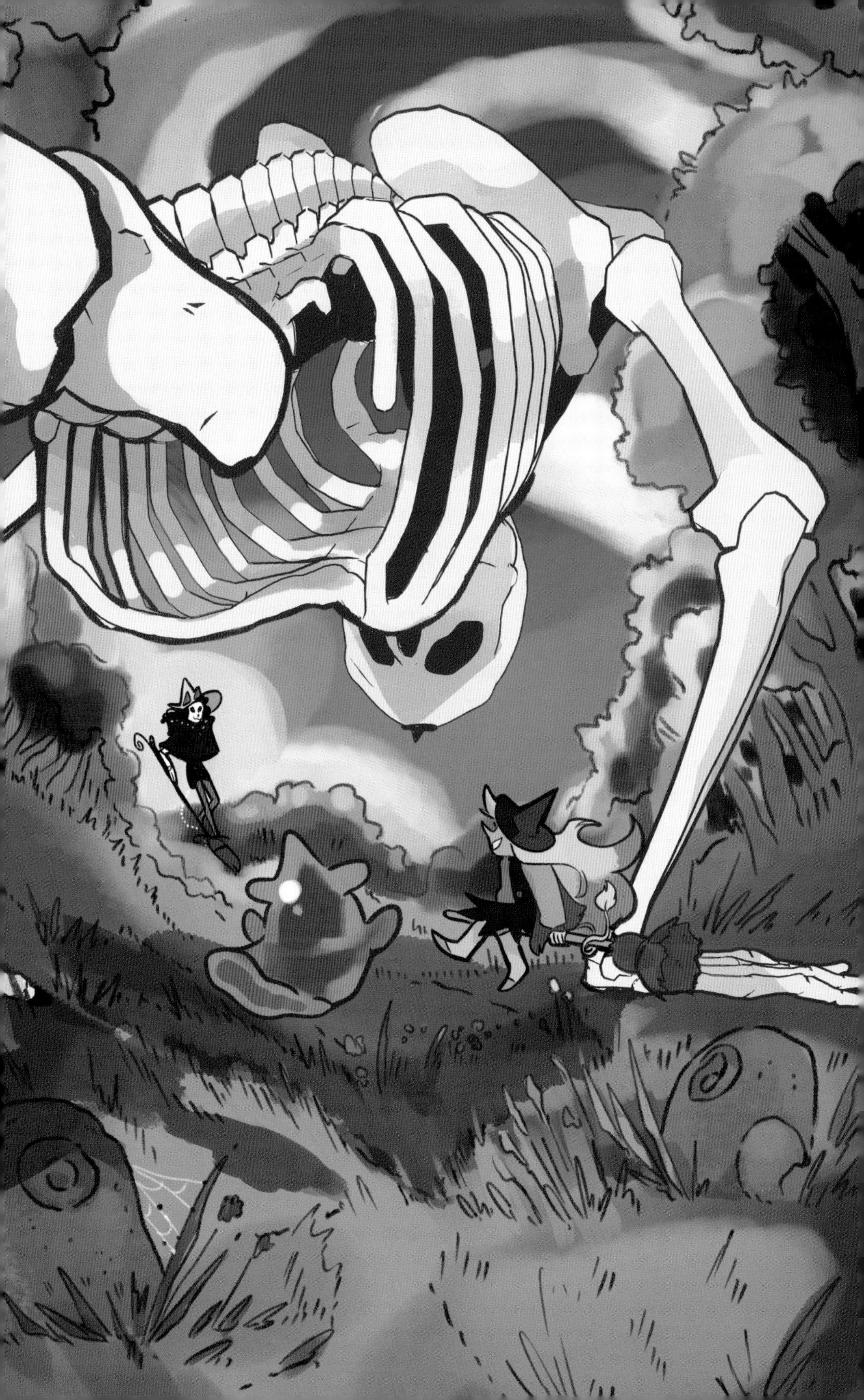

CONCEPT ART

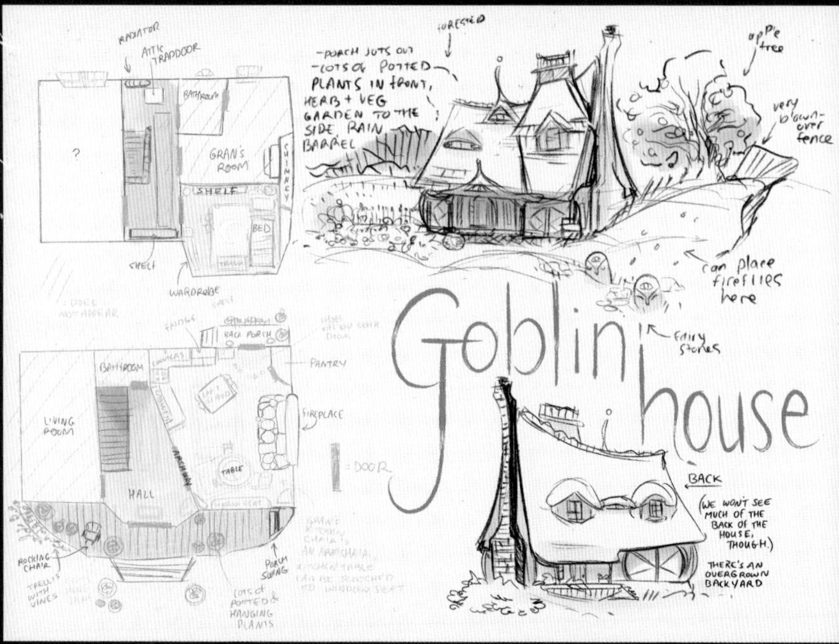
RADIATOR
ATTIC TRAPDOOR
BATHROOM
GRAN'S ROOM
CHIMNEY
SHELF
BED
?
WARDROBE
FRIDGE
BACK PORCH
PANTRY
BATHROOM
COUNTERS
LIVING ROOM
FIREPLACE
TABLE
HALL
ROCKING CHAIR
TRELLIS WITH VINES
PORCH SWING
LOTS OF POTTED & HANGING PLANTS
= DOOR
FORESTED
-PORCH JUTS OUT -LOTS OF POTTED PLANTS IN FRONT, HERB + VEG GARDEN TO THE SIDE, RAIN BARREL
apple tree
very blown-over fence
can place fireflies here
Goblin house
Fairy stones
BACK
(WE WON'T SEE MUCH OF THE BACK OF THE HOUSE, THOUGH.)
THERE'S AN OVERGROWN BACKYARD

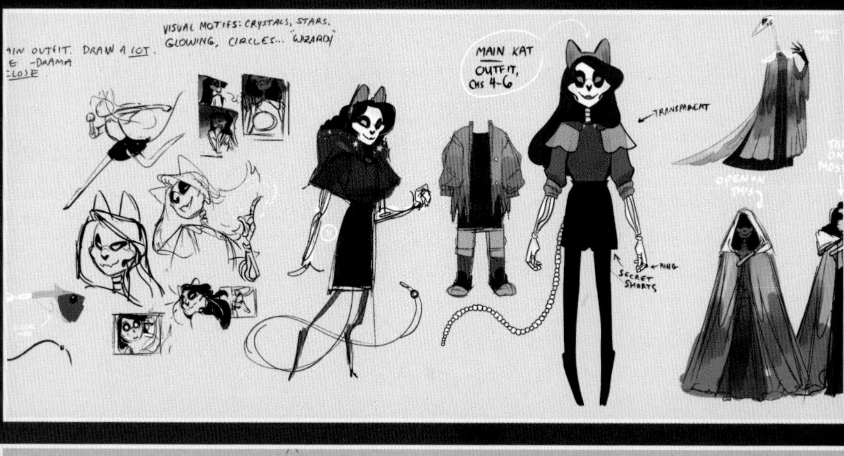
VISUAL MOTIFS: CRYSTALS, STARS, GLOWING, CIRCLES... "WIZARD"
MAIN KAT OUTFIT, CHS 4-6
TRANSPARENT
RING
SECRET SHORTS
OPEN ON THIS

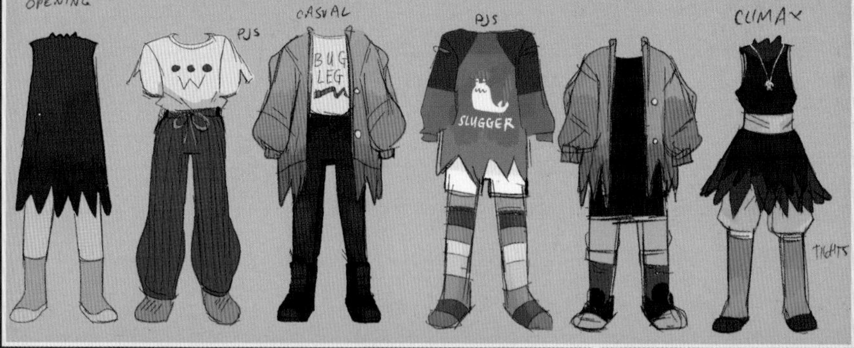
OPENING
PJS
CASUAL
BUG LEG
PJS
SLUGGER
CLIMAX
TIGHTS

Acknowledgments

I'd like to start by thanking my agent, Susan Graham, whose hard work, passion, and great ideas not only shaped this book, but enabled it to exist at all, and for whom I would draw hundreds of chickencats if it meant they'd keep lending me their support. I also owe *Beetle*'s existence to the fantastic work of my editor, Julia "Ghoulia" McCarthy, whose excitement over this story and willingness to put up with my antics deserve particular gratitude.

The staff at Simon & Schuster also deserve my boundless thanks, particularly Rebecca Syracuse, *Beetle*'s phenomenal designer; Jeannie Ng; Shivani Annirood; Chantal Gersch; Devin MacDonald; Justin Chanda; and Reka Simonsen.

If Natalie Riess and Kristen Acampora had not done the flat colors for this book, my hands would have fallen off. It was a treat to paint their work, and I cannot thank them enough. Natalie has the best bug-and-dragon ideas in the world and has been my fierce and wonderful friend for many years. Kristen is one of the kindest, most uplifting, and most hardworking people I have ever met, and I am so grateful to be her friend.

A special mention is also due to Stacey Friedberg, who workshopped a great deal of this book with me early on.

Tremendous thanks to all my friends and family, especially to Kate Dobson for her mentorship; to Smo for coming up with "Worm of Endearment"; to Deborah, TJ, Angelique, and Nick for their support and good ideas and warrior-cats-role-playing chops; and to all my phenomenal, funny, and absurdly skilled friends for appearing in my life and appearing in this book as background creatures. Thank you for the readers and supporters of my webcomic for also cheering *Beetle* on.

When I first wrote the short comic that *Beetle* is based on, I sent it to Zack Morrison, my rival, and asked if it was any good. Their enthusiasm for these characters lit a fire in my heart. I also showed it to my brother, Luke, who was in middle school himself back then, and *he* laughed at it, so I wrote more for him.

For my friends

atheneum

ATHENEUM BOOKS FOR YOUNG READERS
An imprint of Simon & Schuster Children's Publishing Division
1230 Avenue of the Americas, New York, New York 10020

Copyright © 2020 by Aliza Layne
Illustrations colored by Natalie Riess and Kristen Acampora

For information about special discounts for bulk purchases, please contact Simon & Schuster Special Sales at 1-866-506-1747 or business@simonandschuster.com.
The Simon & Schuster Speakers Bureau can bring authors to your live event. For more information or to book an event, contact the Simon & Schuster Speakers Bureau at 1-866-248-3047 or visit our website at www.simonspeakers.com.
Also available in an Atheneum Books for Young Readers hardcover edition
Book design by Rebecca Syracuse
The text for this book was set in Prova.
The illustrations for this book were digitally rendered.
Manufactured in China
0720 SCP
First Atheneum Books for Young Readers paperback edition
2 4 6 8 10 9 7 5 3
CIP data for this book is available from the Library of Congress.
ISBN 978-1-5344-4154-5 (paperback)
ISBN 978-1-5344-4153-8 (hardcover)
ISBN 978-1-5344-4155-2 (eBook)